Self Raised

Or, From the Depths: A Sequel to "Ishmael."

Mrs. E.D.E.N. Southworth

(1876)

TABLE of CONTENTS

CHAPTER I

RECOVERY.

Something I know. Oft, shall it come about

When every heart is full of hope for man,

The horizon straight is darkened, and a doubt

Clouds all. The work the youth so well began

Wastes down, and by some deed of shame is finished.

Ah, yet we will not be dismayed:

What seemed the triumph of the Fiend at length

Might be the effort of some dying devil,

Permitted to put forth his fullest strength

To loose it all forever!

Owen Meredith.

Awful as the anguish of his parting with Claudia had been, it was not likely that Ishmael, with his strength of intellect and will, would long succumb to despair. It was not in Claudia's power to make his life quite desolate; how could it be so while Bee cared for him?

Bee had loved Ishmael as long as Ishmael had loved Claudia. She had loved him when he was a boy at school; when he was a young country teacher; when he was a law-student; and she loved him now that he was a successful barrister. This love, founded in esteem and honor, had constantly deepened and strengthened. In loving Ishmael, she found mental and spiritual development; and in being near him and doing him good she found comfort and happiness. And being perfectly satisfied with the present, Bee never gave a thought to the future. That she tacitly left, where it belongs, to God.

Or if at times, on perceiving Ishmael's utter obliviousness of her own kindly presence and his perfect devotion to the thankless Claudia, Bee felt a pang, she went and buried herself with domestic duties, or played with the children in the nursery, or what was better still, if it happened to be little Lu's "sleepy time" she would take her baby-sister up to her own room, sit down and fold her to her breast and rock and sing her to sleep. And certainly the clasp of those baby-arms about her neck, and the nestling of that baby-form to her bosom, drew out all the heart-ache and soothed all the agitation.

Except these little occasional pangs Bee had always been blessed in loving. Her love, all unrequited, as it seemed, was still the sweetest thing in the world to her; and it seemed thus, because in fact it was so well approved by her mind and so entirely unselfish. It seemed to be her life, or her soul, or one with both; Bee was not metaphysical enough to decide which. She would not struggle with this love, or try to conquer it, any more than she would have striven against and tried to destroy her mental and spiritual life. On the contrary she cherished it as she did her religion, of which it was a part; she cherished it as she did her love of God, with which it was united.

And loving Ishmael in this way, if she should fail to marry him, Bee resolved never to marry another; but to live and die a maiden; still cherishing, still hiding this most precious love in her heart as a miser hides his gold. Whether benign nature would have permitted the motherly little maiden to have carried out this resolution, I do not know; or what Bee would have done in the event of Ishmael's marrying another, she did not know. When Claudia went away, Bee, in the midst of her regret at parting with her cousin, felt a certain sense of relief: but when she saw the effect of that departure upon Ishmael she became alarmed for him; and after the terrible experiences of that day and night Bee's one single thought in life was—Ishmael's good.

On the morning succeeding that dreadful day and night, Ishmael awoke early, in full possession of his faculties. He remembered all the incidents of that trying day and night; reflected upon their effects; and prayed to God to deliver him from the burden and guilt of inordinate and sinful affections.

Then he arose, made his toilet, read a portion of the Scriptures, offered up his morning prayers, and went below stairs.

In the breakfast parlor he found Bee, the busy little house-keeper, fluttering softly around the breakfast table, and adding a few finishing touches to its simple elegance.

Very fair, fresh, and blooming looked Bee in her pale golden ringlets and her pretty morning dress of white muslin with blue ribbons. There was no one else in the room; but Bee advanced and held out her hand to him.

He took her hand, and retaining it in his own for a moment, said:

"Oh, Bee! yesterday, last night!"

"'Upbraid not the past; it comes not back again.' Ishmael! bury it; forget it; and press onward!" replied Bee sweetly and solemnly.

He raised her hand with the impulse to carry it to his lips; but refraining, bowed his forehead over it instead, and then gently released it. For Ishmael's affection for Bee was reverential. To him she appeared saintly, Madonna-like, almost angelic.

"Let me make breakfast for you at once, Ishmael. It is not of the least use to wait for the others. Mamma, I know, is not awake yet, and none of the gentlemen have rung for their hot water."

"And you, Bee; you will also breakfast now?"

"Certainly."

And she rang and gave her orders. And the coffee, muffins, fried fresh perch, and broiled spring chickens speedily made their appearance.

"Jim," she said to the waiter who set the breakfast on the table, "tell cook to keep some of the perch and pullets dressed to put over the fire the moment she hears the judge's bell ring, so that his breakfast may be ready for him when he comes down."

"Very well, miss," answered Jim, who immediately left the room to give the order; but soon returned to attend upon the table.

So it was a tete-a-tete meal, but Bee made it very pleasant. After breakfast Ishmael left Bee to her domestic duties and went up into the office to look after the letters and papers that had been left for him by the penny postman that morning.

He glanced over the newspapers; read the letters; selected those he would need during the day; put the others carefully away; tied up his documents; took up his hat and gloves, and set out for his daily business at the City Hall.

In the ante-chamber of the Orphans' Court Room he met old Wiseman, who clapped him on the shoulder, exclaiming:

"How are you this morning, old fellow? All right, eh?"

"Thank you, I am quite well again," replied Ishmael.

"Ah ha! nothing like good brandy to get one up out of a fit of exhaustion."

"Ah!" exclaimed Ishmael, with a shudder.

"Well, and have you thought over what we were talking of yesterday?"

"It was—" Ishmael began, and then hesitated.

"It was about your going into partnership with me."

"Oh, yes! so it was! but I have not had time to think of it yet."

"Well, think over it today, will you, and then after the court has adjourned come to my chambers and talk the matter over with me. Will you?"

"Thank you, yes, certainly."

"Ah, well! I will not keep you any longer, for I see that you are in a hurry."

"It is because I have an appointment at ten," said Ishmael courteously.

"Certainly; and appointments must be kept. Good morning."

"Good morning, Mr. Wiseman."

"Mind, you are to come to my chambers after the court has adjourned."

"I will remember and come," said Ishmael.

And each went his way.

Ishmael had not yet seriously thought of Lawyer Wiseman's proposal. This forenoon, however, in the intervals of his professional business, he reflected on it.

The proposed partnership was unquestionably a highly advantageous one, in a worldly point of view. Lawyer Wiseman was undoubtedly the best lawyer and commanded the largest practice at the Washington bar, with one single exception—that of the brilliant young barrister whom he proposed to associate with himself. Together, they would be invincible, carrying everything before them; and Ishmael's fortune would be rapidly made.

So far the offer was a very tempting one; yet the more Ishmael reflected on it the more determined he became to refuse it; because, in fact, his conscience would not permit him to enter into partnership with Lawyer Wiseman, for the following reasons: Lawyer Wiseman, a man of unimpeachable integrity in his private life, declined to carry moral responsibility into his professional business. He was indiscriminate in his acceptation of briefs. It mattered not whether the case presented to him was a case of injustice, cruelty, or oppression, so that it was a case for law, with a wealthy client to back it. The only question with Lawyer Wiseman being the amount of the retaining fee. If his client liberally anointed Lawyer Wiseman's eyes with golden ointment, Lawyer Wiseman would undertake to see and make the judge and jury see anything and everything that his client wished! With such a man as this, therefore, whatever the professional advantages of the association might be, Ishmael could not enter into partnership.

And so when the court had adjourned Ishmael walked over to the chambers of Mr. Wiseman on Louisiana Avenue, and in an interview with the old lawyer courteously declined his offer.

This considerably astonished Mr. Wiseman, who pressed Ishmael for the reasons of his strange refusal.

And Ishmael, being urged, at length candidly confessed them.

Instead of being angry, as might have been expected, the old lawyer was simply amused. He laughed at his young friend's scruples, and assured him that experience would cure them. And the interview having been brought to a close, they shook hands and parted amicably.

Ishmael hurried home to dine and spend the evening with the family.

On the Monday following, at the order of Judge Merlin, preparations were commenced for shutting up the town house and leaving Washington for Tanglewood; for the judge swore that, let anyone whatever get married, or christened, stay in the city another week he could not, without decomposing, for that his soul had already left his body and preceded him to Tanglewood, whither he must immediately follow it.

Oh, but Bee had plenty of work to look after that week—the packing up of all the children's clothes, and of all the household effects—such as silver plate, cut-glass, fine china, cutlery, etc., that were to be sent forward to Tanglewood.

She would have had to overlook the packing of the books also, but that Ishmael insisted on relieving her of that task, by doing it all with his own hands, as indeed he preferred to do it, for his love of books was almost—tender. It was curious to see him carefully straighten the leaves and brush the cover and edges of an old book, as conscientiously as he would have doctored a hurt child. They were friends and he was fond of them.

Ishmael continued steadily in the performance of all his duties, yet that he was still suffering very much might be observed in the abiding paleness and wasting thinness of his face, and in a certain languor and weariness in all his movements.

Bee in the midst of her multifarious cares did not forget his interests; she took pains to have his favorite dishes appear on the table in order to tempt him to take food. But, observing that he still ate little or nothing, while he daily lost flesh, she took an opportunity of saying to him in the library:

"Ishmael, you know I am a right good little doctress; I have had so much experience in nursing father and mother and the children; so I know what I am talking about, when I tell you that you need a tonic."

"Oh, Bee! if you did but really know, little sister!"

"I do know, Ishmael, I know it all!" she said gently.

"'Out of the heart are the issues of life!' Bee, mine has received a paralyzing blow."

"I know it, dear Ishmael; I know it; but let your great mind sustain that stricken heart until it recovers the blow. And in the meantime try to get up your strength. You must have more food and more rest, and in order to secure them you must take a tonic in the morning to give you an appetite, and a sedative at night to give you sleep. That was the way we saved mamma after little Mary died, or, indeed, I think she would have followed her."

Ishmael smiled a very wan smile as he answered:

"Indeed, I am ashamed of this utter weakness, Bee."

"Why should you be? Has Providence given you any immunity from the common lot? We must take our human nature as it is given to us and do the best we can with it, I think."

"What a wise little woman you are, Bee."

"That's because I have got a good memory. The wisdom was second- handed, Ishmael, being just what I heard you yourself say when you were defending Featherstonehaugh:

Ishmael smiled.

"And, now, will you follow my advice?"

"To the letter, dear Bee, whenever you are so good as to advise me. Ah, Bee, you seem to comprise in yourself all that that I have missed of family affection, and to compensate me for the unknown love of her mother, sister, friend."

"Do I, Ishmael? Oh, I wish that I really did!" said Bee, impulsively; and then she blushed deeply at suddenly apprehending the construction that might he put upon her words.

But Ishmael answered those words in the spirit in which they were uttered:

"Believe me, dearest Bee, you do. If I never feel the want of home affections it is because I have them all in you. My heart finds rest in you, Bee. But oh, little sister, what can I ever render to you for all the good you have done me from my childhood up?"

"Render yourself good and wise and great, Ishmael, and I shall be sufficiently happy in watching your upward progress," said Bee.

And quietly putting down on the table a bunch of grapes that she had brought, she withdrew from the office.

CHAPTER II

HERMAN AND ISHMAEL.

With a deep groan he cried—"Oh, gifted one,

I am thy father! Hate me not, my son!"

—Anon.

Nor are my mother's wrongs forgot;

Her slighted love and ruined name,

Her offspring's heritage of shame,

Shall witness for thee from the dead

How trusty and how tender were

Thy youthful love—paternal care!

—Byron.

Her exit was almost immediately followed by the entrance of Mr. Brudenell. He also had noticed Ishmael's condition, and attributed it to overwork, and to the want of rest, with change of air. He was preparing to leave Washington for Brudenell Hall. He was going a few days in advance of Judge Merlin and the Middletons, and he intended to invite Ishmael to accompany him, or to come after him, and make a visit to Brudenell. He earnestly desired to have Ishmael there to himself for a week or two. It was with this desire that he now entered the library.

Ishmael arose from his packing, and, smiling a welcome, set a chair for his visitor.

"You are not looking well, Mr. Worth," said Herman Brudenell, as he took the offered seat.

"I am not well just at present, but I shall be so in a day or two," returned Ishmael.

"Not if you continue the course you are pursuing now, my young friend. You require rest and change of air. I shall leave Washington for Brudenell Hall on Thursday morning. It would give me great pleasure if you would accompany me thither, and remain my guest for a few weeks, to recruit your health. The place is noted for its salubrity; and though the house has been dismantled, and has remained vacant for some time, yet I hope we will find it fitted up comfortably again; for I have written down to an upholsterer of Baymouth to send in some furniture, and I have also written to a certain genius of all trades, called the 'professor,' to go over and see it all arranged, and do what else is needed to be done for our reception."

Ishmael smiled when he heard the name of the professor; but before he could make any comment, Mr. Brudenell inquired:

"What do you say, Mr. Worth? Will you accompany me thither, or will you come after me?"

"I thank you very much, Mr. Brudenell. I should like to visit Brudenell Hall; but—"

"Then you will come? I am very glad! I shall be alone there with my servants, you know, and your society will be a god-send to me. Had you not better go down at once when I do? I go by land, in a hired carriage. The carriage is very comfortable; and we can make the journey in two days, and lay by during the heat of both days. I think the trip will be pleasant. We can reach Brudenell Hall on Friday night, and have a good rest before Sunday, when we can go to the old country church, where you will be likely to meet the faces of some of your old friends. I think we shall be very comfortable, keeping bachelor-hall together at Brudenell Hall this summer, Mr. Worth," said Herman Brudenell, who longed more than tongue could tell to have Nora's son at home with him, though it might be only for a short time.

"I feel your kindness very much indeed, Mr. Brudenell; and I should be very, very happy to accept your hospitable invitation; but—I was about to say, it really is quite impossible in the existing state of my business for me to go anywhere at present," said Ishmael courteously.

"Indeed? I am very sorry for that. But the reasons you give are unanswerable, I know. I am seriously disappointed. Yet I trust, though you may not be able to come just at present, you will follow me down there after a little while—say in the course of a few days or weeks—for I shall remain at the hall all summer and shall be always delighted to receive you. Will you promise to come?"

"Indeed, I fear I cannot promise that either, for I have a very great pressure of business; but if I can possibly manage to go, without infringing upon my duties, I shall be grateful for the privilege and very happy to avail myself of it; for—do you know, sir?—I was born in that neighborhood and passed my childhood and youth there. I love the old place, and almost long to see the old hut where I lived, and the hall where I went to school, and the wooded valley that lies between them, where I gathered wild-flowers and fruits in summer and nuts in winter, and—my mother's grave," said the unconscious son, speaking confidentially, and looking straight into his father's eyes.

"Ishmael," said Herman Brudenell, in a faltering voice, and forgetting to be formal, "you must come to me: that grave should draw you, if nothing else; it is a pious pilgrimage when a son goes to visit his mother's grave."

There was something in this new friend's words, look, and manner that always drew out the young man's confidence, and he said, in a voice trembling with emotion:

"She died young, sir; and oh! so sorrowfully! She was only nineteen, two years younger than I am now; and her son was motherless the hour he was born."

Violent emotion shook the frame of Herman Brudenell. He had not entered the room with any intention of making a disclosure to Ishmael; but he felt now that—come life, come death, come whatever might of it—he must claim Nora's son.

"Ishmael," he began, in a voice shaken with agitation, "I knew your mother."

"You, sir!" exclaimed the young man in surprise.

"Yes, I knew her and her sister, naturally, for they were tenants of mine."

"I knew that they lived on the outskirts of the Brudenell estate; but I did not know you were personally acquainted with them, sir; for I thought that you had resided generally in Europe."

"Not all the time; I was at Brudenell Hall when—you were born and your mother went to heaven, Ishmael."

Some of the elder man's agitation communicated itself to the younger, who half arose from his seat and looked intently at the speaker.

"I knew your mother in those days, Ishmael. She was not only one of the most beautiful women of her day, but one of the purest, noblest, and best."

Herman Brudenell hesitated. And Ishmael, who had dropped again into his seat, bent eagerly forward, holding his breath while he listened.

Herman continued.

"You resemble her in person and character, Ishmael. All that is best and noblest and most attractive in you, Ishmael, is derived under Divine Providence from your mother."

"I know it! Oh, I know it!"

"And, Ishmael, I loved your mother!"

"Oh, Heaven!" breathed the young man, in sickening, deadly apprehension; for well he remembered that this Mr. Herman Brudenell was the husband of the Countess of Hurstmonceux at the very time of which he now spoke.

"Ishmael, do not look so cruelly distressed. I loved her, she loved me in return, she crowned my days with joy, and—"

A gasping sound of suddenly suspended breath from Ishmael.

"I made her my wife," continued Herman Brudenell, in a grave and earnest voice.

"It was you then!" cried Ishmael, shaking with agitation.

"It was I!"

Silence like a pall fell between them.

"Oh, Ishmael! my son! my son! speak to me! give me your hand!" groaned Herman Brudenell.

"She was your wife! Yet she died of want, exposure, and grief!" said Nora's son, standing pale and stony before him.

"And I—live with a breaking heart! a harder fate, Ishmael. Since her death, I have been a wifeless, childless, homeless wanderer over the wide world! Oh, Ishmael! my son! my son! give me your hand!"

"I am your mother's son! She was your wife, you say; yet she never bore your name! She was your wife; yet her son and yours bears her maiden name! She was your wife; yet she perished miserably in her early youth; and undeserved reproach is suffered to rest upon her memory! Oh, sir! if indeed you were her husband and my father, as you claim to be, explain these things before I give you my hand! for when I give my hand, honor and respect must go with it," said Ishmael in a grave, sweet, earnest tone.

"Is it possible that Hannah has never told you? I thought she would have told you everything, except the name of your father."

"She told me everything that she could tell without violating the oath of secrecy by which she was bound; but what she told me was not satisfactory."

"Sit down then, Ishmael, sit down; and though to recall this woeful history will be to tear open old wounds afresh, I will do so; and when you have heard it, you will know how blameless we both—your mother and myself—really were, and how deep has been the tragedy of my life as well as hers—the difference between us being that hers is a dead trouble, from which she rests eternally, while mine is a living and life-long sorrow!"

Ishmael again dropped into his chair and gave undivided attention to the speaker.

And Mr. Brudenell, after a short pause, commenced and gave a narrative of his own eventful life, beginning with his college days, and detailing all the incidents of his youthful career until it culminated in the dreadful household wreck that had killed Nora, exiled his family and blasted his own happiness forever.

Ishmael listened with the deepest sympathy.

It was indeed the tearing open of old wounds in Herman Brudenell's breast; and it was the inflicting of new ones in Ishmael's heart. It was an hour of unspeakable distress to both. Herman did not spare himself in the relation; yet in the end Ishmael exculpated his father from all blame. We know indeed that in his relations with Nora he was blameless, unless his fatal haste could be called a fault. And so for his long neglect of Ishmael, which really was a great sin, and the greatest he had ever committed, Ishmael never gave a thought to that, it was only a sin against himself, and Ishmael was not selfish enough to feel or resent it.

Herman Brudenell ended his story very much as he had commenced it.

"And since that day of doom, Ishmael, I have been a lonely, homeless, miserable wanderer over the wide world! The fabled Wandering Jew not more wretched than I!" And the bowed head, blanched complexion, and quivering features bore testimony to his words.

CHAPTER II

FATHER AND SON.

For though thou work'st my mother ill

I feel thou art my father still!

—Byron.

Yet what no chance could then reveal,

And no one would be first to own,

Let fate and courage still conceal,

When truth could bring reproach alone.

—Milnes.

Ishmael had been violently shaken. It was with much effort that he controlled his own emotions in order to administer consolation to one who was suffering even more than he himself was, because that suffering was blended with a morbid remorse.

"Father," he said, reaching forth his hand to the stricken man; but his voice failed him.

Herman Brudenell looked up; an expression of earnest love chasing away the sorrow from his face, as he said:

"Father? Ah, what a dear name! You call me thus, Ishmael? Me, who worked your mother so much woe?"

"Father, it was your great misfortune, not your fault; she said it on her death-bed, and the words of the dying are sacred," said Ishmael earnestly, and caressing the pale, thin hand that he held.

"Oh, Nora! Oh, Nora!" exclaimed Herman, as all his bosom's wounds bled afresh.

"Father, do not grieve so bitterly; and after all these years so morbidly! God has wiped away all tears from her eyes. She has been a saint in glory these many years!"

"You try to comfort me, Ishmael. You, Nora's son?" exclaimed Herman, with increased emotion.

"Who else of all the world should comfort you but Nora's son?"

"You love me, then, a little, Ishmael?"

"She loved you, my father, and why should not I?"

"Ah, that means that you will love me in time; for love is not born in an instant, my son."

"My heart reaches out to you, my father: I love you even now, and sympathize with you deeply; and I feel that I shall love you more and more, and as I shall see you oftener and know you better," said the simply truthful son.

"Ishmael! this is the happiest hour I have known since Nora's death, and Nora's son has given it to me."

"None have a better right to serve you."

"My son, I am a prematurely old and broken man, ruined and impoverished, but Brudenell Hall is still mine, and the name of Brudenell is one of the most ancient and honored in the Old and New World! If you consent, Ishmael, I will gladly, proudly, and openly acknowledge you as my son. I will get an act of the Legislature passed authorizing you to take the name and arms of Brudenell. And I will make you the heir of Brudenell Hall. What say you, Ishmael?"

"Father," said the young man, promptly but respectfully, "no! In all things I will be to you a true and loving son; but I cannot, cannot consent to your proposal; because to do so would be to cast bitter, heavy, unmerited reproach upon my sweet mother's memory! For, listen, sir: you are known to have been the husband of the Countess Hurstmonceux for more years than I have lived in this world; you are known to have been so at the very time of my birth; you could not go about explaining the circumstances to everyone who would become acquainted with the facts, and the consequences would be what I said! No, father, leave me as I am; for, besides the reasons I have given, there is yet another reason why I may not take your name."

"What is that, Ishmael?" asked Brudenell, in a broken voice.

"It is, that in an hour of passionate grief, after hearing my mother's woeful story from the lips of my aunt, I fell upon that mother's grave and vowed to make her name—the only thing she had to leave me, poor mother!—illustrious. It was a piece of boyish vainglory, no doubt, but it was a vow, and I must try to keep it," said Ishmael, faintly smiling.

"You will keep it; you will make the name of Worth illustrious in the annals of the country, Ishmael," said Mr. Brudenell.

There was a pause for a little while, at the end of which the latter said:

"There is another way in which I may be able to accomplish my purpose, Ishmael. Without proclaiming you as my son, and risking the reproach you dread for your dear mother's memory, I might adopt you as my son, and appoint you as my heir. Will you make me happy by consenting to that measure, Ishmael?" inquired the father, in a persuasive tone.

"Dear sir, I cannot. Oh, do not think that I am insensible to all your kindness, for indeed I am not! I thank you; I love you; and I deeply sympathize with you in your disappointment; but—"

"But what, my son? what is the reason you cannot agree to this last proposal?" asked Mr. Brudenell, in a voice quivering with emotion.

"A strong spirit of independence, the growth of years of lonely struggle with the world, possesses and inspires me. I could not for an hour endure patronage or dependence, come they from where or how they might. It is the law of my life," said Ishmael firmly, but affectionately.

"It is a noble law, and yours has been a noble life, my son. But—is there nothing, nothing I can do for you to prove my affection, and to ease my heart, Ishmael?"

"Yes!" said the young man, after a pause. "When you return to England, you will see—Lady Vincent!" The name was uttered with a gasp. "Tell her what you have told me—the history of your acquaintance with my mother; your mutual love; your private marriage, and the unforeseen misfortune that wrecked your happiness! Tell her how pure and noble and lovely my young mother was! that her ladyship may know once for all Nora Worth was not"—Ishmael covered his face with his hands, and caught his breath, and continued—"not, as she said, 'the shame of her own sex and the scorn of ours'; that her son is not 'the child of sin,' nor 'his heritage dishonor!'" And Ishmael dropped his stately head upon his desk, and sobbed aloud; sobbed until all his athletic form shook with the storm of his great agony.

Herman Brudenell gazed at him—appalled. Then, rising, he laid his hand on the young man's shoulder, saying:

"Ishmael! Ishmael! don't do so! Calm yourself, my son; oh, my dear son, calm yourself!"

He might as well have spoken to a tempest. Sobs still shook Ishmael's whole frame.

"Oh, Heaven! oh, Heaven! Would to the Lord I had never been born!" cried Herman Brudenell, in a voice of such utter woe that Ishmael raised his head and struggled hard to subdue the storm of passion that was raging in his bosom. "Or would that I had died the day I met Nora, and before I had entailed all this anguish on you!" continued Herman Brudenell, amid groans and sighs.

"Don't say so, my father! don't say so! You were not in fault. You were as blameless as she herself was; and you could not have been more so," said Ishmael, wiping his fevered brow, and looking up.

"My generous son! But did Claudia—did Lady Vincent use the cruel words you have quoted, against your mother and yourself?"

"She did, my father. Oh, but I have suffered!" exclaimed Ishmael, with shaking voice and quivering features.

"I know you have; I know it, Ishmael; but you have grandly, gloriously conquered suffering," said Mr. Brudenell, with enthusiasm.

"Not quite conquered it yet; but I shall endeavor to do so," replied the young man, who had now quite regained his self-possession.

And another pause fell between them.

Ishmael leaned his head upon his hand and reflected deeply for a few moments. Then, raising his head, he said:

"My father, for her sake, our relationship must remain a secret from all the world, with the few exceptions of those intimate friends to whom you can explain the circumstances, and even to them it must be imparted in confidence. You will tell Lady Vincent, that her ladyship may know how false were the calumnies she permitted herself to repeat; and Judge Merlin and Mr. Middleton, whose kindness has entitled them to the confidence, for their own satisfaction."

"And no one else, Ishmael?"

"No one else in the world, my father. I myself will tell Uncle Reuben. And in public, my father, we must be discreet in our intercourse with each other. Forgive me if I speak in too dictatorial a manner; I speak for lips that are dumb in death. I speak as my dead mother's advocate," said Ishmael, with a strange blending of meekness and firmness in his tone and manner.

"And her advocate shall be heard and heeded, hard as his mandate seems. But, ah! I am an old and broken man, Ishmael. I had hoped, in time, to claim you as my son, and solace my age in your bright youth. I am grievously disappointed. Oh! would to Heaven I had taken charge of you in your infancy, and then you would not disclaim me now!" sighed Mr. Brudenell.

"I do not disclaim you, father. I only deprecate the publicity that might wound my mother's memory. And you are not old and broken, my father. How can you be—at forty-three? You are in the sunny summer noon of your life. But you are harassed and ill in mind and body; and you are very morbid and sensitive. You shun society, form no new ties with your fellow-creatures, and brood over that old sad tragedy long passed. Think no more of it, father; its wounds are long since healed in every heart but yours; my mother has been in heaven these many years; as long as I have been on earth; my birthday here was her birthday there! Therefore, brood no more over that sad time; it is forever past and gone. Think of your young love as much as you please; but think of her in heaven. It is not well to think forever of the Crucifixion and never of the Ascension; forever of the martyrdom that was but for a moment, and never of the glory that is from everlasting to everlasting. Nora was martyred; her martyrdom was as the grief of a moment; but she has ascended and her happiness is eternal in the heavens. Think of her so. And rouse yourself. Wake to the duties and pleasures of life. Look around upon and enjoy the beauty of the earth, the wisdom of man, the loveliness of woman, and the goodness of God. If you were a single man I should say 'marry again'; but as you are already a married man, though estranged from your wife, I say to you, seek a reconciliation with that lady. You are both in the prime of life."

"What! does Nora's son give me such advice?" inquired Brudenell, with a faint, incredulous smile.

"Yes, he does; as Nora herself in her wisdom and love would do, could she speak to you from heaven," said Ishmael solemnly Brudenell slowly and sorrowfully shook his head.

"The Countess of Hurstmonceux can nevermore be anything to me," he said.

"My father! have you then no kindly memory of the sweet young lady who placed her innocent affections upon you in your early manhood, and turning away from all her wealthy and titled suitors, gave herself and her fortune to you?"

Slowly and bitterly Herman Brudenell shook his head. Ishmael, still looking earnestly in his face continued:

"Who left her native country and her troops of friends, and crossed the sea alone, to follow you to a home that must have seemed like a wilderness, and servants that were like savages to her; who devoted her time and spent her money in embellishing your house and improving your land, and in civilizing and Christianizing your negroes; and who passed the flower of her youth in that obscure neighborhood, doing good and waiting patiently long, weary years for the return of the man she loved."

Still the bitter, bitter gesture of negation from Herman.

"Father," said Ishmael, fixing his beautiful eyes on Brudenell's face and speaking earnestly, "it seems to me that if any young lady had loved me with such devotion and constancy, I must have loved her fondly in return. I could not have helped doing so!"

"She wronged me, Ishmael!"

"And even if she had offended me—deeply and justly offended me—I must have forgiven her and taken her back to my bosom again."

"It was worse than that, Ishmael! It was no common offense. She deceived me! She was false to me!"

"I cannot believe it!" exclaimed Ishmael earnestly.

"Why, what ground have you for saying so? What can you know of it?"

"Because I do not easily think evil of women. My life has been short and my experience limited, I know; but as far as my observation instructs me, they are very much better than we are; they do not readily yield to evil; their tendencies are all good," said Ishmael fervently.

"Young man, you know a great deal of books, a great deal of law; but little of men, and less of women. A man of the world would smile to hear you say what you have just said, Ishmael."

"If I am mistaken, it is a matter to weep over, not to smile at!" said Ishmael gravely, and almost severely.

"It is true."

"But to return to your countess, my father. I am not mistaken in that lady's face, I know. I have not seen it since I was eight years old; but it is before me now! a sweet, sad, patient young face, full of holy love. Among the earliest memories of my life is that of the young Countess of Hurstmonceux, and the stories that were afloat concerning herself and you. It was said that every day at sunset she would go to the turnstile at the crossroads on the edge of the estate, where she could see all up and down two roads for many miles, and there stand watching to catch the first glimpse of you, if perhaps you might be returning home. She did this for years and years, until people began to say that she was crazed with hope deferred. It was at that very stile I first saw her. And when I looked at her lovely face and thought of her many charities—for there was no suffering from poverty in that neighborhood while she lived there—I felt that she was an angel!"

"Aye! a fallen angel, Ishmael!"

"No, father! no! my life and soul on her truth and love! Children are good judges of character, you know! And I was but eight years old on the occasion of which I speak! I was carrying a basket of tools for the 'professor,' whose assistant I was; and who would have carried them himself only that his back was bent beneath a load of kitchen utensils, for we had been plastering a cistern all day and in coming home took these things to mend in the evening. And as we passed down the road we saw this lovely lady leaning on the stile. And she called me to her and laid her hand on my head and looked in my face very tenderly, and turning to the professor, said: 'This child is too young for so heavy a burden.' And she took out her purse and would have given me an eagle, only that Aunt Hannah had taught me never to take money that I had not earned."

"Grim Hannah! It is a marvel she had not starved you with her scruples, Ishmael! But what else passed between you and the countess?"

"Not much! but if she was sorry for me, I was quite as sorry for her."

"There was a bond of sympathy between you which you felt without understanding at the time!"

"There was; though I mistook its precise character. Seeing that she wore black, I said: 'Have you also lost your mother, my lady, and are you in deep mourning for her?' And she answered, 'I am in deep mourning for my dead happiness, child!'"

"For her dead honor, she might have said!"

"Father! the absent are like the dead; they cannot defend themselves," said Ishmael.

"That is true; and I stand rebuked! And henceforth, whatever I may think, I will never speak evil of the Countess of Hurstmonceux."

"Go farther yet, dear sir! seek an explanation with her, and my word on it she will be able to confute the calumnies, or clear up the suspicious circumstances or whatever it may have been that has shaken your confidence in her, and kept you apart so long."

"Ishmael it is a subject that I have never broached to the countess, and one that I could not endure to discuss with her!"

"What, my father? Would you forever condemn her unheard? We do not treat our worst criminals so!"

"Spare me, my son! for I have spared her!"

"If by sparing her you mean that you have left her alone, you had better not spared her; you had better sought divorce; then one of two things would have happened—either she would have disproved the charges brought against her, or she would have been set free! either alternative much better than her present condition."

"I could not drag my domestic troubles into a public courtroom, Ishmael!"

"Not when justice required it, father?—But you are going down into the neighborhood of Brudenell Hall! You will hear of her from the people among whom she lived for so many years, and who cherish her memory as that of an angel of mercy, and—you will change your opinion of her."

Herman Brudenell smiled incredulously, and then said:

"Apropos of my visit to Brudenell Hall! I hope, Ishmael, that you will be able to join me there in the course of the summer?"

"Father, yes! I promise you to do so. I will be at pains to put my business in such train as will enable me to visit you for a week or two."

"Thanks, Ishmael! And now, do you know I think the first dinner bell rang some time ago and it is time to dress?"

And Herman Brudenell arose, and after pressing Ishmael's hand, left the library.

The interview furnished Ishmael with too much food for thought to admit of his moving for some time. He sat by the table in a brown study, reflecting upon all that he had heard, until he was suddenly startled by the pealing out of the second bell. Then he sprang up, hurried to his chamber, hastily arranged his toilet, and went down into the dining room, where he found all the family already assembled and waiting for him.

CHAPTER IV

BEE.

And coldly from that noble heart,

In all its glowing youth,

His lore had turned and spurned apart

Its tenderness and truth—

Let him alone to live, or die—

Alone!—Yet, who is she? Some guardian angel from the sky,

To bless and aid him?—Bee!

—Anon.

Ishmael received many other invitations. One morning, while he was seated at the table in his office, Walter Middleton entered, saying:

"Ishmael, leave reading over those stupid documents and listen to me. I am going to Saratoga for a month. Come with me; it will do you good."

"Thank you all the same, Walter; but I cannot leave the city now," said Ishmael.

"Nonsense! there is but little doing; and now, if ever, you should take some recreation."

"But I am busy with getting up some troublesome cases for the next term."

"And that's worse than nonsense! Leave the cases alone until the court sits; take some rest and recreation and you will find it pay well in renewed vigor of body and mind. I that tell you so am an M. D., you know."

"I thank you, Dr. Middleton, and when I find myself growing weak I will follow your prescription," smiled Ishmael, rising and beginning to tie up his documents.

"And that's a signal for my dismissal, I suppose. Off to the City Hall again this morning?" inquired Walter.

"Yes; to keep an appointment," replied Ishmael. And the friends separated.

Later in the day, when the young attorney had returned and was spending his leisure hour in going on with the book-packing, Judge Merlin entered and threw himself into a chair and for some moments watched the packer.

"What is that you are doing now, Ishmael? Oh, I see; doctoring a sick book!"

"Well, I dislike to see a fine volume that has served us faithfully and seen hard usage perish for the want of a moment's attention; it is but that which is required when we have the mucilage at hand," he said, smiling and pointing to the bottle and brush, and then deposited the book in its packing-case.

"But that is not what I come to talk to you about. Have you found a proper room for an office yet?"

"Yes; I have a suite of rooms on the first floor of a house on Louisiana Avenue. The front room I shall use for a public office, the middle one for a private office, and the back one, which opens upon a pleasant porch and a garden, for a bedchamber; for I shall lodge there and board with the family," replied Ishmael.

"That seems to be a pleasant arrangement. But, Ishmael, take my advice and engage a clerk immediately;—you will want one before long, anyhow—and put him in your rooms to watch your business, and do you take a holiday. Come down to Tanglewood for a month. You need the change. After the wilderness of houses and men you want the world of trees and birds. At least I do, and I judge you by myself."

Ishmael smiled, thanked his kind friend cordially, and then, in terms as courteous as he could devise, declined the invitation, giving the same reasons for doing so that he had already given first to Mr. Brudenell and next to Walter Middleton.

"Well, Ishmael, I will not urge you, for I know by past experience when you have once made up your mind to a course of conduct you deem right, nothing on earth will turn you aside from it. But see here! why do you go through all that drudgery? Why not order Powers to pack those books?"

"Powers is a pearl in his own way; but he cannot pack books; and besides, he has no respect for them."

"No feeling, you mean! he would not dress their wounds before putting them to bed in those boxes!"

"No."

"Well, 'a wilfu' mon maun ha' his way,'" said the judge, taking up the evening paper and burying himself in its perusal. That same night, while Ishmael, having finished his day's work, was refreshing himself by strolling through the garden, inhaling the fragrance of flowers, listening to the gleeful chirp of the joyous little insects, and watching the light of the stars, he heard an advancing step behind him, and presently his arm was taken by Mr. Middleton, who, walking on with him, said:

"What are you going to do with yourself, Ishmael?"

"Put myself to work like a beaver!"

"Humph! that will be nothing new for you. But I came out here to induce you to reconsider that resolution. I wish to persuade you to join us at Beacon House. That high promontory stretching far out to sea and exposed to all the sea breezes will be the very place to recruit your health at. Come, what say you?"

Ishmael's eyes grew moist as he grasped Mr. Middleton's hand and said:

"Three invitations of this sort I have already had—this is the fourth. My friends are too kind. I know not how I have won such friendship or deserved such kindness. But I cannot avail myself of the pleasant quarters they offer me. I cannot, at present, leave Washington, except at such a sacrifice of professional duties as they would not wish me to make. Mr. Middleton, I thank you heartily all the same."

"Well, Ishmael, I am sorry to lose your company; but not sorry for the cause of the loss. The pressure of business that confines you to the city during the recess argues much for your popularity and success. But, my dear boy, pray consider my invitation as a standing one, and promise me to avail yourself of it the first day you can do so."

"Thank you; that I will gladly do, Mr. Middleton."

"And when you come, remain with us as long as you can without neglecting your duty."

"Indeed I will."

At that moment a light rustle through the bushes was heard and Bee joined them, saying:

"Papa, if I were to tell you the dew is falling heavily and the grass is wet, and it is not good for you or Ishmael to be out here, you might not heed me. But when I say that uncle has gone with General Tourneysee to a political pow-wow, and mamma and myself are quite alone and would like to amuse ourselves with a game of whist, perhaps you will come in and be our partners."

"Why, certainly, Busy Bee; for if anyone in this world deserves play after work it is you," replied Mr. Middleton.

"Right face! forward! march!" then said Bee; and she led her captives out of the night air and into the house.

Early the next morning Ishmael was surprised by a fifth invitation to a country house. It was contained in a letter from Reuben Gray, which was as follows:

"Woodside,—Monday Morning. "My Deer Ishmael:—Hannah and me, we hav bin a havin of a talk about you. You see the judge he wrote to me a spell back, a orderin of me to have the house got reddy for him comin home. And he menshunned, permiskuously like, as you was not lookin that well as you orter. But Hannah and me, we thort as how is was all along o that botheration law business as you was upset on your helth. And as how you'd get better when the Court riz. But now the Court is riz, and pears like you aint no ways better from all accounts. And tell you how we knowed. See Hannah and me, we got a letter from Mrs. Whaley as keeps the 'Farmers.' Well she rote to Hannah and me to send her up some chickins and duks and eggs and butter and other fresh frutes and vegetubbles, which she sez as they doo ask sich onlawful prices for em in the city markits as she cant conshuenshusly giv it. So she wants Hannah and me to soopli her. And mabee we may and mabee we maynt; but that's nyther here nur there. Wot Hannah and me wants to say is this—as how Mrs. Whaley she met you in the street incerdentul. And she sez as how she newer saw no wun look no wusser than you do! Now, Ishmael, Hannah and me, we sees how it is. Youre a-killin of yourself jest as fast as ever you can, which is no better than Susanside, because it is agin natur and agin rillijun to kill wunself for a livin. So Hannah and me, we wants you to drap everythink rite outen your hands and kum home to us. Wot you want is a plenty of good kuntre air and water, and nun o your stifeld up streets and pizen pumps. And plenty o good kuntre eetin and drinkin and nun o your sickly messes. So you kum. Hannah and me is got a fine caff and fat lamm to kill soon as ever you git here. And lots o young chickins and duks. And the gratest kwontity o frute, peeehes, peers, plums, and kanterlopes and warter millions in plenty. And the hamberg grapes is kummin on. And we hav got a noo cow, wun o the sort cawld durrums, which she doo give the richest milk as ever you drinked and if ennything will set you up it is that. And likewise we hav got the noo fashund fowls as people are all runnin mad about. They cawl em shank hyes pun count o there long leggs, which they is about the longest as ever you saw. And the way them fowls doo stryde and doo eet is a cawshun to housekeepers. They gobble up everything. And wot doo you think. You know Sally's brestpin, as Jim bawt her for a kristmus gift. Well she happened to drap it offen her buzzum, inter the poultry yard, and soons ever she mist it she run rite out after it; but the shank-hye rooster he run fastern she did with his long legs and gobbled it rite down, afore his eyes. And the poor gals bin a howlin and bawlin and brakin of her poor hart ebout it ever since. She wanted us—Hannah and me to kill the shank-hye; to git the brestpin; but as we had onlee a pare on em we tolde her how it was too vallabel for that. But Hannah and me we give the shank hye a dose of eepeekak, in hope it would make him throw up the brestpin; but it dident; for the eepeekak set on his stomik like an angel, as likewise did the brestpin; and Hannah and me thinks he diggested em both. Well, they aint daintee in their wittels them shank hyes. Now bee shure to kum, Ishmael. Hannah and me and the young uns and Sally will awl be so glad to see you and you can role in clover awl day if you like. And now I have ralely no more noose to tell you; only that I rote this letter awl outen my own hed without Hannah helpin of me. Dont you think as Ime improvin? Hannah and the little uns and Sally jine me in luv to you mi deer Ishmael. And Ime your effectshunit frend till deth do us part. "Reuben Gray.

"Post Cript. Ive jist redd this letter to Hannah. And she doo say as every uther wurd is rote rong. I dont think they is; becawse Ive got a sartain roole to spell rite; which is—I think how a word sownde and then I spell it accordin. But law, Ishmael! ever sense Hannah has been teechin them young uns o ourn to reede there primmers, shes jest got to be the orfullest Bloo Stokkin as evver was. Dont tell her I sed so tho, for she ralely is wun of the finest wimmin livin and Ime prowd of her and her young uns. So no more at present onle kum. "R.G."

Grateful for this kind invitation as he had been for any that had been given him, Ishmael sat down immediately and answered the letter, saying to Reuben, as he had said to others, that he would thankfully accept his offered hospitality as soon as his duties would permit him to do so.

The last day of the family's sojourn in town came. On the morning of that day Mr. Brudenell took leave of his friends and departed, exacting from Ishmael a renewal of his promise to visit Brudenell Hall in the course of the summer. On that last day Ishmael completed the packing of the books and sent them off to the boat that was to convey them to the Tanglewood landing. And then he had all his own personal effects conveyed to his new lodgings. And finally he sought an interview with Bee. That was not so easily obtained, however. Bee was excessively busy on this last day. But Ishmael, with the privilege of an inmate, went through the house, looking for her, until he found her in the family storeroom, busy among the jars and cans, and attended by her maids.

"Come in, Ishmael, for this concerns you," she said pleasantly.

And Ishmael entered, wondering what he could be supposed to have to do with preserved fruits and potted meats.

Bee pointed to a box that was neatly packed with small jars, saying:

"There, Ishmael—there are some sealed fruits and vegetables, and some spiced meats and fish, and a bachelor's lamp and kettle, in that case which Ann is closing down. They are yours. Direct Jim where to find your lodgings, and he will take them there in the wheelbarrow. And there is a keg of crackers and biscuits to go with them."

"Dearest Bee, I am very grateful; but why should you give me all these things?" inquired Ishmael, in surprise.

"Because you are going away from home, and you will want them. Yes, you will, Ishmael, though you don't think so now. Often business will detain you out in the evening until after your boarding-house supper is over. Then how nice to have the means at hand to get a comfortable little meal for yourself in your own room without much trouble. Why, Ishmael, we always put up such a box as this for Walter when he leaves us. And do you think that mamma or I would make any difference between you?"

"You have always been a dear—yes, the dearest of sisters to me! and some day, Bee—" He stopped, and looked around. The maids were at some distance, but still he felt that the family storeroom was not exactly the place to say what was on his heart for her, so he whispered the question:

"How long will you be engaged here, dear Bee?"

"Until tea time. It will take me quite as long as that to get through what I have to do."

"And then, Bee?"

"Then I shall be at leisure to pass this last evening with you, Ishmael," answered Bee, meeting his wish with the frankness of pure affection.

"And will you walk with me in the garden after tea? It will be our last stroll together there," he said rather sadly.

"Yes; I will walk with you, Ishmael. The garden is lovely just at sunset."

"Thank you, dearest Bee. Ah! how many times a day I have occasion to speak these words!"

"I wish you would leave them off altogether, then, Ishmael. I always understand that you thank me far more than I deserve."

"Never! How could I? 'Thank you!' they are but two words. How could they repay you, Bee? Dearest, this evening you shall know how much I thank you. Until then, farewell." He pressed her hand and left her.

Now Ishmael was far too clear-sighted not to have seen that Bee had fixed her pure maidenly affections upon him, and to see also that Bee's choice was well approved by her parents, who had long loved him as a son. While Ishmael's hands had been busy with the book-packing his thoughts had been busy with Bee and with the problem that her love presented him. He had loved Claudia with an all-absorbing passion. But she had left him and married another, and so stricken a deathblow to his love. But this love was dying very hard, and in its death-struggles was rending and tearing the heart which was its death-bed.

And in the meantime Bee's love was alive and healthy, and it was fixed on him. He was not insensible, indifferent, ungrateful for this dear love. Indeed, it was the sweetest solace that he had in this world. He felt in the profoundest depths of his heart all the loveliness of Bee's nature. And most tenderly he loved her—as a younger sister. What then should he do? Offer to Bee the poor, bleeding heart that Claudia had played with, broken, and cast aside as worthless? All that was true, noble, and manly in Ishmael's nature responded:

"God forbid!"

But what then should he do? Leave her to believe him insensible, indifferent, ungrateful? Strike such a deathblow to her loving heart as Claudia had stricken to his? All that was generous, affectionate and devoted in Ishmael's nature cried out: "No! forbid it, angels in heaven!"

But what then could he do? The magnanimity of his nature answered:

"Open your heart to her; that she may know all that is in it; then lay that heart at her feet, for accepting or rejecting."

And this he resolved to do. And this resolution sent him to beg this interview with Bee. Yet before going to keep it he determined to speak to Mr. Middleton. He felt certain that Mr. Middleton would indorse his addresses to his daughter; yet still his fine sense of honor constrained him to seek the consent of the father before proposing to the daughter. And with this view in mind immediately upon leaving Bee he sought Mr. Middleton.

He found that gentleman walking about in the garden, enjoying his afternoon cigar. In these afternoon promenades Mr. Middleton, who was the shorter and slighter as well as the older man, often did Ishmael the honor of leaning upon his arm. And now Ishmael went up to his side and with a smile silently offered the usual support.

"Thank you, my boy! I was just feeling the want of your friendly arm. My limbs are apt to grow tired of walking before my eyes are satiated with gazing or my mind with reflecting on the beauty of the summer evening," said Mr. Middleton, slipping his arm within that of Ishmael.

"Sir," said the young man, blushing slightly, "a selfish motive has brought me to your side this afternoon."

"A selfish motive, Ishmael! I do not believe that you are capable of entertaining one," smiled Mr. Middleton.

"Indeed, yes, sir; you will say so when you hear of it."

"Let me hear of it, then, Ishmael, for the novelty of the thing."

The young man hesitated for a few moments and then said:

"Mr. Middleton—Mr. Brudenell has, I believe, put you in possession of the facts relative to my birth?"

"Yes, my dear Ishmael; but let me assure you that I did not need to be told of them. Do you remember the conversation we had upon the subject years ago? It was the morning after the school party when that miserable craven, Alfred Burghe, disgraced himself by insulting you. You said, Ishmael, 'My mother was a pure and honorable woman! Oh, believe it!' I did believe it then, Ishmael; for your words and tones and manner carried irresistible conviction to my mind. And every year since I have been confirmed in my belief. You, Ishmael, are the pledge of your parents' honor as well as of their love. 'Men do not gather grapes of thorns, nor figs of thistles,'" said Mr. Middleton earnestly.

"And yet, sir, I have suffered and may again suffer reproach that neither myself nor my parents deserved," said Ishmael gravely.

"You never will again, Ishmael. You have overcome the world."

"Thank you! thank you, sir! I purposely reminded you of this old injustice. You do not regard me the less for having suffered it?"

"The less! No, my boy; but the more, for having overcome it!"

"Again I thank you from the depths of my heart. You have known me from boyhood, Mr. Middleton; and you may be said to know my character and my prospects better than anyone else in the world does; better, even, than I know them myself."

"I think that quite likely to be true."

"Well, sir, I hope in a few years to gain an established reputation and a moderate competency by my practice at the bar."

"You will gain fame and wealth, Ishmael."

"Well, sir, if ever by the blessing of Heaven I do attain these distinctions, taking everything else into consideration, would you, sir, would you then—"

"What, Ishmael? Speak out, my boy?"

"Accept me as a son?"

"Do you want me to give you Bee?" gravely inquired Mr. Middleton.

"When I shall be more worthy of her, I do."

"Have you Bee's consent to speak to me on this subject?"

"No, sir; I have not yet addressed Miss Middleton. I could not venture to do so without your sanction. It is to obtain it that I have come to you this evening. I would like very much to have an understanding with Miss Middleton before we part for an indefinite time."

Mr. Middleton fell into deep thought. It was some minutes before he spoke. When he did, it was to say:

"Ishmael, Bee is my eldest daughter and favorite child."

"I know it, sir," answered the young man.

"Parents ought not to have favorites among their children; but how can I help it? Bee is almost an angel."

"I know it, sir," said Ishmael.

"Oh, yes; you know it! you know it!" exclaimed Mr. Middleton, half laughing and not far from crying; "but do you know what you do when you ask a father to give up his best beloved daughter?"

"Indeed I think I do, sir; but—daughters must some time or other become wives," said Ishmael, with a deprecating smile.

"Yes, it is true!" sighed Mr. Middleton. "Well, Ishmael, since in the course of nature I must some day give my dear daughter up, I would rather give her to you than to any man on earth, for I have a great esteem and affection for you, Ishmael."

"Indeed, sir, it is mutual!" replied the young man, grasping the hand of his friend.

"It is just the state of feeling that should exist between father-and son-in-law," said Mr. Middleton.

"I have your sanction, then, to speak to Bee?"

"Yes, Ishmael, yes; I will give her to you! But not yet, my dear boy; for several reasons not just yet! You are both very young yet; you are but little over twenty-one; she scarcely nineteen; and besides her mother still needs her assistance in taking care of the children; and I—must get used to the idea of parting with her; so you must wait a year or two longer, Ishmael! She is well worth waiting for."

"I know it! Oh, I know it well, sir! I have seen women as beautiful, as amiable, and as accomplished; but I never, no, never met with one so 'altogether lovely' as Bee! And I thank you, sir! Oh, I thank you more than tongue can tell for the boon you have granted me. You will not lose your daughter, sir; but you will gain a son; and I will be a true son to you. sir, as Heaven hears me! And to her I will be a true lover and husband. Her happiness shall be the very first object in my life, sir; nothing in this world over which I have the slightest control shall be suffered to come into competition with it."

"I am—I am sure of that, my boy!" replied Mr. Middleton, in a broken voice.

"And I do not presume to wish to hurry either you or her, sir; I am willing to wait your leisure and hers; all I want now is to have an understanding with Bee, and to be admitted to the privileges of an accepted lover. You could trust me so far, sir?"

"Trust you so far! Why, Ishmael, there is no limit to my trust in you!"

"And Mrs. Middleton, sir?"

"Why, Ishmael, she loves you as one of her own children; and I do think you would disappoint and grieve her if you were to marry out of the family. I will break the matter to Mrs. Middleton. Go find Bee, and speak to her of this matter, and when you have won her consent, bring her to me that I may join your hands and bless your betrothal."

Ishmael fervently pressed the hand of his kind friend and left him.

Of course Bee, who was still busy with her maids in the store-room, was not to be spoken to on that subject at that hour. But Ishmael went up to his own room to reflect.

Perhaps the whole key to Ishmael's conduct in this affair might have been found in the words he used when pleading with his father the cause of the Countess of Hurstmonceux; he said:

"It seems to me, if any young lady had loved me so, I must have loved her fondly in return; I could not have helped doing so."

And he could not. There was something too warm, generous, and noble in Nora's son to be so insensible as all that.

His inspiration also instructed him that not the beautiful and imperious Claudia, but the lovely and loving Bee was his Heaven-appointed wife.

He was inspired when in his agony that dreadful night he had cried out: "By a woman came sin and death into the world, and by a woman came redemption and salvation! Oh! Claudia, my Eve, farewell! And Bee, my Mary, hail!"

And now that he was about to betroth himself to Bee, and make her happy, he himself felt happier than he had been for many days. He felt sure, too, that when his heart should recover from its wounds he should love Bee with a deeper, higher, purer, and more lasting affection than ever his fierce passion for Claudia could have become.

CHAPTER V

SECOND LOVE.

The maiden loved the young man well,

And pined for many a day,

Because that star-eyed, queenly belle

Had won his heart away.

But now the young man chooses well

Between the beauteous pair,

The proud and brilliant dark-haired belle,

And gentle maiden fair.

—M. F. Tupper

After tea Ishmael, having missed Bee from the drawing room, went out into the garden, expecting to find her there. Not seeing her, he walked up and down the gravel walk, waiting for her appearance.

Presently she came up, softly and silently, and joined him.

"Thanks, dearest Bee," he said, as he drew her arm within his own.

"It is a beautiful evening, Ishmael; I have never seen the garden look more lovely," said Bee.

And it was indeed a beautiful evening and a lovely scene. The sun had just set; but all the western horizon and the waters of the distant river were aflame with crimson fire of his reflected rays; while over the eastern hills the moon and stars were shining from the dark gray heavens. In the garden, the shrubs and flowers, not yet damp with dew, were sending forth their richest fragrance; the latest birds were twittering softly before settling themselves to sleep in their leafy nests; and the earliest insects were tuning up their tiny, gleeful pipes before commencing their evening concert.

"This garden is a very pleasant place, quite as pleasant as Tanglewood, if uncle would only think so," said Bee.

"Yes, it is very pleasant. You do not like the plan of returning to the country, Bee?" said Ishmael.

"No, indeed, I do not; breaking up and parting is always a painful process." And Bee's lips quivered and the tears came into her eyes.

Ishmael pressed the little hand that lay light as a snowflake on his arm, drew it closer within his embrace, and turned down the narrow path that led to the remote arbor situated far down in the angle of the wall in the bottom of the garden.

He led her to a seat, placed himself beside her, took her hand, and said:

"It is here, dearest Bee—here in the scene of my humiliation and of my redemption—that I would say to you all I have to say; that I would lay my heart open before you, and place it at your feet, for spurning, or for blessing."

She looked up at him with surprise, but also with infinite affection in her innocent and beautiful eyes. Then, as she read the truth in his earnest gaze, her eyes fell, and her color rose.

"And dearest Bee, I have your father's sanction for what I do, for without it I would not act."

Her eyes were still fixed upon the ground, but her hand that he clasped in his throbbed like a heart. And oh! he felt how entirely she loved him; and he felt that he could devote his whole life to her.

"Dearest of all dear ones, Bee, listen to me. Not many days have passed, since, one evening, you came to this arbor, seeking one that was lost and found—me!"

She began to tremble.

"You know how you found me, Bee," he said sadly and solemnly.

"Oh, Ishmael, dear!" she cried, with an accent of sharp pain, "do not speak of that evening! forget it and let me forget it! it is past!"

"Dearest girl, only this once will I pain you by alluding to that sorrowful and degrading hour. You found me—I will not shrink from uttering the word, though it will scorch my lips to speak it and burn your ears to hear it—you found me—intoxicated."

"Oh, Ishmael, dear, you were not to blame! it was not your fault! it was an accident—a misfortune!" she exclaimed, as blushes burned upon her cheeks and tears suffused her eyes.

"How much I blamed, how much I loathed myself, dearest Bee, you can never know! Let that pass. You found me as I said. Actually and bodily I was lying on this bench, sleeping the stupid sleep of intoxication; but morally and spiritually I was slipping over the brink of an awful chasm.

Bee, dearest Bee! dearest saving angel! it was this little hand of yours that drew me back, so softly that I scarcely knew I had been in danger of ruin until that danger was past. And, Bee, since that day many days of storm have passed, but the face of my saving angel has ever looked out from among the darkest clouds a bright rainbow of promise. I did not perish in the storm, because her sweet face ever looked down upon me!"

Bee did not attempt to reply; she could not; she sat with her flushed and tearful eyes bent upon the ground.

"Love, do you know this token?" he inquired, in a voice shaking with agitation, as he drew from his bosom a little wisp of white cambric and laid it in her lap.

"It is my—my—" she essayed to answer, but her voice failed.

"It is your dear handkerchief," he said, as he took it, pressed it to his lips, and replaced it in his bosom. "It is your dear handkerchief! When you found me as you did, in your loving kindness you laid it over my face—mine! so utterly unworthy to be so delicately veiled! Oh, Bee, if I could express to you all I felt! all I thought! when I recognized this dear token and so discovered who it was that had sought me when I was lost, and dropped tears of sorrow over me! and then covered my face from the blistering sun and the stinging flies—if I could tell you all that I suffered and resolved, then you would feel and know how earnest and sincere is the heart that at last—at last, my darling, I lay at your beloved feet."

She looked up at him for a moment and breathed a single word—a name that seemed to escape her lips quite involuntarily—"Claudia!"

"Yes, my darling," he said, in tones vibrating with emotion, "it is as you suppose, or rather it was so! You have divined my secret, which indeed I never intended to keep as a secret from you. Yes, Bee; I loved another before loving you. I loved her whom you have just named. I love her no longer. When by her marriage with another my love would have become sinful, it was sentenced to death and executed. But, Bee, it died hard, very hard; and in its violent death-throes it rent and tore my heart, as the evil spirit did the possessed man, when it was driven out of him. Bee, my darling," said Ishmael, smiling for the first time since commencing the interview, "this may seem to you a very fanciful way of putting the case; but is a good one, for in no other manner could I give you to understand how terrible my sufferings have been for the last few weeks, how completely my evil passion has perished; and yet how sore and weak it has left my heart. Bee, it is this heart, wounded and bleeding from a dead love, yet true and single in its affection for you, that I open before you and lay at your feet. Spurn it away from you, Bee, and I cannot blame you. Raise it to your own and I shall love and bless you."

Bee burst into tears.

He put his arm around her and drew her to his side and she dropped her head upon his shoulder and wept passionately. Many times she tried to speak, but failed. At last, when she had exhausted all her passion, she raised her head from its resting-place. He wiped the tears from her eyes and stooping, whispered:

"You will not reject me, Bee, because I loved another woman once?"

"No," she answered softly, "for if you loved another woman before me, you could not help it, Ishmael. It is not that I am concerned about."

"What then, dearest love? Speak out," he whispered.

"Oh, Ishmael, tell me truly one thing;" and she hid her face on his shoulder while she breathed the question: "Isn't it only for my sake, to please me and make me happy, that you offer me your love, Ishmael?" She spoke so low, with her face so muffled on his shoulder, that he scarcely understood her; so he bent his head and inquired:

"What is it that you say, dear Bee?"

She tried to speak more clearly, for it seemed with her a point of principle to put this question; but her voice was, if possible, lower and more agitated than before, so that he had to stoop closely and listen intently to catch her words as she answered:

"Do you not offer me your love, only because—because you have found out—found out somehow or other that I—that I loved you first?"

He clasped her suddenly close to his heart, and whispered eagerly:

"I offer you my love because I love you, best and dearest of all dear ones!" And he felt at that moment that he did love her entirely.

She was sobbing softly on his shoulder; but presently through her tears she said:

"And will my love do you any good, make you any happier, compensate you a little for all that you have missed in losing that brilliant one?"

He held her closely to his heart while he stooped and answered:

"Dearest, your love has always been the greatest earthly blessing Heaven ever bestowed upon my life! I thank Heaven that the blindness and madness of my heart is past and gone, and I am enabled to see and understand this! Your love, Bee, is the only earthly thing that can comfort all the sorrows that may come into my life, or crown all its joys. You will believe this, dearest Bee, when you remember that I never in my life varied from the truth to anyone, and least of all would I prevaricate with you. I love you. Bee, let those three words answer all your doubts!"

Brightly and beautifully she smiled up at him through her tears.

"All is well, then, Ishmael! For all that I desire in this world is the privilege of making you happy!"

"Then you are my own!" he said, stooping and kissing the sparkling tears that hung like dew-drops on the red roses of her cheeks; and holding her to his heart, in profound religious joy and gratitude, he bowed his head and said:

"Oh, Father in Heaven! how I thank thee for this dear girl! Oh, make me every day more worthy of her love, and of thy many blessings!"

And soon after this Ishmael, happier than he ever thought it possible to be in this world, led forth from the arbor his betrothed bride.

He led her at once to the house and to the presence of her parents, whom he found in their private sitting room.

Standing before them and holding her hand, he said:

"She has promised to be my wife, and we are here for your blessing."

"You have it, my children! You have it with all my heart! May the Lord in heaven bless with his choicest blessings Ishmael and Beatrice!" said Mr. Middleton earnestly.

"Amen," said Mrs. Middleton.

Later in the evening Judge Merlin was informed of the engagement. And after congratulating the betrothed pair he turned to Mr. and Mrs. Middleton and said:

"Heaven knows how I envy you your son-in-law."

The gratified parents smiled, for they were proud of Ishmael, and what he would become. But Walter Middleton grinned and said:

"Heaven may know that, Uncle Merlin; but I know one thing!"

"What is that, Jackanapes?"

"I know they may thank Bee for their son-in-law, for she did all the courting!"

The panic-stricken party remained silent for a moment, and then Judge Merlin said:

"Well, sir! I know another thing!"

"And what is that, uncle?"

"That it will be a long time before you find a young lady to do you such an honor!"

Everybody laughed, not at the brilliancy of the joke, for the joke was not brilliant, but because they were happy; and when people are happy they do honor to very indifferent jests.

But Bee turned a ludicrously appalled look upon her lover and whispered:

"Oh, Ishmael! suppose he had known about that little bit of white cambric. He would have said that I had 'thrown the handkerchief' to you! And so I did! it is a dreadful reflection!"

"That handkerchief was a plank thrown to the drowning, Bee. It saved me from being whelmed in the waves of ruin. Oh, dearest, under heaven, you were my salvation!" said Ishmael, with emotion.

"Your comfort, Ishmael—only your comfort. Your own right- mindedness, 'under heaven,' would have saved you."

This was the last and the happiest evening they all spent at the city home together. Early in the morning they separated.

Judge Merlin and his servants started for Tanglewood, and Mr. and Mrs. Middleton and their family for The Beacon, where Ishmael promised as soon as possible to join them. Walter Middleton left for Saratoga. And, last of all, Ishmael locked up the empty house, took charge of the key, and departed to take possession of his new lodgings—alone, but blessed and happy.

CHAPTER VI

AT WOODSIDE.

Who can describe the sweets of country life

But those blest men that do enjoy and taste them?

Plain husbandmen, though far below our pitch

Of fortune placed, enjoy a wealth above us:

They breathe a fresh and uncorrupted air,

And in sweet homes enjoy untroubled sleep.

Their state is fearless and secure, enriched

With several blessings such as greatest kings

Might in true justice envy, and themselves

Would count too happy if they truly knew them.

—May.

Ishmael was settled in his new apartments on the first floor of a comfortable house on Louisiana Avenue. The front room opening upon the street, and having his name and profession engraved upon a silver plate attached to the door, was his public office; the middle room was his private office; and the back room, which opened upon a pleasant porch leading into the garden, was his bed-chamber.

The house was kept by two sisters, maiden ladies of venerable age, who took no other boarders or lodgers.

So, upon the whole, Ishmael's quarters were very comfortable.

The rapid increase of his business justified him in taking a clerk; and then in a week or two, as he saw this clerk over-tasked, he took a second; both young men who had not been very successful barristers, but who were very good office lawyers.

And Ishmael's affairs went on "swimmingly."

Of course there were hours when he sadly missed the companionship of the congenial family circle with whom he had been so long connected; but Ishmael was not one to murmur over the ordinary troubles of life. He rather made the best of his position and steadily looked on the bright side.

Besides, he maintained a regular correspondence with his friends. That correspondence was the only recreation and solace he allowed himself.

Almost every day he wrote to Bee, and he received answers to every one of his letters—answers full of affection, encouragement, and cheerfulness.

And at least once a week he got letters from Judge Merlin, Mr. Middleton, and Mr. Brudenell, all of whom continued to urge him to pay them visits as soon as his business would permit. Only one more letter he got from Reuben Gray; for letter writing was to poor Reuben a most difficult and dreaded task; and this one was merely to say that they should expect Ishmael down soon.

From Judge Merlin's letters it appeared that Lord and Lady Vincent had extended their tour into Canada East, and were now in the neighborhood of the "Thousand Isles," but that they expected to visit the judge at Tanglewood some time during the autumn; after which they intended to sail for Europe.

Ishmael continued to push his business for six or seven weeks, so that it was near the first of September before he found leisure to take a holiday and pay his promised visits.

Two weeks was the utmost length of time he could allow himself. And there were four places that seemed to have equal claims upon his society. Where should he go first? Truly Ishmael was embarrassed with the riches of his friendships.

At Woodside were Hannah and Reuben, who had cared for him in his orphaned infancy, and who really seemed to have the first right to him.

And at Tanglewood Judge Merlin was alone, moping for the want of his lost daughter and needing the consolation of a visit from Ishmael.

At the Beacon was his betrothed bride, who was also anxious to see him.

And finally, at Brudenell Hall was Herman Brudenell; and Herman Brudenell was—his father!

After a little reflection Ishmael's right-mindedness decided in favor of Woodside. Hannah had stood in his mother's place towards him, and to Hannah he would go first.

So, to get there by the shortest route, Ishmael took passage in the little steamer "Errand Boy," that left Georgetown every week for the mouth of the river, stopping at all the intervening landing-places.

Ishmael started on Friday morning and on Saturday afternoon was set ashore at Shelton, whence a pleasant walk of three miles through the forest that bordered the river brought him to Woodside.

Clean and cheerful was the cottage, gleaming whitely forth here and there from its shadowy green foliage and clustering red roses. The cottage and the fence had been repainted, and the gravel walk that led from the wicket-gate to the front door had been trimmed and rolled. And very dainty looked the white, fringed curtains and the green paper blinds at the front windows.

Evidently everything had been brightened up and put into holiday attire to welcome Ishmael.

While his hand was on the latch of the gate he was perceived from within, and the front door flew open and all the family rushed out to receive him—Reuben and Hannah, and the two children and Sally and the dog—the latter was as noisy and sincere in his welcome as any of the human friends, barking round and round the group to express his sympathy and joy and congratulations.

"I told Hannah how you'd come to us fust; I did! Didn't I, Hannah, my dear?" said Reuben triumphantly, as he shook both Ishmael's hands with an energy worthy of a blacksmith.

"Well, I knew he would too! It didn't need a prophet nor one to rise from the dead to tell us that Ishmael would be true to his old friends," said Hannah, pushing Reuben away and embracing Ishmael with a—

"How do you do, my boy? You look better than I expected to see you after your hard year's work."

"Oh, I am all right, thank you, Aunt Hannah. Coming to see you has set me up!" laughed Ishmael, cordially returning her embrace.

"You, Sally! what are you doing there? grinning like a monkey? Go directly and make the kettle boil, and set the table. And tell that Jim, that's always loafing around you, to make himself useful as well as ornamental, and open them oysters that were brought from Cove Banks to-day. Why don't you go? what are you waiting for?"

"Please 'm, I hav'n't shook hands long o' Marse Ishmael yet," said Sally, showing all her fine ivories.

Ishmael stepped forward and held out his hand, saying, as he kindly shook the girl's fat paw:

"How do you do, Sally? You grow better looking every day! And I have got a pretty coral breastpin in my trunk for you, to make up for that one the shanghai swallowed."

"Oh, Marse Ishmael, you needn't have taken no trouble, not on my account, sir, I am sure; dough I'm thousand times obleege to you, and shall be proud o' de breas'pin, 'cause I does love breas'pins, 'specially coral," said Sally, courtesying and smiling all over her face.

"Well, well," said Hannah impatiently, "now be off with you directly, and show your thankfulness by getting supper for your Marse Ishmael as quick as ever you can. Never mind the table—I'll set that."

Sally dropped another courtesy and vanished.

"Where did you say your trunk was, Ishmael?" inquired Gray, as they walked into the house.

"He never said it was anywhere; he only said he had a coral breastpin in it for Sally," put in the literal Hannah.

"My trunk is at the Steamboat Hotel in Shelton, Uncle Reuben. I could not at once find a cart to bring it over, for I was too anxious to see you all to spend time looking for one. So I left it with the landlord, with orders to forward it on Monday."

"Oh, sho! And what are you to do in the meantime? And Sally'll go crazy for a sight of her breastpin! So I'll just go out and make Sam put the horse to the light wagon, and go right after it; he'll jest have time to go and get it and come back afore it's dark," said Reuben; and without waiting to hear any of Ishmael's remonstrances, he went out immediately to give his orders to Sam.

Hannah followed Ishmael up to his own old room in the garret, to see that he had fresh water, fine soap, clean towels, and all that was requisite for his comfort.

And then leaving him to refresh himself with a wash, she returned downstairs to set the table for tea.

By the time she had laid her best damask table-cloth, and set out her best japan waiter and china tea-set, and put her nicest preserves in cut glass saucers, and set the iced plumcake in the middle of the table, Ishmael, looking fresh from his renewed toilet, came down into the parlor.

She immediately drew forward the easiest arm-chair for his accommodation.

He sat down in it and called the two children and the dog, who all gathered around him for their share of his caresses.

And at the same moment Reuben, having dispatched Sam on his errand to Shelton, came in and sat down, with his big hands on his knees, and his head bent forward, contemplating the group around Ishmael with immense satisfaction.

Hannah was going in and out between the parlor and the pantry bringing cream, butter, butter-milk, and so forth.

Ishmael lifted John upon his knees, and while smoothing back the flaxen curls from the child's well-shaped forehead, said:

"This little fellow has got a great deal in this head of his! What do you intend to make of him, Uncle Reuben?"

"Law, Ishmael, how can I tell!" grinned Reuben.

"You should give him an education and fit him for one of the learned professions; or, no; I will do that, if Heaven spares us both!" said Ishmael benevolently; then smiling down upon the child, he said:

"What would you like to be when you grow up, Johnny?"

"I don't know," answered inexperience.

"Would you like to be a lawyer?"

"No."

"Why not?"

"'Cause I wouldn't."

"Satisfactory! Would you like to be a doctor?"

"'No."

"Why?"

"'Cause I wouldn't."

"'As before.' Would you like to be a parson?"

"No."

"Why?"

"'Cause I wouldn't."

"Sharp little fellow, isn't he, Ishmael? Got his answer always ready!" said the father, rubbing his knees in delight.

Ishmael smiled at Reuben Gray and then turned to the child and said:

"What would you like to be, Johnny?"

"Well, I'd like to be a cart-driver like Sam, and drive the ox team!"

"Aspiring young gentleman!" said Ishmael, smiling.

"There now," said Hannah, who had heard the latter part of this conversation, "that's what I tell Reuben. He needn't think he is going to make ladies and gentlemen out of our children. They are just good honest workman's children, and will always be so; for 'what's bred in the bone will never come out in the flesh'; and 'trot mammy, trot daddy, the colt will never pace.' Cart-driver!" mocked Hannah, in intense disgust.

"Nonsense, Aunt Hannah! Why, don't you know that when I was Johnny's age my highest earthly ambition was to become a professor of odd jobs, like the renowned Jim Morris, who was certainly the greatest man of my acquaintance!"

While they were chatting away in this manner Sally brought in the coffee and tea, which was soon followed by dishes of fried oysters, stewed oysters, fried ham, and broiled chicken, and plates of waffles, rolls, and biscuits, and in fact by all the luxuries of a Maryland supper.

Hannah took her place at the head of the table and called her family around her.

And all sat down at the board. Even the dog squatted himself down by the side of Ishmael, where he knew he was sure of good treatment. Sally, neatly dressed, waited on the table. And presently Jim, who had a holiday this Saturday evening and was spending it with Sally, came in, and after shaking hands with "Mr. Ishmael" and welcoming him to the neighborhood, stood behind his chair and anticipated his wants as if he, Jim, had been lord-in-waiting upon a prince.

When supper was over and the service cleared away, Ishmael, Reuben, Hannah, and the children, who had been allowed to sit up a little longer in honor of Ishmael's visit, gathered together on the front porch to enjoy the delicious coolness of the clear, starlit, summer evening.

While they were still sitting there, chatting over the old times and the new days, the sound of wheels were heard approaching, and Sam drove up in the wagon, in which was Ishmael's trunk and a large box.

Jim was called in from the kitchen, where he had been engaged in making love to Sally, to assist in lifting the luggage in.

The trunk and the box were deposited in the middle of the parlor floor to be opened,—because, forsooth, all that simple family wished to be present and look on at the opening.

Ishmael's personal effects were in the trunk they guessed; but what was in the box? that was the riddle and they could not solve it. Both the children pressed forward to see. Even the dog stood with his ears pricked, his nose straight and his eyes fixed on the interesting box as though he expected a fox to break cover from it as soon as it was opened.

Ishmael had mercy on their curiosity and ended their suspense by ripping off the cover.

And lo! a handsome hobby-horse which he took out and set up before the delighted eyes of Johnny.

He lifted the tiny man into the saddle, fixed his feet in the stirrups, gave him the bridle, and showed him how to manage his steed.

"There, Johnny," said Ishmael, "I cannot realize your aspirations in respect to the driver's seat on the ox-cart, but I think this will do for the present."

"Ah, yes!" cried the ecstatic Johnny, "put Molly up behind! put Molly up behind and let her sit and hold on to me! My horse can carry double."

"Never mind! I've got something for Molly that she will like better than that," said Ishmael, smiling kindly on the little girl, who stood with her finger in her mouth looking as if she thought herself rather neglected.

And he unlocked his trunk and took from the top of it a large, finely painted, substantially dressed wooden doll, that looked as if it could bear a great deal of knocking about without injury.

Molly made an impulsive spring towards this treasure, and was immediately rendered happy by its possession.

Then Sally was elevated to the seventh heaven by the gift of the coral breastpin.

Hannah received a handsome brown silk dress and Reuben a new writing-desk, and Sam a silver watch, and Jim a showy vest-pattern.

And Ishmael, having distributed his presents, ordered his trunk to be carried upstairs, and the box into the outhouse.

When the children were tired of their play Hannah took them off to hear them say their prayers and put them to bed.

And then Ishmael and Reuben were left alone.

And the opportunity that Ishmael wanted had come.

He could have spoken of his parents to either Hannah or Reuben separately; but he felt that he could not enter upon the subject in the presence of both together.

Now he drew his chair to the side of Gray and said:

"Uncle Reuben, I have something serious to say to you."

"Eh! Ishmael! what have I been doing of? I dessay something wrong in the bringing up of the young uns!" said Reuben, in dismay, expecting to be court-martialed upon some grave charge.

"It is of my parents that I wish to speak, Uncle Reuben."

"Oh!" said the latter, with an air of relief.

"You knew my mother, Uncle Reuben; but did you know who my father was?"

"No," said Reuben thoughtfully. "All I knowed was as he married of your mother in a private manner, and from sarcumstances never owned up to it; but left her name and yourn to suffer for it—the cowardly rascal, whoever he was!"

"Hush, Uncle Reuben, hush! You are speaking of my father!"

"And a nice father he wur to let your good mother's fair name come to grief and leave you to perish a'most!"

"Uncle Reuben, you know too little of the circumstances to be able to judge!"

"Law, Ishmael, it takes but little knowledge and less judgment to understand, as when a feller fersakes his wife and child for nothink, and leaves 'em to suffer undesarved scandal and cruel want, he must be an unnatural monster and a parjured vilyun!"

"Uncle Reuben, you are unjust to my father! You must listen to his vindication from my lips, and then you will acquit him of all blame. But first I must tell you in confidence his name—it is Herman Brudenell!"

"There now!" exclaimed Reuben, dropping his pipe in his astonishment; "to think that I had that fact right afore my eyes all my life and never could see it! Well, of all the blind moles and owls, I must a been the blindest! And to think as I was the very first as warned the poor girl agin him at that birthday feast! But, law, arter that I never saw them together agin, no, not once! So I had no cause to s'picion him, no more nor others! Well and now, Ishmael, tell me all how and about it! Long as it was him, Mr. Herman, there must a been something uncommon about it, for I don't believe he'd do anythink dishonorable, not if he knowed it!"

"Not if he knew it! You are right there, Uncle Reuben," said Ishmael, who immediately related the tragic story of his parents' marriage, ending with the family wreck that had ruined all their happiness.

"Dear me! dear, dear me! what a sorrowful story for all hands, to be sure! Well, Ishmael, whoever was most to be pitied in former times, your father is most to be pitied now. Be good to him," said Reuben.

"You may be sure that I will do all that I can to comfort my father, Uncle Reuben. And now a word to you! Speak of this matter to me alone whenever you like; or to Aunt Hannah alone whenever you like; but to no others; and not even to us when we are together! for I cannot bear that this old tragic history should become the subject of general conversation."

"I know, Ishmael, my boy, I know! Mum's the word!" said Reuben.

And the entrance of Hannah at that moment put an end to the conversation.

There was one subject upon which Ishmael felt a little uneasiness—the dread of meeting Claudia.

He knew that she was not expected at Tanglewood until the first of October; for so the judge had informed him in a letter that he had received the very night before he left Washington. And this was only the first of September; and he intended to give himself but two weeks' holiday and to be back at his office by the fourteenth at farthest, full sixteen days before the expected arrival of Lord and Lady Vincent at Tanglewood.

Yet this dread of meeting Claudia haunted him. His love was dead; but as he had told Bee, it had died hard and rent his heart in its death-struggles, and that heart was sore to the touch of her presence.

The judge's letter wherein he had spoken of the date of his daughter and son-in-law's visit had been written several days previous to this evening, and since that, news might have come from them, speaking of some change of plan, involving an earlier visit.

These Ishmael felt were the mere chimeras of imagination. Still he thought he would inquire concerning the family at Tanglewood.

"They are all well up at the house, I hope, Uncle Reuben?" he asked.

"Famous! And having everything shined up bright as a new shilling, in honor of the arrival of my lord and my lady, who are expected, come first o' next mont'."

"On the first of October? Are you sure?"

"On the first of October, sharp! Not a day earlier or later! I was up to the house yes'day afternoon, just afore you come; and sure enough the judge, he had just got a letter from the young madam,—my lady, I mean,—in which she promised not to disappoint him, but to be at Tanglewood punctually on the first of October to a day!"

Reuben, a hard-working man, who was "early to bed and early to rise," concluded this speech with such an awful, uncompromising yawn that Ishmael immediately took up and lighted his bedroom candle, bid them all good-night, and retired.

He was once more in the humble little attic room where he had first chanced upon a set of old law books and imbibed a taste for the legal profession.

There was the old "screwtaw," as Reuben called it, and there was the old well-thumbed volumes that had constituted his sole wealth of books before he had the range of the well-filled library at Tanglewood.

And there was the plain deal table standing within the dormer window, where he had been accustomed to sit and read and write; or, whenever he raised his head, to gaze out upon the ocean-like expanse of water near the mouth of the Potomac.

After all, this humble attic chamber had many points of resemblance with that more pretentious one he had occupied in Judge Merlin's elegant mansion in Washington. Both were on the north side of the Potomac. Each had a large dormer window looking southwest and commanding an extensive view of the river; within the recess of each window he had been accustomed to sit and read or write.

The only difference was that the window in the Washington attic looked down upon the great city and the winding of the river among wooded and rolling hills; while the window of the cottage here looked down upon broad fields sloping to the shore, and upon the vast sea-like expanse of water stretching out of sight under the distant horizon.

The comparison between his two study-windows was in Ishmael's mind as he stood gazing upon the shadowy green fields and the starlit sky and water.

Not long he stood there; he was weary with his journey; so he offered up his evening prayers and went to bed and to sleep.

Early in the morning he awoke, and arose to enjoy the beauty of a summer Sunday in the quiet country. It was a deliciously cool, bright, beautiful autumnal morning.

Ishmael looked out over land and water for a little while, and then quickly dressed himself, offered up his morning prayers and went below.

The family were already assembled in the parlor, and all greeted him cordially.

The table was set, and Sally, neat in her Sunday clothes and splendid in her coral brooch, was waiting ready to bring in the breakfast.

And a fine breakfast it was, of fragrant coffee, rich cream, fresh butter, Indian corn bread, Maryland biscuits, broiled birds, boiled crabs, etc.

And Ishmael, upon whom the salt sea air of the coast was already producing a healthful change, did ample justice to the luxuries spread before him.

"For church this morning, Ishmael?" inquired Reuben.

"Yes; but I must walk over to Tanglewood and go with the judge. He would scarcely ever forgive me if I were to go anywhere, even to church, before visiting him."

"No more he wouldn't, that's a fact," admitted Reuben.

CHAPTER VII

AT TANGLEWOOD.

Are not the forests, waves and skies, a part

Of me and of my soul as I of them?

Is not the love of these deep in my heart

With a pure passion? Should I not contemn

All objects if compared with these? and stem

A tide of sufferings, rather than forego

Such feelings for the hard and worldly phlegm

Of those whose eyes are only turned below,

Gazing upon the ground, with thoughts that dare not glow?

—Byron.

After breakfast Ishmael took his hat, and, promising to return in the evening, set out for Tanglewood to spend the day and go to church with the judge.

How he enjoyed that Sunday morning walk through the depths of the forest that lay between Woodside and Tanglewood.

He reached the house just as the judge had finished breakfast. He was shown into the room while the old man still lingered in sheer listlessness over his empty cup and plate.

"Eh, Ishmael! is that you, my boy? Lord bless my soul, how glad I am to see you! Old Jacob was never so glad to see Joseph as I am to see you!" was the greeting of the judge, as he started up, overturning his chair and seizing both his visitor's hands and shaking them vigorously.

"And I am very glad indeed to see you again, sir! I hope you have been well?" said Ishmael warmly, returning his greeting.

"Well? Hum, ha, how can I be well? What is that the poet says?

I miss Claudia, Ishmael. I miss her sadly."

"Lady Vincent will be with you soon, sir," observed Ishmael, in as steady a voice as he could command.

"Yes, she will come on the first of October and stop with me for a month. So her letter of Wednesday received yesterday says. And then I shall lose her forever!" complained the judge, with a deep sigh.

"Ah, but you must look on the bright side, sir! You are independent. You have time and money at your own disposal; and no very strong ties here. You can visit Lady Vincent as often and stay with her as long as you please," smiled Ishmael cheerfully.

"Why, so I can! I never thought of that before! I may certainly pass at least half my time with my daughter if I please!" exclaimed the old man, brightening up.

"Are you going to church this morning, sir?" inquired Ishmael.

"You are, of course!" said the judge; "for you take care never to miss morning service! So I must go!"

"Not on my account. I know the road," smiled Ishmael.

"Oh, in any case I should go. I promised to go and dine at the parsonage, so as to attend afternoon service also. And when I mentioned to Mr. Wynne that I was expecting you down he requested me, if you arrived in time, to bring you with me, as he was desirous of forming your acquaintance. So you see, Ishmael, your fame is spreading."

"I am very grateful to you and to Mr. Wynne," said Ishmael, as his heart suddenly thrilled to the memory that Wynne was the name of the minister who had united his parents in their secret marriage.

"Has Mr. Wynne been long in this parish?" he inquired.

"Some three or four months, I believe. This is his native State, however. He used to be stationed at the Baymouth church, but left it some years ago to go as a missionary to Farther India; but as of late his health failed, he returned home and accepted the call to take charge of this parish."

Ishmael looked wistfully in the face of the judge and said:

"It was very kind in Mr. Wynne to think of inviting me. Why do you suppose he did it?"

"Why, I really do suppose that the report of your splendid successes in Washington has reached him, and he feels some curiosity to see a young man who in so short a time has attained so high a position."

"No, it is not that," said Ishmael, with a genuine blush at this great praise; "but do you really not know what it is?"

"I do not, unless it is what I said," replied the judge, raising his eyebrows.

"He married my parents, and baptized me; he knows that I bear my mother's maiden name; and he was familiar with my early poverty and struggles for life; he left the neighborhood when I was about eight years old," said Ishmael, in a low voice.

The judge opened his eyes and drooped his head for a few moments, and then said:

"Indeed! Your father, when he told me of his marriage with your mother, did not mention the minister's name. Everything else, I believe, he candidly revealed to me, under the seal of confidence; this omission was accidental, and really unimportant. But how surprised Brudenell will be to learn that his old friend and confidant is stationed here."

"Yes."

"And now I can thoroughly understand the great interest Mr. Wynne feels in you. It is not every minister who is the confidant in such a domestic tragedy as that of your poor mother was, Ishmael. It is not only the circumstances of your birth that interest him in you so much, but those taken in connection with your recent successes. I should advise you to meet Mr. Wynne's advances."

"I shall gratefully do so, sir."

"And now I really do suppose it is time to order the carriage, if we mean to go to church to-day," said the judge, rising and touching the bell.

Jim answered it.

"Have the gray horses put to the barouche and brought around. And put a case of that old port wine in the box; I intend to take it as a present to the parson. I always considered port a parsonic wine, and it really is in this case just the thing for an invalid," said the judge, turning to Ishmael as Jim left the room.

In twenty minutes the carriage was ready, and they started for the church, which was some five miles distant. An hour's drive brought them to it.

A picturesque scene that old St. Mary's church presented. It was situated in a clearing of the forest beside the turnpike road. It was built of red brick, and boasted twelve gothic windows and a tall steeple. The church-yard was fenced in with a low brick wall, and had some interesting old tombstones, whose dates were coeval with the first settlement of the State.

Many carriages of every description, from the barouche of the gentleman to the cart of the laborer, were scattered about, drawn up under the shade of the trees. And saddle-horses and donkeys were tied here and there. And groups of negroes, in their gay Sunday attire, stood gossiping among the trees. Some young men, as usual, were loitering at the church door.

The judge's carriage drew up under the shade of a forest tree, and the judge and Ishmael then alighted, and leaving the horses in the care of the coachman went into the church.

The congregation were already assembled, and soon after Judge Merlin and his guest took their seats the minister entered and took his place at the reading-desk and the services commenced.

There was little in this Sunday morning's service to distinguish it from others of the same sort. The minister was a good man and a plodding country parson. He read the morning prayers in a creditable but by no means distinguished manner. And he preached a sermon, more remarkable for its practical bearing than for its eloquence or originality, his text being in these words: "Faith without works is dead."

At the conclusion of the services, while the congregation were leaving the church, the minister descended from his pulpit and advanced towards Judge Merlin, who was also hastening to meet his pastor.

There was a shaking of hands.

Judge Merlin, who was an eminently practical man in all matters but one, complimented the preacher on his practical sermon.

And then without waiting to hear Mr. Wynne's disclaimer, he beckoned Ishmael to step forward, and the usual formula of introduction was performed.

"Mr. Wynne, permit me—Mr. Worth, Mr. Wynne!"

And then were two simultaneous bows and more handshaking.

But both the judge and Ishmael noticed the wistful look with which the latter was regarded by the minister.

"He is comparing likenesses," thought the judge.

"He is thinking of the past and present," thought Ishmael.

And both were right.

Mr. Wynne saw in Ishmael the likeness to both his parents, and noted how happily nature had distinguished him with the best points of each. And he was wondering at the miracle of seeing that the all-forsaken child, born to poverty, shame, and obscurity, was by the Lord's blessing on his own persevering efforts certainly rising to wealth, honor, and fame.

Mr. Wynne renewed his pressing invitation to Judge Merlin and Mr. Worth to accompany him home to dinner.

And as they accepted the minister's hospitality the whole party moved off towards the parsonage, which was situated in another clearing of the forest about a quarter of a mile behind the church.

The parson was blessed with the parson's luck of a large family, consisting of a wife, several sisters and sisters-in-law, and nieces, and so many sons and daughters of all ages, from one month old to twenty years, that the judge, after counting thirteen before he came to the end of the list, gave up the job in despair.

Notwithstanding, or perhaps because of, this, for "the more, the merrier," you know, the family dinner passed off pleasantly. And after dinner they all returned to church to attend the afternoon service.

And when that was ended Judge Merlin and Ishmael took leave of the parson and his family and returned home.

When they reached Tanglewood and alighted, the judge, who was first out, was accosted by his servant Jim, who spoke a few words in a low tone, which had the effect of hurrying the judge into the house.

Ishmael followed at his leisure.

He entered the drawing room and was walking slowly and thoughtfully up and down the room, when the sound of voices in the adjoining library caught his ear and transfixed him to the spot.

"Yes, papa, I am here, and alone—strange as this may seem!"

It was the voice of Claudia that spoke these words.

CHAPTER VIII

WHY CLAUDIA WAS ALONE.

Be not amazed at life. 'Tis still

The mode of God with his elect:

Their hopes exactly to fulfill,

In times and ways they least expect.

Who marry as they choose, and choose,

Not as they ought, they mock the priest,

And leaving out obedience, lose

The finest flavor of the feast.

—Coventry Patmore.

Ishmael stood transfixed to the spot—for a moment, and then, breaking the spell with which the sound of Claudia's voice had bound him, he passed into the hall, took his hat from the rack, and said to Jim, who was still in attendance there:

"Give my respects to your master, and say that I have an engagement this evening that obliges me to withdraw. And give him my adieus."

"But, Mr. Ishmael, sir, you will wait for tea. Lady Vincent is here, sir, just arrived—" began Jim, with the affectionate freedom of a petted servant.

But Ishmael had left the hall, to keep his promise of spending the evening with Reuben and Hannah.

Claudia, standing by her father's side in the library, had also heard the sound of Ishmael's voice, as he spoke to the servant in the hall; and she suddenly ceased talking and looked as if turned to stone.

"Why, what is the matter, my dear?" inquired the judge, surprised at the panic into which she had been cast.

"Papa, he here!" she said.

"Who?"

"Ishmael!"

"Yes. Why?"

"Papa, make some excuse and get rid of him. I must not, cannot, will not, meet him now!" she exclaimed, in a half breathless voice of ill-suppressed excitement.

The judge looked at his daughter wistfully, painfully, for a moment, and then, as something like the truth in regard to Claudia's feelings broke upon him, he replied very gravely:

"My dear, you need not meet him; and he has saved me the embarrassment of sending him away. He has gone, if I mistake not."

"If you 'mistake' not. There must be no question of this, sir! See! and if he has not gone, tell him to go directly!"

"Claudia!"

"Oh, papa, I am nearly crazy! Go!"

The judge stepped out into the hall and made the necessary inquiries.

And Jim gave Ishmael's message.

With this the judge returned to Claudia.

"He is gone. And now, my dear, I wish to know why it is that you are here alone? I never in my life heard of such a thing. Where is Vincent?"

"Papa, I am nearly fainting with fatigue. Will you ring for one of the women to show Ruth my room? I suppose I have my old one?" she said, throwing herself back in her chair.

"Why—no, my dear; I fancy I saw Katie and the maids decorating the suite of rooms on the opposite side of the hall on this floor for you. I'll see."

"Anywhere, anywhere—'out of the world,'" sighed Claudia, as the judge sharply rang the bell.

Jim answered it.

"Tell Katie to show Lady Vincent's maid to her ladyship's chamber, and do you see the luggage taken there."

Jim bowed and turned to go.

"Stop," said the judge. "Claudia, my dear, what refreshment will you take before going up? A glass of wine? a cup of tea?" he inquired, looking anxiously upon the harassed countenance and languid figure of his daughter.

"A cup of coffee, papa, if they have any ready; if not, anything they can bring quickest."

"A cup of coffee for Lady Vincent in one minute, ready or not ready!" was the somewhat unreasonable command of the judge.

Jim disappeared to deliver all his master's orders.

And it seemed that the coffee was ready, for he almost immediately reappeared bearing a tray with the service arranged upon it.

"Is it strong, Jim?" inquired Claudia, as she raised the cup to her lips.

"Yes, miss—ma'am—my ladyship, I mean!" said poor Jim, who was excessively bothered by Claudia's new title and the changes that were rung upon it.

The coffee must have been strong, to judge by its effects upon Claudia.

"Take it away," she said, after having drunk two cupfuls. "Papa, I feel better; and while Ruth is unpacking my clothes I may just as well sit here and tell you why, if indeed I really know why, I am here alone. We were at Niagara, where we had intended to remain throughout this month of September. All the world seemed to know where we were and how long we intended to stay; for you are aware how absurdly we democratic and republican Americans worship rank and title; and how certain our reporters would be to chronicle the movements of Lord and Lady Vincent," said Claudia, with that air of world-scorn and self-scorn in which she often indulged.

"Well, Lady Vincent cannot consistently find fault with that," said the judge, with a covert smile.

"Because Lady Vincent shares the folly or has shared it," said Claudia; "but Lord Vincent did find fault with it; great fault—much greater fault than was necessary, I thought, and grumbled incessantly at our custom of registering names at the hotels, and at 'American snobbery and impertinence' generally."

"Bless his impudence! Who sent for him?"

"Papa, we should have quarreled upon this subject in our honeymoon, if I had had respect enough for him to hold any controversy with him."

"Claudia!"

"Well, I cannot help it, papa! I must speak out somewhere and to someone! Where so well as here in the woods; and to whom so well as to you?"

"You have not yet told me why you are here alone. And I assure you, Claudia, that the fact gives me uneasiness; it is unusual— unprecedented!"

"I am telling you, papa. One morning while we were still at Niagara I was sitting alone in our private parlor, when our mail was brought in—your letter for me, and three letters for 'my lord.' Of the latter, the first bore the postmark of Banff, the second that of Liverpool, and the third that of New York. They were all superscribed by the same hand; all were evidently from the same person. After turning them over and over in my hand, and in my mind, I came to the conclusion that the first dated was written to announce the writer as starting upon a journey; the second to announce the embarkment at Liverpool; and the third the arrival at New York; and that these letters, though posted at different times and places, had by the irregularities of the ocean mails happened to arrive at their final destination the same day. Lord Vincent has a mother and several sisters; yet I felt very sure that the letters never came from either of them, because in fact I had seen the handwriting of each in their letters to him. While I was still wondering over these rather mysterious letters my lord lounged into the room.

"I handed him the letters, the Banff one being on the top. As soon as he saw the handwriting he gave vent to various exclamations of annoyance, such as I had never heard from a gentleman, and scarcely ever expected to hear from a lord. 'Bosh!' 'Bother!' 'Here's a go!' 'Set fire to her,' etc., being among the most harmless and refined. But presently he saw the postmarks of Liverpool and New York on the other letters, and, after tearing them open and devouring their contents, he gave way to a fury of passion that positively appalled me. Papa, he swore and cursed like a pirate in a storm!"

"At you?"

"At me? I think not," answered Claudia haughtily; "but at some person or persons unknown. However, as he forgot himself so far as to give vent to his passion in my presence, I got up and retired to my chamber. Presently he came in, gracefully apologized for his violence,—did not explain the cause of it, however,—but requested me to give orders for the packing of our trunks and be ready to leave for New York in one hour."

"Did he give you no reason for his sudden movement?"

"Not until I inquired; then he gave me the general, convenient, unsatisfactory reason 'business.' In an hour we were off to New York. But now, papa, comes the singular part of the affair. When we reached the city, instead of driving to one of the best hotels, as had always been his custom, he drove to quite an inferior place, and registered our names—'Captain and Mrs. Jenkins.'"

"What on earth did he do that for?"

"How can I tell? When I made the same inquiry of him he merely answered that he was tired of being trumpeted to the world by these 'impertinent Yankee reporters!' The next day he left me alone in that stupid place and went out on his 'business,' whatever that was. And when he returned in the evening he told me that the 'business' was happily concluded, and that we might as well go on to Washington and Tanglewood to pay our promised visit to you. I very readily acceded to that proposition, for, papa, I was pining to see you."

"My dear child!" said the judge, with emotion.

"So next morning we started for the Philadelphia, Baltimore, and Washington station. We were in good time, and were just comfortably seated in one of the best cars when Lord Vincent caught sight of someone on the platform. And papa, with a muttered curse he started up and hurried from the car, throwing behind to me the hasty words, 'I'll be back soon.' Five, ten, fifteen minutes passed, and he did not come. And while I was still anxiously looking for him the train started. It was the express, and came all the way through. And that is why myself and attendants are here alone."

"All this seems very strange, Claudia," said the judge, with a troubled countenance.

"Yes, very."

"What do you make of it? Of course you, knowing more of the circumstances, are better able to judge than I am."

"Papa, I do not know."

"Who was it that he caught sight of on the platform?"

"A tall, handsome, imperious-looking woman between thirty and forty years of age, I should say; a sort of Cleopatra; very dark, very richly dressed. She was looking at him intently when he caught sight of her and rushed out as I said."

"And you can make nothing of it?"

"Nothing. I do not know whether he missed the train by design or accident; or whether he is at this moment on board the cars steaming to Washington or on board one of the ocean packets steaming to Liverpool."

"A bad, bad business, Claudia; all this grieves me much. You have been but two months married, and you return to me alone and your husband is among the missing; a bad, bad business, Claudia," said the judge very gravely.

"Not so bad as your words would seem to imply, papa. At least I hope not. I am inclined to think the detention was accidental; and that Lord Vincent will arrive by the next boat," said Claudia.

"But how coolly and dispassionately you speak of an uncertainty that would drive any other woman almost mad. At this moment you do not know whether you are abandoned or not, and to be candid with you, you do not seem to care," said the judge austerely.

"Papa, what I paid down my liberty for,—this rank, I mean—is safe! And so whether he goes or stays I am Lady Vincent; and nothing but death can prevent my becoming Countess of Hurstmonceux and a peeress of England," said Claudia defiantly, as she arose and drew her shawl around her shoulders and looked about herself.

"What is it that you want, my dear?" inquired the judge.

"Nothing. I was taking a view of the old familiar objects. How much has happened since I saw them last. It seems to me as if many years had passed since that time. Well, papa, I suppose Ruth has unpacked and put away my clothes by this time, and so I will leave you for the present."

And with a weary, listless air Claudia left the room and turned to go upstairs.

"Not there, not there, my dear, I told you. The rooms on this floor have been prepared for you," said the judge, who had followed her to the door.

With a sigh Claudia turned and crossed the hall and entered the "parlor-chamber," as the large bedroom adjoining the morning room was called.

Ruth was hanging the last dresses in the wardrobe, and Jim was shouldering the last empty trunk to take it away.

"I have left out the silver gray glace, for you to wear this evening, if you please, my lady," said Ruth, indicating the dress that lay upon the bed.

"That will do, Ruth," answered her mistress, whose thoughts were now not on dresses, but on that time when Ishmael, for her sake, lay wounded, bleeding, and almost dying on that very bed.

CHAPTER IX

HOLIDAY.

Ha! like a kind hand on my brow

Comes this fresh breeze.

Cooling its dull and feverish glow,

While through my being seems to flow

She breath of a new life—the healing of the seas.

Good-by to pain and care! I take

Mine ease to-day;

Here where these sunny waters break,

And ripples this keen breeze. I shake

All burdens from the heart, all weary thoughts away.

With every nerve, vein, and artery throbbing with excitement Ishmael hurried away from the house that contained Claudia.

The solitary walk through the thick woods calmed his emotion before he reached Woodside.

He found a tidy room, a tempting tea-table, and smiling faces waiting to welcome him.

"That's my boy!" exclaimed Reuben, coming forward and grasping his hand; "I told Hannah to keep the tea back a spell, 'cause I knowed you wouldn't disappoint us."

"As if I ever thought you would, Ishmael! Reuben is always prophesying things that can't fail to come true, like the rising of the sun in the east every day, and so forth. And he expects to get credit for his foresight," said Hannah, taking her seat before the steaming tea-pot and calling upon the others to sit down.

"Well, that was rayther a surprise, as met you and the judge, when you comed home from church, wasn't it?" inquired Reuben, as he began to cut slices from the cold ham.

"You knew of the arrival, then?" questioned Ishmael.

"Why, bless you, yes! Why, laws, you know the carriage passed right by here, and stopped to water the horses afore going on to Tanglewood. But look here! There was nobody in it but Mrs. Vincent—blame my head—I mean Mrs. Lord Vincent—and her city maid."

"Lady Vincent, Reuben. How many times will I have to tell you that?" said Hannah impatiently.

"All right, Hannah, my dear; I'll remember next time. Ishmael, my boy, I think you got all your interlects from Hannah. You sartainly didn't get 'em from me. Well as I was a-saying of, there was no one inside except Mrs. Lord—I mean Mrs. Lady Vincent and her city waiting-maid. And on the outside, a-sitting alongside o' the driver, was a gentleman, as Jim as happened to be here introduced to me as Mr. Frisbie, Lord Vincent's vallysham, whatever that may be."

"Body-servant, Reuben," said his monitress.

"Servant! Well, if he was a servant, I don't know nothink! Why, there ain't a gentleman in S'Mary's county as dresses as fine and puts on as many airs!"

"That is quite likely, Uncle Reuben; but for all that, Frisbie is Lord Vincent's servant," said Ishmael.

"Well, hows'ever that may be, there he was alongside o' the driver. But what staggers of me is, that there wa'n't no Lord Vincent nowhere to be seen! He was 'mong the missin'. And that was the rummest go as ever was. A new bride a-comin' home to her 'pa without no bridegroom. And so I jest axed Mr. Frisbie, Esquire, and he told me how his lordship missed the trail. What trail! And what business had he to be offen the trail, when his wife was on it? That's what I want to know. And, anyways, it's the rummest go as ever was. Did you hear anythink about it, Ishmael?"

"I chanced to overhear Lady Vincent say to her father—that she was alone. That was all. I did not even see her ladyship."

"Well, now, that's another rum go. Didn't wait to see her. And you sich friends? Owtch! Oh! Ah! What's that for, Hannah? You've trod on my toe and ground it a'most to powder! Ah!"

"If your foot is as soft as your head, no wonder every touch hurts it!" snapped Mrs. Gray.

"Law, what a temper she have got, Ishmael!" said poor Reuben, carressing his afflicted foot.

Hannah had effected the diversion she intended, and soon after gave the signal for rising from the table. And she took good care during the rest of the evening that the subject of Lord and Lady Vincent should not be brought upon the tapis.

The next morning being Monday, Ishmael accompanied Reuben in his rounds over his own little farm and the great Tanglewood estate, to see the improvements. The "durrum" cow and calf and the "shank-bye" fowls received due notice. And the first ripe bunches of the "hamburg" grapes were plucked in the visitor's honor.

In the afternoon they went down to the oyster banks and amused themselves with watching Sam rake the oysters and load the cart.

They returned to a late tea.

It was while they were sitting out on the vine-shaded porch, enjoying their usual evening chat under the star-lit sky, that they heard the sound of approaching wheels.

And a few moments afterwards a carriage drew up at the gate.

Reuben walked up to see who was within it. And Ishmael heard the voice of Lord Vincent inquiring:

"Is this the best road to Tanglewood?"

"Well, yes, sir; I do s'pose it's the best, if any can be called the best where none on 'em is good, but every one on 'em as bad as bad can be!" was the encouraging answer.

"Drive on!" said Lord Vincent. And the carriage rolled out of sight into the forest road.

After all, then, the viscount had not absconded. He probably had missed the train. But why had he missed it? That was still the question.

On Tuesday morning Ishmael took leave of Hannah and Reuben, promising to stop and spend another day and night with them on his return to Washington; and mounted on a fine horse, borrowed from Reuben, with his knapsack behind him, he started for the Beacon.

It was yet early in the forenoon when he arrived at that cool promontory where the refreshing sea breezes met him.

As he rode up to the house, that you know fronted the water, he saw Bee, blooming and radiant with youth and beauty, out on the front lawn with her younger sisters and brothers.

Their restless glances caught sight of him first; and they all exclaimed at once:

"Here's Ishmael, Bee! here's Ishmael, Bee!" and ran off to meet him.

Bee impulsively started to run too, but checked herself, and stood, blushing but eager, waiting until Ishmael dismounted and came to greet her.

She met him with a warm, silent welcome, and then, looking at him suddenly, said:

"You are so much better; you are quite well. I am so glad, Ishmael!"

"Yes, I am well and happy, dearest Bee—thanks to you and to Heaven!" said Ishmael, warmly pressing her hands again to his lips, before turning to embrace the children who were jumping around him.

Then they all went into the house, where Mr. and Mrs. Middleton met him with an equally cordial welcome.

"And how did you leave the family at Tanglewood? Family, said I? Ah! there is no family there now; no one left but the old judge. How is he? And when is Claudia and her lordling expected back?" inquired Mr. Middleton, when they were all seated near one of the sea-view windows.

"The judge is well. Lord and Lady Vincent are with him," replied Ishmael.

And then in answer to their exclamations of surprise he told all he knew of the unexpected arrival.

A luncheon of fruit, cream, cake, and wine was served, and the welcome guest was pressed to partake of it.

Ishmael tasted and enjoyed all except the wine—that, faithful to his vow, he avoided, and was rewarded by a sympathetic look from Bee.

This was one of the bright days of Ishmael's life. Nowhere did he feel so much at home or so happy as with these kind friends. They had an early seaside dinner—fish, crabs, oysters, and water-fowl, forming a large portion of the bill of fare. Luscious, freshly gathered fruits composed the dessert. After dinner, as the evening was clear and bright, the wind fresh and the waters calm, they went for a sail down to Silver Sands, and returned by starlight.

Ishmael remained all the week at the Beacon. And it was a week of rare enjoyment to him. He passed nearly all the time with Bee and her inseparable companions, the children. He helped them with the lessons in the schoolroom in the morning; he went nutting with them in the woods, or strolled with them on the beach; and he gave himself up to the task of amusing them during the hour after the lamp was lighted that they were permitted to sit up.

All this was due partly to his desire to be with his betrothed, and partly to his genial love to children.

About the middle of the week, as they were all seated at breakfast one morning, missives came from Tanglewood to the Beacon—invitations to dine there the following Wednesday evening. These invitations included Mr. and Mrs. Middleton, Beatrice, and Ishmael.

"You will go, of course, Worth?" said Mr. Middleton.

"I am due at Brudenell Hall on Tuesday evening, and I must keep my appointment," said Ishmael.

"Well, I suppose that settles it, for I never knew you to break an appointment, under any sort of temptation," said Mr. Middleton.

And Bee, who well understood why, even had Ishmael's time been at his own disposal, he should not have gone to Tanglewood, silently acquiesced. On this day Ishmael sought an interview with Mr. and Mrs. Middleton, and besought them, as his present income and future prospects equally justified him in taking a wife, to fix some day, not very distant, for his marriage with Bee.

But the father and mother assured him, in the firmest though the most affectionate manner, that at least one year, if not two, must elapse before they could consent to part with their daughter.

Ishmael most earnestly deprecated the two years of probation, and finally compromised for one year, during which he should be permitted to correspond freely with his betrothed, and visit her at will.

With this Ishmael rested satisfied.

The remainder of the week passed delightfully to him.

Mrs. Middleton took the children off Bee's hands for a few days, to leave her to some enjoyment of her lover's visit.

And every morning and afternoon Ishmael and Bee rode or walked together, through the old forest or along the pebbly beach. Sometimes they had a sail to some fine point on the shore. Their evenings were passed in the drawing room, with Mr. and Mrs. Middleton, and were employed in music, books, and conversation.

And so the pleasant days slipped by and brought the Sabbath, when all the family went together to the old Shelton church.

Monday was the last day of his visit, and he passed it almost exclusively in the society of Bee. In the evening Mr. and Mrs. Middleton left them alone in the drawing room, that they might say their last kind words to each other unembarrassed by the presence of others.

And on Tuesday morning Ishmael mounted his horse and started for Brudenell.

CHAPTER X

ISHMAEL AT BRUDENELL

God loves no heart to others iced,

Nor erring flatteries which bedim

Our glorious membership in Christ,

Wherein all loving His, love Him.

—M. F. Tupper.

It was a long day's ride from the Beacon to Brudenell Hall. The greater length of the road lay through the forest. It was, in fact, the very same route traversed, five years before, by Reuben Gray, when he brought Hannah and Ishmael from the Hill Hut to Woodside.

Ishmael thought of that time, as he ambled on through the leafy wilderness.

At noon he stopped at a rural inn to feed and rest his horse, and refresh himself, and an hour afterwards he mounted and resumed his journey.

It was near sunset when he came in sight of the bay and the village to which it gave the name of Baymouth. How well he remembered the last time he had been at that village—when he had run that frantic race to catch the sleigh which was carrying Claudia away from him, and had fallen in a swoon at the sight of the steamer that was bearing her off.

How many changes had taken place since then! Claudia was a viscountess; he was a successful barrister; their love a troubled dream of the past.

He rode through Baymouth, looking left and right at the old familiar shops and signs that had been the wonder and amusement of his childhood; and at many new shops and signs that the march of progress had brought down even to Baymouth.

He paused a moment to gaze at Hamlin's book store, that had been the paradise of his boyhood; and he recalled that noteworthy day in August, when, while standing before Hamlin's window, staring at the books, he had first been accosted by Mr. Middleton, afterwards assaulted by Alfred Burghe, and finally defended by Claudia Merlin. Claudia was noble then—but, ah, how ignoble now!

He passed on, unrecognized by anyone, first because the years between the ages of seventeen, when he was last there, and twenty-one, when he was now there, really had wrought serious changes in his personal appearance, and secondly because no one was just then expecting to see Ishmael Worth at all, and least of all in the person of the tall, distinguished-looking, and well-mounted stranger, who came riding through their town and taking the road to Brudenell.

Every foot of that road was rich in memories to Ishmael. Over it he had ridden, in Mr. Middleton's carriage, on that fateful day of his first meeting with Claudia.

Over it he had traveled, weary and footsore, through the snow, to sell his precious book to buy tea for Hannah.

And over it he had again flashed in Mr. Middleton's sleigh, happy in the possession of his recovered treasure.

Twilight was deepening into dark when he reached that point in the road where the little footpath diverged from it and led up to the Hill Hut.

No! he could not pass this by. The path was wide enough to admit the passage of a horse. He turned up it, and rode on until he came in sight of the hut.

It was but little changed. It is astonishing how long these little lonely dilapidated houses hold on if let alone.

He alighted, tied his horse to a tree, and walked up behind the house, where, under the old elm, he saw the low headstone gleaming dimly in the starlight.

He knelt and bowed his head over it for a little while. Then he arose and stood with folded arms, gazing thoughtfully down upon it. Finally he murmured to himself: "Not here, but risen;" and turned and left the spot.

He went to the tree where he had tied his horse, remounted, and rode on his way.

Again he passed down the narrow path leading back to the broad turnpike road that wound around the brow of the hills to Brudenell Hall.

Here also every yard of the road was redolent of past associations.

How often, while self-apprenticed to the Professor of Odd Jobs, he had passed up and down this road, carrying a basket of tools behind his master.

At length he came to the cross-roads, and to the turnstile, where he had once seen and been accosted by the beautiful Countess of Hurstmonceux.

He rode past this spot, and taking the lower arm of the road entered upon the Brudenell grounds.

A very short ride brought him to the semi-circular avenue leading to the house.

It was now quite dark; but the front of the house was lighted up, holding forth, as it were, its hands in welcome.

As he rode up and dismounted a servant took his horse.

And as he walked up the front steps Mr. Brudenell came out of the front door and, holding out his hand, said cordially:

"You are welcome, my dear Ishmael! I received your letter this morning, and have been looking for you all afternoon!"

"And I am very glad to get here at last, sir," said Ishmael, returning the fervent pressure of his father's hands.

"Come up, my boy! Felix, go before us with the light to the room prepared for Mr. Worth," he said to a mulatto boy who was waiting in the hall.

Felix immediately led the way upstairs to a large back room, whose windows overlooked the star-lit, dew-spangled garden, and which Ishmael at once recognized as the happy schoolroom of his boyhood, now transformed into his bedroom. He welcomed the old familiar walls with all his heart; he was glad to be in them.

Mr. Brudenell himself took care that Ishmael had everything he was likely to want, and then he left him.

When Ishmael had changed his dress he went below to the drawing room, where he found his father waiting. The late dinner was immediately served.

Old Jovial, who on account of his age and infirmity had been left to vegetate on the estate, waited on the table.

He stole wistful glances at the strange young man who was his master's guest, and who somehow or other reminded him of somebody whom he felt he ought to remember, but knew he could not.

At length Ishmael, attracted by his covert regards, looked at him in return, and in spite of his bowed and shrunken form and thinned and whitened hair, recognized the old friend of his boyhood, and exclaimed, as he offered his hand:

"Why, Jovial, it is never you!"

"Mr. Ishmael, sir, it's never you!" returned the old man with a grin of joyful recognition.

They shook hands then and there.

And old Jovial showed his increased regard for the guest by continually proffering bread, vegetables, meat, poultry, pepper, salt, in short, everything in succession over and over again, thereby effectually preventing Ishmael from eating his dinner, by compelling his constant attention to these offerings; until at length Mr. Brudenell interfered and brought him to reason.

The next morning Mr. Brudenell proposed to Ishmael to go out for a day's shooting. And accordingly they took their fowling-pieces, called the dogs and started for the wooded valley where game most abounded.

They spent the day pleasantly, bagged many birds and returned home to a late dinner; and the evening closed as before.

"What would you like to do with yourself this morning, Ishmael?" inquired Mr. Brudenell, as they were seated at breakfast on Thursday.

"I wish to go in search of a valued old friend of mine, known in this neighborhood as the Professor of Odd Jobs," was the reply.

"Oh, Morris. Yes. You will find him, I fancy, in the old place, just on the edge of the estate," replied Mr. Brudenell.

And when they arose from the table the latter went out and mounted his horse to ride to the post office, for Herman Brudenell's establishment was now reduced to so small a number of servants that he was compelled to be his own postman. To be plain with you, there were but two servants—old Jovial, who was gardener, coachman, and waiter; and old Dinah, his wife, who was cook, laundress, and chambermaid.

Felix, the lad mentioned in the beginning of this chapter, was scarcely to be called one, upon account of the mental imbecility that confined his usefulness to such simple duties as running little errands from room to room about the house.

So Mr. Brudenell rode off to the post office, and Ishmael walked off to the cottage occupied by Jim Morris.

CHAPTER XI

THE PROFESSOR OF ODD JOBS.

An ancient man, hoary gray with eld.

—Dante.

The little house was situated right at the foot of the hill south of Brudenell Hall.

Ishmael approached it from behind and walked around to the front. He opened the little wooden gate of the front yard and saw seated in the front door, enjoying that early autumn morning, a stalwart old man, whose well-marked features and high forehead were set in a rim of hair and beard as white as snow. A most respectable and venerable-looking form, indeed, though the raiment that clothed it was old and patched. But Ishmael had to look again before he could recognize in this reverend personage the Professor of Odd Jobs.

A curiosity to know whether the professor would recognize him induced Ishmael to approach him as a stranger. As he came into the yard, however, Morris arose slowly, and, lifting his old felt hat, bowed courteously to the supposed stranger.

"Your name is Morris, I believe," said Ishmael, by way of opening a conversation.

But at the first word the professor started and gazed at his visitor, and exclaiming: "Young Ishmael! Oh, my dear boy, how glad I am to see you once more before I die!" burst into tears.

Ishmael went straight into his embrace, and the old odd-job man pressed the young gentleman to his honest, affectionate heart.

"You knew me at once, professor," said Ishmael affectionately.

"Knew you, my boy!" burst out the old man, with enthusiasm. "Why, I knew you as soon as ever you looked at me and spoke to me. I knew you by your steady, smiling eyes and by your rich, sweet voice, young Ishmael. No one has a look and a tone like yours."

"You think so because you like me, professor."

"And how you have grown! And they tell me that you have risen to be a great lawyer? I knew it was in you to do it!" said the professor, holding the young man off and gazing at him with all a father's pride.

"By the blessing of Heaven, I have been successful, dear old friend," said Ishmael affectionately; "but how has it been with you, all these years?" he asked.

"How has it been with me? Ah, young Ishmael—I should say 'Mr. Worth.'"

"Young Ishmael, professor."

"No, no; 'Mr. Worth.' I shall love you none the less by honoring you more. And with me you are henceforth 'Mr. Worth.'"

"As you please, professor. But I hope it has been well with you all these years?"

"Come in, Mr. Worth, and sit down and I will tell you."

The professor led the way into the humble dwelling. It was as neat as ever, with its sanded floor, flag-bottom chairs, and pine tables,—all of the professor's manufacture,—and its bright tinware and clean crockery ranged in order on its well scrubbed shelves.

But its look of solitude struck a chill upon Ishmael's spirits.

"Where are they all, professor?" he inquired.

"Gone, Mr. Worth," answered Morris solemnly, as he placed a chair for his guest.

"Gone! not dead!" exclaimed Ishmael, dropping into the offered seat.

"Not all dead, but all gone," answered the professor sadly, letting himself sink into a seat near Ishmael.

"Your wife?" inquired the young man.

"There—and there," answered the professor, pointing first down and then up; "her body is in the earth; her soul in heaven, I hope."

"And your daughters, professor?" inquired Ishmael, in a voice of sympathy.

"Both married, Mr. Worth. Ann Maria married Lewis Digges, old Commodore Burghe's boy that he set free before he died, and they have moved up to Washington to better themselves, and they're doing right well, as I hear. He drives a hack and she clear starches. They have three children, two girls and a boy. I have never seen one of them yet."

"And your other daughter?"

"Mary Ellen? She married Henry Parsons, a free man, by trade a blacksmith, and they live in St. Inigoes. They have one child, a boy. I haven't seen them either since they have been married."

"And you are quite alone?" said Ishmael, in a tender voice

"Quite alone, young Ishmael," answered the professor, who forgot on this occasion to call his sometime pupil Mr. Worth.

"And how is business, professor?"

"Business has fallen off considerably; indeed I may say it has fallen off altogether."

"I am very sorry to hear it. How is that, professor?"

"Why, you see, Mr. Worth, its falling off is the natural result of time and progress, of which I cannot complain, and at which I ought to rejoice. It was all very well for the neighborhood to patronize a Jack of all trades like me when there was nothing better to be had; but now you see there are lots of regular mechanics been gradually coming down and settling here—carpenters and stone-masons and painters and glaziers and plumbers and tinners and saddlers and shoemakers, and what not. Law, why you might have seen their signs as you rode through Baymouth."

"I did."

"Well, you see these mechanics, they have journeymen and apprentices with their trades at their fingers' ends, and they can do their work not only easier and quicker and better than I can, but even cheaper. So I cannot complain that they have taken the custom of the neighborhood from me."

"Professor, I really do admire the justice and forbearance of your nature."

"Well, young Ishmael, there was another thing. I was getting too old to tramp miles and miles through the country with a heavy pack on my back, as I used to do."

"Well, then, I hope you have saved a little money, at least, old friend, to make you comfortable in your old age," said Ishmael feelingly.

The poor, old odd-job man looked up with a humorous twinkle in his eye, as he replied:

"Why, law, young Ishmael, the idea of my saving money! When had I ever a chance to do it in the best o' days? Why, Ishmael, they say how ministers of the gospel and teachers of youth are the worst paid men in the community; but I think, judging by my own case, that professors are quite as poorly remunerated. It used to take everything I could rake and scrape to keep my family together; and so, young Ishmael, I haven't saved a dollar."

"Is that so?" asked Ishmael, in a voice of pain.

"True as gospel, young Ishmael—Mr. Worth."

"How then do you manage to live, Morris? I ask this from the kindest of feelings."

"Don't I know it, young—Mr. Worth. Well, sir, I do an odd job once in a while yet, for the colored people, and that keeps me from starving," said the professor, with a smile.

Ishmael fell into a deep thought for a while, and then lifting his head, said:

"Well, professor, you have been in your day and generation as useful a man to your fellow-creatures as any other in this world. You have contributed as much to the comfort and well-being of the community in which you live as any other member of it! And you should not and you shall not be left in your old age, either to suffer from want or to live on charity—"

"I may suffer for want, Mr. Worth, but I never will consent to live on charity!" said the odd-job man with dignity.

"That I am sure you never will, professor; though mind! I do not believe it to be any degradation to live by charity when one cannot live in any other way. For if all men are brethren should not the able brother help the disabled brother, and that without humbling him?"

"Yes; but I am not disabled, young—Mr. Worth. I am only disused."

"That is very true. And therefore I spoke as I did when I said just now that you should not suffer from want nor live by charity. Listen to me, professor. I have a proposition to make to you. Your daughters are all married and your work is done; you are alone and idle here. But you are not a mere animal to be tied down to one spot of earth by local attachment. You are a very intelligent man with a progressive mind. You will never stop improving, professor. You have improved very much in the last few years. I notice it in your conversation—"

"I am glad you think so, young—Mr. Worth! but I'm getting aged."

"What of that? You are 'traveling towards the light,' and after improving all your life here you will go on progressing through all eternity."

"Well, sir, that thought ought to be a great comfort to an old man."

"Yes. Now what I want to propose to you is this—I think you love me, professor?"

"Love you, young—Mr. Worth! Why the Lord in heaven bless your dear heart, I love you better than I do anything on the face of the earth, and that's a fact," said the professor, with his face all in a glow of feeling.

And all who knew him might have known that he spoke truth; for though he was not in the least degree deficient in affection for his daughters, yet his love of Ishmael amounted almost to idolatry.

"Dear old friend, I will prove to you some day how high a value I set upon your love. I think, professor, that loving me, as you do, you could live happily with me?"

"What did you say, young—Mr. Worth? I did not quite understand."

"I will be plain, professor. You have lived out your present life here; it is gone. Now, instead of vegetating on here any longer, come into another sphere, a more enlarged and active sphere, where your thoughts as well as your hands will find employment and your mind as well as your body have food."

"How is that to be done, young—Mr. Worth?"

"Come with me to Washington. I have a suite of three very pleasant rooms in the house where I board. Now suppose you come and live with me and take care of my rooms? Your services would be worth a good, liberal salary, from which you would be enabled to live very comfortably and save money."

"What, young Ishmael! Me! I go to Washington and live with you all the time, day and night, under one roof! and live where I can get books and newspapers and hear lectures and debates and see pictures and models, and, in short, come at everything I have been longing to reach all my life?"

"Yes, professor, that is what I propose to you."

"There! I used to say that you'd live to be a blessing to my declining years, young—Mr. Worth (I declare I'll not forget myself again), Mr. Worth! there! Do you really mean it, sir?"

"Really and truly."

"There, then, I am not going to be a hypocrite and pretend to higgle-haggle about it. I'll go, sir; and be proud to do it; it will be taking a new lease of life for me to go. Do you know, I never was in a large city in all my life, though I have always longed to go? Well, sir, I'll go with you. And I will serve you faithfully, sir; for mine will be a service for love more than for money. And I will never forget the proprieties so far as to call you anything else but 'Mr. Worth,' or 'sir,' in the presence of others, sir, though my heart does betray me into calling you young Ishmael sometimes here."

"I shall leave here on Saturday morning. Can you be ready to go with me as soon as that?"

"Of course I can, Mr. Worth. There's nothing for me to do in the way of preparation but to pack my knapsack and lock my door," answered this "Rough and Ready."

"Very well, then, professor, I like your promptitude. Meet me at Brudenell Hall on Saturday morning at seven o'clock, and in the meantime I will find a conveyance for you."

"All right; thank you, sir; I will be ready."

And Ishmael shook hands with the professor and departed, leaving him hopeful and happy.

At the dinner-table that day, being questioned by his father, Ishmael told him of the retainer he had engaged.

"Ah, my dear boy, it is just like you to burden yourself with the presence and support of that poor old man, and persuade him—and yourself, too, perhaps—that you are securing the services of an invaluable assistant. And all with no other motive than his welfare," said Mr. Brudenell.

"Indeed, sir, I think it will add to my happiness to have Morris with me. I like and esteem the old man, and I believe that he really will be of much use to me," replied the son.

"Well, I hope so, Ishmael; I hope so."

There was through all his talk a preoccupied air about Mr. Brudenell that troubled his son, who at last said:

"I hope, sir, that you have received no unpleasant news by this mail?"

"Oh, no; no, Ishmael! but I have had on my mind for several days something of which I wish to speak to you—"

"Yes, sir?"

"Ishmael, since I have been down here I have followed your counsel. I have gone about among my tenants and dependents, and—without making inquiries—I have led them to speak of the long period of my absence from my little kingdom, and of the manner in which Lady Hurstmonceux administered its affairs. And, Ishmael, I have heard but one account of her. With one voice the community here accord her the highest praise."

"I told you so, sir."

"As a wife, though an abandoned one, as mistress of the house, and as lady of the manor, she seems to have performed all her duties in the most unexceptionable manner."

"Everyone knows that, sir."

"But still remains the charge not yet refuted."

"Because you have given her no chance to refute it, sir. Be just! Put her on her defense, and my word for it, she will exonerate herself," said Ishmael earnestly.

Mr. Brudenell shook his head.

"There are some things, Ishmael, that on the very face of them admit of no defense," said Mr. Brudenell, with an emphasis that put an end to the conversation.

Punctually at seven o'clock Saturday the professor, accoutered for a journey, with knapsack on his back, presented himself at the servant's door at Brudenell Hall.

His arrival being announced, Ishmael came out to meet him.

"Well, here I am, Mr. Worth; though how I am to travel I don't know. I have walked, by faith, so far!" he said.

"All right, professor. Mr. Brudenell will lend me an extra horse."

And father and son took leave of each other with earnest wishes for their mutual good.

CHAPTER XII

THE JOURNEY.

Ever charming, ever new,

When will the landscape tire the view?

The fountains fall, the rivers flow,

The woody valleys, warm and low,

The windy summit, wild and high,

Roughly rushing on the sky!

The pleasant seat, the chapel tower,

The naked rock, the shady bower,

The town and village, dome and farm,

Each gave each a double charm,

As pearls upon a woman's arm.

—Dyer.

Ishmael and his aged retainer rode on, down the elm-shaded avenue and out upon the turnpike road. There seemed to be a special fitness in the relations between these two. Ishmael, you are aware, was a very handsome, stately, and gracious young man. And the professor was the tallest, gravest, and most respectable of servants. Ah, their relative positions were changed since twelve years before, when they used to travel that same road on foot, as "boss" and "boy."

Many men in Ishmael's position would have shrunk from all that would have reminded them of the poverty from which they had sprung; and would have avoided as much as possible all persons who were familiar with their early struggles.

But Ishmael did not so. While pressing forward to the duties and distinctions of the future, with burning aspiration and untiring energy, he held the places and persons of the past in most affectionate remembrance.

To a vain or haughty man in Ishmael's situation there could scarcely have occurred a more humiliating circumstance than the constant presence of the poor, old odd-jobber, whose "boy" he had once been.

But Ishmael was neither the one nor the other; he was intellectual and affectionate. His breadth of mind took in his past memories, his present position, and his future prospects, and saw them all in perfect harmony. And his depth of heart found room for the humblest friends of his wretched infancy, as well as for the higher loves of his manhood's prime.

Ishmael was at ease with the old odd-job man, and he would have been at ease with his imperial majesty, had circumstances brought him into the immediate circle of the Czar; because from the depths of his soul he was intensely conscious of the innate majesty of man.

Ishmael had no more need of a servant than a coach has of a fifth wheel. He took the professor into his service for no other purpose than to take care of the poor old man and make him happy, never foreseeing how really useful and important this gray-haired retainer would eventually become to him. He was planning only the professor's happiness, not his own convenience. But he found both.

As they rode along that pleasant September morning he was pleasing himself with thinking how that intelligent old man, starved all his life for mental food, would delight himself amid the intellectual wealth of his new life.

They were approaching the turn-stile at the cross-roads, memorable for the weary watchings of Lady Hurstmonceux.

As they reached the spot and took the road leading to Baymouth Ishmael looked back to the professor, who, as he felt in duty bound to do, rode in the rear of his master, and, as was natural, looked a little serious.

"Do you remember, professor, how often you and I have traveled afoot up and down this road in the exercise of our useful calling of odd- jobbing? Your great shoulders bowed under an enormous load of pots, pans, kettles, umbrellas, and everything that required your surgical skill; and my little back bent beneath the basket of tools?" inquired Ishmael, by way of diverting him.

"Ah, do I not, sir! But why recall those days? You have left them far behind, sir," said the professor, in grave consideration of his master's dignity.

"Because I like to recall them, professor. It quickens my gratitude to the Lord for all his marvelous mercies, and it deepens my love for my friends for their goodness to me then," said Ishmael fervently.

"The Lord knows I don't know who was good to you then! Of course, now, sir, there are multitudes of people who would be proud to be numbered among your friends. But then, of all the abandoned children that ever I saw, you were about the most friendless," said the professor, with much feeling.

"You, for one, were good to me, professor; and I do not forget it."

"Ah, the Lord knows it was but little I could do."

"What you did do was vital to me, professor. My life was but a little flame, in danger of dying out. You fed it with little chips, and kept it alive."

"And it burns great hickory logs now, and warms the world," said the professor, looking proudly and fondly upon the fine young man before him.

"It shall at least warm and shelter your age, professor. And whatever of prosperity the Lord accords me, you shall share."

As he said these words he turned an affectionate look on his retainer, and saw the tears rolling down the old man's cheeks.

"It was but a few, poor crumbs I cast upon the waters, that all this bread should come back to me after many days," he muttered in a broken voice.

"We were really very happy, professor, when we used to trudge the road together, plying our profession; but we are going to be much happier now, because our lives will be enlarged."

The professor smiled assent and they rode on.

They passed through Baymouth, where the professor directed his master's attention to the new signs of the mechanics who had taken his custom from him,

"But it is a true saying, sir, that there never was one door closed but what there was another opened. Many doors were closed against me at once; but just see what a broad, beautiful door you have opened to me, letting me into a glorious new life!"

"Life is what we make of it, professor. To you, who will appreciate and enjoy every good thing in it, no doubt your new life will be very happy," replied Ishmael.

And so conversing they passed through the town and entered the deep forest that lay along the shores of the river between Baymouth and Shelton.

They rode all the morning through the pleasant woods and stopped an hour at noon to rest and refresh themselves and their horses; and then resumed their journey and rode all the afternoon and arrived at Woodside just as the sun was setting.

As before, Reuben, Hannah, Sam, Sally, the children, and the dog, all rushed out to welcome Ishmael.

Much astonished was Hannah to see her old friend, the professor, and much delighted to hear that he was going up to Washington to fill the place of major-domo to Ishmael. For Hannah shared the old woman's superstition, that the young man is never able to take care of himself; and notwithstanding all that had come and gone—notwithstanding that Ishmael had taken care of himself and her too, from the time he was eight years old, for years more, still she thought that he would be all the safer for having "an old head to look after him."

There was plenty of news to tell, too.

As soon as the bounteous supper that Reuben and Hannah always provided for favored guests was over, and they were all gathered around the bright little wood fire that the capricious autumn weather rendered desirable, the budget was opened.

Lord and Lady Vincent were to have an evening reception, at Tanglewood.

And on the first of October they were to sail for Europe.

Lady Vincent was going to take three of the servants with her—old Aunt Katie, Jim, and Sally.

Jim was to go as lady's footman; Sally as lady's maid; and old Aunt Katie in no particular capacity, but because she refused to be separated from the two beings she loved the most of all in the world.

She had nursed Miss Claudia, and she was bound to nurse Miss Claudia's children, she said.

Lady Vincent had decided to take her, and was rather glad to do it.

Lord Vincent, it was supposed, did not like the arrangement, and stigmatized the black servants as "gorillas," but Lady Vincent, it was confidently asserted, never deigned to consult his lordship, or pay the slightest attention to his prejudices. And so matters stood for the present.

All this was communicated to Ishmael by Reuben and Hannah. And in the midst of their talk, in walked one of the subjects of their conversation—Aunt Katie.

She was immediately welcomed and provided with a seat in the chimney-corner. She was inflated with the subject of her expected voyage and glowing with the importance of her anticipated office. She expatiated on the preparations in progress.

"But don't you feel sorry to leave your native home, Aunt Katie?" inquired Hannah.

"Who, me? No, 'deed! I takes my native home along with me when I takes Miss Claudia and Jim and Sally! For what says the catechism?—'tis home where'er de heart is!' And my heart is 'long o' de chillun. 'Sides which I don't want to be allus stuck down in one place like an old tree as can't be moved without killing of it. I'm a living soul, I am, and I wants to go and see somethin' of this here world afore I goes hence and bees no more," said Katie briskly.

Evidently Katie was a progressive spirit, and would not have hesitated to emigrate to Liberia or any other new colony where she could better herself or her children, and begin life afresh at fifty.

At last Katie got up to go, and bade them all a patronizing farewell.

Sally, and Jim, who as usual was spending his evening with her, arose to accompany Katie.

And Ishmael took his hat and walked out after them.

Very much embarrassed they were at this unusual honor, which they could in no wise understand, until at length when they had gone some little way into the woods Ishmael said:

"I have something to say to you three."

"Yes, sir," said Katie, speaking for the rest.

"Katie, you are acquainted with that psychological mystery called presentiment, for I have heard you speak of it," said Ishmael, smiling half in doubt, half in derision of his present feelings.

"Ye-es, sir," answered Katie hesitatingly, "I believe in persentiments; though what you mean by sigh-what's-its-name, I don't know."

"Never mind, Katie, you believe in presentiments?"

"Indeed do I! and got reason to, too! Why, law! the month before Mrs. Merlin, as was Miss Claudia's mother, died. I sperienced the most 'stonishing—"

"Yes, I know. You told me all about that before, Katie."

"Why, so I did, to be sure, sir, when you were lying wounded at the house!"

"Yes. Well, Katie, some such feeling as that of which you speak, vague, but very strong, impels me to say what I am about to say to you all."

"Yes, sir. Listen, chillun!" said Katie, in a voice of such awful solemnity that Ishmael again smiled at what he was inclined to characterize as the absurdity of believing in presentiments.

"You three are going to Europe in attendance upon Lady Vincent."

"Yes, sir. Listen, chillun!" again said Katie, keeping her eyes fixed upon Ishmael and nudging her companions right and left with her elbows.

"You will be all of her friends, all of her native country, all of her past life that she will take with her."

"Yes, sir. Listen, chillun!" and another elbow dig, right and left.

"She is going among strangers, foreigners, possibly rivals and enemies."

"Yes, sir. Listen, chillun—now it's a-comin'!"

"She may need all your devotion. Be vigilant, therefore. Watch over her, care for her, think for her, pray for her; let her honor and happiness be the one charge and object of your lives."

"Yes, sir. Listen, chillun! you hears, don't you?"

A sharp reminder right and left brought out the responses "yes" and "yes" from Jim and Sally.

"And when you are far away you will remember all this that I have said to you; for, as I told you before, I feel, deep in my spirit, that your lady will need your utmost devotion," said Ishmael earnestly.

"You may count on me, for one, Mr. Ishmael, sir; not only to devote myself to my lady's sarvice, but to keep the ole 'oman and Sally in mind to go and do likewise," said Jim, with an air of earnest good faith that could not be doubted.

"That is right. I will take leave of you now. Good-by! God bless you!"

And Ishmael shook hands with them all around, and left them and walked back to the cottage.

The next day, being the Sabbath, he went with Hannah and Reuben and the professor to church. He had almost shrunk from this duty, in his dread of meeting Claudia there; but she was not present. Judge Merlin's pew was empty when they entered, and remained empty during the whole of the morning service.

When the benediction had been pronounced, and the congregation were going out, Ishmael was about to leave his pew when he saw that the minister had come down from the pulpit and was advancing straight towards him to speak to him. He therefore stopped and waited for Mr. Wynne's approach.

There was a shaking of hands and mutual inquiries as to each other's health, and then Mr. Wynne invited Ishmael to accompany him home and dine with him.

Ishmael thanked him and declined the invitation, saying that he was with friends.

Mr. Wynne then smilingly shook hands with Hannah and Reuben and the professor, claiming them all as old friends and parishioners, and extending the invitation to them.

But Hannah pleaded the children left at home, and, with many thanks, declined the honor.

And the friends shook hands and separated.

Very early on Monday morning Ishmael and his gray-haired retainer prepared for their departure for Washington.

Ishmael left two commissions for Reuben. The first was to make his apologies and adieus to Judge Merlin. And the second was to send back the horse, borrowed for the use of the professor, to Mr. Brudenell at Brudenell Hall. Both of which Reuben promised to execute.

After an early breakfast Ishmael and his venerable dependent took leave of Hannah, the children and the dog, and seated themselves in the light wagon that had been geared up for their accommodation, and were driven by Reuben to Shelton, where they arrived in time to catch the "Errand Boy" on its up trip. Reuben took leave of them only half a minute before the boat started.

They had a pleasant run up the river, and reached the Washington wharf early on Wednesday morning, where Ishmael took a carriage to convey himself, servant, and his luggage to his lodgings.

As they drove through the streets the professor, seated on the front seat, bobbed about from right to left, looking out at the windows and gazing at the houses, the shops, and the crowds of people. Nothing could exceed the surprise and delight of the intellectual but childlike old man, who now for the first time in his life looked upon a large city. His enthusiasm at the sight of the Capitol was delicious.

"You shall go all through it some day, as soon as we get settled," said Ishmael.

"There is only one thing that I am doubtful about," said the professor.

"And what is that?"

"That I have not years enough left to live to see all the wonders of the world."

"None of us—not the youngest of us have, professor. But you will live to see a great many. And by the time that you have seen everything that is to be found in Washington, I shall be ready to go to Europe; for I expect to see Europe some time or other, professor, and you shall see it with me."

"Oh!" ejaculated the odd-job man, who seemed to think that the millennium was not far off.

And at that moment the carriage drew up before Ishmael's lodgings. And the driver and the professor carried the luggage into the front hall. And when the carriage was paid and dismissed

Ishmael conducted the professor to the inner office where the two clerks that were in charge of it arose to welcome their principal.

When he had shaken hands with them, he led his retainer into the bedroom, and showed him a small vacant chamber adjoining that, and told him that the latter should be his—the professor's own sanctuary. Then he showed the old man the pleasant garden, all blooming now with late roses, chrysanthemums, dahlias, and other gorgeous autumn flowers, and told him that there he might walk or sit, and smoke his pipe in pleasant weather. And finally he brought the professor back to the front office, where he found his hostesses, Miss Jenny and Miss Nelly Downey, waiting to welcome him. Nice, delicate, refined-looking old maiden ladies they were—tall, thin, and fair complexioned, with fine, gray hair, and cobweb lace caps and pale gray dresses, and having pleasant smiles and soft voices.

After they had shaken hands with their lodger they turned looks of inquiry upon the tall, gray-haired old man that stood behind him.

"This is a very old friend of mine; I have engaged him to take care of my rooms, his name is Morris, but upon account of his skill in many arts he has received from the public the title of professor," said Ishmael, turning an affectionate look upon the old odd-job man.

"How do you do, Professor Morris? We are very glad to see you, I am sure; and we hope you will find yourself comfortable, and also that you will be a comfort to Mr. Worth, who is a very estimable young gentleman indeed," said Miss Jenny, speaking for herself and sister.

"I cannot fail to be both comfortable and happy under this honored roof, my ladies!" said the professor, in a most reverential tone, laying his hand upon his heart and making a profound bow that would have done credit to the most accomplished courtier of the grave and stately old school.

"A nice, gentlemanly old person," said Miss Jenny, nodding her head to her sister. And Miss Nelly said "Yes," and nodded her head also.

"If you can fit up the little chamber adjoining my bedroom for the professor, I will arrange with you for his board," said Ishmael, aside to Miss Jenny.

"Oh, certainly; it shall be done immediately," replied the old lady. And she left the room, followed by her sister, to give orders to that effect.

And before night the professor was comfortably installed in his neatly furnished and well-warmed little room, and Ishmael's apartments were restored to order, and he himself in full career going over the office business of the last two weeks with his clerks.

He found a plenty of work cut out for him to do, and he resolved to be very busy to make up for his idleness during his holiday.

Ishmael did not really wish to tax his old servant with any labor at all. He wished his office to be as much of a sinecure as possible. And he continually urged the professor to go abroad and see the city sights, or to walk in the garden and enjoy his pipe, or rest himself in his own room, or visit his daughter, the hackman's wife.

The professor obediently did all this for a time; but as the days passed Ishmael saw that the old man's greatest happiness consisted in staying with and serving his master; and so he at length permitted the professor to relieve the chamber-maid of her duties in his rooms, and take quiet possession and complete charge of them.

And never were rooms kept in more perfect order. And, best of all, love taught the professor the mystic art of dusting without deranging papers and dementing their owner.

Ishmael's present position was certainly a very pleasant one. He not only found a real home in his boarding-house, and a faithful friend in his servant, but a pair of aunties in his landladies. Every good heart brought in contact with Ishmael Worth was sure to love him. And these old ladies were no exception to the rule. They had no relatives to bestow their affections upon, and so, seeing every day more of their young lodger's worth, they grew to love him with maternal ardor. It is not too much to say that they doted on him. And in private they nodded their heads at each other and talked of its being time to make their wills, and spoke of young Mr. Worth as their heir and executor.

Ishmael for his part treated the old ladies with all the reverential tenderness that their age and womanhood had a right to expect from his youth and manhood. He never dreamed that the "sweet, small courtesies," which it was his happiness to bestow alike on rich and poor, had won for him such signal favor in the eyes of the old ladies. He knew and was happy to know that they loved him. That was all. He never dreamed of being their heir; he never even imagined that they had any property to bequeath. He devoted himself with conscientious zeal to his profession, and went on, as he deserved to go on, from success to success.

CHAPTER XIII

LADY VINCENT'S RECEPTION.

The folds of her wine-dark violet dress

Glow over the sofa fall on fall.

As she sits in the light of her loveliness,

With a smile for each and for all.

Could we find out her heart through that velvet and lace,

Can it beat without rumpling her sumptuous dress?

She will show us her shoulder, her bosom, her face,

But what her heart's like, we must guess.

—O. M.

The evening of Lady Vincent's reception arrived. At an unfashionably early hour Judge Merlin's country house was filled.

All the county families of any importance were represented there. The rustic guests, drawn, no doubt, not more by their regard for Judge Merlin and his daughter than by their curiosity to behold a titled foreigner.

Mr. and Mrs. Middleton and Beatrice came very early, encumbered with several bandboxes; for their long ride made it necessary for them to defer their evening toilet until after their arrival.

They were received and conducted to their rooms by old Aunt Katie. "Lady Vincent," she said, "has not yet left her dressing room."

When their toilets were made, Mr. and Mrs. Middleton came to Bee's door to take her down to the drawing room.

Very beautiful indeed looked Bee, in her floating, cloud-like dress of snow-white tulle, with white moss-roses resting on her rounded bosom and wreathing her golden ringlets; and all her beauty irradiated with the light of a happy love.

Her father smiled proudly and her mother fondly on her as she came out and joined them.

The found the drawing rooms already well filled with guests.

Lord and Lady Vincent stood near the door to receive all comers. To them the Middletons first went.

Very handsome and majestic looked Claudia in her rich robe of royal purple velvet, with her raven black hair crowned with a diadem of diamonds, and diamonds blazing on her neck and arms and at her waist. Strangers looked upon her loveliness with unqualified delight. Her "beauty made them glad." But friends who saw the glittering surface and the alloy beneath it, admired and sighed. Her dark eyes were beaming with light; her oval cheeks were burning with crimson fire. Mrs. Middleton thought this was fever; but Bee knew it was French rouge.

Claudia received her friends with bright smiles and gay words. She complimented them on their good looks and rallied them on their gravity. And then she let them lightly pass away to make room for new arrivals, who were approaching to pay their respects.

They passed through the crowd until they found Judge Merlin, to whose care Mr. Middleton consigned Bee, while he himself, with his wife on his arm, made a tour of all the rooms, including the supper room.

The party, they saw, was going to be a successful one, notwithstanding the fact that the three great metropolitan ministers of fashion had nothing whatever to do with it.

Sam and Jim, with perfect liberty to do their worst in the matters of garden flowers and wax lights, had decorated and illuminated the rooms with the rich profusion for which the negro servants are notorious. The guests might have been in fairy groves and bowers, instead of drawing rooms, for any glimpse of walls or ceilings they could get through green boughs and blooming flowers.

In the supper room old Aunt Katie with her attendant nymphs had laid a feast that might vie in "toothsomeness" if not in elegance with the best ever elaborated by the celebrated caterer.

And in the dancing room the local band of negro musicians drew from their big fiddle, little fiddle, banjo, and bones notes as ear-piercing and limb-lifting, if not as scientific and artistic, as anything ever executed by Dureezie's renowned troupe.

The Englishman, secretly cynical, sneered at all this; but openly courteous, made himself agreeable to all the prettiest of the country belles, who ever after had the proud boast of having quadrilled or waltzed with Lord Vincent.

The party did not break up until morning. The reason of this was obvious—the company could not venture to return home in their carriages over those dangerous country roads until daylight.

It was, in fact, sunrise before the last guests departed and the weary family were at liberty to go to bed and sleep. They had turned the night into day, and now it was absolutely necessary to turn the day into night.

They did not any of them awake until three or four o'clock in the afternoon, when they took coffee in their chambers. And they did not reassemble until the late dinner hour at six o'clock, by which time the servants had removed the litter of the party and restored the rooms to neatness, order, and comfort.

The Middletons had not departed with the other guests. They joined the family at dinner. And after dinner, at the pressing invitation of Judge Merlin, they agreed to remain at Tanglewood for the few days that would intervene before the departure of Lord and Lady Vincent for Europe. Only Bee, the next morning, drove over to the Beacon to give the servants there strict charges in regard to the girls and boys, and to bring little Lu back with her to Tanglewood.

The next week was passed in making the final preparations for the voyage.

And when all was ready on a bright Monday morning, the first of October, Lord and Lady Vincent, with their servants and baggage, departed from Tanglewood.

Judge Merlin, leaving his house to be shut up by the Middletons, accompanied them to see them off in the steamer.

It was quite an imposing procession that left Tanglewood that morning. There were two carriages and a van. In the first carriage rode Lord and Lady Vincent and Judge Merlin. In the second my lord's valet and my lady's three servants. And in the van was piled an inconceivable amount of luggage.

This procession made a sensation, I assure you, as it lumbered along the rough country roads. Every little isolated cabin along the way turned out its ragged rout of girls and boys who threw up their arms with a prolonged "Hooray!" as it passed—to the great disgust of the Englishman and the transient amusement of the judge. As for Claudia, she sat back with her eyes closed and cared for nothing.

The negroes came in for their share of notice.

"Hooray, Aunt Katie, is that you a-ridin' in a coach as bold as brass?" some wayside laborer would shout.

"As bold as brass yourself!" would be the irate retort of the old woman, nodding her head that was adorned with a red and yellow bonnet, from the window.

"Hillo, Jim! that's never you, going to forring parts as large as life?" would sing out another.

"Yes! Good-by! God bless you all as is left behind!" would be Jim's compassionate reply.

"Lord bless my soul and body, what a barbarous country!" would be Lord Vincent's muttered comment. And the judge would smile and Claudia slumber, or seem to do so.

And this happened over and over again all along the turnpike road, until they got to Shelton, where they embarked on the steamer "Arrow" for Baltimore, where they arrived the next day at noon.

They made no stay in the Monumental City. Old Katie's dilated eyes had not time to relieve themselves by one wink over the wonders of the new world into which she was introduced, before, to her "surprise and 'stonishment," as she afterwards expressed it, she found herself "on board the cars, being whisked off somewhere else. And if you would believe her racket, she had to hold the h'ar on her head to keep it from being streamed off in the flight. And she was no sooner set down comfortable in the cars at Baltimore than she had to get up and get outen them at New York. And you better had believe it, chillun, that's all."

Old Aunt Katie must have slept all the way through that night's journey; for it is certain that the cars in which she traveled left Baltimore at eight o'clock in the evening and arrived at New York at six o'clock the next morning.

After their dusty, smoky, cindery ride of ten hours our party had barely time to find their hotel, cleanse and refresh themselves with warm baths and changes of raiment and get their breakfasts comfortably, before the hour of embarkation arrived. For they were required to be on board their steamer at ten o'clock, as she was announced to sail at twelve, meridian.

At ten, therefore, the carriages that had been ordered for the purpose of conveying them to the pier were announced.

Lower and lower sank the heart of the widowed father as the moment approached that was to separate him from his only child. There were times when he so dreaded that moment as to wish for death instead. There were times when he felt that the wrench which should finally tear his daughter from him must certainly prove his death-blow. Yet, for her sake, he bore himself with composure and dignity. He would not let her see the anguish that was oppressing his heart.

He entered the carriage with her and drove to the pier. He drew her arm within his own, keeping her hand pressed against his aching heart, and so he led her up the gang-plank on board the steamer, Lord Vincent and their retinue following. He would not trust himself to utter any serious words; but he led her to find her stateroom, that he might see for himself she would be comfortable on her voyage, and that he might carry away with him a picture of her and her surroundings in his memory. And then he brought her up on deck and found a pleasant seat for her, and sat down beside her, keeping her arm within his and her hand pressed as a balm to his covered bleeding heart.

There he sat, speaking but little, while active preparations were made for sailing. It looked to him like preparations for an execution.

Lord Vincent walked up and down the deck, occasionally stopping to exchange a word with Claudia, or the judge.

At length the signal-bell rang out, every peal striking like a death-toll on the heart of the old man.

And the order was shouted forth:

"All hands ashore!"

The moment of life and death had come. He started up; he strained his daughter to his breast. He gasped:

"God bless you, my dear! Write as soon as you land!"

He wrung the hand of Lord Vincent. "Be good to—" He choked, and hurried from the steamer.

He stood alone on the pier gazing at the receding ship, and at his daughter, who was leaning over the bulwarks, waving her handkerchief. Swiftly, swiftly, receded the ship from his strained sight. First his daughter's face faded from his aching vision; but still he could see the outline of her form. A minute or two and even that grew indistinct and was lost among the rigging. And while he was still straining his eyes to the cracking, in the effort to see her, the signal gun from the steamer was fired. The farewell gun! The ball seemed to strike his own heart. All his strength forsook him; his well-strung nerves suddenly relaxed; his limbs gave way beneath him, and he must have fallen but for the strong arms that suddenly clasped him and the warm bosom that firmly supported him.

Turning up his languid, fainting eyes, he saw—

"Ishmael!"

Yes, it was Ishmael, who with a son's devotion was standing there and sustaining Claudia's forsaken father in the hour of his utter weakness and utmost need.

At first the judge looked at him in surprise and incredulity, which soon, however, gave way before recognition and affection, as he rested on that true breast and met those beautiful eyes bent on him in deepest sympathy.

"Oh, Ishmael, Ishmael, is it you? is it indeed you? You here at need? Oh, my son, my son, would to the Lord that you were indeed my son! It is a grief and folly that you are not!" he exclaimed with emotion.

What could Ishmael reply to these words? Nothing. He could only tenderly support the old man and turn to a gray-haired servant that waited behind him and say:

"Professor, go call a carriage here quickly!"

And Jim Morris started on his errand, with all the crippled alacrity of age and zeal.

"Oh, Ishmael, she has gone! she has gone! My daughter has left me!" he groaned, grasping the hand of his young supporter.

"I know it, sir, I know it. But this hour of parting is the bitterest of all. The heart feels the wrench of separation keenly now."

"Oh, yes, yes!"

"But every coming hour will bring relief. You will cease to look back to the bitter parting, and you will look forward to the happy meeting. And that meeting may be as soon as you please, sir, you know. There is nothing on earth to prevent or even delay your visit to Lady Vincent as soon after she gets settled at home, as you like. This is October. You may spend Christmas with her, you know."

"That is true; that is very true, and Christmas is not so very far off. Ah! I ought not to have given way so, and I should not have done it, only I was quite alone when they sailed. There was no one with me to suggest these comforting thoughts, and I was too much prostrated by the wrench of parting to remember them of myself. Oh, Ishmael! what Providence was it that sent you to my side in this extremity?" inquired the judge, curiosity mingling with his interest in the question.

"I came here," said Ishmael frankly, "with no other purpose than to be with you in your hour of trial. I knew that you would require the presence of some friend."

"Ah, Ishmael! it was just like you to drop all your business and come uncalled, traveling from Washington to New York, with the sole object of sustaining an old friend in the hour of his weakness. So that does not surprise me. But how did you hit the time so well?"

"I knew from Bee's last letter, dated from Tanglewood, the day that Lord Vincent had positively determined to sail. I knew also the name of the only steamer that sailed for Europe on that day. And so, as Bee expressed great regret that her father could not accompany you to New York, and great anxiety because you would be left quite alone after the trial of parting with Claudia, I suddenly resolved to come on. I came on by the same train that brought your party, although not in the same car. I reached the city this morning, and finding that the steamer was to sail at twelve, noon, I walked down to the pier at half-past eleven so as to be ready to meet you when you should come ashore."

"And you took all this thought and trouble for me? Oh, Ishmael, Ishmael, what a sorrow and shame it is that you are not my son!"

"I am your son in reverence, and love, and service, sir; and if I am not in any other way it is because the Lord has willed otherwise," said Ishmael very gravely.

"Did you see Claudia off?" inquired the judge.

"I saw the steamer; I did not see Lady Vincent. I was in the rear of the crowd on the pier and looking out among them that I might not miss you," replied Ishmael. But he did not add that he had sedulously avoided looking at Claudia as she stood beside her husband on the deck waving her handkerchief in adieus to her father.

In a few minutes Jim Morris came up with a comfortable carriage, and the judge, somewhat recovered now, was assisted into it.

"You are coming too, Ishmael, are you not?" said the old man, looking anxiously out of the window.

"Of course I am, sir; for with your permission I will not leave you until we get back to Washington," replied the young man, preparing to spring into the carriage. But suddenly pausing with his hand on the door he inquired:

"Where shall I order the hackman to drive?"

The judge named his hotel, which happened to be the very one at which Ishmael was stopping; and so the young man gave the order and entered the carriage.

The professor climbed up to a seat beside the hackman, and the hack moved on.

As the carriage turned into Broadway and rolled along that magnificent street, the professor, from his elevated seat, gazed with ever-increasing delight and admiration on the wonders of the great city spread before him.

There were moments when honest Jim Morris was inclined to suspect that, some time within the past few weeks, he must have died, been buried, and risen again to some new stage of existence; so wonderful to him seemed the change in his life. He had not had his satisfaction with gazing when the carriage stopped at the hotel.

Ishmael paid off the hack and gave his arm to the judge, and assisted him into the house.

"Ishmael," he said, as soon as they had reached a sitting room, "have you no other business in New York than to look after me?"

"None whatever. I am entirely at your service."

"Then we—But stop. Are you quite ready to return to Washington at any time?"

"Quite ready to go at a moment's warning, if required."

"Then I think we had better take the early train to-morrow morning, for you ought not to be absent from your office, especially during court term, and even I shall be better at home. We shall need to-day and to-night for rest, but we will start to-morrow. What do you think?"

"I think that is altogether the best plan."

As it was now about one o'clock the judge ordered luncheon. And when they had partaken of it, and the judge had drunk several glasses of rich old port, he said:

"Ishmael, I did not get a wink of sleep last night, and this wine has made me drowsy. I think I will go to my chamber and lie down."

Ishmael gave the judge his arm and assisted him to his bed-room, and saw him lie down, and waited until he knew him to be in a deep, refreshing sleep; and then he closed the blinds, and darkened the room, and left him to repose.

In the hall he spoke to one of the waiters, and placing a quarter of an eagle in his hand, requested him to go up and remain near the judge's chamber door until he should awake.

Then Ishmael sought the professor out and said to him:

"Professor, this is your first visit to New York, as it is also mine. Let us make use of the little time we have to see as much as we can."

Jim Morris eagerly jumped at the proposition.

Ishmael sent for a carriage, and they started; the professor this time riding inside with Ishmael, as he always did when they were alone.

They spent the whole afternoon in sight-seeing, and returned at sunset.

The judge had not awakened, nor did he awake until roused by the ear-stunning gong that warned all the guests to prepare for dinner.

He opened his eyes and stared around in bewilderment for a few seconds, and then seeing Ishmael, remembered everything.

"Ah, my boy, now it is all come back to me afresh, and I have got to meet it all over again. I had been dreaming that I was at Tanglewood with my child, and she was neither married nor going to be. Now I have lost her anew," he said, with a deep sigh.

"I know it, sir; but with every sleep and every awakening this impression will be fainter and fainter. You will soon be cheerful and happy again, in the anticipation of going to see her."

"Plague take that gong! how it does belabor and thrash one's tympanum!" said the judge irritably, as he slowly arose to dress for dinner.

After dinner Ishmael persuaded him not to stay in and mope, but to go with him to hear a celebrated traveler and eloquent lecturer, who was to hold forth in one of the churches on the manners and customs of the Laplanders. The professor also had leave to go. And the judge and Ishmael were well entertained and interested, and the professor was instructed and delighted. Evidently the old odd-job man, judging from his past and present experience, thought

They returned to a late supper, and then retired to bed.

Next morning they took the early train for Washington, where they arrived at seven o'clock.

The judge went home with Ishmael and remained his guest for two or three days, while he wrote to Reuben Gray to send up Sam and the carriage for him; and waited for it to come.

Ishmael at the same time took the responsibility of writing to Mr. Middleton, advising him to come up with the carriage in order to bear the judge company in his journey home.

The last day of the week the carriage arrived with Mr. Middleton inside and Sam on the box. And on Monday morning the judge, in better spirits than anyone could have expected him to be, took an affectionate leave of Ishmael, and with Mr. Middleton for company, set out for Tanglewood, where in due time they arrived safely.

We also must bid adieu to Ishmael for a short time and leave him to the successful prosecution of his business, and to the winning of new laurels. For it is necessary to the progress of this story that we follow the fortunes of Claudia, Viscountess Vincent.

CHAPTER XIV

ROMANCE AND REALITY.

If we had heard that she was dead

We hastily had cried,

"She was so richly favored

God will forgive her pride!"

But now to see her living death—

Power, glory, arts, all gone—

Her empire lost and her poor breath

Still vainly struggling on!

—Milnes.

The "Ocean Empress" steamed her way eastward. The month was favorable; the weather bright; the wind fair and the sea calm. Every circumstance promised a pleasant voyage. None but a few unreasonable people grew seasick; and even they could not keep it up long.

There was a very select and agreeable set of passengers in the first cabin.

But Lord and Lady Vincent were the only titled persons present; and from both European and American voyagers received a ridiculous amount of homage.

Claudia enjoyed the worship, though she despised the worshipers. Her spirits had rebounded from their depression. She was Lady Vincent, and in the present enjoyment and future anticipation of all the honors of her rank. She gloried in the adulation her youth, beauty, wealth, and title commanded from her companions on the steamer; hut she gloried more in the anticipation of future successes and triumphs on a larger scale and more extensive field.

She rehearsed in imagination her arrival in London, her introduction to the family of the viscount; her presentation to the queen; and the sensation she would produce at her majesty's drawing room, where she was resolved, even if it should cost her her whole fortune, to eclipse every woman present, not only in the perfection of her beauty, but also in the magnificence of her dresses and the splendor of her jewels. And after that what a season she would pass in London! Whoever was queen of England, she would be queen of beauty and fashion.

And then she would visit with Lord Vincent all the different seats of his family; and every seat would be the scene of a new ovation! As the bride of the heir she would be idolized by the tenants and retainers of his noble family!

She would, with Lord Vincent, make a tour of the Continent; she would see everything worth seeing in nature and in art, modern and antique; she would be presented in succession at every foreign court, and everywhere by her beauty and splendor achieve new successes and triumphs! She would frequent the circles of American ministers, for the express purpose of meeting there her countrywomen, and overwhelming by her magnificence those who had once, dared to sneer at that high flavor of Indian blood which had given luster to her raven hair and fire to her dark eyes! Returning to England after this royal progress on the Continent she would pass her days in cherishing her beauty and keeping up her state.

And the course of her life should be like that of the sun, beautiful, glorious, regnant! each splendid phase more dazzling than any that had preceded it. Was not this worth the price she paid for it?

Such were Claudia's dreams and visions. Such the scenes that she daily in imagination rehearsed. Such the future life she delighted to contemplate. And nothing—neither the attentions of her husband, the conversation of her companions, nor the beauty and glory of sea and sky— could win her from the contemplation of the delightful subject.

Meanwhile in that lovely October weather the "Empress" steamed her way over the sapphire blue sea and neared the cliffs of England.

At length on a fine afternoon in October they entered the mouth of the Mersey River, and two hours later landed at Liverpool.

Soon all was bustle with the custom house officers.

Leaving their luggage in charge of his valet, to be got through the custom house, Lord Vincent hurried Claudia into a cab, followed her, and gave the direction:

"To the Crown and Miter."

"Why not go to the Adelphi? All Americans go there, and I think it the best hotel in the city," said Claudia.

"The Crown and Miter will serve our turn," was the curt reply of the viscount.

Claudia looked up in surprise at the brusqueness of his answer, and then ventured the opinion:

"It is a first-class hotel, of course?"

"Humph!" answered his lordship.

They left the respectable-looking street through which they were driving and turned into a narrow by-street and drove through a perfect labyrinth of narrow lanes and alleys, made hideous by dilapidated and dirty buildings and ragged and filthy people, until at last they reached a dark, dingy-looking inn, whose creaking sign bore in faded letters: "The Crown and Miter."

"It is not here that you are taking me, Lord Vincent?" exclaimed Claudia in surprise and displeasure, as her eyes fell upon this house and sign.

"It certainly is, Lady Vincent," replied his lordship, with cool civility, as he handed her out of the cab.

"Why this—this is worse than the tavern you took me to in New York. I never was in such a house before in all my life."

"It will have all the attractions of novelty, then."

"Lord Vincent, I do beg that you will not take me into this squalid place," she said shrinking back.

"You might find less attractive places than this in the length and breadth of the island," he replied, as he drew her hand within his arm and led her into the house.

They found themselves in a narrow passage, with stained walls, worn oil-cloth, and a smell of meat, onions, and smoke.

"Oh!" exclaimed Claudia, in irrepressible disgust.

"You will get used to these little inconveniences after a while, my dear," said his lordship.

A man with a greasy white apron and a soiled napkin approached them and bowed.

"A bedroom and parlor, and supper immediately," was Lord Vincent's order to this functionary.

"Yes, sir. We can be happy to accommodate you, sir, with a bedroom; the parlor, sir, is out of our power; we having none vacant at the present time; but to-morrow, sir—" began the polite waiter, when Lord Vincent cut him short with:

"Show us into the bedroom, then."

"Yes, sir." And bowing, the waiter went before them up the narrow stairs and led them into a dusky, fady, gloomy-looking chamber, whose carpet, curtains, and chair coverings seemed all of mingled hues of browns and grays, and from their fadiness and dinginess almost indescribable in color.

The waiter set the candle on the tall wooden mantelpiece and inquired:

"What would you please to order for supper?"

"What will you have, madam?" inquired Lord Vincent, referring to Claudia.

"Nothing on earth, in this horrid place! I am heart-sick," she added, in a low, sad tone.

"The lady will take nothing. You may send me a beefsteak and a bottle of Bass' pale ale," said his lordship, seemingly perfectly careless as to Claudia's want of appetite.

"Yes, sir; shall I order it served in the coffee room?"

"No, send it up here, and don't be long over it."

The waiter left the room. And Lord Vincent walked up and down the floor in the most perfect state of indifference to Claudia's distress.

She threw herself into a chair and burst into tears, exclaiming:

"You do not care for me at all! What a disgusting place to bring a woman—not to say a lady—into! If you possessed the least respect or affection for me you would never treat me so!"

"I fancy that I possess quite as much respect and affection for you, Lady Vincent, as you do, or ever did for me," he answered.

And Claudia knew that he spoke the truth, and she could not contradict him; but she said:

"Suppose there is little love lost between us, still we might treat each other decently. It is infamous to bring me here."

"You will not be required to stay here long."

"I hope not, indeed!"

At this moment the waiter entered to lay the cloth for the viscount's supper.

"What time does the first train for Aberdeen leave?" inquired the viscount.

"The first train, sir, leaves at four o'clock in the morning, sir; an uncomfortable hour, sir; and it is besides the parliamentary, sir."

"That will do. See if my people have come up from the custom house."

"Yes, sir; I beg your pardon, sir, what name?" inquired the perplexed waiter.

"No matter. Go look for a fellow who has in charge a large number of boxes and a party of male and female gorillas."

The man left the room to do his errand and to report below that the person in "Number 13" was a showman with a lot of man-monkeys from the interior of Africa.

But Claudia turned to her husband in astonishment.

"Did I understand you to inquire about the train to Aberdeen?"

"Yes," was the short reply.

"But—I thought we were going to London—to Hurstmonceux House—"

"Belgravia? No, my dear, we are going to Scotland."

"But—why this change of plan? My father and myself certainly understood that I was to be taken to London and introduced to your family and afterwards presented to her majesty."

"My dear, the London season is over ages ago. Nobody that is anybody will be found in town until February. The court is at Balmoral, and the world is in Scotland. We go to Castle Cragg."

"But why could you not have told me that before?"

"My dear, I like to be agreeable. And people who are always setting others right are not so."

"Is Lord Hurstmonceux at Castle Cragg?"

"The earl is at Balmoral, in attendance upon her majesty."

"Then why do we not go to Balmoral?"

"The queen holds no drawing rooms there."

Claudia suspected that he was deceiving her; but she felt that it would do no good to accuse him of deception.

The waiter returned to the room, bringing Lord Vincent's substantial supper, arranged on a tray.

"I have inquired below, sir; and there is no one arrived having in charge your gorillas. But there is a person with a panorama, sir; and there is a person with three negro persons, sir," said the waiter.

"He will do. Send up the 'person with three negro persons,'" said the viscount.

And once more the waiter left the room.

In a few moments Lord Vincent's valet entered.

"Frisbie, we leave for Scotland by the four o'clock train, to-morrow morning. See to it."

"Yes, my lord. I beg your lordship's pardon, but is your lordship aware that it is the parliamentary?"

"Certainly; but it is also the first. See to it that your gorillas are ready. And—Frisbie."

"Yes, my lord."

"Go and engage a first-class carriage for our own exclusive use."

"Yes, my lord," said the man, with his hand still on the door, as if waiting further orders.

"Lord Vincent, I would be obliged if you would tell him to send one of my women to me," said Claudia coldly.

"Women? Oh! Here, Frisbie! send the female gorillas up."

"I said one of my women, the elder one, he may send."

"Frisbie, send the old female gorilla up, then."

The man went out of the room. And Claudia turned upon her husband:

"Lord Vincent, I do not know in what light you consider it; but I think your conduct shows bad wit and worse manners."

"Lady Vincent, I am sorry you should disapprove of it," said his lordship, falling to upon his beefsteak and ale, the fumes of which soon filled the room.

But that was nothing to what was coming. When he had finished his supper he coolly took a pipe from his pocket, filled it with "negro-head," and prepared to light it. Then stopping in the midst of his operations, he looked at Claudia and inquired:

"Do you dislike tobacco smoke?"

"I do not know, my lord. No gentleman ever smoked in my presence," replied Claudia haughtily.

"Oh, then, of course, you don't know, and never will until you try. There is nothing like experiment."

And Lord Vincent put the pipe between his lips and puffed away vigorously. The room was soon filled with smoke. That, combined with the smell of the beefsteak and the ale, really sickened Claudia. She went to the window, raised it and looked out.

"You will take cold," said his lordship.

"I would rather take cold than breathe this air," was her reply.

"Just as you please; but I hadn't," he said. And he went and shut down the window.

Amazement held Claudia still for a moment; she could scarcely believe in such utter disregard of her feelings. At last, in a voice vibrating with ill-suppressed indignation, she said:

"My lord, the air of this room makes me ill. If you must smoke, can you not do so somewhere else?"

"Where?" questioned his lordship, taking the pipe from his mouth for an instant.

"Is there not a smoking room, reading room, or something of the sort, for gentlemen's accommodation?"

"In this place? Ha, ha, ha! Well, there is the taproom!"

"Then why not go there?" inquired Claudia, who had no very clear idea of what the taproom really was.

Lord Vincent's face flushed at what he seemed to think an intentional affront.

"I can go into the street," he said.

And he arose and put on his greatcoat and his cap, and turned up the collar of his coat and turned down the fall of his cap, so that but little of his face would be seen, and so walked out. Then Claudia raised the window to ventilate the room, and rang the bell to summon the waiter.

"Take this service away and send the chambermaid to me," she said to him when he came.

And a few minutes after he had cleared the table and left the room the chambermaid, accompanied by old Katie, entered.

"Is there a dressing room connected with this chamber?" Lady Vincent inquired.

"Law, no, mum! there isn't sich a place in the house," said the chambermaid.

"This is intolerable! You may go; my own servants will wait on me."

The girl went out.

"Unpack my traveling bag and lay out my things, Katie," said Lady Vincent, when she was left alone with her nurse.

But the old woman raised her hands, and rolled up her eyes, exclaiming:

"Well, Miss Claudia, child!—I mean my ladyship, ma'am!—if this is Ingland, I never want to see it again the longest day as ever I live!"

"Liverpool is not England, Katie."

"Live-a-pool, is it? More like Die-a-pool!" grumbled old Katie, as she assisted her lady to change her traveling dress for a loose wrapper.

"Now, what have you had to eat, my ladyship?"

"Nothing, Katie. I felt as if I could not eat anything cooked in this ill-looking house."

"Nothing to eat! I'll go right straight downstairs and make you some tea and toast myself," said Katie.

And she made good her words by bringing a delicate little repast, of which Claudia gratefully partook.

And then Katie, with an old nurse's tenderness, saw her mistress comfortably to bed, and cleared and darkened the room and left her to repose.

But Claudia did not sleep. Her thoughts were too busy with the subject of Lord Vincent's strange conduct from the time that he had at Niagara received those three suspicious letters up to this time, when with his face hid he was walking up and down the streets of Liverpool.

That he sought concealment she felt assured by many circumstances: his coming to this obscure tavern; his choosing to take his meals and smoke his pipe in his bedroom; and his walking out with his face muffled—all of which was in direct antagonism to Lord Vincent's fastidious habits; and, finally, his taking a whole carriage in the railway train, for no other purpose than to have himself and his party entirely isolated from their fellow-passengers.

Lord Vincent came in early, and, thanks to the narcotic qualities of the ale, he soon fell asleep.

Claudia had scarcely dropped into a doze before, at the dismal hour of three o'clock in the morning, they were roused up to get ready for the train. They made a hurried toilet and ate a hasty breakfast, and then set out for the station.

It was a raw, damp, foggy morning. The atmosphere seemed as dense and as white as milk. No one could see a foot in advance. And Claudia wondered how the cabmen managed to get along at all.

They reached the station just as the train was about to start, and had barely time to hurry into the carriage that had been engaged for them before the whistle shrieked and they were off. Fortunately Frisbie had sent the luggage on in advance, and got it ticketed.

The carriage had four back and four front seats. Lord and Lady Vincent occupied two of the back seats, and their four servants the front ones. As they went on the fog really seemed to thicken. They traveled slowly and stopped often. And Claudia, in surprise, remarked upon these facts.

"One might as well be in a stage—for speed," she complained.

"It is the parliamentary train," he replied.

"I have heard you say that before; but I do not know what you mean by 'parliamentary' as applied to railway trains."

"It is the cheap train, the slow train, the people's train; in fact, one that, in addition to first- and second-class carriages, drags behind it an interminable length of rough cars, in which the lower orders travel," said his lordship.

"But why is it called the 'parliamentary'?"

"Because it was instituted by act of parliament for the accommodation of the people, or perhaps because it is so heavy and slow."

On they went, hour after hour, stopping every three or four miles, while the fog seemed still to condense and whiten.

At noon the train reached York, and stopped twenty minutes for refreshment. Lord Vincent did not leave the carriage, but sent his valet out to the station restaurant to procure what was needful for his party. And while the passengers were all hurrying to and fro, and looking in at the carriage, he drew the curtains of his windows, and sat back far in his seat.

Claudia would gladly have left the train and spent the interval in contemplating, even if it were only the outside of the ancient cathedral of which she had read and heard so much.

Lord Vincent assured her there was no time to lose in sight-seeing then, but promised that she should visit York at some future period.

And the train started again. They began to leave the fog behind them as they approached the seacoast. They soon came in sight of the North Sea, beside which the railway ran for some hundred miles. Here all was bright and clear. And Claudia for a time forgot all the suspicions and anxieties that disturbed her mind, and with all a stranger's interest gazed on the grandeur of the scenery and dreamed over the associations it awakened.

Here "lofty Seaton-Delaval" was pointed out to her. And Tinemouth, famed in song for its "haughty prioress," and "Holy Isle," memorable for the inhumation of Constance de Beverly.

At sunset they crossed Berwick bridge and entered Scotland.

Claudia was entirely lost in gazing on the present landscape, and dreaming of its past history. Here the association between scenery and poetry was perfect. Nature is ever young—and this was the very scene and the very hour described in Scott's immortal poem, and as Claudia gazed she murmured the lines:

Yes! it was the very scene, viewed at the very hour, just as the poet described it to have been two hundred years before, when

crossed with his knightly train into Scotland. There was the setting sun burnishing the brown tops of the Cheviot hills; gilding the distant ruined towers of Norham Castle, and lighting up the waters of the Tweed.

But there is little time for either observation or dreaming in a railway train.

They stopped but a few minutes at Berwick, and then shot off northward, still keeping near the coast.

Claudia looked out upon the gray North Sea, and enjoyed the magnificence of the coast scenery as long as the daylight lasted.

When it was growing dark Lord Vincent said:

"You had just as well close that window, Claudia. It will give us all cold; and besides, you can see but little now."

"I can see Night drawing her curtain of darkness around the bed of the troubled waters. It is worth watching," murmured Claudia dreamily.

"Bosh!" was the elegant response of the viscount; "you will see enough of the North Sea before you have done with it, I fancy." And with an emphatic clap he let down the window.

Claudia shrugged her shoulders and turned away, too proud to dispute a point that she was powerless to decide.

They sped on towards Edinboro', through the darkness of one of the darkest nights that ever fell. Even had the window been open Claudia could not have caught a glimpse of the scenery. She had no idea that they were near the capital of Scotland until the train ran into the station. Then all was bustle among those who intended to get out there.

But through all the bustle Lord Vincent and his party kept their seats,

"I am very weary of this train. I have not left my seat for many hours. Can we not stop over night here? I should like to see Edinboro' by daylight," Claudia inquired.

"What did you say?" asked Lord Vincent, with nonchalance.

Claudia repeated her question, adding:

"I should like to remain a day or two in Edinboro'. I wish to see the Castle, and Holyrood Palace and Abbey, and Roslyn and Craigmiller, and——"

"Everything else, of course. Bother! We have no time for that. I have taken our tickets for Aberdeen, and mean to sleep at Castle Cragg to-night," replied the viscount.

Claudia turned away her head to conceal the indignant tears that arose to her eyes. She was beginning to discover that her comfort, convenience, and inclination were just about the last circumstances that her husband was disposed to take into consideration. What a dire reverse for her, whose will from her earliest recollection had been the law to all around her!

The train started again and sped on its way through the darkness of the night towards Aberdeen, where they arrived about eight o'clock.

"Here at last the railway journey ends, thank Heaven," sighed Claudia, as the train slackened its speed and crawled into the station. And the usual bustle attending its arrival ensued.

Fortunately for Claudia, the viscount found himself too much fatigued after about sixteen hours' ride to go farther that night. So he directed Mr. Frisbie to engage two cabs to take himself and his party to a hotel.

And when they were brought up he handed Claudia, who was scarcely able to stand, into the first one, and ordered Frisbie to put the "gorillas" into the other. And they drove to a fourth- or fifth-rate inn, a degree or two dirtier, dingier, and darker than the one they had left at Liverpool.

But Claudia was too utterly worn out in body, mind, and spirit to find fault with any shelter that promised to afford her the common necessaries of life, of which she had been deprived for so many hours.

She drank the tea that was brought her, without questioning its quality. And as soon as she laid her head on her pillow she sank into the dreamless sleep of utter exhaustion.

She awoke late the next morning to take her first look at the old town through a driving rain that lashed the narrow windows of her little bedroom. Lord Vincent had already risen and gone out.

She rang for her servants. Old Katie answered the bell, entering with uplifted hands and eyes, exclaiming:

"Well, my ladyship! if this ain't the outlandishest country as ever was! Coming over from t'other side we had the ocean unnerneaf of us, and now 'pears to me like we has got it overhead of us, by the fog and mist and rain perpetual! And if this is being of lords and ladyships, I'd a heap leifer be misters and mist'esses, myself."

"I quite agree with you, Katie," sighed Lady Vincent, as, with the old woman's assistance, she dressed herself.

"It seems to me like as if we was regerlerly sold, my ladyship," said old Katie mysteriously.

"Hush! Where are we to have breakfast—not in this disordered room, I hope?"

"No, my ladyship. They let us have a little squeezed-up parlor that smells for all the world as if a lot of men had been smoking and drinking in it all night long. My lordship's down there, waiting for his breakfast now. Pretty place to fetch a 'spectable cullored pusson to, let alone a lady! Well, one comfort, we won't stay here long, cause I heard my lordship order Mr. Frisbie to go and take two inside places and four outside places in the stage-coach as leaves this mornin' for Ban. 'Ban,' 'Ban'; 'pears like it's been all ban and no blessin' ever since we done lef' Tanglewood."

Lady Vincent did not think it worth while to correct Katie. She knew by experience that all attempts to set her right would be lost labor.

She went downstairs and joined Lord Vincent in the little parlor, where a breakfast was laid of which it might be said that if the coffee was bad and the bannocks worse, the kippered herrings were delicious.

After breakfast they took their places in or on the Banff mail coach; Lord and Lady Vincent being the sole passengers inside; and all their servants occupying the outside. And so they set out through the drizzling rain and by the old turnpike road to Banff.

This road ran along the edge of the cliffs overhanging the sea—the sea, ever sublime and beautiful, even when dimly seen through the dull veil of a Scotch mist.

Claudia was not permitted to open the window; but she kept the glass polished that she might look out upon the wild scenery.

Late in the afternoon they reached the town of Banff, where they stopped only long enough to order a plain dinner and engage flies to take them on to their final destination, Castle Cragg, which in truth Claudia was growing very anxious to behold.

CHAPTER XV

CASTLE CRAGG.

The wildest scene, but this, can show

Some touch of nature's genial glow;

But here, above, around, below,

On mountain or in glen,

Nor tree, nor shrub, nor plant, nor flower.

Nor aught of vegetative power

The weary eye may ken.

For all is rocks at random thrown,

Black waves, bare crags, and banks of stone.

—Scott.

Immediately after dinner they set out again on this last stage of their journey, Claudia and Vincent riding in the first fly and Frisbie and the "gorillas" in the second one. The road still lay along the cliffs above the sea. And Claudia still sat and gazed through the window of the fly as she had gazed through the window of the coach, at the wild, grand, awful scenery of the coast. Hour after hour they rode on until the afternoon darkened into evening.

The last object of interest that caught Claudia's attention, before night closed the scene, was far in advance of them up the coast. It was a great promontory stretching far out into the sea and lifting its lofty head high into the heavens. Upon its extreme point stood an ancient castle, which at that height seemed but a crow's nest in size.

Claudia called Lord Vincent's attention to it.

"What castle is that, my lord, perched upon that high promontory? I should think it an interesting place, an historical place, built perhaps in ancient times as a stronghold against Danish invasion," she said.

"That? Oh, ah, yes! That is a trifle historical, in the record of a score of sieges, storms, assaults, and so on; and a bit traditional, in legends of some hundred capital crimes and mortal sins; and in fact altogether, as you say, rather interesting, especially to you, Claudia. It is Castle Cragg, and it will have the honor to be your future residence."

"Heaven forbid!" exclaimed Claudia, gazing now in consternation upon that drear, desolate, awful rock. "Dread point of Dis" it seemed indeed to her.

"For a season only, my dear, of course," said the viscount, with the queerest of smiles, of which Claudia could make nothing satisfactory.

She continued to look out, but the longer she gazed upon that awful cliff and the nearer she approached it, the more appalled she became. She now saw, in turning a winding of the coast, that the point of the cliff stretched much farther out to sea than had at first appeared, and that only a low neck of land connected it with the main; and she knew that when the tide was high this promontory must be entirely cut off from the coast and become, to all intents and purposes, an island. Approaching nearer still, she saw that the cliff was but a huge, bare, barren rock, of which the castle, built and walled in of the same rock, seemed but an outgrowth and a portion.

If this rock-bound, sea-walled dwelling-place, which had evidently been built rather for a fortification than for a family residence, struck terror to the heart of Claudia, what effect must it have had upon the superstitious mind of poor old Katie, riding in the fly behind, when Mr. Frisbie was so good as to point it out to her with the agreeable information that it was to be her future home.

"What, dat!" exclaimed the old woman in consternation. "You don't mean dat! Well, lord! I'se offen hearn tell of de 'Debbil's Icy Peak,' but I nebber expected to cotch my eyes on it, much less lib on it, I tell you all good!"

"That's it, hows'ever, Mrs. Gorilla," said Mr. Frisbie.

"I keep a-telling you as my family name aint Gorilla, it's Mortimer; dough Gorilla is a perty name, too; it ralely is, on'y you see, chile, it aint mine," said unconscious Katie.

But the darkening night shut out from their view the awful cliff to which, however, they were every moment approaching nearer.

Fortunately as the carriages reached the base of this cliff the tide was low, and they were enabled to pass the neck of land that united the island to the coast and made it a promontory. After passing over this narrow strip they ascended the cliff by a road so steep that it had been paved with flagstones placed edgeways to afford a hold for the horses' hoofs and aid them in climbing. It was too dark to see all this then; but Claudia knew from the inclined position of the carriage how steep was the ascent, and she held her very breath for fear. As for old Katie, in the carriage behind, she began praying.

A solitary light shone amid the darkness above them. It came from a lamp at the top of the castle gate. They reached the summit of the cliff in safety, and Lady Vincent breathed freely again and old Katie's prayers changed to thanksgivings.

They crossed the drawbridge over the ancient moat and entered the castle gate. The light above it revealed the ghastly, iron-toothed portcullis, that looked ready to fall and impale any audacious passenger under its impending fangs. And they entered the old paved courtyard and crossed over to the main entrance of the castle hall.

Here, at length, some of the attendant honors of Lady Vincent's new rank seemed ready to greet her.

The establishment had been expecting its lord and had heard the sound of carriages. The great doors were thrown open; lights flashed out; liveried servants appeared in attendance.

"You got my telegram, I perceive, Cuthbert," Lord Vincent said to a large, red-haired Scot, in plain citizen's clothes, who seemed to be the porter.

"Yes, me laird, though, as ye ken, the chiels at yon office at Banff hae to send it by a special messenger—sae it took a long time to win here."

"All right, Cuthbert, since you received it in time to be ready for us. Light us into the green parlor, and send the housekeeper here to attend Lady Vincent."

"Yes, me laird," answered the man, bowing low before he led the way into a room so elegantly furnished as to afford a pleasant surprise to Claudia, who certainly did not expect to find anything so bright and new in this dark, old castle.

Here she was presently joined by a tall, spare, respectable-looking old woman in a black linsey dress, white apron and neck shawl, and high-crowned Scotch cap.

"How do you do, dame? You will show Lady Vincent to her apartments and wait her orders."

"Eh, sirs! anither ane!" ejaculated the old woman under her breath; then turning to Claudia, with a courtesy she said: "I am ready to attend your leddyship."

Claudia arose and followed her through the vast hall and up the lofty staircase to another great square stone hall, whose four walls were regularly indented by lines of doors leading into the bed chambers and dressing rooms.

And as Claudia looked upon this array, her first thought was that a stranger might easily get confused among them and open the wrong door. And that it would be well to have them numbered as at hotels to prevent mistakes.

The old housekeeper opened one of the doors and admitted her mistress into a beautifully furnished and decorated suite of apartments which consisted of boudoir, bedroom, and dressing room opening into each other, so that, as Claudia entered the first, she had the vista of the three before her eyes. The floors were covered with Turkey carpets so soft and deep in texture that they yielded like turf under the tread. And the heavy furniture was all of black walnut; and the draperies were all of golden-brown satin damask and richly embroidered lace.

The effect of the whole was warm, rich, and comfortable.

Claudia looked around herself with approbation; her spirits rose; she felt reconciled to the rugged old fortress that contained such splendors within its walls; for who would care how rough the casket, so that the jewels it held were of the finest water? Her plans "soared up again like fire."

She passed through the whole suite of rooms to the dressing room, which was the last in succession, and seated herself in an easy-chair beside a bright coal fire.

"The dinner will be served in an hour, me leddy. Will I bring your leddyship a cup of tea before you begin to dress?" inquired the housekeeper.

"If you please, you may send it to me by one of my own women. You are too aged to walk up and down stairs," replied Claudia kindly.

"Hech, sirs! I'm e'en reddy to haud me ain wi' any lassie i' the house," said she, nodding her tall, flapping white sap.

"Will you tell me your name, that I may know in future what to call you?" Claudia asked.

"It's e'en just Mistress Murdock, at your leddyship's bidding. And now I'll gae bring the tea."

"Send my servant Katie to me at the same time," said Lady Vincent, who, when she was left alone, turned again to view the magnificence that surrounded her.

"If ever I spend another autumn on this bleak coast, I shall take care to fill the castle halls and chambers with gay company," she said to herself.

The housekeeper entered with an elegant little tea-service of gold plate, and set it on a stand of mosaic work, by Claudia's side.

While she was drinking her tea Katie entered, smiling with both her eyes and all her teeth.

"Well, my ladyship, ma'am, this looks like life at last; don't it, though?"

"I think so, Katie," said her mistress, sipping her aromatic "oolong."

"I like Scraggy better nor I thought I would."

"You like what?"

"This big jail of a house—Scraggy something or other they call it."

"Castle Cragg."

"Yes, that's it; plague take the outlandish names, I say!"

"Now, Katie, unpack my maize-colored moire antique. I must dress for dinner."

Of course Claudia expected to meet no one at dinner except the disagreeable companion of her journey; but Claudia would have made an elaborate evening toilet had there been no one but herself to admire it.

So she arrayed herself with very great splendor and went downstairs.

In the lower hall she found the porter and several footmen.

"Show me into the drawing room," she said to the former.

Old Cuthbert bowed and walked before her, and threw open a pair of folding doors leading into the grand saloon of the castle. And Claudia entered.

CHAPTER XVI

FAUSTINA.

And she was beautiful, they said;

I saw that she was more—

One of those women women dread,

Men fatally adore.

—Anon.

It was a saloon of magnificent proportions and splendid decorations. And Claudia was sailing across it with majestic gait, in the full consciousness of being the Viscountess Vincent and Lady of the Castle, when suddenly her eyes fell upon an object that arrested her footsteps, while she gazed in utter amazement.

One of the most transcendently beautiful women that she had ever beheld lay reclining in the most graceful and alluring attitude upon a low divan. Her luxuriant form, arrayed in rich, soft, white moire antique and lace, was thrown into harmonious relief by the crimson velvet cover of the divan. She was asleep, or perhaps affecting to be so. One fine, round, brown arm, with its elbow deep in the downy pillow, rose from its falling sleeve of silk and lace, and with its jeweled hand, buried in masses of glittering, purplish black ringlets, supported a head that Rubens would have loved to paint. Those rich ringlets, flowing down, half veiled the rounded arm and full, curved neck and bosom that were otherwise too bare for delicacy. The features were formed in the most perfect mold of Oriental beauty, the forehead was broad and low; the nose fine and straight; the lips plump and full; and the chin small and rounded. The eyebrows were black, arched, and tapering at the points; the eyelashes were black, long, and drooping over half-closed, almond-shaped, dark eyes that seemed floating in liquid fire. The complexion was of the richest brown, ripening into the most brilliant crimson in the oval cheeks and dewy lips that, falling half open, revealed the little glistening white teeth within. While one jeweled hand supported her beautiful head the other drooped over her reclining form, holding negligently, almost unconsciously, between thumb and finger, an odorous tea-rose.

Claudia herself was a brilliant brunette, but here was another brunette who eclipsed her in her own splendid style of beauty as an astral lamp outshines a candle. Cleopatra, Thais, Aspasia, or any other world-renowned siren who had governed kingdoms through kings' passions, might have been just such a woman as this sleeping Venus.

Doubting really whether she slept or not, Claudia approached and looked over her; and the longer she looked the more she wondered at, admired, and instinctively hated this woman.

Who was she? What was she? How came she there?

So absorbed was Claudia in these questions, while gazing at the beautiful and unconscious subject of them, that she did not perceive the approach of Lord Vincent until he actually stood at her side.

Then she looked up at him inquiringly, and pointed at the sleeping beauty.

But instead of replying to her, he bent over the sleeper and whispered:

"Faustina!"

Now, whether she were really sleeping or shamming, the awakening, real or pretended, was beautiful. The drooping, black-fringed eyelids slowly lifted themselves from the eyes—two large black orbs of soft fire; and the plump, crimson lips opened, and dropped two liquid notes of perfect music—the syllables of his baptismal name:

"Malcolm!"

"Faustina, you are dreaming; awaken! remember where you are," he said in a low voice.

She slowly raised herself to a sitting posture and looked around; but every movement of hers was perfect grace.

"Lady Vincent, this is Mrs. Dugald," said the viscount.

Claudia drew back a step, and bent her head with an air of the most freezing hauteur.

Mrs. Dugald also bent hers, but immediately threw it up and shook it back with a smile.

So graceful was this motion that it can be compared to nothing but the bend and rebound of a lily.

But when Claudia looked up she detected a strange glance of intelligence between her two companions. The beauty's eyes flashed from their sheath of softness and gleamed forth upon the man—two living stilettos pointed with death.

His look expressed annoyance and fear.

He turned away and touched the bell.

"Let dinner be served immediately," he said to the servant who answered the summons.

"Dinner is served, my lord," answered the man, pushing aside the sliding doors opening into the dining room.

Lord Vincent waved his hand to Lady Vincent to precede them, and then gave his arm to Mrs. Dugald to follow her.

But when they reached the dining room Mrs. Dugald left his arm, advanced to the head of the table, and stood with her hand upon the back of the chair and her gaze upon the face of the viscount.

"No; Lady Vincent will take the head of the table," said his lordship, giving his hand to Claudia and installing her.

"As you will; but 'where the MacDonald sits, there is the head of the table,'" said Mrs. Dugald, quoting the haughty words of the Lord of the Isles, as she gave way and subsided into a side seat.

Lord Vincent, with a lowering brow, sat down.

Old Cuthbert, who sometimes officiated as butler, placed himself behind his lord's chair, and two footmen waited on the table.

The dinner was splendid in its service, and luxurious in its viands; but most uncomfortable in its company, and it suggested the Scripture proverb: "Better is a dinner of herbs where love is, than a stalled ox and hatred therewith."

Claudia, for one, was glad when it was over, and they were permitted to return to the saloon, where coffee awaited them.

"Mrs. Dugald, will you give me some music?" said Lord Vincent, in the course of the evening.

The beauty arose, and floated away in her soft, swimming gait towards the piano.

Lord Vincent went after her and opened the instrument; and when she sat down he stood behind her chair to turn over the music.

She played a brilliant prelude, and then commenced singing.

Claudia, who, at the proposition that Mrs. Dugald should give Lord Vincent "some music," had shrugged her shoulders and turned her back, was now startled. She turned around—listened. Claudia was a most fastidious connoisseur of music, and she recognized in this performer an artiste of the highest order. Claudia had heard such music as this only from the best opera singers—certainly from no unprofessional performer.

After executing a few brilliant pieces the beautiful musician arose with a weary air and, saying that she was tired, courtesied, smiled, and withdrew from the room.

Lord Vincent walked slowly up and down the floor.

"Who is Mrs. Dugald?" inquired Claudia coldly.

"Mrs. Dugald is—Mrs. Dugald," replied his lordship, affecting a light tone.

"That is no answer, my lord." "Well, my lady, she is a relation of mine. Will that do for an answer?"

"What sort of a relation?"

"A very near one."

"How near?"

"She is my—sister," smiled Lord Vincent.

"Your sister? I know that you have only two sisters, and they are styled 'ladies'—Lady Eda and Lady Clementina Dugald. This is a 'Mrs.' She cannot be your sister, and not even your sister-in-law, since you have no brother."

The viscount coolly lighted his cigar and walked out of the room.

Claudia remained sitting where he had left her, deeply perplexed in mind. Then, feeling too restless to sit still, she arose and began to walk about the room and examine its objects of interest—its pictures, statues, vases, et cetera.

She then went to the windows; the shutters were closed, the blinds down and the curtains drawn, so that she could not look out into the night; but she could hear the thunder of the sea as it broke upon the rock on which the castle was founded.

Tired of that, she went to the music stand, near the piano, and began to turn over the music books.

She picked up one from which Mrs. Dugald had been singing. In turning it over her eyes fell upon the picture of a full-length female form engraved upon the cover. She looked at it more closely. It was the portrait of the woman who had been introduced to her as Mrs. Dugald. But it bore the name: La Faustina, as Norma.

CHAPTER XVII

THE PLOT AGAINST CLAUDIA.

Alas! a thought of saddest weight

Presses and will have vent:

Had she not scorned his love, her fate

Had been so different!

Had her heart bent its haughty will

To take him for its lord,

She had been proudly happy still;

Still honored, still adored.

—Monckton Milnes

Indignation rooted Claudia to the spot.

Instinct had already warned her that she was insulted and degraded by the presence of this strange woman in the house.

Reason now confirmed instinct.

And Claudia was entirely too self-willed and high-spirited to submit to either insult or degradation.

She instantly resolved to demand of Lord Vincent the immediate dismissal of this woman, and to keep her own rooms until her demand was complied with.

This, in fact, was the only truly dignified course of conduct that, under the circumstances, Claudia could have pursued.

With this resolution she withdrew from the drawing rooms, and went upstairs to seek her own apartment.

Here the very accident happened that we mentioned as being so likely to happen to any newcomer to the castle.

As she reached the great hall on the second floor she looked around upon the many doors that opened from its four walls into the many suites of apartments that radiated from it, as from a common center, to the outer walls of the castle keep.

But which was her own door she was puzzled for a moment to decide.

The chandelier that hung from the ceiling gave but a subdued light that helped her but little.

At last she thought she had found her own door; she judged it to be her own because it was partly open and she saw, through the vista of the three rooms, the little coal fire that burned dimly in the last one.

So she silently crossed the hall, walking on the soft deep drugget, into which her footsteps sank noiselessly, as she entered what she supposed to be her own boudoir.

The room was dark, except from the gleam of light that stole in from the chandelier in the hall, and the dull glow of the coal fire that might be dimly seen in the distant dressing room, at the end of the suite.

Claudia, however, had no sooner entered the room and looked around than she discovered that it was not hers. This suite of apartments was arranged upon the same plan as her own—first the boudoir, then the bed chamber, and last the dressing room with the little coal fire; but—the hangings were different; for, where hers had been golden brown, these were rosy red.

And she was about to retire and close the door softly when the sound of voices in the adjoining room arrested her steps.

The first that spoke was the voice of Faustina, in tones of passionate grief and remonstrance. She was saying:

"But to bring her here! here, of all the places in the world! here, under my own very eyes! Ah!"

"My angel, I had a design in bringing her here, a design in which your future honor and happiness is involved," said the voice of Lord Vincent, in such tones of persuasive tenderness as he had never used in speaking to his betrayed and miserable wife.

"My honor and happiness! Ah!" cried the woman with a half-suppressed shriek.

"Faustina, my beloved, listen to me!" entreated the viscount.

"Do not love her! Do not, Malcolm! If you do I warn you that I shall kill her!" wildly exclaimed the woman, interrupting him.

"My angel, I love only you. How can you doubt it?"

"How can I doubt it? Because you have deceived me. Not once, nor twice, nor thrice; but always and in everything, from first to last!"

"Deceived you, Faustina! How can you say so? In what have I ever deceived you? Not in vowing that I love you; for I do! You must know it. How, then, have I deceived you?"

"You promised to make me your viscountess."

"And I will do so. I swear it to you, Faustina."

"Ah, you have sworn so many oaths to me."

"I will keep them all—trust me! I would die for you; would go to perdition for you, Faustina!"

"You will keep all your oaths to me, you say?"

"All of them, Faustina!"

"One of them is, that you will make me your viscountess!"

"Yes, and I will do it, my angel. Who but yourself should share my rank with me? I will make you my viscountess, Faustina."

"How can you do that, even if you wished to do so? She is your viscountess."

"Yes, for a little while; and for a little while only. Until she has served the purpose for which I married her—and no longer," said the viscount.

"Ah! what do you mean?" There was breathless eagerness and ruthless cruelty in the tone and manner in which the woman put this question.

The viscount did not immediately reply.

And Claudia, her blood curdling with horror at what seemed plainly a design against her life, left her position near the door of the boudoir and concealed herself behind the crimson satin hangings; feeling fully justified in becoming an eavesdropper upon conversation that concerned her safety.

"What do you mean?" again whispered the woman, with restrained vehemence.

"'Be innocent of the knowledge, dearest chuck, 'till you approve the deed,'" quoted Lord Vincent.

"But trust me; I am ready to aid you in the deed, and to share with you the danger it must bring, for I love you, Malcolm, I love you! Confide in me! Tell me what you mean," she whispered in low, deep, vehement tones.

"I mean—not what you imagine, Faustina. Turn your face away. Those eyes of yours make my blood run cold. No! We English are not quite so ready with bowl and dagger as you Italians seem to be. We like to keep within bounds."

"I do not understand you, then."

"No, you do not. And you will not understand me any better when I say to you, that I shall get rid of my Indian Princess, not by breaking the law, but by appealing to the law."

"No; it is true; I do not understand you. You seem to be playing with me."

"Listen, then, you bewitching sprite. You reproached me just now with bringing her here, here under your very eyes, you said. Faustina, I brought her here, to this remote hold, that she might be the more completely in my power. That I might, at leisure and in safety, mature my plans for getting entirely rid of her."

"But, Malcolm, why did you marry her at all? Ah, I fear, I fear, it was after all a real passion, though a transient one, that moved you!"

"No; I swear to you it was not! I have never loved woman but you!"

"But why then did you marry her at all?"

"My angel, I told you why. You should have believed me! My marriage was a financial necessity. The earl, my father, chose to take umbrage at what he called my disreputable—"

"Bah!" exclaimed the woman, in contempt.

"Well, let the phrase pass. The Earl of Hurstmonceux chose to take offense at my friendship with your lovely self. And he—did not threaten to stop my allowance unless I would break with you; but he actually and promptly did stop it until I should do so."

"Beast!"

"Certainly; but then what was to be done? I had no income; nothing to support myself; much less you, with your elegant tastes."

"I could have gone on the boards again! I did not love you for your money; you know it, Malcolm."

"I do know it, my angel; and in that respect, as in all others, you were immeasurably above your fancied rival, who certainly loved me only for my rank."

"But why then did you not rather let me return to the boards?"

"Where your beauty brought you so many admirers and me so many rivals?"

"But I preferred you to them all."

"I know it, Faustina."

"Why then not let me go?"

"I could not bear the thought of it, my precious treasure. I preferred to sacrifice myself. The opportunity occurred in this way. You know that I left England as the bearer of dispatches to our minister in the United States."

"Yes."

"The very day after I reached Washington I met at the evening reception at the President's house this Indian Princess, as she was called. I was no sooner presented to her than she began to exercise all her arts of fascination upon me. But my heart was steeled by its love for you against the charms of all others."

"Ah! don't stop to pay compliments; go on."

"Well, but I was good-natured, and I flattered her vanity by flirting with her a little."

"A little!" repeated the woman, curling her beautiful lip.

"Yes, only a little; for I had no idea of seriously addressing her until I discovered that she possessed in her own right one of the largest fortunes in the—world, I was going to say—and I should not have been far wrong, for she had in fact inherited three immense fortunes. This was the way of it. Her mother was the only child of a millionaire, and of course inherited the whole of her father's estate. She had also two bachelor uncles who had made immense fortunes in trade, and who left the whole to their niece, in her own right. She, dying young, bequeathed the whole unconditionally to her daughter."

"Ciel! what good luck! How much is it all put together?"

"About three millions of pounds sterling."

"Ma foi! In what does it consist?"

"It did consist in bank stock, railway shares, lead mines, city houses, iron foundries, tobacco plantations, country seats, gorillas, etc. It now consists in money."

"But what good, if you get rid of her, will it do you? Is it not settled on the lady?"

"No! I took very good care of that. When I saw that she was doing all she could to entrap—not me, for for me she did not care, but—a title, I humored her by falling into the snare. I addressed her. We were engaged. Then her governor talked of settlements. I took a high tone, and expressed astonishment and disgust that any lady who was afraid to trust me with her money should be so willing to confide to me the custody of her person. And the negotiations might have come to an end then and there, had not the lady herself intervened and scornfully waived the question of settlements. She had always ruled her father and everyone else around her in every particular, and she ruled in this matter also. The fact is, that she was determined to be a viscountess at any price, and she is one—for a little while!"

"What a fool!"

"Yes, she was a poor gambler; for it was a game between us. She was playing for a title, I for a fortune; well, she won the title and I won the fortune. Or rather you may call it purchase and sale. She bought a title and paid a fortune for it. For the moment the marriage ring encircled her finger she became the Viscountess Vincent and I became the possessor of her three millions of pounds sterling."

"Ah, that marriage ring! There is another broken oath! You swore to me, once, that no living woman should ever wear a marriage ring of your putting on, except myself!" complained Faustina.

"And I have kept that oath, my angel. If ever you see Lady Vincent without her gloves, look on the third finger of her left hand and see if there is any wedding ring to be found there."

"But you yourself, just now, spoke of the ring on her finger, saying that as soon as it was placed there, you became the possessor of her three millions of pounds sterling."

"I will explain. Listen! I remembered my vow to you. I got the ring purposely too large for her finger; consequently, soon after it was placed on, it dropped off and rolled away. When the ceremony was over the gentlemen searched for it. I found it and concealed it. She never saw it again. Here it is. I give it to you."

Claudia from her hiding place stooped forward until she got a glimpse of the two traitors.

She saw the viscount open his pocketbook and take from an inner compartment her own wedding ring, and place it upon the finger of his companion, saying:

"There, my angel, wear it; it will fit your fat finger, though it was too large for her slender one."

"What will she say when she sees it?" inquired the woman, contemplating the golden circle with a triumphant smile.

"She will not recognize it. All wedding rings are alike. This one has no mark to distinguish it from all other wedding rings."

"And so I have got it!" said the woman, clapping her hands gleefully.

"Yes, my sweet, and you shall have everything else; the three millions of pounds sterling and the title of viscountess included."

"Ah! but how got you all the fortune in money so easily?"

"I sold everything, bank stock, railway shares, city houses, tobacco plantations, lead mines, foundries, gorillas, and all! And I have transferred the whole in simple cash to this country."

"And it is three millions?"

"Three millions."

"Ciel! Now, then, I can have my villa at Torquay, and my yacht, and my—"

"You can have everything you want now, and the rank and position of viscountess as soon as I can get rid of her."

"Ah, yes! but when will that be?"

"Very, very soon, I hope. Just as soon as I can mature my plans."

"But what are they?"

"Scarcely to be breathed even here. The very walls have ears, you know."

"Tell me; what does the earl think of this marriage of yours?"

"So, so; he wrote me a cool letter, saying that he would have preferred that I should have married an Englishwoman of my own rank; but that since the lady was of respectable family and large fortune, he should welcome her as a daughter. And finally, that any sort of a decent marriage was better than—but let that pass!"

"Yes, let it pass. Beast!"

"Never mind, my angel. Your turn will come."

"Ah, surely, yes! But is he not expecting to welcome his wealthy daughter-in-law?"

"Not yet. No, we have come over a full month before we were looked for. The earl is traveling on the Continent. His daughter-in-law will be disposed of before he returns to England."

"Ha, ha, good! But is not miladie amusing herself with the anticipation of being introduced to her noble father-in-law?"

"Ha, ha, ha! yes! You would have been diverted, 'Tina, if you could have heard her talk of her plans when coming over. Ah! but that was good. I laughed in my sleeve."

"Tell me! and I will laugh now."

"Well, she expected to land on the shores of England like any royal bride; to find the Earl of Hurstmonceux waiting to welcome her; to be introduced to my family; to be presented to her majesty; to be feted by the nobility; lionized by the gentry; and idolized by our own tenantry. In short, she dreamed of a grand royal progress through England, of which every stage was to be a glorious triumph! Ha, ha, ha!"

"Ha, ha, ha!" echoed Faustina.

"But instead of entering England like a royal bride, she was smuggled into England like a transported felon, who had returned before her time of penal service in the colonies had expired. Instead of a triumphal entry and progress along the highways, she was dragged ignominiously through the byways! Instead of halting at the palatial Adelphia, we halted at the obscure Crown and Miter."

"Ha, ha, ha! Good! that was very good! But why did you do this? Not that I care for her. I care not. But my curiosity. And it must have inconvenienced you, this squalor."

"Well, it did. But I was resolved she should meet no countrymen; form no acquaintances; contract no friendships; in fine, have no party here in England. The Adelphia was full of American travelers; the Queen's was full of my friends. In either she would have got into some social circles that might have proved detrimental to my purposes. As it was managed by me, no one except the passengers that came over with us, and dispersed from Liverpool all over the Continent, knew anything about her arrival. At the Crown and Miter she was half a mile in distance and half a thousand miles in degree from anyone connected with our circle. No one, therefore, knows her whereabouts; no inquiries will be made for her; we may do with her as we like."

"Oh, ciel! and we will quickly make way with her."

"Quickly."

"But how?"

"Another time I will tell you, 'Tina. Now I must be gone. I must not linger here. It becomes us to be very wary."

"Go, then. But ah! you go to her. Misery! Do not love her! If you do—remember I will kill her! I have sworn it. You say that you will make way with her by the help of the law. Do it soon; or be sure I will make way with her in spite of the law."

"Hush! be tranquil. Trust in me. You shall know all in a few days. Good-night!"

"Ah! you are leaving me. You, that I have not seen for so many months until now—and now have seen but a few minutes alone. And you go to her—her, with whom you have been in company all the time you have been away from me! Ah, I hate her! I will kill her!" exclaimed the woman, in low, vehement tones.

"Faustina, be quiet, or all is lost! You must be my sister-in-law only until you can be my wife. To accomplish this purpose of ours, you must be very, very discreet, as I shall be. Be on your guard always. Treat Lady Vincent with outward respect, as I must do, in the presence of the servants. They must be our future witnesses. Surely you will be enabled to do what I require of you in this respect, when I assure you that I hate my viscountess as deeply as you hate your rival."

"Ha! you?"

"Yes; for in her heart she despises me and adores another. She is unfaithful to me in thought. And it shall go hard, but I will make it appear that she is unfaithful in deed, too, and so send her, dishonored and impoverished, from the castle," said the viscount vindictively.

"Ciel! Is that your plan? I understand now. I trust you, my Malcolm."

"Good-night, then; and don't be jealous."

"Never! I trust you. I shall triumph."

CHAPTER XVIII

IN THE TRAITOR'S TOILS.

Her heart is sick with thinking

Of the misery she must find.

Her mind is almost sinking—

That once so buoyant mind— She cannot look before her,

On the evil-haunted way.

Redeem her! oh! restore her!

Thou Lord of night and day!

—Monckton Milnes.

Overwhelmed with, horror, terror, and indignation, Claudia just tottered from the room in time to escape discovery.

On reaching the hall she saw the door leading into her own suite of apartments wide open and all the rooms lighted up and old Katie moving about, unpacking trunks and hanging up dresses. Katie, it seemed, with something like canine instinct as to locality, had experienced no difficulty in finding her mistress' rooms.

As soon as Lady Vincent entered her dressing room the old woman drew the resting chair and footstool up to the fire, and when Claudia had dropped into the seat she leaned over the back of the chair, and forgetting ceremony, spoke to her nursling as she had spoken to her in the days of that nursling's infancy.

"Miss Claudia, honey, I wants to talk to you downright ser'us, I do."

"Talk on, Katie," sighed Claudia.

"But, 'deed, I'm feared I shall hurt your feelings, honey."

"You cannot do that."

"Well, then, honey—but 'deed you must excuse me, Miss Claudia, because I wouldn't say a word, only I think how it is my bounden duty."

"For Heaven's sake, Katie, say what you wish to without so much preface."

"Well, then, Miss Claudia—laws, honey, I's nussed you ever since you was borned, and been like another mammy to you ever since your own dear mammy went to heaven, and if I haven't got a right to speak free, I'd like to know who has!"

"Certainly; certainly! Only, in mercy, go on!" exclaimed Claudia, who, fevered, excited, and nearly maddened by what she had overheard, could scarcely be patient with her old servant.

"Well, Miss Claudia, honey, it is all about this strange foreign 'oman as is a-wisiting here."

"Ah!" exclaimed Claudia, looking up and becoming at once interested.

"Miss Claudia, honey, that 'oman aint no fitting company for you. She aint."

"Ah! what do you know of her?" inquired Claudia in a low, breathless, eager voice.

"Honey, I cotch my eye on her dis evening. You see dis was de way of it, chile. I was in dis very room; but I hadn't lighted up de lamps, so I was in 'parative darkness, and de big hall was in 'parative light; so dey couldn't see me, but I could see dem, when dey come into de big hall, her and my lordship. And I seen her how she look at him, and smile on him, and coo over him like any turkle dove, as no 'spectable lady would ever do. And so dey walks into dat room, opposite to dis."

"Katie, I do not wish to hear any more of this stuff. You forget yourself, surely!" said Lady Vincent, suddenly waking to the consciousness that she was compromising her dignity in listening to the tale-bearing of a servant, even so old and tried as Katie was.

"Very well, Miss Claudia, honey, you knows best; but take one piece of advice from de best friend you's got on dis side o' de big water. You 'void dat 'oman. Oh, Miss Claudia, chile! wouldn't you keep out'n de way of anybody as had de smallpox or any other deadly plague? Tell me dat!"

"Of course I would."

"Oh, Miss Claudia, honey, listen to me, den! Dere is worser plagues dan de smallpox; more 'fectious and more fatal, too. Moral plagues! De fust plague, Miss Claudia, can only disfigur' de face and kill de body; but de las' plague can disfigur' de heart and kill de soul. Miss Claudia, 'void dat 'oman! She'll 'fect you with the moral plague as is deadly to de heart and soul," said the old woman, with a manner of deep solemnity.

Claudia was moved. She shook as she answered:

"Katie, you mean well; but let us talk no more of this tonight. And whatever your thoughts may be of this evil woman, I must beg that you will not utter them to any one of the other servants."

"I won't, Miss Claudia. I won't speak of her to nobody but you."

"Nor to me, unless I ask you. And now, Katie, bring me my dressing gown and help me to disrobe. I am tired to death."

"And no wonder, honey," said the old woman, as she went to obey.

When she had arranged her young mistress at ease in dressing gown and slippers, in the resting chair, she would still have lingered near her, tendering little offices of affection, but Claudia, wishing to be alone, dismissed her.

Lady Vincent had need of solitude for reflection.

As soon as old Katie had left her alone she clasped her hands and fell back in her chair, exclaiming: "What shall I do? Oh! what shall I do?"

She tried to think; but in the whirl of her emotions, thought was very difficult, almost impossible. She felt that she had been deceived and betrayed; and that her situation was critical and perilous in the extreme. What should she do? to whom should she appeal? how should she escape? where should she go?

Should she now "beard the lion in his den"; charge Lord Vincent with his perfidy, duplicity, treachery, and meditated crime; demand the instantaneous dismissal of Faustina; and insist upon an immediate introduction to his family as the only means of safety to herself? Where would be the good of that? She, a "stranger in a strange land," an inmate of a remote coast fortress, was absolutely in Lord Vincent's power. He would deride her demands and defy her wrath.

Should she openly attempt to leave the castle and return to her native country and her friends? Again, what would be the good of such an attempt? Her departure, she felt sure, would never be permitted.

Should she try to make her escape secretly? That would be difficult or impossible. The castle stood upon the extreme point of its high promontory, overlooking the sea; it was remote from any other dwelling; the roads leading from it were for miles impassable to foot passengers. And besides all this, Claudia was unwilling to take such a very undignified course.

In fact, she was unwilling to abandon her position at all—painful and dangerous as it was; having purchased it at a high price she felt like retaining end defending it.

What then should she do? The answer came like an inspiration. Write to her father to come over immediately to her aid. And get him to bring about her introduction to the Earl of Hurstmonceux's family and her recognition by their circle. This course, she thought, would secure her personal safety and her social position, if not her domestic happiness; for the latter she had never dared to hope.

And while waiting for her father's arrival, she would be "wise as serpents," if not "harmless as doves." She would meet Lord Vincent on his own grounds and fight him with his own weapons; she would beat duplicity with duplicity.

But first to write the letter to her father and dispatch it secretly by the first mail. She arose and rang the bell.

Katie answered it.

"Unpack my little writing desk and place it on this stand beside me."

Katie did as she was ordered.

"Now lock the door and wait here until I write a letter."

Katie obeyed and then seated herself on a footstool near her lady's feet.

Claudia opened her writing desk; but paused long, pen in hand, reflecting how she had better write this letter.

If she should tell her father at once of all the horror of her position the sudden news might throw him into a fit of apoplexy and kill him instantly.

And on the other hand, if she were to conceal all this and merely write him a pressing invitation to come over immediately, he might take his time over it.

Speed Claudia felt to be of the utmost importance to her cause. So, after due reflection, she dipped her pen in ink, and commenced as follows:

"Castle Cragg, near Banff, Buchan, Scotland. "My Dearest Father: We are all in good health; therefore do not be alarmed, even though I earnestly implore you to drop everything that you may have in hand, and come over to me immediately, by the very first steamer that sails after your receipt of this letter. Father, you will comply with my entreaty when I inform you that I have been deceived and betrayed by him who swore to protect and cherish me. My life and honor are both imperiled. I will undertake to guard both for a month, until you come. But come at once to your wronged, though "Loving child, "Claudia."

She sealed the letter very carefully, directed it, and gave it into the hands of her old servant, saying:

"Katie, listen to every word I say, and obey to the very letter. Take this downstairs and give it to Jim privately. Let no one see, or hear, or even suspect what you are doing. Tell him to steal out carefully from the castle and walk to the nearest roadside inn, and hire a horse and ride to Banff, and mail this letter there; and then come back and report progress to you. Now, Katie, do you understand what you have got to do?"

"Yes, Miss Claudia."

"Repeat it to me, then."

Katie rehearsed her instructions.

"That will do. Hurry now and obey them."

When Katie had gone Lady Vincent closed her writing desk, threw herself back in her chair, covered her face with her hands, and wept.

She was startled by the entrance of Lord Vincent.

She hastily dried her eyes, and shifted her position so that her back was to the light and her face in deep shadow.

"You are sitting up late, my lady. I should think you would be tired after your long journey," he said, as he took another armchair and seated himself opposite to her.

"I was just thinking of retiring," answered Claudia, putting severe constraint upon herself.

"But since I find you sitting up, if it will not fatigue you too much, I will answer some questions you asked me concerning Mrs. Dugald," said his lordship.

"Yes?" said Claudia, scarcely able to breathe the single syllable.

"Yes. You inquired of me who she was. I told you she was my sister. You did not believe me; but you should have done so, for I told you the truth. She is my sister."

Scarcely able to restrain her indignation at this impudent falsehood, and fearful of trusting the sound of her own voice, Claudia answered in a low tone:

"I supposed that you were jesting with my curiosity. I knew, of course, that your sisters were titled ladies. Mrs. Dugald is an untitled one, therefore she could not be your sister; nor could she be your sister-in-law, since you are an only son."

"You are mistaken in both your premises: Mrs. Dugald is my sister-in-law, and is a titled lady, since she is the widow of my younger half-brother, the Honorable Kenneth Dugald," said the viscount triumphantly.

"I never heard that your deceased brother had been married," answered Claudia coolly.

"No? Why, bless you, yes! About four years ago he married the beauty over whom all Paris was going raving mad. She was the prima donna of the Italian opera in Paris. But the marriage was not pleasing to the earl, who is severely afflicted with the prejudices of his rank. He immediately disowned his son, the Honorable Kenneth, never speaking to him again during his, Kenneth's, life. And more than that, he carried his resentment beyond the grave; for even after Kenneth died of a fever contracted in the Crimea, and his widow was left unprovided for, and with the pleasant alternative of starving to death or dragging the noble name of Dugald before the footlights of the stage, my father politely informed her that she was at liberty to go on the stage or to go to—hem! It was then that I offered La Faustina an asylum in my house, which she accepted. And I hope, Lady Vincent, that you will be good enough to make her welcome," said Lord Vincent.

Claudia could not reply; the anger, scorn, and disgust that filled her bosom fairly choked her voice.

After a struggle with herself, she managed to articulate:

"How does the earl like your protection of this woman?"

"I wish you would not use that word 'protection,' Claudia. It is an equivocal one."

"Then it is the better suited to describe the relation, which is certainly most equivocal!" Claudia, in spite of all her resolutions, could not for the life of her help replying.

"It is false! And I will not permit you to say it. The position of Mrs. Dugald is not an equivocal one. It is clearly defined. She is my brother's widow. When I invited her to take up her residence in this castle I took care to leave it before she arrived. And I never returned to it until to-day, when I brought you with me. Your presence here, of course, renders the residence of my brother's widow beneath my roof altogether proper."

Claudia had much to do to control her feelings, as she said:

"We will waive the question of propriety, which, of course, is settled by my presence in the house; but you have not yet told me how the earl likes this arrangement."

"I have not seen the earl since the arrangement has been made. I fancy he will like it well, since it relieves him of the burden of having her to support, and saves him from the mortification of seeing her return to the boards."

"Good-night, my lord!" said Claudia abruptly, rising and retiring to her bedroom, for she felt that she could not remain another moment in Lord Vincent's presence, without confronting him with her perfect knowledge of his meditated villainy, and thus losing her only chance of defeating it.

Claudia retired to bed, but, though worn out with fatigue, she could not sleep. This, then, was her coming home! She had sold her birthright, and got not even the "mess of pottage," but the cup of poison.

She lay tossing about with fevered veins and throbbing temples until morning, when, at last, she sunk into a sleep of exhaustion.

She awoke with a prostrating, nervous headache. She attempted to rise, but fell helplessly back upon the pillow. Then she reached forth her hand and rang the bell that hung at the side of her bed.

Katie answered it.

"Did Jim succeed in mailing my letter?" was her first question.

"Yes, my ladyship; but he had to wait ever so long before the tide ebbed to let him cross over to the shore; but he got there all right, and in time to save the mail; but he didn't get back here until this morning."

"Did anyone find out his going?"

"Not a living soul, as I knows of, Miss Claudia."

"Thank Heaven!" said Lady Vincent, with a deep sigh.

Old Katie busied herself with bringing her mistress' stockings, soft slippers, and dressing gown to the bedside; but Claudia said:

"Put them away again, Katie; I shall not rise to-day. I have one of my very bad, nervous headaches. You may bring me a cup of strong coffee."

"Ah, honey, no wonder! I go bring it directly," said Katie, hurrying away with affectionate eagerness to bring the fragrant restorative.

A few minutes afterwards Katie entered with the tray, followed by the housekeeper, Mrs. Murdock, who came with anxious inquiries as to Lady Vincent's health.

"I have a very bad, nervous headache, which is not surprising, after all my fatigue," replied Claudia.

"Nay, indeed, and it is not, me leddy; you should lie quietly in bed to-day, and to-morrow you will be well," said the dame.

"Yes."

"And, me leddy, Mrs. Dugald bid me give her compliments to your leddyship, and ask if she should come and sit with you."

"I cannot receive Mrs. Dugald," said Claudia coldly.

"Ah, then I will say your leddyship is na weel enough to receive company?"

"Say what you please. I cannot receive Mrs. Dugald."

Old Katie had gone into the dressing room to stir the fire, which was to warm the whole suite. Taking advantage of her absence the housekeeper sat down beside Lady Vincent's bed, and, while pouring out her coffee, stooped and nodded and whispered:

"Aye! and sma' blame to your leddyship, gin ye never receive the likes of her."

"What do you know of Mrs. Dugald that you should say so?" was Claudia's cold question. For alas, poor lady, she was in sad straits! She had need to glean knowledge of her dangerous enemy from every possible quarter; but—she felt that she must do so without committing herself, or compromising her dignity.

"Nay, I ken naething! I dinna like the quean! that's all!" said the woman, growing all at once reserved.

"She is the widow of the late Honorable Kenneth Dugald?" said Claudia, in a tone that might be received either as a statement or a question.

"Sae it is said. I ken naething anent it," replied the dame, taking up the tray of empty cups. "Will your leddyship ha' anything more?"

"No, thank you, Mrs. Murdock," replied Claudia, in a very sweet tone, for she felt that in her pride of place she had repulsed the offered confidence of an honest old creature who might have been of great use to her.

"Will I sit wi' your leddyship?" inquired the dame.

"No, I am much obliged to you. I must rest now; but I should be glad if you would come to me later in the day."

"Yes, me leddy," answered the dame, somewhat mollified, as she courtesied and withdrew from the room, leaving Lady Vincent to the care of her own faithful servant.

CHAPTER XIX

CLAUDIA'S TROUBLES AND PERILS.

Like love in a worldly breast

Alone in my lady's chamber

The lamp burns low, suppressed

'Mid satins of broidered amber

Where she lies, sore distressed.

My lady here alone

May think till her heart is broken

Of the love that is dead and done,

Of the day that with no token

For evermore hath gone.

—Owen Meredith.

All day long Claudia lay abed within her darkened chamber, It was a scene of magnificence, luxury, and repose. Scarcely a ray of light stole through the folds of the golden-brown curtains of window and bed. No sound broke the stillness of the air, except the dull, monotonous thunder of the sea upon the rocks below. This at length soothed her nervous excitement and lulled her to repose.

She slept until the evening, and awoke comparatively free from pain.

Her first thought on waking was of the housekeeper, and her first feeling was the desire to see the old creature, and if possible make a friend of her.

Ah! but it was bitterly galling to Lady Vincent's pride to be obliged to stoop to the degradation of questioning a servant concerning the domestic affairs of her own husband's family! But she felt that her life and honor were imperiled, and that she must use such means for her safety as circumstances offered. Mrs. Murdock impressed her as being an honest, truthful, and trustworthy woman. And Claudia wished to discover, by what should seem casual conversation with her, how much or how little truth there might be in Lord Vincent's representations of Mrs. Dugald's position in the family.

She put out her hand and rang the bell that hung just within her reach.

Katie answered it.

"Tell the housekeeper I would like to see her now," said Lady Vincent.

Katie tossed her head and went out. Katie was already jealous of the housekeeper.

In a few minutes Mrs. Murdock entered.

"I hope your leddyship is better," she said, courtesying.

"I am better; do not stand; sit down on that chair beside me," said Claudia kindly.

The dame sank slowly into the offered seat and said: "Will your leddyship please to take onything?"

"Nothing, just yet."

"Can I do naething for you, me leddy?"

"Yes, thank you; you can take that flagon of carmelite water on the stand beside you and bathe my forehead and temples while you sit there," said Claudia slowly and hesitatingly; for she was thinking how best to open the subject that occupied her mind. At length, while the dame was carefully bathing her head, Claudia said, with assumed carelessness:

"Mrs. Dugald is very beautiful."

"Ou, aye, me leddy, she's weel eneugh to look upon, if that was a'," replied the housekeeper dryly.

"Has she been here long?"

"Ever sin' Mr. Kenneth died, me leddy."

"Mr. Kenneth?" echoed Claudia, in an interrogative tone; for she remembered well that Kenneth was the name of Lord Vincent's younger brother, said to have been married to La Faustina; but she wished to hear more without, however, compromising herself by asking direct questions.

"Mr. Kenneth?" she repeated, looking into the housekeeper's face.

"Ou, aye, your leddyship; just the Honorable Kenneth Dugald, puir lad!"

"Why do you say poor lad?"

"I beg your leddyship's pardon. I mean just naething. It's on'y just a way I ha'."

Claudia reflected a moment; and then, though it went sorely against her pride so to speak to a dependent, she said:

"Mrs. Murdock, I am a very young and inexperienced woman; I have been motherless from my infancy; I am 'a stranger in a strange land'; unacquainted even with the members of my husband's family; my meeting with Mrs. Dugald here was unexpected, Lord Vincent never having mentioned her existence to me; my first impression of her was very unfavorable; some words you dropped deepened that impression; and now I feel that there are circumstances with which I ought to be made acquainted and with which you can acquaint me; will you do so?"

"Aye, me leddy, and with the freer conscience that I ken weel his lairdship the airl would approve. Ye ken, me leddy, there were but twa brithers; Laird Vincent and the Honorable Kenneth Dugald?"

"I am aware of that."

"Aweel they were in Paris tegither and fell in somewhere with this quean."

"This—what?"

"This player-bodie, me leddy; who afterwards put the glamour over Mr. Kenneth's eyes to make her Mrs. Dugald."

"Oh," said Claudia to herself, "then that is true; the woman really is the widow of Kenneth Dugald and the sister-in-law of Lord Vincent. Go on, Mrs. Murdock; I am listening."

"Aweel, she had the art, me leddy, to make him marry her. A burning shame it was, me leddy, in one of his noble name, but he did it. He was a minor, ye ken, being but twenty years of age, and sae he could na be lawfu' married in France nor in England, and sae he brought his player-woman to auld Scotland and made her his wife—woe worth the day!"

"This must have been a terrible mortification to the earl?"

"Ye may weel say that, me leddy. His lairdship never saw or spoke to Mr. Kenneth afterwards. But he purchased him a commission in a regiment that was just about to embark for the Crimea, where the young gentleman went, taking his wife with him, and where he died of the fever, leaving his widow to find her way back as she would."

"Poor young man!"

"Aye, puir laddie! nae doubt regret helped the fever to kill him. Aweel, his widow come her ways back to Scotland, as I had the honor to tell your leddyship, and made her appeal to his lairdship the airl for dower. But your leddyship may weel ken that me laird would ha'e naething to say till her. Will I bathe your leddyship's head ony langer?"

"Yes, please, and go on with what you are telling me."

"Aweel, me leddy, failing to come over the airl, she began to cast her spells over his lairdship my Laird Vincent. This gave the airl great oneasiness, for ye ken he feared this woman that she should bewitch the ane as she had the ither, e'en to the length of making him marry her. And to say naething of ony ither reason against siccan a marriage, we think it wrang for ony mon to wed wi' his brother's widow. Sae the airl took short measures wi' his son, Laird Vincent, and stopped his siller; but got him an appointment to carry out papers to the minister, away yonder in the States. Sae the young laird sent his sister-in-law, as he calls her, up here to bide her lane, telling his feyther, the airl, he could na' turn his brither's widow out of doors. Which, ye ken, me leddy, sounded weel eneugh. Sae hither she cam'. And an unco' sair heart she's gi'e us a' sin' ever she cam'!"

"Has she been here ever since?"

"Nay, me leddy; she left hame last August and did na come back till a month."

Claudia was satisfied. This was the same woman that she had seen on the platform of the railway station at Jersey City.

"Does the earl know of this lady's continued residence beneath his roof?"

"I dinna ken, me leddy. But I'm just thinking his lairdship will na care onything about it ony langer, sin' his son is weel married to yoursel', me leddy."

"The earl liked his son's marriage, then?" inquired Claudia, for upon this point she felt anxious for authentic information.

"Aye, did he! didna it keep the lad out o' danger o' the wiles o' siccan a quean as yon? And now, will I bring your leddyship some refreshment?"

"Yes," said Claudia, "you may bring me a bowl of your oatmeal porridge. I should like to taste your national food."

The housekeeper left the room and Claudia fell into thought. Two important facts she had gained by descending from her dignity to gossip with an upper servant, namely: That La Faustina was really the widow of Kenneth Dugald, and that the Earl of Hurstmonceux was well pleased with his son's marriage to herself, and would therefore be likely to be her partisan in any trouble she might have on account of Mrs. Dugald. She resolved, therefore, to be very wary in her conduct until the arrival of her father, and then to request an introduction to the earl's family. Bitterly galling as it would be to her pride, she even determined to meet Mrs. Dugald in the drawing room and at the table without demur; since she could treat her as the widow of the Honorable Kenneth Dugald without openly compromising her own dignity. Finally she concluded to meet Lord Vincent's treacherous courtesy with assumed civility.

On the third day Lady Vincent felt well enough to join the viscount and Mrs. Dugald at breakfast. Pursuant to her resolution she received their congratulations with smiles, and answered their inquiries as to her health with thanks.

It was a foggy, misty, drizzly day the precursor of a long spell of dark and gloomy weather, that Claudia at length grew to fear would never come to an end.

During this time the monotony of Claudia's life at the castle was really dreadful.

And this was something like it: She would wake about seven o'clock, but knowing that it was hours too early to rise in that house, she would lie and think until she was ready to go mad. At nine o'clock she would ring for her maid, Sally, and spend an hour in dawdling over her toilet. At ten she would go down to breakfast—a miserable, uncomfortable meal of hollow civility or sullen silence. After breakfast she would go into the library and hunt among the old, musty, worm-eaten books for something readable, but without success.

Then, ready to kill herself from weariness of life, she would wrap up in cloak and hood and climb the turret stairs and go out upon the ramparts of the castle and walk up and down with the drizzling mist above and around her and the thundering sea beneath her—up and down—hour after hour—up and down—lashing herself into such excitement that she would be tempted to throw herself from the battlements, to be crushed to death by the rocks or swallowed up by the waves below.

At length, as fearing to trust herself with this temptation, she would descend into the castle again, and go to her own rooms, and try to interest herself in a little needle-work, a little writing, a talk with Katie or with Mrs. Murdock.

At last the creeping hours would bring luncheon, when the same inharmonious party would assemble around the same ungenial table, and eat and drink without enjoyment or gratitude.

After that she would lie down and try to sleep, and then write a letter home, do a little embroidery, yawn, weep, wish herself dead, and wonder how soon she would hear from her father.

The dragging hours would at length draw on the late dinner, when she would make an elaborate toilet, just for pastime, and go to dinner, which always seemed like a funeral feast. Here Claudia formed the habit of drinking much more wine than was good for her: and she did it to blunt her sensibility; to obtund the sharpness of her heartache; to give her sleep.

After dinner they would go into the drawing room, where coffee would be served. And after that, if Mrs. Dugald were in the humor, there would be music. And then the party would disperse. Claudia would go into her own room and pass a long, lonely, wretched evening, sometimes speculating on life, death, and immortality, and wondering whether, in the event of her deciding to walk out of this world with which she was so much dissatisfied, into the other of which she knew nothing, she would be any better off.

At eleven o'clock she always rang for wine and biscuits, and drank enough to make her sleep. Then she would go to bed, sink into a heavy, feverish sleep, that would last until the morning, when she would awake with a headache, as well as a heartache, to pass just such a day as the preceding one.

Such were Claudia's days and nights. Ah! how different to those she had pictured when she sold herself and her fortune for rank and title.

Her days were all so much alike that they could only be distinguished by the change in her dinner dress, and the difference in the bill of fare.

"It is maize-colored moire antique and mutton one day and violet-colored velvet and veal another; that is all!" wrote Claudia in one of her letters home.

That was all! The same leaden sky overhung the land and sea; the same fine, penetrating mist drizzled slowly down and sifted like snow into everything; the same stupid routine of sleeping, walking, dressing, eating, drinking, undressing, and sleeping again, occupied the household.

No visitors ever came to the house, and of course Claudia went nowhere. She was unspeakably miserable, and would have wished for death, had she not been a firm believer in future retribution.

"Misery loves company," it is said. There was one inmate in this unblessed house who seemed quite as miserable as Claudia herself. This was one of the housemaids; the one who had charge of Claudia's own rooms. Lady Vincent had noticed this poor girl, and had observed that she was pale, thin, sad, always with red eyes, and often in tears. Once she inquired kindly:

"What is the matter with you, Ailsie?"

"It's just naething, me leddy," was the weeping girl's answer.

"But I am sure it is something. Can you not tell me? What is it troubles you?"

"Just naething, me leddy," was still the answer.

"Are you away from all your friends? Are you homesick?"

"I ha'e naebody belanging to me, me leddy."

"You are an orphan?"

"Aye, me leddy."

"Then you must really tell me what is the matter with you, my poor child; I will help you if I can."

"Indeed I canna tell you, my leddy. Your leddyship maun please to forgi'e me, and not mind me greeting. It's just naething; it's ony a way I ha'e."

And this was all that Claudia could get out of this poor girl.

Once she inquired of Mrs. Murdock: "What ails Ailsie Dunbar? Her looks trouble me."

"Indeed, me leddy, I dinna ken. The lassie is greeting fra morning till night, and will na gie onybody ony satisfaction about it! But I will try to find out." And that was all Lady Vincent could get out of the housekeeper.

The month of November crept slowly by. And December came, darker, duller, drearier than its predecessor. And now anxiety was added to Claudia's other troubles. She had not heard from her father.

The monotony, deepened by suspense, grew horrible. She wished for an earthquake, or an inundation—anything to break the dreadful spell that bound her, to burst the tomb of her buried life and let in air and light.

Sometimes she overheard the precious pair of friends who shared her home murmuring their sinful nonsense together; and she was disgusted.

And sometimes she heard them in angry and jealous altercation; and she grew insane, and wished from the bottom of her heart that one might murder the other, if it were only to break the horrible monotony of the castle life, by bringing into it the rabble rout of inspectors, constables, coroners, and juries. At length there came a day when that frenzied wish was gratified.

CHAPTER X

A LINK IN CLAUDIA'S FATE.

For who knew, she thought, what the amazement,

The irruption of clatter and blaze meant.

And if, in this minute of wonder,

No outlet 'mid lightning and thunder,

Lay broad and her shackles all shivered,

The captive at length was delivered?

—Robert Browning.

Claudia had awakened one morning with one of those nervous headaches that were becoming habitual to her. She had taken a narcotic sedative and gone to sleep again, and slept throughout the day.

It was night when she awoke again, and became immediately conscious of an unusual commotion in the castle—a commotion that reached her ears, even over the thick drugget with which the stairs and halls were covered, and through the strong doors and heavy hangings with which her chamber was protected. Whether it was this disturbance that had broken her rest, she did not really know. She listened intently. There was a swift and heavy running to and fro, and a confusion of tongues, giving voices in mingled tones of fear, grief, rage, consternation, expostulation, and every key of passionate emotion and excitement.

Lady Vincent reached forth her hand and rang the bell, and then listened, but no one answered it. She rang again, with no better success. After waiting some little time she rang a violent peal, that presently brought the housekeeper hurrying into the room, pale as death, and nearly out of breath.

"Mrs. Murdock, I have rung three times. I have never before had occasion to ring twice for attendance," said Lady Vincent, in a displeased tone.

"Ou, me leddy, ye will e'en forgi'e me this ance, when ye come to hear the cause," panted the housekeeper.

"What has happened?" demanded Claudia.

"Ou, me leddy! sic an' awfu' event."

"What is it, then?"

"Just murther—no less!"

"Murder!" exclaimed Claudia, starting up and gazing at the speaker with horror-distended eyes.

"Just murther!" gasped the housekeeper, sinking down in the armchair beside her lady's bed, because in truth her limbs gave way beneath her.

"Who? what? For Heaven's sake, speak!"

"The puir bit lassie—" began the dame; but her voice failed, and she covered her face with her apron and began to howl.

Claudia gazed at her in consternation and horror for a minute, and then again demanded:

"What lassie? Who is murdered? For the Lord's sake try to answer me!"

"Puir Ailsie! puir wee bit lassie!" wailed the woman.

"Ailsie! what has happened to her?" demanded Lady Vincent, bewildered with panic.

"She's found murthered!" howled the housekeeper.

"Ailsie! Heaven of heavens, no!" cried Claudia, wound up to a pitch of frenzied excitement.

"Aye is she; found lying outside the castle wall, wi' her puir throat cut fra ear to ear!" shrieked the dame, covering up her face to smother the cries she could not suppress.

"Mercy of Heaven, how horrible!" exclaimed Lady Vincent, throwing her hands up to her face, and falling back on her pillow.

"Puir Ailsie! puir, bonnie lassie!" howled the dame, rocking her body to and fro.

"Who did it?" gasped Claudia, under her breath.

"Ah! that's what we canna come at; naebody kens."

"I cannot rest here any longer. Ring the bell, Mrs. Murdock, and hand me my dressing gown. I must get up and go downstairs. Good Heavens! a poor, innocent girl murdered in this house, and her murderer allowed to escape!" exclaimed Claudia, throwing the bed-clothes off her and rising in irrepressible excitement.

"Ah, me leddy, I fear, I greatly fear, she was no that innocent as your leddyship thinks, puir bairn! Nae that I would say onything about it, only it's weel kenned noo. Puir Ailsie! she lost her innocence before she lost her life, me leddy. And I greatly misdoubt, he that reft her of the ane reft her of the ither!" sobbed the dame, as she assisted Claudia to put on her crimson silk dressing gown.

"Now give me a shawl; I must go below."

"Nay, nay, me leddy, dinna gang! It's awfu' wark doon there. They've brought her in, and laid her on the ha' table, and a' the constables and laborers are there, forbye the servants. It's nae place for you, me leddy. Your leddyship could na stand it."

"Anyone who has stood six weeks of the ordinary life in this house can stand anything else under the sun!" exclaimed Claudia, wrapping herself in the large India shawl that was handed her, and hurrying downstairs.

She was met by old Katie, who was on her way to answer the bell that had been rung for her, and who, as soon as she saw her mistress, raised both her hands in deprecation, and in her terror began to speak as if Lady Vincent were still a child and she was still her nurse and keeper:

"Now, Miss Claudia, honey, you jes' go right straight back ag'in! Dis aint no place for sich as you, chile. You mustn't go down dar and look at dat gashly objeck, honey. 'Cause no tellin' what de quoncequinces mightn't be. Now mind what your ole Aunt Katie say to you, honey, and turn back like a good chile."

While old Katie was coaxing her Lady Vincent was looking over the balustrade down into the hall below, which was filled to suffocation with a motley crowd, who were pressing around some object extended upon the table, and which Claudia could only make out in the obscurity by the gleam of the white cloth with which it was covered.

Without stopping to answer old Katie, she pushed her aside and hurried below.

The crowd had done with loud talking and an awe-struck silence prevailed, broken only now and then by a half-suppressed murmur of fear or horror.

Forgetting her fastidiousness for once, Lady Vincent pushed her way through this crowd of "unwashed" workmen, whose greasy, dusty, and begrimed clothes soiled her bright, rich raiment as she passed, and among whom the mingled fumes of tobacco, whisky, garlic, and coal-smoke formed "the rankest compound of villainous smells that ever offended nostrils."

Claudia did not mind all this. She pressed on, and they gave way for her a little as she approached the table. Three constables stood around it to guard the dead body from the touch of meddlesome hands. On seeing Lady Vincent with the air of one having authority, the constable that guarded the head of the table guessed at her rank, and officiously turned down the white sheet that covered the dead body, and revealed the horrible object beneath—the ghastly face fallen back, with its chin dropped, and its mouth and eyes wide open and rigid in death; and the gaping red wound across the throat cut so deep that it nearly severed the head from the body. With a suppressed shriek Claudia clapped her hands to her face to shut out the awful sight.

At the same moment she felt her arm grasped by a firm hand, and her name called in a stern voice: "Lady Vincent, why are you here? Retire at once to your chamber."

Claudia, too much overcome with horror to dispute the point, suffered the viscount to draw her out of the crowd to the foot of the stairs. Here she recovered herself sufficiently to inquire:

"What has been done, my lord? What steps have been taken towards the discovery and arrest of this poor girl's murderer?"

"All that is possible has been done, or is doing. The coroner has been summoned; the inspector has been sent for; a telegram has been dispatched to Scotland Yard in London for an experienced detective. Rest easy, Lady Vincent. Here, Mistress Gorilla! Attend your lady to her apartment."

This last order was addressed to Katie, who was still lingering on the stairs, and who was glad to receive this charge from Lord Vincent.

"Come along, Miss Claudia, honey," she said, as soon as the viscount had left them; "come along. We can't do no good, not by staying here no longer. My lordship was right dar. Dough why he do keep on a-calling of me Mrs. Gorilla is more'n I can 'count for. Not dat I objects to de name; 'cause I do like the name. I think's it a perty name, sweet perty name, so soft and musicky; only you see, chile, it aint mine; and I can't think what could put it in my lordship's head to think it was."

Lady Vincent paid no attention to the innocent twaddle of poor old Katie, though at a less horrible moment it might have served to amuse her. She hurried as fast as her agitation would permit her from the scene of the dreadful tragedy, unconscious how closely this poor murdered girl's fate would be connected with her own future destiny. She gained the shelter of her own apartments and shut herself up there, while the investigations into the murder proceeded.

It is not necessary for us to go deeply into the revolting details of the events that followed. The coroner arrived the same evening, impaneled his jury and commenced the inquest. Soon after the inspector came from Banff. And the next morning a skillful detective arrived from London. And the investigation commenced in earnest. Many witnesses were examined; extensive searches were made, and all measures taken to find out some clew to the murderer, but in vain. The police held possession of the premises for nearly a week, and the coroner's jury sat day after day; but all to no purpose, as far as the discovery of the perpetrator of the crime was concerned. This seemed one of the obstinate murders that, in spite of the old proverb to the contrary, will not "out."

On Saturday night the baffled coroner's jury returned their unsatisfactory verdict: "The deceased, Ailsie Dunbar, came to her death by a wound inflicted in her throat with a razor held in the hands of some person unknown to the jury."

And the house was rid of coroner, jury, inspector, detective, country constables and all; and the poor girl's body was permitted to be laid in the earth; and the household breathed freely again.

The same evening Lord Vincent, being alone in his dressing room, rang his bell; and his valet as usual answered it.

"Come in here, Frisbie. Shut the door after you, and stand before me," said his lordship.

"Yes, my lord," answered the servant, securing the door and standing before his master.

Lord Vincent sat with his back to the window and his face in the shadow, while the light from the window fell full on the face of the valet, who stood before him. This was a position Lord Vincent always managed to secure, when he wished to read the countenance of his interlocutor, without exposing his own.

"Well, Frisbie, they are gone," said his lordship, looking wistfully into the face of his servant.

"Yes, my lord," replied the latter, looking down.

"And—without discovering the murderer of Ailsie Dunbar," he continued, in a meaning voice.

"Yes, my lord," replied the valet, with the slightest possible quaver in his tone.

"That must be a very great relief to your feelings, Frisbie," said the viscount.

"I—have not the honor to understand your lordship," faltered Frisbie, changing color.

"Haven't you? Why, that is strange! My meaning is clear enough. I say it must be a very great relief to your feelings, Frisbie, to have the inquest so well over, and all the law-officers out of the house. You must have endured agonies of terror while they were here. I know I should in your place. Why, I expected every day that you would bolt, though that would have been the worst thing you could possibly have done, too, for it would have been sure to direct suspicion towards you, and you would have been certain to be recaptured before you could have got out of England," said Lord Vincent coolly.

"I—I—my lord—I have not the honor—to—to—under——" began the man, but his teeth chattered so that he could not enunciate another syllable.

"Oh, yes! you have the honor, if you consider it such. You understand me well enough. What is the use of attempting to deceive me? Frisbie, I was an eye-witness to the death of Ailsie Dunbar," said his lordship emphatically, and fixing his eyes firmly upon the face of his valet.

Down fell the wretch upon his knees, with his hands clasped, his face blanched, and his teeth chattering.

"Oh, my lord, mercy, mercy! It was unpremeditated, indeed it was! it was an accident! it was done in the heat of passion! and—and—she did it herself!" gasped the wretch, so beside himself with fright that he did not clearly know what he was talking about.

"Frisbie, stop lying. Did it herself, eh? I saw you do the deed. The razor was in your hands. She struggled and begged, poor creature, and cut her poor hands in her efforts to save her throat; but you completed your purpose effectually before I could appear and prevent you from murdering her. Then I kept your secret, since no good could have come of my telling it."

"Mercy, mercy, my lord! indeed it was unpremeditated! It was done in the heat of passion. She had driven me mad with jealousy!"

"Bosh! what do you suppose I care whether you committed the crime in hot blood or cold blood? whether it was the result of a momentary burst of frenzy or of a long premeditated and carefully arranged plan? It is enough for me to know that I saw you do the deed. You murdered that girl, and if the coroner's jury had not been just about the stupidest lot of donkeys that ever undertook to sit on a case, you would be now in jail waiting your trial for murder before the next assizes."

"Mercy, mercy, my lord! I am in your power!"

"Hold your tongue and get up off your knees and listen to me, you cowardly knave. Don't you know that if I had wished to hang you I could have done so by lodging information against you? Nonsense! I don't want to hang you. I think, with the Quaker, that hanging is the worst use you can put a man to. Now, I don't want to put you to that use. I have other uses for you. Get up, you precious knave!"

"Oh, my lord! put me to any use your lordship wishes, and no matter what it is, I will serve you faithfully in it!" said the wretch, rising from his knees and standing in a cowed and deprecating manner before his master.

"It is perfectly clear to me, Frisbie, that you settled that girl to silence a troublesome claimant of whom you could not rid yourself in any other way."

"Your lordship knows everything. It was so, my lord. She was all the time bothering me about broken promises and all that."

"And so you settled all her claims by one blow. Well, you have got rid of the woman that troubled you; and now I mean that you shall help me to get rid of one who troubles me."

"In—in—in the same manner, my lord?" gasped the man, in an accession of deadly terror.

"No, you insupportable fool! I am not a master butcher, to give you such an order as that. Noblemen are not cut-throats, you knave! You shall rid me of my troublesome woman in a safer way than that. And you shall do it as the price of my silence as to your own little affair."

"I am your lordship's obedient, humble servant. Your lordship will do what you please with me. I am absolutely and unreservedly at your lordship's disposal," whined the criminal.

"Well, I should think you were, when I hold one end of a rope of which the other end is around your neck. Come closer and stoop down until you bring your ear to a level with my lips, for I must speak low," said his lordship.

The man obeyed.

And Lord Vincent confided to his confederate a plan against the peace and honor of his viscountess of so detestable and revolting a nature that even this ruthless assassin shrunk in loathing and disgust from the thought of becoming a participator in it. But he was, as he had said, absolutely and unreservedly at the disposal of Lord Vincent, who held one end of the rope of which the other was around his own neck, and so he ended in becoming the confederate and instrument of the viscount.

When this was all arranged Lord Vincent dismissed the valet with the words:

"Now be at ease, Frisbie; for as long as you are faithful to me I will be silent in regard to you."

And as the second dinner-bell had rung some little time before, Lord Vincent stepped before the glass, brushed his hair, and went downstairs.

As soon as he had left the room another person appeared upon the scene. Old Katie came out from the thick folds of a window curtain and stood in the center of the room with up-lifted hands and up-rolled eyes, and an expression of countenance indescribable by any word in our language.

For more than a minute, perhaps while one could slowly count a hundred, she stood thus. And then, dropping her hands and lowering her eyes, she walked soberly up to Lord Vincent's tall dressing-glass, plucked the parti-colored turban off her head and looked at herself, muttering:

"No! it aint white, nor likewise gray! dough I did think, when dat creeping coldness come stealing through to roots of my h'ar, when I heerd dem wilyuns at deir deblish plot, as ebery libbing ha'r on my head was turned on a suddint white as snow; as I've heerd tell of happening to people long o' fright. But dar! my ha'r is as good as new, dough it has had enough to turn it gray on a suddint in dis las' hour! Well, laws! I do think as Marse Ishmael Worth mus' be somefin of a prophet, as well as a good deal of a lawyer! He told me to watch ober de peace and honor of Lady Vincent. Yes, dem was his berry words—peace and honor. Well, laws! little did I think how much dey would want watching ober. Anyways, I've kep' my word and done my duty. And I've found out somefin as all de crowners, and constables and law-fellows couldn't find out wid all deir larnin'. And dat is who kilt poor misfortunate Miss Ailsie, poor gal! And

I've found out somefin worse 'an dat, dough people might think there couldn't be nothing worse; but deir is. And dat is dis deblish plot agin my ladyship. Oh, dem debils! Hanging is too good for my lordship and his sham wally—wally sham! but it's all de same. And now I go right straight and tell my ladyship all about it," said Katie, settling her turban on her head and hurrying from the room.

She met Lady Vincent, elegantly dressed in a rose-colored brocade and adorned with pearls, on her way to the dinner-table.

"Oh, my ladyship, I've found out somefin dreadful! I must tell you all about it!" she exclaimed, in excitement, as she stopped her mistress.

"Not now, Katie. Dinner is waiting. Go into my dressing room and stop there until I come. I will not stay long in the drawing room this evening," said Lady Vincent, who thought that Katie's news would prove to be only some fresh rumors concerning the murder of poor Ailsie.

"My ladyship, you had better stop now and hear me," pleaded the old woman.

"I tell you dinner is waiting, Katie," said Lady Vincent, hurrying past her.

Ah! she had better have stopped then, if she had only known it. Old Katie groaned in the spirit and went to the dressing room as she was bid.

She sat down before the fire and looked at the clock on the chimney piece. It was just seven.

"Dat funnelly dinner will keep my ladyship an hour at the very latest bit. It will be eight o'clock afore she comes back, Laws-a-massy, what shall I do?" grunted the old woman impatiently.

Slowly, slowly, passed that hour of waiting. The clock struck eight.

"She'll be here every minute now," said old Katie, with a sigh of relief.

But minute after minute passed and Claudia did not come. A half an hour slipped away. Old Katie in her impatience got up and walked about the room. She heard the rustle of silken drapery, and peeped out. It was only Mrs. Dugald, in her rich white brocade dress, passing into her own apartments.

"Nasty, wenemous, pison sarpint! I'll fix you out yet!" muttered old Katie between her teeth, with a perfectly diabolical expression of countenance, as she shook her head at the vanishing figure of the beauty; for that was the unlucky way in which poor Katie's black phiz expressed righteous indignation.

"I do wonder what has become of my ladyship. This is a-keeping of her word like a ladyship oughter, aint it now? I go and look for her," said Katie.

But just as she had opened the door for that purpose her eyes fell upon the figure of the viscount, creeping with stealthy, silent, cat-like steps towards the apartments of Mrs. Dugald, in which he disappeared.

"Ah ha! dat's somefin' else. Somefin' goin' on in dere. Well, if I don't ax myself to dat party, my name's not old Aunt Katie Mortimer, dat's all!" said the old woman in glee, as she cautiously stole from the room and approached the door leading into Mrs. Dugald's apartments.

When at the door, which was ajar, she peeped in. The suite was arranged upon the same plan as Lady Vincent's own. As Katie peered in, she saw through the vista of three rooms into the dressing room, which was the last of the suite. Before the dressing-room fire she saw the viscount and Mrs. Dugald standing, their faces towards the fire; their backs towards Katie.

She cautiously opened the door and stepped in, closing it silently behind her. Then she crept through the intervening rooms and reached the door of the dressing room, which was draped around with heavy velvet hangings, and she concealed herself in their folds, where she could see and hear everything that passed.

"How long is this to go on? Do you know that the presence of my rival maddens me every hour of the day? Are you not afraid—you would be, if you knew me!—that I should do some desperate deed? I tell you that I am afraid of myself! I cannot always restrain my impulses, Malcolm. There are moments when I doubt whether you are not playing me false. And at such times I am in danger of doing some desperate deed that will make England ring with the hearing of it," said Mrs. Dugald, with passionate earnestness.

"Faustina, you know that I adore you. Be patient a few days longer—a very few days. The time is nearly ripe. I have at last found the instrument of which I have been so much in need. This man, Frisbie. He is completely in my power, and will be a ready tool. I will tell you the whole scheme. But stop! first I must secure this interview from interruption. Not a word of this communication must be overheard by any chance listener," said Lord Vincent.

And to poor old Katie's consternation he passed swiftly to the outer door of the suite of rooms, locked it and put the key in his pocket and returned to the dressing room, the door of which remained open.

"Dere! if I aint cotch like an old rat in a trap, you may take my hat! Don't care! I gwine hear all dey got to say. An' if dey find me dey can't hang me for it, dat's one good thing! And maybe dey won't find me, if I keep still till my lordship—perty lordship he is—unlocks de door and goes out, and den I slip out myself, just as I slipped in, and nobody none de wiser. Only if I don't sneeze. I feel dreadful like sneezing. Nobody ever had such an unlucky nose as I have got. Laws, laws, if I was to sneeze!" thought old Katie to herself as she lurked behind the draperies.

But soon every sense was absorbed in listening to the villainous plot that Lord Vincent was unfolding to his companion. It was the very same plot that he had communicated to his valet, the atrocity of which had shocked even that cut-throat. It did not shock Faustina, however. She listened with avidity. She co-operated with zeal. She suggested such modifications and improvements for securing the success of the conspiracy, and the safety of the conspirators, as only her woman's tact, inspired by the demon, could invent.

"Oh, the she-sarpint! the deadly, wenemous, pisonous sarpint!" shuddered Katie, in her hiding-place. "I've heern enough this night to hang the shamwally, and send all the rest on 'em to Bottommy Bay. And I'll do it, too, if ever I live to get out'n this room alive."

But at that instant the catastrophe that Katie had dreaded occurred. Katie sneezed—once, twice, thrice: "Hick-ket-choo! Hick-ket-choo! Hick-ket-choo!"

Had a bombshell exploded in that room it could not have excited a greater commotion. Lord Vincent sprang up, and in an instant had the eavesdropper by the throat.

"Now, you old devil, what have you got to say for yourself?" demanded the viscount, in a voice of repressed fury, as he shook Katie.

"I say—Cuss my nose! There never was sich a misfortunate nose on anybody's face—a-squoking out dat way in onseasonable hours!" cried Katie.

"How dare you be caught eavesdropping in these rooms, you wretch?" demanded the viscount, giving her another shake.

"And why wouldn't I, you grand vilyun? And you her a-plotting of your deblish plots agin my own dear babyship—I mean my ladyship, as is like my own dear baby! And 'wretch' yourself! And how dare you lay your hands on me? on me, as has heern enough this precious night to send you down to the bottom of Bottommy Bay, to work in de mud, wid a chain and a weight to your leg, you rascal! and a man with a whip over your head, you vilyun! 'Stead o' standin' dere sassin' at me, you ought to go down on your bare knees, and beg and pray me to spare you! Dough you needn't, neither, 'cause I wouldn't do it! no! not if you was to wallow under my feet, I wouldn't. 'Cause soon as eber I gets out'n dis room I gwine right straight to de queen and tell her all about it; and ax her if she's de mist'ess of England and lets sich goings on as dese go on in her kingdom. And if I can't get speech of the queen, I going to tell de fust magistet I can find—dere! And you, too, you whited salt-peter! you ought dis minute to be pickin' of oakum in a crash gown and cropped hair! And you shall be, too, afore many days, ef eber I lives to get out'n dis house alive!" shrieked Katie, shaking her fist first at one culprit and then at the other, and glaring inextinguishable hatred and defiance upon both. For righteous wrath had rendered her perfectly insensible to fear.

Meanwhile the viscount held her in a death-grip; his face was ghastly pale; his teeth tightly clenched; his eyes starting.

"Faustina, she is as ignorant as dirt, but her threats are not vain. If she leaves this room alive all is lost!" he exclaimed in breathless excitement.

"She must not leave it alive!" said the fell woman.

Katie heard the fatal words, and opened her mouth to scream for help. But the fingers of the viscount tightened around her throat and strangled the scream in its utterance. And he bore her down to the floor and placed his knee on her chest. And there was murder in the glare with which he watched her death-throes.

"Faustina!" he whispered hoarsely, "help me! have you nothing to shorten this?"

She flew to a cabinet, from which she took a small vial, filled with a colorless liquid, and brought it to him.

He disengaged one hand to take it, and then stooped over his victim. And in a few moments Katie ceased to struggle.

Then he arose from his knees with a low laugh, whispering.

"It is all right."

CHAPTER XX

NEWS FOR ISHMAEL.

December's sky is chill and drear,

December's leaf is dun and sere;

No longer Autumn's glowing red

Upon our forest hills is shed;

No more beneath the evening beam

The wave reflects their crimson gleam;

The shepherd shifts his mantle's fold

And wraps him closely from the cold:

His dogs no merry circles wheel,

But shivering follow at his heel;

And cowering glances often cast

As deeper moans the gathering blast.

—Scott.

"Ah what is good must be worked for," wrote the wisest of our sages. Ishmael felt the truth of this, and worked hard.

His first success at the bar had been so brilliant as to dazzle and astonish all his contemporaries; and upon the fame of that success he prospered exceedingly.

But Ishmael well knew that if it needed hard work to win fame, it needed much harder work to keep it.

He felt that if he became idle or careless now, his brilliant success would prove to be but a meteor's flash, instead of the clear and steady planet light he intended it to become.

He read and thought with great diligence and perseverance; and so he often found a way through labyrinths of difficulty that would have baffled any less firmly persistent thinker and worker.

And thus his success, splendid from the first, was gaining permanency every day.

His reputation was established on a firm foundation, and be was building it up strongly as well as highly.

Strangers who had heard of the celebrated young barrister, and had occasion to seek his professional services, always expected to find a man of thirty or thirty-five years old, and were astonished to see one of scarcely twenty-two.

Ishmael was very much admired and courted by the best circles of the Capital; but, though eminently social and affectionate in his nature, he entered only moderately into society. Devotion to company and attention to business were incompatible, he knew.

If there ever happened to be an alternative of a tempting evening party, where he might be sure of meeting many congenial friends on the one hand, and an impending case that required careful preparation on the other, you may rely on it that Ishmael sacrificed pleasure and gave himself up to duty. And this he did, not occasionally, but always; in this way he earned and retained his high position.

And, ambitious young reader, this is the only way.

Thus in useful and successful work Ishmael employed the autumn that Claudia in her distant home was wasting in idleness and repinings.

On the first Monday in December Congress met, as usual. And about the middle of the month the Supreme Court sat.

Therefore Ishmael was not very much surprised when one morning, just after he had brought a very difficult suit to a triumphant termination, he saw his friend Judge Merlin enter his private office.

Ishmael started up joyously to greet his visitor; but stopped short on, seeing how pale, haggard, and feeble the old man looked. And his impulsive exclamation of: "Oh, judge, I am so glad to see you," changed at once to the commiserating words—"How sorry I feel to see you so indisposed! Have you been ill long?" he inquired, as he placed his easiest chair for the supposed invalid.

"Yes, I have been ill, Ishmael, very ill; but not long, and not in body—in mind, Ishmael, in mind!" and the old man sank into the chair and, resting his elbow on the office table, bowed his stricken head upon his hand.

Ishmael drew near and bent over him in respectful sympathy, waiting for his confidence. But as the judge continued overwhelmed and silent, the young man took the initiative, and in A soft and reverential tone said:

"I do hope, sir, that you have met with no serious trouble."

A deep groan was the only answer.

"Can I serve you in any way, sir? You know that I am devoted to your interests."

"Yes, Ishmael, yes. I know that you are the most faithful of friends, as well as the most accomplished of counselors. It is in both characters, my dear boy, that you are wanted to-day."

"Instruct me, sir. Command me. I am entirely at your disposal."

"Even to the extent of going to Europe with me?"

Ishmael hesitated; but only because he was utterly unprepared for the proposal; and then he answered:

"Yes, sir; if it should appear to be really necessary to your interests."

"Oh, Ishmael! I am an old and world-worn man, and I have had much experience; but, indeed, I know not how to break to you the news I have to bring!" groaned the judge.

"If there is any man in the world you can confide in it is surely myself, your friend and your attorney."

"I feel sure of that, Ishmael, quite sure of that. Well, I do not see any better way of putting you in possession of the facts than by letting you read these letters. When you have read them all, you will know as much as I do," said the judge, as he drew from his pocket a parcel of papers and looked over them. "There, read that first," he continued, placing one in Ishmael's hand.

Ishmael opened the letter and read as follows:

"Castle Cragg, near Banff, Buchan, Scotland. "My Dearest Father: We are all in good health; therefore do not be alarmed, even though I earnestly implore you to drop everything you may have in hand and come over to me immediately, by the very first steamer that sails after your receipt of this letter. Father, you will comply with my entreaty when I inform you that I have been deceived and betrayed by him who swore to cherish and protect me. My life and honor are both imperiled. I will undertake to guard both for a month, until you come. But come at once to your wronged but "Loving child, "Claudia."

"Good Heaven, sir, what does this mean?" exclaimed Ishmael, looking up, after he had read the letter.

"I do not clearly know myself. It is what I wish you to help me to find out."

"But—when was this letter received?"

"On Monday last."

"On Monday last," repeated Ishmael, glancing at the envelope; "that was the 5th of December; and it is postmarked 'Banff, October 15th.' Is it possible that this important letter has been seven weeks on its way?"

"Yes, it is quite possible. If yea look at the envelope closely you will see that it is stamped 'Missent,' and remailed from San Francisco, California, to which place it was sent by mistake. You perceive it has traveled half around the world before coming here."

"How very unfortunate! and a letter so urgent as this! Sir, can you give me any idea of the danger that threatens Lady Vincent?" inquired Ishmael, raising his eyes for a moment from his study of the letter.

"Read this second letter; I received it, and a third one, by the very same mail that brought the long-delayed first one," replied the judge.

Ishmael took this letter also, and read:

"McGruder's Hotel, Edinboro', Scotland, "November 25, 184—. "My Dearest Father: I wrote to you about six weeks ago, informing you that I was in sorrow and in danger, and imploring you to come and comfort and protect me. And since that time I have been waiting with the most acute anxiety to hear from you by letter or in person. Expecting this with confidence, I did not think it necessary to write again. But, as so long a time has elapsed, I begin to fear that you have not received my letter, and so I write again. Oh, my father! if you should not be already on your way to my relief—if you should be still lingering at home on the receipt of this letter, fly to me at once! My situation is desperate; my danger imminent; my necessity extreme. Oh, sir! an infamous plot has been hatched against me; I have been driven with ignominy from my husband's house; my name has gone over the length and breadth of England, a by-word of reproach! I am alone and penniless in this hotel; in which I know not how short the time may be that they will permit me to stay. Come! Come quickly! Come and save, if it be possible, your wretched child, "Claudia."

"Heaven of heavens! how can this be?" cried Ishmael, looking up from these fearful lines into the woe-worn face of the judge.

"Oh, I know but little more than yourself. Head this third letter."

Ishmael eagerly took and opened it and read:

"Cameron Court, near Edinboro', "November 27, 184—, "Judge Merlin—Sir: Your unhappy daughter is under my roof. As soon as I heard what had happened at Castle Cragg, and learned that she was alone and unprotected at McGruder's, I lost no time in going to her and offering my sympathy and protection. I induced her to come with me to my home. I have heard her story from her own lips. And I believe her to be the victim of a cunningly contrived conspiracy. Lord Vincent has filed a petition for divorce, upon the ground of alleged infidelity. Therefore I join my urgent request to hers that, if this finds you still in America, you will instantly on its receipt leave for England. I write in great haste to send my letter by the Irish Express so as it may intercept the steamer at Queenstown and reach you by the same mail that carries hers of the 25th; and so mitigate your anxiety by assuring you of her personal safety, with sympathizing friends; although her honor is endangered by a diabolical conspiracy, from which it will require the utmost legal skill to deliver her. "With great respect, sir, I remain, "Berenice, Countess of Hurstmonceux."

"You will go by the first steamer, sir," said Ishmael.

"Certainly. This is Saturday morning; one sails at noon from New York to-day; but I could not catch that."

"Of course not; but the 'Oceana' sails from Boston on Wednesday."

"Yes; I shall go by her. But, Ishmael, can you go with me?" inquired the judge, with visible anxiety.

"Certainly," promptly replied the young man, never hinting at the sacrifices he would have to make in order to accompany his friend on so long a journey.

"Thank you, thank you, my dear Ishmael! I knew you would. You will be of great assistance. Of course we must oppose this rascally viscount's petition, and do our best to unmask his villainy. But how to do it? I was never very quick-witted, Ishmael; and now my faculties are blunted with age. But I have much to hope from your aid in this case. I know that you cannot appear publicly for Lady Vincent; but at the same time you may be of inestimable value as a private counselor. Your genius, acumen, and wonderful insight will enable us to expose this conspiracy, defeat the viscount, and save Claudia, if anything on earth can do so. Thank you, thank you, good and noble young friend!" said the judge, taking and cordially pressing his hand.

"Judge, you know that you are most heartily welcome to all my services. There is no one in the world that I would work for with more pleasure than for you," replied the young man, returning the pressure.

"I know it, my boy. Heaven bless you!"

"And now let us arrange for our journey. As the steamer leaves Boston on next Wednesday morning, we should leave here on Tuesday morning at latest."

"Yes, I suppose so."

"Therefore, you see, we have but three days before us; and, as the Sabbath intervenes, we have really but two for preparation—to-day and Monday."

"That will be sufficient."

"Yes, sir. But, judge, I must run down into St. Mary's, and take leave of my betrothed, before starting on so long a journey."

"Oh, Ishmael, you will not have time. Suppose you should be too late to meet the steamer?"

"I will not be too late, Judge Merlin. I will hire a horse and start this morning. I can get fresh horses at several places on the road, and reach the Beacon before twelve o'clock at night. I can spend the Sabbath there, and go to church with the family. And on Monday morning I will make an early start, so as to be here on Monday night."

"Oh, Ishmael, it will be a great risk."

"Not at all; I shall be sure to come up in time. And, besides, you know I must see Bee before I go," said Ishmael, with that confiding smile that no one could resist.

"Well, well, I suppose it must be so; so go on; but only be punctual."

"I surely will."

"And oh, by the way, Ishmael, tell Mr. Middleton all about it; that is, all we know, which is very little, since neither Lady Vincent nor Lady Hurstmonceux has given us any details."

"Then Mr. Middleton knows nothing of this?"

"Not a syllable. I left the neighborhood without breathing a hint of it to any human being. I did not even think of doing so. Oh, Ishmael, I was in a state of distraction when I left home! Think of it! I had been tormented with anxiety for weeks before the receipt of these letters. For, listen: you know that Claudia sailed on the first of October. Well; I calculated it would take about two weeks for her to reach Liverpool, and about two more weeks for a letter to return. So I made myself contented until the first of November, when, as I expected, I received my first letter from her. It was a very long letter, dated at various times from the sea, and written during the voyage, and mailed at Queenstown. Three days later I received another and shorter letter, merely advising me of her safe arrival in England, and mailed from Liverpool. Still three days later a letter dated Aberdeen, and informing me of her journey to Scotland. A whole week later—for it appeared this last letter was much delayed on its route—I got a short letter from her dated Banff, and telling me that she had arrived that far on her journey, and expected to be at Castle Cragg the same evening. Now these letters were all dated within one or two days of each other, though there was a longer time between the reception of each; a fact, I suppose, to be accounted for by the irregularity of the ocean mails. The last letter, dated October 14th, did not reach me until November 12th. And after that I received no more letters, until I got these three all by one mail. You may judge how intense my anxiety was until these letters came; and how distracted my mind, as soon as I had read them."

"Oh, yes, sir, yes!"

"Therefore, you see, I never thought of what was due to Middleton, or anybody else. So just tell him all about it, but in strict confidence; for Claudia must not become the subject of gossip here, poor child!"

"No, sir; certainly she must not. I will bind Mr. Middleton to secrecy before I tell him anything about it."

"Yes, and—stop a moment! You had better just show him these letters. They will speak for themselves and save you the trouble. Tell him that we know no more than these letters reveal."

"I will do so, Judge Merlin."

"And now, Ishmael, I must return to my hotel, where I expect to meet my old friend, General Tourneysee. When do you start for St. Mary's?"

"Within an hour from this."

"Well, then, call at the hotel on your way and take leave of me."

"I will do so."

"Good-by, for the present," said the judge, shaking hands with his young friend.

As soon as Judge Merlin had left the office Ishmael sank down into his chair and yielded up his mind to intense thought.

It was true, then, the terrible presentiment of evil that had haunted his imagination in regard to Claudia was now realized! The dark storm cloud that his prophetic eye had seen lowering over her had now burst in ruin on her head! How strange! how unexplainable by human reason were these mysteries of the spirit! But Ishmael lost no time in fruitless speculations. He arose quickly and rang the bell.

The professor answered it.

"Morris, I wish you to go around to Bellingby's stables and ask them to send me a good, fresh horse, immediately, to go into the country. I shall want him for three days. Tell them to send me the brown horse, Jack, if he is not in use; but if he is, tell them to send the strongest and fastest horse they have."

"Yes, sir," answered the professor, hurrying off.

Ishmael went up to his chamber and packed his valise, and then returned to the office and summoned his first clerk, told him that he was going into the country immediately, for three days, and that after his return he should start for Europe, to be gone for a few weeks, and gave him instructions regarding the present conduct of the office business, and promised directions respecting the future administration of professional affairs when he should return from the country before starting for Europe.

When he had got through his conference with his clerk, and the latter had left the private office, the professor, who had come back and was waiting his turn, entered.

"Well, Morris?"

"Well, sir, the brown horse will be here as soon as he is fed, and watered, and saddled, and bridled. He is in good condition, sir, and quite fresh, as he hasn't been in use for two days, sir."

"All right, professor, sit down; I have something to tell you."

"Yes, sir? Indeed, sir!" said Jim Morris, taking his seat and feeling sure he should presently hear Mr. Worth was going down into the country for the purpose of marrying Miss Middleton and bringing her home. But the news that he really heard astonished him more than this would have done.

"I shall start for Europe on Wednesday, Morris."

"You don't say so, sir!" exclaimed the old man.

"Yes; sudden business. But I promised you, professor, that if ever I should go to Europe you should go with me, if you should please to do so. Now I will give you your choice. You shall attend me to Europe, or stay here and take care of my rooms while I am gone."

The professor's eyes fairly danced at the idea of crossing the mighty Atlantic and seeing glorious old Europe; but still he had sense of propriety and self-denial enough to say:

"I am willing to do that which will be of the most use to yourself, sir."

"Morris, you would be of great use to me in either position. If you should stay here, I should feel sure that my rooms were safe in the care of a faithful keeper."

"Then, sir, I prefer to stay."

"Yes, but stop a moment. If you should go with me, I should enjoy the trip much more. I should enjoy it myself and enjoy your enjoyment of it also. And, besides, it would be so pleasant to feel that I had an attached friend always with me."

"Then, Mr. Worth, as there is about as much to be said on one side as there is on the other, I'll do whichever you prefer."

"I greatly prefer that you should go with me, professor," said Ishmael, who read the old man's eager desire to travel.

"Then I'll go, sir; and with the greatest of pleasure."

"Can you be ready to leave for Boston on Tuesday morning, to catch the steamer that sails on Wednesday?"

"Law, yes, sir! what's to hinder? Why, I would be ready in ten minutes, sooner than miss going to Europe. What's to do but just pitch my clothes into a trunk and lock it?"

"Well, Morris, I will give you time enough to pack your clothes carefully, and mine also. There is the horse!" exclaimed Ishmael, rising and locking his desk.

"Sure enough, there he is, and looking as gay as a lark, this bright morning. You will have a pleasant ride, sir," said the professor, looking from the window.

"Yes; fetch my overcoat from the passage, Morris."

"Yes, sir; here it is. But won't you take just a bit of luncheon before you go? I am sure the ladies would get it ready for you quick, and glad to do it."

"No, thank you, Morris. You know I ate breakfast only two hours ago, and a very hearty one, too, as I always do. So I shall not require anything until I get to Horsehead," said Ishmael, buttoning up his greatcoat. Then he drew on his gloves and shook hands with the professor.

"Good-by, Morris! God bless you! Think of going to Europe."

"Oh, sir, you may be sure I shan't think of anything else all day, nor dream of anything else all night. To think of my seeing the Tower of London! Well, sir, good-by! And the Lord bless you and give you a pleasant journey," said the professor as he handed his master's hat.

CHAPTER XXI

ISHMAEL'S VISIT TO BEE.

Thank Heaven my first love failed,
As every first love should.

—Palmore.

Ishmael mounted and rode off, calling only at the hotel to say good-by to the judge and renew his promise of a punctual return.

Then he galloped blithely away; crossed the beautiful Anacostia, by the Navy Yard bridge; and gayly took the road to the old St. Mary's.

Gayly? Yes, gayly, notwithstanding all.

To be sure he was sorry for Claudia; and he proved it by consenting, at a great sacrifice of his personal interests, to cross the ocean and go to her assistance. But he had faith in the doctrine that—"Ever the right comes uppermost"; and he believed that she would be delivered from her troubles. And his compassion for Claudia did not prevent him from rejoicing exceedingly in the speedy prospect of meeting Bee. Besides he no longer loved Claudia, except with that Christian kindliness which he cherished for every member of the human family.

You may be sure that the sickly, sentimental, sinful folly of loving another man's wife, even if she had been, before her marriage, his own early passion, was very far below Ishmael's healthy, rational, and honorable nature. No nerve in his bosom vibrated to the sound of Claudia's name. The passion of his heart was perfectly cured; its wounds were quite healed; even its scars were effaced. He could have smiled at the memory of that ill-starred passion now.

He was heart-whole, and his whole heart—his sound, large loving heart—was unreservedly given to Bee.

And therefore, notwithstanding his compassion for the misfortunes of Claudia, he rode gayly on to his anticipated meeting with his betrothed.

It was a fine, frosty, bracing, winter morning; the roads were good; and the horse was fresh; and he enjoyed his ride exceedingly, rejoicing in his youth, health, and happy, well-placed love.

He galloped all the way to Horsehead, where he arrived at noon, took an early dinner, procured a fresh horse and continued his journey.

He rode all the short, bright winter afternoon, and at dusk reached his second stopping-place, where he took an early tea, changed his horse, and started afresh.

Four more hours of riding through the leafless forest, and under the starlit sky, brought him in sight of the water; and a few minutes brought him to the door of the Beacon.

Here he sprung from his saddle; secured his horse to a post; and rushed up the front steps to the hall door and rang. An old servant opened it.

"Oh, Mr. Ishmael, sir! what a surprise! I am so glad to see you, sir."

"Thank you, Ben. How are the family?"

"All well, sir. Walk in, sir. Won't they be delighted to see you!" said the old man, opening a side door leading into the lighted drawing room, and announcing:

"Mr. Worth!"

There was a general jumping up of the party around the fireside, and a hasty rushing towards the visitor.

Mr. Middleton was foremost, holding out both his hands, and exclaiming:

"Why, how do you do? Is this you? This is a surprise! Where did you drop from?"

"Washington, sir," replied Ishmael, returning the handshaking, and then passing on to meet the ready welcome of Mrs. Middleton and the young folks.

"How do you do, Mrs. Middleton? Dearest Bee—it is such joy to meet you!" he said, as he returned the lady's greeting, and pressed the maiden's hand to his lips.

Bee was fairer, fresher, and lovelier than ever, as she stood there, blushing, but delighted to see him.

"How do you do, Worth?" spoke another deep voice.

Ishmael looked up suddenly, and saw his father standing before him. The latter had approached from a distant part of the room.

"Mr. Brudenell—you here? This is indeed a pleasant surprise!" said the young man joyfully.

"Mutually so, I assure you, Ishmael."

"When did you arrive, sir?"

"Only this afternoon. I came up to take the Shelton boat, that goes to Washington on Monday. My dislike to Sunday traveling decided me to come up to-day, and quarter myself on our friend Middleton for the Sabbath, so as to be in readiness to catch the 'Errand Boy' on Monday."

"You were coming to see me, I hope, sir?"

"Not purposely, my dear fellow. I had other business, less pleasant but more pressing. I should have called on you, however, though I could not have stayed long; for I must go by the Monday evening train to Boston, in order to catch the 'Oceana,' that sails on Wednesday morning. I am off by her."

"Indeed, sir!" exclaimed Ishmael, in surprise and delight. "Why, I am going to Europe by the 'Oceana'!"

"You!" responded the elder man, in equal surprise and pleasure. "Why, what on earth should take you to Europe?"

"I go on strictly confidential business with Judge Merlin."

"Merlin going to England, too? Oh, I see!"

The last three words were uttered in a low tone, and with a total change of manner, that struck Ishmael with the suspicion that Mr. Brudenell knew more of Lady Vincent's troubles than anyone on this side of the ocean, except her father and himself, was supposed to know.

"Going to Europe, Ishmael? you and the judge? Well, Merlin did start off at a tangent yesterday from Tanglewood. I suppose he is pining after his child, and has taken a sudden freak to rush over and see her. And as you are the staff of his age, of course, he would not think of undertaking so long a journey without the support of your company. Am I right?" inquired Mr. Middleton jollily.

"Judge Merlin is going to see Lady Vincent, and has invited me to accompany him, and I have accepted the invitation," answered the young man.

"Exactly, precisely, just so. But I wonder how the son of Powhatan, Merlin of Tanglewood, who could scarcely breathe out of the boundless wilderness, will like to sojourn in that cleared-up, trim, tidy, well-packed little island!" laughed Mr. Middleton; while Mr. Brudenell looked down, and slowly nodded his head.

Meanwhile Bee's careful, affectionate eyes noticed that Ishmael was very tired, and she said something in a low voice to her father.

"To be sure—to be sure, my dear. I ought to have thought of that myself. Ishmael, my boy, you have ridden hard to-day; you look fagged. Go right up into your own room now—you know where to find it; it is the same one you occupied when you were here last, kept sacred to you; and

I will send up Ben to rub you down and curry you well; and by the time he has done that Bee will have the provender ready," said Mr. Middleton, whose delight at seeing his welcome visitor hurried him into all sorts of absurdities.

Ishmael smiled, bowed, and withdrew.

Half an hour afterwards, when he returned to the drawing room, looking, as Mr. Middleton said, "well-groomed and much refreshed," Mrs. Middleton touched the bell; the doors leading into the dining room were thrown open; and the guests were invited to sit down to a delicious supper of fresh fish, oysters, crabs, and waterfowl, which had been spread there in honor of Mr. Brudenell's arrival; but which was equally appropriate to Ishmael's welcome presence.

After supper, when they returned to the drawing room, Ishmael found an opportunity of saying aside to his host that he wished to have some private conversation with him that night.

Accordingly, when the evening circle had broken up and each had withdrawn to his or her own apartment, and Ishmael found himself alone in his chamber, he heard a rap at his door, and on bidding the rapper come in, saw Mr. Middleton enter.

"I have come at your request, Ishmael," he said, taking the chair that the young man immediately placed for him.

"Thank you, sir; I wished to confide to you the cause of Judge Merlin's sudden journey to England," said Ishmael gravely.

"Why, to see his daughter!" exclaimed Mr. Middleton, raising his eyebrows.

"Yes, it is to see Lady Vincent. But Mr. Middleton, her ladyship is in great sorrow and greater danger," said the young man, speaking more gravely than before.

"Sorrow and danger! What are you talking of, Ishmael?" inquired Mr. Middleton, knitting his brows in perplexity.

"Lady Vincent is separated from her husband, who has filed a petition for divorce from her," said Ishmael solemnly.

The exclamation of amazement and indignation that burst from Mr. Middleton's lips was rather too profane to be recorded here.

"Yes, sir; it is so," sighed Ishmael.

"Who says this?" demanded Mr. Middleton, in a voice of suppressed fury.

"She herself says it, sir, in a letter to her father, who has commissioned me to impart the facts in confidence to yourself. Here are the letters he received and desired me to hand to you for perusal.

They are numbered one, two, three. Read them in that order, and they will put you in possession of the whole affair, as far as is known to any of us over here."

Mr. Middleton grasped the letters, and one after another devoured their contents.

"This first letter is nearly two months old! Why has it not been acted upon before?" he demanded, in an angry manner, that proved he would have liked to quarrel with somebody.

"It was not received until two days since. It was miscarried and it went half around the world before it reached its proper destination," said Ishmael equably.

"But what does it all mean, then? What plot is this alluded to? And who is in it?"

"Mr. Middleton, we know no more than you now do. We know no more than the letters that you have just read tell us."

"But why, in the name of Heaven, then, could these letters not have been more explicit? Claudia was alone at McGruder's Hotel! Where were her servants? A plot was formed against her! Who formed it? Why could she not have satisfied us upon these subjects?" exclaimed Mr. Middleton vehemently.

"Sir, each letter seems to have been written under the spur of imminent necessity. Perhaps there was no time to enter fully upon the subject; perhaps also it was one that could not be discussed through an epistolary correspondence."

"Perhaps they were all raving mad!" exclaimed Mr. Middleton excitedly. "Now what are you all to do?"

"Judge Merlin and myself are going to England, as I told you. He will support his daughter in opposing Lord Vincent's application for a divorce. I will give them all the assistance in my power to render. Of course, as I am not a member of any English bar, I cannot appear as her public advocate; but I will serve her to the utmost of my ability as a private counselor. I will make myself master of the case and use my best efforts to discover and expose the conspiracy against her. And if I succeed, I will do my best to have the conspirators punished. For in England, fortunately, conspiracy against the life, property, or character of any person or persons is a felony, punishable by penal servitude. Fortunately, also, in the criminal courts of England the peer finds no more favor than the peasant. And if the Lord Viscount Vincent is prosecuted to conviction he will stand as good a chance of transportation to the penal colonies as the meanest confederate he has employed," said Ishmael.

"I wish he may be! I'd make a voyage to Sydney myself for the sake of seeing him working in a chain-gang. I hate the fellow, and always did."

"I never liked him," candidly admitted Ishmael; "but still it is not in the spirit of vengeance, but of stern justice, that I shall devote every faculty of my mind and body to the duty of exposing and convicting him."

"I declare to you, Ishmael, 'vengeance' and 'stern justice' look so much alike to me, that, as the darkies say, I cannot tell 't'other from which.'"

"There is a distinction, however," said Ishmael.

"But, under either name, I hope the villainous Viscount Vincent (I didn't mean to make that alliteration, however) will get his full measure of retribution! You go by the 'Oceana' on Wednesday, you say?"

"Yes, sir."

"Well, success to you! Poor Claudia! I hope she will be vindicated. I will talk farther of this with you to-morrow, after church. Now I see that you are very weary and need repose. Good-night! God bless you, my dear boy."

Very early the next morning Ishmael arose, and after making his toilet and offering up his devotions, he went out to refresh himself by a stroll on the beach that fine winter morning.

Very exhilarating it was to him, coming from the crowded city, to saunter up and down the sands, letting his eyes wander over the broad, sun-lit waters and the winding, wooded shores.

He watched the latest, hardier fish, not yet driven to warmer climes, leap up through the sparkling ripples and disappear again.

He watched the waterfowl start up in flocks from some near brake, and, spreading their broad wings, sail far away over the bright emerald-green waves.

Along the shore he noted the sly, brown squirrel peep at him from her hole, and then hop quickly out of sight; and the hardy little snow-bird light at his feet and then dart swiftly away.

Very dear to Ishmael were all these little darlings of nature. They had been the playfellows of his boyhood; and something of the boy survived in Ishmael yet, as it does in every pure young man. It is only sin that destroys youthfulness.

Sometimes he watched a distant sail disappear below the horizon, and followed her in imagination over the seas, and thought with youthful delight how soon he too would be on the deep blue waves of mid- ocean.

A step and a voice roused him from his reverie.

"Good-morning, Ishmael! I saw you walking here from my window and came out to join you."

"Oh, good-morning, Mr. Brudenell!" exclaimed the young man, turning with a glad smile to meet the elder one.

Mr. Brudenell took the arm of Ishmael, and, leaning rather heavily on it, joined him in his walk.

"I know why Judge Merlin and yourself are going to England," he said.

"I thought you did. But I could not, and cannot now, conceive how you should have found out; since we ourselves knew nothing about the unfortunate affair until a day or two since; and it is one of a strictly private and domestic nature," replied Ishmael.

"Strictly private and domestic? Why, Ishmael, it may have been so in the beginning; but now it is public and patent. All England is ringing with the affair. It is the last sensation story that the reporters have got hold of. It was from the London papers received by the last mail that I learned the news," said Mr. Brudenell, taking from his pocket the "Times," "Post," and "Chronicle."

Ishmael hastily glanced over the accounts of the affair as contained in each of these. But though the articles were long and wordy they afforded him no new information.

They told him what he already knew; that the Viscount Vincent had filed a petition for divorce from his viscountess on the ground of infidelity; that the lady was the daughter of an American chief-justice; that she was a beauty and an heiress; that Lord Vincent had formed her acquaintance at the President's house during his official visit to Washington; that he had married her during the past summer; and after an extended bridal tour had brought her in October to Castle Cragg, when the suspicions that led to subsequent discovery and ultimate separation were first aroused, etc., etc., etc.

"All that is very unsatisfactory. I wish we knew the suspicious circumstances," said Mr. Brudenell.

"I believe there were no suspicious circumstances. I believe the whole affair to be a conspiracy against Lady Vincent," said Ishmael.

"But what motive could the viscount have for conspiracy against her?"

"The motive of getting rid of her, while he retains her fortune, which most unluckily was not settled upon herself."

While Mr. Brudenell stood gazing with consternation upon the speaker, there came flying from the house a negro boy, who said that he was sent to tell them that the breakfast was ready.

They returned to the house and joined the family at the cheerful breakfast table. It was a large party that met in the parlor afterwards to go to church.

And a gig in addition to the capacious family carriage was in attendance.

"Ishmael," said Mr. Middleton, in the kindly thoughtfulness of his nature, "you will drive Bee in the gig. The rest of us will go in the carriage."

"Thank you very much, Mr. Middleton," answered the young man, as he smilingly led his betrothed to the gig, placed her in it and seated himself beside her.

"Go on—go on ahead! We shall not ride over you in our lumbering old coach!" said Mr. Middleton.

Ishmael nodded, took the reins, and started. The road lay along the high banks of the river above the sands.

"How delightful it is to spend this day with you, dear Bee!" he said, as they bowled along.

"Oh, yes! and it is delightful to us all to have you here, Ishmael!" she said; and then, with a slight depression in her tone, she inquired:

"Will you be gone to Europe long?"

"No, dearest Bee. I shall dispatch the business that takes me there as quickly as I can and hasten back," he replied; but he forbore to hint the nature of this business; it was a subject with which he did not wish to wound the delicate ear of Bee Middleton.

"I hope you will enjoy your voyage," she said, smiling on him.

"I wish you were going with me, dearest Bee. I had looked forward to the pleasure of our seeing Europe together when we should go there for the first time. And the continent we will see together; for I shall go no farther than England. I shall reserve France, Italy, Germany, and Russia for our tour next autumn, dear Bee."

She smiled on him with sympathetic delight. But as the road here, quite on the edge of the banks, required the most careful driving, the lovers' conversation ceased for a while.

And presently they were at the Shelton church. The congregation were in luck that day. A celebrated preacher, who happened to be visiting the neighborhood, occupied the pulpit. He preached from the text, "Come up higher." And his discourse was a stirring call upon his hearers to strive after perfection. All were pleased, instructed, and inspired.

When the services were concluded, our party returned home in the same order in which they had come. And as there was no afternoon service, they spent the remainder of the day in the enjoyment of each other's company and conversation.

Bee and Ishmael were mercifully left to themselves, to make the most of the few hours before their separation. They were not morbid sentimentalists—those two young people; they were not fearful, or doubtful, or exacting of each other. If you had chanced to overhear their conversation, you would have heard none of those entreaties, warnings, and protestations that often make up the conversation of lovers about to part for a time, and a little uncertain of each other's fidelity. They had faith, hope, and love for, and in, each other and their Creator. Ishmael never imagined such a thing as that Bee could form another attachment, or go into a decline while he was gone. And Bee had no fears either that the sea would swallow her lover, or that a rival would carry him off.

So at the end of that evening they bade each other a cheerful good-night. And the next morning, when Ishmael had bid farewell to all the family, herself included, and was in the saddle, she sent him off with a brilliant smile and a joyous:

"Heaven bless you, Ishmael! I know you will enjoy the trip."

But when he had ridden away and disappeared down the path leading through the pine woods, Bee turned into the house, ran into her mother's chamber, threw herself into her mother's arms, and burst into a flood of tears.

It is the mother that always comes in for this sort of thing. Women spare men—sometimes; but never spare each other.

"My poor child! but it isn't far, you know!"

"Oh, mamma, such a long way! I never expected to be separated so far from Ishmael."

"My dear, steam annihilates distance. Only think, it is a voyage of but ten days."

"I know. Oh, it was very foolish in me to cry. Thank Heaven, Ishmael didn't see me," said Bee, wiping her eyes, and smiling through her wet eyelashes, like a sunbeam through the rain-sprinkled foliage.

Bee would scarcely have been flesh and blood if she had not indulged in this one hearty cry; but it was the last.

She left her mother's side and went about her household duties cheerfully, and very soon she was as happy as if Ishmael had not come and gone; happier, for she followed him in imagination over the ocean and sympathized in his delight.

CHAPTER XXIII

HANNAH'S HAPPY PROGNOSTICS.

The morn is tip again, the dewy morn,

With breath all incense and with cheek all bloom,

Laughing the night away with playful scorn,

Rejoicing as if earth contained no tomb

And glowing into day.

—Byron.

Ishmael had also keenly felt the parting with Beatrice. But accustomed to self-government, he did not permit his feelings to overcome him. And indeed his mind was too well balanced to be much disturbed by what he believed would be but a short separation from his betrothed.

He rode on gayly that pleasant winter morning, through the leafless woods, until he came to those cross-roads of which we have so often spoken.

Here he paused; for here it was necessary, finally, to decide a question that he had been debating with himself for the last two days.

And that was whether or not he should take the time to go to see Hannah and Reuben and bid them good-by, before proceeding on his long journey.

To go to Woodside he must take the road through Baymouth, which would carry him some miles out of the direct road to Washington, and consume several hours of that time of which every moment was now so precious. But to leave the country without saying farewell to the friends of his infancy was repugnant to every good feeling of his heart. He did not hesitate long. He turned his horse's head towards Baymouth and put him into a gallop. The horse was fresh, and Ishmael thought he would ride fast until he got to Woodside and then let the horse rest while he talked to Hannah.

He rode through Baymouth without drawing rein; only giving a rapid glance of recognition as he passed the broad show-window of Hamlin's bookstore, which used to be the wonder and delight of his destitute boyhood.

It was still early in the morning when he reached Woodside and rode up to the cottage gate. How bright and cheerful the cottage looked that splendid winter morning. The evergreen trees around it and the clusters of crimson rose-berries on the climbing rosevines over its porch, making quite a winter verdure and bloom against its white walls.

Ishmael dismounted, tied his horse, and entered the little gate. Hannah was standing on the step of the porch, holding a tin pan of chicken food in her hands, and feeding two pet bantams that she kept separate from the shanghais, which beat them cruelly whenever they got a chance.

On seeing Ishmael she dropped her pan of victuals and made a dash at him, exclaiming:

"Why, Ishmael! Good fathers alive! is this you? And where did you drop from?"

"From my saddle at your gate, last, Aunt Hannah," said Ishmael, smiling, as he folded her in his embrace.

"But I'm so glad to see you, Ishmael! And so surprised! Come in, my dear, dear boy. Shoo! you greedy, troublesome creeturs. You're never satisfied! I wish the shanghais would swallow you!" cried Hannah, speaking first to Ishmael as she cast her arms around his neck; and next to the bantams that had flown up to her shoulders.

"I am delighted to see you looking so hearty, ma'am. I declare you are growing quite stout," said Ishmael, affectionately surveying his relation.

"Women are apt to, at my age, Ishmael. But come in, my dear boy, come in!"

When they entered the cottage she drew Reuben's comfortable armchair up to the fire; and when Ishmael had seated himself she said:

"And now! first of all—have you had your breakfast?"

"Hours ago, thank you."

"Yes; a road-side tavern breakfast. I know what that is. Here, Sam! Sam! Lord, how I do miss Sally, to be sure!" complained Hannah, as she went to the back door and bawled after her factotum.

"Sit down and give yourself no trouble. I breakfasted famously at the Beacon."

"Oh!" exclaimed Hannah, with a little jealous twinge, "you've been there, have you? That accounts for everything. Well, I suppose it's natural. But when is that affair to come off, Ishmael?"

"If you mean my marriage with Miss Middleton, it will not take place until next autumn, Aunt Hannah, as I believe I have already told you."

"But haven't you been down there to coax the old man to shorten the time?"

"No, ma'am, but with a very different purpose."

"A different purpose? What was it? But, law, here I am keeping you talking in your greatcoat! Take it off at once, Ishmael, and be comfortable. And I will make Sam light a fire and carry some hot water in your room."

"No, ma'am, do not, please. Believe me it is unnecessary, and indeed quite useless. I have but half an hour to stay."

"But half an hour to stay with me! Do you mean to insult me, Ishmael Worth?" demanded Hannah wrathfully.

"Certainly not, dear Aunt Hannah," laughed Ishmael, "but I am going to leave the country, and so—"

"Going to—what?"

"I am going to leave the country quite suddenly, and that is the reason—"

"Ishmael Worth! have you robbed a bank or killed a man that you are going to run away from your native land?" exclaimed Hannah indignantly.

"Neither, ma'am," laughed Ishmael. "I go with Judge Merlin, on professional business—"

"Is that old man going to travel at his age?"

"Yes, because—"

"The more fool he!"

"He goes on very important business."

"Very important fiddle-stick's end! The great old baby is pining after his daughter. And he's just made up this excuse of business because he is ashamed to let people know the real reason—as well he may be! But why he should drag you along with him is more than I can guess."

"He thinks I can be of service to him, and I shall try."

"You'll try to ruin yourself, that's what you'll do!"

"Aunt Hannah, I have but a few minutes left. If you will permit me, I will just give my horse some water and go."

"Go! What, so suddenly? Lord, Lord, and Reuben away out in the field and the children with him! And you'll go away without taking a last farewell of them. I'll call Sam and send for them if you will wait a minute. Sam! Sam! Sam!" cried Hannah, going to the back door and screaming at the top of her voice.

But no Sam was forthcoming.

"Plague take that nigger! I do wish from the very bottom of my heart the deuce had him! Now, what shall I do?" she cried, returning to the room and dropping into her chair.

Fate answered the question by relieving her from her dilemma.

The front door opened and Reuben Gray entered, leading the two children and saying:

"It was too sharp for 'em out there, Hannah, my dear, especially as Molly, bless her, was a-sneezin' dreadful, as if she was a-catchin' a cold in her head; and so I fotch 'em in."

"Reuben, where's your eyes? Don't you see who is in the room? Here's Ishmael!" exclaimed Hannah irately.

"Ishmael! Why, so he is! Why, Lord bless you, boy. I'm so glad to see you!" exclaimed Reuben, with his honest face all in a glow of delight as he shook his guest's hands.

And at the same time the children let go their father's hand, and stood before the young man, waiting eagerly to be noticed.

"Yes, you better look at him! Look at him your fill now, You'll never see him again!" groaned Hannah.

"Never see who again? What are you talking about, Hannah, my dear?"

"Ishmael! He's come to bid a last good-by to us all. He's a-going to leave his native country! He's a-going to foreign parts!"

"Ishmael going to foreign parts!" exclaimed Reuben, gazing in surprise on his young guest.

"Yes, Uncle Reuben, I am going to England with Judge Merlin on business."

"Well, to be sure! that is a surprise! I knowed the judge was a- going to see his darter; but I had no idee that you was a-going 'long of him," said Reuben.

"When do you go? that is what I want to know," cried Hannah sharply.

"We sail in the 'Oceana' from Boston on Wednesday; and that is the reason, Aunt Hannah, why I am so hurried; you see I must reach Washington to-night so as to finish up my business there, and take the early train for the North on Tuesday morning."

"What? you going in one of them steamers? Oh, law!"

"What is the matter, ma'am?"

"I know the steamer'll burst its boiler, or catch afire, or sink, or something! I know it!"

"Lord, Hannah, don't dishearten people that-a-way! Why should the steamer do anything of the kind?" said Reuben, with a doubtful and troubled air.

"Because they are always and for everlasting a-doing of such things. Just think what happened to the 'Geyser'—burst her boiler and scalded everybody to death!"

"Law, Hannah! that was only one in a—"

"And the 'Vesuvius,'" fiercely continued Hannah; "the 'Vesuvius' caught on fire and burned down to the water's edge, and was so found—a floating charcoal, and every soul on board perished."

"Lord, Hannah, you're enough to make anybody's flesh creep. Surely that was only—"

"And then there was the 'Wave,' as struck St. George's bar and smashed all to pieces, and all on board were drowned!"

"Well, but, Hannah, you know—"

"And the 'Boreas,' that was lost in a gale. And the 'White Bear,' that was jammed to smash between two icebergs. And the 'Platina,' that sunk to the bottom with a clear sky and a smooth sea. Sunk to the bottom as if she had been so much lead. And the—"

"Goodness, gracious, me alive! And the Lord bless my soul, Hannah! You turn my very blood to water with your stories. Ishmael, don't you go!"

"Nonsense, Uncle Reuben! You know Aunt Hannah. She cannot help looking on the darkest side. When I was a boy, she was always prophesying I'd be hung, you know. Positively, sometimes she made me fear I might be," said Ishmael, smiling, and turning an affectionate glance upon his croaking relative.

"Yes, it's all very well for you to talk that way, Ishmael Worth. But I know one thing. I know I never heard of any sort of a ship going safe into port more than two or three times in the whole course of my life. And I have heard of many and many a shipwreck!" said Hannah, nodding her head, with the air of one who had just uttered a "knock-down" argument.

"Why, of course, Aunt Hannah. Because, in your remote country neighborhood you always hear of the wreck that happens once in a year or in two years; but you never hear of the thousands upon thousands of ships that are always making safe voyages."

"Oh, Ishmael, hush! It won't do. I'm not convinced. I don't expect ever to see you alive again."

"Law, Hannah, my dear, don't be so disbelieving. Really, now, you disencourage one."

"Hold your tongue, Reuben, you're a fool! I say it, and I stand to it, that steamer will either burst her boiler, or catch on fire, or sink, or something! And we shall never see our boy again."

Here little Molly, who had been attentively listening to the conversation, and, like the poor Desdemona, understood "a horror in the words," if not the words, opened her mouth and set up a howl that was immediately seconded by her brother.

It became necessary to soothe and quiet these youngsters; and Reuben lifted them both to his knees.

"Why, what's the matter with pappy's pets, then? What's all this about?" he inquired, tenderly stroking their heads.

"Cousin Ishmael is going away to be drownded! Boo-hoo-woo!" bawled Molly.

"And be burnt up, too! Ar-r-r-r-r-r!" roared Johnny.

"No, I am not going to be either one or the other," said the subject of all this interest cheerfully, as he took the children from Reuben and enthroned them on his own knees. "I am going abroad for a little while, and I will bring you ever so many pretty things when I come back."

They were reassured and stopped howling.

"How is your doll, Molly!"

"Her poor nose is broke."

"I thought so." Well, I will bring you a prettier and a larger doll, that can open and shut its mouth and cry."

"Oh-h!" exclaimed Molly, making great eyes in her surprise and delight.

"Now, what else shall I bring you, besides the new doll?"

"Another one."

"What, two dolls?"

"Yes."

"Well, what else?"

"Another one, too."

"Three dolls! goodness! but tell me what you would like beside the three dolls?"

"Some more dolls," persisted Molly, with her finger in her mouth.

"Whew! What would you like, Johnny?" inquired Ishmael, smiling on the little boy.

"I'd like a hatchet all of my own. I want one the worst kind of a way," said Johnny solemnly.

"Shall I bring him a little box of dwarf carpenter tools, Uncle Reuben?" inquired Ishmael doubtfully.

"Just as you please, Ishmael. He can't do much damage with them inside, because Hannah is always here to watch him; and he may hack and saw as much as he likes outside," said Reuben.

These points being settled, and the children not only soothed, but delighted, Ishmael put them off his knees and arose to depart.

He kissed the children, shook hands with Reuben and embraced Hannah, whose maternal tenderness caused her to restrain her emotions and forbear her croakings, lest she should frighten the children again.

When he got outside he found Sam standing by the horse, having just given him water, and being in the act of removing the empty bucket.

Ishmael shook hands with him also, got into the saddle, and, amid the fervent blessings of Reuben and Hannah, recommenced his journey.

CHAPTER XXIV

THE JOURNEY.

Love, hope, and joy, fair pleasure's smiling train;

Hate, fear, and grief, the family of pain;
These mixed with art and to due bounds confined,

Make and maintain the balance of the mind;

The lights and shades whose well-accorded strife

Give all the strength and color to our life

—Pope.

Ishmael's ride up to the city was, upon the whole, as much enjoyed as the ride down had been. It is true that, in the first instance, he had been going to see Bee; and now he was coming away from her; but he had passed one whole day and two pleasant evenings in her society, and he could live a long time on the memory of that visit.

He soon struck into his old direct path, and calling at the same places where he had changed horses on his journey down, he re-changed them on his way up.

At Horsehead, where he stopped to take tea, he recovered his favourite brown horse Jack, which was in excellent condition and carried him swiftly the rest of the way to Washington.

It was ten o'clock when he drew rein at the door of his office, dismounted, and rang.

The professor opened the door.

"Well, Morris, all right here?" was Ishmael's cheerful greeting.

"All right, sir, now that you have come. We have been a little anxious within the last hour or two, sir; especially the judge, who is here."

"Judge Merlin here?"

"Yes, sir. He came over to wait for you. And the two young gentlemen are also here, sir. They came back after tea. I heard them say to the judge that they thought it quite likely you would have some last things to say to them to-night, and so they would wait."

"Quite right. Morris. Now take my horse around to the stables and then return as fast as you can," said Ishmael, as he passed the professor and entered the office.

The judge and the two young clerks occupied it.

The former was walking up and down the floor impatiently. The latter were seated at their desks.

The judge turned quickly to greet his young friend.

"Oh, Ishmael, I am so relieved that you have come at last. I have been very anxious for the last few hours."

"Why so, sir?" inquired Ishmael, as he shook hands with the old man. "Did you not know that I would be punctual when I gave you my word to that effect?"

"Oh, yes; but there are such things as accidents, you know, and an accident would have been very awkward on the eve of a voyage. And you are late, you are late, you see!"

"Yes," said Ishmael, as he passed on to speak to his young clerks and thank them for their thoughtfulness in waiting.

Then, while divesting himself of his greatcoat, he explained to the judge the cause of his short delay—the detour he had made to bid good-by to his old friends, Hannah and Reuben. By the time he had done this, and seated himself, the professor returned from the livery stables; but he only reported the safe delivery of the horse and then passed through the office into the house.

In a few minutes he returned, saying:

"Mr. Worth, the ladies bid me say that they had kept supper waiting for you, and they hope you will do them the favor to come in and partake of it, as it is your last evening at home for some time. And they will also be very much gratified if your friends will come and sup with you on this occasion."

"Will you come, judge? And you, too, gentlemen?" inquired Ishmael, turning to his companions, who all three bowed assent.

"Return to the ladies and say that I thank them very much for their kindness, and that we will come with pleasure," he said to the professor.

And then with a smile and a bow, and a request to be excused for a few minutes, Ishmael passed into his bedroom to make some little change in his toilet for the evening.

When he rejoined his friends they went into the supper-room, where they found an elegant and luxurious feast laid; and the two fair old ladies, in their soft, plain, gray mousseline dresses and delicate lace caps, waiting to do the honors. These maiden ladies, with their refinement, intelligence, and benevolence, had completely won the affections of Ishmael, who loved them with a filial reverence.

There was no one else present in the room except themselves and a waiter.

"My dear Mr. Worth," said the elder lady, approaching and taking his hand, "we hear that you are going to Europe. How sudden, and how we shall miss you! But we hope that you will have a pleasant time."

"Yes, indeed!" joined in her sister, coming up to shake hands; "we do so! and I am sure in church, yesterday, when we came to that part of the litany in which we pray for 'all who travel by land or by water,' I thought of you and bore you up on that prayer. And I shall continue to do it until you get back safe."

"And so shall I," added the elder.

"Thank you! thank you!" said Ishmael, fervently shaking both their hands. "I am sure if your good wishes and pious prayers can effect it, I shall have a pleasant and prosperous voyage."

"That you will," they simultaneously and cordially responded.

"And now permit me to introduce my friends: Judge Merlin, Mr. Smith, Mr. Jones."

The gentlemen bowed and the ladies courtesied, and they presently sat down to supper. The conversation turned on the projected voyage.

"Judge, you will have an unexpected fellow-passenger—an old friend," said Ishmael.

"Ah! who is he?" sighed the judge, who never spoke now without a sigh.

"Mr. Brudenell is going over in the 'Oceana.'"

"Indeed! What takes him over?"

"I do not know; unless it is the desire of seeing his mother and sisters. He did not tell me, and I did not ask him. In fact, we had so short a time together there was no opportunity."

"Oh! you have seen him? Where did you meet him? And where is he now?"

"I met him at the Beacon, en route for Washington. He left there this morning, to embark on the 'Errand Boy,' which expects to reach the city to-morrow, in time for the express train North."

"Ah! coming by the 'Errand Boy,' is he? That's a risk, under all the circumstances, for the 'Errand Boy' is sometimes three or four hours behind time. And if he should miss the early train to-morrow morning he can never be in time to meet the Boston steamer, that is certain. Why couldn't he have dashed up on horseback with you?"

"I fancy, sir, he was not strong enough to bear such a forced ride as I was obliged to undertake."

As it was eleven o'clock when they arose from the supper-table the judge almost immediately took his leave, having previously arranged with Ishmael to join him at his hotel the next morning, to proceed from there to the station.

The two young clerks remained longer, to go over certain documents with their employer, and receive his final instructions. When they had departed, Ishmael went into his bedroom, where he found the professor waiting for him.

"At last!" said the latter, as his master entered.

"What, Morris, you up yet? Do you know what time it is?" demanded Ishmael, in surprise.

"Yes, sir; it is two o'clock in the morning."

"Then you know you ought to have been in bed, hours ago."

"Law, Mr. Worth—I couldn't have slept, sir, if I had gone to bed. I'm rising sixty years old, but I am just as much excited over this voyage to England as if I was a boy of sixteen. To think I shall see St. Paul's Cathedral, sir! Aint the thought of that enough to keep a man's eyes open all night? And to think it is all through you, young Ish—Mr. Worth. If it wasn't for you, I might be vegetating on, in that cabin, in old St. Mary's, with no more chance of improving my mind than the cattle that browse around it. God bless you, sir!"

"Ah, professor, if at your age I have such a fresh, young, evergreen heart, and such an aspiring, progressive spirit as yours, I shall think the Lord has blessed me. But now go to bed, old friend, and recruit your strength for the journey. Though 'the spirit is willing, the flesh is weak,' you know. The soul is immortal, but the body is perishable; so you must take care of it."

"Yes, sir, I will, just because you tell me. But I want to show you first what preparations I have made for the voyage, to see if you approve them. You see, sir, when you went off to St. Mary's so sudden, and left me to pack up your clothes, it just struck me that there must be many things wanted on a sea-voyage as is not wanted on land; but of course I didn't know exactly what they were. So after cogitating a while, I remembered that the judge had been to Europe several times, and would know all about it, and so I just made bold to go and ask him. And he told me what you would require. And I went and got it, sir. Please, look here," said the professor, raising the lid of a trunk.

"You are very thoughtful, Morris. You are a real help to me," said Ishmael, smiling.

"You see, here are the warm, fine, dark flannel shirts, to be worn instead of linen ones on the voyage. And here is a thick woolen scarf. And here is your sea cap. And oh, here is your sea suit—of coarse pepper and salt. And if you believe me, sir, I went and gave the order to your tailor on Saturday morning, and told him the necessity for haste, and he sent the clothes home before twelve o'clock at night. I'm only afraid they'll hang like a bag on you, sir, as the tailor had nothing but your business suit to measure them by, though, to be sure, the fit of a sea suit isn't much matter, sir."

"Certainly not. You are a treasure to me, Morris; but if you do not go to bed now and recruit your strength, my treasure may be endangered."

"I'm going now, sir; only I want to call your attention to the books I have put into your trunk, sir. I thought as we could only take a very few, I had better put in the Bible, and Shakspeare, and Milton, sir."

"An admirable selection, Morris. Good-night, dear old friend."

"Good-night, sir; but please take notice I have put in a chess board and set of chessmen."

"All right, professor. Good-night," repeated Ishmael

"Yes, sir; good-night! And there's a first-rate spy-glass, as I thought you'd like to have to see distant objects."

"Thank you, professor. Good-night!" reiterated Ishmael, scarcely able to restrain his laughter.

"Good-night, sir. And there's some—well, I see you're laughing at me."

"No, no, professor! or, if I was, it was in sympathy and pleasure; not in derision—Heaven forbid! Your boyish interest in this voyage is really charming to me, professor. But you must retire, old friend; indeed you must. You know we will have plenty of time to look over these things when we get on board the steamer," said Ishmael, taking the old man's hand, cordially shaking it, and resolutely dismissing him to rest.

And Ishmael himself retired to bed and to sleep, and being very much fatigued with his long ride, he slept soundly until morning.

Though the professor was too much excited by the thoughts of his voyage to sleep much, yet he was up with the earliest dawn of morning, moving about softly in his master's room, strapping down the trunks and laying out traveling clothes and toilet apparatus.

The kind old maiden ladies also bestirred themselves earlier than usual this morning, that their young favorite should enjoy one more comfortable breakfast before he left.

And so when Ishmael was dressed and had just dispatched the professor to the stand to engage a hack to take them to the station, and while he was thinking of nothing better in the way of a morning meal than the weak, muddy coffee and questionable bread and butter of the railway restaurant, he received a summons to the dining room, where he found his two hostesses presiding over a breakfast of Mocha coffee, hot rolls, buckwheat cakes, poached eggs, broiled salmon, stewed oysters, and roast partridges.

Our young man had a fine healthy appetite of his own, and could enjoy this repast as well as any epicure alive; but better than all to his affectionate heart was the motherly kindness that had brought these two delicate old ladies out of their beds at this early hour to give him a breakfast.

They had their reward in seeing how heartily he ate. There was no one at the table but himself and themselves; and they pressed the food upon him, reminding him how long a journey he would have to make before he could sit down to another comfortable meal.

And when Ishmael had breakfasted and thanked them, and returned to his rooms to tie up some last little parcels, they called in the professor, who had now come back, and they plied him with all the luxuries on the breakfast table.

And when to their great satisfaction the old man had made an astonishing meal and risen from the table, they beckoned him mysteriously aside and gave a well-filled hamper into his charge, saying:

"You know, professor, it is a long journey from Washington to Boston, and in going straight through you can't get anything fit to eat on the road; and so we have packed this hamper for your master. There's ham sandwiches and chicken pie, and roast partridges and fried oysters, and French rolls and celery, and plenty of pickles and pepper and salt and things. And I have put in some plates and knives and napkins, all comfortable."

The professor thanked them heartily on the part of his master; and took the hamper immediately to the hack that was standing before the door.

Ishmael had already caused the luggage to be carried out and placed on the hack, and now nothing remained to be done but to take leave of the two old ladies. He shook hands with them affectionately, and they blessed him fervently. And as soon as he had got into the hack and it had driven off with him, they turned and clasped each other around the neck and cried.

Truly Ishmael's good qualities had made him deeply beloved.

When the hack reached the hotel, Ishmael found Judge Merlin, all greatcoated and shawled, walking up and down before the door with much impatience. His luggage had been brought down.

"You see I am in time, judge."

"Yes, Ishmael. Good morning. I was afraid you would not be, however. I was afraid you would oversleep yourself after your hard ride. But have you breakfasted?"

"Oh, yes! My dear old friends were up before day to have breakfast with me."

"I tell you what, Ishmael, they are really two charming old ladies, and if ever I get right again and spend another winter in this city, I will try to get them to take me to board. They would make a home for a man," said the judge.

While they were talking the porters were busy putting Judge Merlin's luggage upon Ishmael's hack.

"You have not heard whether the 'Errand Boy' has reached the wharf?" inquired Ishmael.

"Not a word. There has been no arrival here this morning from any quarter, as I understand from the head waiter."

"I am really afraid Mr. Brudenell will miss the train."

"If he does he will miss the voyage also. But we must not risk such a misfortune. Get in, boy, get in!" said the judge, hastily entering the hack.

Ishmael followed his example. The professor climbed up to a seat beside the driver and the hack moved off. They reached the railway station just in time. In fact they had not a moment to lose.

They had just got seated in the cars, and were expecting the signal whistle to shriek out every instant, when Ishmael, who was seated nearest the window, saw a gentleman in a great-coat, and with his shawl over his arm, and his umbrella and hat-box in his hand, hurrying frantically past.

"There is Mr. Brudenell now!" he exclaimed with pleasure, as he tapped upon the window to attract that gentleman's attention.

Mr. Brudenell looked up, nodded quickly, and darted on, and the next moment hurried in at the end door of the car and came down to them just as the signal whistle shrieked out and the train started.

Ishmael reserved the seat in front of himself and the judge, and invited Mr. Brudenell to take it.

The latter gentleman dropped into his place and then held out his hand to greet his fellow-passengers.

"So you are going with us to England. I am very glad of it," said the judge, though in fact he looked very pale and worn, as if he never could be glad again in this world.

"Yes," said Mr. Brudenell, "I am very glad indeed to be of your party. Good-morning, Worth!"

"Good-morning, sir! You were very fortunate to catch the train."

"Very! I was within half a minute of missing it. I had a run for it, I assure you."

"I beg your pardon, sir! Have you breakfasted?" here inquired the professor, in all the conscious importance of carrying a hamper.

"Ah, professor! how do you do? You are never going to Europe?" exclaimed Mr. Brudenell, in surprise.

"Yes, sir. I go wherever my master leads, sir. Mr. Worth and his humble servant will never be separated till death do them part. But about your breakfast, sir?"

"Why, truly, no, I have not breakfasted, unless a cup of suspicious-looking liquid called coffee, drunk at the railway table, could be called breakfast."

The professor sat his hamper on his knees, opened it, and began to reveal its hidden treasures.

Ishmael laughed, expressed his surprise, and inquired of Morris what cook shop he patronized.

And then the professor explained the kind forethought of the old ladies who had provided these luxuries for his journey.

"I declare I will live with them if they will let me, if ever I spend another winter in Washington! One could enjoy what is so often promised, so seldom given—'the comforts of a home'—with those old ladies," said the judge fervently.

Mr. Brudenell made a very satisfactory meal off half a dozen French rolls, a roasted partridge and a bottle of claret. And then while he was wiping his mouth and the professor was repacking the hamper and throwing the waste out of the window, Judge Merlin turned to Mr. Brudenell, and, with an old man's freedom, inquired:

"Pray, sir, may I ask, what procures us the pleasure—and it is indeed a great pleasure—of your company across the water?"

A shade of the deepest grief and mortification fell over the face of Herman Brudenell, as bending his head to the ear of his questioner, and speaking in a low voice, he replied:

"Family matters, of so painful and humiliating a nature as not to be discussed in a railway car, or scarcely anywhere else, in fact."

"Pardon me," said the judge, speaking in the same low tone; "some malignant star must reign. Had you asked the same question of me, concerning the motives of my journey, I might have truly answered you in the very same words."

And the old man groaned deeply; while Ishmael silently wondered what the family matters could be of which Mr. Brudenell spoke.

A modern railway journey is without incident or adventure worth recording, unless it be an occasional disastrous collision. No such calamity befell this train. Our travelers talked, dozed, eat, and drank a little through their twenty-four hours' journey. At noon they reached Philadelphia, at eve New York, at midnight Springfield, and the next morning Boston.

It was just sunrise as they arose and stretched their weary limbs and left the train. They had but an hour to spare to go to a hotel and refresh themselves with a bath, a change of clothes, and a breakfast before it was time to go on board their steamer.

They were the last passengers on board. Fortunately, at this season of the year there are comparatively but few voyagers. The best staterooms in the first cabin, to use a common phrase, "went a-begging."

And Judge Merlin, Mr. Brudenell, and Ishmael were each accommodated with a separate stateroom "amidships."

The professor was provided with a good berth in the second cabin.

There were about thirty other passengers in the first cabin, as many in the second, and quite a large number in the steerage.

CHAPTER XXV

THE VOYAGE.

Thalatta! Thalatta!

I greet thee, thou ocean eternal!

I give thee ten thousand times greeting,

My whole soul exulting!

—Heine.

It was a splendid winter morning, and Boston harbor, with its shipping, presented a magnificent appearance, lighted up by the rising sun, as the "Oceana" steamed out towards the open sea.

Our three friends stood in the after part of the deck, gazing upon the dear native land they were leaving behind them. The professor waited in respectful attendance upon them.

A little way from the shore the signal gun was fired; the farewell gun! how it brought back to the father's memory that moment of agony when the signal gun of another steamer struck the knell of his parting with his only daughter, and seemed to break his heart!

He was going to Claudia now, but oh! how should he find her? Who could tell?

Still there was hope in the thought that he was going to her, and there was exhilaration in the wide expanse of sparkling waters, in the splendid winter sky, in the fresh sea-breeze, and in the swift motion of the steamer.

His eyes, however, with those of all his party, were fixed upon the beloved receding shore; for so smooth as yet was the motion of the steamer that it did not seem to be so much the "Oceana" that was sailing eastward, as the shore that was receding and dropping down below the western horizon.

They stood watching it until all the prominent objects grew gradually indistinct and became blended in each other; then until the dimly diversified boundary faded into a faint irregular blue line; then until it vanished. Only then they left the deck and went down into the cabin to explore their staterooms.

Ishmael found the professor, who had gone down a few minutes before him, busy unpacking his master's sea trunk, and getting him, as he said:

"Comfortably to housekeeping for the next two weeks."

When Ishmael entered the professor was just in the act of setting up the three books that comprised the sea library, carefully arranging them on a tiny circular shelf in the corner. One of the stateroom stewards who stood watching the "landlubber's" operations sarcastically said:

"How long, friend, do you expect them books to stand there?"

"Until my master takes them down, sir," politely answered the professor.

"Well, now, they'll stand there maybe until we get out among the big waves; when, at the first lurch of the ship, down they'll tumble upon somebody's head."

"'Sufficient unto the day—'" said the professor, persevering in his housekeeping arrangements. All that day there was nothing to threaten the equilibrium of the books. A splendid first day's sail they had. The sky was clear and bright; the sea serene and sparkling; the wind fresh and fair; and the motion of the steamer smooth and swift. Our travelers, despite the care at the bottom of their hearts, enjoyed it immensely. Who, with a remnant of hope remaining to them, can fail to sympathize with the beauty, glory, and rapture of Nature in her best moods?

At dinner they feasted with such good appetites as to call forth a jocose remark from a fellow-passenger who seemed to be an experienced voyager. He proved, in fact, to be a retired sea-captain, who was making this voyage partly for business, partly for pleasure. He was an unusually tall and stout old gentleman, with a stately carriage, a full, red face, and gray hair and beard.

"That is right. Go it while you're well, friends! For in all human probability this is the last comfortable meal you will enjoy for many a day," he said. Those whom he addressed looked up in surprise and smiled in doubt.

The splendid sunny day was followed by a brilliant starlight night, in which all the favorable circumstances of the voyage, so far, continued.

After tea the passengers went on deck to enjoy the beauty of the evening.

"What do you think, Captain Mountz?" inquired a gentleman, "will this fair wind continue long?"

"What the deuce is the wind to me? I'm a passenger," responded the irresponsible retired captain.

They remained on deck enjoying the starlit glory of the sea and sky until a late hour, when, fatigued and sleepy, they went below and sought their berths. To new voyagers there is in the first night at sea something so novel, so wild, so weird, so really unearthly, that few, if any, can sleep. They have left the old, still, safe land far behind, and are out in the dark upon the strange, unstable, perilous sea. It is a new element, a new world, a new life; and the novelty, the restlessness, and even the dangers, have a fascination that charms the imagination and banishes repose. A few voyages cure one of these fancies; but this is how a novice feels.

And thus it was with Ishmael. Fatigued as he was, he lay awake in his berth, soothed by the motion of the vessel and the sound of the sea, until near morning, when at length he fell into a deep sleep. It was destined to be a brief one, however.

Soon every passenger was waked up by the violent rolling and tossing of the ship; the creaking and groaning of the rigging; the howling and shrieking of the wind, and the rising and falling of the waves.

All the brave and active passengers tumbled up out of their berths and dressed quickly, while the timid and indolent cowered under their sheets and waited the issue.

Ishmael was among the first on deck. Day was dawning.

Here all hands were on the alert: the captain swearing his orders as fast as they could be obeyed. One set of men were rapidly taking in sail. Another set were seeing to the life boats. The sea was running mountains high; the ship rolling fearfully; the wind so fierce that Ishmael could scarcely stand.

He saw old Captain Mountz on deck, and appealed to him.

"We are likely to have a heavy gale?"

"Oh, a capful of wind! Only a capful of wind!" contemptuously replied that "old salt," who, by the way, through the whole of the tempestuous voyage could not be induced to acknowledge that they had had a single gale worth noticing.

But the wind increased in violence and the sea arose in wrath, and to battle they went, with their old irreconcilable hatred. And yet, notwithstanding the fury of wind and wave, the sun arose upon a perfectly clear sky.

Ishmael remained on deck watching the fierce warring of the elements until the second breakfast bell rung, when he went below.

Neither Judge Merlin nor Mr. Brudenell was at the breakfast table. In fact there was no one in the saloon, except Captain Mountz and two or three other seasoned old voyagers.

The remainder of the passengers were all dreadfully ill in their berths. The prediction of the old captain was fulfilled in their cases at least; they had eaten the last comfortable meal they could enjoy for many days.

As soon as Ishmael had eaten his breakfast he went below in search of the companions of his voyage.

He found the judge lying flat on his back, with his hands clasping his temples, and praying only to be let alone.

The stateroom steward was standing over him, bullying him with a cup of black tea, which he insisted upon his taking, whether or no.

"If he drinks it, sir, he will have something to throw up; which will be better for him than all this empty retching. And after he has thrown up he will be all right, and be able to get up and eat his breakfast and go on deck," said the man, appealing to Ishmael.

"Ishmael, kick that rascal out of my room, and break his neck and throw him overboard!" cried the judge, in anguish and desperation.

"Friend, don't you know better than to exasperate a seasick man? Leave him to me until he is better," said Ishmael smiling on the well-meaning steward.

"But, sir, if he would drink this tea he would throw up and—"

"Ishmael, will you strangle that diabolical villain and pitch him into the sea?" thundered the judge.

The "diabolical villain" raised his disengaged hand in deprecation and withdrew, carrying the cup of tea in the other.

"And now, Ishmael, take yourself off, and leave me in peace. I hate you! and I loathe the whole human race!"

Ishmael left the stateroom, meditating on the demoralizing nature of seasickness.

He next visited Mr. Brudenell, whom he found in a paroxysm of illness, with another stateroom steward holding the basin for him.

"Ugh! ugh! ugh!" moaned the victim. "This heaving, rising, falling sea! And this reeling, pitching, tossing ship! If it would only stop for one moment! I should be glad of anything that would stop it—even a fire!"

"I am sorry to see you suffering so much, sir! Can I do anything for you?" inquired Ishmael sympathetically.

"Ugh! ugh! ugh! No! Hold the basin for me again, Bob! No, Ishmael, you can do nothing for me! only do go away! I hate anyone to see me in this debasing sickness! for it is debasing, Ishmael! Ugh! the basin, Bob! quick!"

Ishmael backed out in double-quick time.

And next he found his way to the second cabin, to the bedside of the professor.

Apparently Jim Morris had just suffered a very severe paroxysm; for he lay back on his pillow with pale, sharp, sunken features and almost breathless lungs.

"I am sorry to see you so ill, professor," said Ishmael tenderly, laying his hand on the old man's forehead.

"It is nothing, Mr. Ishmael, sir, only a little seasickness, as all the passengers have. I dare say it will soon be over. I am only concerned because I can't come and wait on you," said the professor, speaking faintly, and with a great effort.

"Never mind that, dear old friend. I can wait on myself very well; and on you, too, while you need attention."

"Oh, Mr. Ishmael, sir! You are much too kind; but I shall be all right in a little time, and am so glad you are not sick, too."

"No; I am not sick, Morris. But I am afraid that you have been suffering very much," said Ishmael, as he noticed the old man's pallid countenance.

"Oh, no, Mr. Ishmael! Don't disturb yourself. I shall be better soon. You see, when I was very bad they persuaded me to drink a pint of sea-water, which really made me much worse, though it was all well meant. But now I am better. And I think I will try to get up on deck. Why, law, seasickness aint pleasant, to be sure; but then it is worth while to bear it for the sake of crossing the sea and beholding the other hemisphere," said Jim Morris, trying to smile over his own illness and Ishmael's commiseration.

"God bless you, for a patient, gentle-spirited old man and a true philosopher! When you are able to rise, Morris, I will give you my arm up on deck and have a pallet made for you there, and the fresh air will do you good."

"Thank you, thank you, Mr. Ishmael! It is good to be ill when one is so kindly cared for. Isn't there a gale, sir?"

"Yes, Morris, a magnificent one! The old enemies, wind and sea, are in their most heroic moods, and are engaged in a pitched battle. This poor ship, like a neutral power, is suffering somewhat from the assaults of both."

"I think I will go and look on that battlefield," smiled the professor, trying to rise.

Ishmael helped him, and when he was dressed gave him his arm and took him up on deck, at the same time requesting one of the second-cabin stewards to follow with a rug and cushion.

This man, wondering at the affectionate attention paid by the stately young gentleman to his sick servant, followed them up and made the professor a pallet near the wheel-house, on the deck.

When, with the assistance of the steward, Ishmael had made his old retainer comfortable, he placed himself with his shoulders against the back of the wheel-house to steady himself, for the ship was rolling terribly, and he stood gazing forth upon the stormy surface of the sea.

A magnificent scene! The whole ocean, from the central speck on which he stood to the vast, vanishing circle of the horizon, seemed one boundless, boiling caldron. Millions of waves were simultaneously leaping in thunder from the abyss and rearing themselves into blue mountain peaks, capped with white foam, and sparkling in the sunlight for a moment, to be swallowed up in the darkness of the roaring deep the next. A lashing, tossing, heaving, foaming, glancing rise and fall of liquid mountains and valleys, awful, but ravishing, to look on.

Ishmael stood leaning against the wheel-house, with his arms folded and his eyes gazing out at sea. His whole soul was exalted to reverence and worship, and he murmured within himself:

"It is the Lord that commandeth the waters; it is the glorious God that maketh the thunder!

"It is the Lord that ruleth the sea; the voice of the Lord is mighty in operation; the voice of the Lord is a glorious voice!"

As for the professor, he lay propped up at his master's feet, and looking forth upon the mighty war of wind and wave. The sight had subdued him. He was content only to exist and enjoy.

CHAPTER XXVI

THE STORM.

Colder and louder blew the wind,

A gale from the northeast;

The snow fell hissing in the brine;

And the billows foamed like yeast.

Down came the storm and smote amain,

The vessel in its strength;

She shuddered and paused like a frightened steed,

Then leaped her cable's length.

And fast through the midnight, dark and drear,

Through the whistling sleet and snow,

Like a sheeted ghost the vessel swept,

Toward the reef of Norman's Woe.

—Wreck of the "Hesperus."

Ishmael remained upon the quarterdeck, gazing out upon the stormy glory of the sea and sky until he was interrupted by the most prosaic, though the most welcome of sounds—that of the dinner-bell.

Then he went below.

On his way to the saloon he stopped at the entrance of the second cabin; called one of the stewards, and while putting a piece of money in his hand, requested him to take a bowl of soup up to the old man on deck, and to see that he wanted nothing.

Then Ishmael paid a visit to each of his suffering companions.

First he opened the door of Judge Merlin's stateroom, and found that gentleman with his face sulkily turned to the wall, and in a state of body and mind so ill and irritable as to make all attempts at conversation with him quite dangerous to the speaker.

Next Ishmael looked in upon Mr. Brudenell, whom he luckily found fast asleep. And then, after having given the stateroom stewards a strict charge concerning the comfort of these two victims, Ishmael passed on to the dining saloon. It was nearly empty. There were even fewer people gathered for dinner than there had been for breakfast.

The tables had the storm-guards upon them, so that each plate and dish sat down in its own little pen to be kept from slipping off in the rolling of the ship. But this arrangement could not prevent them from occasionally flying out of their places when there was an unusually violent toss.

At the table where Ishmael sat there was no one present except the old retired merchantman, Captain Mountz, who sat on the opposite side, directly under the port lights. And with the rolling of the ship these two diners, holding desperately onto the edge of the table, were tossed up and down like boys on a see-saw plank.

The mingled noise of wind and wave and ship was so deafening as to make conversation difficult and nearly impossible. And yet Ishmael and the captain seemed to feel in courtesy compelled to bawl at each other across the table as they see-sawed up and down.

"The gale seems to have knocked down all our fellow passengers and depopulated our saloon," cried Ishmael, soaring up to the sky with his side of the table.

"Yes, sir, yes, sir; a lot of land-lubbers, sir; a lot of lubbers, sir! Gale? Nothing but a capful of wind, sir! Nothing but a capful of wind!" roared the captain, sinking down to the abyss on his side of the table.

Here the steward, seizing a favorable moment, deftly served them with soup. And nothing but the utmost tact and skill in marine legerdemain enabled this functionary to convey the soup from the tureen to the plates. And when there, it required all the attention and care of the diners to get it from plate to lip. And, after all, more than half of it was spilled.

"Thank goodness, that is over! The solids won't give us so much trouble," said the captain, handing his empty plate to the steward.

The second course was served. But the motion of the ship increased so much in violence that the two diners were compelled to hold still more firmly on to the edge of the table with one hand, while they ate with the other, as they were tossed up and down.

"You're a good sailor, sir!" bawled the captain as he pitched down out of sight.

"Yes, thank Heaven!" shouted Ishmael, flying up.

Then came a tremendous lurch of the ship.

"Oh, I must see that wave!" cried the captain, imprudently climbing up to look out from the port-light above him.

He had scarcely attained the desired position when there came another, an unprecedented toss of the ship, and the unlucky captain lay sprawling on the top of the table—with one wide-flung hand deep in the dish of mashed turnips and the other grasping the roast pig, while his bullet head was butted into Ishmael's stomach.

"Blast the ship!" cried the discomfited old man—very unnecessarily, since there was "blast" enough, and to spare.

"'Only a capful of wind,' captain! 'Only a capful of wind,'" said Ishmael, in a grave, matter-of-fact way, as he carefully assisted the veteran to rise.

"Humph! humph! humph! I might have known you would have said that. Ha! glad none of the women are here to see me! I s'pose I've done for the mashed turnips and roast pig; and I shouldn't wonder if I had knocked your breath out of your body, too, sir," sputtered the old man, trying to recover his feet, a difficult matter amid the violent pitching of the ship.

"Oh, you've not hurt me the least," said Ishmael, still rendering him all the assistance in his power.

But this mishap put an end to the dinner. For the captain's toilet sadly needed renovating, and the table required putting right.

Ishmael went up on deck—a nearly impossible feat for any landsman, even for one so strong and active as Ishmael was, to accomplish with safety to life and limb, for the ship was now fearfully pitched from side to side, and wallowing among the leaping waves.

High as the wind was—blowing now a hurricane—the sky was perfectly clear, and the sun was near its setting.

Ishmael found his old servant sitting propped up against the back of the wheel-house, looking out at one of the most glorious of all the glorious sights in nature—sunset at sea.

"As soon as the sun has set you must go down and turn in, Morris. The wind is increasing, and it is no longer safe for a landsman like you to remain up here," said his master.

"Mr. Ishmael, sir, you must just leave me up here to my fate. As to getting me down now, that is impossible; I noticed that it took both your hands, as well as both your feet, to help yourself up," replied the professor.

"What! do you mean to stay on deck all night?"

"I see no help for it, sir; I should be pitched downstairs and have my neck broken, or be washed into the sea and get drowned, by any attempt to go below."

"Nonsense, Morris; the sun has gone down now; follow his example. I will take you safely," said Ishmael, offering his arm to the old man in that kind, but peremptory, way that admitted of no denial.

A sailor near at hand came forward and offered his assistance. And between the two the professor was safely taken down to the second cabin and deposited in his berth.

A German Jew, who shared the professor's stateroom, saw the party coming, and exclaimed to a fellow-passenger:

"Tere's tat young shentleman mit his olt man again. Fader Abraham! he ish von shentleman; von drue shentleman!"

"A 'true gentleman,' I believe you, Isaacs. Why, don't you know who he is? He is that German prince they've been making such a fuss over, in the States. I saw his name in the list of passengers. Prince—Prince Edward of—of Hesse—Hesse something or other, I forget. They are all Hesses or Saxes up there," said his interlocutor.

"No, no," objected the Jew. "Dish ish nod he. I know Brince Etwart ven I see him. He ish von brince, but nod von shentleman. He svears ad hish mens."

The near approach of the subject of this conversation prevented farther personal remarks. But when Ishmael had seen his old follower comfortably in bed, the Jew turned to him and, as it would seem, for the simple pleasure of speaking to the young man whom he admired so much, said:

"Zir; te zhip rollts mush. Tere vill pe a gread pig storm."

"I think so," answered Ishmael courteously.

"Vell, if zhe goesh down do te boddom tere vill pe von lesh drue shentleman in de vorlt, zir. Ant tat vill be you."

"Thank you," said Ishmael, smiling.

"Ant tere vill pe von lesh Sherman Shew in te vorlt. Ant tat vill pe me."

"Oh, I hope there is no danger of such a calamity. Good-night!" said Ishmael, smiling upon his admirer and withdrawing from the cabin.

Ishmael took tea with the old captain, who came into the saloon and sat down in a perfectly renovated toilet, as if nothing had happened.

But when I say they took tea, I mean that they took quite as much of it up their sleeves and down their bosoms as into their mouths. Drinking tea in a rolling ship is a sloppy operation.

After that the captain produced a chess-board, ingeniously arranged for sea-service, and the two gentlemen spent the evening in a mimic warfare that ended in a drawn battle.

"The gale seems to be subsiding. The motion of the ship has not been so violent for the last half hour, I think," said Ishmael, as they arose from the table.

"No; if it had been, we could not have played chess, even on this boxed board," was the reply.

"I hope we shall have fine weather now. What do you say, captain?"

"I say as I said before. I am a passenger, and the weather is nothing to me. But if you expect we are going to have fine weather because the wind has lulled—humph!"

"We shall not, then?"

"We shall have a twister, that is what we shall have—and before many hours. And I shouldn't wonder if we had a storm of snow and sleet to cap off with. Good-night, sir!" And with this consoling prophecy the old man withdrew.

Ishmael went to his berth and slept soundly until morning. When he awoke he found the ship rolling, pitching, tossing, leaping, falling, and fairly writhing and twisting like a living creature in mortal agony.

He fell out of his berth, pitched into his clothes, slopped his face and hands, raked his hair, and tumbled on deck. In other words, by sleight of hand and foot, he made a sea-toilet and went up.

What a night!

The sky black as night; the sea lashed into a foam as white as snow; the waves running mountain high from south to north; the wind blowing a hurricane from east to west; the ship subjected to this cross action, pitching onward in semicircular jerks, deadly sickening to see and feel.

"I suppose this is what you call a 'twister,'" said Ishmael, reeling towards the old captain, who was already on deck.

"Yes; just as I told you! You see that gale blew from the south for about forty-eight hours and got the sea up running north. And then, before the sea had time to subside, the wind chopped round and now blows from due east. And the ship is rolled from side to side by the waves and tossed from stem to stern by the wind. And between the two actions she is regularly twisted, and that is the reason why the sailors call this sort of thing a 'twister.' And this is not the worst of it. This east wind will be sure to blow up a snowstorm. We shall have it on the Banks."

"This has gone beyond a gale. I should call this a hurricane," said Ishmael.

"Hurricane? hurricane? Bless you, sir, no, sir! capful of wind! capful of wind!" said the old man doggedly.

Nevertheless Ishmael noticed that the ship's captain looked anxious and gave his orders in short, peremptory tones.

The predicted snowstorm did not come on during that short winter's day, however. The "twister" "twisted" vigorously; twisted the ship nearly in two; twisted the souls, or rather the stomachs, nearly out of the bodies of the seasick victims. Even the well-pickled "old salt," Captain Mountz, felt uncomfortable. And it was just as much as Ishmael could do to keep himself up and avoid succumbing to illness. Those two were the last of the passengers that attempted to keep up. And they were very glad when night came and gave them an excuse for retiring.

The predicted snowstorm came on about midnight. When Ishmael dressed and struggled out of his stateroom in the morning, he found it just the nearest thing to an impossibility to go up on deck. The wind was still blowing a hurricane; the sea leaping in the wildest waves; the ship pitching, tossing, and jerking as before; and in addition to all this, the snow was falling thick and fast, and freezing as it fell, and every part of the deck and rigging was covered with a slippery, shining coating of ice.

Those who find it dangerous to walk on a motionless pavement in sleety weather may now imagine what is was to climb the ice-sheathed steps of this pitching ship.

Ishmael managed to get up on deck somehow; but he found the place deserted of all except the man at the wheel and the officer of the watch. Even the old sea lion, Captain Mountz, was among the missing.

There was little to be seen. He stood on the deck of a tossing ship of ice, in the midst of a high wind, a boiling sea, and a storm of snow; he could not discern an object a foot in advance of him.

And so, after a few words with the well-wrapped-up officer of the watch, he went below to look after the companions of his voyage.

Judge Merlin and Mr. Brudenell, like all the other passengers, were so ill as still to hate the sight of a human being. Leaving them in the care of the stateroom steward, Ishmael went to see after his old retainer. The professor was up, clothed, and in his right mind.

"You see I made an effort, Mr. Ishmael, sir, and a successful one, so far as getting on my feet was concerned. When I woke up this morning it occurred to me, like a reproach, that I had come with you, sir, to wait on you and not to be waited on by you—which latter arrangement was a sort of turning things topsy-turvy—"

"I ding sho doo," interrupted the German Jew, whose name was Isaacs.

"And so," continued the professor, "I made an effort to get up and do my duty, and I find myself much better for it."

"I am glad you are well enough to be up, Morris, but indeed, you need have suffered no twinges of conscience on my account," said Ishmael, smiling.

"I know your kindness, sir, and that makes it more incumbent on me to do my duty by you. Well, sir, I've been to your stateroom; but finding you gone, and everything dancing a hornpipe there, I tried to get up on deck to you, but there, sir, I failed. And, besides, while I was doing my best, a stout old gentleman, a sea captain I take him to be, blasted my eyes, and ordered me to go below and not break my blamed neck. And so I did."

"That was Captain Mountz. He meant you well, Morris. You did quite right to obey him."

Soon after this Ishmael went to his stateroom, took a volume of Shakspeare, and then ensconsed himself in a corner of the saloon, where he sat and read until dinner-time.

The progress of the steamer was very slow. The day passed heavily. And again when night came everyone was glad to go to bed and to sleep.

CHAPTER XXVII

THE WRECK.

And ever the fitful gusts between

A sound came from the land;

It was the sound of the tramping surf,

On the rocks and the hard sea-sand.

The breakers were right beneath her bows,

She drifted a dreary wreck,

And a whooping billow swept the crew

Like icicles from her deck.

She struck where the white and fleecy waves

Looked soft as carded wool,

But the cruel rocks, they gored her sides,

Like the horns of an angry bull.

—Wreck of the "Hesperus."

When Ishmael awoke in the morning he was surprised to find that the motion of the ship was much lessened. And when he went up on deck he was pleased to discover that the wind had fallen and the sea was going down.

There was but one trouble—the thick fog; but that might be expected on the Banks of Newfoundland.

Old Captain Mountz was pacing up and down the deck with the firm tread of a man who felt himself on solid ground.

"Good-morning, captain! A pleasant change this," was Ishmael's greeting.

"Oh, aye, yes! for as long as it will last," was the dampening reply.

"Why, you don't think the wind will rise again, do you?"

"Don't I? I tell you before many hours we shall have a strong sou'wester, that will do its best to drive us ashore on these Banks," was the discouraging answer.

But by this time Ishmael had grown to understand the old sailor, and to know that he generally talked by the "rules of contrary"; for whereas he would not permit the late gale to be anything more than a "capful of wind," he now declared the fine weather to be nothing less than the forerunner of a hurricane.

So Ishmael did not feel any very serious misgivings, but went downstairs to breakfast with a good appetite.

Here another pleasant surprise greeted him: Judge Merlin and Mr. Brudenell, recovered from their seasickness, were both at breakfast; and notwithstanding the weight of care that oppressed their hearts they were both, from the mere physical reaction from depressing illness, in excellent spirits.

They arose to greet their young friend.

"How do you do, how do you do, Ishmael?" began Judge Merlin, heartily shaking his hand. "I really suppose now that you think I owe you an apology? But the fact is you owe me one. Didn't you know better than to intrude on the privacy of a seasick man? Didn't you know that a victim hates the sight of one who is not a victim? And that a seasick man or a rabid dog is better let alone, eh?"

"I beg your pardon, sir; I did not know it; but now that you enlighten me, I will not offend again," laughed Ishmael.

Mr. Brudenell's greeting was quieter, but even more cordial than that of the judge.

Before breakfast was over they were joined by others of their fellow-passengers, whom they had not seen since the first day out.

Among the rest was a certain Dr. Kerr, a learned savant, professor in the University of Glasgow, who had been on a scientific mission to the United States, and was returning home. He was a tall, thin old gentleman, in a long, black velvet dressing-gown and a round, black velvet skullcap. And he entered readily into conversation with our party on the subject of the late gales, and from that diverged into the subject of meteorology. There were no ladies present at breakfast.

The whole party soon adjourned to the deck, and notwithstanding the fog, enjoyed the pleasure of a promenade and conversation as they only can who have been deprived of such privileges for many days.

At dinner the long absent ladies reappeared; among the rest, the wife and daughters of the Scotch professor; and with the freedom of ocean steamer traveling, all well-dressed and well-behaved first-cabin passengers soon became acquainted and sociable, if not intimate.

Mrs. Dr. Kerr had happened to hear of Mr. Worth as one of the most promising young barristers of the time; and finding him in the company of Chief Justice Merlin, and approving him on short acquaintance, and knowing that he was unmarried, and not knowing that his heart, hand, and honor were irretrievably engaged, she singled him out as a very desirable match for one of her four penniless daughters, and paid such court to him as Ishmael, in the honesty and gratitude of his heart, repaid with every attention.

Mrs. Dr. Kerr, complaining of the tediousness of the voyage, and the dullness of her own circle, invited Ishmael and his party to spend the evening and play whist in the ladies' cabin—forbidden ground to all gentlemen who had no ladies with them, unless indeed they should happen, as in this case, to be invited.

All the gentlemen of our party availed themselves of this privilege, and the evening passed more pleasantly than any other evening since they had been at sea.

The fog lasted for three days, during which, as the wind was fair and the sea calm, the passengers, well wrapped up, enjoyed the promenade of the deck during the day, and the social meetings in the dining saloon, or the whist parties in the ladies' cabin during the evening.

And lulled by this deceitful calm, they were happy in the thought that the voyage was nearly half over, and in the anticipation of a prosperous passage over the remaining distance, and a safe arrival in port.

On the evening of the third day of the fog, however, a vague and nameless dread prevailed among the passengers. No one could have told whence this dread arose, or whither it pointed. Those well acquainted with the locality knew that the steamer was upon the Banks of Newfoundland, and that those Banks were considered rather unsafe in a fog.

Some others, who were in the secret, also knew that the captain had not left the quarterdeck, either to eat or to sleep, for forty-eight hours; for they had left him on deck at a late hour at night, and found him there at an early hour of the morning. And they had seen strong coffee carried up to him at short intervals. That was all. For sailors never think of danger until that danger, whatever it might be, is imminent; and never speak of it until it becomes necessary to do so, in order to save life.

Thus the passengers on board the "Oceana," on the night of the 20th of December, were totally ignorant of the real nature of the perils that beset them, although, as I said, an undefined misgiving and a sense of insecurity oppressed their hearts.

At ten o'clock that night the weather was thick, foggy, and intensely cold, with a heavy sea and a high wind.

The captain and first mate were on deck, where a number of the hardier and more anxious passengers were collected to watch.

In the dining saloon were gathered around the tables those inveterate gamblers who seem to have no object, either in the voyage of the ocean or the voyage of life, except the winning or losing of money.

In the ladies' cabin there were two social whist parties, formed of the ladies of the Scotch professor's family and the gentlemen of our set.

They were playing with great enjoyment, notwithstanding that little undercurrent of vague uneasiness of which I spoke, when the Scotchman, who had been on the deck all the evening, came down into the cabin, wearing a long face.

But the whist-players were too much interested in their game to notice the lugubrious expression of the old man, until he came to the table, and in a tone of the most alarming gravity exclaimed:

"Don't be frightened!"

Every lady dropped her cards and turned deadly pale with terror. Every gentleman looked up inquiringly at this judicious speaker.

"What is there to be frightened at, sir?" coldly inquired Ishmael.

"Well, you know our situation—But, ladies, for Heaven's sake, be composed. Your sex are noted for heroism in the midst of danger—"

Here, to prove his words good, one of the ladies shrieked, fell back in her chair, and covered her face with her hands.

"These ladies are not aware of any danger, sir, and I think it quite needless to alarm them," said Ishmael gravely.

"My good young friend, I don't wish to alarm them; I came down here on purpose to exhort them to coolness and self-possession, so necessary in the hour of peril. Now, dear ladies, I must beg that you will not suffer yourselves to be agitated."

"There is really, sir, no present cause for agitation, except, if you will pardon me for saying it, your own needlessly alarming words and manner," said Ishmael cheerfully, to reassure the frightened women, who seemed upon the very verge of hysterics.

"No, no, no, certainly no cause for agitation, ladies—certainly not. Therefore don't be agitated, I beg of you. But—but—don't undress and go to bed to-night. Lie down on the outside of your berths just as you are; for, look you—we may all have to take to the lifeboats at a minute's warning," said the doctor, his long, pale face looking longer and paler than ever under his round, black skullcap.

A half-smothered shriek burst simultaneously from all the women present.

"I trust, sir, that your fears are entirely groundless. I have heard no apprehensions expressed in any other quarter," said Ishmael. And although he never begged the ladies not to be "frightened," yet every cheerful word he spoke tended to calm their fears.

"What cause have you for such forebodings, doctor?" inquired Mr. Brudenell.

"Oh, none at all, sir. There is no reason to be alarmed. I hope nobody will be alarmed, especially the ladies. But you see the captain has not been able to make an observation for the last three days on account of the fog; and it is said that no one accurately knows just where we are; except that we are on the Banks, somewhere, and may strike before we know it. That is all. Now don't be terrified. And don't lose your presence of mind. And whatever you do, don't take off your clothes; for if we strike you mayn't have time to put them on again, and scanty raiment, in an open boat, on a wintry night at sea, wouldn't be pleasant. Now mind what I tell you. I shall not turn in myself. I am going on deck to watch."

And having succeeded in spreading a panic among the women, the old man took himself and his black skullcap out of the cabin. Exclamations of surprise, fear, and horror followed his departure.

There was no more card-playing; they did not even finish their game; they felt it to be sacrilegious to engage in even a "ladies' game" of whist, on the eve of possible shipwreck, perhaps on the brink of eternity.

Ishmael gathered up and put away the cards and set himself earnestly to calm the fears of his trembling fellow-passengers; but they were not to be soothed. Then he offered to go up on deck and make inquiries as to the situation, course, and prospects of the ship; but they would not consent to his leaving them; they earnestly besought him to stay; and declared that they found assurance and comfort in his presence.

At length he took the Bible and seated himself at the table, and read to them such portions as were suited to their condition. He read for more than an hour, and then, hoping that this had composed their spirits, he closed the book and counseled them to retire and take some rest; and promised to station himself outside the cabin door and be their vigilant sentinel, to warn them of danger the instant it should become necessary.

But no! they each and all declared sleep to be impossible under the circumstances. And they continued to sit around the table with their arms laid on its top and their heads buried In them, waiting for—what? Who could tell?

Meanwhile the ship was borne swiftly on by wind and wave—whither? None of these frightened women knew.

Eight bells struck—twelve, midnight; and Ishmael renewed his entreaties that they would take some repose. But in vain; for they declared that there could be no repose for their bodies while their minds were suffering such intense anxiety.

One bell struck, and there they sat; two bells, and there they still sat; and there was but little conversation after this. Three bells struck, and they sat on, so motionless that Ishmael hoped they had fallen asleep on their watch and he refrained from addressing them. Four bells struck. It was two o'clock in the morning, and dead silence reigned in the ladies' cabin. Everyone except Ishmael had gone to sleep.

Suddenly through the stillness a cry rang—a joyous cry. It was the voice of the man on the lookout, and it shouted forth:

"Land ho!"

"Where away?" called another voice.

"On her lee bow!"

"What do you make of it?"

"Cape Safety lighthouse!"

A shout went up from the passengers on deck. A simultaneous, involuntary, joyous three times three.

"Hurrah! Hurrah! Hurrah!"

A devout thanksgiving ascended from Ishmael's heart:

"Thank God!" he fervently exclaimed.

It was indeed an infinite relief.

Then he turned to wake up his wearied fellow-passengers, who had fallen asleep in such uneasy attitudes—arms folded, on the top of the table and heads fallen on the folded arms.

"Ladies! dear ladies! dear Mrs. Kerr! you may retire to rest now. We have made Cape Safety," he said, going from one to another and gently rousing them.

They were a little bewildered at first; and while they were still trying to understand what Ishmael was saying, the Scotch professor burst into the cabin and enlightened them by a coup-de-main.

"You may all undress and go to bed now, and sleep in peace, without the least fear of a shipwreck."

"Eh, pa! is it so—are we safe?" cried the elder daughter.

"Safe as St. Paul's. We know where we are now. We have made Cape Safety Lighthouse. Go to bed and sleep easy. I'm going now. Come along, Jeanie," said the doctor to his old wife.

"Not until I have shaken hands with this good young gentleman. I don't know what would have become of us, doctor, after you frightened us so badly, if it had not been for him. He stayed with us and kept up our hearts. God bless you, young sir!" said Mrs. Dr. Kerr, fervently pressing Ishmael's hands.

Ishmael himself was glad to go to rest; so he only stopped long enough to bid good-night to Judge Merlin and Mr. Brudenell, who had just awakened to a sense of security, and then he went to his stateroom and turned in.

Thoroughly wearied in mind and body, he had no sooner touched his pillow than he fell into a deep sleep—a sleep that annihilated several hours of time.

He slept until he was aroused by a tremendous shock—a shock that threw him, strong, heavy, athletic man as he was, from his stateroom berth to the cabin floor. He was on his feet in a moment, though stunned, confused, and amazed. The poor ship was shuddering throughout her whole frame like a living creature in the agony of death.

Men who had been violently thrown from their berths to the floor were everywhere picking themselves up and trying to collect their scattered senses. Crowds were hurrying from the cabins and saloons to the deck. The voices of the officers were heard in quick, anxious, peremptory orders; and those of the crew in prompt, eager, terrified responses.

And through all came shrieks of terror, anguish, and despair.

"The ship has struck!" "We are lost!" "God have mercy!" were the cries.

Ishmael hurried on his clothes and rushed to the deck. Here all was panic, confusion, and unutterable distress. The fog had cleared away; day was dawning; and there was just light enough to show them the utter hopelessness of their position.

The steamer bad struck a rock, and with such tremendous force that she was already parting amidships; her bows were already under water and the sea was breaking over her with fearful force.

How had this happened, with the lighthouse ahead? Was it really a lighthouse, or was it a false beacon?

No one could tell; no one had time to ask. Everybody was fast crowding to the stern of the ship, the only part of her that was out of water. Some crawled up, half drowned; some dripping wet; some scarcely yet awake, acting upon the blind impulse of self-preservation.

Two of the lifeboats had been forcibly reft away from the side of the ship by the violence of the shock and carried off by the sea. Only two remained, and it was nearly certain that they were not of sufficient capacity to save the crew and passengers.

But the danger was imminent—a moment's delay might be fatal to all on board the wreck; not an instant was to be lost.

The order was quickly given:

"Get out the lifeboats!"

And the sailors sprang to obey.

At this moment another fatality threatened the doomed crew—it was what might have been expected: the steerage passengers, mostly a low and brutalized order of men, in whom the mere animal instinct of love of life and fear of death was predominant over every nobler emotion, came rushing in a body up the deck, and crying with one voice:

"To the lifeboats! to the lifeboats! Let us seize the lifeboats, and save ourselves!"

Everyone else was panic-stricken. It is in crises like this that the true hero is developed. With the bound of a young Achilles Ishmael seized a heavy iron bar and sprang to the starboard gangway, where the two remaining boats were still suspended; and standing at bay, with limbs apart, and eyes threatening, and his fearful weapon raised in his right hand, he thundered forth:

"Who tries to pass here dies that instant! Stand off!"

Before this young hero the, crowd of senseless, rushing brutes recoiled as from a fire.

He pursued and secured his victory with a few words:

"Are you men? If so, before all, let helpless childhood, and feeble womanhood, and venerable age be saved; and then you. I demand of you no more than I am willing to do myself. I will be the last to leave the wreck. I will see you all in safety before I attempt to save my own life."

So great is the power of heroism over all, that even these brutal men, so selfish, senseless, and impetuous a moment before, were now subdued; nay, some of them were inspired and raised a hurrah.

Fear of a possible reaction among the steerage passengers, however, caused old Captain Mountz, Judge Merlin, Mr. Brudenell, Dr. Kerr, Jem Morris, the Jew, and several others to come to the support of Ishmael. Among the rest the captain of the steamer came.

"Young man, you have saved all our lives," he said.

Ishmael slowly bowed his head.

"I hope that God has saved you all," he answered.

The sailors were now busy getting down the lifeboats. It was but the work of a very few minutes.

"Let the ladies and children be brought forward," ordered the captain. And the women and children, some screaming, some weeping, and some dumb with terror, were lowered into one of the boats.

"Now the nearest male relatives of these ladies to the same boat," was the captain's next order.

And Dr. Kerr and about a dozen other gentlemen presented themselves, and were lowered into the boat, where they were received with hysterical cries of mingled joy and fear by the women.

And all this time the sea was dashing fearfully over the wreck, and at every interval the planks of the deck upon which they clung were felt to swell and sway as if they were about to part.

"Now the old men!" shouted the captain.

Ishmael took Judge Merlin by the arm, and with gentle coercion passed them on to the sailors, who lowered him into the boat.

Then Captain Mountz and several other old men, and many who were not old, but were willing to appear so "for this occasion only," followed and were passed down into the boat.

Then Ishmael looked around in concern. The professor was lingering in the background.

"Come here, Morris! You certainly fall under the head of "'old men,'" he said, taking the professor by the elbow and gently pushing him forward.

"No, young Ishmael, no! I cannot go! The boat is as full as it can be packed now—or at least it won't hold more than one more, and you ought to go; and I will not crowd you out," urged the old man, with passionate earnestness.

And all this time the sea was thundering over the wreck and entirely drenching everybody, and nearly drowning some.

"Morris, I shall not in any case enter that boat. There is no time, when scores of lives are in imminent danger, to argue the point. But—as you never disobeyed me in your life before, I now lay my commands on you to go into that boat," said Ishmael, with the tone and manner of a monarch.

With a cry of despair the professor let himself drop into the lifeboat to be saved.

The boat was now really as full as it could possibly be crammed with safety to its passengers. And it was detained only until a cask of fresh water and a keg of biscuit could be thrown into it, and then it gave way for the second lifeboat to come up to the gangway.

This second boat was rapidly filled. But when it was crowded quite full there remained upon the breaking wreck Ishmael and ten of the younger steerage passengers.

"Come! come!" shouted the captain of the steamer, who was in the second boat. "Come, Mr. Worth! There is room for one more! There is always room, for one more."

"If there is room for one more, take one of these young men, my companions," replied Ishmael gravely.

"No! no! if we cannot take all, why take one of their number, instead of taking you, Mr. Worth? Come! come! do not keep us here! It is dangerous!" urged the captain.

"Pass on! I remain here!" answered Ishmael steadfastly.

"But that is madness. What good will it do? Come, quick! climb up on the bulwarks and leap down into the boat! You are young and active, and can do it! quick!"

"Give way! I shall remain here," replied Ishmael, folding his arms and planting himself firmly on the quaking deck, over which the sea incessantly thundered.

"Ishmael! Ishmael! My son! my son! for Heaven's sake—for my sake,—come!" cried Mr. Brudenell, holding out his arms in an agony of prayer.

"Father," replied the young man, in this supreme moment of fate not refusing him that paternal title; "father," he repeated, with impassioned fervor, "father, every one of these men has precedence of me, in the right to be saved. For when I intervened between them and the lifeboats they were about to seize I promised them that I would see every one of them in safety before attempting to save myself. I promised them that I would be the very last man to leave the wreck. Father, they confided in me, and I will keep my word with them."

"But you cannot save their lives!" cried Mr. Brudenell, with a gesture of desperation.

"I can keep my word by staying with them," was the firm reply.

While Ishmael spoke there was a rapid consultation going on among his companions on the wreck. Then one of them spoke for the rest:

"Go and save yourself, young gentleman. We give you back your promise."

Ishmael turned and smiled upon them with benignity, as he replied sweetly:

"I thank you, my friends. I thank you earnestly. You are brave and generous men. But from such a pledge as I have given, you have no power to release me."

"Ishmael! Ishmael, for Bee's sake!" cried Judge Merlin, stretching his arms imploringly towards the young man. "For Bee's sake, Ishmael! Think of Bee!"

"Oh, I do! I do think of her!" said the young man, in a voice of impassioned grief. "God bless her! God forever bless her! But not even for her dear sake must I shrink from duty. I honor her too much to live to offer her the dishonored hand of a craven. Tell her this, and tell her that my last earthly thought was hers. We shall meet in eternity."

"Ishmael, Ishmael!" simultaneously cried Judge Merlin and Mr. Brudenell, as they saw a tremendous sea break in thunder over the wreck, which was instantly whirled violently around as in the vortex of a maelstrom.

"Give way! give way! quick! for your lives! The wreck is going and she will draw down the boats!" shouted Ishmael, waving his arm from the whirling deck.

The sailors on board the lifeboats laid themselves vigorously to their oars, and rowed them swiftly away from the whirling eddy around the settling wreck. The passengers on board the boats averted their heads or veiled their eyes—they could not look upon the death of Ishmael,

But as the boats bounded away, something leaped from one of them with the heavy plunge of a large dog into the water, and the next instant the old gray head of Jim Morris was seen rising from the foaming waves. He struggled towards the deck, clambered up its sides and sunk at Ishmael's feet, embracing his knees, weeping and crying:

"Young Ishmael! master! master! Oh, let me die with you!" Speechless from profound emotion, Ishmael stooped and raised the old man and clasped him to his bosom with one arm, while with the other he waved adieu to the rapidly receding lifeboats.

CHAPTER XXVIII

A DISCOVERY.

Why stand ye thus amazed? me thinks your eyes

Are fixed in meditation; and all here

Seem like so many senseless statues,

As if your souls had suffered an eclipse

Betwixt your judgments and affections.

—Swetnam

We must return to Claudia, and to that evening when she was accosted by Katie on the stairs.

On that occasion Claudia went down to dinner without feeling the least anxiety on the subject of Katie's promised communication. She supposed, when she thought of it at all, that it was some such idle rumor as frequently arose concerning the discovery of some suspected person implicated in the murder of Ailsie Dunbar.

The dinner that evening happened to be more protracted than usual.

And when they arose from the table Mrs. Dugald, contrary to her custom, immediately retired to her private apartments. Claudia was also about to withdraw, when the viscount said to her:

"Excuse me, Lady Vincent; but I must request the favor of a few moments' conversation with you."

"Very well, my lord," answered Claudia, bowing coldly.

He led the way to the drawing room and Claudia followed. Coffee was already served there, and old Cuthbert was in attendance to hand it around.

"You may go, Cuthbert. We can wait on ourselves." said Lord Vincent, as he led his wife to a seat and took one for himself near her.

When the old servant had left the room the viscount turned to Claudia and said:

"Lady Vincent, I have been obliged to solicit this interview because I have much to say to you, while you give me very few opportunities of saying anything."

Claudia bowed a cold assent and remained silent.

"It is of Mrs. Dugald that I wish to speak to you."

"I am listening, my lord," replied Claudia haughtily.

"Lady Vincent, this arrogant manner towards me will not serve any good purpose. However, it is not on my own score that I came to complain, but on Mrs. Dugald's; that lady's position in this house is a very delicate one."

"So delicate, my lord, that I think the sooner she withdraws from it the better it will be."

"You do! It is the to that end, then, I presume, that you have treated her with so much scorn and contempt?" said his lordship angrily.

"My lord, with all my faults, I am no hypocrite; and with all my accomplishments I am no actress."

"What do you mean by that, my lady?"

"I mean that I have not been able to treat your—sister-in-law—with the respect that I could not feel for her," replied Claudia, with disdain.

"No, madam!" exclaimed Lord Vincent, turning pale with rage. "You have treated that lady with the utmost contumely. And I have demanded this interview with you for the express purpose of telling you that I will not submit to have the widow of my brother treated with disrespect in my own house and by my own wife!"

Claudia arose with great dignity and answered:

"My lord, since you desired this interview for the purpose of expressing your wishes upon this point; and, since you have expressed them, I presume the object of our meeting has been accomplished and I am at liberty to withdraw. Good-night."

"Not so fast, not so fast, Lady Vincent! I have not done with you yet, my lady. The will that I have just spoken must be obeyed. Mrs. Dugald must be treated by you, as well as by others, with the courtesy and consideration due to her rank and position. Many abuses must be reformed. And among them is this—your constant refusal to appear in public with her. Ever since your arrival here Mrs. Dugald has been a prisoner in the house, because she cannot go out alone; and she will not go out, attended by me, unless you are also of the party, for fear that evil-minded people will talk."

Claudia's beautiful lip curled with scorn as she answered:

"Mrs. Dugald's scruples do credit to her—powers of duplicity."

"You wrong her. You always wrong her; but, by my soul, you shall not continue to do so! Listen, Lady Vincent! Mr. and Mrs. Dean, the celebrated tragedians, are playing a short engagement at Banff. Mrs. Dugald and myself wish to go and see them. It will be proper for you to be of the party. I desire that you will be prepared to go with us to-morrow evening."

Claudia's face flushed crimson with indignation.

"Excuse me, my lord. I cannot possibly appear anywhere in public with Mrs. Dugald," she haughtily replied.

"If you fail to go with us, you will rue your scorn in every vein of your heart, my lady. However, I will not take your final answer to- night; I will give you another chance in the morning. Au revoir!" he said, with an insulting laugh, as he lounged out of the room.

Claudia remained where he had left her, transfixed with indignation, for a few minutes. And then she began to walk up and down the room to exhaust her excitement before going upstairs to her dressing room, where she supposed that Katie was awaiting her.

She walked up and down the floor some fifteen or twenty minutes, and then left the saloon and sought her own apartments. She had just reached the landing of the second floor, on which her rooms were situated, when she was startled by a low, half-suppressed cry of "Murd—," which was quickly stopped, and immediately followed by a muffled fall and a low scuffling, and the voice of Lord Vincent muttering vehemently: "Faustina!" and other words inaudible to the hearer.

"Ah! they are quarreling as usual!" said Claudia to herself, with a scornful smile, as she crossed the hall and entered her own suite of apartments.

"I have kept you waiting, Katie; but I could not help it, my good woman," she said cheerfully, as she entered her dressing room. But there was no reply. She looked around her in surprise. Katie was nowhere to be seen; the room was empty. The lamp was burning dimly and the fire was smoldering out.

Claudia raised the light of the lamp, and, seating herself in her easy-chair before the fire, stirred the coals into a blaze and began, to warm her feet and hands.

"'The old creature has grown weary of waiting, I suppose, and has gone down to her supper," she said to herself. And she sat waiting patiently for some time before she rang her bell.

Sally answered it.

"Go down, Sally, and tell Katie that I am here and ready to see her now," said Lady Vincent.

Sally went on this errand, but soon returned and said:

"If you please, ma'am, Aunt Katie aint nowhere downstairs. I s'pects she's done gone to bed."

Claudia suddenly looked up to the ormolu clock that stood upon the mantel shelf.

"Why, yes!" she said, "it is nearly eleven o'clock. I had no idea that it was so late. Of course she has gone to bed."

"Mus' I go call her up, ma'am?"

"No, Sally; certainly not. But there was something that she said she had to tell me. Something, I fancy, it was, about the murder of that poor girl. Has anything new been discovered in relation to that affair, do you know?"

"No, ma'am, not as I has hearn. 'Deed it was only jes now we was all a-talking about it in de servants' hall, and Mr. Frisbie he was a-mentioning how misteerious it was, as we could hear nothing. And jes then your bell rung, ma'am, and I came away."

"Well, Sally, you must help me to disrobe, and then you may go."

The waiting maid did her duty and retired.

And Claudia, wrapped in her soft dressing gown and seated in her easy-chair before the fire, gave herself up to thought.

She was thinking of her meeting with Katie on the stairs. Since it was no new rumor connected with the murder, she was wondering what could be the nature of the communication Katie had to make to her. She recalled the anxious, frightened, indignant countenance of the old woman, and in her memory that expression seemed to have a more significant meaning than it had had to her careless eyes at the time of seeing it.

What could it be that Katie had to tell her? Of course Claudia did not know; she soon gave up trying to conjecture; but felt impatient for the morning, when the mystery should be revealed.

Other anxious thoughts also troubled her; thoughts of the dangers to which she was exposed from the hatred of Lord Vincent, the jealousy of Mrs. Dugald, and the depravity of both; thoughts of her father's long and strange silence; thoughts of the insult she had received that evening in being commanded to chaperon Mrs. Dugald to the theater; thoughts of the mysterious sounds she had heard from Mrs. Dugald's room, and which she was so far from connecting with any idea of Katie that she attributed them solely to a quarrel between her two precious companions; and lastly the ever-recurring thoughts of that mysterious discovery which old Katie had made, and which she was so eager to impart to her lady. Ever Claudia's thoughts, traveling in a circle, came back to this point.

Wearied with fruitless speculation she still sat on, watching the decaying fire and listening to the thunder of the sea as it broke upon the rocks at the base of the castle. At length she got up, drew aside the heavy window curtains, opened the strong oaken shutters and looked out upon the expanse of the gray and dreary sea, dimly visible under the cloudy midnight sky.

At last she closed the window and went to bed. But she could not sleep. She lay wakeful, restless, anxious, through the long hours of the middle night, and through the gray dawn of morning and the early flush of day. A little before her usual hour of rising she rang the bell.

Sally answered it.

"Is Katie up?" she inquired.

"No, ma'am. Mus' I wake her?"

"Certainly not. Let her have her sleep out, poor creature. And do you stop and help me to dress."

And so saying Claudia arose and made an elegant morning toilet; for Claudia, like Mary Stuart, would have "dressed" had she been a lifelong, hopeless captive.

When her toilet was made she directed Sally to bring her a cup of strong coffee; and when she had drunk it she sat down to wait with what patience she could for the awakening of old Katie.

Poor Claudia, with all her faults, was kind to her dependents and considerate of their comforts. And so, anxious as she was to hear the communication old Katie had to make to her, she was resolved not to have the old woman's rest broken.

She sat by the window of her dressing room, looking out upon the boundless sea from which the sun was rising, and over which a solitary sail was passing. She sat there until the breakfast bell rang. And then she went below.

She was the first in the breakfast room, and she remained there standing before the fire full ten minutes before anyone else appeared.

Lord Vincent was the next to come in. And Claudia actually started when she saw the awful pallor of his face. Every vestige of color had fled from it; his brow, cheeks, and even lips were marble white; his voice shook in saying "good-morning," and his hand shook in lifting the "Banff Beacon" from the table.

While Claudia was watching him in wonder and amazement, there came a flutter and a rustle, and Mrs. Dugald entered the room all brightness and smiles.

She gave one quick, wistful glance at the viscount, and then addressed him in a hurried, anxious tone, speaking in the Italian language and saying:

"Rouse yourself! Look not so like an assassin. You will bring suspicion!"

"Hush!" answered the viscount, with a quick glance towards Claudia, which warned La Faustina that the American lady might be supposed to understand Italian.

Claudia did understand it, and was filled with a vague sense of horror and amazement.

They sat down to the table. Lord Vincent followed Mrs. Dugald's advice and tried to "rouse" himself. And after he had two or three cups of coffee he succeeded.

Faustina was as bright as a paroquet and as gay as a lark. She prattled on in a perpetual, purling stream of music. Among other things she said:

"And do we go to see Mr. and Mrs. Dean in 'Macbeth' tonight, mon ami?"

"Yes; and Lady Vincent goes with us," answered Lord Vincent emphatically.

"I beg your pardon, my lord. I have already declined to do so," said Claudia, speaking with forced coolness, though her heart was burning, her cheeks flaming, and her eyes flashing with indignation.

"You will think better of it, my lady. You will go. Cuthbert, pass the eggs."

"I shall not, my lord," replied Claudia.

"Why will you not? Pepper, Cuthbert."

"For the reason that I gave you last night. Your lordship cannot wish me to repeat it here."

"Oh, a very particular reason you gave me! The salt, Cuthbert," said his lordship, coolly breaking the shell of his egg.

"A reason, my lord, that should be considered sufficiently satisfactory to relieve me from importunity on the subject," answered Claudia.

"If miladie does not wish to go, we should not urge her to do so," observed Mrs. Dugald, as she slowly sipped her chocolate.

"Certainly not. And now I think of it, you can send over for Mrs. MacDonald to come and go with us. The old lady enjoys the drama excessively and will be glad to come. So you shall be sure of your intellectual treat, Faustina."

"That will be so nice!" exclaimed Mrs. Dugald, clapping her hands in childish glee.

Claudia arose from the table and withdrew to her own apartments. She was revolted by the fulsome manners of the strange woman who shared her dwelling, and she was drawn toward the secret, whatever it was, that old Katie wished to impart to her.

When she entered the rooms she found them all arranged tidily by the neat hands of Sally, who since the death of poor Ailsie had had the care of them.

"Sally, has not Katie been up yet?" inquired Lady Vincent.

"No, ma'am; I don't think she's awake yet; I reckon she's a- oversleepin' of herself. And I would 'a' waked her up, only, ma'am, you bid me not to do it."

"What, do you mean to say that she has not yet made her appearance?" demanded Claudia, in alarm.

"Nobody aint seen nothing 'tall of her this morning, ma'am."

"Go to her room at once and see if she is ill. She may be, you know. Go in quietly, so that you will not awaken her if she should be asleep," said Claudia, in alarm, for she suddenly remembered that people of Katie's age and habit sometimes die suddenly and are found dead in their beds.

Sally went on her errand, and Claudia stood waiting and listening breathlessly until her return.

"Laws, ma'am, Aunt Katie's done got up, and made her bed up and put her room to rights, and gone downstairs," said Sally, as she entered the room.

"Then go at once, and if she has had her breakfast send her up to me. Strange she did not come."

Sally departed on this errand also, but she was gone longer than on the first. It was nearly half an hour before she returned. She came in with a scared face, saying:

"Ma'am, it's very odd; but the servants say as ole Aunt Katie hasn't been down this morning."

"Hasn't been down this morning? And is not in her room either?" cried Claudia, in amazement.

"No, ma'am!" answered Sally, stretching her big eyes.

Lady Vincent sharply rang the bell.

The housekeeper promptly answered it, entering the room with an anxious countenance.

"Mrs. Murdock, is it true that my servant Katie has not been seen this morning?"

"Me leddy, she has nae been seen, puir auld bodie, sin' last e'en at the gloaming. She didna come to supper, though Katie isna use to be that careless anent her bit and sup, neither."

"Not seen since last evening at dusk!" exclaimed Claudia, in consternation.

"Na, me leddy, ne'er a bit o' her, puir bodie!"

"Go, Mrs. Murdock, and send the maids to look for her in every place about the castle where she is in the habit of going. And send the men outside to examine the premises. She may be taken with a fit somewhere, and die for want of assistance," said Lady Vincent, in alarm.

"And sae she may, me leddy! That is true enough," replied the dame, nodding her head emphatically as she hurried out on this mission.

Claudia sat down before her dressing-room fire and tried to wait the issue patiently. To be sure, she thought Katie might be in the stillroom, or the linen closet, or the bathroom, and there could be no reasonable cause of uneasiness. But why, then, did she not come up? Well, she might have been busy in some one of the above- mentioned places; and she might have been waiting until she thought her mistress should have got through breakfast; and perhaps she might come now very soon; might even enter at any moment. Such were the thoughts that coursed through Claudia's brain, as she tried to sit still before her little fire.

For more than an hour Claudia waited, and then she impatiently rang the bell. It brought Mrs. Murdock into the room.

"Has Katie been found yet?"

"Na, me leddy, not a bit of her. The servants are still seeking her."

"But this is very strange and alarming."

"It just is, me leddy. And I canna but fear that some ill has happened till her, puir soul!"

"I will go down and assist in the search," said Lady Vincent, rising anxiously.

"Na, me leddy, dinna gang, ye canna do ony good. The lasses are seeking in every nook and cranny in the house; and if she is biding in it they will find her. And the lads hae gone outside to seek in the grounds, whilk same is sune done; for the castle yard and grounds are nae that expansive, as your leddyship kens." "But I cannot sit here, waiting in idleness. It drives me half frantic! Who can say what may not have happened to poor Katie?"

"Nae, me leddy, dinna fash yo'sel'! She may e'en just ha' gone her ways over to Banff, or some gait, and may be back sune. I'll gae see if they ha' brought in ony news."

"Go, then, Mrs. Murdock, and let me know the instant you hear anything definite," said Claudia, sinking back in her chair.

Mrs. Murdock left the room, and another hour of suspense passed. And then, uncalled, the housekeeper came up again, and said:

"It is a' in vain, me leddy. The servants have sought everywhere, within and without the castle, and they can na find the auld bodie at a'! And your leddyship's ain footman, Jamie, ha' come fra Banff and brought the morning mail, and he has na seen onything o' his mither on the road."

"Good Heavens! but this is strange and very dreadful. Send Jim up to me at once."

The housekeeper went to obey. And Jim soon stood in the presence of his mistress.

"Any letters from America, Jim?" inquired Lady Vincent anxiously, and for a moment forgetting poor old Katie's unknown fate.

"No, my lady, not one. There was no foreign mail to-day."

"Another disappointment! Always disappointments!" sighed Claudia. And then reverting to the subject of Katie's disappearance, she said:

"What is this about your mother, Jim? When did you see her last? And have you any idea where she can be gone?"

Jim suddenly burst into tears; for we know that he loved his old mother exceedingly; and he sobbed forth the words:

"Oh, my lady, I am afeared as somebody has gone and made way with her as they did with poor Ailsie!"

"Gracious Heaven, Jim, what a horrible idea! and what an utterly irrational one. Who could possibly have any motive for harming poor old Katie?"

"I don't know, my lady. But, you see, my poor mother was always a-watching and a-listening about after his lordship and that strange lady. And I know they noticed it, and maybe they have done made way with mother—My lady! oh! you are fainting! You are dying!" cried Jim, suddenly breaking off, and rushing towards his mistress, who had turned deadly pale, and fallen back in her chair.

"No, no! water, water!" cried Lady Vincent, struggling to overcome her weakness.

Jim flew and brought her a full glass. She quaffed its contents eagerly, and sat up, and tried to collect her panic-stricken faculties. She had received a dreadful shock. Jim's words had given the key to the whole mystery. In one terrible moment the ghastly truth had burst upon her. She understood, now, the whole. She could combine the circumstances: Katie's agitated meeting with her on the stairs; the communication which the poor faithful old creature seemed so eager to make, and which must have related to some discovery that she had made; the mysterious noises heard in Mrs. Dugald's apartments; the guilty paleness of the viscount at the breakfast table; the strange words spoken in Italian by Faustina; the mysterious disappearance of Katie; all, all these pointed to one dreadful deed, from the bare thought of which all Claudia's soul recoiled in horror.

"Jim!" she gasped, in a choking voice.

"My lady!"

"At what hour last evening did you see your mother?"

"Just a little after sunset. The last dinner bell had rung; and I brought some coal up to put on your ladyship's fire, and I set it on the outside of the door, intending to take it in as soon as your ladyship came out to go down to dinner. Well, I was standing there waiting with the coal when I saw my lord's dor open and Mr. Frisbie come out, with such a face! Oh, my lady! I don't know how to describe it; but it had a cruel, cowardly, desperate look—as if he would have cut someone's throat to save himself a shilling! He passed on downstairs without ever seeing me. And the next minute my lord came out of the same room, with—I beg your pardon, my lady—a look of wicked triumph on his face. He was even laughing, like he had done something that pleased him. And he happened to look up and see me, and he growled:

"'What are you doing there, fellow?'

"And I bowed down to the ground a'most, and answered:

"'I have brought up coal for my lady's rooms, my lord.'

"'Very well,' he said, and he went on.

"Next thing, I was tuk right off my feet, by seeing of my own mother come right out'n that same room. And she came out, did the old woman, with her eyes rolled up and her arms lifted high, looking as she a'most always does when she hears anything dreadful; looking just for all the world as she did the day she heard of poor Ailsie's murder. Well, my lady, I felt sure as she had been a-hiding of herself in my lord's room, and had discovered something horrible. And so I called to her in a low voice:

"'Mother!'

"But she shook her head at me, and ran down the stairs, and stood waiting. And just at that minute your ladyship came out of your room. You may remember, my lady, seeing me standing there with the coal as you came out?"

"Yes, Jim, I remember," replied Lady Vincent.

"Well, my lady, I saw mother stop you, and I heard a whispered conversation, in which she seemed to beg you to do something that you hadn't time to attend to, for you went downstairs and left her."

"I was on my way to dinner, you remember; but I bade Katie go into my dressing room and await me there. When I went up after dinner, however, I found that she had not followed my directions. She was not in my apartments, nor have I seen her since."

"I beg pardon, my lady; but, indeed, poor mother did obey your ladyship. She came upstairs again, and she took the coal hod out'n my hands, and said—said she:

"'You go right straight downstairs, Jim, and I'll tend to my ladyship's fires myself.' And I said:

"'Mother,' said I, 'what's the matter?' And she whispered to me:

"'I done hear somethin' awful, Jim; but I must tell my ladyship before I tells anyone else.'

"'Was it about poor Ailsie's death?' said I.

"'Worse 'an dat,' she answered; and then she went in and shut the door in my face. And I come away. And that was the last time as ever I see my poor, dear old mother. She never come down to supper, nor likewise to play cards in the servants' hall in the evening, as she is so fond of doing. And surely, my lady, I was not uneasy, because I knew she often stayed in your ladyship's rooms until late; and as I had seen her go into them myself that evening, I was feeling full sure that she was with you. And so I went to bed in peace. And this morning, as I got up and went to the post office before any of the woman servants were astir, of course I didn't expect to see her. But the first thing as I heard when I come back, was as she was a-missing! And oh, my lady, I'm sure, I'm dead sure, as somebody has made way with her!" exclaimed Jim, bursting into a fresh flood of tears.

"Don't despair, Jim; we must hope for the best," replied Lady Vincent, in whose bosom not a vestige of hope remained.

But Jim only answered with his tears.

"Compose yourself, boy; and go and say to Lord Vincent that I request to see him in my boudoir."

Jim went out with a heavy heart to do his errand; but returned with an answer that Lord Vincent was engaged.

"I will not be baffled in this way!" muttered Claudia to herself. Then speaking aloud she inquired: "Where is his lordship, and upon what is he engaged?"

"He is sitting in the library, with a bottle of brandy and a box of cigars on the table by him; he is smoking and drinking."

"'Smoking and drinking' at twelve o'clock in the day!" muttered Claudia to herself, with a motion of disgust. Then speaking up, she said: "Go downstairs, Jim, and assist in the search for your poor mother; I will ring when I want you."

CHAPTER XXIX

A DEEP ONE.

An evil soul producing holy witness,

Is like a villain with a smiling face.

A goodly apple, rotten at the core.

—Shakespeare.

And when her footman had retired Claudia gave herself up to severe and painful thought upon what she had just heard. And the more she reflected on the circumstances the more firmly convinced she became that poor old Katie had suffered foul play; though of what precise nature or by whom exactly dealt she could not decide. Whether Katie had been kidnaped and sent away; or immured in one of the underground dungeons of the castle; or murdered; or whether the perpetrators of either of these crimes were Lord Vincent and Faustina; or Lord Vincent and Frisbie; or Faustina and Frisbie; or finally, whether all three were implicated, she could not determine. And the whole question overwhelmed her with horror. Was this ancient and noble castle really a den of thieves and assassins? One frightful murder had already been committed. Another had perhaps been perpetrated. Was even her own life safe in such a cut-throat place? She feared not; and she knew that she must act with exceeding caution and prudence to insure her safety. What then should she do? What became her duty in these premises? Clearly she could not leave the faithful servant, who had probably lost life or liberty in her service, to such a fate. And yet for Lady Vincent to stir in the matter would be to risk her own life.

No matter! Claudia, with all her faults, was no coward.

And with a sudden resolution she arose and went downstairs and into the library, where Lord Vincent sat drinking and smoking.

"Lady Vincent, I believe I sent you word that I was engaged," said the viscount, as soon as he saw her.

"Not very particularly engaged, I believe, my lord," said Claudia, resolutely advancing toward him.

"I was smoking. And I understood that you disliked smoke," said Lord Vincent, throwing away the end of his cigar.

"There are crises in life, my lord, that make us forget such small aversions. One such crisis is at hand now," answered Claudia gravely.

"Will your ladyship explain?" he demanded, placing a chair for her. Evidently the brandy or something or other had strung up Lord Vincent's nerves.

Claudia took the seat, and sitting opposite to him, fixed her eyes upon his face and said:

"Are you aware, Lord Vincent, that my servant Katie has been missing since yesterday afternoon?"

"Indeed? Where has the old creature taken herself off to? She has not eloped with one of our canny Scots, has she?" inquired the viscount, coolly lighting another cigar and puffing away at it.

"Such jesting, my lord, is cruelly out of place! It has not been many days since a very horrid murder was committed on these premises. The murderer has eluded detection. And apparently such impunity has emboldened assassins. I have too much cause to fear that my poor old servant has shared Ailsie Dunbar's fate!"

Before Claudia had finished her sentence Lord Vincent had dropped his cigar and was gazing at her in ill-concealed terror.

"What cause have you for such absurd fears? Pray do you take the castle of my ancestors to be the lair of banditti?" he asked in a tone of assumed effrontery, but of real cowardice.

"For something very like that indeed, my lord!" answered Claudia, with a terrible smile.

"I ask you what cause have you for entertaining these preposterous suspicions?"

"First of all, the assassination of Ailsie Dunbar and the successful concealment of her murderer. Secondly, the mysterious disappearance of my servant Katie, just at a time when it was desirable to some parties to get her out of the way," said Claudia emphatically, and fixing her eyes firmly on the face of the viscount, that visibly paled before her gaze.

"What—what do you mean by that?"

"My lord, I will tell you. Yesterday afternoon, as I was descending to dinner, old Katie met me on the stairs and with a frightened face told me that she had made an important discovery that she wished to communicate to me. I directed her to go to my dressing room and wait there until my return from dinner, when I fully intended to hasten at once to her side and hear what she had to say—"

"Some 'mare's nest' of a new rumor concerning the murderer of Ailsie Dunbar, I suppose," said the viscount, with a feeble attempt to sneer.

"No, my lord, I rather think it was something concerning my own safety. But I never knew; for you may recollect that on last evening your lordship detained me in conversation some time after dinner. When I went to my dressing room Katie was not there. I thought she had grown sleepy and had gone to bed, and so I felt no anxiety on that score. But this morning, my lord, she is missing. She is nowhere to be found."

"Oh, I dare say she has gone visiting some of the country people with whom she has picked acquaintance. She will turn up all right by and by."

"I fear not, my lord."

"Why do you 'fear not'?"

"Because there are other very suspicious circumstances connected with the disappearance of Katie, that since her evanishment have recurred to my memory, or been brought to knowledge."

"Pray, may one ask without indiscretion, what these suspicious circumstances are?"

"Certainly, my lord; it was to report them that I came here. First, then, last evening on my return towards my own room I was a little startled by hearing a scream, quickly smothered, and then a fall and a scuffling, soon silenced. These sounds came from the apartment of Mrs. Dugald—"

"The demon!" burst involuntarily from the unguarded lips of Lord Vincent.

Claudia heard, but continued to speak as though she had not heard.—"I caught one single word of the conversation that ensued. It was—'Faustina!' and it was your voice that uttered it. I therefore supposed at the time, my lord, that you were only having one of your customary slight misunderstandings with your—sister-in-law."

"Yes, yes, yes, yes, that was it! She was suffering from an attack of hysterics; and I had to go in and control her a little. She has been subject to these attacks ever since the death of her husband, poor woman," said he, in a quavering voice.

Claudia eyed him closely and continued:

"That was the circumstance that recurred to my memory with so much significance when Katie was reported missing this morning. Then, upon making inquiries as to where and by whom she was last seen, another very significant circumstance was brought to my knowledge; that she was seen last evening to issue from your rooms immediately after you and your valet left them; and it appears to have been just after that she met me on the steps."

"Flames of—! What was she doing in my rooms?" exclaimed the viscount, losing all self-command for the moment and turning ghastly white with the mingled passions of rage and terror.

"I do not know, my lord; probably her duty, a part of which is to keep your linen in order. But whatever took her to your rooms, on that occasion, or detained her there, it is very evident that while there she made some frightful discovery which she wished to communicate and would have communicated to me had she not been—prevented," said Claudia firmly.

Lord Vincent was tremendously agitated, but struggled hard to regain composure. At last he succeeded.

"Who told you that she was seen coming from my rooms? What spy, what eavesdropper, what mischief-maker have you in your employ that goes about my house—watching, listening, and tale-bearing? If I detect such a culprit in the act I will break his or her neck, and that you may rely upon!" he said.

"Have you broken Katie's neck?" inquired Lady Vincent.

"Ha, ha, ha! If I had caught her hiding in my rooms I should have done so beyond all doubt! Luckily for her I did not do so, as you must be aware, since you say she was seen coming out of them."

"Yes; but she was never seen to leave the castle!"

"Lady Vincent, what is it that you dare to insinuate?"

"My lord, I insinuate nothing. I tell you plainly that I feel myself to be—not in a nobleman's castle, but in a brigand's fastness; and that I suspect my poor old servant has been foully made way with."

"Lady Vincent, how dare you!"

"You may glare at me, my lord, but you shall not intimidate me. I have seen one murdered woman in the house; I do strongly suspect the presence of another, and I know not how soon my own life may fall a sacrifice to the evil passions of the fiend that rules your fate. I have been silent in regard to my deep wrongs for a long time, my lord. But now that my poor servant has fallen a victim to her fidelity, I can be silent no longer! I am here alone, helpless, and in your power! Yet I must make my protest, and trust in God's mercy to deliver me, and what is left of mine, from the hands of the spoiler!" said Claudia solemnly.

Sometimes necessity compels people to think and act with great rapidity; to rally their faculties and charge a difficulty at a moment's notice.

This was the case with the Viscount Vincent now. Very quickly he collected his mind, formed his resolution, and acted upon it.

"Lady Vincent," he said, in a kinder tone than he had yet used, "your words shock and appall me beyond all measure. Your suspicions wrong me cruelly, foully; I know nothing whatever of the fate of your woman; on my soul and honor, I do not! But if you really suspect that anyone had an interest in the taking off of that poor old creature, tell me at once to whom your suspicions point, and I will do my very utmost to discover the truth. By all my hopes of final redemption and salvation, I will!" he added, looking earnestly in her face.

Claudia gazed at him in utter amazement. Could this be true? she asked herself. Could a man look so full in her face, speak so earnestly, and swear by such sacred things, while telling a falsehood? To one of Claudia's proud nature it was easier to believe a man guilty of murder than of lying and perjury. She was thoroughly perplexed.

Lord Vincent saw the effect his words had had upon her, and he was encouraged to follow up his success.

"Whom do you suspect, Claudia?" he inquired.

She answered honestly.

"My lord, I will tell you truly. I suspect you."

"Me!" he exclaimed, with a laugh of incredulity. Never were honest scorn and righteous indignation more forcibly expressed. "Me! Why, Claudia, in the name of all the insanities in Bedlam, why should you suspect me? What interest could I possibly have in getting rid of your amusing gorilla?"

"My lord, I hope that I have wronged you; but I feared that Katie had become possessed of some secret of yours which you wished to prevent her from divulging."

"And for that you thought I would have taken her life?"

"For that reason I thought you would have made away with her—by kidnaping and sending her out of the country, or by immuring her in one of the dungeons of the castle, or even by—"

"Speak out! 'Cutting her throat,' why don't you say?"

"Oh, Lord Vincent, but this is horrible, horrible!" shuddered Claudia.

"Ha, ha, ha! Well, upon my life, my lady, you are excessively complimentary to me! But I am willing to believe that the tragic event of last week has shattered your nervous system and disturbed the equilibrium of your mind. But for that I should hardly know how to pardon your absurd insults. Have you anything more to say to me, Lady Vincent?"

"Only this, my lord; that if I find I have wronged you by this dreadful suspicion, as perhaps I have, I shall be glad, yes, overjoyed, to acknowledge it and beg your pardon. And, in the meantime, I must ask you to keep your word with me, and investigate the disappearance of Katie!"

"I will do so willingly, Lady Vincent. And now a word with you. Will you not change your mind and go with us to Mr. and Mrs. Dean to-night?"

"No, my lord," replied Claudia, in a tone that admitted of no further discussion of the question.

And thus they parted.

For some time after Claudia left the library Lord Vincent remained sitting with his brows contracted, his mouth clenched, and his eyes fixed upon the ground. He was in deep thought. Handsome man as he was, villain was written all over his face, form, and manner in characters that even a child could have read; and, therefore, no one was to be pitied who, having once seen Lord Vincent, suffered themselves to be deceived by him.

Presently he arose, bent toward the door and peered out, and, seeing that the coast was clear, he went out with his stealthy, cat-like step, and stole softly to the room of Mrs. Dugald.

She was in her boudoir.

He entered without knocking, locked the door behind him, and went and sat down by her side.

"What now?" she inquired, looking up.

"What now? Why, all is lost unless we act promptly!"

"I said it."

"Faustina, she has missed Katie!"

"That was a matter of course."

"But she suspects her fate."

"What care we what she suspects? She can prove nothing," said Mrs. Dugald contemptuously.

"Faustina, she can prove everything if she follows up the clew she has found. Listen. She was in the hall, near the door, when the deed was done! She heard the struggle and the cry and a part of our conversation."

"We shall all be guillotined!" cried the woman, starting to her feet and standing before him in deadly terror.

"We have no guillotining in England; but hanging is equally or even more disagreeable."

"How can you talk so when my bones are turning to gristle and my heart to jelly with the fright!" cried Mrs. Dugald.

"I jest to reassure you. If we act with promptitude there will be no danger; not in the least. I have thrown her off the scent for the present; I have told her that the noise, the struggle, the cry, and the exclamation she heard were nothing but this—that you were suffering from an attack of hysterics, and that I was trying to control and soothe you. I told her that I knew nothing whatever of the fate of her gorilla; and I did not spare the most solemn oaths to assure her of the truth of my statement."

"Good! but was she assured?"

"Not fully. She is confused, bewildered, perplexed, thrown out of her reckoning and off the track; and before she has time to recover herself, collect her faculties, and get upon the scent again, we must act. We must draw the net around her. We must place her in a position in which her character as a witness against you would he totally vitiated. To do this we must hasten the denouement of the plot."

"That plot which will rid me of my rival and make me—me—Lady Vincent!" exclaimed the siren, her eyes sparkling with anticipated triumph.

"Yes, my angel, yes! And I would it were to-morrow!"

"Ah, but, in the meanwhile, if I should be found out and guillotined!" she cried, with a shudder.

"Hanged, my angel, hanged; not guillotined! I told you we do not guillotine people in England."

"Ah—h—h!" shrieked the guilty woman, covering her face with her hands.

"But I tell you there is no danger, my love; none at all, if we do but act promptly and firmly. The time is ripe. The plot is ripe. She herself walks into the trap, by insisting on staying at home this evening, instead of accompanying us to the theater. I have sent the carriage for Mrs. MacDonald. She will come to luncheon with us, and afterwards go with us to the play. My lady will remain at home, by her own request."

"Does Frisbie know the part he is to play?"

"Yes; but not the precise hour of his debut. That I shall teach him to-day. He will be well up in his lesson by this evening, you may depend."

"Ah, then we shall finish the work to-night!"

"We shall finish it to-night."

"But Mrs. MacDonald—will she not be in the way?"

"No; as I shall arrange matters, she will be of the greatest use and help to us, without knowing it. First, as a most respectable chaperon for you, and, secondly, as a most indubitable witness of the fall of Lady Vincent."

"Good! good! I see! To-night, then, she shall be cast down from her proud pedestal. And to-morrow—"

"To-morrow she shall be dismissed from the castle."

"But then I shall have to go, too. I could not stay—the world would talk."

"No, Faustina, you shall not go. I shall go and leave you here, and invite Mrs. MacDonald to remain and bear you company until—until I shall be free, my angel, to return and make you my wife."

She clapped her hands with great glee and eagerly demanded:

"And when will that be? Oh, when will that be? How soon? how soon?"

"It may be weeks; it may be months; for the Divorce Courts are proverbially slow. But the time will come at length; for I have taken every measure to insure perfect success."

CHAPTER XXX

A NIGHT OF HORROR.

He threw his sting into a poisonous libel

And on the honor of—oh God!—his wife,

The nearest, dearest part of all men's honor,
Left a base slur to pass from month to mouth,

Of loose mechanics with all foul comments,

Of villainous jests and blasphemies obscene;

While sneering nobles in more polished guise

Whispered the tale and smiled upon the lie.

—Byron.

Claudia passed a weary day. She did not cease in her efforts to discover some clew to the disappearance of old Katie. But all her efforts were fruitless of success.

Early in the afternoon the carriage that was sent for Mrs. MacDonald returned, bringing that lady.

Claudia did not go down into the drawing room to receive her; she considered Mrs. Dugald's companion, whatever her pretensions might be, no proper associate for Lady Vincent. She met the visitor, however, at dinner, which was served some hours earlier than usual in order to give the play-going party time enough to reach their destination before the rising of the curtain. She found Mrs. MacDonald to be a thin, pale, shabby woman, about forty years of age; one of those poor, harmless, complacent creatures who, when they can de so without breaking any law of God or man, are willing to compromise a good deal of their self-respect to secure privileges which they could not otherwise enjoy.

And though Mrs. MacDonald was a descendant of the renowned "Lords of the Isles," and was as proud of her lineage as any aristocrat alive, yet she did not hesitate to accept an invitation, to go to the theater with Lord Vincent, who was called a "fast" man, and Mrs. Dugald, who was more than a suspected woman. Claudia treated this lady with the cold politeness that the latter could neither enjoy nor complain of. Immediately after dinner the party left for Banff.

Few good women have ever been so distressingly misplaced as Claudia was; therefore few could understand the hourly torture she suffered from the mere presence of her vicious companions, or the infinite sense of relief she felt in being rid of them, if only for one evening. She felt the atmosphere the purer for their absence, and breathed more freely than she had done for many days.

She soon left the drawing room, whose atmosphere was infected and disturbed with memories of Mrs. Dugald, and retired to her own boudoir, where all was comparatively pure and peaceful.

A deep bay-window from this room overhung the sea. There was a softly cushioned semicircular sofa around this window, and a round mosaic table within it.

Claudia drew aside the golden-brown curtains and sat down to watch the gray expanse of ocean, over which the night was now closing.

While gazing abstractedly out at sea she was thinking of Katie. Now that the darkening influence of Mrs. Dugald's and Lord Vincent's presence was withdrawn from her sphere, she was enabled to think clearly and decide firmly. Now that the viscount no longer stood before her, exercising his diabolical powers of duplicity upon her judgment, she no longer believed his protestations of ignorance in regard to Katie's fate. On the contrary, she felt convinced that he knew all about it. She did not now suppose, what her first frenzied terrors had suggested, that Katie had been murdered, but that she had been abducted, or confined, to prevent her from divulging some secret to the prejudice of the viscount of which she had become possessed. For Claudia had read the viscount's character aright, and she knew that though he would not hesitate to break every commandment in the Decalogue when he could do so with impunity, yet he would not commit any crime that would jeopardize his own life or liberty. Therefore she knew he had not murdered Katie; but she believed that he had "sequestrated" her in some way.

Having come to this conclusion, Claudia next considered what her own duty was in the premises. Clearly it was for her to take every measure for the deliverance of her faithful servant, no matter how difficult or repugnant those measures should be.

Therefore she resolved that early the next morning she would order the carriage and go on her own responsibility and lodge information with the police of the mysterious disappearance of her servant and the suspicious circumstances that attended her evanishment. Claudia knew that the eye of the police was still on the castle, because it was believed to hold the undetected murderer of Ailsie Dunbar, and that, therefore, their action upon the present event would be prompt and keen. She knew, also, that the investigation would bring much exposure and scandal to the castle and its inmates; and that it would enrage Lord Vincent and result in the final separation of herself and the viscount. But why, she asked herself, should she hesitate on that account?

The price for which she had sold herself had not been paid. She had her empty title, but no position. She was not a peeress among peeresses; not a queen of beauty and of fashion, leading the elite of society in London. Ah, no! she was a despised and neglected wife, wasting the flower of her youth in a remote and dreary coast castle, and daily insulted and degraded by the presence of an unprincipled rival.

Claudia was by this time so worn out in body and spirit, so thoroughly wearied and sickened of her life in the castle, that she only desired to get away with her servants and pass the remainder of her days in peaceful obscurity.

And her contemplated act of complaining to the authorities was to be her first step towards that end. Having resolved upon this measure, Claudia felt more at ease. She drew the curtains of her window, and seated herself in her favorite easy-chair before the bright, sea-coal fire, and rang for tea. Sally brought the waiter up to her mistress, and remained in attendance upon her.

"Has anything been heard of Katie yet?" inquired Lady Vincent.

"No, ma'am, nothing at all," answered Sally through her sobs.

"Don't cry; tell them when you go down, to keep up the search through the neighborhood; and if she is not forthcoming before to-morrow morning, I will take such steps as shall insure her discovery," said Lady Vincent, as she sipped her tea.

Sally only wept in reply.

"Remove this service now. And you need not come up again this evening unless you have news to bring me of Katie, for I need to be alone," said Lady Vincent, as she sat her empty cup upon the waiter.

Sally took the service from the room.

And the viscountess wheeled her chair around to the fire, placed her feet upon the fender, and yielded her wearied and distracted spirit up to the healing and soothing influences of night and solitude. As she sat there, the words of a beautiful hymn glided into her memory. Often before this evening, lying alone and wakeful upon her bed,—feeling the great blessing night brought her, in isolating her entirely from her evil companions, and drawing her into a purer sphere, feeling all the sweet and holy influences of night around her,—she had soothed her spirit to rest repeating the words of Mr. Longfellow's hymn:

Oh, Holy Night! from thee I learn to bear

What souls have borne before,

Thou lay'st thy fingers on the lips of care

And they complain no more.

Peace! Peace! Orestes-like I breathe this prayer,

Descend with broad-winged flight,

The welcome, the thrice prayed-for, the most fair,

The best beloved Night!"

She repeated it now. And it soothed her like a benediction,

A solitary night in her own boudoir would not seem to promise much enjoyment; yet Claudia was happier, because more peaceful now than she had ever seen since her first arrival at Castle Cragg.

She sat on, letting the hours pass calmly and silently over her, until the clock struck ten. Then to her surprise she heard a knocking at the outer hall door, followed by the sound of an arrival, and of many footsteps hastening up the stairs.

Claudia arose to her feet in astonishment, and at the same moment heard the voice of the viscount without, saying in ruffianly tones:

"Burst open the door then! Don't you see it is locked on the inside?" And with a violent kick the door of Claudia's boudoir, which certainly was not locked, was thrown open, and Lord Vincent, with inflamed cheeks and blood-shot eyes, strode into the room, followed by Mrs. Dugald, Mrs. MacDonald, and old Cuthbert.

"Keep the door, sir! Let no one pass out!" roared the viscount to his butler, who immediately shut the door and placed himself against it.

"My lord!" exclaimed Claudia, in indignant amazement, "what is the meaning of this violence?"

"It means, my lady, that you are discovered, run to earth, entrapped, cunning vixen as you are!" exclaimed the viscount, with an air of vindictive triumph.

Mrs. Dugald laughed scornfully.

Mrs. MacDonald turned up her chin contemptuously.

Old Cuthbert groaned aloud.

Claudia looked from one to the other, and then said:

"My lord, you and your friends appear to have been supping on very bad wine; I would counsel you to retire and sleep off its effects."

"Ha, ha, my lady! You take things coolly! I compliment you on your self-possession!" sneered the viscount.

Her heart nearly bursting with anger, Claudia threw herself into her chair, and with difficulty controlling her emotions, said:

"Will your lordship do me the favor to explain your errand in this room, and then retire with your party as speedily as possible?"

"Certainly, my lady, that is but reasonable, and is also just what I intended to do," said the viscount, bowing with mock courtesy.

And he drew a letter from his pocket and held it in his hand, while he continued to speak, addressing himself now to the whole party assembled in Lady Vincent's boudoir.

"It is necessary to premise, friends, that my marriage with this lady was a hasty, ill-advised, and inconsiderate one; unacceptable to my family, unfortunate for myself, humiliating in its results. For some weeks past my suspicions were aroused to the fact that all was not right between the viscountess and another member of my establishment. Cuthbert, keep that door! Let no one rush past!"

"Ah, me laird; dinna fash yoursel'! I'll keep it!" groaned the old man, putting his back firmly against the door.

"Lord Vincent," exclaimed Claudia haughtily, "I demand that you retract your words. You know them to be as false—as false as—yourself. They could not be falser than that!"

"I will prove every word that I have spoken to be true!" replied the viscount. Then continuing his story, he said: "This morning certain circumstances strengthened my suspicions. Among others the persistence with which her ladyship, though in good health, and with no other engagement at hand, resolved and adhered to her resolution to remain at home and miss the rare opportunity of seeing Mr. and Mrs. Dean in their great parts of Macbeth and Lady Macbeth. Suspecting that her ladyship had some unlawful design in thus denying herself an amusement of which I know her to be excessively fond, and preferring to spend the evening at home, of which I know she is excessively tired, I ordered my faithful old servant, Cuthbert, to watch—not his mistress, Lady Vincent, but another individual—"

Here old Cuthbert interrupted the speaker with deep groans.

Claudia remained sitting in her chair, with her face as pale as death, her teeth firmly set, and her eyes fiercely fixed upon the face of the man who was thus maligning her honor.

He continued:

"How well my suspicions were founded, and how faithfully old Cuthbert has performed his duty, you will soon see. It appears that we had but just started on our drive, when Cuthbert, watching the motions of the suspected person, saw him steal towards Lady Vincent's apartments. The old man glided after him, and, unseen himself, saw him, the miscreant, enter Lady Vincent's boudoir."

"It is as false as Satan! Oh, you infamous wretch, what form of punishment would be ignominious enough for you!" cried Claudia, springing to her feet, her eyes flaming with consuming wrath.

But the viscount approached and laid his hand upon her shoulder, and forced her down into her seat again.

And Claudia, too proud to resist, where resistance would be but a vain, unseemly struggle, dropped into her chair and sat perfectly still—a marble statue, with eyes of flame.

The viscount, with fiendish coolness, continued:

"Cuthbert watched and listened on the outside of the door for some time, and then, thinking that the intruder had no intention of leaving the room, he went and wrote a note, and sent it by one of the grooms, mounted on a swift horse, to me. Ladies, you both saw the boy enter the theater and hand me this note. Your interest was aroused, but I only told you that I was summoned in haste to my lady's apartments, and begged you to come with me—"

"And I thought her ladyship was perhaps ill, and needed experienced help, or I should certainly not have followed your lordship into this room," said Mrs. MacDonald, who, however, made no motion to withdraw.

Mrs. Dugald's insulting laugh rang through the room.

"I beg pardon, madam; I know this is not a pleasant scene for a lady to take part in, but I needed witnesses, and necessity has no law. If you will permit me, I will read the note I received," said the viscount, with a diabolical sneer, as he unfolded the paper. He read as follows:

"'It is a' as your lairdship suspicioned. If your lairdship will come your ways hame at ance, you will find the sinful pair in me leddy's boudoir.'"

The note had neither name nor date.

"You know," pursued Lord Vincent, "that we hurried home; you saw me speak aside with Cuthbert in the hall; in that short interview he informed me that he had remained upon the watch, and that the villain had not yet left Lady Vincent's apartments; that he was still within them!"

"Oh, Cuthbert! I believed you to be an honest old man! It is awful to find you in league with these wretches!" exclaimed Claudia, in sorrowful indignation.

"Ou, me leddy! I'd rather these auld limbs o' mine had been streaket in death, ere I had to use them in siccan uncanny wark! But the Lord's will be dune!" groaned the old man, is such sincere grief that Claudia was thoroughly perplexed.

And all this time the viscount was continuing his cool, devlish monologue.

"It was for this reason, ladies, that I burst open the door and called you in; and it was to prevent the escape of the fellow that I placed Cuthbert on guard at the door. Now, my lady, that you understand the cause of the 'violence' of which you just now complained, you will please to permit me to search the room. You cannot complain that I have acted with unseemly haste. I have proceeded with great deliberation. In fact, your accomplice has had abundant time to escape, if he had the means."

"Lord Vincent, these outrages shall cost you your life!" exclaimed Claudia, in the low, deep, stern key of concentrated passion.

"All in good time, my lady," sneered the viscount, commencing the humiliating search. He looked in the recess of the bay window; peeped behind curtains; opened closets: and finally drew a large easy-chair from the corner of the room.

"Pray, whom do you expect to find concealed in my apartment, my lord?" demanded Claudia, white with rage.

"My respectable valet, the good Mr. Frisbie. And here he is!" replied the viscount sarcastically.

And to Claudia's horror and amazement he drew the trembling wretch from his concealment and hurled him into the center of the room, where he stood with dangling arms and bending legs, pale and quaking, but whether with real or assumed fear Claudia could not tell.

"How came this fellow in my room?" she demanded, in consternation.

"Aye, sure enough! how did he come here?" sneered Lord Vincent.

Mrs. Dugald laughed.

Mrs. MacDonald raised both her hands in horror.

"Come! perhaps he'll tell us why he came here! Confess, you scoundrel! Say what brought you here!" exclaimed the viscount, suddenly changing his tone from cool irony to burning rage, as he seized and shook his valet.

"Oh, my lord, I will! I will! only let go my collar!" gasped the man, shaking or affecting to shake.

"Confess, then, you rascal! What brought you here?"

"Oh, my lord, mercy! mercy! I will confess! I will!"

"Do it, then, you villain!"

"Oh, my lord, I—I come—at—at my lady's invitation, my lord!"

"You came at Lady Vincent's invitation?" cried the viscount, shaking the speaker.

"Y-y-yes, my lord!" stammered the valet.

"You—came—at my invitation?" demanded Lady Vincent haughtily, fixing her eyes of fire on the creatures's dace.

"Yes, my lady, you know I did! It is no use for us to deny it now! Ah, my lady, I alwasy warned you that we should be found out, and now sure enough we are!" replied Frisbie.

Claudia clasped her hands and raised her eyes to Heaven with the look of one who would have called down fire upon the heads of these fiends in human form.

Lord Vincent continued to question his valet.

"Does Lady Vincent makes a practice of inviting you to her apartments?"

"Y-y-yes, my lord!"

"How often?"

"Wh-wh-whenever your lordship's abscence seems to make it safe."

"Then I am to understand that you are a favored suitor of Lady Vincent's?"

"Yes, yes, my lord! Oh, my lord, I know I have done very wrong. I know I—"

"Do you know that you deserve death, sir?" demanded the viscount, in a voice of thunder.

"Oh, my lord, mercy! mercy! I know I am a great sinner! I could kill myself for it, if it wasn't for fear of losing my soul! All I can do now is to repent and confess! I do repent from the bottom of my heart; and I will confess everything! Yes, I will tell your lordship all about it and throw myself on your lordship's mercy! cried this remorseless villain.

"Enough! I wish to hear no more from you just at present. Your confession would be scarcely fir for the ears of these ladies. your testimony must be reserved for a future occasion," said the viscont. And then turning to Claudia with the coolest and most insulting hauteur, he said:

"And now! what have you to say to all this, my lady?"

Claudia advanced into the center of the room; her step was firm; her head erect; her cheeks burning; her eyes blazing; her whole form dilated and lifted to grandeur; she looked a very Nemesis—a very Goddess of Retribute Justice, as throwing her consuming glance around upon the group, who fairly quailed before her, she said:

"What have 'I to say to all this'? I say, Lord Vincent, be assured that you shall die for these insults! I say that I know this to be a foul conspiracy against my honor, and as feeble as it is foul! Oh, reptiles! base, venomous reptiles! Do you really suppose that the honor of a pure woman is of such a weak and sickly nature as to be destroyed by the poison of your calumnies? Fools! I shall leave this place for London tomorrow! I shall go at once to the American Legation and see our American minister, who is an old friend of my father. I will tell him all that has taken place and come to my knowledge, since I have lived under this accursed and polluted roof. I will advise with him as to the best measures to be taken for the discovery of my poor old servant, Katie, and for the unmasking and prosecuting to conviction the wretches who have conspired against my honor. What! I am the daughter of Randolph Merlin! The blood of an Indian king, who never spared a foe, burns along my veins! Take heed—beware—escape while you may! My lord, your fate shall find you, even though it follow you to the farthest ends of the earth! You are warned! And now, as a few moments since, my request that you would withdraw your accomplices from the room was disregarded, I must retire to my chamber."

And with the air and manner of an outraged queen, Claudia left the boudoir.

"Friends," said Lord Vincent, turning to his female companions, "your testimony will be hereafter required in this case. I beg you, therefore, in the name of justice, to make a mental note of what you have seen and heard to-night. Remember Lady Vincent's strange conduct in declining to accompany us to the theater and resolving to stay at home; remember the note that was brought me in my box and our unexpected return home; remember particularly that the door leading into Lady Vincent's apartments was fastened on the inside, and that I had to break it open; remember also that we found the wretch, Frisbie, concealed in the room, and that he made a full confession."

"It is not likely that we shall forget it, my lord!" said Mrs. MacDonald gravely.

"No! what horror!" cried Mrs. Dugald.

"And now, ladies, I will no longer detain you from your necessary rest," said the viscount, ringing the bell, which the housekeeper, looking amazed, scandalized, and full of curiosity, answered.

"Murdock, show this lady, Mrs. MacDonald, to the blue suite of rooms, and place yourself at her service. Madam, pray order any refreshments you may require. Good-night, madam. Sister, good-night!"

"Good-night! good-night, my lord! I shall pray that you shall be able to bear this great misfortune with the fortitude becoming a man," said Mrs. MacDonald.

"Good-night, brother!" said Mrs. Dugald.

When the "ladies," attended by the housekeeper, had left the room and were quite out of hearing, Lord Vincent turned to his accomplice and whispered:

"You did that capitally, Frisbie. You would make an excellent actor. Anyone on earth, looking at you this evening and not knowing the truth, would have thought you were dying of mortification and terror—you shook and faltered so naturally."

"Oh, my lord!" returned the valet, in modest deprecation of this praise.

"You did; but now I wish you to tell me. How did you manage to awaken the suspicions of old Cuthbert? How did you manage to draw his eyes upon you—and draw him on to watch you until you entered the room without seeming to know that you were watched?"

"I tell you, my lord, that part of my task was hard. But I contrived to do it by pretending to watch him, and affecting to dodge out of sight every time he saw me. This excited his curiosity, and caused him to conceal himself in order to watch me. When I knew that he had done this, I began to creep towards my lady's apartments, knowing full well that he was stealing after me."

"But how did you contrive to get into the boudoir?"

"I wore list slippers, and your lordship knows that the thick carpets return no echo to the footstep, and that the doors open and shut silently. First I peeped through the keyhole, and I saw that her ladyship was sitting within the curtained recess of the hay window, looking out at sea, her attention being absorbed there, and her back being towards the door. So I just softly opened the door, entered the room, closing it after me and concealed myself behind your lordship's own great easy-chair, that I knew was never drawn from its dark corner,"

"For the good reason that the owner is never there to occupy it," sneered the viscount.

"Just so, my lord. And now I have told your lordship exactly how I managed matters, so as to make old Cuthbert our accomplice without his ever suspecting it."

"Old Cuthbert must think you a grand rascal."

"He does me great honor, your lordship."

"There! now go about your business, Frisbie. Of course you must get away from here by the morning's first light. It must be supposed that you have been kicked out. Remain in the neighborhood of Banff. You will be wanted as a witness."

"Yes, my lord; but in the meantime-I have saved nothing. I have no means."

"Oh, you mercenary rascal! You have saved your neck from the gallows, if you have saved nothing else. But here are ten pounds for present needs; and I will take care not to see you want for the future. Now be off with you. Your longer stay will excite surprise and conjecture."

"Your lordship is too good!" said the caitiff, bowing himself out.

Lord Vincent soon after left the boudoir and went downstairs. In the hall he found old Cuthbert up and waiting.

"You here yet, Cuthbert? Why don't you go to bed?"

"Ou, me laird, I couldna sleep wi' the thought o' siccan dishonor befa'ing the house!" groaned the old man.

"The dishonor attaches but to one person, and the house will be rid of it when she is cast forth," said the viscount.

"Ou, me laird! for pity, dinna do that! Send her ways back to her ain countrie. She's but a wee bit lassie after a'! And she's awa' fra fayther and mither, and a' her folk! And 'deed I canna bring mysel' to think that ill o' her, neither! 'deed no!"

"Cuthbert, are you out of your senses? What are you talking about? The man was found concealed in her room, and being discovered, confessed his guilt," said Lord Vincent.

"Aye, me laird, but she denied all knowledge of him; and she looked grand wi' the majesty of truth, me laird. Folk dinna look that way when they're leeing. And the lad Frisbie looked just as if he were leeing. Folk dinna look as he looked when they're telling the truth."

"Cuthbert, you are an old dolt! We do not depend on Frisbie's word, exclusively. We have the fact of finding him in the room."

"I misdoubt he e'en just hid himsel' in there for the purpose of robbery, unbeknownst to the leddy. And then cast the blame on her to help to shield himsel', the villain!"

"Cuthbert, you are in your dotage!" exclaimed the viscount angrily.

"It may be sae, my laird; but I canna think shame o' the leddy! Nay, I canna! Howbeit! richt or wrong, the shame has come till her. Sae, me laird, in marcy take an auld man's counsel, and e'en just gie her her dower, and send her her ways to her feyther's house."

"Cuthbert, your brain is softening. Hark ye! Get yourself off to bed."

"Aye, me laird," said the old man meekly, as he withdrew to his den; "but I canna think sin o' the leddy! nay, nay, I canna!"

When all the house was still Lord Vincent stole to the apartments of Mrs. Dugald.

"Oh! I have been waiting for you so long and so impatiently," she said, as she placed him a chair at her dressing-room fireside.

"I came as soon as all was quiet. Oh, Faustina, how I am sinking my soul in sin and infamy for your sake!" exclaimed Lord Vincent, as a momentary qualm of shame sickened his heart.

"Do you repent it, then?" she inquired, with a glance that brought him to her feet, a slave once more, "do you repent it?"

"No, my angel, no! though we go to perdition, we go together! And it is joy and glory to lose myself for you—for you!" he exclaimed passionately, and attempting to embrace her.

"Ha! stop! beware! You are not free yet—nor am I your wife!" exclaimed the artful woman, withdrawing herself from his advances.

"But I shall be free soon, and you shall be my wife. You know it, Faustina. You know that I am your slave. You can do with me as you please. Then why be so cruel as to refuse me even one kiss?"

"That I may have nothing to reproach myself with in after time—when I shall be Lady Vincent. That you may not have to blush for your second viscountess, as you have had to blush for your first."

"Oh, Faustina, how coldly cruel and calculating you sometimes seem to me! Why do I love you so insanely that you possess my very soul? Why is it, beautiful witch?"

"Because I love you so much, mon ami."

"You do, you do! You really love me, 'Tina?"

"Oh, I do! You know I do! more than life!"

"Then let Satan have me after death! I do not care!" replied this desperate fool.

"Hush! this is a dangerous topic. It makes me reel. Give me a glass of water, Malcolm, and let us talk of something else," said the wily siren.

When she had drunk the water the viscount brought her she said:

"There is a question I have been dying to ask you all day, but I could get no good chance without the risk of being overheard—and that would have been ruin."

"What is the question, Faustina?"

The woman turned so deadly white that her black eyes gleamed like great balls of jet from a face of stone, as sinking her voice to the lowest key, she said:

"What have you done with it?"

"With what, Faustina?"

"With the dead body of the black woman?"

The viscount slowly lowered his finger and significantly pointed downward.

"Down there?" whispered Faustina.

The viscount nodded.

"Where we left it?"

"Yes."

"Oh, but that is not safe. There is suspicion. Suppose there should be a search; suppose there should be a discovery?" cried the woman in alarm. For she, who was not afraid of committing the worst crimes, was terribly afraid of meeting their consequences.

"Be at ease. I shall not leave her there long; the sea is near at hand," whispered the viscount.

"Yes, you may cast her into the sea; but the sea sometimes casts back its dead—especially when they have been murdered," shuddered the woman.

"The sea will not cast her back," said the viscount significantly.

"Oh. you will tie a heavy weight to her body! But when will you do it? Oh, I am in agony, until that is removed!"

"Be still! I hope to have an opportunity of removing it tonight."

"But you cannot do it alone. Let me help you. I would rather help you."

"No, I can and will do it without your help. Do you think, my angel, that I would permit you to engage in such dreadful work?"

"I helped you to stop her breath," said the woman hoarsely.

"That was a work of necessity that presented itself suddenly before us. This is different."

"But I would rather help. I would rather be present. I would rather see, for then I should know to a certainty that it was gone," she insisted.

"Can you not trust me?"

"No, no, I cannot trust anyone when my head is in danger of the guillotine."

"I tell you there are no guillotines in England."

"The other thing, then, which is worse, because it is more disgraceful. Hanging by the neck until one is dead! Ugh! No, I cannot trust you, Malcolm, where so much is at stake," said the woman, with a terrible shudder.

"You have no confidence in me then? And yet you say you love me. Why, confidence is the very soul of love."

"Oh, yes, I love you, Malcolm. I love you more than words can tell. And it is for your safety as well as for my own that I am so cautious. And I have confidence in you, Malcolm. Only, being alone, you may not be able to do the work effectually. I must help you. The house is all still; everybody has retired; can we not go now and remove it?"

"No, not now; there is a vessel lying at anchor close under the shore. We must wait until she moves off."

"And the vessel may lay there a whole week. And in the meantime what becomes of the body?" exclaimed Faustina, her eyes wild with apprehension.

"I am assured by those who know, that the vessel will sail with the first tide to-morrow morning. So be tranquil. And now, Faustina, there is another subject which we must settle to-night. Lady Vincent leaves the castle early to-morrow morning. That is necessary; and though it cleaves my heart in two to part with you, I must do it for a season. The world must have no cause to talk of you and me, Faustina; of you, especially, for of you it would be the most likely to talk."

"Why of me?" inquired the ex-opera singer testily.

"Because, my dearest, you have more beauty and genius and fame than the world ever forgives in a woman," answered the viscount artfully.

"Oh!" said the siren, with an air of arch incredulity.

"And now, Faustina, it shall be for you to decide. Shall you remain here, with Mrs. MacDonald for a companion and chaperon, while I go to London to take the preliminary steps towards the divorce; or shall you go to Brighton or Torquay, or any other watering-place on the South Coast?"

Mrs. Dugald was very astute; she answered promptly:

"Oh, I will remain here. And then you will not be jealous. There is no one here to admire me except Mrs. MacDonald and old Cuthbert and Murdock."

"Bless you! Bless you! I do believe you love me because you anticipate my wishes so readily," said this devotee fervently.

"And now you must go, and say good-night! It is two o'clock in the morning and I am tired to death. And mind about that below, you know. And the first safe opportunity you have, come to me to help you remove it. Mind!" said Faustina, raising her finger.

"I will mind. Good-night! What, no kiss, even for good-night?" he said, as she recoiled from his offered salute.

"No. I reserve my kisses for my husband," she answered archly. Thus this evil woman, steeped to the lips in sin, affected the prude with the man she wished to secure. And while making and receiving the most ardent protestations of love, disallowed the very slightest caress.

The viscount, baffled and dissatisfied, but more determined than ever to marry this tantalizing beauty, left the room and retired to his own chamber.

Mr. Frisbie's work was over there, and Mr. Frisbie himself was absent, of course.

CHAPTER XXXI

THE CASTLE VAULT.

It was more dark and lone, that vault,

Than the worst dungeon cell,

A hermit built it for his fault,

In penitence to dwell:

This den, which chilling every sense

Of feeling, hearing, sight,

Was called the Vault of Penitence,

Excluding air and light.

'Twas by an ancient prelate made

The place of burial for such dead

As having died in mortal sin

Might not be laid the church within.

'Twas next a place of punishment;

Where if so loud a shriek were sent,

As reached the upper air,

The hearers blessed themselves and said

The spirits of the sinful dead

Bemoaned their torments there.

—Scott.

There was opening from Lord Vincent's dressing room a bay window, having a balcony on the outside, overhanging the sea. The viscount took a night telescope, opened the window, and stepped out upon the balcony. He adjusted the glass and swept the coast. Nothing was to be seen but the solitary vessel that lay at anchor almost under the castle walls.

"The coast is clear," said the viscount to himself, as he re-entered the room and replaced the telescope.

Then wrapping himself in a large maud and pulling a slouched hat over his eyes, he left the room, descended the stairs and went out.

He took the way down to the sands at the extreme base of the promontory. The path that led down the side of the cliff was steep, slippery, and very dangerous even at noonday. And this was one of the darkest hours of the night that precedes the dawn. And the path was more perilous than ever. But the viscount was Highland-bred, and his step was as sure on the steep mountain edge as on the level plain. He reached the foot of the precipice in safety and stood upon the sands and drew from his pocket a small whistle, which he placed to his lips and blew a shrill call.

It was answered from the vessel at anchor. And soon a boat was put off from her side, and rowed swiftly to the shore.

"Is that you, Costo?" inquired the viscount of the man who jumped ashore.

"No, senor; it is Paolo."

"The mate?"

"Yes, senor."

"Where is Costo?"

"On board the vessel, senor."

"What have you brought this time?"

"Cuban tobacco, Jamaica spirits, and some rich West Indian fabrics for ladies' dresses. A cask of spirits and a box of cigars have gone up to the castle. Old Mr. Cuthbert took them in."

"All right; but I have some business now at hand that Cuthbert must know nothing about. For instance, he is in ignorance, and must remain in ignorance, of my visit to the beach to-night."

"We can be silent as the grave, senor."

"Have you had any trouble from the coastguard?"

"No, senor; how could we? Is not your excellency the protector of the poor?"

The viscount laughed.

"It is true," he said, "that the guards at the nearest station are in my power, and know better than to pry too closely into the concerns of any vessels that run into my castle cove; but beyond their domain I cannot protect you; so be cautious."

"We are cautious, senor. So cautious that we shall sail with the first tide."

"For Havana?"

"For Havana, senor."

"Well, now I wish you to take me to the vessel. I must see the captain."

"Surely, senor," said the obsequious mate, as the viscount stepped into the boat.

"Give way, men! Back to the brigantine," said the mate. And the men laid themselves to their oars, and soon reached the vessel's side.

Lord Vincent was received with the greatest respect by the captain, who came obsequiously to the starboard gangway to meet him.

"Let us go into your cabin at once, Costo; I have business to discuss with you," said the viscount.

"Surely, senor," replied the captain, leading the way down to a small, snug cabin.

It was flanked each side by two comfortable berths, and furnished with a buffet at one end and a round table and two chairs in the center.

"Will the senor deign to seat himself?" said the captain, offering one of these chairs to the visitor and taking the other himself.

There were decanters of spirits, glasses, cigars, pipes, and tobacco on the table.

"Will the senor deign to taste this rum, which is of fine quality, and try one of these cigars, which are at once so strong and so delicate of aroma?"

For an answer the viscount poured out a liberal portion of the spirits and quaffed it almost at a draught, and then lighted a cigar and commenced smoking. He smoked away for a few minutes, during which Costo waited respectfully for him to open communications.

At length the viscount spoke:

"Costo, in your island of Cuba able-bodied men and women of the negro race command good prices, do they not?"

"Yes, senor—great prices, since your illustrious statesmen have abolished the African slave-trade over all the ocean."

"For instance, how much would a fine young man, of say twenty-one years of age, bring?"

"From two to five thousand dollars, according to his health, good looks, and accomplishments. I have known a likely boy of fourteen to sell for three thousand dollars. He is now one of the best cooks on the island."

"Humph! then I should say the one I speak of would bring near the highest price you have named. How much would a healthy, handsome girl of eighteen bring?"

"Mulatress or quadroon?"

"Oh, neither. She is a negress, black as the blackest satin, but with a skin as smooth and soft—a Venus carved in jet."

"From a thousand to two thousand dollars, perhaps, as she is a negress but if she were a mulatress she would bring more, or if a quadroon most of all—other things being equal."

"And how much would a stout, healthy, strong-minded woman of fifty bring?"

"That depends upon other circumstances, senor. If, together with her health and intelligence, she should be a good housekeeper and nurse, as women of her age are apt to be, why, then she might bring from nine to twelve hundred dollars."

"Well, Costo, I have three such negroes as I have just described to dispose of."

"Yes, senor? But you are English and this is England!" exclaimed the buccaneer in amazement.

"Scotch—and Scotland. But, no matter—it amounts to the same thing. Will you buy my negroes at a bargain?"

"Pardon, senor, but I do not understand. I thought there was no buying and selling of slaves in England."

"Of course there is not. And there is no free trade in England. Both negro-trading and smuggling are illegal. Yet, as you manage to drive a pretty profitable business in the latter, you might speculate a little in the former. Eh?"

"But, pardon, senor. I am not in the slave-trade."

"What of that? When such a splendid opportunity of doing a fine stroke of business offers, you might step aside from your regular routine of trade to make a considerable sum of money, might you not?"

"If the senor would condescend to explain himself I might understand the affair he proposes to me. I do not yet comprehend how he can have slaves to sell in England," said the captain respectfully.

"Perhaps another would not be able to understand how you manage to import articles upon which heavy duty is laid, free of all duty whatever?" said the viscount, indulging in a sneer.

"If the senor would deign to make his meaning clear?"

"Well, the senor will endeavor to do so. Though more depends upon your perspicacity than his perspicuity. Can you comprehend that when I was on a visit to the States I married a young American lady, who owned a large number of slaves, who, of course, passed into my possession from the marriage day?"

"Oh, yes, senor; that is easily understood."

"Three of these slaves, the three of which I have just spoken, being favorites of their mistress, attended her to this country."

"And became free from the moment they touched English ground, senor; for such is English law."

"We are not talking of law—though I suppose there is as much law for slavery as there is for smuggling. But the less you and I say about law the better. So just suppose we leave law entirely out of the argument."

"With all my heart, senor; if the senor desires it to be left out."

"'The senor' does. So now, then, we shall get along better, These three negroes are at Castle Cragg. At your own estimation, the lot must be worth eight thousand dollars—sixteen hundred pounds in our money; now you shall have them for six hundred pounds—that is, three thousand dollars of your money; and you will thereby make a profit of one thousand pounds, or five thousand dollars, which is nearly two hundred per cent. Come, what do you say?"

"Senor, we are to leave law out of the argument?"

"Of course."

"Then, if I had these negroes on board this vessel, which is to sail with the morning tide, I would give the senor his price for them."

"You shall have them all on board within the hour."

"Good! but, pardon, senor, a thought strikes me!"

"What is it?"

"Since these negroes are favorite servants of the illustrious Senora?"

"What then?"

"She will not consent to part with them."

"Her consent is as unnecessary as the sanction of the law. It is just because they are favorite servants—petted, pampered, and spoiled servants—that I wish to part with them. Such servants are nuisances in the family circle."

"The senor is right, always right! but—shall we have any difficulty with the negroes?"

"None whatever. You will take them in their beds."

"Will they not make an outcry and bring the house upon us?"

"My excellent but too cautious friend, did you never hear of chloroform?"

"Surely, senor."

"It is one of the greatest blessings modern science has conferred upon us. It not only saves much pain in surgical operations, but in other operations it actually saves life. The experienced burglar now, when he enters a house for the purpose of robbery, instead of cutting the throat of a wakeful inmate, simply administers chloroform, and soothes his restlessness so perfectly that he falls into a happy state of insensibility, while he, the burglar, pursues his calling undisturbed and at leisure."

"Well, senor?"

"Well, don't you understand? I will conduct you and such of your men as you can trust to the castle; admit you secretly; lead you to the bedside of the negroes, who are sure at this hour to be in a deep sleep; administer the chloroform to send them into a deeper one; and so transport them to the vessel."

"And by that time we will be ready to raise anchor and sail. And when our sleepers awake we shall be safely on our way to Cuba."

"Exactly. But no time is to be lost. Will you go now?" inquired the viscount, rising.

"Certainly," said the captain, and he went on deck to order the boat manned to go on shore.

In a few minutes it was reported ready, and the captain, the mate, and two sailors whom they supposed they could rely upon, entered it. In a very few minutes they reached the shore and left the boat.

"Leave the two sailors here with the boat; the mate will be sufficient for our purpose," said the viscount.

The captain gave the necessary directions to the boatmen. Lord Vincent, Captain Costo, and Paolo went up the narrow pass leading to the top of the cliff and entered the castle courtyard.

"Your boots are heavy; they might awaken the household, even at this hour of its deepest sleep; you must put them off here," whispered the viscount.

It was no sooner said than done. The men cast off both shoes and stockings and stood in their bare feet.

"We must keep them dry to put on again," said the mate, as he stuffed the stockings into the boots.

Then, silent as death, they stole into the castle and glided along the dark, deserted halls and up its staircases.

The viscount paused before the door of Mrs. Dugald's boudoir, and taking the maid's pass-key from its hiding place, softly unlocked and entered the room, beckoning his companions in crime to follow.

Silently he stole across the room, drew aside the crimson-satin hangings, exposed the oak-paneled walls, and touched a spring.

A secret door opened, revealing a narrow flight of stairs. Making a sign for his companions to follow, he descended.

Down many narrow flights of stairs, through many winding labyrinths, along many dark passages, the sailors followed their leader, until far down in the deepest foundations of the castle they reached a large, circular stone crypt, with many rusted iron doors around it, leading into little dungeons. On one side of this horrible place was a rude stone altar with an iron crucifix. In the center was a block. It was probably a vault which in the old and dark ages had been used for a place of secret imprisonments, executions, and burials.

Lord Vincent flashed his lantern around upon the scene and then went up to one of the grated doors, unfastened it, and entered the dungeon.

It was a small stone cavity, a hard hole, where it seemed impossible for a human being to live and breathe for an hour. And yet poor old Katie, with the wonderful tenacity of life which belongs to the pure African, had clung to existence there ever since the hour when, seeming dead, she had been dragged from the apartments of Faustina to this hideous vault.

So you see he had deceived Faustina into the belief that Katie had died in the vault from the effects of chloroform.

By the dim light of the lantern her form could now be seen squatted in the corner of the dungeon. Her knees were drawn up, her arms folded on them, and her head buried in them. She had fallen asleep; probably after long watching and fasting and the effects of mental and physical exhaustion. The entrance of the viscount did not awaken her.

"This is the woman; I was obliged to confine her here for a violent assault upon a lady of my family. She is fast asleep; but to attempt to remove her might awaken her; so we will make all sure by sending her into a deeper sleep," whispered the viscount, drawing from his pocket first a bottle of chloroform and then a piece of sponge, which he proceeded to saturate with the liquid.

But it required tact to apply it. Katie's face was buried in her arms. So he first put the lantern out of the way where it could not shine upon her, and then went and gently lifted Katie's head with one hand while he applied the sponge near her nose with the other.

"Yes, chile; I tink so too—my ladyship—whited saltpetre—Bottomy Bay," muttered Katie, who was sleeping the deep sleep of her race, and probably dreaming of her lady and her lady's dangers.

The viscount laid her head back on his own breast, put the chloroform sponge to her nose, and fitted his own slouch hat over her face in such a manner as to confine the fumes.

Poor old Katie's wide nostrils soon inhaled the whole of the deadly vapor, which acted with unusual power upon her exhausted frame, so that she speedily lay as one dead.

"Take her up! make haste! There is a shorter way out of this vault; but I could not bring you here by it because it is fastened on this side," said the viscount, leaving the den.

The captain and mate went in, and raised old Katie's unresisting form in their arms, and followed the viscount, who led them from the vault into a long stone passage, at the end of which was a door, fastened on the inside with a chain and padlock.

The viscount unlocked this door, which opened out into a rocky cave, through which they passed to an intricate, winding, and rugged labyrinth, which finally led out into the open air, on the beach near which the boat was left.

The captain and mate laid down their burden, and stretched their limbs, and took a long breath. The viscount beckoned the boatmen to approach, and they came. Then turning to the captain, he said:

"You had better order these men to take this woman immediately to the boat, and carry her across to the vessel, and lock her up in some place of safety. Then they can return for us; and in the meantime we will return to the castle for the other two."

"Yes, senor," said the captain; and he promptly gave the order.

The viscount waited until he saw Katie safely in the boat and half across on her way to the vessel, and then he beckoned his companions to follow him, and led the way back to the castle.

This time he conducted them to an old turret that had been appointed to the use of Lady Vincent's servants; it was remote from the sleeping apartments of the other domestics. The locks were without keys.

"We will take the man first," said Lord Vincent, softly opening an old oaken door and leading them into a small circular room, scantily furnished, where, upon a rude bedstead, lay poor Jim in a profound sleep. He was a fine subject for their villainous practices. He was lying on his back, with his head stretched back over his pillow, his eyes fast closed, and his mouth wide open. One touching incident in the appearance of this poor fellow was the presence of two large tears on his cheeks. He had probably lain awake all night, and just cried himself to sleep over the fate of his mother, whom his loyal heart loved so faithfully.

The viscount applied the chloroform, and Jim's sleep sunk into insensibility. The captain and the mate then raised him in their arms and bore him from the room and through the many passages and down the many stairs, and along the great hall to the outside of the castle.

They had a hard time getting him down the cliff. But they accomplished the task at last. They found the boat returned and the boatmen waiting patiently for their arrival.

"Captain, the tide serves," said one of these men.

"I know it, Jacques. We will sail in half an hour. Where did you put the woman?"

"I locked her in your cabin for the present, captain."

"Did she recover her senses?"

"No, captain."

"The devil! I hope she won't die."

"No danger, Costo; they lie insensible under the influence of chloroform sometimes for hours, and then recover in a better condition than they were before," said the viscount, hazarding an opinion on a subject of which he knew very little. "But, now, order the sailors to convey this man to the vessel and then return once more for us."

"Pardon, senor. We had better bind him first. If he should recover before he reaches the vessel he might jump out and make his escape," replied the captain, drawing a large silk handkerchief from his pocket and tying the hands of the captive firmly behind his back.

"Lend me yours, Paolo," he next requested, holding his hands out for the required article.

With this second handkerchief twisted into a rope the captain firmly tied together the feet of the captive.

Jim was now as effectually bound as if his fetters had been iron or rope; but he was beginning to show signs of recovery. The viscount saw this and applied the chloroform again, and Jim relapsed into insensibility. In this condition he was conveyed into the boat and rowed swiftly to the vessel.

Meanwhile Lord Vincent and his confederates in crime retraced their steps up the cliff.

"We must be very quick this time, for the household will soon be astir," whispered Lord Vincent eagerly, as he noticed on the eastern horizon the faint dawn of the late winter morning.

They entered the castle, which, luckily for them, was still buried in repose, and wound their circuitous way back to the turret where the last victim, poor Sally, lay.

The viscount opened the oaken door and preceded his companions into her chamber.

But, oh, horror! Sally was awake and up! She was seated on the side of her bed and in the act of putting on her shoes. On seeing the viscount enter she raised her eyes and gazed in dumb amazement.

He lost no time. Like a wild beast he sprang upon her before she could utter a cry.

Throwing one arm around her throat, with his hand upon her mouth, he forced her head back against his breast and applied the chloroform until she succumbed to its fatal power and sunk like a corpse in his arms.

Then his two accomplices took her, and by the same winding route of halls, stairs, and passages carried her out of the castle and down to the beach, where the boat was waiting to receive her. They put her into it, and the viscount, the captain, and the mate followed. In three minutes they reached the vessel, and all went on board, taking the captive girl with them.

The viscount accompanied the captain to his little office and received the six hundred pounds in gold which was the price of this last infamy.

Then the accomplices shook hands and parted.

The sailors rowed the viscount back to the shore, and then returned to their vessel. The viscount stood on the beach, watching the brigantine until she raised her anchor and made sail. And then, as it was growing light, he turned and climbed the cliff and entered the castle, wearing a smile of triumph.

CHAPTER XXXII

THE END OF CLAUDIA'S PRIDE.

Is she saved by pangs that pained her?

Is there comfort in all it cost her?

Before the world had gained her,

Before the Lord had lost her,

Or her soul had quite disdained her?

For her soul—(and this is the worst

To bear, as we well know)—

Has been watching her from the first

As closely as God could do,

And herself her life has curst!

Talk of the flames of hell,

We build, ourselves, I conceive,

The fire the fiend lights.—Well!

Believe or disbelieve,

We know more than we tell.

Owen Meredith.

After a sleepless night, whose lonely anguish would have driven almost any woman who was compelled to endure it mad, Claudia arose and rung her bell.

No one answered it.

Too impatient to wait for the tardy attendance of her servants, Claudia thrust her feet into slippers, drew on her dressing-gown, and went and opened the window-shutters to let in the morning light. Then she rang again.

Still no one obeyed the summons.

She was not alarmed. Even with the knowledge of what had gone before, she felt no uneasiness. She went to the dressing glass and loosened her hair, and let it fall all over her shoulders to relieve her burning head. And then she bathed her face in cold water. She was impatient to make her toilet and leave the castle.

She knew that all was over with her worldly grandeur; that all her splendid dreams had vanished forever; that obscurity, perhaps deepened by degradation, was all that awaited her in the future.

Wounded, bruised, and bleeding as her heart was, she felt glad to go; glad to leave the abode of splendid discord, misery, and crime, for any quiet dwelling-place. For she was utterly worn out in body, mind, and spirit.

She no longer desired wealth, rank, admiration, or even love; she only longed for peace; prayed for peace.

She knew a turbulent future threatened her; but she feebly resolved to evade it. She knew that Lord Vincent would sue for a divorce from her; would drag her name before the world and make it a by-word of scorn in those very circles of fashion over which she had once hoped to reign; she would not oppose him, she thought; she had no energy left to meet the overwhelming mass of testimony with which he had prepared to crush her. If her father should come over and defend her cause—well and good. She would let him do it; but as for her, she would go away, and seek peace.

You see, Claudia was in a very different mood of mind from that of the night previous, which had inspired her with such royal dignity and heroic courage to withstand and awe her accusers.

There had come the natural reaction from high excitement, and feats which had appeared easy, in the hour of her exalted indignation, seemed now impossible. She could now no more go to the American minister, and tell him her story, and claim his assistance, than she could have run into a burning fire. But, thank Heaven, she could go from the castle.

She rang her bell a third time, and more sharply than before. After a few minutes it was answered by the housekeeper, who entered with her customary respectful courtesy.

"She has not heard of last night's scandal," thought Claudia, as she noticed the dame's unaltered manner.

"I have rung three times, Mrs. Murdock. Why has not my maid come up?" she inquired.

"Indeed, me leddy, I dinna ken. I ha' na seen the lass the morn," answered the woman.

"What! You do not mean to say that Sally has not made her appearance this morning?"

"Indeed and she ha' na, me leddy."

"Mrs. Murdock, pray go at once to her room and see if she is there."

The housekeeper went away; and after an absence of fifteen minutes returned to say that Sally was not in her room.

"But I dinna think she is far awa', me leddy; because her bed is all tumbled as if she was just out of it. And her shoes and clothes are lying there, just as she put them off."

"I will dress and go and make inquiries myself. This house is a place of mysterious disappearances. I wonder if the beach below is of quicksand, and does it swallow people up alive?"

"I dinna ken, me leddy," gravely answered the dame.

"Mrs. Murdock, can you help me to dress?"

"Surely, me leddy," said the housekeeper, approaching Claudia with so much respectful affection that the unhappy lady said once more to herself:

"She knows nothing of last night's work."

And then Claudia, who was much too high-spirited and sincere to receive attentions rendered by the dame in ignorance of that night's scandal which she might not have so kindly rendered had she known of them, said:

"Mrs. Murdock, do you know what happened last night?"

"Aye, surely, me leddy, I ken a' about it, if your leddyship means the fause witness o' that de'il Frisbie," said the housekeeper, growing red with emotion.

"It was a false witness! a base, wicked, infamous calumny! I think the more highly of you, Mrs. Murdock, for so quickly detecting this. And I thank you," said Claudia, with difficulty restraining the tears, which for the first time since her great wrong were ready to burst from her eyes.

"Ou, aye, me leddy! It did na require the Witch of Endor to see the truth of that business. Ye'll see I ken Laird Vincent and Frisbie and the player-quean, wha is worst o' a'! And I hanna served ye, me leddy, these twa months without keening yer ladyship as well. And sae I ken the differ, me leddy. I ken the differ—-"

"Oh, Mrs. Murdock, in this deep desolation I find some comfort in your faith in me!"

"And sae I dinna believe a word the fause knave Frisbie says. And neither does auld Cuthbert, honest man! But wae's me, me leddy, whate'er our convictions may be, we canna disprove the lees o' yon de'il."

"No, we cannot," said Claudia, with a sigh of despair; "and unless Providence intervenes to save me, I am lost."

"Aweel, me leddy, ye maun just hope that he will intervene. Na, na, dinna greet sae sairly!" the good woman entreated, for Claudia had burst into a flood of tears, and was weeping bitterly.

This refreshed her spirit and cleared her brain. Presently, wiping her eyes and looking up, she said:

"Mrs. Murdock, I cannot meet those wretches at breakfast. Send me some coffee; and order the carriage to be at the door in an hour; also send Sally, who must be at hand by this time, to help me pack."

The dame went on this errand, and after a short absence returned, bringing Claudia's breakfast on a tray.

"Where is Sally?" inquired Lady Vincent, as the housekeeper arranged the breakfast on a little table.

"She hanna come yet, me leddy," said the housekeeper, who remained and waited on Lady Vincent at breakfast.

Claudia could eat but little. To all her own sources of trouble was now added alarm, on account of Sally. What if the hapless girl had shared old Katie's fate? was the question that now began to torture her.

"Have you seen my footman this morning, Mrs. Murdock?" she inquired.

"Nae, me leddy; the lad aye gaes to Banff for the mail about this hour."

"When he comes send him to me at once. And now please take the service away. And when you go downstairs institute a search for my maid. And do you, if you can do so conveniently, return and help me to pack."

"Aye, me leddy," replied the woman, as she lifted the tray and carried it away.

In a few minutes she returned and assisted Lady Vincent to fill one large trunk.

"That is all I shall take with me. I shall leave the remainder of my wardrobe in your care, Mrs. Murdock, and I must request you to see them packed and sent on to Edinboro', where I shall stop before deciding on my future steps," said Lady Vincent.

"Aye, me leddy; ye may be sure I will do a' in my power to serve your leddyship."

"And now pray see if Jim has returned from the post office."

Mrs. Murdock went; but returned with startling news:

"The lad Jamie has na got back, me leddy; and it e'en appears that he has na gane. I just asked ane o' the stable lads what time it was when Jamie took the horse to gang to the post office, and the lad said that Jamie had na come for the horse at a'!"

Claudia sprang up and gazed at the speaker in consternation; and then sunk down in her chair, and covered her face with her hands and groaned.

"Dinna do that, me leddy—dinna do that!"

"Oh, Mrs. Murdock! don't leave me! don't lose sight of me, or I shall vanish too; swallowed up in this great ruin!" she cried, with a shudder.

There was a rap at the door. Mrs. Murdock opened it. Lord Vincent's footman stood there.

"My lord sends his compliments to my lady, and says that the carriage is waiting to take her from the castle; the tide is rising, which will render the road impassable for several hours; and he hopes she will take that fact into consideration and not delay her departure."

"'Delay'? I am only too glad to go. But oh, my poor faithful servants. Mrs. Murdock, tell the man to send someone up here to carry my trunk down," said Lady Vincent, hastily putting on her sable cloak and tying on her bonnet.

Her heart ached at the thought of abandoning her servants; and she only reconciled herself to the measure by reflecting that to lodge information with the detective police at Banff would really be the best means she could possibly take for their recovery.

When two of the men servants had carried down her trunk, Lady Vincent shook hands with the kind-hearted housekeeper, and prepared to follow them. In taking leave of Mrs. Murdock she said:

"I thank you sincerely for your kindness to the strangers that came to your land. You are really the only friend that I and my unfortunate servants have met since our arrival in this country; and I shall not forget you!"

The housekeeper wept.

"When my poor servants reappear, if they ever should do so, you will be so good as to send them to me at Edinboro'. Send them to the railway office, where I will leave my address."

"Aye, me leddy, I will na forget," sobbed the old dame.

Claudia pressed her hand, dropped it, and went below.

In crossing the central hall towards the principal entrance Claudia suddenly stopped as though the Gorgon's head had blasted her sight. For Lord Vincent stood near the open door, as if to witness and triumph over her expulsion. With a strong effort she conquered her weakness and approached the door. The viscount made a low and mocking bow and stepped aside. Claudia confronted him.

"My lord," she said, "you think you have very successfully conspired against my honor; but if there is justice on earth, or in heaven, you will yet be exposed and punished."

Lord Vincent made her an ironical bow; but no other reply.

"Where are my servants?" she inquired solemnly.

"I am not their manager, my lady, that I should be conversant with their movements," answered the viscount.

"My lord, you well know where they are. And if Heaven should bless my efforts this morning, the world shall soon know."

"My lady, the way is open; the north wind rather piercing. Will you please to pass out and let me close it?" said his lordship, holding the door wide open for her exit.

"Will you tell me where my servants are?" persisted Claudia.

"I do not know, my lady. They have probably stolen the plate and gone. I will ask the butler, and if it is so, I will put the constables on their track," said Lord Vincent, bowing and waving his hand towards the door.

"I leave you to the justice of Heaven, evil man!" replied Claudia, as she passed through and left the castle. She entered the carriage and was driven off.

Lord Vincent closed the door behind her and then went into the breakfast room, where the cloth was already laid. Neither Mrs. MacDonald nor Mrs. Dugald had yet come down. They seemed to be sleeping late after their disturbed night.

Presently, however, they entered—Mrs. MacDonald looking very much embarrassed, Faustina pale as death. Lord Vincent received them with grave politeness, and they all sat down to the table.

It was then Lord Vincent said:

"Mrs. MacDonald, Lady Vincent has this morning left this house upon which she has brought so much dishonor. It is also necessary for me to go to London to take measures for the dissolution of my marriage. I am, therefore, about to ask of you a great favor."

"Ask any you please, my lord. I am very anxious to be of service to you in this awful crisis. And I will gladly do all in my power to help you," replied this very complaisant lady.

"I thank you, madam. I thank you very much. The favor I had to ask of you is this—that you will kindly remain here with Mrs. Dugald, until some plan is formed for her future residence."

"Surely, my lord, I will remain with great pleasure," answered this needy lady, who was only too glad to leave for a season the straitened home of her married sister, and take up her abode in this plentiful establishment.

"Again I thank you, madam; thank you cordially on the part of my widowed sister as well as on my own part," said the viscount courteously.

And this point being settled, the party dispersed.

Mrs. MacDonald retired to her own apartments to write a note to her sister, requesting that her effects might be forwarded to Castle Cragg.

Mrs. Dugald went to her boudoir to await there in feverish impatience the arrival of the viscount.

He did not keep her long in suspense; he soon entered, locked the door behind him, and seated himself beside her.

"She is gone—really gone?" whispered Faustina, in a low, eager, breathless voice.

"Yes, my angel; you heard me say so."

"Really and truly gone?"

"Really and truly."

"Oh, I am so glad! And her servants? Ah, I always hated those blacks! She has not left them behind?"

"Certainly not," answered the viscount evasively.

"Ah, what a relief! The house is well rid of them."

"It is, indeed, my love."

"But—but—but—the dead body?" whispered the woman in a husky voice, while her eyes dilated with terror.

"It is gone."

"Where? how?"

"I tied a heavy weight to its feet and sunk it in the depths of the sea," replied the viscount, who felt no scruples in deceiving anyone, least of all his accomplice in crime.

And this shows the utter falsity of the absurd proverb that asserts "there is honor among thieves." There can be no honor and no confidence in any league wherein the bond is guilt.

Lord Vincent was completely under the influence of Mrs. Dugald, whom he worshiped with a fatal passion—a passion the more violent and enduring because she continually stimulated without ever satisfying it. Up to this time she had never once permitted the viscount to kiss her. Thus he was her slave; but, like all slaves, he deceived his tyrant. He had deceived Mrs. Dugald from the first; he habitually deceived her.

In this instance he persuaded her that old Katie died under the influence of the chloroform that she had helped to administer on that fatal night when the old negress had been discovered eavesdropping behind the curtain in Mrs. Dugald's apartments.

What his motive could have been for this deception it would be difficult to say; perhaps it was for the purpose of gaining some power over her; perhaps it was from the pleasure of torturing her and seeing her terrors—for his passion for the woman was by no means that pure love which seeks first of all the good of its object; and, finally, perhaps it was from the mere habit of duplicity.

However that might be, he had persuaded her that Katie was dead, dead from the effects of the chloroform they had forced her to take.

And now that he had really committed a felony by selling the three negroes to a West Indian smuggler, he was not inclined to confess the truth. For not upon any account would he have confided to his companion in guilt the secret of a criminal transaction in which she had not also been implicated. He could not have trusted her so far as to place his liberty in her keeping. Therefore he preferred she should believe Katie's body had been sunk in the depths of the sea; and that Sally and Jim had accompanied their lady in her departure from the castle. It is true, the household servants might soon disabuse her mind of the mistake that the lady's maid and footman had gone with their mistress. But if they should do so, the viscount knew he could easily plead ignorance as to the fact; and say that all he knew was, she had not left them at the castle.

Mrs. Dugald listened to his account of the disposition of old Katie's body with deep delight. She clapped her little hands in her usual silly manner and exclaimed eagerly:

"That is good; oh, that is good! But are you sure it will stay down there? Great Heaven, if it should rise against us!"

"There is no danger, love, no danger."

"We should all be guillotined!" she repeated for the twentieth time since that night. And she shuddered through all her frame.

"Hanged, my dearest, not guillotined; hanged by the neck till we are dead," said the viscount, smiling.

"Ah, but you look like Mephistopheles when you say that!" she shrieked, covering her face with her hands.

"But there is no danger, none at all, I assure you. And now, my angel, I must leave you; I ordered the brougham to be at the door at twelve precisely to take me to Banff to meet the Aberdeen coach. And I have some preparations to make. Come down into the drawing room and wait to take leave of me, that is a dear."

"Oh, yes, yes! but before you go, promise me! You will write every day?"

"Every day, my angel," said the viscount, bowing over her hand, before he withdrew from the room.

His preparations were soon made. Old Cuthbert performed the duties of valet. And punctually at twelve o'clock the viscount took leave of his evil demon and her chaperon and departed for Banff, where he took the coach to Aberdeen, at which place he arrived in time to catch the night train up to London.

CHAPTER XXXIII

THE COUNTESS OF HURSTMONCEUX.

The beauteous woe that charms like faded light,

The cheek so pure that knows no youthful bloom,

Well suiteth her dark brow and forehead white,

And in the sad endurance of her eye

Is all that love believes of woman's majesty.

—Elliott.

In the meantime Lady Vincent reached Banff. She drove at once to the principal hotel, where she engaged a room into which her luggage was carried. With a gratuity to the coachman who had driven her she dismissed the carriage, which returned immediately to the castle.

Then she ordered a fly and drove to the police station—at that time a mean little stone edifice, exceedingly repulsive without and excessively filthy within.

A crowd of disreputable-looking ragamuffins of both sexes and all ages obstructed the entrance. Surely it was a revolting scene to one of Lady Vincent's fastidious nature and refined habits. But she did not shrink from her duty. She made her way through this disgusting assemblage, and found just within the door a policeman, to whom she said:

"I wish, if you please, to see your inspector."

"You will have to wait in the outer room, then, miss, because he is engaged now," replied the man curtly; for the beauty of the woman, the costliness of her apparel, and the fact of her having come unattended to a place like that, filled the mind of the officer with evil suspicions concerning her.

He opened a door on the left and let the visitor pass into the anteroom—a wretched stone hall, whose floor was carpeted with dirt and whose windows were curtained with cobwebs. A bench ran along the wall at one end, on which sat several forlorn, stupefied, or desperate-looking individuals waiting their turn to be examined. Two or three policemen, walking up and down, kept these persons in custody.

Claudia could not sit down among them; she walked to one of the windows and looked out.

She waited there some time, while one after another the prisoners were taken in and examined. Some returned from examination free, and walked out unattended and wearing satisfied countenances. Others came back in the custody of policemen and with downcast looks.

It seemed long before the inspector was at leisure to receive her. At length, however, the policeman she had seen at the door came up and said:

"Now, miss!"

Claudia arose and followed him to another room—a small, carpeted office, where Inspector Murray was seated at a desk.

He was a keener observer of character than the policeman had proved himself to be; and so, despite the suspicious circumstances which had awakened that worthy's doubts, Inspector Murray recognized in his visitor a lady of rank. He arose to receive her and handed her a chair, and then seated himself and respectfully waited for her to open her business.

Lady Vincent felt so much embarrassed that it was some time before she spoke. At length, however, she took courage to say:

"My errand here is a very painful one, sir."

The inspector bowed and looked attentive.

"Indeed it is of so strange and distressing a nature that I scarcely know how to explain it," she said.

"I beg you will feel no hesitation in making your communication, madam. We are accustomed to receive strange and distressing complaints."

"Sir," said Claudia, gently preparing the way, "you have not failed, then, in the course of your professional experience, to observe that crime is not an inmate of the houses of the impoverished and the degraded only, but that it may be found in the mansions of the rich and the palaces of the nobility."

"Without a doubt, madam."

"Then you will be the less shocked when I inform you that the circumstances which have driven me to seek your aid occurred recently in Castle Cragg, in the family of Lord Vincent."

"It is not the murder that was lately committed there to which you allude?" gravely inquired the inspector.

"Oh, no, not that murder; but I greatly fear there has been another one," replied Claudia, with a shudder.

"Madam!" exclaimed the inspector, in astonishment.

"I fear it is as I have hinted, sir," persisted Claudia.

"But who has been murdered?"

"I suspect that a harmless old female servant, named Katie Mortimer who became aware of a dangerous secret, has been."

"And—by whom?"

"I fear by a woman called Faustina Dugald and a man named Alick Frisbie."

Now, it is very difficult to surprise or startle an inspector of police. But Mr. Murray was really more than surprised or startled. He was shocked and appalled, as his countenance betrayed when he dropped his pen and fell back in his chair.

"Madam," he said, "do you know what you are saying?"

"Full well, sir; and I entreat you to receive my statement in detail and act upon it with promptitude. Your own investigations will discover how much cause I have for my suspicions," said Claudia firmly.

The inspector drew some writing paper before him, took up his pen, and said:

"Proceed, madam, if you please."

Claudia commenced her statement, but was almost immediately interrupted by the inspector, who said:

"Your name, madam, if you please."

Claudia started and blushed at her own forgetfulness; though, in truth, it had never occurred to her to introduce herself by name to an inspector of police. Now, however, she perceived how necessary it was that her name should attend her statement.

"I am Lady Vincent," she replied.

There was an instantaneous change in the inspector's manner. His deportment had been respectful from the first, because he had recognized his visitor as a lady; but his manner was obsequious now that he heard she was a titled lady.

"I beg your ladyship's pardon," he said. "I had no idea that I was honored with the presence of Lady Vincent. Pray, my lady, do not inconvenience yourself in the least by going over these painful things at the present hour, unless you feel that it is really necessary. I could wait on your ladyship at your residence and receive your communication there."

"Sir, I thank you for your courtesy, but I prefer to make my statement now and here," replied Claudia.

The inspector dipped his pen in ink and looked attentive.

Claudia proceeded with her communication. She related all the circumstances that had come to her knowledge respecting the disappearance of Katie, and the inspector took down her words.

Then she mentioned the more recent evanishment of Sally and Jim; but she alluded to these facts only as collateral circumstances; she could not believe that the two last named had lost their lives.

When the inspector had taken down the whole of her statement she arose to go.

The inspector also arose.

"Will you investigate this matter immediately?" she said.

"I will do so to-day, my lady," replied Mr. Murray, bowing deferentially.

"Can I be of any assistance to you in pursuing your inquiry into this affair?"

"Not at present, I thank your ladyship," replied the inspector, with a second bow.

"Then I will bid you good-morning."

"I beg your ladyship's pardon; but would your ladyship deign to leave your address with me? We might need your ladyship's personal testimony."

"Certainly," said Claudia. "I shall go to Edinboro' to-day, where I shall remain at the best hotel, if you know which that is, for a few days; before I leave I will write and advise you of my destination. And now there is one important part of my errand that I had nearly forgotten. It was to ask you to advertise for the missing servants, and to authorize you to offer a reward of two hundred pounds for any information that may lead to their recovery."

"I will do it immediately, my lady," replied Inspector Murray, as he obsequiously attended Lady Vincent to the door and put her into the fly.

She drove quickly back to her hotel, where she had only time to take a slight luncheon before starting in the eleven o'clock coach for Aberdeen, where, after four hours' ride through a wildly picturesque country, she arrived just in time to take the afternoon train to Edinboro'. It was the express train, and reached the old city at seven o'clock that evening.

Among the many hotels whose handbills, pasted on the walls of the railway station, claimed the attention of travelers, Claudia selected "MacGruder's," because it was opposite Scott's monument.

She took a cab and drove there. She liked the appearance of the house, and engaged a comfortable suite of apartments, consisting of a parlor, bed chamber, and bathroom, and ordered dinner.

Now, by all the rules of tradition, Claudia, ignominiously expelled from her husband's house, deprived of her servants' attendance, far from all her friends, alone in a strange hotel in a foreign city, with a degrading trial threatening her—Claudia, I say, ought to have been very unhappy. But she was not. She was almost happy.

Her spirits rebounded from their long depression. Her sensations were those of escape, freedom, independence. She felt like a bird freed from its cage; a prisoner released from captivity; a soul delivered from purgatory. Oh, she was so glad—so glad to get away entirely, to get away forever—from the hold of sin, that Castle Cragg, where she had been buried alive so long; where she had lived in torment among lost spirits; where the monotony had been like the gloom of the grave, and the guilt like the corruption of death!

She had passed through the depths of Hades, and was happy—how happy!—to rise to the upper air again and see the stars. This, only, was enough for the present. And she scarcely thought of the future. Whatever that unknown future might bring her, it would not bring back Castle Cragg, Lord Vincent, Faustina, or Frisbie.

After she had refreshed herself with a bath and a change of dress, she went into the parlor, where she found a warm fire, a bright light, and a neatly laid table.

And whatever you may think of her, she really enjoyed the boiled salmon, roasted moor-hen, and cabinet custard she had ordered for dinner. After the service was removed she sat comfortably in her easy-chair before the fire, and reflected on her future movements.

She liked her quarters in this hotel very much. The rooms were clean and comfortable; the servants were polite and attentive; the meals delicately prepared and elegantly served.

And she resolved to remain here for the present; to write to her father by the first American mail; and while waiting for his answer, beguile the interval by seeing everything that might prove interesting in the city and in the surrounding country.

And in a locality so rich in historical monuments as this was, she was sure of interesting occupation for the month that must intervene before she could hear from her father in answer to the letter which she meant to write.

She had brought with her from Castle Cragg all the ready money she had; it was something more than two hundred pounds; so that there was nothing to fear from financial embarrassments.

After settling this matter to her satisfaction, Claudia, feeling very tired, went to bed, and having lost two nights' rest, immediately fell into a deep and dreamless sleep, that lasted, unbroken, until morning.

Her first sensation on awakening from this sleep of oblivion to the consciousness of her altered circumstances was—not humiliation at her own unmerited dishonor—not dread of the impending, degrading trial—but pleasure at the recollection that she was free; that she was away from Castle Cragg; that she would not have to meet Lord Vincent and Faustina at breakfast; that she would never have to meet them again.

Ah! only those who have been compelled for months to breathe the vitiated atmosphere of guilt can appreciate the excess of Claudia's joy at her deliverance. It was a joy that not even the distressing circumstances that surrounded her, and the trial that awaited her, had any power to destroy.

To one who knew her position, without being able to enter into her feelings, it would have seemed an extravagant, an unnatural, an insane joy. Perhaps she was a little insane; she had had enough trouble to derange her reason.

She arose gladly. She had a motive for rising now; formerly, at Castle Cragg, she had none, because she had nothing to do. Now she had to order her breakfast, write to her father, and drive round to see the old city.

She dressed herself quickly and went into the parlor. The windows were already opened, the fire lighted, and the breakfast table was laid.

She went to the windows and looked out. The morning was clear and bright. It seemed to her that even Nature sympathized in her deliverance. The winter sun shone down brightly upon Scott's monument, that stood within its inclosure in the middle of the space before her windows. Yes, she was pleased with her quarters.

She rang the bell and ordered breakfast, which was quickly served. When she had finished her morning meal and sent the service away, she got her writing-case from her trunk and sat down to write to her father and give him a detailed account of her misfortunes.

But she found a difficulty in arranging her thoughts; her mind was in too excitable a condition to admit of close application. She commenced, and discarded letter after letter.

Finally, she gave up trying to write for the present. There was time enough; the foreign mail, as she had ascertained, did not close until six o'clock in the evening. She thought a drive through the old city would work off her excitement and tranquilize her nerves. She rang and ordered a fly, and drove out.

First she went to Holyrood, and soon lost all consciousness of her own present and individual troubles in dreaming of all those princes, heroes, and beauties of history who had lived and sinned or suffered within those old palace walls.

She went into Queen Mary's rooms, and fell into a reverie over that fatal bed-chamber, which remains to this day in the same condition in which it was left by the hapless queen about three hundred years ago. She saw the steep, dark, narrow, secret staircase, with its opening concealed behind the tapestry, up which the assassins of Rizzio had crept to their murderous work. She saw the little turret closet in which the poor queen was at supper with her ladies when the minstrel was surprised and massacred in her presence.

She went into the great picture gallery, where hung the portraits of the Scottish kings—each mother's royal son painted with a large curled proboscis—"a nose like a door-knocker," as someone described it. With one exception—that of James IV., the hapless hero of Flodden field. It was a full-length portrait, life-sized, and full of fire. Claudia stood and gazed upon it with delight. She was charmed by its beauty and by the lines that it brought distinctly to her recollection. Whether this was really a faithful portrait of King James or not, it certainly was an accurate likeness of the hero described by the poet:

Yes, there he stood before her, pictured to the very life; all luminous with youth and love, chivalry and royalty; bending graciously from the canvas, smiling upon the spectator, and seeming about to step forward and take her hand.

Claudia turned away from this picture, feeling at the same moment both pleased and saddened. She had spent three hours dreaming amongst the ancient halls and bowers of Holyrood, and now she felt that it was time for her to return to the hotel, especially as the palace was beginning to be filled with the usual daily inflowing of sight-seers, and she felt somewhat fatigued and worried by the crowd.

So she went out and re-entered her cab, and was driven back to the hotel. Here an unexpected misfortune awaited her. As she left the cab she put her hand in her pocket to take out her purse and pay the cabman.

It was gone!

She turned sick with apprehension, for the loss of this purse, which contained all the money which she had brought with her, was, under the circumstances, a serious calamity.

She hurried again into the cab and searched it thoroughly; but no purse was to be found.

Then the truth burst upon her; she had been robbed of it by someone in the crowd of visitors in Holyrood Palace; her pocket had probably been picked while she stood in the picture gallery dreaming before the portrait of King James. How she reproached herself for her carelessness in taking so considerable an amount of money with her.

She was excessively agitated; but she managed to control herself sufficiently to speak calmly to the waiter, and say:

"Be good enough to pay this man and put the item in my bill"

The waiter obeyed and discharged the cab; for, of course, the name of Lady Vincent was as yet a passport to credit. Then she hurried to her room in a state of great agitation that nearly deprived her of all power to think or act. She rang the bell, which brought a waiter to her presence.

"I would like to see the landlord of this hotel," she said.

"I beg your pardon, my lady, but the proprietor lives out of town," returned the man.

"Then send the clerk of the house, or the head waiter, or whoever is in charge here."

"I will send the clerk, my lady," said the waiter, retiring.

The clerk soon made his appearance.

"Sir," said Claudia, "I sent for you to say, that while I was seeing Holyrood Palace, this forenoon, my pocket was picked of my purse, which contained a considerable amount of money; and I wish to ask you what steps I should take for its recovery?"

"Have you any idea of the sort of person that robbed you, my lady?"

"Not the slightest; all I know is that I had the purse with me when I paid the guide on entering the palace, and then I missed it when I reached home; and all I suspect is that it was purloined from me while I was in the picture gallery, standing before the portrait of James IV."

"In what form was the money, my lady?"

"Five and ten pound Bank of England notes."

"Were the numbers taken?"

"Oh, no; I never thought of taking the numbers."

"Then, my lady, I very much fear that it will be difficult or impossible to recover the money. However, I will send for a detective, and we will make an effort."

"Do, sir, if you please."

The clerk retired.

In a few moments Detective Ogilvie waited on Lady Vincent, and received her statement in regard to the robbery, promised to take prompt measures for the discovery of the thief, and retired.

Then suddenly Claudia remembered her letter to her father It was now near the close of the short winter day. Her interview with the detective had occupied her so long that she had barely time to scribble and send off the few urgent lines with which the reader is already acquainted. Then she dined and resigned herself to repose for the remainder of the evening.

While she sat in her easy-chair luxuriating in indolence and solitude before the glowing fire, the thought suddenly occurred to her that she was not really so badly off as the loss of her purse had first led her to suppose. She recollected that she had several costly rings upon her fingers; diamonds, rubies, and emeralds—the least valuable of which was worth more than the purse of money which had been stolen from her; and if she should be driven to extremity she could part with one of these rings; but then, on calm consideration of the subject, she had really no fears of being driven to extremity. She was Lady Vincent, and her credit was as yet intact before the world. This was a first-class hotel, and would supply her with all that she might require for the month that must intervene before her father's arrival.

She would spend this interval in seeing Edinboro' and its environs, and when her father should come she would persuade him to take her to the Continent, and afterwards carry her back to her native country, and to her childhood's home, to pass the remainder of her life in peace and quietness.

Dreaming over this humble prospect for the future, Claudia retired to bed, and slept well.

The next morning, as soon as she had breakfasted, she ordered a carriage from the stables connected with the hotel and drove to Edinboro' Castle, where she spent two or three hours among its royal halls and bowers, dreaming over the monuments of the past.

She lingered in the little cell-like stone chamber where Queen Mary had given birth to her son, afterwards James VI. She read the pathetic prayer carved on the stone tablet above the bedstead, and said to have been composed by the unhappy queen in behalf of her newborn infant.

In the great hall of the castle she paused long before a beautiful portrait of Mary Stuart, that was brought from Paris, where it had been painted, and which represented the young queen in her earliest womanhood, when she was the Dauphiness of France. And Claudia thought that this portrait was the only one, among all that she had ever seen of Mary Stuart, which came up to her ideal of that royal beauty, who was even more a queen of hearts than of kingdoms.

At length, weary of sight-seeing, she re-entered her carriage and returned home. While she was in her bedchamber taking off her bonnet, a card was brought to her.

"This must be a mistake—this cannot be for me; I have no acquaintances in the town," she said, without taking the trouble to glance at the card.

"I beg your ladyship's pardon, but the countess inquired particularly for Lady Vincent," replied the waiter who had brought the card.

"The countess?" repeated Claudia, and she took it up and read the lightly penciled name:

"Berenice, Countess of Hurstmonceux."

"Say to Lady Hurstmonceux that I will be with her in a few minutes," said Claudia.

"'Berenice, Countess of Hurstmonceux,'" she repeated when the man had retired; "that is the widow of the late earl, and the forsaken wife of Herman Brudenell. What on earth brings her here? And how did she know of my presence in the city, and even in this house? However, I shall know soon, I suppose."

And so saying, Claudia made a few changes in her toilet, and went into the parlor.

Standing, looking from the window, was a lady dressed in a black velvet bonnet and plumes, a black silk gown, and a large sable cloak and muff.

As Claudia entered, this lady turned around and lifted her veil, revealing a beautiful, pale face, with large, deep-fringed, mournful dark eyes, and soft, rippling, jet-black hair. At the first glance Claudia was touched by the pensive beauty of that lovely face.

Yes! at the age of forty-five the Countess of Hurstmonceux was still beautiful. She had passed a serene life, free alike from carking cares and fashionable excesses, and so her beauty had been well preserved. It would have taken a keen observer to have detected the few wrinkles that had gathered in the corners of her fine eyes and plump lips, or to have found out the still fewer silver threads that lay hidden here and there among her dark tresses.

Claudia advanced to greet her, holding out her hand, and saying:

"The Countess of Hurstmonceux, I presume?"

"Yes," replied the visitor, with a sweet smile.

"I am Lady Vincent; and very happy to see you. Pray be seated," said Claudia, drawing forward a chair for her visitor.

"My dear Lady Vincent, I only learned this morning of your arrival in town, and presuming upon my slight connection with the family of the present Earl of Hurstmonceux, I have ventured to call on you and claim a sort of relationship," said Berenice kindly.

"Your ladyship is very good, and I am very glad to see you," said Claudia cordially. Then suddenly recollecting her own cruel position, and feeling too proud as well as too honest to appear under false colors, she blushed, and said:

"I cannot think how your ladyship could know that I was here; but I am sure that when you did me this honor of calling, you did not know the circumstances under which I left Castle Cragg."

A tide of crimson swept over the pale face of Berenice; it arose for Claudia, not for herself, and she replied:

"My dear, wronged lady, I know it all."

"You know all—all that they allege against me, and you call me wronged?" exclaimed Claudia, in pleased surprise.

"I know all that they allege against you, and I believe you to be wronged. Therefore, my dear, I have come to-day to offer you all the service in my power," said Berenice sweetly.

Claudia suddenly caught her hand and clasped it fervently.

"And now, my dear Lady Vincent, will you permit me to explain myself and inform you how I became acquainted with the circumstances of your departure from Castle Cragg, and your arrival at this house?" inquired Berenice.

"Oh, do! do!" replied Claudia.

"You must know, then, that a few of my old domestics, who served the late earl and myself while we lived at Castle Cragg, still remain there in the service of the present earl's family, which is always represented at the castle by Lord Vincent. Among them there are two who, it appears, became very much attached to your ladyship. I allude to the housekeeper, Jean Murdock, and the major-domo, Cuthbert Allan."

"Yes, they were very kind; but, after all, it was old Cuthbert who sent that note to Lord Vincent, which brought him from the play at midnight to burst into my room and find his wretched valet hidden there," replied Claudia gravely.

"Yes; Cuthbert saw the valet steal into your room and sent word to his master, as in duty bound. But, after witnessing the scene of his discovery, Cuthbert's mind instantly cleared your ladyship of suspicion and rushed to the conclusion that the miserable valet concealed himself in your boudoir unknown to you and for the purpose of robbery. I, for my part, believe he was placed there with the connivance of Lord Vincent, and that old Cuthbert was made to play a blind part in that conspiracy."

"I knew, of course, that it was a conspiracy, but really wondered to find the honest old man in it."

"He was a blind tool in their hands. But I was about to tell you how the facts of your departure from the castle and your arrival in this hotel came to my knowledge. In brief, I received a letter from old Cuthbert this morning, in which he related the whole history of the affair, as it was known to him. He expressed great sorrow for the part he had been obliged to bear in the business, and the most respectful sympathy for your ladyship. He said his 'heart was sair for the bonnie leddy sae far frae a' her friends and living her lane in Edinboro' toun.' And he begged me to find you out and protect you. To this letter was added a postscript by Jean Murdock. It was a warm, humble, respectful encomium upon your ladyship, in which she joined her prayers to those of Cuthbert.that I would seek you out and succor you."

As Berenice spoke, blushes dyed the cheeks of Claudia, and tears dropped from her eyes. She was softened by the kindness of those two old people, and their patronage humiliated her.

Something of the nature of her emotions the countess must have divined, for she took the hand of Claudia and said:

"Believe me, dear Lady Vincent, I did not need urging to come to you. I needed only to know that you were in town and alone. As soon as I read the letters I sent for the morning paper to look for the arrivals at the various hotels, to see if I could find your name among them. I could not, and so I was about to lay aside the paper and send for the one of the day before, when my eye happened to light on a paragraph in which I found your name. It was the robbery of your purse at Holyrood Palace. There I learned your address. And I came away here immediately."

Claudia's fingers tightened on the hand of the countess which she still retained in hers.

"How much I thank you, Lady Hurstmonceux, you can never know; because you have never felt what it is to be a stranger in a foreign country, with your fame traduced and not one friend to stand by your side and sustain you," she said.

Again that crimson tide swept over the pale face of Berenice; but this time it was for herself, and she answered:

"Oh, yes, yes! I have known just that. Ten years in a foreign country, forsaken, shunned, traduced, without one friend to speak comfort to an almost breaking heart—It is past. I have overlived it. The God of my fathers has sustained me. Let us speak no more of it." And crimson as she had been for a moment she was as pale as marble now.

Claudia laid her hand caressingly upon the shoulder of Berenice and looked in her face with that mute sympathy which is more effective than eloquent words. Something, indeed, she had heard of this before, but the rumor had left no impression on her mind; though she blamed herself now for the momentary forgetfulness.

"Let us speak of yourself and your plans for the future," said the countess.

"My plans are simple enough. I have written to my father. I shall remain here until his arrival," said Claudia.

There was a pause between them for a few minutes, during which the countess seemed in deep thought, and then this still beautiful woman, smiling, said:

"I am old enough to be your mother, Lady Vincent, and in the absence of your father, I hope you will trust yourself to my guardianship. It is not well, under present circumstances, that you should remain alone at a public hotel. Come with me and be my guest at Cameron Court. It is a pretty place, near Roslyn Castle, and despite all the evil in the hearts of men, I think I can make your visit there pleasant and interesting."

Claudia burst into tears; the proud Claudia was softened, almost humbled by this unexpected kindness.

"God bless you!" was all that she could say. "I will gladly go."

"I am your mother, in the meantime, Claudia, you know," said Lady Hurstmonceux, touching the bell.

"You are my guardian angel!" sobbed Claudia.

"Lady Vincent's bill, if you please," said the countess to the waiter who answered the bell, and who immediately bowed and disappeared.

But Claudia grasped the arm of the countess and exclaimed in alarm:

"I had forgotten. I cannot leave the hotel yet, because I cannot pay the bill. My lost purse contained all the money that I brought from Castle Cragg." "What of that? I am your mother, Claudia, until you hear from your father; and your banker until you recover your money. Now, my dear, go put on your bonnet, while I settle with the waiter. My carriage is at the door, and we will go at once. I will send my own maid in a fly to pack up your effects and bring them after us."

"How much my father will thank and bless you!" said Claudia, as she left the room to prepare herself.

Lady Hurstmonceux paid the bill, and left half a sovereign in the hands of the chambermaid, bidding her take care of Lady Vincent's effects until they should be sent for.

And when Claudia came out, equipped for her ride, they went below stairs.

A handsome brougham, painted dark green, drawn by fine gray horses, with silver mountings on their harness and with a coachman and footman in gray-and-green livery stood before the door.

And the countess and her protegee entered it and were driven towards the Cameron Court.

CHAPTER XXXIV

THE RESCUE.

The tide has ebbed away;

No more wild surging 'gainst the adamant rocks,

No swayings of the sea-weed false that mocks

The hues of gardens gay;

No laugh of little wavelets at their play!

No lucid pools reflecting Heaven's brow—

Both storm and cloud alike are ended now.

The gray, bare rocks sit lone;

The shifting sand lies so smooth and dry

That not a wave might ever have swept by

To vex it with loud moan.

Only some weedy fragments blackening grown

To dry beneath the sky, tells what has been;

But desolation's self has grown serene.

—Anon.

We must now relate what happened to Ishmael and his companions after they were deserted by the lifeboats. When they were out of sight he dropped his eyes and bent his head in prayer for himself and his fellow-sufferers, and thus awaited his fate.

But, oh, Heaven of heavens! what is this? Is it death, or—life?

The wreck that had been whirling violently around at the mercy of the furious sea was now lifted high upon the crest of a wave and cast further up upon the reef, where she rested in comparative safety.

So suddenly and easily had this been done that it was some minutes before the shipwrecked men could understand that they were for the present respited from death.

It was Ishmael who now inspired and confirmed their hopes.

"Friends," he exclaimed, in a deep, earnest, solemn voice, as he looked around upon them, "let us return thanks to the Lord, for we are saved!"

"Yes; saved from immediate death by drowning, but perhaps not saved from a slow death of starvation," observed a "doubting Thomas" of their number.

"The Lord never mocks his servants with false hopes. We are saved!" repeated Ishmael emphatically, but with the deepest reverence.

For some hours longer the wind raved and the sea roared around the wreck; but even the highest waves could not now wash over it. As the sun arose the mist cleared away and the wreck gradually dried. About noon the sea began to subside. And at sunset all was calm and clear.

Ishmael and his companions now suffered from only two causes-hunger and cold-the sharpest hunger and the most intense cold; for every single atom and article that could be possibly used for food or covering had been washed out of the wreck and swept off to sea. And all day long they had been fasting and exposed to all the inclemency of that severe season and climate. And during the ensuing night they were in danger of death from starvation or freezing. But they huddled closely together and tried to keep life within them by their mutual animal heat; while Ishmael, himself confident of timely rescue, kept up their hopes. It was a long and trying night.

But it ended at last. Day dawned; the sun arose. Then Ishmael saw some fragments of the wreck that had been tossed upon the rocks and left there by the retiring waves. Among them was a long spar. This he directed the men to drag up upon the deck. The men, who were weak from hunger and numb from cold, could scarcely find power to obey this order. But when they did, Ishmael took off his own shirt and fastened it to the end of the spar, which he immediately set up in its position as a flag-staff. They had no glass, and therefore could not sweep the horizon in search of a sail. But Ishmael had an eagle's piercing glance, and his fine eyes traveled continually over the vast expanse of waters in the hope of approaching rescue.

At last he cried out:

"A sail from the eastward, friends!"

"Hurrah! but are you sure, sir?" broke from half a dozen lips, as all hands, forgetting cold and hunger, weakness and stiffness, sprang upon their feet and strained their eyeballs in search of the sail; which they could not yet discern.

"Are you quite certain, sir?" someone anxiously inquired.

"Quite. I see her very plainly."

"But if she should not see our signal!" groaned "doubting Thomas."

"She sees it. She is bearing rapidly down upon us!" exclaimed Ishmael.

"I see her now!" cried one of the men.

"And so do I!" said another.

"And so do I!" added a third.

"She is not a sail-boat, she is a steamer," said a fourth, as the ship came rapidly towards the wreck. "She is the 'Santiago,' of Havana," said Ishmael, as she steamed on and came within hailing distance.

Then she stopped, blew off her steam, and sent out a boat. While it was cleaving the distance between the ship and the rocks a man on the deck of the former shouted through his trumpet:

"Wreck ahoy!"

"Aye, aye!" responded Ishmael, with all the strength of his powerful lungs.

"All safe with you?"

"All safe!"

As the boat was pushed up as near as it could with safety be brought to the wreck, the frozen and famished men began to climb down and drop into it. When they were all in, even to the professor, Ishmael stepped down and took his place among them with a smile of joy and a deep throb of gratitude to God, For, ah! the strong young man had loved that joyous and powerful life which he had been so prompt to offer up on the shrine of duty; and he was glad and thankful to return to life, to work, to fame, to love, to Bee!

The boatmen laid themselves to their oars and pulled vigorously for the steamer. They were soon alongside.

The men made a rush for her decks. They wanted to be warmed and fed. Ishmael let them all go before him, and then he followed and stepped upon the steamer.

And the next moment he found himself seized and clasped in the embrace of—Mr. Brudenell!

"Oh, my son, my brave and noble son, you are saved! God is kinder to me than I deserve!" he cried.

"One moment, Brudenell! Oh, Ishmael, thank Heaven, you are safe!" fervently exclaimed another voice—that of Judge Merlin, who now came forward and warmly shook his hand.

"Ant dere ish—von more—drue shentlemans—in te vorlt!" sobbed the German Jew, seizing and pressing one of Ishmael's hands.

Captain Mountz, Doctor Kerr, and in fact all Ishmael's late fellow-passengers, now crowded around with earnest and even tearful congratulations.

And meanwhile dry clothes and warm food and drink were prepared for the shipwrecked passengers. And it was not until Ishmael had changed his raiment and eaten a comfortable breakfast that he was permitted to hear an explanation of the unexpected appearance of his friends upon the deck of the steamer.

It happened that the passengers in the lifeboats, after suffering severely with cold and with the dread of a slow death from exposure for twelve hours, were at last picked up by the "Santiago," a Spanish steamer bound for Havana. That after their wants had been relieved by the captain of the "Santiago" they had told him of the imminently perilous condition In which they had left the remnant of the crew and passengers. And the captain had altered the course of the ship in the forlorn hope of yet rescuing those forsaken men. And the Lord had blessed his efforts with success. Such was the story told by Mr. Brudenell and Judge Merlin to Ishmael.

"But, oh, my dear boy, what a fatal delay! Just think of it! This steamer is bound for Havana. And this very day, when we ought to be landing on the shores of England, we find ourselves steaming in an opposite direction for the West India Islands," said Judge Merlin.

"Oh, sir, trust still in Heaven," answered Ishmael. "Think how marvelously the Lord has delivered us from danger and death! This very delay that seems so fatal may be absolutely necessary to our final success."

The words of Ishmael proved prophetic. For had it not been for their shipwreck and the consequent alteration in their course, their voyage to England would have been taken in vain.

The "Santiago" steamed her way southward, and in due course of time, without the least misadventure, reached the port of Havana.

It was Sunday, the first of January, when they arrived.

"We shall have no trouble with the Custom House officers here," laughed Ishmael, as he gave his arm to Judge Merlin and went on shore, leaving all the passengers who had not been shipwrecked, and lost their luggage, to pass the ordeal he and his friends had escaped.

They went at once to the hotel which had been recommended to them by the captain of the "Santiago."

And as this was Sunday, and there was no English Protestant church open, they passed the day quietly within doors.

On Monday Judge Merlin's first care was to go to the American consul and get the latter to accompany him to a banker, from whom he procured the funds he required in exchange for drafts upon his own New York bankers.

While Judge Merlin was gone upon this errand Ishmael went down to the harbor to make inquiries as to what ships were to sail in the course of the week for Europe.

He found that he had a choice between two. The "Mary," an English sailing ship, would leave on Wednesday for London. And the "Cadiz," a screw steamer, would sail on Saturday for the port whose name she bore.

Ishmael mentally gave preference to the swift and sure steamer, rather than the uncertain sailing packet; but he felt bound to refer the matter to Judge Merlin before finally deciding upon it.

With this purpose he left the harbor and entered the city. He was passing up one of the narrow granite-paved streets in the neighborhood of the grand cathedral where lie the ashes of Columbus, when he was startled by hearing quick and heavy footsteps and a panting, eager voice behind him:

"Marse Ishmael! Marse Ishmael Worth! Oh, is it you, sir, dropped from the clouds to save me! Marse Ishmael! Oh, stop, sir! Oh, for de Lord's sake, stop!"

Ishmael started and turned around, and, to his inexpressible amazement, stood face to face with old Katie.

"Oh, Marse Ishmael, honey, is dis you? Is dis indeed you, or only de debbil deceiving of me!" she exclaimed, panting for breath as she caught him by the greatcoat, and grasping him as the drowning grasp a saving plank.

"Katie!" exclaimed Ishmael, in immeasurable astonishment. "Yes, honey, it's Katie. Yes, my dear chile, ole Katie an' no ghose, nor likewise sperit, dough you might think I is! But oh, Marse Ishmael! is you, you? Is you reely an' truly you, and no, no 'ception ob de debbil?"

"Katie!" repeated Ishmael, unable to realize the fact of her presence.

"Hi! what I tell you? Oh, Marse Ishmael, chile, don't go for to 'ny your old Aunt Katie, as nussed you good when you lay out dere for dead at Tanglewood! don't!" said the poor creature, clinging to his coat. "Katie!" reiterated Ishmael, unable to utter another word.

"Laws a massy upon top of me, yes! I keep on telling you, chile, I is Katie! don't 'ny me; don't 'ny me in my 'stress, Marse Ishmael, if ebber you 'spects to see hebben!" she said, beginning to cry.

"I do not deny you, Katie; but I am lost in amazement. How on earth came you here?" asked Ishmael, staring at her.

"I didn't come on earth at all. I come by de sea. Oh, Marse Ishmael! I done died since I lef' you! done died and gone to the debbil! been clar down dar in his place, which it aint 'spectable to name! done died and gone dere and come to life again, on a ship at sea."

"Who brought you here, Katie?" questioned Ishmael, thoroughly perplexed.

"De debbil, honey! de debbil, chile! Sure as you lib it was de debbil! Oh, Marse Ishmael, honey, stop long o' me! Don't go leabe me, chile, don't! Now de Lor' has sent you to me, don't go leabe me. You is all de hopes I has in de world!" she cried, clinging with desperate perseverance to his coat.

"I will not leave you, Katie. I have not the least intention of doing so. But all this is quite incomprehensible. Where is your mistress? She is never here?" said Ishmael.

"I dunno. I dunno nuffin 'bout my poor dear babyship—ladyship, I mean; only my head is so 'fused! Oh, lor', don't go break away from me! don't, Marse Ishmael!"

"I will not desert you, Katie, be assured that I will not; but let go my coat and try to compose yourself. Don't you see that you are collecting a crowd around us?" expostulated Ishmael.

But Katie hung fast, saying:

"'Deed I can't! 'Deed I can't, Marse Ishmael! If I let go of you I shall wake up an' find you is all a dream, an' I'll be as bad off as ebber," persisted Katie, taking Ishmael more firmly into custody than ever.

He laughed; he could not help laughing at the ludicrous desperation of his captor. But his astonishment and wonder were unabated; and he saw that Katie could not give a lucid explanation of her presence on the island, or at least not until her excitement should have time to subside.

Besides the crowd of negroes, mulattoes, and creoles, men, women, and children, who had gathered around them, with open eyes and mouths, was still increasing.

"Katie," he said, "we cannot talk in the middle of the street with all these people staring at us. So come with—"

"Oh, lor', Marse Ishmael," interrupted Katie, "don't you mind dese poor trash! Dey can't speak one word o' good Christian talk, nor likewise understand a Christian no mor'n dumb brutes. Dey is no better nor barbariums, wid dere o's and ro's ebery odder word. Don't mind dem herrin's."

"But, Katie, they have eyes. Come with me to the hotel. You will find your old master there."

"Who? My ole—" began Katie, opening her mouth, which remained open as if incapable of closing again, much less of uttering another syllable.

"Yes, Judge Merlin is here."

"My ole—Well, Lor'!"

"Come, Katie."

"My ole—If ebber I heard de like! What de name o' sense he doin' here? An' same time, what you doin' here yourself, Marse Ishmael?"

"Katie, it is a long story. And I fancy we both, you and I, have much to tell. Will you come with me to my hotel?"

"Will I come, Marse Ishmael? Why wouldn't I come den? Sure I'll come. I don't mean to do nuffin else; nor likewise let go of you, nor lose sight of you, de longest day as eber I lib, please my 'Vine Marster, don't I; so dere!" replied the old creature, tightening her clasp upon Ishmael's coat.

"Oh, Katie, Katie, but that would be too much of a good thing," said Ishmael, smiling.

"Dey done sent me arter pines. Fetch pines! I don't care as ebber I see a pine again as long as ebber I lib. I gwine to my own ole—, De Lor'! but de thought o' he being here!" cried Katie, breaking off in the middle of her speech again to give vent to her amazement.

"Now, Katie, you must walk by my side; but, really, you must let go my coat," said Ishmael kindly, but authoritatively.

"If I do, you promise me not to run away?" said Katie half pleadingly and half threateningly.

"Of course I do."

"Nor likewise wake me up to find it all a dream?"

"Certainly not, Katie."

"Well, den, I trust you, Marse Ishmael—I trust you," said Katie, releasing her hold on him. "'Dough, 'deed and 'deed," she added doubtingly, "so many queer things is happened of since I done left my ole—Goodness gracious me! to think o' he being here!—marster; and so many people and so many places has 'peared and dis'peared, dat, dere! I aint got no conference in nothing."

"I hope that you will recover your faith with your happiness, Katie. And now come on, my good woman," said Ishmael, who felt extremely anxious to get from her, as soon as they should reach the hotel, some explanation of her presence on the island, and some news of her unfortunate mistress.

They walked on as rapidly as the strength of the old woman would allow, for Ishmael would not permit her to put herself out of breath. When they reached the hotel Ishmael told Katie to follow him, and so led her to her master's apartments.

They stopped outside the door.

"You must remain here until I go in and see if the judge has returned from his ride from the bank. And if he has, I must prepare him for your arrival here; for your master has aged very much since you saw him last, Katie, and the surprise might hurt him," whispered Ishmael, as he turned the doorknob and went in.

The judge had just returned. He was seated at the table, counting out money. "Ha, Ishmael, my boy, have you got back?" he asked, looking up from his work.

"Yes, sir; and I have the choice of two packets to offer you. The brig 'Mary' sails for London on Wednesday; the steamer 'Cadiz' sails for the port of Cadiz on Saturday. The choice remains with you," said Ishmael, putting down his hat and seating himself.

"Oh, then we will go by the 'Cadiz'; though she sails at a later day, and for a farther port, we shall reach our destination sooner, going by her, than we should to go in a sailing packet bound direct for London."

"I think so too, sir; there is no certainty in the sailing packets. I hope you succeeded at the bank?"

"Perfectly; our consul, Tourneysee, went with me, to identify me and vouch for my solvency, and I got accommodated without any difficulty whatever. And now I must insist upon being banker for our whole party until we reach England."

"I thank you, sir, in behalf of my father as well as myself," said Ishmael.

"Now, let me see—nine hundred and seventy, eighty, ninety, an hundred—that is one thousand. I will lay that by itself," muttered the judge, still counting his money.

"I met an old acquaintance down in the city," said Ishmael, gradually feeling his way towards the announcement of Katie.

"Ah!" said the judge indifferently, and going on with his counting.

"An old friend, indeed, I may say," added Ishmael emphatically.

"Yes," replied the judge absently, and continuing to count.

"Judge Merlin," inquired Ishmael, in a meaning tone, "have you no curiosity to know who it was that I met near the quays?"

"No," said the old man, counting diligently; "some fellow you knew in Washington, I suppose, my boy. Why, the Lord bless you, I stumbled over half a dozen acquaintances on my way to the consulate and the bank. Among them Frank Tourneysee, who is staying here with his brother for the benefit of his health. He is a consumptive, poor man! crossed in love; or something;

"Sir, it was no casual acquaintance or ordinary friend that I met," said Ishmael, in so grave a voice that the judge looked up from his work and stared in wonder, not at the words, but at the manner of the speaker.

"It was no man, but a woman, sir," continued Ishmael, fixing his eyes wistfully upon the face of the old man.

"It was Claudia!" cried the judge, in an ear-piercing voice, jumping at once at the most improbable conclusion, as he started up, pale as death, and gazed with breathless anxiety upon the grave face of Ishmael.

"No, Judge Merlin," answered the young man, as he gently replaced him in his seat; "no, it was not Lady Vincent; but it is one who, I hope, can give us later news of her."

"Who—who was it then?" gasped the old man, trembling violently.

Ishmael poured out a glass of water and handed it to the judge, saying calmly:

"It was old Katie whom I met."

"Katie!" cried the judge, in astonishment, and holding the glass of water suspended in his hand.

"Katie. But drink your water, Judge Merlin; it will refresh you."

"Katie! But where is her mistress?" demanded the old man, in burning anxiety.

"I do not know, sir; Katie was too much excited by the shock of her meeting with me and hearing that you were on the island to give any coherent account of herself."

"But—how came she here if not in attendance upon her mistress? And—what should have brought Claudia here?—unless she should have been on her voyage home to me, and got wrecked and brought here, as we have been, which is not likely."

"No; that is too improbable to have happened, I should think. But drink the water, sir, let me beg of you."

"I will. I will, Ishmael, when I have qualified it a little!" said the judge, tottering to his feet and going to a buffet upon which stood some Jamaica rum. He mixed a strong glass of spirits and water, drank it, and returned to his seat, saying, as he sank into it with a deep sigh of refreshment:

"I feel better. Where is Katie? And how in the world came she here? And what news does she bring of her mistress?"

"Katie is outside that door, sir, waiting for you to receive her."

"Let her come in, then, Ishmael."

CHAPTER XXXV

A FATHER'S VENGEANCE.

Haste me to know it; that I, with wings as swift

As meditation or the thoughts of love,

May sweep to my revenge!

—Shakespeare.

Ishmael went to the door and admitted Katie. The old woman made an impulsive rush towards her master, but stopped and burst into a passion of tears so violent that she was scarcely able to stand.

"Sit down, Katie. Sit down and compose yourself. Your master will not take it amiss that you sit in his presence," said Ishmael, pushing a low, soft chair towards the woman, while he glanced inquiringly towards the judge.

"Certainly not; let her rest; sit down, Katie. How do you do?" said the judge, going towards his old servant and holding out his hands.

"Oh, marster! Oh, marster!" sobbed Katie, sinking into the seat and clinging to her master's venerable hands, upon which her tears fell like rain.

The judge gently withdrew his hands, but it was only that he might use them for Katie's relief.

He poured out a glass of the same restorative that he had found so effectual in his own case, and he made her drink it.

Poor Katie was unused to such stimulants, and she immediately felt its effects. Her eyes sparkled threateningly as she set the empty glass down upon the table.

"Ah!" she exclaimed, with indescribable force of spite; "ah, the whited saltpeter! Now I send her to de penumtenshury; now I send her dere to pick oakum in a crash gown and cropped hair, and an oberseer wid a big whip to drive her!"

"What is she talking of? What does she mean by whited saltpeter?" inquired the judge.

"'Whited sepulchre' is Katie's Scripture name for a hypocrite, I suppose," suggested Ishmael.

"Not on'y for a hypocrite, Marse Ishmael! Not on'y for a hypocrite; but for a pi'son, 'ceitful, lyin' white nigger!" said Katie, with her eyes snapping.

"Katie, Katie, you are using ugly words," remonstrated the judge.

"Not half so venomous ugly as dem I applies 'em to, begging your pardon, ole marse," said the woman, with a positive nod of her head.

"Where did you leave your lady?" inquired the judge, who had been almost dying of anxiety to ask this question, but had refrained on account of Katie's excessive agitation. "Where did you leave your mistress?"

"Le'me see. Where did I leave her ag'in? Oh! I 'members exactly now. 'Deed I got good reason to 'member dat night, if I never 'members anoder day nor night of my life."

"Tell us, Katie," said Ishmael.

"Well, den, I done lef her on de grand staircase o' de castle a- goin' down to dinner. And she looked beautiful in her rosy more antics, just like a lamb dressed for the sacrifice, 'cordin' to de Scriptur'. And she unsuspicionin' anything and me dyin' to tell her, on'y she wouldn't stop to listen to me."

"To tell her what, Katie?"

"Why, laws, honey, 'bout de debblish plot as my lordship and dat whited saltpeter and de shamwalley plotted ag'in her—ag'in her, my own dear babyship—ladyship, I meant to say."

"There was a plot, then?" inquired Ishmael, with forced calmness, for he wished quietly to draw out the woman's story without agitating and confusing her. "There was a plot then?"

"Oh, wasn't dere? De blackest plot ag'in my ladyship as ebber de old debbil hisse'f could o' put in anybody's head. And I heard it all! And I heard it all good, too."

"What was it, Katie? Can you tell us?" inquired Ishmael, while the judge bent his pale, careworn, and anxious face nearer the speaker.

"Well, Marse Ishmael, you know how solemn you cautioned me to watch ober my ladyship, don't you, sir?"

"Yes, Katie; yes."

"Well, I beared what you said in mind. And de dear knows as my poor dear ladyship did 'quire to be watched ober worse nor anybody I ebber seed. It seems like you was a prophet, Marse Ishmael, 'cause how you know how she was going to be sitterated."

"Never mind, Katie. Go on and tell us of the plot," said Ishmael, while Judge Merlin's face grew sharp and peaked in his silent anguish of suspense. But both knew that it was best to let Katie tell her story in her own way.

"Well, Marse Ishmael, sir, I laid to heart what you telled me so solemn, and I did watch ober my ladyship, and I watched ober her good! And she didn't know it, nor likewise nobody else. And berry soon I saw as my ladyship was 'rounded by inimies. And as dat whited saltpeter was a'tryin' to take her husband away from her. And den ag'in I say plain 'nough as my lordship was willin' 'nough for to be tuk, for dat matter. So I watched him and de whited saltpeter."

"But who is it that you call the whited sepulchre, Katie?" demanded the judge.

"Why, who but his sisser-in-law! his sisser-in-law what lib long o' him; yes! and libbed long o' him afore ebber my poor, dear, 'ceived ladyship ebber see him!"

"But who was this lady, and what was her name?" asked the judge.

"She warn't no lady! She was an oppry singer, as was no better 'an she should be, and as had misled away my lordship's younger brother, who married of her, and died, and serve him right, de 'fernally fool! And den ebber since he died she done lib long o' my lordship at de castle. And her name is Mrs. Doogood, which is a 'fernally false, 'cause she nebber does no good! But my lordship, whenebber he's palabering ob his sof' nonsense to her, he call her, so he do, Fustunner! I s'pose 'cause, when she quarrel wid him, she make fuss 'nough to stun a miller."

"And this woman you say was my daughter's enemy?"

"Well, I reckon, marster, as you would call her sich, ef you heerd de plot she and my lordship and de shamwalley made up 'gin my ladyship."

"Yes, but, Katie, you have not yet told us the plot," said Ishmael.

"Well, I gwine do it now, right off, Marse Ishmael! Well, you see I kept on watchin' of 'em, till one day, it happened as a poor gal, one o' de housemaids, was found wid her t'roat cut unnerneaf of de castle wall—"

At this announcement Judge Merlin started and looked at Ishmael, but the young man made a sign that the judge should say nothing that might interrupt the thread of Katie's narrative. Katie continued:

"And de offercers ob de law tuk possession ob de castle to 'quire inter who was de murderers ob de poor gal. But de more dey 'quired inter it, de more dey couldn't find it out! And arter dey'd stayed dere a whole week 'quiring, dey was furder off from findin' out nor ebber. So dey all up and sent in a werdick as de gal was foun' wid her t'roat cut and nobody knowed who did it. Dat was de werdick. Which dey needn't o' stayed 'quiring and eaten' and drinkin' on us a whole week to tell us dat. 'Cause we knowed dat much afore. How-so-ebber, home 'dey all went and let de poor gal be buried. And I happened to be in de big hall and to cotch my eye on my lordship, as he said to his wally sham:

"'Frisbie, I shall want you in my room presently; so don't be out o' de way.'

"And I cotch my eye on Mr. Frisbie, too, and I see how he turned sort o' white round de gills, and he say:

"'I'll be at hand, my lord.'

"I says:

"'And so will I be at hand, my lord.'

"And sure 'nough, I goes and steals inter my lordship's dressing room, unbeknown to anybody, and I hides myself ahind one ob dem thick curtains! And presently sure 'nough my lordship he comes in and rings for Mr. Frisbie. Marse Ishmael, honey, would you mind givin' of your poor old Aunt Katie another tumbler o' rum? 'Deed I don't beliebe as I can go on wid de story widout somet'ing to s'port me."

"So much rum is not good for you, Katie, but I will give you a glass of water," said Ishmael.

"Oh, honey, no, don't, please! I don't like water in de winter time, it allers gibs me a cold in the stummick. But rum warms me."

Judge Merlin, who was much too anxious that Katie should continue her story to be fastidious as to the means he took to that end, poured out and administered to the old creature a small portion of the spirits.

"Thanky, marster! thanky, chile! You'se got some feelin' for ole folks, you has! Dese young people, dey aint got no 'sideration, dey aint. Dat make me feel good all ober! now I gwine on. Well, Mr. Frisbie, he answers my lordship's bell and he comes in, so he does. And den—oh! Marse Ishmael!—my lordship 'cuses ob him o' bein' de murderer! and tells him how he, my lordship, seen him, Mr. Frisbie, do de deed! Well Frisbie, he fell on his two knees and begged for marcy. And oh! marster! my lordship promised to hide his crime on conditions—such conditions, Marse Ishmael!"

"What were they, Katie?" inquired Judge Merlin, in a dying voice, for a suspicion of something like the truth made him reel.

"My lordship promised de shamwalley he would save him from de gallows if he would help him to get rid ob Lady Vincent."

There was an irrepressible exclamation of horror from Ishmael and a low cry of anguish from Judge Merlin. But neither ventured to speak, lest by doing so he should confuse Katie, who continued her story.

"And so my lordship plotted wid de shamwalley, how he, de shamwalley, was to 'tend to be fond o' my ladyship, and follow arter her, and do sly things to draw de eyes o' de household on her, make dem all s'picion her, and talk about her—"

"What! my daughter! Claudia Merlin!" exclaimed the judge, in a voice of thunder, as he started to his feet and stood staring at the speaker.

"Oh, ole marse, for de Lord's sake, don't! You scare away all de little sense dem debbils has lef' me!" cried Katie, shuddering.

"His wretched lackey!" vociferated the judge. "By all the fiends in flames, I'll shoot that scoundrel Vincent with less remorse than I would a mad dog!"

"Oh, marster, yes! shoot him or hang him, jus' which ebber you thinks bes'! On'y don't roar so loud; for 'deed it's awful to hear you! And besides, if you do, I can't go on and tell you no more, and you ought to hear it all, you know," shivered Katie.

"She is right, sir! Pray compose yourself. Do you not see how important it is that we should have a clear statement of facts from this eye- and ear-witness of the conspiracy against Lady Vincent's honor? Try to listen coolly, sir! as coolly as if you were on the bench. Be—not the father, but the judge," earnestly remonstrated Ishmael, as he gently constrained his old friend to sit down again.

"Don't you know that I will kill that man?" exclaimed the judge, as he sank into his seat.

"I know that you will do just what a Christian gentleman should do in the premises," gravely replied Ishmael.

"Go on! what next?" demanded the judge, in a voice that utterly upset Katie, who had to recover her composure before she could continue her statement. At last she said:

"Well, den, arter dey had 'ranged dat plot dey lef' de room. And I come out and waylaid my ladyship to tell her all about it and put her on her guard. And I met her on de stairs jus' as I telled you afore, and she looking like an angel o' beauty; but she wouldn't stop to listen to me. She tole me to go to her dressing room and wait for her there. And she walked downstairs like any queen, so she did, and dat was de las' as ebber I see ob my ladyship."

Here Katie paused for breath. Ishmael made a sign to Judge Merlin not to speak. Then Katie went on.

"I goed to de dressin' room; and I waited and waited hour arter hour, but my ladyship she nebber come. But while I was a-peeping t'rough de door, a-watching for her, in comes dat whited saltpeter and goes into her 'partments. And den soon arter comes my lordship, takin' long, sly steps, like a cat as is gwine to steal cream. And he goes into Fustunner's rooms."

Katie paused, drew a long breath, and went on.

"You may be sure, marster, as I knowed he war a-going in dere to talk ober his debblish plot long o' her. So I jus' took a leaf out'n my lordship's own book and I creeps along jus' as sly as he could and I peeps t'rough de keyhole, and I sees as how dey wasn't in de outermos' room, but in de innermos', dough all the doors was open in a row and I seen clear t'rough to de dressin'-room fire, where dey was bof a-standing facin' of it, wid deir backs towards me. So I opens de door sof', an' steals in t'rough all de rooms to de las' one, and hides myse'f in de folds ob de curtain as was drawed up one side o' de door. So, sure 'nough, he was a-tellin' of her 'bout de plot ag'n my ladyship, and how dey would 'trive t'rough de wallysham to make her appear guilty, so he could get a 'vorce from her, and keep her fortin, and marry Fustunner!"

"Flames and furies!" burst forth the judge, starting to his feet; but Ishmael firmly, though gently, put him down again, and made an imploring sign that he should control his passion and listen in calmness.

It took Katie some little time to get over this last startling shock before she could continue her story.

"Now, Marse Ishmael, if you don't keep ole marster quiet, 'deed I gwine shut up my mouf, 'cause he's wuss on anybody's narves dan an elected battery," she said.

"Go on, Katie, go on!" commanded Ishmael, as he stood by Judge Merlin's chair and kept his arm over the old man's shoulders.

"Well, den, he keep still. 'Deed I 'fraid he tears me up nex' time he jump at me."

"Have no uneasiness, Katie. Go on!"

"Well, dat whited saltpeter—oh, but she's deep!—'proved obde plot, and clapped her hands like a fool, and den she 'proved on de plot, too, for she planned out how dey should all make a party to go to de play, and pertend to inwite my ladyship to go 'long too, which they knowed she wouldn't do. And how dey should go widout her; and how de shamwalley should hide himse'f in my ladyship's room, unbeknownst to her; and how dey should all come back and bust open de door and find him in dere; and how he should 'fess a lie as my ladyship invited him dere, and was in de habit ob so doing—"

Here Ishmael had hard work to keep Judge Merlin down in his seat, and restrain the old man's demonstrations within the limits of making awful faces and tearing out his own gray hair by the roots.

Katie meanwhile continued:

"Well, marster, jus' when I had heerd dat much—cuss my nose!—I beg your pardon, Marse Ishmael, but—I sneezed! And nex' minute my lordship had me by de t'roat, and den he began cussin' and swearin', an' sassin' at me hard as ebber he could. But didn't I gib him good as he sent, soon as ebber he let go my t'roat? Well, childun, I jus' did! But den, when dey foun' out I had heern ebberyt'ing, and knowed all deir 'fernally tricks, and mean to 'form on dem, dey got scared, dey did! And my lordship ax what was to be done? And de whited saltpeter said how I mus'n't be let to leabe de room alibe. So when I heerd dat, I got scared; and anybody would in my place. So I opened my mouf to scream. But lor', childun, he squeezed my t'roat till I loss my breaf as well as my voice. But I heerd him ax her ag'in what was to be done? For, you see, de 'fernally fool seemed to 'pend on her for ebberyt'ing. And he ax her couldn't she help him? And she rushed about de room and fotch somefin, and he put it to my nose, and—I went dead!"

"It must have been chloroform," suggested Ishmael.

"Dunno what it was; but I'm sure I should know de truck ag'in. For of all de grape winyards and apple orchids and flower gardens as ebber smelt lovely, dat truck smelt de loveliest. And of all de silvery flutes and violins and pineannas and bells as ebber rung out for a wedding, dat truck did ring de silveriest t'rough my brain. And of all de 'luminations as ebber was 'luminated for de presiden's 'lection, dat truck did 'luminate my eyes. And tell you what, childun, dough dey was a-murdering of me wid it, de 'ceiving truck sent me right to hebben afore it sent me dead!"

"What next?" inquired Ishmael.

"Well, nex' thing when I come to life ag'in, I found myself in a dark, narrow, steep place, going down—bump! bump! bump! and den faster—bumpetty—bumpetty—bumpetty—bump! till I t'ought ebbery blessed bone in my body would have been broke! And I t'ought how two debbils had hold of my soul, a-dragging it down to—you know where," said Katie, rolling her eyes mysteriously.

"Proceed," said Ishmael.

"Well, when dey got me to de bottom, dey drag me along a wet, hard, stony floor, so dey did; and I 'fraid to draw my bref! Oh, marster! I couldn't tell you how far dey dragged me, till dey stopt. Den a voice said:

"'Finish her here!'—and dat was Fustunner's voice. And den anoder voice answered and said:

"'She's done for already.' And dat was my lordship's voice.

"And den I knowed as dey wa'n't debbils—leastways not spiritual debbils—as had my soul, dragging it down to—you know where; but human debbils, as was takin' of me down in some deep wault to kill me. So I t'ought de best t'ing I could do was to sham dead. So I kep' my eyes shet and held my breaf, and shammed hard as I could. But somehow or 'noder I don't t'ink I 'ceived my lordship. I t'ink I on'y 'ceived her. Anyways, he pitched me neck and crop into a dark, stony, wet cell, and locked de door on me, and den dey bof went away."

Here Katie paused and remained silent so long that Ishmael felt obliged again to set her going by saying:

"Well, Katie, what followed?"

"Why, nothing but darkness; blackness of darkness, Marse Ishmael, so thick it 'peared like I could feel it with my hands. I did get up on my feet and feel all around, and dere was nothing below, or 'round, or ober me but wet stone wall. And de place was so small, as I could stand dere and reach any part of de wall on any side ob me widout taking of a step. And wa'n't dat a perty place to put a Christian 'oman into? Deed, I beliebe I should o' gib up de ghose, if I had had de t'ought to t'ink about myself. But I hadn't. I t'ought only of my poor, dear ladyship up dere 'sposed to de treachery ob dem debbils wid nobody to warn her, nor likewise purtect her, poor dear baby! And when I t'ought of dat, seemed to me as my poor heart would 'a' bust. And I beliebe it would, on'y dere came a divurtisement. For you see, I sets myself down in my 'spair, on de cole stone floor; and soon as ebber I does dat, a whole passel o' rats come a-nosin' and a-smellin' at me, and nibblin' my shoes 's if dey'd like to 'vour me alibe; and it tuk all my time and 'tention to dribe dem away."

"That was horrible, Katie," said Ishmael, in a tone of sympathy.

"Well, so it was, Marse Ishmael; but for all dat somehow I was right down glad to see de rats— dey was alibe, and arter dey come, 'peared like de place wasn't so much like a grabe; 'sides which dey was company for me down dere in de dark, and dey gi' me somefin to do, keepin' dem offen me."

"But, Katie, were you not afraid of being abandoned there and left to die?"

"Well, honey, I s'pose I should ha' been ef I had t'ought of it. But, you see, I nebber t'ought o' nothin' but my poor, dear, desolate ladyship, as I telled you before."

"Yes; I can easily understand that, Katie. Lady Vincent's situation was even much worse than your own," said Ishmael.

"Oh, the infernal scoundrel! I'll kill him! I'll shoot him like a dog, if I have to follow him all over the world and spend my life in the pursuit!" broke forth Judge Merlin.

There ensued a short pause in the conversation, and then Ishmael, speaking in a low, calm tone, inquired:

"How long did you remain in that dungeon, Katie?"

"'Deed, Marse Ishmael, chile, I dunno; cause, you see, I hadn't no ways o' keepin' 'count o' de time; for, you see, noonday was jus' as dark as midnight in dat den. So how I gwine tell when day broke, or when night come ag'in? or how many days broke, or how many nights come?"

"Then you have really no idea of how long you remained there?"

"Not a bit! 'Cause, you see, Marse Ishmael, 'pears to me, judging by my feelin's, as I must a stayed dere about seben years. But den I don't s'pose I stayed dat long neider, 'cause I know I nebber had nothin' to eat nor drink all de time I was dere; which, you know I couldn't a' fasted seben years, down dere, could I?"

"Not with safety to life and health, Katie," smiled Ishmael.

"Well, den, if it wasn't seben years, it was as long as ebber anybody could lib dere a-fastin'!"

"How did you get out at last, Katie?"

"Well, now, Marse Ishmael, begging of your pardon, dat was the curiousest t'ing of all! I dunno no more how I come out'n dat dark den, nor de man in de moon! I t'ink it was witchcraft and debbilment, dat's what I t'ink," whispered Katie, rolling her eyes mysteriously.

"Tell us what you do know, however," said Ishmael.

"Well, all I know is jus' dis: I had to keep my eyes open day and night to dribe de rats away. And tired and sleepy as I was, I dar'n't go to sleep, for fear as dey would 'vour me alibe. Last, hows'eber, I was so dead tired, and so dead sleepy, dat I couldn't keep awake no longer, and so I fell fas' asleep, and now, Marse Ishmael, listen, 'cause I gwine to tell you somethin' wery 'stonishin'! Sure as I'm a-libbin' 'oman, standin' here afore your eyes, when I drapped asleep I was in dat dark den, unner de groun', and when I waked up I was in a ship sailin' on de big sea! Dere! you may beliebe me or not, as you choose, but dat is de trufe!"

Judge Merlin and Ishmael exchanged glances and then the latter said:

"The case is a perfectly clear one to me, sir. While she slept she was made to inhale chloroform, and while under its influence she was conveyed from her prison to the ship, very likely a smuggler; and was brought here and sold for a slave."

"Dere! dere! If Marse Ishmael wort aint hit de nail right on de head! To be sure it mus' a been chloe-fawn! And 'pears to me I has a faint membry as how I was dreaming o' de same sweet scents and silver bells and rosy lights as I had 'sperienced once afore. To be sure it mus' a been chloe-fawn! And as for de rest, Marse Ishmael, it is all true as gospel! Sure 'nough, dey did fetch me to dis island and dey did sell me for a slabe," said old Katie.

"But hadn't you a tongue in your head? Couldn't you have told the people here that you were free?" demanded Judge Merlin impatiently.

"An' sure, didn't I do it? Didn't I pallaber till my t'roat was sore? And didn't poor Jim and Sally pallaber till deir t'roats was sore? And didn't all t'ree of us pallaber togeder till we mos' wore out our tongues? Didn't do no good, dough! 'Cause you see, de people here is sich barbariums dat dey cannot unnerstan' one word o' good Christian talk."

"And if they had understood you, Katie, as some of them probably did, it would not have served you; your unsupported words would have never been taken. As you are aware, my dear judge, if you will take time to reflect," added Ishmael, turning to Judge Merlin,

"Certainly, certainly," replied the latter.

"But, Katie, you mentioned Sally and Jim. Is it possible that they also were kidnaped?" inquired Ishmael.

"You better beliebe it, honey! 'Cause it's true as gospel, chile! Now I gwine to tell you all about it. One o' de fust tings I t'ought when I woke up and stared around to find myself aboard dat vessel on de water, was dat I had died in dat cell and dat de angels was a-takin' my soul across de Riber ob Jordan to the City ob de New Jerusalem 'cordin' to de Scriptur'. On'y you see, chile, I wasn't dat downright sure and sartain as I myse'f was a saint prepared for hebben; nor likewise did de man as sat smoking and drinking at de table look like the chief ob de angels."

"In what part of the ship were you when you recovered your consciousness?" inquired Ishmael, who wished to have a clear idea of the "situation."

"In de cap'n's cabin, Marse Ishmael. And dat was de cap'n, dough I didn't know who he was, nor where I was, at de time. So I up and ax him:

"'Please, marster, if you please, sir, to tell me is I to go to hebben or t'other place?'

"'Oh! you've come to, have you?' says he, and he takes a pipe from de table and he whistles.

"And den a bad-lookin' man comes down. And says de captain to him:

"'Jack, bundle dis 'oman out'n here and put her into the steerage.'

"And de ill-lookin' man he says to me:

"'Come along, blacky!'

"And so I up and followed him to de deck, 'cause why not? What was de use o' resistin'? 'Sides which, I t'ought by going farder I might fine out more. And sure 'nough so I did! for soon as ebber I got on deck, de fuss person I see was Jim. Which soon as ebber I see him, and he see me, he run, de poor boy, and cotch me 'round de neck, and hugged and kissed me, and said says he:

"'Oh, my mammy! is dis you?'

"And says I:

"'Yes, Jim, it's me! I died down dere, in a wault, in de bottom o' de castle. When did you die, Jim?'

"'Am I dead, mammy?' says he.

"'Why, to be sure you are,' says I, 'else how you come here?'

"'And dat's true enough,' says he. 'On'y I didn't know I was dead till you told me, mammy. Well, if I'm dead, I s'pose I must 'a' died sudden. Cause I know I was well and hearty enough; on'y dat I was troubled 'bout you, mammy; and I went to sleep in my bed and when I waked up I was here.'

"Well, while Jim was talkin' I heerd de man, Jack, say:

"'Go along den, you cuss! dere's your frien's.'

"And I looked up and dere he was a-pushing Sally along towards us!

"'And, oh, Sally,' says I, 'are you dead too?'

"'No, Aunt Katie, I aint dead; but I'm stole! And I s'pects you all is too!' And den she boo-hoo-ed right out.

"'Sally,' says I, 'you is dead!'

"'No, I aint, Aunt Katie, I's stole!' she said, crying as if her heart would break.

"'Sally,' says I, 'you's dead! Now don't 'ny it! 'Cause what would be de use? For if you aint dead, how came you here?'

"'I know how I come here well enough. I was stole out'n my bed and brought here. And my lordship help de t'ieves to steal me. I saw him.'

"'Mammy,' says Jim, 'I reckon Sally's in de right ob it. And 'deed I hopes she is; 'cause you see if she aint dead, why no more are we; and if she was stole, why, it's like as we was too!' And den turnin' round to Sally, he says, says he:

"'Sally, tell us what happened to you.'

"So Sally she told us how she hadn't been able to sleep de night afore; and how towards mornin' she t'ought she would get up and dress herse'f. And jus' as she was a-puttin' on her shoes, all ob a sudden de door opens and in walks my lordship, follyed by two men! which she was so 'stonished she could do nothing but stare, 'till my lordship sprung at her t'roat and put somefing to her nose, as made her faint away. Which ob course it mus' a been chloe-fawn."

"Of course," said Ishmael; "but go on with your statement."

"Well, and Sally tole me how, when she come to herself, she was in dis wessel. But she says she wasn't 'ceived one bit. She 'membered eberyting. And she could swear to de men as stole her, which dey was my lordship—and a perty lordship he is!—and de captain o' de wessel and de fust mate."

"Sally will be a most invaluable witness against those felons Judge Merlin, if she can be found and taken to England," whispered Ishmael.

The old man nodded assent. And Katie continued:

"Well, childun, afore I heerd Sally's 'scription o' how dey sarved her, I could a sword as we was all dead, and on our woyage cross de riber of Jordan. But arter dat I was open to conwiction; which you know, Marse Ishmael, I was allers ob a lib'ral, 'lightened turn o' mind! And so I gib in as we was all alibe."

"Well, and what then, Katie? How did you reconcile yourself to your lot?"

"Well, Marse Ishmael, you know how it is wid us poor cullered folks, as can't eben call our childun our own? Well, seeing as we was in de hand o' de spoiler, we laid low and said nothin'. What would a been de use o' makin' a fuss dere? We couldn't get out'n de wessel if dey'd let us, 'less we had gone inter de water. So we 'signed ourselves to carcumstances and did de bes' we could till we arribed out here to dese Wes' Stingy Islands and was put up for sale. Den we spoke; but we might jus' as well a held our tongues; for as I telled you afore, dese barbariums don't unnerstan' one blessed word o' good Christian talk. And so, Marse Ishmael, spite o' all we could say, poor Jim was knocked down to a sinner-done as libe in de country, which sinner-done took him off dere. And Sally she was sole to a sinner-done as libs near de Captain General's palace. Dese barbariums calls all de ladies and gemmen sinner-dones an' sinner-doners. And I was give away to a 'fernal low shopkeeper near de quays."

"Now, Judge Merlin," said Ishmael, "that we have heard her story, we must take very prompt measures."

"What would you do, Ishmael?"

For all answer, Ishmael rang the bell and ordered a carriage to be brought to the door immediately. That done, he turned to the judge and said:

"We must take Katie with us, ask Mr. Brudenell to accompany us, and drive first to the office of our consul. We shall require official assistance in the recovery of these servants. We must be quick, for we must get all this business settled in time for the sailing of the 'Cadiz,' in which we must return to England, and take these negroes with us. We must at any cost; even if we have to purchase them back at double the money for which they were sold. For you see that their testimony is all we require to overthrow Lord Vincent and vindicate his wife."

"Oh, the infernal villain! Do you think, Ishmael, that I shall be contented with simply overthrowing him in the divorce court? No! By all that is most sacred, I will kill him!" thundered the judge.

"We will not have any divorce trial," said Ishmael firmly. "We will not have your daughter's pure name dragged through the mire of a divorce court; we will have Lord Vincent and his accomplices arrested and tried; the valet for murder, and the viscount and the opera singer for conspiracy and kidnaping. We have proof enough to convict them all; the valet will be hanged; and the viscount and the opera singer sentenced to penal servitude for many years. Will not that be sufficient punishment for the conspirators. And is it not better that the law should deal out retributive justice to them, than that you should execute unlawful vengeance?" inquired the young man.

"But my daughter! My daughter!"

"Your daughter shall be restored to you; her dower recovered; her name preserved; and her honor perfectly, triumphantly vindicated."

CHAPTER XXXVI

ON THE VISCOUNTS TRACK.

Vengeance to God alone belongs;

But when I think of all my wrongs

My blood is liquid flame!

—Marmion.

While Ishmael and Judge Merlin still conversed the carriage was announced. A message was dispatched to Mr. Brudenell; but the messenger returned with the news that the gentleman had gone out.

Therefore Ishmael and the judge, taking Katie with them, entered the carriage and gave the order to be driven to the American consul's office.

The way was long, the carriage slow, and the judge boiling over with rage and impatience.

It was well for Judge Merlin that he had Ishmael Worth beside him to restrain his passion and guide his actions.

During the ride the young lawyer said:

"In conducting this affair, Judge Merlin, Lady Vincent's welfare must be our very first consideration."

"Oh, yes, yes!"

"To do her any good we must act with promptitude."

"Of course."

"But to act with promptitude, great sacrifices must be made."

"What sacrifices?"

"In the first place, you must lay aside your desire for vengeance upon the villainous kidnapers who brought your old servants here and sold them."

"Ah, but, Ishmael, I cannot bear to let them go unpunished."

"Believe me, no crime ever goes unpunished. These men, sooner or later, will be brought to justice. But if you attempt to prosecute them, you will be detained here for days, weeks, and perhaps even months. For, once having laid so grave a charge against any man, or set of men, you would be compelled to remain as a prosecuting witness against them. And the delay would be almost fatal to Lady Vincent, suffering as she must be the most extreme agony of suspense."

"I see! I see! Poor Claudia! she must be my only thought! I must leave the smuggler to the justice of Heaven. But it is a sacrifice, Ishmael."

"A necessary one, sir; but there is still another that you must make in order to hasten to the rescue of Lady Vincent."

"And that?"

"Is the sacrifice of a large sum of money. A large sum, even for a man of fortune like yourself, judge."

"And that fortune is not nearly so considerable as it is supposed to be, Ishmael. When I had paid over my daughter's dower, I left myself but a moderate independence."

"Nevertheless, judge, if it should take the whole of your funded property, you will gladly devote it to the vindication of your daughter's honor. We must be in England with our witnesses in time to arrest Lord Vincent and his accomplices before he has an opportunity of bringing on the divorce suit."

"Certainly."

"To do this you will have to expend a large sum of money in the repurchasing of the negroes; for you must be aware that their present owners, having bought them in good faith, will not relinquish them without a struggle, which would involve you in a long lawsuit, the issue of which would be very doubtful; for you must be aware that there are many knotty points in this case. Now, I put the question to you, whether you can, with safety to Lady Vincent, remain here for weeks or months, either as prosecutor in the criminal trial of the smugglers or as plaintiff in a civil suit with the purchasers of Lady Vincent's servants?"

"I cannot."

"Then do not attempt either to punish the kidnapers or wrest the slaves from the hands of their present owners. Our plan will be simply this: Take the consul with us to identify us, go to these owners, explain the facts, and offer to repurchase the negroes at once. They will, no doubt, gladly come to terms, rather than risk a lawsuit in which they would probably lose their purchase-money."

"I see. Yes, Ishmael. You are wise and right, as you always are," said the judge, with an air of conviction.

"All this business may be arranged in time for us to take passage on the 'Cadiz,' that sails on Saturday. Now, here we are at the consul's office," said Ishmael, as the carriage stopped at the door of the American consulate.

Leaving Katie in the carriage they alighted and entered. The consul was engaged, so that they were detained in the anteroom nearly half an hour; at the end of which four or five gentlemen were seen to issue from the inner room, and then the doorkeeper, with a bow, invited Judge Merlin's party to pass in.

Philip Tourneysee, the American consul for Havana at that time, was the eldest son of that General Tourneysee whom the reader has already met at the house of Judge Merlin in Washington. He had sought his present appointment because a residence in the West Indies had been recommended for his health. He was a slight, elegant, refined-looking man, with a clear complexion, bright auburn hair, and dark hazel eyes. The fine expression of his countenance alone redeemed it from effeminacy.

On seeing Judge Merlin enter with his party he arose smilingly to receive them.

"You are surprised to see me here again so soon, Philip," said the judge, as he seated himself in the chair placed for him by the consul.

"I cannot see you too often, judge," was the courteous answer.

"Hem! This is my friend, Mr. Worth, of the Washington bar. Mr. Worth, Mr. Tourneysee, our consul for the port of Havana," said the judge, with all his old-fashioned formality.

The gentlemen thus introduced bowed, and the consul offered a chair to his second visitor and then seated himself and looked attentive.

"We have come about the most awkward business that ever was taken in hand," said the judge; "the strangest and most infamous, also, that ever came before a criminal tribunal. But let that pass. What would you say, for instance, to the fact of an English nobleman turning slave-trader—and not only slave-trader, but slave-stealer?"

The consul looked perplexed and incredulous.

"I will tell you all about it," said the judge, who immediately commenced and related to the astonished consul the history of the abduction and sale of the three negroes by Lord Vincent, and their subsequent transportation to Cuba and second sale at Havana by the smugglers.

"You will, of course, cause instant search to be made for the guilty parties, and I will certainly give you every assistance in my power, both in my public capacity and as your private friend. We will go to work at once," said the consul warmly, placing his hand upon the bell.

"No," said the judge, arresting his motion. "I have consulted with my friend and counsel, Mr. Worth, and we have decided that the smugglers, who are, after all, but the subordinates in this guilty confederacy, must go unpursued and unpunished for the present."

"How?" inquired the consul, turning to Ishmael, as if he doubted his own ears.

"Yes, sir," said Ishmael calmly, "circumstances into which it is not necessary that we should now enter, render it absolutely necessary that we should be in England as soon as possible. It is equally necessary that we should take the negroes with us, not only as witnesses against their first abductor as to the fact of the abduction, but also as to other transactions of which they were cognizant previous to that event. We must therefore avoid lawsuits which would be likely to detain us here. We cannot delay our departure either to prosecute the smugglers for kidnaping, or to sue the purchasers for the recovery of the negroes. We must leave the smugglers to the retribution of Providence, and we must pay the purchasers for the negroes we wish to carry away with us. What, therefore, we would ask of your kindness is this—that you will go with us to the purchasers of these negroes and identify us, so as to smooth the way for a negotiation of our difficulties."

"Certainly, certainly. Let me see. I have an appointment here at two o'clock, but at three I will join you at any place you may name."

"Would our hotel be a convenient rendezvous for you?"

"Perfectly."

"Then we will detain you no longer," said Ishmael, rising.

The judge followed his example.

And both gentlemen shook hands with the consul and departed.

"I think," said Ishmael, as they took their seats in the carriage, "that we should take Katie immediately back to her owner. I understand from her that he is a man in the humbler walks of life, and therefore I think that he might be willing to close with us for a liberal advance upon the price paid the smuggler."

"Do so, if you please, Ishmael; I trust entirely to your discretion," answered the judge.

"Katie," said Ishmael to the old woman, who had never left the carriage, "can you direct us the way to find the man who bought you?"

"Not to save my precious life, couldn't I, honey. Because you see, I nebber can t'ink o' de barbareous names dey has to de streets in dis outlan'ish place. But I knows where I is well 'nough. An' I knows where it is—de shop, I mean. And so if you'll put me up alongside ob de driver I can point him which way to go an' where to stop," said Katie.

This proposition was agreed to. The carriage was stopped and Katie was let out and enthroned upon the seat beside the coachman, a Spaniard, whom she proceeded to direct more by signs and gestures than by words.

After a very circuitous route through the city they turned into a narrow street and stopped before a house partly confectionery and partly tobacco shop.

They alighted and went in, and found the proprietor doing duty behind his counter.

The study of the Spanish language had been one of the few recreations Ishmael had allowed himself in his self-denying youth. He had afterwards improved his opportunities by speaking the language with such Spaniards as he met in society in Washington. He therefore now addressed the tobacconist in that tongue, and proceeded to explain the business that brought himself and his friend to the shop.

The tobacconist, who was the ordinary, small, lean, yellow specimen of the middle class of Cubans, courteously invited the "senors" into the back parlor, where they all seated themselves and entered more fully into the subject, Ishmael acting as interpreter between the judge and the tobacconist, whose name they discovered to be Marinello.

Marinello expressed himself very much shocked to find that his purchase of the woman was illegal, if not positively felonious; and that an appeal to the law would probably deprive him of his bargain, and possibly criminate him as the accomplice of the slave stealer.

He said that he had given eight hundred dollars for the woman Katie, who had been extolled by the trader as a most extraordinary cook. And a "most extraordinary" one, he declared, he found her to be, for she did not appear to know beef from mutton or rice from coffee. And in fact she was good for nothing; for even if he sent her on an errand, as on this occasion, she would stay forever and one day after, and charge her sloth upon her infirmities. She had been a bitter bargain to him.

Judge Merlin smiled; he knew Katie to be one of the best cooks in this world and to be in the enjoyment of perfect health, and so he supposed that the cunning old woman had taken a lesson from the sailor's monkey, who could talk, but wouldn't, for fear he should be made to work. And that she had feigned her ignorance and ill health to escape hard labor for one who she knew could have no just claim to her services.

Ishmael, speaking for Judge Merlin, now explained to the tobacconist that this woman Katie had been a great favorite with the mistress from whom she was stolen; that they were on their way to see that lady, that they wished to take the woman with them; that they would rather repurchase her than lose time by suing to recover her; and finally, that they were willing to give him back the money that he had paid for Katie, provided that he would deliver her up to them at once.

Marinello immediately came to terms and agreed to all they proposed. He accompanied them back to the hotel, where he received eight hundred dollars and left Katie.

"That is a 'feat accomplished,'" said Ishmael gayly, as he returned to Judge Merlin's room, after seeing Marinello out; "and now we may expect Mr. Tourneysee every moment."

And in fact while he spoke the door was opened and Mr. Tourneysee was announced.

"I am up to time," he said, smiling, as he entered.

"With dramatic punctuality," said Ishmael, pointing to the clock on the mantel-piece, which was upon the stroke of three.

"Yes," said the consul, smiling.

"We have done a good stroke of business since we left you. We have bought Katie back from her new master at the same price he gave for her, and he was very glad to get out of the affair so happily," said Ishmael.

"Ah! that was prompt indeed. I wish you equal good speed with the other purchasers of stolen slaves. By the way, where do we go first?"

"I think we had best call on the lady who bought the girl Sally; from her—Sally, I mean—we might learn the name and residence of the gentleman who bought Jim, and of which we are at present in ignorance."

"Who is the lady, and where does she live?"

"We do not know her name either; Katie could not tell us; but she lives in the city, and Katie can direct the coachman where to drive. And now as the carriage is at the door, I think we had better start at once."

"I think so, too," said the judge.

And accordingly the whole party went downstairs and re-entered the carriage, with the exception of Katie, who again mounted the box beside the driver for the purpose of directing him.

Katie, who could not, if it were to save her life, remember the name of any place or person in that "barbareous" land, as she called it, yet possessed the canine memory of localities; so she directed the coachman through the shortest cut of the city towards the beautiful suburb Guadaloupe, and then to an elegant mansion of white granite, standing within its own luxuriant grounds.

On seeing the carriage draw up and stop before the gate of this aristocratic residence, the young consul suddenly changed color and said:

"This is the palace of the Senora Donna Eleanora Pacheco, Countess de la Santa Cruz."

"You know this lady?" inquired the judge.

Mr. Tourneysee bowed.

The porter threw open the great gate, and the carriage rolled along a lovely shaded avenue, up before the white marble facade of the palace, where it stopped.

"If you please, I will send your cards in with my own. As I am known to the senora, it may insure you a speedier audience."

"We thank you very much," said Ishmael, placing his own and the judge's cards in the hands of the consul, who alighted, went up the marble steps to the front door, and rang.

A footman opened the door, took in the cards, and after a few moments returned.

"The countess will see the senors," was the message that the consul smilingly brought back to his friends in the carriage.

Then all alighted and went into the house.

The same footman, a jet black young negro, in gorgeous livery of purple and gold, led them into a small, elegantly furnished reception room, where, seated on a sofa, and toying with a fan, was one of the loveliest little dark-eyed Creoles that ever was seen.

She did not rise, but extended her hand with a graceful gesture and gracious smile to welcome her visitors.

Tourneysee advanced, with a deep and reverential bow, that would have done honor to the gravest and most courteous hidalgo of that grave and courteous people.

"Senora," he said, with great formality, "I have the honor to present to your ladyship Chief Justice Merlin, of the United States Supreme Court. Judge Merlin, the Countess de la Santa Cruz."

The judge made a profound bow, which the lady acknowledged by a gracious bend of the head.

With the same serious and stately formality, which was certainly not natural to the young Marylander, but which was assumed, in deference to the grave character of Spanish etiquette, Mr. Tourneysee next presented:

"Mr. Worth, of the Washington bar."

The low obeisance of this visitor was received with even a more gracious smile than had been vouchsafed to that of the judge.

When they were seated, in accordance with the lady's invitation, the conversation turned upon the ordinary topics of the day: the weather; the opera; the last drawing room at the Government Palace; the new Captain General and his beautiful bride, etc., etc., etc.

The judge fidgeted; Ishmael was impatient; the consul perplexed. It was necessary to speak of the affair that brought them there. Yet how was it possible without offense to introduce any topic of business in that bower of beauty, to that indolent Venus, whose only occupation was to toy with her fan; whose only conversation was of sunshine, flowers, music, balls, and brides?

Clearly neither the judge nor the consul had the courage to obtrude any serious subject upon her. The disagreeable task was at length assumed by Ishmael, who never permitted himself to shrink from a duty merely because it was an unpleasant one.

Taking advantage, therefore, of a break in the conversation, he turned to the lady and, speaking with grave courtesy, said:

"Will the senora pardon me for beseeching her attention to an affair of great moment which has brought us to her presence?"

The "senora" lifted her long, curled lashes until they touched her brows, and opened wide her large, soft, dark eyes in childish wonder. "An affair of great moment!" What could it be? A masked ball? a parlor concert? private theatricals? a—what? She could not imagine. Dropping her eyelids demurely, she answered softly:

"Proceed, senor."

Ishmael then briefly explained to her the business upon which they had come.

The senora was as sensible as she was beautiful, and as benevolent as she was sensible. She listened to the story of the negroes' abduction with as much sympathy as curiosity, and at the end of the narrative she exclaimed:

"What villains there are in this world!"

Ishmael then delicately referred to their wish to purchase the girl Sally.

The senora promptly assented to the implied desire.

"It was my steward, Miguel Manello, who bought her for me. I did not particularly want her. And I find her of very little use to me. She cannot understand one word that is said to her. And she does nothing from morning until night but weep, weep, weep tears enough to float away the house."

"Poor girl!" muttered Ishmael.

"So if the senor wishes to recover her he can take her now, or at any time."

Ishmael delicately hinted at the purchase money.

"Oh, I know nothing about such matters. I will send my steward to wait on the senor at his hotel this evening. The senor can then arrange the matter with him."

Ishmael expressed his thanks, arose, and bowed as if to take leave. But the lady waved her hand, and said in a sweet but peremptory manner:

"Be seated, senor."

With another inclination of the head, Ishmael resumed his seat. The lady rang a silver bell that stood on a stand at his right hand and brought to her presence the gorgeous, sable footman.

"Serve the senors with refreshments," was the order given and promptly obeyed.

An elegant little repast was set before them, consisting of delicious coffee, chocolate, fresh fruits, cakes, and sweetmeats. And only when they had done full justice to these delicacies would their hostess permit them to retire.

Again Ishmael bowed with profound deference, expressed his thanks on the part of himself and his friends, and finally took leave.

On going from the room they noticed a person, who, from the extreme quietness of her manner, had escaped their observation until this moment. She was a woman of about sixty years of age, clad in the habit of a lay-sister of the Benedictine Order, and seated within a curtained recess, and engaged in reading her "office." She was probably doing duty as duenna to the beautiful widow.

CHAPTER XXXVII

STILL ON THE TRACK.

One sole desire, one passion now remains,

To keep life's fever still within his veins,—

Vengeance! Dire vengeance on the wretch who cast

On him and all he loved that ruinous blast.

—Moore.

Our party drove back to the hotel to await the coming of the steward with Sally. Mr. Brudenell had not yet returned.

Ishmael sent for the clerk of the house and bespoke proper accommodations for the servants.

But Katie rebelled, and protested that she would not leave her old master until bedtime, when she should insist upon his locking her in her bedroom and taking charge of the key, for fear she should be bewitched and stolen again.

At about six o'clock Miguel Manello arrived, having Sally in charge. According to instructions left with the waiters they were immediately shown up to the apartments of Judge Merlin.

Miguel Manello, a little, dried-up, mahogany-colored old man with blue-gray hair, came in, bowing profoundly.

Sally followed him, but suddenly stopped, opened her mouth and eyes as wide as they could be extended, and stood dumb with astonishment.

As she could not speak a word of Spanish, nor the steward of English, she could not be made to understand where he was bringing her. So she had not the remotest suspicion that she was approaching her master until she actually stood in his presence. Astonishment makes people break into exclamations; but Sally it always struck speechless. So it had been with her when the viscount and his accomplices entered her room that night of the abduction. So it was with her now that she was brought unexpectedly to the presence of the beloved old master whom she had never hoped to see again on this side of the grave.

How long she might have remained standing there, dumfounded, had she not been interrupted, is not known; for old Katie made a dash forward, caught her in an embrace, kissed her, burst into tears, and said:

"Oh, Sally, it is all come right! Ole marster done come here and he gwine to buy us all back and take us to my ladyship, and we gwine be witness ag'in my lordship and de shamvally—which I hopes dey'll be hung, and likewise de whited saltpeter as is de wuss ob de t'ree!"

The tears began to steal down poor Sally's cheeks and she looked appealingly from old Katie to Judge Merlin and Ishmael, as if to entreat confirmation of the good news.

"It is all quite true, Sally. You are to return to England with us, and then, I hope, we shall all come back to old Maryland, never to leave it again," said Ishmael.

"Oh, Marse Ishmael, dat would be like coming out'n purgatory into heaben! Thank de Lord!" fervently exclaimed the girl, while tears—tears of joy—now streamed down her cheeks.

"There, now, Sally; go with your aunty into the next room, and have a glorious old talk, while we settle some business with the steward," said Ishmael, pointing to the door of the anteroom.

When they had retired he beckoned the steward to approach. Miguel Manello advanced with a series of genuflexions, and laid upon the table a document which proved to be a bill of sale for the girl, Sally.

"The senor will perceive," he said, "that I paid the trader twelve hundred dollars for the negress. My mistress, the Senora Donna Eleanora Pacheco, has instructed me to deliver the girl up to the senor at his own price. But the senor will not, perhaps, object to paying the same sum I paid for the girl."

"Certainly not," answered Ishmael.

Judge Merlin produced the money, and the sale was immediately effected. The steward took up his hat to depart, but Ishmael made a sign for him to stop.

"You were present at the sale of this girl?"

"Assuredly, senor; since I purchased her."

"There was an old woman sold at the same time?"

"Yes, senor; the one that I found in here."

"Exactly. There was also a young man?"

"Yes, senor."

"Can you tell me who became his purchaser?"

"Certainly, senor. He was bought by the Senor Don Filipo Martinez, who lives in the Suburb Regla."

"Can you give me directions how to find the place?"

"Certainly, senor. I will write it down, if the senor will permit me the use of his writing-case."

Ishmael placed a chair at the table, and signed for the steward to take it. Miguel Manello sat down, wrote out the directions, handed them to Ishmael, and then with a deep bow took his leave.

When they were alone Ishmael said:

"The Suburb Regla is on the other side of the harbor. We cannot with propriety visit it this evening. In the morning we will set out early. We must either make a long circuit by land, or else take the shorter cut across the harbor. I think the last mentioned the best plan."

"I agree with you," said the judge; "but I fear we are greatly trespassing on the time and the official duties of our friend," he added, turning with a smile to the consul.

"Oh, not at all! I am sufficiently attentive to my business to afford to take a day now and then, when necessity demands it," replied Mr. Tourneysee pleasantly, as he arose and bid his friends good-evening.

He had scarcely left the scene when the door opened and the truant, Herman Brudenell, entered.

"You are a pretty fellow to back your friends. Here we have been overwhelmed with business and beset with adventures, and you gone!" exclaimed the judge, whose spirits were much elated with the successes of the day. "Give an account of yourself, sir!" he added.

"Well," said Mr. Brudenell, throwing himself into a chair and setting his hat upon the table with a wearied, but cheerful air, "I have been walking around the city to see all that was interesting in it. I visited the cathedral, where the ashes of Columbus repose; saw the Government Palace; the Admiralty; the Royal Tobacco Factory; several interesting old churches, and so forth. Last of all, I ran up against a very dear friend of mine, whose acquaintance I made at the court of Queen Isabella when I was at Madrid, some years ago. And Don Filipo insisted on my returning home with him to the Suburb Regla, where he has a beautiful house standing in the midst of equally beautiful grounds. Well, I dined there; and I got away as soon after dinner as I decently could."

"'Don Filipo? Suburb Regla?'" repeated Judge Merlin, as his thoughts ran upon the purchaser of the negro boy Jim.

"Yes. Do you know him? Senor Don Filipo Martinez—"

"No, not personally; we have heard of him, though. Sit still, Brudenell, I have got something to tell you. We have met some old acquaintances also since you left us," said the judge.

"Ah, who are they? The Tourneysees, I presume."

"We have met the Tourneysees of course; but we have met others."

"Then you will have to tell me, judge, for I should never be able to guess among your thousands of friends and acquaintances who were the individuals encountered here."

"What would you say to me if I should tell you that Ishmael met our old Katie in the street and brought her hither?"

"I should say that you or I were mad or dreaming," said Mr. Brudenell, staring at the judge.

"And yet I tell you the sober truth. That infamous villain, Malcolm, Lord Vincent, taking advantage of the opportunities afforded by his residence on a remote part of the sea coast, and his connection with a crew of smugglers, actually succeeded in kidnaping Lady Vincent's three servants and selling them to the trader, who brought them to this island and sold them again."

"Am I awake?" exclaimed Mr. Brudenell, in amazement.

"As much as any of us, I suppose. There are times when I fancy myself in a strange dream."

"What could have been the man's motive for such a crime?"

"Partly, no doubt, cupidity; for he is as mean as marsh mud! partly revenge; for he hates these negroes for their devotion to their mistress; but mostly caution; for one of these negroes became possessed of a secret compromising the reputation, and even the personal liberty of the viscount."

"Good Heavens! I never heard of such a transaction in all my life. Do give me the particulars of this affair."

"By and by. Just now I must tell you that, with the aid of our consul, who has just left us, we have ferreted out the purchasers of the negroes, and we have just repurchased two of them—old Katie and Sally; who are at this present moment in the next room, enjoying their reunion."

"But—why the deuce did you repurchase these negroes, when, by appealing to the law, and proving their felonious abduction and illegal sale, you might have recovered possession of them without paying a dollar?"

"Yes, I might; but then again I mightn't, as the children say. In the first impetuosity of my anger, at discovering these crimes, I would have instantly sued for the recovery of the negroes, and sought out and prosecuted the traders, had it not been for Ishmael. God bless that young man, how much I owe him! He interposed his warning voice and wise counsels. He indicated several questionable features in the case, that would make the issue of any lawsuit that I might bring for the recovery of the negroes very uncertain. He reminded me that if I involved myself in any lawsuit, either civil or criminal, it would detain me on the island for weeks or months, while it is of the utmost importance that I should be at the side of my injured child. I could but acknowledge the truth and justice of his argument, and therefore I have, at some sacrifice of money and temper, repurchased the negroes."

"And looking at the affair from Ishmael's point of view, I think you have done quite right, sir," said Mr. Brudenell.

"And there is another consideration," put in Ishmael. "Judge Merlin mentioned to you, as one of the motives that instigated Vincent to the perpetration of the crime, the fear of the negroes, who had become possessed of a secret involving the liberty of the viscount. This secret was neither more nor less than the knowledge of a conspiracy formed by the viscount and two of his accomplices against the honor of Lady Vincent. Thus, you see, it is absolutely necessary that these negroes should be taken to England without delay as witnesses—"

"In the divorce trial, certainly."

"No; not in the divorce trial; though their testimony in such a trial would be conclusive for the lady. But we wish, if possible, to prevent the divorce trial. We will not have the daughter of Randolph Merlin assailed in such unseemly manner. No woman, however innocent she may be, comes out unscarred from such a struggle; for the simple reason that the bare fact of such a suit having brought against her attaches a life-long reproach to her."

"There is truth in what you say, Ishmael, but I do not see how the trial is to be avoided, since Lord Vincent is determined to sue for a dissolution of his marriage."

"In this way, sir. By placing Lord Vincent hors-du-combat at the very onset. When we reach Edinboro' our first visit will be to a magistrate's office, where we will lodge information and cause warrants to be issued for the arrest of Lord Vincent and his accomplices upon the charge of conspiracy and kidnaping. Do you suppose that Lord Vincent, lodged in jail and awaiting his trial for abduction and conspiracy, will be in a condition to prosecute his suit for divorce?"

"Certainly not. I see that you are right, Ishmael. But poor Claudia! In any case, how she must suffer."

"Heaven comfort her! Yes. But we chose the least of two evils for her. Delivered from the fiend who has tormented her for so long a time, and restored to her native country and to the bosom of her family, we will hope that Lady Vincent's youth will enable her to rally from the depressing influences of these early troubles, and that she will yet regain her peace and cheerfulness."

"Heaven grant it, Heaven grant it!" said the judge fervently. "Oh, Ishmael," he continued, "when I think that I shall have my child back again, I almost feel reconciled to the storm of sorrow that must drive her for shelter into my arms. Is that selfish? I do not know. But I do know that I shall love her more, indulge her more than I ever did before. She must, she shall be, satisfied and happy with me."

Ishmael pressed his hand in silent sympathy, and then to divert his thoughts from a subject fraught with so much emotion he said:

"It occurs to me, judge, to say that Mr. Brudenell will probably be able very much to facilitate our negotiations with his friend, Don Filipo."

"Yes, I should think he would," replied the judge, with difficulty tearing his thoughts from the image of his daughter restored to his home, sitting by his fireside, or at the head of the table; "yes, I should think Brudenell would be able to smooth our way in that quarter."

"What is that, Ishmael? What are you both talking of in connection with myself and friend?" demanded Mr. Brudenell.

"Why, sir, your friend, Senor Don Filipo Martinez, is just precisely the same gentleman who became the purchaser of the boy Jim. We intend to pay him a visit to-morrow, for the purpose of trying to repurchase the boy. It is rather a delicate matter to propose to a Spanish hidalgo; and therefore we feel very much pleased to find that he is a friend of yours, and we hope that your introduction will recommend us to a favorable hearing."

"Certainly, I will go with you and introduce you. But I do not think your cause needs my advocacy; and I am very much mistaken in my estimation of Don Filipo's character, if when he has heard all the facts he does not at once deliver the negro boy into your hands and decline to accept any payment."

"But to that I would never consent," said the judge.

"I do not see how you can help it, if you cannot get your witness on any other terms. Don Filipo is a Spanish nobleman; he has high ideas of honor. The manner in which he will look upon this affair will be probably this—he will see that he has been deceived into the purchase of stolen property, and into a sort of unconscious complicity with the thieves. He will drop the property 'like a hot potato,' as the Irish say. In other words, he would consider his honor ineffaceably stained by either keeping the boy on the one hand or receiving any payment on the other. Don Filipo would lose ten times the amount of the purchase money rather than suffer the shadow of a shade of reproach to rest for one instant on his 'scutcheon."

"I think if it is as Mr. Brudenell says, judge, that you had better not make any difficulty about this 'point of honor' with the Senor Don Filipo. Get the negro back on his own terms. Afterwards, when you reach England you can easily and delicately remunerate him by sending him a complimentary present of equal or greater value than the purchase money he refuses, supposing that he does refuse it," said Ishmael.

"He will refuse it," persisted Mr. Brudenell.

"That will do, Ishmael. You have shown me a way out of this difficulty. And now suppose we ring for supper? We have had nothing since breakfast except the light repast set before us by the Senora Donna—et cetera."

Ishmael touched the bell, which brought up a waiter. Judge Merlin ordered supper to be served immediately. When it was ready he called in Katie and Sally to wait on the table—to remind him of old times, he said.

After supper he sent for the housekeeper and gave his two female servants into her charge, requesting her to see that their wants were supplied. And Katie, now that she had Sally with her, went away willing enough without insisting on being locked in her bedchamber for safe-keeping. And soon after this our wearied party separated and retired to rest.

The next morning, directly after an early breakfast, they set off for the Suburb Regla, calling on their way at the office of the consul, to discharge that gentleman from the duty of accompanying them; a measure now rendered unnecessary by the presence of Mr. Brudenell, and the fact of the latter being an intimate friend of Don Filipo, and therefore quite competent to indorse these strangers.

Mr. Tourneysee was excessively busy, and was very glad to be released from his promise to attend his friends. He gave them, however, his best wishes for their success, bid them adieu, and suffered them to depart.

It was about eleven o'clock in the forenoon when they reached the residence of Don Filipo. It was an imposing edifice, built of white granite, and standing within its own spacious grounds. A broad avenue, paved with granite, and shaded with tropical trees, led up to the front of the house.

Arrived here, Mr. Brudenell alighted from his carriage, rang the doorbell, and sent in the cards of his party with his own. In a few minutes they were admitted by a mulatto footman, in rich though plain livery, who conducted them to a handsome library, where Don Filipo stood ready to receive them.

The Senor Don Filipo Martinez, Marquis de la Santo Espirito, was not a creole. That any spectator might know at a glance. He was, as has been said, a Spanish hidalgo, of the glorious old Castilian order. He had been born and brought up near the Court of Madrid; he had graced an enviable position about the person of his sovereign; and lately, he had been sent out to fill a responsible office in the government of the island. He was even now talked of as the next Captain General.

He was a very distinguished-looking man, somewhat past middle age, with a tall, finely proportioned though very spare form; a long, thin face, Roman nose, piercing black eyes, heavy black eyebrows, olive complexion, and iron-gray hair and beard.

He advanced with grave and stately courtesy to welcome his visitors, whom Mr. Brudenell presented in due order.

When they were all seated, Mr. Brudenell undertook at once to introduce the subject of the business upon which they had come.

Don Filipo gave the speaker his most serious attention, and heard the narrative with surprise and mortification, somewhat modified by his habitual and dignified self-restraint.

At its conclusion, he turned to Judge Merlin, and said:

"I am deeply grieved, senor, in having done you, however unconsciously, so great a wrong. I must pray you to accept my apologies, and the only atonement I can make you—the restitution of your slave."

"Sir, I am pained that you should accuse yourself so unjustly; I cannot feel that you have done me any wrong, or owe me any apology, or restitution. I shall be very glad to get the boy back; and I thank you heartily for your willingness to give him up. But I am quite willing and ready to refund to you the purchase money paid for him," said Judge Merlin.

"Senor, it is impossible for me to receive it," answered Don Filipo gravely.

"But, sir, I cannot think of permitting you to be the loser by this transaction. I really must insist upon you accepting the purchase money."

"Senor, it is impossible for me to do so," very gravely replied Don Filipo.

"But, my dear sir, pray reflect. You have actually disbursed a large sum of money in the purchase of this boy. I do but offer you your own. I pray you accept it."

"It is impossible, senor," very, very gravely replied the Spaniard.

And at that moment Judge Merlin caught the eye of Ishmael fixed upon him with an anxious gaze. This gaze caused Judge Merlin to glance up at the face of his interlocutor.

The countenance of Don Filipo had assumed a severe and haughty aspect, although his words and tones were still courteous and gentle, as he repeated:

"It is impossible, senor."

And then Judge Merlin seemed to understand that to continue to press money upon this proud old Castilian nobleman would be simply to insult him.

With a deep bow, he said:

"I yield the point to you, Senor Don Filipo. And must remain your debtor for this great favor."

The stern face of the old Castilian melted into a fascinating smile, as he offered his hand to the judge, and said courteously:

"I esteem myself happy in being able to restore to the senor his slave. The boy is absent now exercising my favorite saddle horse; but as soon as he returns he shall be sent to the senor."

Our party then arose to depart; but Don Filipo would not allow them to go before they had partaken of a tempting repast of cakes, fruits, sweetmeats, and wine.

Then, with a real regret at parting with this "fine old Spanish gentleman," they took leave and returned to their hotel.

In the course of the afternoon Jim arrived in the custody of Don Filipo's steward, and was regularly delivered over to the safe-keeping of Judge Merlin.

The meeting of poor Jim with his old master and friends, and with his mother and his sweetheart, was at once so touching and so absurd, that it inclined the spectator at the same time to tears and laughter.

"Now," said Judge Merlin, as they sat together in his rooms that evening, "our work is over. And this is Tuesday evening, and we cannot sail until Saturday morning! What the deuce shall we do with the three intervening days?"

"To-morrow," answered Ishmael, "we had better see to providing ourselves with an outfit for the voyage. Remember that since our wardrobe was lost on the 'Oceana,' we have had nothing but the single change provided us by the captain of the 'Santiago.'"

"True, we must have an outfit. The purchase of that will occupy one day; but there will be still two left to dispose of."

"On Thursday we can spend the morning in seeing whatever is interesting in the city and its suburbs, and in the evening you know we are engaged to dine with Mr. Tourneysee."

"Exactly! But what shall we do on Friday?"

"Continue our sight-seeing through the city in the morning, and have Mr. Tourneysee and the Senor Don——"

"Et cetera, to dine with us in the evening. Is that what you mean, Ishmael?"

"Yes, sir."

"That will do then. Now we will go to bed," said the judge, rising and taking his bedroom candle.

And that was the signal for the party to disperse and go to rest.

The remainder of the week was passed in the manner sketched out by Ishmael. Nevertheless the three days of waiting seemed to the anxious father of Claudia three years in length. On Saturday morning our whole party, consisting now of three gentlemen and four servants, embarked on the "Cadiz" for Europe.

Mr. Tourneysee and Don Filipo "Et cetera," as the judge called him, accompanied them to the steamer, and remained with them to the latest possible moment. Then with many fervent wishes for their prosperity in the voyage, the two gentlemen took leave of our party and went on shore. The steamer sailed at nine o'clock. When it was well under way Ishmael looked around among his fellow-passengers, and was pleased to recognize many of the companions of his disastrous voyage on the "Oceana." Among the others was the family of Dr. Kerr. Later in the day, as Ishmael and his shadow, the professor, were standing leaning over the bulwarks of the ship and watching the setting sun sink into the water, leaving a trail of light upon the surface of the sea, he heard a familiar voice exclaim:

"Fader Abraham! Tere ish tat yunk shentleman ant hish olt man again!"

And Ishmael turned and saw the German Jew standing near him. Ishmael smiled and held out his hand; and Isaacs came and grasped it, expressing his pleasure in having "von drue shentleman" for his fellow-passenger once more. And from this day quite a friendship grew up between the young Christian and the old Jew. Without making the least effort to do so, Ishmael won his entire confidence.

Isaacs, reserved and uncommunicative with everyone else, seemed to find pleasure in talking to Ishmael.

Among other voluntary revelations, Isaacs informed Ishmael that he was going to England to see his niece, who was "von gread laty." She was the daughter, he said, of his only sister, who had been the wife of a rich English Jew. She had married an Englishman of high rank; but her husband, as well as her father and mother, was dead; all were dead; and she was living in widowhood and loneliness; and, ah! a great wrong had been done her! And here the Jew would sigh dismally and shake his head.

Now Ishmael, in the delicacy of his nature, would receive all the Jew's voluntary communications and sympathize with all his complaints, without ever asking him a question. And thus, as the Jew never happened to mention the name of his niece, and Ishmael never inquired it, he remained in ignorance of it.

The voyage of the "Cadiz," considering the season of the year, might be said to have been very prosperous. The weather continued clear, with a light wind from the northwest, alternating with calms. Our party having served out their time at seasickness on the "Oceana," were not called to suffer any more from that malady on this voyage.

On the fourteenth day out they arrived at Cadiz, whence they took a steamer bound for Liverpool, where they landed on the first of February, late in the night.

They went to a hotel to spend the remaining hours in sleep. And the next morning, after a hurried breakfast, eaten by candlelight, they took the express train for Edinboro'.

CHAPTER XXXVIII

CLAUDIA AT CAMERON COURT.

Sweet are the paths—oh, passing sweet,

By Esk's fair streams that run

O'er airy steep, thro' copsewood deep,

Impervious to the sun.

There the rapt poet's step may rove,

And yield the muse the day;

There beauty led by timid love

May shun the tell-tale ray.

—Scott.

Cameron Court, the favorite seat of Berenice, Countess of Hurstmonceux, was situated about seven miles south of Edinboro', on the north banks of the Esk. It was an elegant modern edifice, raised upon the ruins of an ancient castle, overhanging a perpendicular precipice, with a sheer descent of several hundred feet to the river. It looked down upon the course of the Esk, winding between rocks of lofty height, whose sides were fringed with a tangled mass of shrubs, ferns, and thistles, and whose summits were crowned with thickets of hazel, pine, and birch. On still higher ground, behind the house, and sheltering it from the northern blast, stood a thick wood of cedar, beech, and fir trees. Many winding footpaths led through this wood, and down the rocks and along the edge of the river. A wilder, more picturesque and romantic spot could scarcely have been found for a dwelling-place.

In summer, green with foliage, bright with blooming flowers, and musical with singing birds and purling brooks, it was beautiful! But in winter, bound in ice, mantled with snow, and gemmed with frost, it was sublime!

Such was the aspect of the place without; while within were collected all the comforts, luxuries, and elegances that wealth, taste, and intellect could command.

Within a short distance of this charming residence stood Craigmillar Castle, an old ruin, memorable from having been the first residence of Mary Queen of Scots after her return from France; and also her favorite retreat when driven to seek repose from the clashing antagonisms of her court at Holyrood.

Nearer still, on the banks of the Esk, stood Roslyn Castle and Chapel, famous in song and story for "the lordly line of high St. Clair"; and Hawthornden, remarkable for its enormous artificial caves, hewn out of the solid foundation rocks, and used as a place of refuge during the barbarous wars of by-gone ages; and many other interesting monuments of history and tradition.

To this attractive home Lady Hurstmonceux had brought Claudia late one winter afternoon.

At that hour, between the thickness of the Scotch mist and the low, gathering shadows of the night, but little could be seen or surmised of the scenery surrounding the house.

But Claudia keenly appreciated the comfort and elegance of the well-warmed and brightly lighted rooms within.

Not that they were more luxurious or more splendid than those she had left forever behind at Castle Cragg, but they were—oh, so different!

There all the magnificence was tainted with the presence of guilt; here all was pure with innocence. There she had been "under the curse"; here she was "under the benediction." There she had been tormented by a devil; here she was comforted by an angel. And this is scarcely putting the comparison, as it existed in her experience, too strongly.

Even when she had been alone and unprotected at the hotel, she had experienced a rebound of spirits from long depression, a joyous sense of freedom—only from the single cause of getting away from Castle Cragg and its sinful inmates. But now, added to that were the pleasure of friendship, the comfort of sympathy, and security of protection. Relief, repose, satisfaction— these were the sensations of Claudia in taking up her temporary abode at Cameron Court. The very first evening seemed a festive one to her, who had been so lonely, so wretched, and so persecuted at Castle Cragg.

The countess took her to a bright, cheerful suite of apartments on the second floor, whose French windows opened upon a balcony overlooking the wild and picturesque scenery of the Esk.

And when she had laid off her bonnet and wrappings her hostess took her down to a handsome dining room, where an elegant little dinner for two was served.

Ah! very different was this from the horrible meals at Castle Cragg, or even from the lonely ones at Magruder's Hotel.

Berenice possessed the rare gift of fascination in a higher degree than any woman Claudia had ever chanced to meet. And she exerted herself to please her guest with such success that Claudia was completely charmed and won.

After dinner they adjourned to a sumptuous apartment, called in the house "my lady's little drawing room." Here everything was collected that could help to make a winter evening pass comfortably and pleasantly.

The Turkey carpet that covered the floor was a perfect parterre of brilliant flowers wrought in their natural colors; and its texture was so fine and thick that it yielded like moss to the footstep. Crimson velvet curtains, lined with white satin and fringed with gold, draped the windows and excluded every breath of the wintry blast. Many costly pictures, rare works of art, covered the walls. A grand piano-forte, a fine harp, a guitar, and a lute were at hand. Rich inlaid tables were covered with the best new books, magazines, and journals. Indian cabinets were filled with antique shells, minerals, ossifications, and other curiosities, Marble stands supported vases, statuettes, and other articles of vertu. Lastly, two soft, deep, easy-chairs were drawn up before the glowing fire; while over the mantelpiece a large cheval glass reflected and duplicated all this wealth of comfort.

With almost motherly tenderness the beautiful countess placed her guest in one of these luxurious chairs and put a comfortable foot cushion under her feet. Then Berenice took the other chair. Between them, on a marble stand, stood a vase of flowers and the countess' work-box. But she did not open it. She engaged her guest in conversation, and such was the charm of her manners that the evening passed like a pleasant dream.

And when Claudia received the kiss of Berenice and retired for the night, it was with the sweet feeling of safety added to her sense of freedom. And when she awoke in the morning, it was to greet with joy her new life of sympathy, security, and repose.

As soon as she rang her bell she was attended by a pretty Scotch girl, who informed her that her ladyship's luggage had arrived, and had been placed in the hall outside her apartments to await her ladyship's orders.

Claudia, when she was dressed, went to look after it and found, to her surprise, not only her large trunk from Magruder's, but also her numerous boxes from Castle Cragg.

Upon inquiry she discovered that the boxes had been forwarded from the castle to the hotel, and sent on with the trunk.

She did not stop to inspect any part of her luggage, but went downstairs into the breakfast parlor, where she found Lady Hurstmonceux presiding over the table, and waiting for her.

Berenice arose and met her guest with an affectionate embrace, and put her into the easiest chair nearest the fire; for it was a bitter cold morning, and the snow lay thick upon the ground and upon the tops of the fir trees that stood before the windows, like footmen with powdered heads.

On turning up her plate Claudia found a letter.

"It is from Jean Murdock, dear. Read it; it refers no doubt to the boxes she has forwarded," said Lady Hurstmonceux.

Claudia smiled, bowed, broke the seal, and read as follows:

"Castle Cragg, Thursday Morning. "Me Leddy: I hae the honor to forward your leddyship's boxes fra the castle. I hope your leddyship will find a' richt. There hae been unco ill doings here sin your leddyship left. Me laird hae gane his ways up to Lunnun; but hae left the player bodie, Guid forgie him, biding her lane here. And she has guided us a' a sair gate sin' she hae held the reins. Auld Cuthbert wouldna bide here longer gin it wer' na for the luve o' the house; na mare would I. I must tell your leddyship about the visit of the poleece, whilk I understand were sent by your leddyship's ain sel'. They cam' the same day your leddyship left. Me laird was going away; and me laird's carriage stood at the door; and just as he was stepping into the carriage they cam' up and spake till him. And then his lairdship laughed, and invited them to enter the house, and walk into the library. And he sent Auld Cuthbert to fetch me. And when I went into the library, his lairdship said till me:

"'Murdock, these people have come about some gorillas that are said to be missing. What about them?'

"'If your lairdship means the puir negro bodies, I dinna ken; I hae nae seen ane of them the day,' I answered. An noo, me leddy, ye maun e'en just forgie' an auld cummer like mesel' gin she writes you a' that followed, e'en though it should cut you to the heart; for ye ought to ken weel the ways o' your bitter ill-wishers. Aweel, then, and when I had answered me laird, he turned to the poleecemen and said:

"'The truth is, Mr. Murray, that you have been deceived by a vera artful party. I may just as well tell you now what in a few days will be the talk of every taproom in the United Kingdom. When I was in America I was regularly taken in by a beautiful adventuress, whom I found—worse luck—in the best circles there. I married the creature and brought her to this castle, which she has dishonored.' And here, me leddy, he gave the poleeceman an exaggerated account of the finding of Frisbie in your leddyship's room. And then he rang the bell, and sent for the player bodie and her friend, who cam' in and confeermed a' that he tauld the poleeceman. And then me laird spake up and said that the negroes had run off wi' a large quantity of jewelry and plate; that he had nae doubt but your leddyship had gi'e them commission to purloin it; that your leddyship's visit and compleent to the poleece was naught but a blind to deceive them; and finally that he demanded to have a warrant issued for the arrest of the negroes on the charge of theft.

"Aweel, me leddy, ye ken that your leddyship and your puir serving bodies are strangers here, and me laird and a' his family are well kenned folk, and, mare than that, they are o' the auld nobility—mare the shame for me laird, na better to do honor till his race. And sae the lang and short o' it is, he talked over the poleecemen, sae that instead of pursuing their investigations in the castle, they went off with me laird to have warrants out for the apprehension of the puir negro folk, whilk I believe to be as innocent of theft as I mysel' or auld Cuthbert. And noo, me leddy, I hae telled ye a', thinking till mesel' that ye ought to ken it. And sae maun e'en just commit your ways to the Lord, and put your trust intil him. Auld Cuthbert and mesel' pray for your leddyship ilka day, that ye may be deleevered fra the spoilers, and fra a' those wha gang about to wark you wae. Me laird hae gane his ways up to Lunnun, as I tauld your leddyship. And the player quean and her cummer hae possession o' the house, and guide a' things their ain gait, wae's me! Gin I suld hear onything anent your leddyship's puir negro folk, I will mak' haste to let your leddyship ken. Auld Cuthbert begs permission to send his duty and his prayers for your leddyship's happiness. And I mysel' hae the honor to be your honorable leddyship's "Obedient humble servant to command, "Jean Murdock."

When Claudia had finished reading this letter she passed it with a sad smile to Lady Hurstmonceux, who, as soon as she had in her turn perused it, tossed it upon the table, saying, scornfully:

"'Whom the gods wish to destroy they first make mad!' Lord Vincent appears to me to have lost his reason. He thinks that he is weaving a net of circumstantial evidence around you for your ruin, when he is, in fact, only involving himself in intricacies of crime which must inevitably prove his destruction."

"I cannot, oh, I cannot, see it in the same light that you do! It seems to me that he has succeeded in making me appear guilty," said Claudia, with a shudder.

"Ah, let us not talk of it, since talking will do no good; at least not now. When your father comes, then we will talk and act," said the countess soothingly, as she set a cup of fragrant coffee before her guest.

Now I do not know whether you care to be informed how Claudia passed her time during the five weeks of her sojourn at Cameron Court, so I shall make the description of her visit a short one.

In the first place, you may be sure, from what you have already seen of Lady Hurstmonceux, that she would not allow her guest to mope.

As soon as the snow ceased to fall and the sky cleared, with a sharp northwest wind that froze the river hard, the countess took her guest out to learn the exhilarating art of skating, and in this way they employed an hour or two of each morning. The remainder of the day would be passed in needlework, reading, music, and conversation.

When the weather moderated and the ice was unsafe for skating, they substituted riding and driving excursions, and visited all the remarkable places in the neighborhood.

They visited Roslyn Castle and went down into those fearful vaults, three tiers under ground, and listened to the guide who told them traditions of the princely state kept up by the ancient lords of Roslyn, who had noblemen of high degree for their carvers and cupbearers; and of those ladies of

Roslyn, who never moved from home without a train of two hundred waiting gentlewomen and two hundred mounted knights.

They visited Roslyn Chapel and admired the unequaled beauty of its architecture, and gazed at the wondrous chef d'oeuvre—the "apprentice's pillar"—and heard the story how a poor but gifted boy, hoping to please, had designed and executed the work during the absence of his master, who, on returning and seeing the beautiful pillar, fell into a frenzy of envious rage and slew his apprentice.

They visited the ruins of Craigmillar Castle and stood in the little stone den, seven feet by four, which is known as "Queen Mary's bedroom." They saw those deep, dark dungeons where in the olden times captives pined away their lives forgotten of all above ground; they saw the "execution room," with its condemned cell, its chains and staples, its instruments of torture, its altar and its block.

It was indeed a

where, in those savage times, great criminals and innocent victims were alike condemned unheard, and secretly shrived, beheaded, and buried.

They passed on to a still more terrible dungeon among those dread vaults—a circular stone crypt surrounded by tall, deep, narrow niches, in which human beings had been built up alive.

With a shudder Claudia turned from all these horrors to the countess:

"It is said that our country has no past, no history, no monuments. I am glad of it. Better her past should be a blank page than be written over with such bloody hieroglyphics as these. When I consider these records and reflect upon the deeds of this crime-stained old land, I look upon our own young nation as an innocent child. Let us leave this place. It kills me, Berenice."

On Sunday morning at the breakfast table Lady Hurstmonceux proposed, as the day was fine, that they should drive into Edinboro' and attend divine services at St. Giles' Cathedral, interesting from being the most ancient place of worship in the city; a richly endowed abbey and ecclesiastical school in the Middle Ages; and at a later period, after the Reformation, the church, from which. John Knox delivered his fierce denunciation of the sins and sinners of his day.

All this Berenice told Claudia at the breakfast table, seeking to draw her thoughts away from the subject of her own position.

But at the invitation from Lady Hurstmonceux to attend a Christian place of worship Claudia looked up in surprise and exclaimed impulsively:

"But I thought—"

And there she stopped and blushed.

Lady Hurstmonceux understood her, smiled, and answered:

"You thought that I was a Jewess. Well, I was born and brought up in the Jewish faith. But it is now many years, Lady Vincent, since I embraced the Christian religion."

"I am very glad! I am very, very glad! Ah! I am but a poor, unworthy Christian myself, yet I do rejoice in every soul converted to Christ," said Claudia warmly, clasping the hand of her hostess; and, while holding it, she continued to say: "I do love to live in an atmosphere of Christianity, and I hate to live out of it. That was one reason, among others, why I was so unutterably wretched at Castle Cragg. They were such irredeemable atheists. There was never a visit to church, never a prayer, never a grace, never a chapter from the Bible, never any sort of acknowledgment of their Creator, never the slightest regard to his laws. Lord Vincent and Mrs. Dugald would sit down and play cards through a whole Sabbath evening, as upon any other. Oh, it was dreadful. Looking back upon my life among them, I wonder—yes, wonder—how I ever could have lived through it! Coming from that place to this, Lady Hurstmonceux, is like coming from something very like hell to something very like heaven."

"You were tortured in many ways, my poor Claudia. You are now off the rack, that is all. And now, I suppose, we are to go to St. Giles'?"

"If you please, yes; I should like to do so."

Lady Hurstmonceux rang the bell and ordered the carriage. And then the friends arose from the breakfast table and retired to prepare for church.

They enjoyed a beautiful drive of seven miles through a wildly picturesque country, and entered the town and reached the church in time for the opening of the services.

The preacher of the day was a very worthy successor of John Knox, having all the faith and hope, and a good deal more of charity than that grand old prophet of wrath had ever displayed.

This was the first divine worship that Claudia had engaged in for many months. It revived, comforted, and strengthened her.

She left the church in a better mood of mind than she had perhaps ever experienced in the whole course of her life. Her inmost thought was this:

"God enriched my life with the most bountiful blessings. But by sins turned them all into curses and brought my sorrows upon me. I will repent of my sins, I will accept my sorrows. God from his own mercy and not from my deserts has brought me thus far alive through my troubles; he has raised up a friend to succor me. I will bow down in penitence, in humility, in gratitude before him, and I will try to serve him truly in the future, and I will trust all that future to him."

They reached home to a late dinner, and spent the evening in such serious reading and conversation and sacred music as befitted the day. Not one dull hour had Claudia experienced during her residence at Cameron Court.

On Monday, which was another fine winter day, the countess said to her guest:

"This is the day of each week that I always devote to my poor. Would you like to drive around with me in the pony chaise and make acquaintance with the peasantry of Scotland? You will find them a very intelligent, well-educated class."

"Thank you, I should enjoy the drive quite as much as any that we have yet taken," said Claudia.

And accordingly after breakfast the ladies set out upon their rounds. Berenice did not go empty-handed. Hampers of food and bundles of clothing filled up every available space in the carriage. It was a very pleasant drive. To every cottage that the countess entered she brought relief, comfort, and cheerfulness.

The children greeted her with glad smiles; the middle-aged with warm thanks; and the old with fervent blessings. Not from one humble homestead did she turn without leaving some token of her passage; with one family she would leave the needed supply of food; with another the necessary winter clothing; with another, wine, medicine, or books. With others, very poor, she would leave a portion of all these requisites.

Finally, when the sun was sinking to his setting behind the Pentland Hills, she returned home with her guest.

"I must thank you for a very pleasant day, Lady Hurstmonceux. One of the pleasantest I have ever passed in my life. For I have witnessed and I have felt more real pleasure to-day than I ever remember to have experienced before. You have conferred much happiness to-day. If you dispense as much on every Monday, as I suppose you do, the aggregate must be very great," said Claudia, with enthusiasm, as they sat together at tea that evening in "my lady's little drawing room."

For some minutes Berenice did not reply, and when she did, she spoke very seriously.

"If there is one thing more than another for which I thank God, it is for making me one of his stewards. Do you suppose, Claudia, that I hold all the wealth that he has entrusted to me, as my own, to be used for my own exclusive benefit? Oh, no! I feel that I am but his almoner, and I am often ashamed of taking as I do, the lion's share of the good things," she added, glancing around upon the luxuries that encompassed her.

The next day Lady Hurstmonceux proposed another excursion.

"I will not take you to visit any romantic old ruin this morning; but to vary the programme I will take you to see an interesting living reality."

And accordingly the carriage was ordered and they drove out to New Haven, a fishing village within three miles of Edinboro', and yet as isolated and as primitive in its manners and customs as the most remote hamlet in the country.

There Claudia was amused and interested in watching the coming in of the fishing boats, and observing the picturesque attire of the fish-wives, and listening to the deafening clatter of their tongues as they chaffered with the fishermen, while lading their baskets.

This was another pleasant day for Claudia.

But it would stretch this chapter to too great a length to describe each day of her sojourn at Cameron Court.

Let it suffice to say in general terms that the countess kept her guest usefully employed or agreeably entertained during the whole of her visit. There was neither a tedious nor a fatiguing hour in the five weeks of her sojourn.

Every Sunday they attended divine worship at "St. Giles' Cathedral," commonly called "John Knox's church." Every Monday they went their rounds among the poor. Other days in the week they visited interesting and remarkable places in and around Edinboro'. And thus cheerfully passed the days.

CHAPTER XXXIX

SUSPENSE.

Wait, for the day is breaking,

Tho' the dull night be long,

Wait, Heav'n is not forsaking

Thy heart—be strong! be strong!

—Anon.

As the time approached when Claudia might reasonably expect a reply to the letter she had written to her father, she naturally became very anxious.

Would he answer that last urgent appeal by letter or in person? that was the question she was forever asking of herself.

And the response of her heart was always the same; he would lose no time in writing, he would hasten at once to her relief.

Ah! but if he should be ill, or—even dead? What then? Claudia's anxiety grew daily more acute.

She had heard nothing of the fate of her negroes. She learned by a second letter from Jean Murdock that Mrs. Dugald still remained at Castle Cragg, "lording it o'er a'," as the housekeeper expressed it. And she saw by the "Times" that Malcolm, Viscount Vincent, had filed a petition for divorce from his viscountess. That was all.

The fourth week had nearly gone by when one morning, on coming to the breakfast table, Claudia found lying beside her plate a foreign letter.

At the very first glance at its superscription she recognized her father's firm handwriting, and with an irrepressible cry of joy she snatched it up.

It was the short letter Judge Merlin had hastily penned on the eve of his journey to Washington. It merely stated that he had just that instant taken her letters from the post office; and that, in order to save the immediately outgoing mail, he answered them without leaving the office, to announce to her that he should sail for England on the "Oceana," that would leave Boston on the following Wednesday. And then, with strong expressions of indignation against Lord Vincent, sorrow for Claudia's troubles, and affection for herself, the letter closed.

"Oh, Berenice, Berenice! I am so happy; so very happy!" exclaimed Claudia wildly. "My father has written to me! he is well! he is coming! he is coming! he will be here in a few days! in a very few days! for this letter was written in the post office, to save the very last mail that came by the steamer immediately preceding the 'Oceana'! Oh, Berenice, I could cry with joy!"

"I congratulate you with all my heart, dear Claudia. Yes, I should think your father would now be here in two or three days, at farthest," said Lady Hurstmonceux.

"And oh, how shall I get ovor the interval? Ah, Berenice, indulge me! Let us go down, to Liverpool to meet my father!"

"My dear, I would do so in a moment, only I think it the worst plan you could pursue. In your circumstances, dearest Claudia, we must not go journeying through the country. We must live very quietly. And besides, though the 'Oceana' may reasonably be expected in two or three days, there is no reason in the world why she might not arrive to-day, or to-night. In which case, by going down to Liverpool, we shall be most likely to miss your father, who would be steaming up here."

"Certainly, certainly! I see the reasonableness of your views; but how, then, shall I get over the intervening time?"

"I might propose for you excursions to many interesting places in the vicinity of Edinboro' which you have not seen; but that we must not go far from home, while expecting Judge Merlin. We must not happen to be absent when your father arrives."

"Oh, no! we must not risk such a thing, I know. Well, I will wait as patiently as I can."

"And I will tell you what you may do, meantime. To-day you shall superintend in person the preparation of a suite of rooms for your father. You shall let my housekeeper into the secret of all his little tastes, and they shall be considered in the arrangements. That will occupy one day. To-morrow, you know, is Sunday, and we must go to church. That will occupy the second. The next day, Monday, we will make our weekly round among the poor. That will occupy the third day, to the exclusion of everything else. For if there is one employment more than another that will make us forget our personal anxieties, it is ministering to the wants of others. And, in all human probability, before Monday evening Judge Merlin will be here."

"Yes, yes! Oh, my dear father! I can scarcely realize that I shall see him so soon," said Claudia, with emotion.

The countess' programme was carried out. Claudia spent that day in superintending the arrangements of a handsome suite of rooms for her father.

On Sunday they went to church. But the text was an unfortunate one for Claudia's spirits. It was taken from James iv. 13: "Ye know not what shall be on the morrow." And the subject of the discourse was on the vanity of human expectations and the uncertainty of human destiny. Claudia returned home greatly depressed; but that depression soon yielded to the cheerfulness of Lady Hurstmonceux's manner.

On Monday they made their rounds among the poor; and Claudia forgot her anxieties and felt happy in the happiness she saw dispensed around her.

Yes, the programme of the countess was carried out, but her previsions were not realized. Judge Merlin did not come that evening, nor on the next morning, nor on the next evening.

On Wednesday morning Claudia, as usual, seized the "Times" as soon as it was brought in, and turned eagerly to the telegraphic column. But there was no arrival from America. Glancing farther down the column, she suddenly grew pale and exclaimed:

"Oh, Berenice!"

"What is it, dear?" inquired the countess.

Claudia read aloud the paragraph that had alarmed her:

"The 'Oceana' is now several days overdue. Serious apprehensions are entertained for her safety."

"Do not be alarmed, my dear. At this season of the year the steamers are frequently delayed beyond their usual time of arrival," said the countess, with a cheerfulness that she was very far from really feeling.

"But if there should have been an accident!"

"My dear, that line of steamers has never had an accident. And their good fortune is not the effect of luck, but of the great care bestowed by the company and its officers upon the safety of those who trust to them their lives and goods. Reassure yourself, Claudia."

But that was easier said than done. Three or four more of anxious days and nights passed, during which Claudia watched the papers for the arrival of the ocean steamers; but all in vain, until the Saturday morning of that week, when, as usual, she opened the "Times" and turned to the telegraphic column.

She could scarcely repress the cry of anguish that arose to her lips on reading the following:

"Arrival of the ocean steamers. The screw propeller 'Superior,' with New York mails of the 15th, has reached Queenstown. On the Banks of Newfoundland she passed the wreck of a large steamer, supposed to be the 'Oceana.'"

"Oh, Berenice! Oh, Berenice! Can this be true? Oh! Speak a word of hope or comfort to me!" cried Claudia, wringing her hands in the extremity of mental agony.

"My dear, let us still hope for the best. There is no certainty that it is the wreck of the 'Oceana.' There is no certainty that the 'Oceana' is wrecked at all. She is delayed; that is all which is known. And that is often the case with the ocean steamers at this season of the year, as I told you before," said the countess, trying to inspire Claudia with a hope that she herself scarcely dared to indulge.

But Claudia's face was drawn with anguish.

"Oh, the suspense, the terrible agony of suspense! It is worse than death!" she cried.

The countess essayed to comfort her, but in vain.

All that day, and for many succeeding ones, Claudia was like a victim stretched upon the rack. The torture of uncertainty was harder to endure than any certainty; it was, as she said, "worse than death," worse than despair! Some two weeks passed away, during which her very breath of life seemed almost suspended in the agony of hope that could not die.

At length one morning, on descending to the breakfast parlor, she found Lady Hurstmonceux reading the "Times."

"Any news?" inquired Claudia, in a faint voice.

The countess looked up. Claudia read the expression of her face, which seemed to say, prepare for good news.

"Oh, yes, there is! there is!" exclaimed Claudia, suddenly snatching the paper, and turning to the telegraphic column, and then, with a cry of joy, sinking into her seat.

"Let me read it to you, my dear, you are incapable of doing so," said Berenice, gently taking the paper from her hand and reading aloud the following paragraph:

"News of the 'Oceana.'—The Oriental and Peninsular Steam Packet Company's ship 'Albatross' has arrived at Liverpool, bringing all the passengers and crew of the 'Oceana,' wrecked on the banks of Newfoundland. They were picked up by the 'Santiago,' bound for Havana, and taken to that port, whence they sailed by the 'Cadiz' for the port of Cadiz, whence lastly they were brought by the 'Albatross' to Liverpool. Among the passengers saved were Chief Justice Merlin of the United States Supreme Court, Ishmael Worth, Esquire, a distinguished member of the Washington bar, and Professor Erasmus Kerr, of the Glasgow University. The shipwrecked passengers have all arrived in good health and spirits, and have already dispersed to their various destinations."

"This is too much joy! Oh, Berenice, it is too much joy!" cried Claudia, bursting into tears and throwing herself into the arms of Lady Hurstmonceux, and weeping freely on the sympathetic bosom of that faithful friend.

"Claudia, dear," whispered that gentle lady, "go to your room and shut yourself in, and kneel and return thanks to God for this his great mercy. And so shall your spirits be calmed and strengthened."

Claudia ceased weeping, kissed her kind monitress, and went and complied with her counsel. And very fervent was the thanksgiving that went up to Heaven from her relieved and grateful heart. She had finished her prayers and had arisen from her knees and was sitting by her writing-table indulging in a reverie of anticipation, when a bustle below stairs attracted her attention.

She listened.

Yes, it was the noise of an arrival!

With a joyous presentiment of what had come to the house, Claudia rushed out of the room and down the stairs to the lower entrance hall, and the next moment found herself clasped to the bosom of her father.

For a few moments neither spoke. The embrace was a fervent, earnest, but silent one.

The judge was the first to break the spell.

"Oh, my child! my child! Thank God that I find you alive and well!" he exclaimed, in a broken voice.

"Oh, my father, my dear, dear father!" began Claudia; but she broke down, burst into tears, and wept upon his bosom.

He held her there, soothing her with loving words and tender caresses, as he had been accustomed to do when she was but a child coming to him with her childish troubles. When Claudia had exhausted her passion of tears, she looked up and said:

"But, papa, you have not been in the drawing room yet? You hare not seen Lady Hurstmonceux?"

"No, my dear, I have but just arrived. Claudia, immediately upon my landing I took the first train north, and reached Edinboro' this morning. I sent my party on to Magruder's Hotel and took a fly and drove immediately out here. I have but just been admitted to the house and sent my card in to the hostess. And, ah, I see that my messenger has returned."

A servant in livery came up, bowed, and said:

"My lady directs me to say to you, sir, that she will see you immediately in the drawing room, unless you would prefer to go first to the apartments which are prepared for you, sir."

The judge hesitated, and then turned to his daughter and whispered the inquiry:

"How do I look, Claudia? Presentable?"

Lady Vincent ran her eyes over the traveler and answered:

"Not at all presentable, papa. You look just as one might expect you to do—black with smoke and dust and cinders, as if you had traveled in the train all night."

"Which of course I did."

"And I think you would be all the better for a visit to your rooms, papa. Come, I will show you the way, for I am as much at home here as ever I was at dear old Tanglewood. James," she said, turning to the footman who had brought the message, "you need not wait. I will show my papa his rooms; but you may order breakfast for him, for I dare say he has had none. Come, papa!"

And so saying Claudia marshaled her father upstairs to the handsome suite of apartments that had been made ready for him. When he had renovated his toilet, he declared himself ready to go below and be presented to his hostess. Claudia conducted him downstairs and into "my lady's little drawing room."

CHAPTER XL

FATHER AND DAUGHTER.

How deep, how thorough felt the glow

Of rapture, kindling out of woe;

How exquisite one single drop

Of bliss, that sparkling to the top

Of misery's cup, is keenly quaffed

Though death must follow soon the draught.

—Moore.

The countess was sitting on one of the armchairs near the fire when Claudia led the judge up before her, saying only:

"Lady Hurstmonceux, my father."

The countess arose and held out her hand with a smile of welcome, saying:

"It gives me much joy to see you safe, after all your dangers, Judge Merlin. Pray sit near the fire."

The judge retained her hand in his own for a moment, while he bowed over it and answered:

"I thank you for your kind expressions, dear Lady Hurstmonceux. But, oh! what terms shall I find strong enough to thank you for the noble support you have given my daughter in her great need?"

"Believe me, I was very happy to be serviceable to Lady Vincent," replied the countess gently. Then, turning to Claudia, she said:

"Your father has probably not had breakfast."

"No; but I assumed the privilege of ordering it for him," replied the latter.

"The 'privilege' was yours without assumption, my dear. You did exactly right," said the countess.

"I see that my daughter is quite at home with you, madam," observed the judge.

"Oh, I adopted her. I told her that I should be her mother until the arrival of her father," replied Lady Hurstmonceux, smiling.

At this moment the footman put his head in at the door to say that the judge's breakfast was served. Lady Hurstmonceux led the way to the breakfast parlor, and then saying:

"You will make your father comfortable here, Claudia, I hope," she bowed and left them alone together.

Claudia sat down to the table and began to pour out the coffee. James, the footman, was in attendance.

"Dismiss the servant, my dear," said the judge, as he took his seat as near to his daughter as the conveniences of the table would allow.

"You may retire, James. I will ring if you are wanted."

The man bowed and went out. The father and daughter looked up; their eyes met and filled with tears.

"Oh, my child, how much we have to say to each other!" sighed the judge.

"Yes, but, dear papa, drink your coffee first. You really look as though you needed it very much," replied Claudia affectionately.

The judge complied with her advice; though, if the truth must be told, he ate and drank indiscreetly fast in order to get through soon and be at liberty to talk to his daughter. When he arose from the table Claudia rang the bell for the service to be removed, and then led the way again to my lady's little drawing room.

It was deserted. Lady Hurstmonceux had evidently left it that the father and daughter might converse with each other unembarrassed by the presence of a third person.

"My dear," said the judge, as he seated himself on the sofa beside his daughter, wound his arm around her shoulders, and looked wistfully into her face, "do you know that I am surprised to see you looking so well? You must possess a great deal of fortitude, Claudia, to have passed through so much trouble as you have and show so few signs of suffering as you do."

"Ah, papa! if you had arrived a few days ago and seen me then, you would have had good cause to say I looked well. But, for the last week, the intense anxiety I have felt on your account has worn me considerably."

"My poor girl! Yes, I know how that must have been. The news of the shipwreck arrived long before we reached England, and everyone must have given us up for lost."

"I did not. Oh, no! I could not! I still hoped; but, oh, with what an agony of hope!"

"Such hope, my child, is worse than despair."

"Oh, no! I thought so then. I do not think so now; now that I have you beside me."

"Now that it is ended. But, oh, my dear child, how hard it was for you to have anxiety for my fate added to all your other troubles!"

"Papa, anxiety for your fate was my only trouble," said Claudia gravely.

"How! what! your only trouble, Claudia? I do not understand you in the least."

"All my other troubles had passed away. And now that anxiety is at an end, that trouble is also passed away and I have none."

"None, Claudia? How you perplex me, my dear."

"None, papa! I left them all behind at Castle Cragg."

"I do not—cannot comprehend you, my dear."

"No, papa, you cannot comprehend me; no one could possibly comprehend me who had not been placed in something like my own position. But—can you not imagine that when a victim has been stretched upon the rack and tortured by executioners, it is comfort enough simply to be taken off it? Or when a sinner has been in purgatory tormented by fiends, it is heaven enough only to be out of it? Oh, papa, that is not exaggeration! That is something like what I suffered at Castle Cragg; something like what I enjoy in being away from it. Think of it, papa," said Claudia, gulping down the hysterical sob that arose to her throat; "think of it! me, an honorable woman, the daughter of Christian parents, to find myself living in the house, sitting at the table in daily communication with creatures that no honest man or pure woman would ever willingly approach! Think of me being not only in the company, but in the power, and at the mercy of such wretches!"

"'Think,' Claudia! I have thought until my brain has nearly burst. Oh, I shall—no matter what I shall do! I will threaten no longer, but, by all my hopes of salvation, I will act. The remorseless monster! the infamous villain! I do not know how you lived through it all, Claudia!"

"I do not know myself, papa. Oh, sir, I never fully realized my life at Castle Cragg until I got away from it and could look back on it from a distance. For the trouble then grew around me gradually; slowly astonishing me, if you can conceive of such a thing; benumbing my heart; stupefying my brain; deadening my sensibilities; else I could not have endured it so quietly. Ah, it would have ended in death, though—death of the body, perhaps death of the soul! But still I knew enough, felt enough, to experience and appreciate the infinite relief. of being delivered from it. Oh, papa, looking back upon that home of horror, that den of infamy, I understand in what hell consists—not in consuming fire, but in the company of devils! Oh, sir, if you could once place yourself in my position and feel what it was for me to leave that polluted atmosphere of sensuality, treachery, and hatred, and to come into this pure air of refinement, truth, and love, you would understand how it is that I can feel no trouble now!"

"I do; but still I wonder to see you so well."

"Oh, sir, you know, severe as my tortures were, they were only superficial, only skin-deep; they did not reach the springs of my spirits. That is the reason why, in being relieved, I am so perfectly at ease."

"Then you never loved that scoundrel, Claudia?"

"No, father, I never loved him. Therefore, the memory of his villainy does not haunt me, as otherwise it might. Not loving him, I ought never to have married him. If I had not, I should have escaped all the suffering."

"Ah, Claudia, would to Heaven you never had married him," sighed the judge, without intending to cast the least reproach on his daughter.

She felt the reproach, however, and exclaimed, with passionate earnestness:

"Oh, father, do not blame me—do not! I could not help it! Oh, often I have examined my conscience on that score and asked myself if I could! And the answer has always come—no, with my nature, my passions, my pride, my ambition, I could not help doing as I have done!"

"Could not help marrying a man you could not love, Claudia?"

"No, papa, no! There were passions in my nature stronger than love. These spurred me on to my fate. I was born with a great deal of pride, inherited from—no one knows how many ancestors. This should have been curbed, trained, directed into worthy channels. But it was not. I was left to develop naturally, with the aid only of intellectual education. I did develop, from a proud, frank, high-spirited girl into a vain, scheming, ambitious woman. I married for a title. And this is the end. How true is it that 'pride goeth before a fall and a haughty temper before destruction!'"

"Oh, Claudia, Claudia, every word you speak wounds me like a sword- thrust! It was my 'theory' that did it all, I said I would let my trees and my daughter grow up as nature intended them to do. And what is the result? Tanglewood has grown into an inextricable wilderness that nothing but a fire could clear, and my daughter's life has run to waste!" groaned the judge, covering his face with his hands.

"Papa, dear, dearest papa, do not grieve so! I did not mean to give you pain. I did not mean to breathe the slightest reflection upon so kind a father as you have always been to me. I meant only to explain myself a little. But I wish I had not spoken so. Forget what I have said, papa," said Claudia, tenderly caressing her father.

"Let it all pass, my dear child," said the judge, embracing her.

"And, papa, my life has not run to waste; do not think it. I told you that my troubles had not touched the springs of my soul; they have not. Is not my mind as strong and my heart as warm and my spirit as sweet as ever? Papa, this day I am a better woman for all the troubles I have passed through. I have never before been much comfort to you, my poor papa; but I will go with you to Tanglewood and make your home happier than it has ever been since mamma died. And you will find that my life shall be redeemed from waste."

"Claudia, are you sure that you do not love that rascal—not even a little?"

"Papa, I do not even hate him; now judge if I ever could have loved him."

But the judge was no metaphysician, and he looked puzzled.

"Papa, if I ever had loved that man, do you not suppose that his unfaithfulness, neglect, and insults, to say nothing of his last foul wrong against me, would have turned all my love into hatred? But I never loved him, therefore all that he could do would not provoke my hatred. Papa, he is as much below my hatred as my love."

"Oh, Claudia, Claudia, that you should be compelled to speak so of one whom you made your husband!"

"Papa, dear, you asked me a question and I have replied to it truthfully."

"My dear, I had a motive for putting that question. I wished to know whether a spark of love for that man survived in your heart to make his punishment a matter of painful interest to you. For to vindicate you, Claudia, it may become necessary to prosecute him with the utmost rigor of the law; necessary, in fact, to disgrace and ruin him," said the judge solemnly.

"Papa, dear, what are you talking about? Prosecute him to the utmost extent of the law? Disgrace and ruin him? Why, it appears to me that you do not know the circumstances, as of course you cannot. He has schemed so successfully, papa, that he has everything his own way. All the evidence, the false but damning evidence, is in his favor and against me. It seems to me, reflecting coolly upon the circumstances, to be quite impossible that he should be punished or I should be vindicated—in this world at least."

"Claudia, I know more of these circumstances than you think I do. I know more of them than you do; and I repeat that, in order to vindicate your honor fully, it may be necessary to prosecute Malcolm, Lord Vincent, with the utmost rigor of the law; to bring him to the felon's dock; to send him to the hulks. Now, are you willing that this should be done?"

Claudia turned very pale and answered:

"Let the man have justice, papa, if it places him on the scaffold."

"There are two courses open to us, Claudia. The first is—simply to let him alone until he brings his suit for divorce, and then to meet him on that ground with such testimony as shall utterly defeat him and destroy his plea. In that case you will be vindicated from the charge that he has brought against you, but not from the reproach that, however undeserved, will attach to a woman who has been the defendant in a divorce trial, and he will go unpunished. The second course is to prosecute him at once in the criminal court for certain of his crimes that have come to my knowledge, and so put him out of the possibility of suing for a divorce. And in that case your honor would go unquestioned, and he would be condemned to a felon's fate—penal servitude for years. Now, Claudia, I place the man's destiny in your hands. Shall we defend ourselves against him in a divorce court, or shall we prosecute him in a criminal court?"

"Papa," said Claudia, hesitating, and then speaking low, "what does Ishmael advise?"

"Ishmael? How did you know that he was with me, my dear?"

"I saw his name in the list of passengers, and I knew that he had come on with you as your private counselor."

"Yes, he did, at a vast sacrifice of his business; but then I never knew Worth to shrink from any self-sacrifice."

"What is his advice?" asked Claudia, in a low voice.

"He does more than advise; in this matter he dictates—I had almost said he commands; at least he insists that the divorce suit shall not be permitted to come on; that it shall be stopped by the arrest of Lord Vincent upon criminal charges that we shall be able to prove upon him. And that after the conviction of the viscount you shall bring suit for a divorce from him; for that it would not be well that your fate should remain linked to that of a felon."

"Then, papa, let it be as Mr. Worth says; and if the prosecution should place the viscount on the scaffold—let it place him there."

"It will not go so far as that, my dear—not in this century. If he had lived in the last century, and amused himself as he has done in this, he would have swung for it, that is certain."

"Papa, what is it that you have found out about him? Was he implicated in the death of poor Ailsie Dunbar? And, if so, how did you find it out? Tell me."

"My dearest, we have both much to tell each other. But I wish to hear your story first. Remember, Claudia, those alarming letters you sent me were very meager in their details. Tell me everything, my child; everything from the time you left me until the time you met me again."

"Papa, dear, it is a long, grievous, terrible story. I do not know how you will bear it. You are sensitive, excitable, impetuous. I scarcely dare to tell you. I fear to see how you will bear it. I dread its effects upon you."

"Claudia, my dearest, conceal nothing; tell me all; and I promise to restrain my emotions and listen to you calmly."

Upon this Claudia commenced the narrative of her sufferings from the moment of parting with her father at Boston to the moment of meeting with him at Cameron Court. The reader is already acquainted with the story, and does not need to hear Claudia's narration. Judge Merlin also knew much of it; as much as old Katie had been able to impart to him; but he wished to hear a more intelligent version of it from his daughter. It was, as she had said, a long, sorrowful, terrible story; such as it was not in the nature of woman to recite calmly. Some parts of it were told with pale cheeks, faltering tones, and falling tears; other parts were told with fiery blushes, flashing eyes, and clenched hands.

At its conclusion Claudia said:

"There, papa, I have hidden nothing. I have told you everything. Now at last you will believe me when I tell you how perfectly relieved I feel only to be out of that purgatory—only to be away from those fiends! Now at last you will see how it is that I can say without ruth, 'Let Malcolm, Lord Vincent, have justice, though that justice consign him to penal servitude, or to the gallows!' But, papa, when I said I had no trouble left, I spoke in momentary forgetfulness of my poor servants; Heaven forgive me for it! Though, really, uncertainty about their fate is the only care I have."

"My dear," said the judge, who had comported himself with wonderful calmness through the trying hour of Claudia's narration; "my dear, cast that care to the winds. Your servants are safe and well and near at hand."

"'Safe and well, and near at hand!' Oh, papa, are you certain—quite certain?" exclaimed Claudia, in joy modified by doubt.

"Quite certain, my dearest, since I myself lodged them at Magruder's Hotel this morning," said the judge.

"Oh, thank Heaven!" exclaimed Claudia fervently. "But, papa, tell me all about it. When, where, and how were they found?"

"About three weeks ago, in Havana, by Ishmael," answered the judge, speaking directly to the point.

His daughter looked so amazed that he hastened to say:

"It is easily understood, Claudia. You mentioned in the course of your narrative that you suspected the viscount of having spirited away the negroes. Your suspicion was correct. Through the agency of chloroform he abducted the negroes and got them on board a West Indian smuggler, that took them to Havana and sold them into slavery. When we went there on the 'Santiago,' we found, recognized, and recovered them."

"And what was his motive—the viscount's motive, I mean—for selling my poor negroes into slavery, and thereby committing a felony that would endanger his reputation and liberty? It could not have been want of money. The highest price they would bring could scarcely be an object to the Viscount Vincent. What, then, could have been his motive?"

"What you mentioned that you suspected it to be, Claudia: to get rid of dangerous witnesses against himself. But I had better tell you the whole story," said the judge; and with that he began and related the history of the conspiracy entered into by the viscount, the valet, and the ex-opera singer, and overheard by Katie; the discovery and seizure of the eavesdropper; and the abduction and sale of the negroes.

At the conclusion of this narrative he said

"So you see, Claudia, that we have got this man completely in our power. Look at his crimes. First, complicity in the murder of Ailsie Dunbar; secondly, conspiracy against your honor; thirdly, kidnaping and slave-trading. The man is already ruined; and you, my dear, are saved."

"Oh, thank Heaven, thank Heaven, that at least my name will be rescued from reproach!" cried Claudia earnestly, clasping her hands and bursting into tears of joy, and weeping on her father's bosom.

"Yes, Claudia," he whispered, as he gently soothed her; "yes, my child—thank Heaven first of all! for there was something strangely providential in the seemingly dire misfortune that was the cause of our being taken to Havana. For if we had not gone thither, we should never have found the negroes; and if we had not found them, it would have been difficult, or impossible, to have vindicated you."

"Oh, I know it. And I do thank Heaven."

"And, after Heaven, there is one on earth to whom your thanks are due—Ishmael Worth. Not because he was the first to find the negroes, for that was an accident, but because he sacrificed so much in order to attend me on this voyage; and because he has been of such inestimable value to me in this business. Claudia, but that I had him with me in Havana, I should not now be by your side. But that I had him with me, I should have plunged myself headlong into two law cases that would have detained me in Havana for an indefinite time. But that I had him with me to restrain, to warn, and to counsel I should have prosecuted the smugglers for their share in the abduction of the negroes, and I should have sued the owners for the recovery of them. But I yielded to Ishmael's earnest advice, and by the sacrifice of a sum of money and a desire of vengeance, I got easy possession of the negroes and brought them on here. You owe much to Ishmael Worth, Claudia."

"I know it, oh, I know it! May Heaven reward him!"

"And now our witnesses are at hand; and before night, Claudia, warrants shall be issued for the arrest of the Viscount Vincent, Alick Frisbie, and Faustina Dugald."

"They can have no suspicion of what is coming upon them, and therefore will have no chance to escape."

"Not a bit. We shall come upon them unawares."

"How astonished they will be."

"Yes—and how confounded when confronted with my witnesses."

"Papa, I am not malicious, but I think I should like to see their faces then."

"My dearest Claudia, you will have to imagine them. You will not be an eye-witness of their confusion. You will not be required either at the preliminary examination or at the trial, and it would not be seemly that you should appear at either."

"Oh, I know that, papa. And I am very glad that I shall not be wanted. But will the testimony of those three negroes be sufficient to convict the criminals?"

"Amply. But that testimony will not be unsupported. We shall summon the steward and housekeeper of Castle Cragg. And now, my dear, I must leave you, if the warrants are to be issued to-day," said the judge, rising.

"So soon, papa?"

"It is necessary, my dear."

"But, at any rate, you will be back very shortly?"

"I do not know, my child."

"The countess expects you to make Cameron Court your home while you remain in the neighborhood."

"Lady Hurstmonceux has not said so to me, Claudia."

"She has had no fit opportunity. Wait till you start to go."

"By the way, I must take leave of my kind hostess," said the judge, looking around the room as if in search of something or somebody.

Claudia touched the bell. A footman entered.

"Let the countess know that the judge is going."

The servant bowed and withdrew, and Lady Hurstmonceux entered.

"Going so soon, Judge Merlin?" she said.

"Just what my daughter has this moment asked. Yes, madam; and you will acknowledge the urgency of my business, when I tell you it is to lodge information against Lord Vincent and his accomplices, and procure their immediate arrest, upon the charge of certain grave crimes that have come to my knowledge, and that I am prepared to prove upon them."

"You astonish me, sir. I certainly had reason to suspect Lord Vincent and his disreputable companions, but I am amazed that in so short a time you should have ferreted out so much."

"It was accident, madam; or rather," said the judge, gravely bending his head, "it was Providence. My daughter will explain the circumstances to you, madam. And now, will you permit me once more to thank you for your great goodness to me and mine, and to bid you good-morning?"

"I hope it will be only good-morning, then, judge, and not good-by. I beg that you will return and take up your residence with us while you remain in Scotland," said the countess, with her sweetest smile.

"I should be delighted as well as honored, madam, in being your guest, but I am off to Banff by the midday train."

"Off to Banff?" repeated Berenice and Claudia, in a breath.

"Certainly."

"What is that for?" inquired Claudia.

"Why, my dear, there is where I must lodge information against the viscount and his accomplices. There is where the crimes were committed, and where the warrants must be issued."

"Oh, I see."

"I had forgotten. I was thinking; or rather without thinking at all, I was taking it for granted that it could be all done in Edinboro'," smiled the countess.

"Madam, I must still leave my daughter a pensioner on your kindness for a few days," said the judge, with a bow.

"You say that as if you supposed it possible for me to permit you to do anything else with her," laughed the countess, holding out her hand to the judge. He raised it to his lips, bowed over it, and resigned it, all in the stately old-time way. Then he turned to his daughter, embraced her, and departed.

"Now, Claudia, tell me what the judge has found out about Vincent. Was he implicated in that murder? I shouldn't wonder if he was," said the countess impatiently.

"That is just what I thought; but that is not the case. Oh, Berenice, what a revelation it is; but I will tell you all about it," said Claudia,

And when they were cozily seated together beside the drawing-room fire Claudia related the story her father had told her of the conspiracy against her own honor, the abduction and sale of the negroes, and the recognition and recovery of them.

"I am not surprised at anything in that story but the providential manner in which the servants were recovered. I believe the viscount capable of any crime, or restrained only by his cowardice. If he should hesitate at assassination, I believe that it would not be from the horror of blood-guiltiness, but from the fear of the gallows. I hope that no weak relenting, Claudia, will cause either you or your father to spare such a ruthless monster."

"No, Berenice, no. I have said to my father, 'Let Lord Vincent have justice, though that justice place him in the felon's dock, in the hulks, or on the scaffold.' No, I do not believe it would be fair to the community to turn such a man loose upon them."

While Lady Hurstmonceux and Lady Vincent conversed in this manner, Judge Merlin drove to Edinboro'.

He reached Magruder's Hotel, where he had left Ishmael Worth, the professor, and the three negroes.

Ishmael had lost no time; he had seen that the whole party had breakfast; and then he had gone himself and engaged a first-class carriage in the express train that started for Aberdeen at twelve, noon.

They were now therefore only waiting for Judge Merlin. And as soon as the judge arrived the whole party started for the station, which they reached in time to catch the train. Three hours' steaming northward and they ran into the station at Aberdeen. The stage was just about starting for Banff. They got into it at once, and in three more hours of riding they reached that picturesque old town.

Merely waiting long enough to engage rooms at the best hotel and deposit their luggage there, they took a carriage and drove to the house of Sir Alexander McKetchum, who was one of the most respected magistrates of Banff.

Judge Merlin introduced himself and his party, produced his credentials, laid his charge, and presented his witnesses.

To say that the worthy Scotch justice was astonished, amazed, would scarcely be to describe the state of panic and consternation into which he was thrown.

Long he demurred and hesitated over the affair; again and again he questioned the accusers; over and over again he required to hear the statement; and slowly and reluctantly at last be consented to issue the warrants for the apprehension of Lord Vincent, Alick Frisbie, and Faustina Dugald.

Ishmael took care to see that these warrants were placed in the hands of an efficient policeman, with orders that he should proceed at once to the arrest of the parties named within them.

And then our party returned to their hotel to await results.

CHAPTER XLI

ARREST OF LORD VINCENT AND FAUSTINA.

Our plots fall short like darts that rash hands throw

With an ill aim that have so far to go,

Nor can we long discovery prevent,

We deal too much among the innocent.

—Howard.

Lord Vincent was at Castle Cragg. Unable to absent himself long from the siren who was the evil genius of his life, he had come down on a quiet visit to her. A very quiet visit it was, for he affected jealously to guard the honor of one who in truth had no honor to lose. The guilty who have much to conceal are often more discreet than the innocent who have nothing to fear.

Mrs. MacDonald was still at the castle, playing propriety to the beauty. A very complacent person was Mrs. MacDonald.

This precaution deceived no one. The neighboring gentry rightly estimated the domestic life at Castle Cragg and the character of its inmates, and refrained from calling there.

This avoidance of her society by the county families galled Faustina.

"What do they mean by it?" she said to herself. "I am the Honorable Mrs. Dugald. Ah, they think I have lost myself. But they shall know better when they see me the Viscountess Vincent, and afterwards, no one knows how soon, Countess of Hurstmonceux and Marchioness of Banff! Ah, what a difference that will make!"

And Faustina consoled herself with anticipations of a brilliant future, in which she would reign as a queen over these scornful prudes. But Faustina reckoned without Nemesis, her creditor. And Nemesis was at the door.

It was a wild night. The snowstorm that had been threatening all day long came down like avalanches whirled before the northern blast. It was a night in which no one would willingly go abroad; when everyone keenly appreciated the comfort of shelter.

Very comfortable on this evening was Mrs. Dugald's boudoir. The crimson carpet and crimson curtains glowed ruddy red in the lamplight and firelight. The thundering dash of the sea upon the castle rock below came, softened into a soothing lullaby, to this bower of beauty.

Lord Vincent and Mrs. Dugald were seated at an elegant and luxurious little supper that would have satisfied the most fastidious and dainty epicure. Three courses had been removed. The fourth—the dessert—was upon the table. Rare flowers bloomed in costly vases; ripe fruits blushed in gilded baskets; rich wines sparkled in antique flasks.

On one side of the table Faustina reclined gracefully in a crimson velvet easy-chair. The siren was beautifully dressed in the pure white that her sin-smutted soul, in its falsehood, affected. Her robe was of shining white satin, trimmed with soft white swan's-down; fine white lace delicately veiled her snowy neck and arms; white lilies of the valley wreathed her raven hair and rested on her rounded bosom.

She looked "divine," as her fool of a lover assured her. Yes, she looked "divine"—as the devil did when he appeared in the image of an angel of light.

How did she dare, that guilty and audacious woman, to assume a dress that symbolized purity and humility?

Lord Vincent lolled in the other armchair on the opposite side of the table, and from under his languid and half-tipsy eyelids cast passionate glances upon her.

Mrs. Macdonald had withdrawn her chair from the table and nearer the fire, and had fallen asleep, or complacently affected to do so; for Mrs. MacDonald was the soul of complacency. Mrs. Dugald declared that she was a love of an old lady.

"What a night it is outside! It is good to be here," said Faustina, taking a bunch of ripe grapes and turning towards the fire.

"Yes, my angel," answered the viscount drowsily, regarding her from under his eyelids. "What a bore it is!"

"What is a bore?" inquired Faustina, putting a ripe grape betweenher plump lips.

"That we are not married, my sweet."

"Eh bien! we soon shall be."

"Then why do you keep me at such a distance, my angel?"

"Ah, bah! think of something else!"

The viscount poured out a bumper of rich port and raised it to his lips.

"Put that wine down, Malcolm, you have had too much already."

He obeyed her and set the glass untasted on the board.

"That's a duck; now you shall have some grapes," she said, and, with pretty, childish grace, she began to pick the ripest grapes from her bunch and to put them one by one into the noble noodle's mouth.

"It is nice to be here, is it not, mon ami?" she smilingly asked.

"Yes, sweet angel!" he sighed languishingly.

"And when one thinks of the black dark and sharp cold and deep snow outside, and of travelers losing their way, and getting buried in the drifts and freezing to death, one feels so happy and comfortable in this warm, light room, eating fruit and drinking wine."

"Yes, sweet angel! but you won't let me have any more wine," said the viscount drowsily.

"You have had more than enough," she smiled, putting a ripe grape between his gaping lips.

"Just as you say, sweet love! You know I am your slave. You do with me as you like," he answered stupidly.

"Now," said Faustina, her thoughts still running on the contrast between the storm without and the comfort within, "what in this world would tempt one to leave the house on such a night as this?

"Nothing in the world, sweet love!"

"Malcolm, I do not think I would go out to-night, even in a close carriage, for a thousand pounds."

"No, my angel, nor for ten thousand pounds should you go."

"I like to think of the people that are out in the cold, though. It doubles my enjoyment," she said, as she put another fine grape in his mouth.

"Yes, sweet love!" he answered drowsily, closing his fingers on her hand and drawing her forcibly towards him.

"Ah! stop!" she exclaimed, under her breath, and directing his attention to Mrs. MacDonald, who sat with her eyes closed in the easy-chair by the chimney corner.

"She is asleep," said the viscount, in a hoarse whisper.

"No, no! you are not certain!" whispered Faustina.

"Come, come! sit close to me!" exclaimed the viscount, with fierce vehemence, drawing her towards him.

"You forget yourself! You are drunk, Malcolm!" cried Faustina, resisting his efforts.

At that moment there came a rap at the door; it was a soft, low tap, yet it startled the viscount like a thunderclap. He dropped the hand of Faustina and demanded angrily:

"Who the fiend is there?"

There was no answer, but the rap was gently repeated.

"Speak, then, can't you? Who the demon are you?" he cried.

"Why don't you tell them to come in?" said Faustina, in a displeased tone.

"Come in, then, set fire to you, whoever you are!" exclaimed Lord Vincent.

The door was opened and old Cuthbert softly entered.

"What the fiend do you want, sir?" haughtily demanded the viscount; for he had lately taken a great dislike to old Cuthbert, as well as to every respectable servant in the house, whose humble integrity was a tacit rebuke to his own dishonor; and least of all would he endure the intrusion of one of them upon his interviews with Faustina.

"What brings you here, I say?" he repeated,

"An' it please your lairdship, there are twa poleecemen downstairs, wi' a posse at their tails," answered the old man, bowing humbly.

"What is their business here?"

"I dinna ken, me laird."

"Something about that stupid murder, I suppose."

Faustina started; she was probably thinking of Katie.

"I dinna think it is onything connected wi' Ailsie's death, me laird."

"What then? What mare's nest have they found now, the stupid Dogberries?"

"I canna tak' upon mesel' to say, me laird. But they are asking for yer lairdship and Mistress Dugald."

"Me!"

This exclamation came from Faustina, who turned deadly pale, and stared wildly at the speaker. Indeed her eyes and her face could be compared to nothing else but two great black set in a marble mask.

"Me!"

"Aye, mem, e'en just for yer ain sel', and na ither, forbye it be his lairdship's sel'," replied the old man, bowing with outward humility and secret satisfaction, for Cuthbert cordially disapproved and disliked Faustina.

"Horror! I see how it is! The dead body of the black woman has been cast up by the sea, as I knew it would be, and we shall be guillotined—no!—hanged, hanged by the neck till we are dead!" she cried, wringing and twisting her hands in deadly terror.

"I wish to Heaven you may be, for an incorrigible fool!" muttered the viscount, in irrepressible anger; for, you see, his passion for this woman was not of a nature to preclude the possibility of his falling into a furious passion with her upon occasions like this. "What madness has seized you now?" he continued. "There is no danger; you have no cause to be alarmed. They have probably come about the murder of Ailsie Dunbar, Satan burn them! Cuthbert, what are you lingering here for? Go, see what it is!"

The old man bowed lowly, and left the room.

"Faustina!" exclaimed the viscount, as soon as Cuthbert had gone, "your folly will be the ruin of us both some day—will lead to discovery! Can you not let the black woman, as you call her, rest? Why will you be so indiscreet?"

"Oh, it is you who are indiscreet now," exclaimed Faustina, clasping her hands and glancing towards Mrs. MacDonald, whose sleep seemed too deep to be real.

"Try to govern yourself, then!" said the viscount.

"Ah, how can I, when I am quaking like a jelly with my terror?"

"You should not undertake dangerous crimes unless you possess heroic courage," said the viscount.

"Mon Dieu! it is you who will ruin us!" cried Faustina, stamping her small feet and pointing to Mrs. MacDonald.

The viscount laughed.

And at this moment old Cuthbert re-entered the room.

"Well?" asked Lord Vincent.

"If you please, me laird, they say they maun see yer lairdship's sel' and the leddy," said the old man.

"What the blazes do they want with us? Was ever anything so insolently persistent? Go and tell the fellows that I cannot and will not see them to-night! And if they are disappointed it will serve them right for coming out on such a night as this, They must have been mad!"

"Verra weel, me laird. I'll tell them," said the old man, departing.

"Compose yourself, Faustina, this business has no reference to you, I assure you. When they asked for us, they merely wished to see us to put some questions about the case of Ailsie Dunbar," said the viscount, who had not the slightest suspicion that there was, or could be, a warrant out for his arrest. He fancied himself entirely secure in his crimes. He believed the negroes to be safe beyond the sea; sold into slavery in a land of which they did not even understand the language, and from which they never would be allowed to return. He believed Claudia to be crushed under the conspiracy he had formed against her. He believed her father to be far away. And so he considered himself safe from all interruptions of his iniquities. What was there, in fact, to arouse his fears? What had he to dread?

Nothing, he thought.

And he was still laughing at Faustina's weakness as he stood with his back to the fire, when once more the door opened and old Cuthbert reappeared, wearing a frightened countenance and followed by two policemen.

Faustina shrieked with terror, covered her face with her hands, and shrunk back in her chair. Mrs. MacDonald, aroused by the shriek from her real or feigned sleep, opened her eyes and stared.

But Lord Vincent, astonished and indignant, strode towards the door and demanded of his old servant:

"What means this intrusion, sir? Did I not order you to say to these persons that I would not see them to-night? How dare you bring them to this room?"

"'Deed, me laird, I could na help it! When I gi'e them yer lairdship's message they e'en just bid me gang before, and sae they followed me up, pushing me to the right and left at their ain will," said Cuthbert sullenly.

Lord Vincent turned to the intruders and haughtily demanded:

"What is the meaning of this conduct, fellows? Were you not told that I would not see you to-night? How dare you push yourselves up into the private apartment of these ladies? Leave the room and the house instantly."

"We will leave the room and the house, my lord; but, when we do so, you and that lady must go with us," said the taller of the two policemen, advancing into the room.

"What?" demanded the viscount.

"Mon Dieu!" shrieked Faustina.

"Gracious, goodness, me, alive!" exclaimed Mrs. MacDonald.

"You are wanted," answered the policeman, whose name by the way was McRae.

"What do you mean, fellow? Leave the room, I say, before I order my servant to kick you out!" fiercely cried the viscount.

The policeman immediately stepped up to the side of his lordship and laid his hand upon his shoulder, saying:

"Malcolm Dugald, Lord Vincent, you are my prisoner."

"Your prisoner, you scoundrel! hands off, I say!" cried the viscount.

"I arrest you in the Queen's name, for the abduction and selling into slavery of the three negroes, Catherine Mortimer, James Mortimer, and Sarah Sims," said McRae, taking a firmer hold of his captive.

"Let go my collar, you infernal villain, and show me your warrant!" thundered Lord Vincent, wrenching himself from the grasp of the policeman.

McRae calmly produced his warrant and placed it in the hands of the viscount.

Lord Vincent, astonished, terrified, but defiant, held the document up before his dazed eyes and tried to read it. But though he held it up with both hands close to his blanched face, it trembled so in his grasp that he could not trace the characters written upon it.

While he held it thus, McRae slyly drew something from his own pocket, approached the viscount and—click! click—the handcuffs were fastened upon the wrists of his lordship!

Down fluttered the warrant from the relaxed fingers of the viscount, while his face, exposed to view, seemed set in a deadly panic as he gazed upon his captor.

"Look to him, Ross," said McRae, addressing his comrade and pointing to the viscount.

Then he stepped up to the cowering form of Mrs. Dugald, who had shrunk to the very back of her deep velvet chair. Laying his hand upon her shoulder he said:

"Faustina Dugald, you are my prisoner. I arrest you, in the Queen's name, upon the charge of having aided and abetted Lord Vincent in the abduction of—"

"Oh, horror! let me go, you horrid brute!" cried Faustina, suddenly finding her voice, interrupting the officer with her shrieks and springing from under his hand.

She rushed towards the passage door with the blind impulse of flight and tore it open, only to find herself stopped by a posse of constables drawn up without. They had come in force strong enough to overcome resistance, if necessary.

"Give yourself up, Faustina. It is the best thing you can do," said the viscount.

She stared wildly like a hunted hare, and then turned and made a dash towards her bedroom door, but only to be caught in the arms of McRae, who stepped suddenly thither to intercept her mad flight.

He held her firmly with one hand, while with the other he drew something from his pocket and suddenly snapped the handcuffs upon her wrists.

She burst into passionate tears.

"I am sorry to do this, madam, but you forced me to it," said McRae gravely and kindly.

She was a pitiable object as she stood there, guilty, degraded, and powerless. Her wreath of lilies had been knocked off and trampled under foot in the scuffle. The bouquet of lilies that rested on her bosom was crushed. Her lace and swan's-down trimmings were torn. Her hair was disheveled, her face pale, and her eyes streaming with tears.

"Why do they make me a prisoner?" she sobbed.

"I told you, madam, it was for your share in the abduction of—"

"Abduction! abduction! I don't know what you mean by abduction! I did not kill the black negro person! I did not put her into the sea! It was Lord Vincent! I never helped him! No, not at all! He would not let me! And if he would, I should not have done it! He did it all himself! And it is cruel to make a poor, small, little woman suffer for what a big man does!" she cried, amid piteous tears and sobs.

"Faustina! Faustina! what are you saying?" exclaimed the viscount, in consternation.

"The truth, my lord viscount; you know it! The truth, messieurs, I assure you! Lord Vincent killed the black negro woman and threw her into the sea! And I had nothing to do with, it! I did not even know it until all was over! And I will tell you all about it, messieurs, if you will only take these dreadful things off my poor, little, small wrists and let me go! It is cruel, messieurs, to fetter and imprison a poor, small little woman, for a big man's crime! Let me go free, messieurs, and I will tell you all about him," pleaded this weeping creature, who for the sake of her own liberty was willing to give her lover up to death.

But you need not be surprised at this; for I told you long ago that there can be no honor, faith, or love among thieves, let the biographers of the Jack Shepherds and Nancy Sykeses say what they please to the contrary. "Do men gather grapes of thorns, or figs of thistles?" The criminal is the most solitary creature upon earth; he has no ties—for the ties of guilt are nothing; they snap at the lightest breath of self-interest.

Faustina's plea dismayed her accomplice and disgusted her captor.

"Madam," said the latter, "you had better hold your peace. Your words criminate yourself as well as Lord Vincent."

"How do they criminate myself? Oh, mon Dieu! what shall I do, since even my denials are made to tell against me!" she whimpered, wringing her hands.

"Faustina, be silent!" said the viscount sternly.

"My lord, we are ready to remove you," said McRae, advancing toward the viscount.

"Where do you intend to take us then?" demanded the viscount, with a blush of shame, though with a tone of defiance.

"To the police station house, for the night. In the morning you will be brought before the magistrate for examination."

"To your beast of a station house?" said the viscount.

The policeman bowed.

"Ah, mon Dieu! will he take us out into the snow to-night? I cannot go! I should freeze to death! I should perish in the storm! It would be murder!" cried Faustina, wringing her hands.

"You see it would be barbarous to drag a lady out in this horrible weather. Can you not leave her here for the night? and if you consider yourself responsible for her safe-keeping, can you not remain and guard her?" inquired his lordship, speaking, however, quite as much, or even more, for himself than for Faustina; for he was well aware that, if she were left, he would be also left.

"My lord, it is impossible. I could not be answerable for my prisoner's safety if she were permitted to remain here all night, no matter how well guarded she might be. It was only a few weeks ago that a prisoner—a young girl she was, charged with poisoning—persuaded me to hold her in custody through the night in her own chamber. I did so, placing a policeman on guard on the outside of each door. And yet, during the night she succeeded in making her escape down a secret staircase and through a subterranean passage, and got clear off. It was in just such an ancient place as this, my lord. I came near losing my office by it; and I made a resolution then never to trust a prisoner of mine out of my sight until I got him or her, as the case might be, safe under lock and key in my station house."

"But, mon Dieu! mon Dieu! what will become of me?" wailed Faustina.

"It will kill her. She is very tender," urged Lord Vincent.

"Your lordship may order your own close carriage for her use. She may wrap up in all her furs. And though she may still suffer a good deal from the long, cold ride, she will not freeze, I assure you," said McRae.

"Ah, but what do you take me for at all? I say that I did not kill the black negro woman; Lord Vincent did it."

"Madam, neither you nor my lord are accused of murder," said McRae.

"Ah! what, then, do you accuse us of?"

"You will hear at the magistrate's office, madam," said the policeman, losing patience.

"I say, what—whatever it was, Lord Vincent did it!"

"Faustina, be silent! If no remnant of good faith leads you to spare me, spare yourself at least," said the viscount.

"Will you order your carriage?" said McRae.

"Cuthbert, go down and have the close carriage brought around. Put the leopard skins inside and bottles of hot water," ordered the viscount.

"Madam, you had better summon your maid and have your wrappings brought to you, and anything else you may wish to take with you," advised McRae.

"Oh, mon Dieu! mon Dieu! must I leave this beautiful place to go to a horrid prison. Oh, mon Dieu, mon Dieu!" wept Faustina, wringing her hands.

"Shall I ring for your maid?" inquired McRae.

"No, you monster!" shrieked Faustina. "Do you think I want Desiree, whose ears I boxed this morning, to come here to see me marched off to prison? She would be glad, the beast! she would laugh in her sleeve, the wretch! Madame MacDonald, will you get my bonnet and sables?" she said, turning to her companion.

"Yes, my dear, suffering angel, I will do all that you wish me to do. Ah! you remind me of your countrywoman, Queen Marie Antoinette, when she was dragged from the luxurious Tuileries to the dreary temple," whined sympathizing Complacency.

"Good Heaven! woman, do not speak of her. She was guillotined!" cried Faustina, with a shiver of terror.

"But you shall not be, my dear; you shall come out clear; and they who have accused you shall be made ashamed," said Mrs. MacDonald, as she passed into Faustina's dressing room.

Presently she came forth, bearing a quilted silk bonnet, a velvet sack, a sable cloak, a muff and cuffs, and warm gloves and fur-lined boots, and what not; all of which she helped Faustina to put on. While she was kneeling on the floor and putting on the beauty's boots she said:

"I think some of these men might have the modesty to turn their backs, if they canna leave the room. Ah, my poor dear! now you remind me of my own countrywoman, poor Queen Mary Stuart, when she complained on the scaffold of having to undress before so many men! Now you have to dress before so many."

"Oh, God, you will be the death of me, with your guillotined women! You turn my flesh to jelly, and my bones to gristle, and my heart to water!" cried Faustina, with a dreadful shudder, as she rose to her feet, quite ready, as far as dress was concerned, for her journey.

"Will my poor, dear, suffering angel have anything else?" said Mrs. MacDonald.

"Yes. Oh, dear, that I should have to leave this sweet place for a nasty prison! Yes, you may get together all that fruit and nuts and cake and wine, and don't forget the bonbons, and have them put in the carriage, for I don't believe I could get such things in the horrid prison! And, stay— put me a white wrapper and a lace cap in my little night-bag; and stop—-put that last novel of Paul de Kock in also. I will be as comfortable as I can make myself in that beast of a place."

"Blessed angel! what a mind you have; what philosophy; what fortitude! You now remind me of your illustrious compatriot, Madame Roland, who, when dragged from her elegant home to the dreadful prison of the Conciergerie, and knowing that in a few days she must be dragged from that to the scaffold, yet sent for her books, her music, her birds, and her flowers, that she might make the most of the time left," said Mrs. MacDonald, as she zealously gathered up the desired articles.

"Silence! I shall dash my brains out if you speak to me of another headless woman!" shrieked Faustina, stopping both her ears.

Old Cuthbert put his head in to say that the carriage was ready. Lord Vincent ordered him to load himself with the luxuries that had been provided for Faustina and put them into the carriage, and then in returning to fetch him his overshoes, cloak, and hat. All of these orders were duly obeyed.

When all was ready Lord Vincent shook hands with Mrs. MacDonald was saying:

"We must all bow to the law, madam; but this is only a passing cloud. We shall be liberated soon. And I hope we shall find you here when we return."

"Ye may be sure of that, my lord. And may Heaven grant you a speedy deliverance," she answered.

Faustina next came up to bid her good-by.

"Good-by! Good-by! my sweet, suffering angel. Bear up under your afflictions; fortify your mind by thinking of the martyred queens and heroines who have preceded you," said Mrs. MacDonald, weeping as she embraced Faustina.

"Good Heaven, I shall think of none of them! I shall think only of myself and my deliverance!" said Faustina, breaking from her.

They went downstairs, marshaled by the policemen. They entered the carriage, two policemen riding inside with them, and one on the box beside the coachman. And thus they commenced their stormy night journey.

CHAPTER XLII

A BITTER NIGHT.

St. Agnes' Eve—ah, bitter chill it was!

The owl, for all his feathers, was acold,

The hare limped trembling thro' the frozen grass;

And silent was the flock in woolly fold!

—Keats.

A freezing night. Faustina shook as with an ague-fit, and her teeth chattered like a pair of castanets, as she crouched down in one corner of the back seat and huddled all her wrappings close about her. But the cold still seemed to penetrate through all her furs and velvets and woolens and enter the very marrow of her bones.

Beside her sat the viscount, silent, grim, and still, as though he were congealed to ice. Before her sat the two policemen, well wrapped up in their greatcoats and thick shawls.

All were silent except Faustina. She shook and moaned and chattered incessantly. Such a mere animal was this wretched woman that she was quite absorbed in her present sufferings. While enduring this intense cold she could not look forward to the terrors of the future.

"It's insufferable!" she exclaimed, fiercely stamping her feet; "can you not make this beast of a carriage closer, then? My flesh is stone and my blood is ice, I tell you."

One window had been left open a little way, to let a breath of air into the carriage, which, crowded with four persons, was otherwise stifling. But the viscount now raised both his fettered hands and closed up the window. The arrangement did not prove satisfactory. It deprived the sufferers of air without making them any warmer. Faustina shook and moaned and chattered all the same.

"Oh, wretches!" she exclaimed, in furious disgust; "open the window again! I am suffocated! I am poisoned! They have all been eating garlic and drinking whisky!"

The window was opened at her desire, but as they were then crossing the narrow isthmus of rock that connected the castle steep with the land, the wind, from that exposed position, was cutting sharp, and drove into the aperture the stinging snow, which entered the skin like needle points.

"Ah, shut it! shut it! It kills me! It is infamous to treat a poor little lady so!" she cried, bursting into tears.

Again the window was closed; but not for any length of time. Apparently she could neither bear it open nor shut. So, shaking, moaning, and complaining, the poor creature was taken through that long and bitter night journey which ended at last only at the station house of Banff.

Half dead with cold, she was lifted out of the carriage by the two policemen who stood upon the sidewalk, where she remained, shaking, chattering, and weeping tears that froze upon her cheeks as they fell.

She could see nothing in that dark street but the gloomy building before her, dimly lighted by its iron lamp above the doorway.

There she remained till the viscount was handed out.

"Cuthbert," said his lordship to the old man, who had exposed himself to the severe weather of this night and driven the carriage for the sake of being near his master as long as possible, "Cuthbert, take the carriage around to the 'Highlander' and put up there for the night. We shall want it to take us back to the castle to-morrow, after this ridiculous farce is over."

"Verra weel, me laird," replied old Cuthbert, touching his hat with all the more deference because his master was suffering degradation.

"Ah! is it so? Will we really get back to the castle to-morrow?" whimpered Faustina, shaking, chattering, and wringing her hands.

"Of course we will," replied his lordship.

"Ah, but how shall I get through the night? I must have a good fire and a comfortable bed, and something warm to drink. Will you see to it, Malcolm?" she whiningly inquired.

"Don't be a fool!" was the gentlemanly reply; for the viscount burned with half-suppressed rage against the woman. whose fatal beauty had led him into all this disgrace.

She burst into a passion of tears.

"That is the reward I get for all my love!" she exclaimed.

"Faustina, for your own sake, if not for any other's, exercise some discretion!" exclaimed the viscount angrily.

"Villain!" she screamed, in fury, "I had no discretion when I listened to you!"

"I wish to Heaven you had had then! I should not have been in this mess," he replied.

"Ah!" she hissed. "If my hands were not fettered I would tear your eyes!"

"Sweet angel!" sneered the viscount, in mockery and self-mockery.

"Thsche!" she hissed, "let me at him!"

The viscount laughed, a hard, bitter, scornful laugh.

And at it they went, criminating and recriminating, until the empty carriage was driven away, and the policemen took them by the shoulders and pushed them into the station house.

They found themselves in a large stone hall, with iron-grated windows. It was partially warmed with a large, rusty stove, around which many men of the roughest cast were gathered, smoking, talking, and laughing. The walls were furnished with rude benches, upon which some men sat, some reclined, and some lay at full length. The stone floor was wet with the slop of the snow that had been brought in by so many feet and had melted. In one of these slops lay a woman, dead drunk.

"Ah! Good God! I cannot stay here!" cried Faustina, gathering up her skirts, as well as she could with her fettered hands, and looking around in strong disgust.

The viscount laughed in derision; he was angry, desperate, and he rejoiced in her discomfiture.

"Eh, Saunders! take these two women in the women's room," said McRae, beckoning a tall, broad-shouldered, red-headed Scot to his assistance.

"Hech! it will take twa o' the strongest men here to lift yon lassie," replied the man, lumbering slowly along towards the prostrate woman, and trying to raise her. If he failed in lifting her, he succeeded in waking her, and he was saluted for his pains with a volley of curses, to which he replied with a shake or two.

"Oh, horror! I will not stay here!" cried Faustina, stamping with rage.

"Attend to her, Christie. Dunlap, help Saunders to remove that woman," said McRae.

Two of the policemen succeeded in raising the fallen woman, and leading her between them into an adjoining room. The man addressed as "Christie" would have taken Faustina by the arm, and led her after them, but that she fiercely shook herself from his grasp.

"Follow then and ye like, lass; but gae some gait ye maun, ye ken," said the man good-naturedly.

She glanced around the dreary room, upon the grated windows, the sloppy floor, the rusty stove, and the wretched men, and finally seemed to think that she could not do better than to leave such a repulsive scene.

"Go along, then, and I will follow, only keep your vile hands off me," said Faustina, gathering up her dainty raiment and stepping carefully after her leader. As she did so she turned a last look upon Lord Vincent. The viscount had thrown himself upon a corner of one of the benches, where he sat, with his fettered hands folded together, and his head bent down upon his breast, as if he were in deep despair.

"Imbecile!" was the complimentary good-night thrown by his angel, as she passed out of the hall into the adjoining room. This—the women's room—was in all respects similar to the men's hall, being furnished with the like grated windows, rusty iron stove, and rude benches. Along, on these benches, or on the floor, were scattered wretched women in every attitude of self-abandonment; some in the stupor of intoxication; some in the depths of sorrow; some in stony despair; some in reckless defiance.

The men who had come in with the drunken woman deposited her on one of the benches, from which she quickly rolled to the floor, where she lay dead to all that was passing around her. Her misfortune was greeted with a shout of laughter from the reckless denizens of this room; but that shout was turned into a deafening yell when their eyes fell upon Faustina's array.

"Eh, sirs! wha the deil hae we here fra the ball?" they cried, gathering around her with curiosity.

"Off, you wretches!" screamed Faustina, stamping at them.

"Hech! but she hae a temper o' her ain, the quean," said one.

"Ou, aye, just! It will be for sticking her lad under the ribs she is here," surmised another.

"Eh, sirs, how are the mighty fa'en!" exclaimed a third, as they closed around her, and began to closely examine her rich dress.

"Rabble! how dare you?" screamed Faustina, fiercely twitching herself away from them.

"Eh! the braw furs and silks! the town doesna often see the loike o' them," said the first speaker, lifting up the corner of the rich sable cloak.

"Wretch, let alone!" shrieked Faustina, stamping frantically.

The uproar brought Policeman Christie to the scene.

"Take me away from this place directly, you beast! How dare you bring me among such wretches?" screamed the poor creature.

"My lass, I hae na commission to remove you. I dinna ken what ye hae done to bring yoursel' here; but here ye maun bide till the morn," said Christie kindly and composedly.

"I will not, I say! What have I done to be placed among these vile wretches?" she persisted, stamping.

"I dinna ken, lassie, as I telled ye before; but joodging by your manners, I suld say ye hae guided yoursel' an unco' ill gait. But howe'er that will be, here ye maun bide till the morn. And gin ye will heed guid counsel, ye'll haud your tongue," said Christie, at the same time good-naturedly setting down the hamper that contained Faustina's luxuries. She did not want it. She threw herself down upon one of the benches and burst into a passion of tears.

The women gathered around the hamper, and quickly tore off the lid and made themselves acquainted with its contents.

But Faustina did not mind. She was too deeply distressed to care what they did. The contents of the hamper were now of no use to her. The "good fire, the comfortable bed, the warm beverage" that she had vehemently demanded were unattainable, she knew, and she cared for nothing else now.

While Faustina, regardless that her famished fellow-prisoners were devouring her cakes, fruits, and wine, gave herself up to passionate lamentations, another scene was going on in the men's hall.

Lord Vincent sat gnawing his nails and "glowering" upon the floor in his corner. From time to time the door opened, letting in a gust of wind, sleet, and snow, and a new party of prisoners; but the viscount never lifted his eyes to observe them.

At length, however, he looked up and beckoned Constable McRae to his side.

"Here, you, fellow! I would like to see your warrant again. I wish to know who is my accuser."

"Judge Randolph Merlin, my lord, of the United States Supreme Court," answered McRae, once more taking out his warrant and submitting it to the inspection of his prisoner.

"Ha, ha, ha!" laughed the viscount affectedly. "Randolph Merlin! He has come to the country, I suppose, to look after his daughter; and finding that these negroes are among the missing, has pretended to get up this charge against me! It will not answer his purpose, however. And I only wonder that any magistrate in his senses should have issued a warrant for the apprehension of a nobleman upon his unsupported charge."

"Pray excuse me, my lord, but the charge was not unsupported," said McRae respectfully.

"How—not unsupported?"

"No, my lord. The judge had for witnesses the three negroes, and—"

"The three negroes!" exclaimed the viscount, recoiling in amazement; but quickly recovering his presence of mind, he added: "Oh! aye! of course! they ran off with my plate, and I suppose they have succeeded in effectually secreting it and eluding discovery. And now I suspect they have been looked up by their old master and persuaded to appear as false witnesses against me. Ha, ha, ha! what a weak device! I am amazed that any magistrate should have ventured upon such testimony to have issued a warrant for my apprehension."

"I beg your pardon, my lord; but theirs was not the only testimony. There were several gentlemen present, fellow-voyagers of Judge Merlin, who testified to the finding of the negroes in a state of slavery in Cuba; their testimony corroborates that of the negroes," said McRae.

Lord Vincent went pale as death.

"What does that mean? Oh, I see! it is all a conspiracy," he said, with an ineffectual effort at derision.

But at that moment there was a bustle outside; the door was thrown open, and another prisoner was brought in by two policemen.

"What is the matter? Who is it now?" inquired McRae, going forward.

"We have got him, sir," said a constable.

"Who?" demanded McRae.

"The murderer, sir!" answered the policeman, at the same moment dragging into view the assassin of Ailsie Dunbar, the ex-valet of Lord Vincent, Alick Frisbie.

Heavily fettered, his knees knocking together, pale and trembling, the wretch stood in the middle of the floor.

"Where did you take him?" inquired McRae.

"At the 'Bagpipes,' Peterhead," replied the successful captor.

"Pray, upon what charge is he arrested?" inquired the viscount, in a shaking voice, that he tried in vain to make steady.

"A trifle of murder, among other fancy performances," said McRae.

At this moment Frisbie caught sight of his master and set up a howl, through which his words were barely audible:

"Oh, my lord, you will never betray me! You will never be a witness against me! You will never hang me! You promised that you would not!"

"Hold your tongue, you abominable fool! What the fiend are you talking about? Do you forget yourself, sir?" roared the viscount, furious at the fatal folly of his weak accomplice.

"Oh, no, my lord, I do not forget myself! I do not forget anything. I beg your lordship's pardon for speaking, and I will swear to be as silent as the grave, if your lordship will only promise not to—"

"Will you stop short where you are, and not open your mouth again, you insufferable idiot!" thundered the viscount.

Frisbie gulped his last words, whined and crouched like a whipped hound, and subsided into silence.

And soon after this McRae and the other officers who were off duty for the remainder of the night went home and the doors were closed.

A miserable night it was to all within the station house, and especially to that guilty man and woman who had been torn from their luxurious home and confined in this dreary prison. All that could revolt, disgust, and utterly depress human nature seemed gathered within its walls. Here were drunkenness, deadly sickness, and reckless and shameless profanity, all of the most loathsome character. And all this was excruciating torture to a man like Lord Vincent, who, if he was not refined, was at least excessively fastidious. There was no rest; every few minutes the door was opened to receive some new prisoner, some inebriate, or some night-brawler picked up by the watch, and brought in, and then would ensue another scene of confusion.

An endless night it seemed, yet it came to an end at last, The morning slowly dawned. The pale, cold, gray light of the winter day looked sadly through the falling snow into the closely-grated, dusty windows. And upon what a scene it looked. Men were there, scattered over the floor and upon the benches in every stage of intoxication; some stupid, some reckless, some despairing; some sound asleep; some waking up and yawning, and some walking about impatiently.

As the day broadened and the hour arrived for the sitting of the police magistrate, the policemen came in and marched off the crowd of culprits to a hall in another part of the building, where they were to be examined. Even the women were marched out from the inner room after the men. It seemed that all the lighter offenders were to be disposed of first.

Lord Vincent and Frisbie were left alone in charge of one officer.

"When are we to be examined?" demanded the viscount haughtily of this man.

"I dinna ken," he answered, composedly lighting his pipe and smoking away.

Lord Vincent paced up and down the wet and dirty stone floor, until at length the door opened and McRae, the officer who arrested him, entered.

"Ah, you have come at last. I wish to be informed why we have been left here all this time? Everyone else has been removed," exclaimed the viscount.

"My lord, those poor creatures who were brought here during the night were not arrested for any grave offense. Some were brought in only to keep them from perishing in the snowstorm, and others for drunkenness or disorder. The sitting police magistrate disposes of them. They will mostly be discharged. But you, my lord, are here upon a heavy charge, and you are to go before Sir Alexander McKetchum."

"Why, then, do you not conduct me there? Do you mean to keep me in this beastly place all day?"

"My lord, your examination is fixed for ten o'clock; it is only nine now," said McRae, passing on to the inner room, from which he presently appeared with Faustina.

Wretched did the poor creature look with her pale and tear-stained face, her reddened eyes and disheveled hair; and her rich and elegant white evening dress with its ample skirts and lace flounces bedraggled and bedabbled with all the filth of the station house.

"I have had a horrid night! I have been in worse than purgatory. I have not closed my eyes. I wish I was dead. See what you have brought me to, Malcolm! And—only look at my dress!" sobbed the woman.

"Your dress! That is just exactly what I am looking at. A pretty dress that to be seen in. What the demon do you think people will take you for?" sneered his lordship.

"I do not know! I do not care! poor trampled lily that I am!"

"Poor trampled fool! Why didn't you change that Merry Andrew costume for something plainer and decenter before you left the castle?"

"Why didn't you tell me to do it, then? I never thought of it. Besides, I didn't know what this beast of a station house was like. No carpets, no beds, no servants. And I'm dying for want of them all. And now I must have my breakfast. Why don't you order it, Malcolm?" she whimpered.

"I am afraid they do not provide breakfasts any more than they do other luxuries for the guests of this establishment," replied the viscount, with a malignant laugh.

"But I shall starve, then," said the poor little animal, bursting into tears.

"I cannot help it," replied the viscount, very much in the same tone as if he had said: "I do not care."

But here McRae spoke:

"My lord, there is nearly an hour left before we shall go before the magistrate. If you wish, therefore, you can send out to some hotel and order your breakfast brought to you here."

"Thank you; I will avail myself of your suggestion. Whom can I send?" inquired the viscount.

"Christie, you can go for his lordship," said McRae to his subordinate, who had just entered the hall.

Christie came forward to take the order.

"What will you have?" inquired Lord Vincent, curtly addressing his "sweet angel."

"Oh, some strong coffee with cream, hot rolls with fresh butter, and broiled moor hen with currant jelly," replied Faustina.

Lord Vincent wrote his order down with a pencil on a leaf of his tablets, tore it out and gave it to Christie, saying:

"Take this to the 'Highlander' and tell them to send the breakfast immediately. Also inquire for my servant, Cuthbert Allan, who is stopping there, and order him to put my horses to the carriage and bring them around here for my use."

The man bowed civilly and went out to do this errand.

In about half an hour he returned, accompanied by a waiter from the "Highlander," bringing the breakfast piled up on a large tray, unfolded the cloth and spread it upon one of the benches and arranged the breakfast upon it.

"Did you see my servant?" inquired Lord Vincent of his messenger.

"Yes, me laird, and gi'e him your order. The carriage will be round," replied the man.

As the viscount and his companion drew their bench up to the other bench upon which their morning meal was laid, Mr. Frisbie, who had been sitting in a remote corner of the hall with his head buried on his knees, got up and humbly stood before them, as if silently offering his services to wait at table.

"He here!" exclaimed Faustina, in amazement.

"Yes, he is in the same boat with us. Go sit down, Frisbie; we don't need you," said Lord Vincent. And the ex-valet retired and crouched in his corner like a repulsed dog.

Trouble did not take away the appetite of Mrs. Dugald. It does not ever have that effect upon constitutions in which the animal nature largely preponderates. She ate, drank, and wept, and so got through a very hearty repast. Lord Vincent, having swallowed a single cup of coffee, which constituted the whole of his breakfast, sat and watched her performances with unconcealed scorn.

Before Faustina got through Officer McRae began impatiently to consult his large silver turnip.

"It is time to go," he said at length.

But Faustina continued to suck the bones of the moor hen, between her trickling tears.

"We must not keep the magistrate waiting," said McRae.

But Faustina continued to suck and cry.

"I am sorry to hurry you, madam; but we must go," said McRae decisively.

"Ah, bah! what a beastly place! where a poor little lady is not permitted to eat her breakfast in peace!" she exclaimed, throwing down the delicate bone at which she had been nibbling, and fiercely starting up.

As she had not removed her bonnet and cloak during the whole night she was quite ready.

As they were going out Lord Vincent pointed to Frisbie and inquired:

"Is not that fellow to go?"

"No; he is in upon a heavier charge, you know, my lord. Your examination precedes his," said McRae, as he conducted his prisoners into the street, leaving Mr. Frisbie to solace himself with the remnants of Faustina's breakfast, guarded by Christie.

The viscount's carriage was drawn up before the door.

"Is it hame, me laird I" inquired old Cuthbert, touching his hat, from the coachman's box.

"No. You are to take your directions from this person," replied his lordship sullenly, as he hurried into the carriage to conceal himself and his fettered wrists from the passers-by.

McRae put Mrs. Dugald into the carriage, and then jumped up and seated himself on the box beside the coachman, and directed him where to drive.

The snow was still falling fast, and the streets were nearly blocked up.

CHAPTER XLIII

FRUITS OF CRIME.

Ay, think upon the cause—

Forget it not: when you lie down to rest,

Let it be black among your dreams; and when

The morn returns, so let it stand between

The sun and you, as an ill-omened cloud,

Upon a summer's day of festival.

—Byron.

After a drive of about twenty minutes through the narrow streets the carriage stopped before the town hall. McRae jumped down from the box and assisted his prisoners to alight.

"Will I wait, me laird?" inquired old Cuthbert, in a desponding tone.

"Certainly, you old blockhead!" was the courteous reply of the viscount, as he followed his conductor into the building.

McRae, who had Mrs. Dugald on his arm, led the way through a broad stone passage, blocked up with the usual motley crowd of such a place, into an anteroom, half filled with prisoners, guarded by policemen, and waiting their turn for examination, and thence into an inner room, where, in a railed-off compartment at the upper end, and behind a long table, sat the magistrate, Sir Alexander McKetchum, and his clerk, attended by several law officers.

"Here are the prisoners, your worship," said McRae, advancing with his charge to the front of the table.

Sir Alexander looked up. He was a tall, raw-boned, sinewy old Gael, with high features, a lively, red face, blue eyes, white hair and side whiskers, and an accent as broad as Cuthbert's own. He was apparently a man of the people.

"Malcolm, lad, I am verra sorry to see your father's son here on such a charge," he said.

"I am here by your warrant, sir! it is altogether a very extraordinary proceeding!" said the viscount haughtily.

"Not mare extraordinary than painful, lad," said the magistrate.

"Who are my accusers, sir?" demanded the viscount, as if he was in ignorance of them.

"Ye sall sune see, me laird. Johnstone, have the witnesses in this case arrived?" he inquired, turning to one of his officers.

"Yes, your worship."

"Then bring them in."

Johnstone departed upon his errand; and the magistrate turned his eyes upon the prisoners before him.

"Eh, it is a bonnie lassie, to be here on such a charge," he muttered to himself, as he looked at Faustina, standing, trembling and weeping, before him. Then beckoning the officer who had the prisoners in charge:

"McRae, mon, accommodate the lady with a chair. Why did ye put fetters on her? Surely there was no need of them."

"There was need, your worship. The 'lady' resisted the warrant, and fought like a Bess o' Bedlam," said McRae, as he set a chair for Faustina.

"Puir bairn! puir, ill-guided bairn!" muttered the old man between his teeth. But before he could utter another word Johnstone re-entered the room, ushering in Judge Merlin, Ishmael Worth, and the three negroes.

"Good Heaven!" exclaimed Faustina, in horror, as her eyes met those of Katie; "it is the ghost of the black negro woman raised from the dead!"

Katie heard this low exclamation, and replied to it by such grotesque and awful grimaces as only the face of the African negro is capable of executing.

"No, it is herself. There are no such things as ghosts. It is herself, and I have been deceived," muttered Faustina to herself. And then she fell into silence.

Perhaps Lord Vincent had not altogether credited McRae's statement, made to him at the station house, for certainly his eyes opened with consternation on seeing this party enter the room.

Johnstone marshaled them to their appointed places on the right hand of the magistrate.

On turning around Ishmael met full the eyes of the viscount. Ishmael gravely bowed and averted his head. He could not be otherwise than courteous under any circumstances; and he could not bear to look upon a fellowman in his degradation, no matter how well that degradation was deserved.

Judge Merlin also bowed, as he looked upon his worthless son-in-law; but the judge's bow was full of irony as his face was full of scorn.

The magistrate looked up from the document he was reading and acknowledged the presence of the new arrivals with a bow. Then turning to the prisoner he said:

"Malcolm, lad, this is an unco ill-looking accusation they hae brought against you; kidnaping and slave-trading, na less—a sort of piracy, ye ken, lad! What hae ye to say till it?"

"What have I to say to it, sir? Why, simply that it has taken me so by surprise that I can find nothing to say but that I am astounded at the effrontery of any man who could bring such a charge against me, and at the fatuity, if you will excuse my terming it so, of any magistrate who could issue a warrant against me upon such a charge," said the viscount haughtily.

"Nay, nay, lad! nay, nay! I had guid grounds for what I did, as ye shall hear presently, and noo, gen ye hae na objection, we will proceed wi' the investigation——"

"But I have an objection, sir! I tell you this has taken me utterly by surprise. I am totally unprepared for it. I must have time, I must have counsel," said the viscount with much heat.

"Then I maun remand ye for another examination," replied Sir Alexander McKetchum coolly.

"But I object to that, also. I object to be kept in confinement while there is nothing proved against me, and I demand my liberty," said the viscount insolently.

"Why dinna ye demaund the moon and stars, laddie? I could gi'e them to ye just as sune," replied Sir Alexander.

"You have no right to detain me in custody!" fiercely broke forth Lord Vincent.

"Whisht, lad, I hae no richt to set you at leeberty."

Here old Katie, whose eyes had been snapping whole volleys of vindictive fire upon the prisoners, broke out into words before Judge Merlin or Ishmael could possibly prevent her.

"Don't you let him go, ole marse! he's one nasty, 'ceitful, lyin', white nigger as ebber libbed! He did do it, and he needn't 'ny it, not while I'm standin' here! Don't you let him go, ole marse! he's cunnin' as de debbil, and he'd run away, sure as ebber you's born! You take my 'vice and don't you let him go! he artful as ole Sam!"

"Katie, Katie, Katie!" remonstrated Ishmael, in a low voice.

"So he is, den! and he knows it himse'f, too! Yes, you is, you grand vilyun! Ah, ha! 'member how you stood dere cussin' and swearin' and callin' names, and sassin' at me, hard as ebber you could! Oh, ho! I telled you den how it was goin' to be! You didn't beliebe me, didn't you? Berry well, den! Now you see! now it's my turn!"

"Katie, be silent!" ordered Judge Merlin in a low tone.

"Yes, marse, yes, chile, I gwine be silent arter I done ease my mind speaking. Umph, humph!" she said, turning again to the unhappy prisoner. "Umph, humph! thought you and dat whited salt-peter was gwine gobern de world all your own way, didn't you? Heave me down in de wault to sleep long o' de rats, didn't you? Ah, ha! where you sleep las' night—and where you gwine to sleep to-night? Not in your feathery bed, dat's sartain! Send me 'cross de seas, to lib long ob de barbariums in de Stingy Islands, didn't you? Oh, ho! where you gwine be sent 'cross de seas? Not on a party ob pleasure, dat sartain, too! Ebber hear tell ob Bottommy Bay, eh? Dere where you gwine. Tell you good."

Here Sir Alexander, who had been gazing in speechless astonishment upon what seemed to him to be an incomprehensible phenomenon, recovered himself, found his voice, and said to Judge Merlin, very much as if he were speaking of some half-tamed wild animal:

"Keep that creature quiet or she must be removed."

"Katie," said Ishmael gently, "you would not like to be taken from the courtroom, would you?"

"No! 'cause I don't want to be parted from my lordship. I lubs him so well!" replied Katie, with a vindictive snap of her eyes.

"Then you must be silent," said Ishmael, "or you will be sent away."

"Look here, ole marse!" said Katie, addressing the bench, "he had his sassagefaction sassin' at me dere at Scraggy! now it's my turn! And I gwine gib it to him good, too. Say, my lordship! sold me to a low life 'fectioner to work in de kitchen—didn't you! Umph-humph! What you gwine to work at? not crickets, dat's sartain! Ebber try to take your recreation in de quarries wid a big ball and chain to your leg, eh? And an oberseer wid a long whip, ha?" she grinned.

"Sir, if you have been sufficiently well entertained with this exhibition of gorilla intelligence and malignity, will you have the goodness to put a stop to the performance and proceed with the business of the day?" asked Lord Vincent arrogantly.

"Aye, lad! though, as ye ask for a short delay of proceeding, in order to get your counsel, which is but reasonable, there is no business on hand but just to remand you and your companion—puir lassie!—back to prison, for future examination," said the magistrate. Then turning to a policeman, he said: "If that strange creature becomes disorderly again, remove her from the room."

"Nebber mind, ole marse! he no call for to take de trouble. I done said all I gwine to say and now I gwine to shut up my mouf tight. I'd scorn to hit a man arter he's down," said Katie, bridling with a lofty assumption of magnanimity. And as she really did shut her mouth fast, the point of expulsion was not pressed.

"And noo, lad, naething remains but to send you back," said Sir Alexander.

"I remarked to you before, sir, that I object to be remanded to prison, since nothing is proved against me. I totally object!" said the viscount stubbornly.

"Aye, lad, it appears too that ye object to maist things in legal procedure; the whilk is but natural, ye ken, for what saith the poet?

replied the magistrate, with a touch of caustic humor.

"But, sir, I am ready to give bail to any amount."

"It will na do, lad. The accusation is too grave a one. Nae doubt ye would gi'e me bail, and leg bail to the boot o' that. Na, Malcolm, ye hae had your fling, lad, and noo yee'll just hae to abide the consequences," replied the magistrate, taking up a pen to sign a document that his clerk laid before him.

"Then I hope, sir, that since we are to be kept in restraint, we shall be placed in something like human quarters; and not in that den of wild beasts, your filthy police station," said the viscount.

"Ou, aye, surely, lad. Ye shall be made as comfortable as is consistent wi' your safe-keeping. Christie, take the prisoners to the jail, and ask the governor to put them in the best cells at his disposal, as a special favor to mysel'. And ask him also in my name to be kind and considerate to the female prisoner—puir lassie!" said the magistrate, handing the document to the policeman in question.

"Ole marse—" began Katie, breaking her word, and addressing the bench.

"The court is adjourned," said the magistrate, rising.

"But, ole marse—" repeated Katie.

"Remove the prisoners," he said, coming down from his seat.

"Yes, but, ole marse—" she persisted.

"Dismiss the witnesses!" he ordered, passing on.

"Laws bless my soul alive, can't a body speak to you?" exclaimed Katie, catching hold of his coat and detaining him.

"What is it that you want, creature?" demanded Sir Alexander, in astonishment.

"Only one parting word to 'lighten your mind, ole marse! Which it is dis: Just now you called dat whited salt-peter here a pure lassie, which, beggin' your pardon, is 'fernally false, dough you don't know it! 'cause if she's pure, all de wus ob de poor mis'able gals ye might pick up out'n de streets is hebbenly angels, cherrybims, and serryfims. Dere now, dat's de trufe! Don't go and say I didn't tell you!" And Katie let go his coat.

And with a bow to Judge Merlin and his party as he passed them, Sir Alexander left the room.

The prisoners were removed—Faustina weeping, and the viscount affecting to sneer.

Judge Merlin and Ishmael went forth arm-in-arm. Of late the old man needed the support of the young one in walking. Sorrow and anxiety, more than age and infirmity, had bowed and weakened him. As the friends walked on, their conversation turned on the case in hand.

"The magistrate seems disposed to be very lenient," said the judge, in a discontented tone of voice.

"Not too lenient, I think, sir. He is evidently very kindly disposed towards the prisoner, with whose family he seems to be personally acquainted; but, notwithstanding all that, you observe, he is conscientiously rigid in the discharge of his magisterial duties in this case. He would not accept bail for the prisoner, although by stretching a point he might have done so," replied Ishmael.

"I wonder if he knew that? I wonder if he really knew the extent and limit of his power as a magistrate? I doubt it. I fancy he refused bail in order to keep on the safe side of an uncertainty. For, do you know, he impressed me as being a very illiterate man. Why, he speaks as broadly as the rudest Scotch laborer I have met with yet! He must be an illiterate man."

"Oh, no, sir; you are quite mistaken in him. Sir Alexander McKetchum is a ripe scholar, an accomplished mathematician, an extensive linguist, and last of all, a profound lawyer. He graduated at the celebrated law school of Glasgow University; at least so I'm assured by good authority," replied Ishmael.

"And speaks in a lingo as barbarous as that of our own negroes!" exclaimed the judge.

Ishmael smiled and said:

"I have also been informed that his early life was passed in poverty and obscurity, until the death of a distant relation suddenly enriched him and afforded him the means of paying his expenses at the University. Perhaps he clings to his rustic style of speech from the force of early habit, or from affection for the accent of his childhood, or from the spirit of independence, or from all three of these motives, or from no motive at all. However, with the style of his pronunciation we have nothing whatever to do. All that we are concerned about is his honesty and ability as a magistrate; and that appears to me to be beyond question."

"Oh, yes, yes, I dare say, he will do his duty. I am pleased that he refused bail and remanded the prisoners."

"Yes, he did his duty in that matter, though it must have been a very disagreeable one. And now, sir, as the prisoners are remanded and we have nothing more to detain us in Banff, had we not better return immediately to Edinboro'?" suggested Ishmael; for you see, ever since the news of his daughter's misfortunes had shaken the old man's strength, it was Ishmael who had to watch over him, to think for him and to shape his course.

"Y—yes; perhaps we had. But when I return to Edinboro', I go to Cameron Court," said the judge hesitatingly.

"The best place for you, sir, beyond all question."

"Yes; and by the way, Ishmael, I am charged with an invitation from the Countess of Hurstmonceux to yourself, inviting you to accompany me on my visit to her ladyship. Do you think you would like to accept it?"

"Very much indeed. I have a very pleasant remembrance of Lady Hurstmonceux, though I doubt whether her ladyship will be able to recollect me," said Ishmael with a smile.

The judge was somewhat surprised at this ready acquiescence. After a short hesitation, he said:

"Do you know that Claudia is staying at Cameron Court?"

"Why, certainly. It was for that reason I favored your going there. It is, besides, under the circumstances, the most desirable residence for Lady Vincent."

This reply was made in so calm a manner that any latent doubt or fear entertained by the judge that there might be something embarrassing or unpleasant to Ishmael in his prospective meeting with Claudia was set at rest forever.

But how would Claudia bear this meeting? How would she greet the abandoned lover of her youth? That was the question that now troubled the judge.

It did not trouble Ishmael, however. He had no doubts or misgivings on the subject. True, he also remembered that there had been a long and deep attachment between himself and Claudia Merlin; but it had remained unspoken, unrevealed. And Claudia in her towering pride had turned from him in his struggling poverty, and had married for rank and title another, whom she despised; and he had conquered his ill-placed passion and fixed his affections upon a lovelier maiden. But that all belonged to the past. And now, safe in his pure integrity and happy love, he felt no sort of hesitation in meeting Lady Vincent, especially as he knew that, in order to save her ladyship effectually, it was necessary that he should see her personally.

But Ishmael never lost sight of the business immediately in hand. Their walk from the town hall towards their hotel took them immediately past the Aberdeen stage-coach office. Here Ishmael stopped a moment, to secure places for himself and company in the coach that started at eleven o'clock.

"We shall only have time to reach the hotel and pack our portmanteaus before the coach will call for us. It is a hasty journey; but then it will enable us to catch the afternoon train at Aberdeen, and reach Edinboro' early in the evening," said Ishmael.

And the judge acquiesced.

When they entered the inn, they found that the professor and the three negroes were there before them.

Ishmael gave the requisite orders, and they were so promptly executed that when, a few minutes later, the coach called, the whole party was ready to start. The judge and Ishmael rode inside, and the professor and the three negroes on the outside; and thus they journeyed to Aberdeen, where they arrived in time to jump on board the express train that left at two o'clock for Edinboro'. They reached Edinboro' at five o'clock in the afternoon, and drove immediately to Magruder's Hotel. Here they stopped only long enough to change their traveling dresses and dine. And then, leaving the three negroes in charge of the professor, they set out in a cab for Cameron Court. It was eight o'clock in the evening when they arrived and sent in their cards.

The countess and Claudia were at tea in the little drawing room when the cards were brought in.

"Show the gentlemen into this room," said Lady Hurstmonceux to the servant who had brought them.

And in a few minutes the door was thrown open and—"Judge Merlin and Mr. Worth" were announced.

The countess arose to welcome her guests.

But Claudia felt all her senses reel as the room seemed to turn around with her.

Judge Merlin shook hands with his hostess and presented Ishmael to her, and then, leaving them speaking together, he advanced to embrace his daughter.

"My dearest Claudia, all is well. We have settled the whole party, the viscount, the valet, and the woman. They are lodged in jail, and are safe to meet the punishment of their crimes," he said, as he folded her to his bosom.

But oh! why did her heart beat so wildly, throbbing almost audibly against her father's breast?

He held her there for a few seconds; it was as long as he decently could, and then, gently releasing her, he turned towards Ishmael, and beckoning him to approach, said:

"My daughter, here is an old friend come to see you. Welcome him."

Ishmael advanced and bowed gravely.

"I am glad to see you, Mr. Worth," said Claudia in a low voice, as she held out her hand.

He took it, bowed over it, and said:

"I hope I find you well, Lady Vincent."

And then as he raised his head their eyes met; his eyes—those sweet, truthful, earnest, dark eyes, inherited from his mother—were full of the most respectful sympathy. But hers—oh, hers!

She did not mean to look at him so; but sometimes the soul in a crisis of agony will burst all bounds and reveal itself, though such revelation were fraught with fate. Grief, shame, remorse, and passionate regret for the lost love and squandered happiness that might have been hers, were all revealed in the thrilling, pathetic, deprecating gaze with which she once more met the eyes of her girlhood's young worshiper, her worshiper no longer.

Only for an instant did she forget herself; and then Claudia Merlin was repressed and Lady Vincent reinstated. Her voice was calm as she replied:

"It is very kind in you, Mr. Worth, to some so long a distance, at so great a cost to your professional interests, for the sake of obliging my father and serving me."

"I would have come ten times the distance, at ten times the cost, to have obliged or served either," replied Ishmael earnestly, as he resigned her hand, which until then he had held.

"I believe you would. I know you would. I thank you more than I can say," she answered.

"Have you been to tea, Judge Merlin?" inquired the countess hospitably.

"No, madam; but will be very glad of a cup," answered the judge, pleased with any divertisement.

Lady Hurstmonceux rang, and ordered fresh tea and toast and more cups and saucers. And the party seated themselves. And thus the embarrassment of that dreaded meeting was overgot.

While they sipped their tea the judge exerted himself to be interesting. He gave a graphic account of the scene in the magistrate's office; the assumption of haughty dignity and defiance on the part of the viscount; the pitiable terrors of the ex-opera singer; the vindictive triumph of Katie; and the broad accent, caustic humor, and official obstinacy of the magistrate. Ishmael, when appealed to, assisted his memory. Claudia was gravely interested. But Lady Hurstmonceux was excessively amused.

They were surprised to hear that further proceedings were deferred; but they at last admitted that they would be obliged to be patient under "the law's delays."

After tea, fearing that her guests were in danger of "moping," Lady Hurstmonceux proposed a game of whist, saying playfully that it was very seldom she was so fortunate as to have the right number of evening visitors to form a rubber.

And as no one gainsaid their hostess, the tea service was taken away, the table cleared, and the cards brought. They seated themselves and cut for partners; and Claudia and her father were pitted against Lady Hurstmonceux and Ishmael.

Do you wonder at this? Do you wonder that people who had just passed through scenes of great trouble, and were on the eve, yes, in the very midst of a fatal crisis, people whose minds were filled with sorrow, humiliation, and intense anxiety, should gather around a table for a quiet game of whist; yes, and enjoy it, too?

Why, if you will take time to reflect, you will remember that such things are done in our parlors and drawing rooms every day and night in our lives. Our thoughts, our passions, our troubles, are put down, covered over, ignored, and we—play whist, get interested in honors and odd tricks, and win or lose the rub; or do something equally at variance with the inner life, that lives on all the same.

Our party spent a pleasant week at Cameron Court.

Ishmael occupied himself with making notes for the approaching trials, or with visiting the historical monuments of the neighborhood.

Judge Merlin devoted himself to his daughter.

Lady Hurstmonceux studied the comfort of her guests, and succeeded in securing it.

And thus the days passed until they received an official summons to appear before Sir Alexander McKetchum at the examination of Lord Vincent and Mrs. Dugald.

CHAPTER XLIV

NEMESIS.

With pallid cheeks and haggard eyes,

And loud laments and heartfelt sighs,

Unpitied, hopeless of relief,

She drinks the cup of bitter grief.

In vain the sigh, in rain the tear,

Compassion never enters here;

But justice clanks the iron chain

And calls forth shame, remorse, and pain.

—Anon

The same carriage that brought Lord Vincent and Mrs. Dugald to the town hall conveyed them from that place to the county jail.

There Lord Vincent finally dismissed it, sending it home to the castle, and instructing Cuthbert to pack up some changes of clothing and his dressing-case and a few books and to bring them to him at the prison.

Mrs. Dugald at the same time stopped crying long enough to order the old man to ask Mrs. MacDonald to put up all that might be necessary to her comfort for a week, and dispatch it by the same messenger that should bring Lord Vincent's effects.

These arrangements concluded, the carriage drove away and Policeman McRae conducted his prisoners into the jail. He took them first into the warden's room, where he produced the warrant for their commital and delivered them up.

The warden, "Auld Saundie Gra'ame," as he was familiarly styled, was a tall, gaunt, hard-favored old Scot, who had been too many years in his present position to be astonished at any description of prisoner that might be confined to his custody. In his public service of more than a quarter of a century he had had turned over to his tender mercies more than one elegantly dressed female, and many more than one titled scamp. So, without evincing the least surprise, he simply took the female prisoner, named in the warrant "Faustina Dugald," to be—just what she was—a fallen angel who had dropped into the clutches of the law; and the male prisoner, named in the warrant "Malcolm Dugald, Viscount Vincent," to be—what he was—a noble rogue, guilty of being found out.

While he was reading the warrants, entering their names in his books, and writing out a receipt for their "bodies," Lord Vincent stood with his fettered hands clasped, his head bowed upon his chest, and his countenance set in grim endurance; and Faustina stood wringing her hands, weeping, and moaning, and altogether making a good deal of noise.

"Whisht, whisht, bairnie! dinna greet sae loud! Hech! but ye mak' din eneugh to deave a miller!" expostulated the warden, as he handed the receipt to McRae and turned his regards to the female prisoner.

But the only effect of his words upon Faustina was to open the sluices of her tears and make them flow in greater abundance.

"Eh, lassie, 'tis pity of you too! But hae ye ne'er been tauld that the way o' the transgreesor is haird? and the wages o' sin is deeth?" said the "kindly" Scot.

"But I do not deserve death! I never did kill anybody myself!" whimpered Faustina.

"Wha the de'il said ye did? I was quoting the Book whilk I greatly fear ye dinna aften look into, or ye would na be here noo."

"But I have no right to be here. I never did anything, I, myself, to deserve such treatment. It was Lord Vincent's fault. It was he who brought me to this!" whined Faustina.

"Nae doobt! nae doobt at a'! He's ane o' the natural enemies o' your sex, ye ken. And ye suld o' thocht o' that before ye trusted him sae far."

"I did not trust him at all. And I do not know what you mean by your insinuations, you horrid old red-headed beast!" cried Faustina.

"Whisht! whisht! haud your tongue, woman! Dinna be sae abusive! Fou' words du nae guid, as I aften hae occasion to impress upon the malefactors that are brocht here for safe-keeping," said the jailer, as he turned and looked around upon the underlings in attendance. Then beckoning one of the turnkeys to him, he said:

"Here, Cuddie, tak' this lass into the north corridor o' the women's ward; and when ye hae her safe in the cell, ye maun knock off the irons fra her wrists. Gang wi' Cuddie, lass; an dinna be fashed; he's nae a bad chiel."

Cuddie, a big, honest, good-natured looking brute, took a bunch of great keys from their hook on the wall and signing for his prisoner to follow him, turned to depart.

But Faustina showed no disposition to obey the order. And McRae, who had lingered in the room, now turned to the warden and said:

"If you please, sir, Sir Alexander McKetchum desired me to request you to put these prisoners into as comfortable quarters as you could command, consistent with their safe custody."

"Sir Alexander would do weel to mind his ain business. Wha the de'il gi'e him commission to dictate to me?" demanded the old Scot wrathfully.

"Nay, sir, he only makes the request as a personal favor," said McRae deprecatingly.

"Ou, aye, aweel, that's anither thing. Though there's nae muckle of choice amang the cells, for that matter; forbye it's the four points o' the compass, nor', sou', east, and wast. The jail is square and fronts nor', and the cells range accordingly. There's nae better than the nor' corridor o' the women's ward. Tak' the lass awa, Cuddie."

Cuddie laid his hand not unkindly on the shoulder of his prisoner, and Faustina, seeing at last that resistance was quite in vain, followed him out.

"Noo, Donald, mon," said the jailer, beckoning another turnkey, "convey his lairdship to the sou-wast corner cell in the men's ward. It has the advantage of twa windows and mare sunshine than fa's to the lot o' prison cells in general. And when ye get him there relieve him o' his manacles."

The officer addressed took down his bunch of keys, and turned to his prisoner. But Lord Vincent did not wait for the desecrating hand of the turnkey to be laid upon his shoulder. With a haughty gesture and tone he said:

"Lead the way, fellow; I follow you."

And Donald bowed and preceded his prisoner as if he had been a head-waiter of a fashionable hotel, showing an honored guest to his apartments.

When they were gone the old warden turned to the policeman:

"Will it gae hard wi' them, do ye think, McRae?"

"I think it will send them to penal servitude for twenty years or for life."

Meanwhile Cuddie conducted his prisoner through long lines of close, musty, fetid passages, and up high flights of cold, damp stone stairs, to the very top of the building, where the women's wards were situated.

Here he found a stout old woman, in a linen cap, plaid shawl, and linsey gown, seated at an end window, with her feet upon a foot-stove, and her hands engaged in knitting a stocking.

She was Mrs. Ferguson, the female turnkey.

"Here, mither, I hae brocht you anither prisoner," said Cuddie, coming up with his charge.

The old woman settled her spectacles on her nose, and looked up, taking a deliberate survey of the newcomer, as she said:

"Hech! the quean is unco foine; they be braw claes to come to prison in. Eh, Cuddie, I wad suner hae any ither than ane o' these hizzies brocht in."

"But, mither, the word is that she maun be made comfortable," said Cuddie.

"Ou, aye—nae doobt! she will be some callant's light o' luve, wha hae a plenty o' siller!" replied the old woman scornfully, as she rose from her place and led the way to the door of a cell about halfway down the same corridor.

"Ye'll pit her in here. It will be as guid as anither," she said.

Cuddie detached a certain key from his bunch and handed it to her. She opened the door, and they entered. The cell was a small stone chamber, six feet by eight, with one small grated window, facing the door. On the right of the window was a narrow bed, filling up that side of the cell; on the left was a rusty stove; that was all; there was no chair, no table, no strip of carpet on the cold stone floor; all was comfortless, desolate.

Faustina burst into a fresh flood of tears as she threw herself upon the wretched bed.

"Let me tak' aff the fetters," said Cuddie gently.

Faustina arose to a sitting position, and held up her hands.

Cuddie, with some trouble, got them off, but so awkwardly that he bruised and grazed her wrists in doing so, while Faustina wept piteously and railed freely. Cuddie was too good-natured to mind the railing, but the dame fired up:

"Haud your growlin', ye ne'er-do well! Gin ye had your deserts, for a fou'-mouthed jaud, ye'd be in a dark cell on bread and water!"

"Whisht! whisht, mither! Let her hae the length o' her tongue, puir lass! It does her guid, and it does me na hurt. There, lass—thc airns arc aff, and if you'll o'ny put your kershief aroun' your bonnie wrists they'll sune be weel eneugh."

"Take me away! take me away from that horrid ol woman!" cried Faustina, turning her wrath upon the dame and appealing to Cuddie.

"Whisht! dinna ye mind her. She's a puir dolted auld carline," said Cuddie, in a voice happily too low to reach the ear of said "carline."

"Ye maunna guid her siccan a sair gait, mither," said Cuddie, as they left the cell.

"I doobt she has guided hersel' an uco' ill ane," retorted the dame.

Faustina was left sitting on the side of the hard bed, weeping bitterly. She did not throw off her bonnet or cloak. She could not make herself at home in this wretched den. Besides, it was bitterly cold; there was no fire in the rusty stove and she wrapped her sables more closely around her.

She remained there in the same position, cowering, shivering and weeping, for two or three miserable hours, when she was at length broken in upon by the old dame, who brought in her prison dinner—coarse beef broth, in a tin can, with an iron spoon, and a thick hunk or oatmeal bread on a tin plate.

"What is that!" ask Faustina.

"Your dinner. Is it na guid o' the authorities to feed the like o' you for naething?"

"My dinner! ugh! Do you think I am going to swallow that swill—fit only for pigs?" exclaimed Faustina, in disgust.

"Hech, sirs! what's the warld comming to? It is guid broose, verra guid broose, that many an honest woman would be unco glad to hae for hersel' and her puir bairns, forbye you!" said the dame wrathfully.

"Take it away! the sight of it makes me ill!"

"Verra weel; just as you please. I'll set it here, till ye come to your stomach," said the dame, setting the can and plate down upon the stone floor, for there was no other place to put them.

"I want a fire—I am frozen!" cried Faustina.

"Why did na ye say sae before?" growled the dame, going out.

In a few minutes she came back, bringing coals and kindlings and lighted the fire, and then retreated as sullenly as she had entered. Faustina drew near the stove, and sat down upon the floor to hover over it.

When she grew warm her eyes began to glitter dangerously. She turned herself around and surveyed the place. Like the frozen viper thawed to life, her first instinct was to bite.

"I would like to set fire to the prison!" she said.

But a moment's reflection proved to her the folly of this impulse. If she should use the fire in her stove for such incendiary purposes, herself would be the only thing burned up; the cell of stone and its furniture of iron would escape with a smoking.

She put off her bonnet and her sables—the first time since the night before, and she threw herself upon the bed, and lay there in a torment until six o'clock in the evening, when the door was once more unlocked by the dame, who brought her the prison supper—a tin can of oatmeal porridge.

"Here's your parritch; ye may eat it or leave it, just as ye please," said the woman, setting the can on the floor.

"I want some tea! I will have none of your filthy messes! Bring me some tea!" cried Faustina.

"I wish ye may get it, lassie, that's a'," answered the dame, as she went out and locked the door behind her.

That was the last visit Faustina had that night. She lay on her hard bed, weeping, moaning, and lamenting her fate, until the last light of day died out of the narrow window, and left the cell in darkness, but for the dim red ray in the corner, that showed where the fire in the rusty stove burned. And still she lay there, until the pangs of hunger began to assail her. These she bore some time before she could overcome her repugnance to the prison fare. At length, however, she arose and groped her way about the stone floor until she found the can of beef broth, which, upon trying, she discovered to taste better than it looked. She ate it all; then she ate the hunk of bread; and finally she finished with the oatmeal porridge. And, then, without undressing, she threw herself on the outside of her bed; and, overcome with fatigue, distress, and vigilance, she fell into a deep sleep that lasted until the morning.

It might have lasted much longer, but she was aroused about seven o'clock, by the entrance of her keeper, bringing her breakfast.

"Eh!" said the dame, glancing at the empty cans, "but I thocht ye would come to your stomach. Here's your breakfast."

Faustina raised herself up and gazed around in a bewildered way, but she soon recollected herself, and looked inquiringly at her keeper.

"It's your breakfast," said the latter; "it's guid rye coffee, sweeted wi' treacle, and a braw bit o' bannock."

"I want water and soap and towels," said Faustina, in an angry, peremptory manner.

"Ou, aye, nae doobt; and ye would like a lady's maid, and perfumery 'till your toilet. Aweel, there is a stone jug and bowl of water, and a hempen clout ahint the stove, gin that will serve your purpose," said the dame, setting down the breakfast, and gathering the empty cans from the floor as she left the cell.

Faustina, poor wretch, made such a toilet as her rude providings enabled her to do, and then, with what appetite she might, made her morning meal. And then she sat on the edge of her bed and cried and wished herself dead.

At about eleven o'clock she heard footsteps and voices approaching the cell. And the door was opened by the turnkey, who ushered in Mrs. MacDonald, followed by a servant from the castle, bringing a large box and a basket.

The servant set down his burdens and retired with the turnkey, who immediately locked the door.

And not until then, when they were left alone, did this precious pair of female friends rush into each other's arms, Faustina bursting into tears and sobbing violently on the bosom of Mrs. MacDonald, and Mrs. MacDonald wheedling, caressing, and soothing Faustina.

"Mine pet, mine darling, mine bonny bairn," were some of the epithets of endearment bestowed by the lady upon her favorite.

"Oh, madame, what a purgatory of a place, and what demons of people!" Faustina cried.

"Yes, my sweet child, yes, I know it! but bear up!"

"Nothing fit to eat, or drink, or sleep on, or sit down, or even to wash with; and no one to speak a civil word to me!" wailed Faustina, still dwelling upon present inconveniences rather than, thinking of the future perils.

"Yes, my dear, yes, I know; but now, sit you down and see what I have brought you," said Mrs. MacDonald, gently forcing Faustina to seat herself upon the side of the bed.

"Look at my poor dress," said Faustina, pointing down to the delicate white evening dress in which she had been arrested, and which was now crumpled, torn, and stained.

"Eh, but that's a woeful sight! But I thought of it, my bairn, and I have brought you a plain black silk and white linen collars and sleeves. Let me help you to change your dress, and I will take that white one home with me."

Faustina agreed to this, and when the change was effected she certainly presented a more respectable appearance.

Mrs. MacDonald next unpacked the large basket, taking from it a dressing-case, furnished with every requisite for the toilet; a work-box, with every convenience for a lady's busy-idleness; and a writing-desk, with every necessary article for epistolary correspondence.

"Now where shall I put them?" she inquired, looking around upon the bare cell.

"Ah, the beastly place!" exclaimed Faustina; "there is no table, no stand; you will have to leave them on the floor or set them on the window sill."

Mrs. MacDonald ranged them on the floor, against the wall, under the window.

And then she rolled up the spoiled evening dress and crowded it into the empty basket. Next she took the trunk and pushed it under the bed, saying:

"In that trunk, my dear, you will find every requisite change of clothing. The basket I will take back."

"Ah, but I want many more things beside clothing. I want tea and coffee. I want bed linen and china; and—many more things," said Faustina impatiently,

"And you shall have everything you want, my dear. Your purse is in your writing desk. There are a hundred and forty guineas in it. Money will buy you all you want. And I will see it brought," said Mrs. Dugald, going to the cell door and rapping.

Dame Ferguson came and unlocked it.

"I wish to come out," said Mrs. MacDonald.

"Aye, me leddy," said the dame, courtesying and making way for the visitor to pass; for the carriage, with the Hurstmonceux arms emblazoned upon its panels, the servant in the livery of the Earl of Hurstmonceux, and the haughty air of the lady visitor, all impressed the female turnkey with a feeling of awe.

"I wish to speak with you, dame," said Mrs. MacDonald.

"Aye, me leddy, and muckle honor till me!" replied the woman, with another low courtesy, as she led the way to her seat at the window at the extreme end of the corridor.

"I wish to bespeak your attention to the lady I have just left," said Mrs. MacDonald.

"Aye, me leddy! Ye will be ane o' the beneevolent leddies wha gang about, seeking for the lost sheep o' the house o' Israel, meaning sic puir misguided lasses as yon! Ye'll be aiblins, ane o' the leddy directors o' the Magdalen Hospital?" said Mrs. Ferguson.

"The—what? I don't know what you mean, woman. I am speaking to you of a lady-the Honorable Mrs. Dugald."

"A leddy? The Honorable Mistress Dugald? Ou! aye! forgi'e me, your leddyship. I'm e'en but a puir, auld, doitted bodie. I e'en thocht ye were talking o' yon misguided quean in the cell. The Honorable Mistress Dugald. She'll be like yoursel', intereested in yon lassie; and aiblins ain o' the leddy direectors o' the Magdalen."

"I think you are a fool. The misguided lassie, as you have the impudence to call her, is no misguided lassie at all. She is the Honorable Mrs. Dugald, of Castle Cragg," said Mrs. MacDonald impatiently.

"Wha—she—the lass in yon cell, the Honorable—Mistress—Dugald?"

"Herself!"

"Hech, that's awfu'l"

"So I wished to give you a hint to treat her with the consideration due to her rank."

"Eh, sirs! but that's awfu'!" repeated the dame, unable to overget her astonishment.

"She has money enough to pay for all that she requires and to reward those who are kind to her besides," continued Mrs. MacDonald.

"Nae doobt! nae doobt! bags o' gowd and siller! bags o' gowd and siller! What a puir, auld, doitted, fule bodie I was, to be sure," said the dame, in a tone of regret.

"Now, I want to know whether she cannot have a few comforts in her cell, if she is able and willing to pay for them, and to reward her attendants for bringing them?"

"And what for no? The bonny leddy sail hae a' that she craves, whilk is consistent wi' her safe-keeping."

"And certainly her friends would ask no more."

"What would her leddyship like to begin wi'?"

"She is to remain here for a week; therefore she would like to have her cell fitted up comfortably. She will want a piece of carpeting to cover the floor; some nice fine bedding and bed linen; a toilet service of china; a single dinner and tea service of china; and a silver fork and spoon. Can you recollect all these articles?"

"What for no?"

"But stay, I forgot; she will want a small table and an easy-chair and footstool. Can you remember them all?"

"Ilk a ane!"

"Twenty pounds, I should think, would cover the whole expense. Here is the money; take it and send out and get the things as soon as you can," said Mrs. MacDonald, putting two ten-pound notes in the hand of the dame.

"I'll has them all in by twal' o' the clock," answered the dame zealously. "Be guid till us! The Honorable Mrs. Dugald! Yon quean! Who'd hae thocht it? But what will be the reason they pit the bonny leddy in prison? It's wonderfu'! It canna be for ony misdeed?"

"No, dame, it is for no misdeed. Ah! you have not read history, or you would know that ladies of the highest rank, even queens and princesses, have been sometimes put in prison."

"Guid be guid till us! For what crime, gin your leddyship pleases?"

"For no crime at all. They have been accused of treason, or conspiracy, or something."

"And sic will be the case wi' this puir leddy?"

"Yes," said Mrs. MacDonald, whose regard for the truth was not of the strictest description.

"And what did they do wi' the puir queens?"

"Cut off their heads."

"Hech! that was awfu'! And what will they do wi' this puir leddy?"

"Release her after a while, because they can prove nothing against her, and because she has powerful friends."

"Eh, but that's guid."

"And those friends will well reward such of the officers of the prison as shall be kind to her during her incarceration," said Mrs. MacDonald meaningly. "And now I will trouble you to unlock the door and admit me for a few minutes to see Mrs. Dugald."

"Surely, me leddy," said the dame, with alacrity.

When Mrs. MacDonald found herself once more alone with her friend she said:

"You will have everything you may require for your comfort in the course of a few hours; and you will have no more trouble from the insolence of your attendant. I have arranged all that. And now, my dear, I am going to see the viscount. What message have you for him?"

"None at all. I hate him; he has brought me to this! And he deceived me about the black woman's death and nearly frightened me into illness. Ah! the beast!" exclaimed Faustina, with a vehemence of spite that quite astounded her visitor.

"My dear," she said, after she had in some degree recovered her composure and collected her faculties, "that there is something very dreadful in this arrest no one can doubt; some charge of kidnaping in which you are both said to be implicated. But let us hope that the charge will be disproved; let us say that it will; in which case, will it be well for you to quarrel with the viscount? Think of it, and send him some kind message."

"I cannot think, and I will not send him any message," persisted Faustina.

"Then I must think for you. Good-by for a little while, my pet. I will be with you again before I leave town," said Mrs. MacDonald, as she left the cell.

She proceeded immediately to the warden's office, and requested permission to visit the Viscount Vincent in his cell.

"Auld Saundie Gra'am," as he was called, beckoned the turnkey of the ward in which the viscount was confined, and ordered him to conduct the lady to Lord Vincent's cell. The man took down his bunch of keys and, with a bow, turned and preceded Mrs. MacDonald upstairs to a corridor on the second floor, flanked each side with grated doors.

The visitor followed her conductor up the whole length of this corridor to a corner door, which he unlocked to admit the visitor. As soon as she passed in he locked the door on her and remained waiting on the outside.

Mrs. MacDonald found herself in the presence of Lord Vincent. As the cell occupied by the viscount was in the angle of the building it possessed the advantage of two small windows, one with a southern and one with a western outlook. And the sun shone in all day long, giving it a more cheerful aspect than usually belongs to such dreary places. It was furnished with the usual hard narrow bed and rusty iron stove. Besides this, it had the unusual convenience of a chair, upon which the viscount sat, and a table at which he wrote.

In one corner of the cell was old Cuthbert, kneeling down over an open trunk from which he was unpacking his master's effects. As Mrs. MacDonald entered the viscount arose, bowed, and handed her to the solitary chair with as much courtly grace as though he had been doing the honors of his own drawing-room.

"I find you more comfortable, or rather, as I should say, less uncomfortable, than I found Mrs. Dugald, poor child," said the visitor, after she sank into a seat.

"Yes, thanks to the chance that left my pocketbook in my pocket," answered the prisoner, with a defiant smile, as he seated himself on the side of the cot.

"I found her with scarcely the decent necessities of life; but I have sent out to purchase for her what is needful, poor angel."

The smile died out of the viscount's face, which became pale, cold, and hard as marble. He made no reply.

"She sent you many kind messages," began Mrs. MacDonald; but the viscount interrupted her.

"Madam," he said, "I wish never to hear that woman's name mentioned in my hearing again."

"Eh, but that is strange! You will have had a misunderstanding."

"A misunderstanding! I tell you, madam, that her base cowardice, her shameful treachery, and her utter selfishness have disgusted me beyond measure."

"Eh, me! friends should na quarrel that length either. You have both had your tempers severely tried. When you get out of this trouble you will be reconciled to each other."

"Never! I loathe that woman! And if I were free to-day, my first act should be to hurry to Castle Cragg and bar the doors against her re-entrance there. And my second should be to send all her traps after her."

Finding at length that it was worse than useless to speak one word in favor of Faustina while the viscount was in his present mood of mind, Mrs. MacDonald turned the conversation by:

"Well, my lord, I hope you have taken proper precautions for your defense at the preliminary examination."

"I have engaged counsel, who is even now at work upon my case."

"And I trust, my lord, that you have summoned the earl. His presence here would be a tower of strength to you."

"I am aware of that. I do not, however, know exactly where to put my hand down upon my father. I telegraphed to his London bankers to-day to know his address. The answer came that he was at St. Petersburg at the last advices. I shall cause a telegram to be sent to him there, in the care of our minister. It may or may not find him."

"And now, my lord, what can I do for you?" said Mrs. MacDonald, rising.

"Nothing, whatever, my dear madam, except to return to the castle and remain there and keep it warm for me against I get back," said the viscount courteously, rising to see his visitor to the door of the cell—a distance of eight feet from the spot where they stood.

Mrs. MacDonald went back to the cell of Faustina, where she remained until the comforts she had sent her were brought in. Then she superintended their arrangement, and even assisted with her own hands in the laying down of the strip of carpet, the making of the bed, and the adjusting of the table.

"There, my dear," she said, when all was done; "I think you are now as tidy and as comfortable as it is possible to be in such a place as this."

"Thank you," said Faustina; "but since you have been in here this last time you have not once mentioned Lord Vincent's name. I suppose you have a reason for your reticence. I suppose he has been speaking ill of me. It would be like him, to bring me into this trouble and then malign me."

"No, my darling, he has not breathed a syllable of reproach against you. He has spoken of you most considerately. He has charged me with many affectionate messages to you," said this disinterested peacemaker, whose personal interests were all at stake in the quarrel between the viscount and his fellow-prisoner.

"I don't want to hear his messages. I hate the sound of his name, and I wish I had never seen the sight of his face. But, Mrs. MacDonald, I thank you for the kindness you have shown me," said Faustina.

Mrs. MacDonald kissed her by way of answer. And then she sent out and ordered a luxurious little dinner, which was promptly brought and served in the cell. And after dinner they had a dessert of fruit, and after that coffee, just as they bad been accustomed to have these things at Castle Cragg.

Coffee cup in hand, Mrs. MacDonald remained chatting with her friend until the hour arrived for locking up the prison for the night. Then, with a promise to return the next day, and to come every day, she took leave and departed, returning to Castle Cragg in the family carriage, driven by old Cuthbert.

This day was a fair sample of all the days passed in prison by the Viscount Vincent and Mrs. Dugald up to the time of the preliminary examination before the magistrate.

The viscount occupied himself with writing, making notes for his defense, or holding consultation with his counsel. As he had plenty of ready money, he did not want any comfort, convenience, or luxury that money could provide. The earl, his father, however, did not arrive, and had not even been heard from.

Faustina passed her days in prison in eating, drinking, sleeping, and repining. Mrs. MacDonald came in every day to see her, and always stayed and dined with her. Mrs. MacDonald rather liked the daily airing she got in her ride to and fro between the castle and the prison. She liked also the epicurean dinners that Faustina would buy and pay for, and thus she was a miracle of constancy and fidelity.

Old dame Ferguson was their attendant. She also was bought with money. And from having been the arrogant mistress of her prisoner, she was now the humble slave of her "leddyship,"—that being the title to which she had advanced Mrs. Dugald.

Thus the days passed, bringing at length the important morning upon which the preliminary examination was to be held, in which it was to be decided whether these prisoners should be honorably discharged or whether they should be committed to jail to stand their trial upon the charge of kidnaping and conspiracy.

The Earl of Hurstmonceux had not yet been heard from; but the Viscount Vincent had prepared himself with the best defense possible to be got up in his case.

Judge Merlin and his witnesses had been duly notified to appear; and they were now in town, lodging at the very house from which the prisoners obtained their recherche meals.

CHAPTER XLV

THE VISCOUNT'S FALL.

They that on glorious ancestors enlarge

Produce their debt instead of their discharge.

—Young.

The viscount ordered his carriage to be in readiness to convey him to the magistrate's office. Old Cuthbert was punctual. And accordingly on the morning in question Lord Vincent, and Faustina, attended by Mrs. MacDonald, and the policemen that had them in custody, entered the carriage and were driven to the town hall.

Here again, as on a former occasion, the viscount, in alighting, ordered the coachman to keep the carriage waiting for him. Then he and his party passed through the same halls and ante-chambers, guarded by policemen, and entered the magistrate's office.

Sir Alexander McKetchum was already in his seat on the little raised platform. His clerk sat at a table below him. On his right hand stood several officers of the law. On his left hand stood Judge Merlin, Ishmael Worth, and the witnesses that had been summoned for the prosecution.

The Policeman McRae led his charge up in front of the magistrate, and taking off his hat, said:

"Here are the prisoners, your worship."

Lord Vincent, as with the purpose of proving himself a gentleman at least in external manners, even under the most trying circumstances, advanced and bowed to the magistrate.

Sir Alexander acknowledged his salute by a nod, and then said:

"Noo, then, as ye are here, me laird, we may as weel proceed wi' the investigation."

"I beg your pardon, sir; I am expecting my counsel," said the viscount.

"Aweel! I suppose we maun wait a bit," said the magistrate.

But at this moment the counsel for the prisoner hurried into the office.

"We have waited for you, Mr. Bruce," said the viscount reproachfully.

"I am very sorry that you should have been obliged to do so, my lord! But the truth is, I have been to the telegraph office, to send a message of inquiry at the last moment to your lordship's London bankers, to ask if the Earl of Hurstmonceux had yet been heard from. I waited for the answer, which has but just arrived, and which has proved unsatisfactory."

"The earl has not written to his London bankers, then?"

"No, my lord."

"Are you ready for the examination?"

"Quite, my lord."

"Aweel, then, I suppose we may proceed," said Sir Alexander.

"At your worship's convenience," replied Mr. Bruce, with a bow.

And thereupon the proceedings commenced. The magistrate took up the warrant that had been issued for the arrest of the prisoners, and read it to them aloud. Then addressing them both, he said:

"Malcolm, Laird Vincent, and you, Faustina Dugald, are herein charged wi' having felonious conspired against the guid character o' Claudia, Viscountess Vincent, and to farther said conspiracy, wi' having abducted and sold into slavery the bodies of three negroes, named herein—Catherine Mortimer, James Mortimer, and Sarah Sims; whilk are felony against the peace and dignity o' the Queen's majesty, and punishable by penal servitude, according to the statute in sich cases made and provided. What hae ye to say for yoursel's in answer to this charge?"

"I deny it in toto. And I think it infamous that I should be called to answer such an insulting charge," said the viscount with a fine assumption of virtuous indignation.

"And sae do I think it infamous; I agree wi' ye there, lad! But as to whilk pairty the infamy attaches to, there we may differ," said the magistrate, nodding.

The viscount drew himself up in haughty silence, as though he disdained farther reply.

"And noo, Faustina Dugald, what hae ye to say for yoursel'?"

"I did not conspire! I did not abduct! I did not sell into slavery any negro bodies! I did not do anything wrong! Not I myself!" cried Faustina vehemently,

"There, there, that will do. We will hear the testimony on this case. Let Ishmael Worth, of Washington, come forward," said the magistrate.

Ishmael advanced, bowed to the magistrate, and stood waiting.

"Ross, administer the oath," said the magistrate.

The clerk took a copy of the Holy Scriptures and held them towards Ishmael, at the same time dictating the oath, according to the custom of such officials.

But Ishmael, at the very onset, courteously interrupted him by saying gently:

"I am conscientiously opposed to taking an oath; but I will make a solemn affirmation of the truth of what I am about to state."

There was some objection made by the counsel for the prisoners, some hesitation upon the part of the clerk, some consultation with the magistrate; and finally it was decided that Mr. Worth's solemn affirmation should be accepted in lieu of an oath.

"I am sorry," said Ishmael courteously, "to have made this difficulty about a seemingly small matter; but in truth, no point of conscience is really a small matter."

"Certainly no," responded the magistrate.

Ishmael then made his formal affirmation, and gave in his testimony. First of all he identified the negroes—Catherine Mortimer, James Mortimer, and Sarah Sims—as the servants, first of Judge Randolph Merlin, of Maryland, and of his daughter Claudia, Lady Vincent. Then he testified to the fact of the finding of the negroes, each in a state of slavery, in the island of Cuba; their recovery by Judge Merlin; and their return, in his company, to Scotland.

At the conclusion of this evidence the counsel for the prisoners made some sarcastic remarks about the reliability of the testimony of a witness who refused to make his statement upon oath; but he was sharply rebuked for his pains by the magistrate.

"Judge Randolph Merlin will please to come forward," was the next order of the clerk.

"I have no conscientious scruples about taking an oath, though I certainly honor the scruples of others. And I am ready to corroborate upon oath the testimony of the last witness," said Judge Merlin, advancing and standing before the magistrate. The oath was duly administered to him, and he began his statement.

He also identified the three negroes as his own family servants, who were transferred to his daughter's service on the occasion of her marriage with Lord Vincent, and who were taken by her to Scotland. He likewise testified to the facts of finding the three negroes in the city of Havana in a condition of slavery, and the repurchasing and transporting them to Scotland.

The counsel for the accused took various exceptions to the evidence given in by this witness; but his exceptions were set aside by the magistrate as vexatious and immaterial.

Then he cross-examined the witness as severely as if the case, instead of being in a magistrate's office, were before the Lords Commissioners of the Assizes. But this cross-examination only had the effect of emphasizing the testimony of the witness, and impressing the facts more firmly upon the mind of the magistrate. And then, as the counsel could make nothing by perseverance in this course, he permitted the witness to sit down.

"Catherine Mortimer will come forward," said the clerk.

"That's me! I's got leabe to talk at last!" said old Katie, with a malignant nod at the accused. And she stepped up, folded her arms upon her bosom, threw back her head, and stood with an air of conscious importance most wonderful to behold.

"Your name is Catherine Mortimer?" said the clerk.

"Yes, young marse—yes, honey, dat my name—Catherine Mortimer. Which Catherine were the name giben me by my sponsibles in baptism; and Mortimer were de name 'ferred upon me in holy matrimony by my late demented 'panion; which he was de coachman to ole Comedy Burghe, as fought de Britishers in the war of eighteen hundred and twelve."

"What the de'il is the woman talking about?" here put in the magistrate.

"She is giving testimony in this case," sarcastically answered the counsel for the accused.

"My good woman, we don't want to hear any of your private history previous to the time of your first landing on these shores. We want to know what happened since. Your name, you say, is Catherine Mortimer—"

"Hi, young marse, what I tell you? Sure it is; Catherine Mortimer, 'spectable widder 'oman, 'cause Mortimer, poor man, died of 'sumption when he was 'bout forty-five years of age, which I hab libed ebber since in 'spectable widderhood, and wouldn't like to see de man as would hab de imperance to ax me to change my condition," said Katie, rolling herself from side to side in the restlessness of her intense self-consciousness.

"Catherine Mortimer, do you understand the nature of an oath?" inquired the clerk.

"Hi, young marse, what should 'vent me? Where you think I done been libbin all my days? You mus' think how I's a barbarium from the Stingy Isles!" replied Katie indignantly.

"I ask you—do you understand the nature of an oath, and I require you to give a straightforward answer," said the clerk.

"And I think it's berry 'sultin' in you to ax a' spectable colored 'oman any such question. Do I understan' de natur' ob an oaf? You might 's well ax me if I knows I's got a mortal soul to be save'! Yes, I does unnerstan' de natur' ob an oaf. I knows how, if anybody takes a false one, which it won't be Catherine Mortimer, they'll go right straight down to de debbil—and serbe 'em right!"

"Very well, then," said the clerk. And he put a small Bible into her hand and dictated the usual oath, which she repeated with an awful solemnity of manner that must have carried conviction of her perfect orthodoxy to the minds of the most skeptical cavilers.

"Your name, you say, is Catherine Mortimer?" said the clerk, as if requiring her to repeat this fact also under oath.

The repetition of the question nettled Katie.

"My good g'acious alibe," she said, "what I tell you? You think you gwine catch me in a lie by 'peating of questions ober and ober in dat a way? Now look here, young marse, I aint been tellin' of you no lies, and if I was a-lying, you couldn't catch me dat a way, 'cause I'se got too good a membery, dere! So, now I tell you ag'in my name is Catherine Mortimer, and like-wise it aint Gorilla, as my lordship and his shamwally used to call me. I done found out what dat means now! It means monkey! which is a 'fernally false! 'cause my fambily aint got no monkey blood in 'em. 'Dough I'd rather be a monkey dan a lordship, if I couldn't be no better lordship den some!" said Katie, with a vindictive nod of her head towards the viscount.

"What is the creature discoorsing anent?" inquired the perplexed magistrate.

"She is giving in her evidence," replied the counsel for the accused.

"You dry up! Who's you? Mus' be my lordship's new shamwally making yourself so smart. Reckon I'll give evidence enough to fix you and my lordship out!" snapped Katie.

"Now, then, tell us what you know of this case," said the clerk.

"What I know ob dis case? Why, in de fus' place, I know how my lordship dere—and a perty lordship he is—and de oder shamwally, which I don't see here present, and dat whited saltpeter, ought ebery single one ob dem to be hung up as high as Harem. Dere! dat what I know; and I hope you'll do it, ole marse!" said Katie vindictively.

"Whisht, whisht, my good woman! Ye are no here to pronounce judgment, but to gi'e testimony. Confine yoursel' to the facts!" said the magistrate.

But this order was more easily made than obeyed. It was very difficult for Katie to confine herself to the statement of facts, for the reason that she seemed to imagine herself prosecutor, witness, judge, jury, and executioner all rolled into one. It took all the tact of the clerk to get from her what could be received as purely legal evidence.

Katie's testimony would be nothing new to the reader. Her statement under oath to the magistrate was the same in effect that she had made to Judge Merlin. And although it was rather a rambling narrative, mixed up with a good deal of bitter invective against the accused, and gratuitous advice to the bench, and acute suggestions of the manner of retribution that ought to be measured out to the culprits, yet still the shrewd magistrate managed to get from it a tolerably clear idea of the nature of the conspiracy formed against the honor of Lady Vincent and the motive for the abduction of the negroes. And although the counsel for the accused labored hard to get this evidence set aside, it was accepted as good.

"James Mortimer," called the clerk.

And Jim walked forward and stood respectfully waiting to be examined.

The clerk, after putting the same questions to Jim that he had put to Jim's mother, and receiving the most satisfactory answers, administered the usual oath and proceeded with the examination.

Jim said he was the son of the last witness, and he corroborated the statements made by her, as far as his own personal experience corresponded with hers. And although he was severely cross-examined, he never varied from his first story, and his testimony was held good.

"Sarah Sims," was the next called.

And Sally advanced modestly and stood respectfully before the magistrate.

Having satisfactorily answered the preliminary questions that were put to her, she took the prescribed oath with a deep reverence of manner that prepossessed everyone, except the accused and their counsel, in her favor.

And then she gave her testimony in a clear, simple, concise manner, that met the approval of all who heard her. The counsel for the accused cross-examined her with ingenuity, but without success.

Sally's testimony was decidedly the most conclusive of any given by the three negroes. And she was allowed to sit down.

Then the counsel for the accused arose and made a speech, in which he ingeniously sought to do away with the effect of all the evidence that had been given in against the prisoners. He took exception to Ishmael's evidence because Mr. Worth had declined to give it under oath; to Judge Merlin's, because, he said, that ancient man was so well stricken with years as to be falling into his dotage; to old Katie's, because most decidedly he declared she was totally unreliable, being half monkey, half maniac, and whole knave; to Jim's, because he averred him to be wholly under the influence of others; to Sally's, for the same reason. It would be monstrous, he said, to send a nobleman and a lady to trial upon such evidence as had been given in by such witnesses as had appeared there. And he ended by demanding that his clients should be instantly and honorably discharged from custody, and particularly that they should not be remanded.

And he sat down.

"Dinna ye fash yersel', laddie! I hae na the least intention to remaund the accused. I s'all commit them for trial," said the magistrate. Then looking down upon his clerk, he said:

"Ross, mon, mak' out the warrants."

A perfect storm of remonstrance, strange to witness in a magistrate's office, arose. The lawyer sprang upon his feet and vehemently opposed the committal. Lord Vincent indignantly exclaimed against the outrage of sending a nobleman of the house of Hurstmonceux to trial. Faustina went into hysterics, and was attended by Mrs. MacDonald.

Meanwhile the clerk coolly made out the warrants and placed them in the hands of McRae for execution. That prompt policeman proceeded to take possession of his prisoners. But the storm increased; Faustina's screams awoke the welkin; Lord Vincent's loud denunciation accompanied her in bass keys; the lawyer's wild expostulations and gesticulations arose above all.

Sir Alexander had borne all this tempestuous opposition very patiently at first; but the patience of the most long-suffering man may give out. Sir Alexander's did.

"McRae, remove the prisoners. And, laddie," he said to the denunciatory lawyer, "gin ye dinna haud your tongue, I'll commit yoursel' for contempt!"

Lord Vincent, seeing that all opposition must be worse than vain, quietly yielded the point and followed his conductor. But Faustina's animal nature got the ascendency, and she resisted, fought and screamed like a wildcat. It took half a dozen policemen to put her into the carriage, and then the handcuffs had to be put on her.

As soon as quiet was restored another case was called on. It was that of Frisbie, the ex-valet, charged with the murder of Ailsie Dunbar.

CHAPTER XLV

THE FATE OF THE VISCOUNT.

Oh, vanity of youthful blood,

So by misuse to poison good.

Reason awakes and views unbarred

The sacred gates she wished to guard,

Sees approach the harpy law,

And Nemesis beholds with awe,

Ready to seize the poor remains

That vice has left of all his gains.

Cold penitence, lame after-thought,

With fear, despair, and horror fraught,

Call back the guilty pleasures dead,

Whom he has robbed and whom betrayed!

—Bishop Hoadley.

When the carriage containing the prisoners reached the jail, they were taken out to be conducted to the warden's office. The viscount, who was in a mood of suppressed fury, was attended by Policeman McRae and followed by old Cuthbert, broken-hearted by the dishonor of his master.

Faustina, who had raged herself into a state of exhaustion and consequently of quietude, was attended by policeman Christie and supported by Mrs. MacDonald who tenderly soothed and flattered her.

It was a busy day in the warden's office, and the warden had but little time to bestow on these interesting prisoners.

"And sae they ha'e committed ye for trial, me laird, mair's the pity; and the puir lassie too; me heart is sair for her," said Auld Saundie Gra'ame, as they were led up to his desk to have their names re-entered upon the prison-books.

"It was a most unwarrantable proceeding! a monstrous abuse of office! an outrage that should be punished by immediate impeachment!" burst forth the viscount, in a fury.

"As to that, me laird, I ha'e never yet seen the prisoner enter these wa's wi' ony verra great esteem for the authorities that sent him here," dryly replied Auld Saundie.

Then turning to an under-warden he said:

"Ye'll convey the prisoners back to the cells occupied by them before."

And Faustina was carried back to the woman's ward, followed by the sympathizing Mrs. MacDonald, who promised to remain with her until the hour of closing up.

And the viscount, attended by Cuthbert, was conducted to his corner cell, there to abide until the day of trial.

Old Cuthbert remained with his master until he was summoned to drive Mrs. MacDonald back to the castle.

Several days passed. Every morning Mrs. MacDonald, driven by Cuthbert in the family carriage, came to town, to spend the day in the cell with Faustina, while Cuthbert remained in attendance upon the viscount. And every evening she returned to the castle.

The Earl of Hurstmonceux did not come. But news at length came of him. His bankers wrote that he was out on his yacht, his exact latitude being unknown.

Lord Vincent, now that he was fully committed for trial, really did not seem to be anxious for his father's return. Perhaps he would rather not have met the earl under the present circumstances. He held daily consultations with his counsel. These were entirely confidential. Being assured by Mr. Bruce that it was essentially necessary the counsel should be in possession of all the facts, the prisoner made a tolerably clean breast of it, at least so far as the abduction of the negroes was concerned; he exercised some little reticence in the matters of his relations with Faustina and his conspiracy against Lady Vincent.

Mr. Brace of course put the fairest construction upon everything; but still he could not help feeling the darkest misgivings as to the result of the approaching trial. And the viscount, rendered keenly observant by intense anxiety, detected these doubts in the mind of his counsel, and became daily more despairing.

He looked forward to the dishonor of a public trial with burning indignation; to the possible, nay probable, conviction and sentence that might follow with shrinking dread, and to the execution of that sentence with stony horror.

Penal servitude! Great Heaven! penal servitude for him, so high- born, so fastidious, so luxurious in all his habits! Penal servitude for him, the Viscount Vincent!

He had often made one of a party of sight-seers, visiting the prisons, the hulks, the quarries, where the prisoners were confined at work. He had seen them in the coarse prison garb, working in chains, under the broiling sun of summer, and under the bitter cold of winter. He had seen them at their loathsome meals and in their stifling sleeping pens. He had gazed upon them with eyes of haughty, cold, unsympathizing curiosity. To him and his friends they formed but a spectacle of interest or amusement, like a drama.

And now to think that he might, nay, probably would, soon make one of their shameful number! The Viscount Vincent working in chains; gazed at by his former companions; pointed out to curious strangers! That was the appalling picture forever present to his imagination.

How bitterly he deplored the crimes that had exposed him to this fate. How deeply he cursed the siren whose fatal beauty had lured him to sin. How passionately he longed for death, as the only deliverance from the memory of the past, the terrors of the present, the horrors of the future. Day and night that appalling future stared him in the face. Day and night the picture of himself working in chains, pointed out, stared at, was before his mind's eyes.

By day it obtruded between him and the face of any visitor that might be with him. Even when in consultation with his counsel his mind would wander from the subject in hand, and his imagination would be drawn away to the contemplation of that dread picture.

By night it would rise up in the darkness and nearly drive him mad.

He could not eat, he could not sleep. He passed his days in pacing to and fro in his narrow cell, and his nights in tossing about upon his restless bed. His sufferings were pitiable, and his worst enemy must have felt sorry for him.

His condition moved the compassion of the warden, and every indulgence that was in the power of old Saundie to bestow was granted to him. And as he was not yet absolutely convicted, but only waiting his trial, these indulgences were considerable. Old Cuthbert was allowed to visit him freely during the day, and to bring him anything in the way of food, drink, clothing, books, stationery, etc., that he required. And very little supervision was exercised over these matters.

Meantime as the Assizes were sitting, and the docket was not very full, it was thought that the trial would soon come on.

On the Wednesday following the committal of the viscount the trial of the murderer, Frisbie, which stood before that of his master on the docket, did come on. The detective police had been busy during the interval between Frisbie's arrest and arraignment, and they had succeeded in collecting a mass of evidence and a number of witnesses besides old Katie.

Frisbie, however, was defended by the best counsel that mere money could procure. There are many among the best lawyers who will not take up a bad case at any price. But Frisbie, as I said, had the best among the unscrupulous that money could buy. His master of course paid the fees. His counsel very gratuitously instructed him to plead "Not Guilty," and of course he did plead "Not Guilty." And his counsel did the best thing they could to establish his innocence. But the evidence against him was conclusive. And on the morning of the second day of his trial Frisbie was found guilty and sentenced to death. But a short period between sentence and execution was then allowed in Scotland. The execution of Frisbie was fixed for the Monday following his conviction.

From the hour that Frisbie had been brought to trial the viscount had experienced the most vehement accession of anxiety. He refused all food during the day, and he paced the floor of his cell all night. And well he might; for he knew that on that trial revelations would be made under oath that would not tend to whiten Lord Vincent's character.

On Thursday noon Mr. Bruce entered his cell.

"Is the trial—" began the viscount; but he could not get on; his intense emotion choked him.

"The trial is over; the jury brought in their verdict half an hour ago," replied the counsel gravely.

"And Frisbie is—For Heaven's sake speak!" gasped the viscount.

"Frisbie is convicted!" said the lawyer.

Lord Vincent, pale before, turned paler still as he sank into the chair and gazed upon the lawyer, who was greatly wondering at the excessive emotion of his client.

"When is the execution fixed to take place?"

"On Monday, of course."

"Is there—can there be any hope of a pardon for him?"

"Not the shadow of a hope."

"Or—of a commutation of his sentence?"

"It is madness to think of it."

"Is there no chance of a respite?"

"I tell you it is madness, and worse than madness, to imagine such a thing as a pardon, a commutation, or even a respite for that wretch. The crime brought home to him was one of the darkest dye—the base assassination of the girl that loved and trusted and was true to him. To fancy any mercy possible for that miscreant, except it be the infinite, all-embracing, all-pardoning mercy of God, is simply frenzy."

"And the execution is to take place on Monday. The time is very short," said the viscount, falling into a reverie.

The lawyer began to speak of the viscount's own affairs; he mentioned several circumstances connected with the viscount's case that had become known to himself only through the testimony of certain witnesses on Frisbie's trial, and he wished to consult the viscount upon them.

But Lord Vincent seemed to act very strangely; he was absent-minded, stupid, distracted—in fact altogether unfit for consultation with his counsel.

And so, after a few unsuccessful attempts to rouse him, gain his attention, and fix it upon the subject at issue, the lawyer arose, said that he would call again the next morning, and bowed and left the cell.

The shame the viscount suffered was in the knowledge of the dishonorable facts relating to himself that had been brought to light on Frisbie's trial; the great dread he felt was that Frisbie, at the near approach of death, would open his heart and make a full confession; and his horrible certainty was that such a confession was all that was wanted to ensure his own conviction.

Again on this Thursday night he could not sleep, but paced the narrow limits of his cell the whole night through, in unutterable agony of mind. Never was the appalling vision of himself in the shameful prison garb, working in chains, pointed out as an interesting object and gazed at by curious strangers, so awfully vivid as upon this night.

The next morning, when his old servant Cuthbert entered the cell as usual, he was frightened at his master's dreadful looks.

"Will I call a doctor to your lairdship?" inquired the old man.

"No, Cuthbert; I am not ill. I am only suffering for want of rest. I have not been able to sleep since Frisbie's arraignment. He is convicted, you know."

"Aye, me laird, I ken a' anent it. My brither Randy was on the jury, and he tauld me it a' ower a pot o' ale in the taproom o' the 'Highlander,' where I was resting while my horses fed," said the old man gravely.

A dark, crimson flush overspread the face of the viscount. Cuthbert had heard all about it. Cuthbert had heard, then, those disgraceful revelations concerning himself. He need not have blushed before Cuthbert. That loyal-hearted old servant could not have been brought to believe such evil of his beloved young master, as all that came to. And his next words proved this.

"There must 'a' been a deal o' fause swearing, me laird," he said.

The viscount looked up and caught at the words.

"Yes, Cuthbert, a great deal of false swearing, indeed, as far as I am concerned, in that testimony."

"Aye, me laird! I tauld them so in the taproom. There was a wheen idle loons collected there, drinking and smoking and talking anent the business o' their betters. And they were a' unco' free in their comments. But when they mentioned your lairdship's name in connection wi' sic infamy, I tauld them a' weel that they were a pack o' fause knaves to believe sic lees."

"Yes. The execution is to take place on Monday morning, Cuthbert."

"Aye, me laird. I hope the puir, sinfu' lad will mak' guid use o' the short time left him and repent o' a' his misdeeds, and seek his peace wi' his Maker," said the old man solemnly.

The viscount heaved a heavy sigh; a sigh that seemed laden with a weight of agony.

"Cuthbert," he said, "you know that I may not go to see the condemned man, being a prisoner myself; but you, being a fellow- servant, and at liberty, may be permitted to do so. I wish to charge you with a note to deliver to him; but you must deliver it secretly, Cuthbert; secretly, mind you."

"Yes, me laird."

The viscount sat down to his little table and wrote the following note:

"Frisbie: While there is life there is hope; therefore make no confession; for if you do, that confession will destroy your last possibility of pardon or commutation. "Vincent."

He folded and sealed this note and delivered it to Cuthbert, saying:

"Conceal it somewhere about your person, and go to the warden's office and ask leave to see your old fellow-servant, and no doubt you will get it. And when you see him deliver this note secretly, as I told you."

"Verra weel, me laird," said the old man, going and knocking on the door of the cell to be let out. The turnkey opened the door, released him, and locked it again. And the viscount, left alone, paced up and down the floor in unutterable distress of mind. An hour passed and then Cuthbert re-entered the cell, wearing a frightened visage.

"Well, Cuthbert, well! did you find an opportunity of delivering the note?"

"Yes, me laird, I did," said the old man hesitatingly.

"Secretly?"

"Y-yes, me laird!"

The viscount looked relieved of a great fear. He saw the great disturbance of his servant's face, but ascribed it to the effect of his interview with the condemned man, and sympathy for his awful position, and he inquired:

"How did Frisbie look, Cuthbert?"

"Like a ghaist; na less! pale as deeth; trembling like a leaf about to fa'! and waefully distraught in his mind!"

"Did he get an opportunity of reading my note while you were with him?"

"Oh, me laird, I maun just tell you! I hope there was na ony great secret in that same note."

The viscount started and stared wildly at the speaker, but then everything alarmed Lord Vincent now.

"What do you mean?" he asked:

"Oh, me laird! I watched my opportunity, and I gi'e him the note in secrecy, as your lairdship tauld me; and I stooped and whispered till him in his lugs to keep the note till he was his lane, and read it then. But the doitted fule, gude forgi'e me, didna seem to compreheend; but was loike ane dazed. He just lookit at me and then proceeded to open the note before my face. Whereupon the turnkey lad takit it out fra his hand, saying that the prisoner, being a condemned man, maunna receive ony faulded paper that hadna passit under the observation of the governor, because sic faulded packets might contain strychnine or other subtle poison. And sae he took possession o' your note, me laird, before the prisoner could read a word of it; and said he maun carry it to the governor whilk I suppose he did."

To see the consternation of the viscount was dreadful.

"Oh, Cuthbert, Cuthbert, the cowardice of that miserable wretch will ruin me!" he exclaimed bitterly.

"Oh, me laird, dinna rail at the puir sinfu' soul for cowardice. Sure mesel' would be a coward gin I had the waefu' woodie before my ees. 'Deed, me laird, and me heart is sair for the mischance o' the note."

"It cannot be mended now, Cuthbert."

The time was drawing near for the closing of the prison doors, and the old man took a dutiful leave of his master and departed.

On his way downstairs he was called into the warden's office, and while there he was severely reprimanded for conveying letters to the convict, and forbidden under pain of punishment to repeat the offense. The old man bore the rebuke very patiently, and at the lecture that was bestowed upon him he humbly bowed and took his leave.

This night the viscount, exhausted by long vigilance and fasting and by intense anxiety, threw himself upon his bed and slept for a few hours. The next morning, Saturday, in his restless trouble he arose early. And in the course of the day he questioned everyone who came into his cell concerning the state of mind of the condemned man.

Some could give him no news at all; others could tell him something; but they differed in their accounts of Frisbie—one saying that he had asked for the prison chaplain, who had gone in to him; a second that he was very contrite; a third that he was only terribly frightened; a fourth that he was as firm as a rock, declined to confess his guilt and persisted in declaring his innocence. The viscount endeavored to believe the last statement.

The miserable day passed without bringing anything more satisfactory to Lord Vincent. And the night that followed was a sleepless one to him.

Sunday came; the last day of life that was left to the wretched valet. On Sunday it was obligatory upon all the prisoners confined in that jail to attend divine service in the prison chapel. They had no choice in this matter; unless they were confined to their beds by illness they were obliged to go.

On this particular Sunday no prisoner felt disposed to place himself on the sick list. Quite the contrary. For, on the other hand, many prisoners who were really ill, in the infirmary, declared themselves well enough to get up and go to chapel.

The reason of their sudden zeal in the performance of their religious duties was simply this: The "condemned sermon," as it was called, was to be preached that day. And the condemned man, who was to be executed in the morning, was to be present under guard. And people generally have a morbid curiosity to gaze upon a man who is doomed to death.

Lord Vincent was ill enough to be exempt from the duty of appearing in the chapel, and haughty enough to recoil from mixing publicly with his fellow-prisoners; but he was intensely anxious to see Frisbie and judge for himself, from the man's appearance, whether he seemed likely to make a confession.

And so, when the turnkey whose duty it was to attend to this ward came around to unlock the doors and marshal the prisoners in order to march them to the chapel, Lord Vincent, without demur, fell into rank and went with them.

The chapel was small, and the prisoners present on this day filled it full. The set to which Lord Vincent belonged were marched in among the last. Consequently they sat at the lower end of the chapel.

Lord Vincent's height enabled him to look over the heads of most persons present. And he looked around for Frisbie. At length he found him.

The condemned pew was immediately before the pulpit, facing the preacher. In it sat Frisbie, unfettered, but guarded by two turnkeys, one of whom sat on each side of him. But Frisbie's back was towards Lord Vincent, and so the viscount could not possibly get a glimpse of the expression of his face.

He next looked to see if he could find the selfish vixen who had lured him to his ruin, and whom he now hated with all the power of hatred latent in his soul. But a partition eight feet high, running nearly the whole length of the chapel and stopping only within a few feet of the pulpit, separated the women's from the men's side of the church, so that even if she had been present he could not have seen her.

"The wages of sin is death."

Such was the text from which the sermon was preached to the prisoners that day. But the viscount heard scarcely one word of it. Intensely absorbed in his own reflections, he paid no attention to the services. At their close he bent his eyes again upon the form of Frisbie.

His perseverance was rewarded. As they arose to leave the chapel Frisbie also arose and turned around. And the viscount got a full view of his face—a pale, wild, despairing face.

"He is desperately frightened, if he is not penitent. That is the face of a man who, in the forlorn hope of saving his life, will deny his guilt until the rope is around his neck, and then, in the forlorn hope of saving his soul, confess his crime under the gallows," said the viscount to himself, as he was marched back to his cell.

In that the viscount wronged Frisbie. The great adversary himself is said to be not so black as he is painted.

That same night, that last solemn night of the criminal's life, the prison chaplain stayed with the wretched man. Mr. Godfree was a fervent Christian; one whose faith could move mountains; one who would never abandon a soul, however sinful, to sink into perdition while that soul remained in its mortal tenement. Such men seem to have a Christ-conferred power to save to the uttermost.

He kept close to Frisbie; he would not permit himself to be discouraged by the sinfulness, the cowardice, and the utter baseness of the poor wretch. He pitied him, talked to him, prayed with him.

With all his deep criminality Frisbie was certainly not hardened. He listened to the exhortations of the chaplain, he wept bitterly, and joined in the prayers. And in the silence of that night he made a full confession to the chaplain, with the request that it might be made public the next day.

He confessed the murder of Ailsie Dunbar; but he denied that the crime had been premeditated, as it had been made to appear at the trial. He killed her in a fit of passion, he said; and he had never known an hour's peace since. Remorse for the crime and terror for its consequences had made his life wretched. His master, Lord Vincent, he said, had been an eye-witness to the murder; but had withheld himself from denouncing him, because he wanted to use the power he had thus obtained to compel him to enter a conspiracy against Lady Vincent. And here followed a full account of the plot and its execution.

Frisbie went on to say that nothing but the terrors of death induced him to become a party to that base conspiracy against the honor of a noble lady, and that he had suffered almost as much remorse for his crimes against Lady Vincent as for his murder of Ailsie Dunbar.

All this Mr. Godfree took down in short-hand from the lips of the conscience-stricken man.

And then, as Frisbie expressed the desire to spend the remainder of the night in devotion, Mr. Godfree decided to remain with him. He read aloud to the convict portions of Scripture suited to his sad case; he prayed fervently with him for the pardon of his sins; and then he sang for him a consoling hymn.

Oh, strangely sounded that sacred song arising in the deep silence of the condemned cell. So the night passed there.

But how did it pass in the viscount's cell? Sleeplessly, anxiously, wretchedly, until long after midnight, when he fell asleep. He was awakened by a sound of sawing, dragging, and hammering, that seemed to be in the prison yard beneath his windows. It continued a long time, and effectually banished slumber from his weary eyes.

What could they be doing at that unusual hour? he asked himself. And he crept from his bed and peeped through the grated window. But the night was over-clouded and deeply dark from that darkness that precedes the dawn. He could see nothing, but he could hear the sound of voices amid the noise of work; although the words, at the distance his window was from the ground, were inaudible.

He lay down again no wiser than he had risen up. After an hour or two the noise ceased, and he dropped into that sleep of prostration that more resembles worn-out nature's swooning than healthy slumber.

CHAPTER XLVII

THE EXECUTION.

What shall he be, ere night?—Perchance a thing

O'er which the raven flaps her funeral wing.

—Byron.

It was broad daylight when the viscount was again awakened, and this time by the solemn tolling of the prison bell. He sprang out of bed and looked out of the window and recoiled in horror. There in the angle of the prison yard stood the gallows, grimly painted black. That was what the carpenters had been at work on all night.

And the tolling of the prison bell warned him that the last hour of the condemned man had come; that he was even now leaving his cell for the gallows. Lord Vincent staggered back and fell upon his bed. In the fate of Frisbie he seemed to feel a forewarning of the certain retribution that was lying in wait for himself.

There came a sound of footsteps along the passage. They paused before his cell. Someone unlocked the door. And, to the viscount's astonishment, the procession that was on its way to the gallows entered his presence. There was Frisbie, still unbound, but guarded by a half a dozen policemen and turnkeys, and attended by the undersheriff of the county, and the warden and the chaplain of the prison.

Lord Vincent stared in astonishment, wondering what brought them there; but he found no words in which to put the question.

The chaplain constituted himself the spokesman of the party.

"My lord, this unhappy man wishes to see you before he dies; and the sheriff has kindly accorded him the privilege," said Mr. Godfree.

Lord Vincent looked from the chaplain to the prisoner in perplexity and terror. What could the condemned man, in the last hour of his life, want with him?

Frisbie spoke:

"My lord, I am a dying man; but I could not meet death with guilty secrets on my soul. My lord, I have told everything, the whole truth about the death of poor Ailsie, and the plot against my lady. I could not help it, my lord. I could not leave the world with such wrong unrighted behind me. I could not so face my Creator. I have come to tell you this, my lord, and ask you to forgive me if, in doing this, I have been compelled to do you harm," said the man, speaking humbly, deprecatingly, almost affectionately.

"God forgive you, Frisbie, but you have ruined me!" was the somewhat strange reply of the viscount, as he turned away; for it seemed to those who heard him that he was asking the Lord to forgive the sinner, not for his sins, but for his confession of them.

The procession of death left the cell; the door was locked, and the viscount was alone again—alone, and in utter, irremediable despair.

He sat upon the side of the bed, his hands clasped and his chin dropped upon his breast until the bell of the prison chapel suddenly ceased to toll. Then he looked up. It was all over. The judicial tragedy had been enacted. And he arose and went to the grated window and looked out.

No, oh, Heaven, it was not all over! That group around the foot of the gallows; that cart and empty coffin; that shrouded and bound figure, convulsed and swaying in the air—blasted his sight. With a loud cry he dashed his hand up to his eyes to shut out the horrible vision, and fell heavily upon the floor. He lay there as one dead until the turnkey brought his breakfast. Then he got up and threw himself upon the bed. He eagerly drank the coffee that was brought to him, for his throat was parched and burning; but he could not swallow a mouthful of solid food.

"Bring me the afternoon paper as soon as it is out," he said to the turnkey, at the same time handing him a half-crown. The man bowed in silence and took his breakfast tray from the table and withdrew.

For some reason or other, perhaps from the fear of coming in contact with the preparations for the execution, Mrs. MacDonald did not present herself at the prison until nearly noon, so that the prison clock was actually on the stroke of twelve when old Cuthbert was admitted to his master's cell. On entering and beholding his master, the old man started and exclaimed in affright:

"Gude guide us, me laird, what has come over ye?"

"Nothing, Cuthbert, but want of rest. What is that you have in your hand?"

"The evening paper, me laird, that ane o' the lads gi'e me to bring your lairdship."

"Have you looked at it?" demanded the viscount anxiously, for he could not bear the idea of his old servant's reading the confession of Frisbie, that was probably in that very paper. "Have you looked at it, I ask you?" he repeated fiercely.

"Nay, no, me laird. I hanna e'en unfaulded it," said the old man simply, handing the paper.

The viscount seized it, threw himself on the chair, and opened it; but instead of reading the paper he looked up at old Cuthbert, who was standing there watching his master, with the deepest concern expressed in his venerable countenance.

"There, get about something; do anything! only don't stand there and stare at me, as if you had gone daft!" angrily exclaimed Lord Vincent.

The old man turned meekly, and began to put things straight in the cell. The viscount searched and found what he had feared to see. Ah! well might he dread the eye of old Cuthbert on him while he read those columns.

Yes, there it was; the account of the last hours of Alick Frisbie by the pen of the chaplain! the night in the cell, the scene of the execution, and, last of all, the confession of the culprit with all its shameful revelations. The viscount, with a feverish desire to see how deeply he himself was implicated, and to know the worst at once, read it all. How far he was implicated indeed! He was steeped to the very lips in infamy.

Why, the crime for which Frisbie had suffered death, the murder of that poor girl, committed in a paroxysm of passion, and repented in bitterness, and confessed in humility, seemed only a light offense beside the deep turpitude, the black treachery, of that long premeditated, carefully arranged plot against Lady Vincent, in which the viscount was the principal and the valet only the accomplice. The plot was revealed in all its base, loathsome, revolting details. The reader knows what these details were, for he has both seen them and heard of them. But can he imagine what it was to the viscount to have them discovered, published, and circulated?

When Lord Vincent had read this confession through he knew that all was forever over with him; he knew that at that very hour hundreds of people were reading that confession, shuddering at his guilt, scorning his baseness, and anticipating his conviction; he knew as well as if he had just heard the sentence of the court what that sentence would be. Penal servitude for life!

Deep groans burst from his bosom.

"Me laird, me laird, you are surely ill," said the old man anxiously, coming forward.

"Yes, Cuthbert, I am ill; in pain."

"Will I call a doctor?"

"No, Cuthbert; a doctor is not necessary; but attend to me a moment. They let you bring me anything you like unquestioned, do they not?"

"Aye, surely, me laird; for you are no under condemnation yet; but only waiting for your honorable acquittal."

"Cuthbert, I think you have a brother who is a chemist in town, have you not?"

"Ou, aye, me laird. Joost Randy, honest man."

The viscount sat down and wrote a line on a scrap of paper and gave it to the old man.

"Now, Cuthbert, take this to your brother. Be sure that you let no one see that bit of paper, and when you get the medicine that I have written for, put it in your bosom and don't take it out until you come back to me and we are alone. Now, Cuthbert, I hope you will be more canny over this affair than you were over the affair of the note I sent to Frisbie, which you permitted to fall into the hands of Philistines."

"Ah, puir Frisbie, puir lad! Gude hae mercy on him! I'll be carfu', me laird; though it was no me, but puir Frisbie himsel', that let the bit note drap. But I'll be carefu', me laird, though 'deed I dinna see the use o' concealment, sin' naebody ever interferes wi' onything I am bringing your lairdship."

"But they might interfere with this because it is medicine; for they might think that no one but the prison doctor has a right to give medicine here."

"Ou, aye—I comprehend, me laird, that sic might be the case where the medicament is dangerous. But will this be dangerous?"

"Why, no; it is nothing but simple laudanum. You know how good laudanum is to allay pain; and that there is no danger at all in it."

"No, me laird, gin ane doesna tak' an ower muckle dose."

"Certainly, if one does not take an overdose; but I have knowledge enough not to do that, Cuthbert."

"Surely, me laird. I'll gae noo and get it," replied the old man, taking up his hat, and knocking at the door to be released. The turnkey opened promptly, and Cuthbert departed on his errand.

When the viscount was left alone he resumed his restless pacing up and down the narrow limits of his cell and continued it for a while. Then he sat down to his little table, drew a sheet of paper before him, and began to write a letter.

He was interrupted by the unlocking of his cell door. Hastily he turned the paper with the blank side up and looked around. It was Mr. Bruce, his counsel. The lawyer looked unusually grave.

"Well," he said, as soon as he was left alone with his client, "the poor devil Frisbie is gone."

"Yes," responded the viscount, in a low voice.

"That is an ugly business of the confession."

"Very; the man was mad," said the viscount.

"Not unlikely; but I wish we may be able to persuade the jury that he was so; or else to induce the judges to rule his evidence out altogether."

"Can that be done? I mean can the judges be induced to rule out the confession as evidence?" inquired the viscount, sudden hope lighting up his hitherto dejected countenance.

"I fear not; I fear that our chance is to persuade the jury that the man was insane or mendacious—in a word, to impeach his rationality or his truthfulness, one or the other; we must decide which stand we are to take, which call in question."

"You might doubt either his sanity or his truth with equally good cause. He was always a fool and always a liar. When is the trial to come on?"

"That is just what I came to speak to you about. It is called for to-morrow at ten."

"To-morrow at ten?"

"Yes."

"Are you quite ready with the defense?"

"I was until this nasty business of Frisbie's confession turned up. I shall have to take a copy of the paper containing it home with me to-night, and study it, to see how I can pull it to pieces, and destroy its effects upon the jury. Have you got it here?" said Mr. Bruce, taking up the afternoon paper that lay upon the table.

"Yes."

"Have you done with it?"

"Yes."

The lawyer folded up the paper and put it in his pocket, and took his hat to depart.

"Mr. Bruce," said the viscount earnestly, "I am about to ask you a question, which I must entreat you to answer truthfully: What are the chances of my acquittal?"

The lawyer hesitated and changed color. The eyes of the viscount were fixed earnestly upon him. The eyes of the counsel fell.

"I see; you need not reply to my question. You think my chance a bad one," said Lord Vincent despondently.

"No, my lord; I did not mean to give you any such impression," said Mr. Bruce, recovering himself and his professional manners. "Before this troublesome confession of Frisbie's your chance was an excellent one—"

"But since?"

"Well, as I say, that is an ugly feature in the case; but I will do my best. And to say nothing of my own poor abilities, my colleagues, Stair and Drummond, are among the most successful barristers in the kingdom. They are always safe to gain a verdict where there is a verdict possible to be gained."

"Yes; I know that I have the best talent in the Three Kingdoms engaged in my defense," said the viscount; but he said it with a profound sigh.

"I will look in upon you again early to-morrow morning, before we go into court," said Mr. Bruce, as he bowed himself out.

This interview with his counsel had only tended to confirm the fears of the viscount and deepen his despondency, for, notwithstanding the guarded words of the lawyer, Lord Vincent saw that he had well-nigh given up all for lost. With a deep groan he sat down to the table and resumed the writing of his letter. He had not written many minutes when he was startled by the opening of the door. He hastily concealed his writing under a piece of blotting paper, and nervously turned to see who was the new intruder.

It was old Cuthbert, come back from his errand.

As soon as the door was closed upon them, the old man approached his master.

"Have you got the medicine, Cuthbert?"

"Aye, me laird," replied the servant, taking a bottle, rolled in a white paper, from his pocket, and handing it to his master. Some instinct made the viscount conceal the bottle in his own bosom.

"And here, me laird, are two letters the turnkey gave me to hand to your lairdship. He tauld me they had just been left at the warden's office for you," said Cuthbert, laying two formidable-looking epistles before his master.

Lord Vincent recognized in the superscription of the respective letters the handwriting of his counsel, Mr. Drummond and Mr. Stair. He hastily opened them one after the other. Several banknotes for a large amount rolled out of each. Surprised, he rapidly cast his eyes over each in turn. And his face turned to a deadly whiteness. The two letters were in effect the same. It seemed as though the writers, though not in partnership, had acted in concert on this occasion. They each respectfully begged leave to return their retaining fees and retire from the defense of the viscount. Since reading the confession of the convict, Alick Frisbie, they could not conscientiously act as counsel for Lord Vincent. Such was the purport, if not the exact words of the two letters.

"Me laird, me laird, ye are ill again!" said old Cuthbert, anxiously approaching his master.

"Yes; the pain has returned."

"Will ye no tak' some o' the medicine noo?"

"No, Cuthbert; not until I retire for the night," answered the viscount; but he withdrew the bottle from his bosom, and took it to the wash-basin and washed off the label and then threw it—the label—into the fire.

Cuthbert watched him, and wondered at this proceeding, but was too respectful to express surprise or make inquiries. And at this moment the turnkey entered with Lord Vincent's supper, that had been brought from the "Highlander"; and while he arranged it on the table he warned Cuthbert that the prison doors were about to be closed for the night, and that Mrs. MacDonald was waiting for him to drive her back to the castle. Upon hearing this the old man took a respectful leave of his master and departed. The turnkey remained in attendance upon the prisoner, kindly pressing him to eat.

But Lord Vincent swallowed only a little tea, and then pushed the food from him. The turnkey took away the service, locked the prisoner in for the night, and went to the warden's office.

"Weel, Donald, what is it, mon?" inquired the warden.

"An ye please, sir, I'm no easy in my mind about me Laird; Vincent," said the turnkey.

"Why, what ails me laird?"

"Why, sir, he is joost like ane distraught!"

"On, aye, it will be the confession o' the malefactor, Frisbie, that has fasht him; as weel it may!"

"He's war nor fasht; he looks joost likely to do himsel' a mischief," said Christie, shaking his head.

"Heeh! an that be sae we maun be carefu'! Are there any sharp-edged or pointed instruments in his cell?"

"Naught but his penknife. I was minded to bring it away, but I did na."

"Eh, then we will pay him a visit in his cell," said the warden, rising.

The turnkey led the way upstairs, and they entered the prisoner's cell. The viscount, who was sitting at the table with his head leaning upon his hand, looked up at this unusual visit. His face was deadly pale; but beyond that the warden noticed nothing amiss in his appearance, and that paleness was certainly natural in a prisoner suffering from confinement and anxiety. There is usually but scant ceremony observed between jailer and prisoner; nevertheless, in this case Auld Saundie Gra'ame actually apologized for his unseasonable visit.

"Me laird," he said, "I hae a verra unpleasant duty to perform here. Donald reports that ye are no that weel in your mind. And sic being the case, I maun, in regard to your ain guid and safety, see till the removal of a' edged tools and sic like dangerous weapons."

"Take away what you please; I have no objection," said the viscount indifferently.

Whereupon the warden and turnkey made a thorough search of the room; took away his razors and scissors from his dressing-case, and his penknife and his eraser from his writing desk.

"I shall take guid care of a' these articles, me laird, and return them to you safe, ance you are out o' these wa's," said the warden.

The viscount made no reply.

"And ye maun ken that I only remove them to prevent ye doin' yoursel' a mischief in your despondency," he continued.

The viscount smiled with a strange, derisive, triumphant expression; but still did not reply in words.

"And gin ye will heed guid counsel, ye will na gi'e yoursel' up to despair. Despair is an unco ill counselor, and the de'il is aye ready to tak' advantage of its presence. Guid nicht, me laird, and guid rest till ye," said Auld Saundie, as he withdrew himself and his subordinate from the cell, and locked his prisoner in finally for the night.

When he got back to his office he summoned all of his officers around him and spoke to them.

"Lads, I ha'e sair misgivings anent yon Laird Vincent. Ye maun be verra carefu'! Ye mauna let his mon Cuthbert tak' onything in, until it ha'e passed muster under me ain twa een. And you, Donald, maun aye gang in wi' Cuthbert or ony ither, gentle or simple, wha gaes to see me laird, and bide in the cell wi' them to watch that the visitor gi'es naething unlawfu' or daungerous to the prisoner. An ounce o' prevention, ye ken, lads, is better than a pund o' cure!"

And having given this order, the warden dismissed his subordinates to their various evening duties.

Yes, an ounce of prevention is better than a pound of cure! But it is a pity the honest warden had not known when to apply the preventive agent.

Meanwhile, how had Faustina borne her imprisonment?

Why, excellently. Not that she had any patience, or courage, or fortitude, for she had not the least bit of either, or any other sort of heroism. But, as I said before, she was such a mere animal that, so long as she was made comfortable in the present, she felt no trouble on the score of the past or the future.

After her first fit of howling, weeping, and raging had exhausted itself, and she had seen that her violence had no other effect than to injure her cause, she resigned herself to circumstances and made herself as comfortable as possible in her cell. The expenditure of a few pounds had procured her everything she wanted, except her liberty; and that she did not feel the want of, as a creature with more soul might have done.

Any chance visitor who might have gone into Faustina's cell would have been astonished to see it fitted up as a tiny boudoir, and would have required to be told that there was no law to prevent a prisoner, unconvicted and waiting trial, from fitting up her cell as luxuriously as she pleased to do, if she had money to pay the expense and friends to take the trouble. And Faustina had freely spent money and freely used Mrs. MacDonald.

The floor of her cell was covered with crimson carpet, the festooned window with a lace curtain, and ornamented with a bouquet of flowers. A soft bed, with fine linen and warm coverlids, stood in one corner; a toilet table and mirror draped with lace, in another; a small marble washstand, with its china service, in a third; and a French porcelain stove in the fourth. A crimson-covered easy-chair and tiny stand filled up the middle of the small apartment.

And here, always well dressed, Faustina sat and read novels, or worked crochet, and gossiped with Mrs. MacDonald all day long. And here her epicurean meals, shared by her friend and visitor, were brought.

And here Mrs. MacDonald petted and soothed and flattered her with the hopes of a speedy deliverance.

CHAPTER XLVIII

NEWS FOR CLAUDIA.

Oh, in their deaths, remember they are men,

Strain not revenge to wish their tortures grievous.

—Addison.

Death—even the most serene and beautiful death, coming to a good old man at the close of a long, beneficent life—is awful. Sudden and violent death, falling upon a strong young man in the midst of his sins and follies, is horrible. But perhaps the most appalling aspect under which the last messenger can appear is that of a deliberately inflicted judicial death.

Such a doom, pronounced upon the greatest sinner that ever lived, must move the pity of his bitterest enemy.

The family at Cameron Court formed a Christian household. They received the news of Frisbie's conviction with solemn, compassionate approbation. Justice approved the sentence; but mercy pitied the victim. And they passed the day of his execution in a Sabbath stillness.

They were glad when the day was over; glad when the late evening mail brought the afternoon papers from Banff, announcing that the tragedy was finished; glad to read there that the sinner had repented, confessed, and died, hoping in the mercy of the Father, through the atonement of sin.

Each one breathed a sigh of infinite relief to find that this sinner had not endangered his soul by impenitently rushing from man's temporal to God's eternal condemnation.

No one failed to see the immense importance of Frisbie's dying confession as evidence for the prosecution in the approaching trial of the Viscount Vincent and Faustina Dugald; or the fatal effect it must have upon the accused; yet no one spoke of it then and there. The day of stern retributive justice was not the time for unseemly triumph.

They separated for the night, gravely and almost sadly.

Claudia went up to her room, where her women, Katie and Sally, reinstated in her service, were in attendance. Sally, as usual, was silent and humble; Katie, equally as usual, talkative and dictatorial.

"And so de shamwally is hung at last! serbe him right; and I hopes it did him good; an' I wish it was my lordship an' de whited salt-peter along ob him!" she said, folding her arms ever her fat bosom and rolling herself from side to side with infinite satisfaction.

"For shame, Katie, to triumph so over a dead man! I should have thought a good Christian woman like you would have prayed for him before he died," said Claudia gravely.

"'Deed didn't I! An' I aint gwine to do it nuther. I aint gwine to bother my Hebbenly Master 'bout no sich grand vilyan! dere now!"

"Oh, Katie, Katie, I am afraid you are a great heathen!"

"Well, den, I just ruther be a heathen dan a whited salt-peter, or a shamwally, or a lordship either, if I couldn't do no more credit to it dan some," said Katie, having, as usual, the last word.

Claudia longed to be alone on this night; so she soon dismissed her attendants, closed up her room, put out all her lights, and lay down in darkness, solitude, and meditation.

Strange! but on this night her thoughts, and even her sympathies, were with Lord Vincent in his prison cell. Why should she think of him? Why should she pity him? She had never loved him, never even fancied that she loved him, even in the delusive days of courtship; or in the early days of marriage; and she had despised and shunned him in the miserable days of their estranged life at Castle Cragg. Why, then, as she lay there in the darkness, silence, and solitude of her own chamber, should her imagination hover over him? Why did she contemplate him in sorrow and in compassion?

Because in that dreary cell she saw the twofold man—the man that he ought to have been, and the man that he was; because she was his wife, and though she had never loved him, yet with better treatment she might have been won to do so; and finally, because she was a woman, and therefore full of sympathy with every sort of suffering.

She knew that the dying confession of Frisbie would seal Lord Vincent's fate. And she contemplated that fate as she had never done before.

Penal servitude.

Why it had seemed a mere, empty phrase until now. Now it was an appalling reality brimful of horror, even for the coarsest, dullest, and hardest criminal; but of how much more for him.

Lord Vincent in the prison garb, working in chains; inquired after by curious sight-seers; and pointed out to strangers as the felon- viscount.

She meditated on the effect all this would have on him, in the unspeakable misery it would inflict upon his vain, insolent, self-indulgent organization; and she marveled how he would ever endure it.

And she thought of the dishonor this would reflect upon herself as his wife. And she shrunk shudderingly away from the burning shame of living on, the wife of a felon.

In the deep compassion she could not but feel for him, and in the intense mortification she anticipated for herself, she earnestly wished that in some manner he might escape the degrading penalty of his crimes.

In these harassing thoughts and distressing feelings Claudia lay tossing upon her restless bed until long after midnight, when at length she dropped into a deep and dreamless sleep.

Now the circumstance that I am about to relate will be interpreted in a different manner by different people. Rationalists who pin their faith on Sir Walter Scott and his "Demonology" will say it was only an optical illusion; the incredulous, who believe in nothing, will declare it was but a dream; while Spiritualists, who follow Mr. Robert Dale Owen in his "Footprints on the Boundaries of Another World," will be ready to declare that it was the apparition of a spirit; I commit myself to no opinion on the subject.

But when Claudia had slept soundly for three hours she was aroused by hearing her name called; she awoke with a violent start; she sat upright in bed, and stared right before her with fixed eyes, pallid face, and immovable form, as though she were suddenly petrified.

For there at the foot of the bed, between the tall posts, in the division formed by the festoons of the curtains, stood the figure of the Viscount Vincent. His face was pale, still, stern, like that of a dead man; one livid hand clutched his breast, the other was stretched towards her; and from the cold, blue, motionless lips proceeded a voice hollow as the distant moan of the wintry wind through leafless woods:

"Claudia, the debt is paid!"

With these words the vision slowly dissolved to air. Then, and not until then, was the icy spell that bound all Claudia's faculties loosened. She uttered piercing shriek upon shriek that startled all the sleepers in the house, and brought them rushing into her room. Katie and Sally being the nearest, were the first to enter.

"For Marster's sake, my ladyship, what is the matter?" inquired the old woman, while Sally stood by in a dumb terror.

"Oh, Katie, Katie! it was Lord Vincent! He has contrived to make his escape in some manner! He is out of prison! he is in this very house! he was in this room but a minute ago, though I do not see him now! and he spoke to me!"

"My goodness gracious me alibe, Miss Claudia, honey, it couldn't a been he! he's locked up safe in jail, you know! It mus' a been his sperrit!" said superstitious Katie, with the deepest awe.

"Claudia, my dearest, what is the matter? What is all this? What has happened?" anxiously inquired the Countess of Hurstmonceux, as, hastily wrapped in her dressing-gown, she hurried into the chamber and up to Claudia's bedside.

"Come closer, Berenice; stoop down; now listen! The viscount has broken prison! he was here but a moment ago! and he is gone! but his unexpected appearance in this place and at this hour, looking as he did so deathly pale, so livid and so corpse-like, frightened me nearly out of my senses, and I screamed with terror. I—I tremble even yet."

"My dearest Claudia, you have been dreaming. Compose yourself," said Lady Hurstmonceux soothingly.

"My dearest Berenice, it was no dream, believe me. I was indeed asleep, fast asleep; but I was awakened by hearing myself called by name—'Claudia, Claudia, Claudia,' three times. And I opened my eyes and sat up in bed, and saw standing at the foot, looking at me between the curtains, Lord Vincent."

At this moment Judge Merlin, in his dressing-gown and slippers, came slowly into the chamber, looking around in a bewildered way and saying:

"They told me the screams proceeded from my daughter's apartment. What is the matter here? Claudia, my dear, what has happened? What has frightened you?" he inquired, approaching her bedside.

"Oh, my poor papa, have you been disturbed, too? How sorry I am!" said Claudia.

"Never mind me, my dear! What has happened to you?"

"Lady Vincent has been frightened by a disagreeable dream, sir," replied Lady Hurstmonceux, answering for her friend.

"My dear lady, you here!" exclaimed the judge, seeing her for the first time since he entered the room.

"I am a light sleeper," smiled the countess.

"I am very sorry, papa, that I aroused the house in this manner," said Claudia, with real regret in her tone.

"It was not like you to do so, for a dream, my dear," replied the judge gravely.

"It was no dream, papa! it was no dream, as the result will prove."

"What was it then, my dear?"

"It was the Viscount Vincent!"

"The Viscount Vincent!" exclaimed the judge, in astonishment.

"Yes, papa; he has contrived to escape and to enter this house and this very room. It was his sudden appearance that frightened me into the screaming fit that alarmed the household; and for which I am very sorry."

"The Viscount Vincent here! But how on earth could he have escaped from prison?"

"I do not know, papa. I only know by the evidence of my own senses that he has done so."

"My dearest Claudia, believe me, you have been dreaming. Judge Merlin, if you knew the great strength and security of our prisons, you would also know how impossible it would be for any prisoner to escape," said Lady Hurstmonceux, addressing in turn the father and the daughter.

"Berenice, that I have not been dreaming to-morrow will show. For to-morrow you and all concerned will know that Lord Vincent has escaped from prison. But my dear Berenice, and you, my dearest father, promise to me one thing; promise me not to give Lord Vincent up to justice; but to suffer him to get away from the country, if he can do so. That is doubtless all that he proposes to himself to do. And such exile will be punishment enough in itself for him, especially as it will involve the resignation of his rank, title, and inheritance. So let him get away if he can. He can work no further woe for me. Frisbie's dying confession has killed off all his calumnies against me. He is harmless henceforth. So leave him to God," pleaded Claudia.

"I am willing to do, or leave undone, whatever you please, my dear; but—do you really think that you actually did see the viscount, and that you did not only dream of seeing him?" inquired the judge, unable to get over his amazement.

"Yes, papa; I saw him; and to-morrow will prove that I did so," said Claudia emphatically.

Lady Hurstmonceux smiled incredulously, for she did not reflect that there were more ways than one of breaking out of prison.

"But supposing it to have been the viscount; and supposing that he had succeeded in bursting locks and bars and eluding guards and sentinels; why should he have come here, of all places in the world? What could have been his motive in so risking a recapture?" inquired the judge, who seemed inclined to investigate the affair then and there.

"I do not know, papa. I have not had time to think. I was so astonished and even frightened at his mere appearance that I never asked myself the reason of it," answered Claudia.

"Did you not ask him?"

"No, papa. I only screamed."

"Did he not speak to you?"

"Yes, papa."

"What did he say?"

"Papa, I had better tell you just how it happened," answered Claudia, giving the judge a detailed account of the dream, vision, or ghost, as the reader chooses to call it; but which she persisted in declaring to be the viscount himself in the flesh.

"It is most extraordinary! How did he get out? Lady Hurstmonceux, had we not better have the house searched for him?" inquired the judge.

"It shall be done if you please, judge; though I think it unnecessary."

"Papa, no! he went as he came. Let him go. I hope he will be clear of the country before to-morrow morning."

At this moment the clock struck five, although it was still pitch-dark and far from the dawn of day.

"There! I declare it is to-morrow morning already, as the Irish would say. Lady Hurstmonceux, do not let me keep you up any longer. I know your usual hour for rising at this season of the year is eight o'clock. You will have three good hours' sleep before you yet. Papa, dear, go to bed or you will make yourself ill."

"Are you sure you will not have anything before I go, Claudia?" inquired the countess.

"Nothing whatever, dear; I think I shall sleep."

Lady Hurstmonceux stooped and kissed her friend, and then, with a smile and a bow to the judge, she retired from the room.

"Do you think now that you will rest, Claudia?" inquired the judge.

"Yes, papa, yes. Go to rest yourself."

He also stooped and kissed her, and then left the chamber.

"Go to bed, Katie and Sally," said Claudia to her women.

"'Deed 'fore de Lord aint I gwine to no bed to leabe you here by yourse'f. I don't want you to see no more sperrits," replied Katie. And she left the room for a few minutes and returned dragging in her mattress, which she spread upon the floor, and upon which she threw herself to sleep for the remainder of the dark hours.

Lady Vincent submitted to this intrusion, because she knew it would be utterly useless to expostulate. But Sally began to whimper.

"Now, den, what de matter long o' you? You seen a sperrit too?" demanded Katie.

"I's feared to sleep by myse'f, for fear I should see somethin'," wept Sally.

"Den you lay down here by me," ordered Katie.

And thus it was that Lady Vincent's two women shared her sleeping room the remainder of that disturbed night—to be disturbed no longer; for, whether it was owing to the presence of the negroes or not, Claudia slept untroubled by dream, vision, or apparition, until the daylight streaming through one window, that had been left unclosed, awakened her.

It was ten o'clock, however, before the family assembled at the breakfast table, where they were engaged in discussing the affair of the previous night, and in each maintaining his or her own opinion as to its character; Claudia persisting that it was the Viscount Vincent in person that she had seen; Berenice contending that it was a dream; and the judge hesitating between two opinions; Ishmael silent.

"A very few hours will now decide the question," said Claudia, abandoning the discussion and beginning to chip her egg. At this moment came a sound of wheels on the drive before the house, followed by a loud knock at the door.

"There! I should not in the least wonder if that is a detachment of police coming to tell us that Lord Vincent has broken prison, and bringing a warrant to search this house for him," said Claudia, half rising to listen.

A servant entered the room and said:

"Sergeant McRae is out in the hall, asking to see his honor the judge."

"I thought so," said Claudia briskly.

The judge went out to see the sergeant of police.

Claudia and Berenice suspended their breakfast, and waited in intense anxiety the result of the interview.

Some little time elapsed, perhaps fifteen or twenty minutes, though the impatience of the ladies made it seem an hour in length; and then the door slowly opened and the judge gravely re-entered the breakfast room.

"It is as I said. The Viscount Vincent has broken jail and they have come here with a search warrant to look for him!" exclaimed Claudia, glancing up at her father as he approached; but when she saw the expression of profound melancholy in his countenance, she started, turned pale, and cried:

"Good Heaven, papa, what—what has happened?"

"Partly what you have anticipated, Claudia. The Viscount Vincent has broken out of prison, but not in the manner you supposed," solemnly replied the judge, taking his daughter's arm and leading her to a sofa and seating her upon it.

Lady Hurstmonceux, startled, anxious, and alarmed, followed and stood by her and held her hand. And both ladies gazed inquiringly into the disturbed face of the old man.

"There is something—something behind! What is it, papa? The viscount has broken jail, you say! Has he—has he—killed one of the guards in making his escape?" inquired Claudia, in a low, awe-stricken voice.

"No, my dear, he has not done that. He has escaped the tribunal of man to rush uncalled to the tribunal of God," said the judge solemnly.

Claudia, though her dilated eyes were fixed in eager questioning on the face of her father, and though her ears were strained to catch his low-toned words, yet did not seem to gather in his meaning.

"What—what do you say, papa? Explain!" she breathed in scarcely audible syllables.

"The Viscount Vincent is dead!"

"Dead!" ejaculated Claudia.

"Dead!" echoed the countess.

"Dead, by his own act!" repeated the judge.

Claudia sank back in the corner of the sofa and covered her face with her hands—overcome, not by sorrow certainly, but by awe and pity.

Berenice sat down beside the newly made widow, and put her arms around her waist, and drew her head upon her bosom. Judge Merlin stood silently before them. The only one who seemed to have the full possession of his faculties was Ishmael.

He quietly dismissed the gaping servants from the room, closed the doors, and drew a resting-chair to the side of his old friend, and gently constrained him to sit down in it. And then he was about to glide away when the judge seized his hand and detained him, saying imploringly:

"No, no, Ishmael! no, no, my dearest young friend! do not leave us at this solemn crisis."

Ishmael placed his hand in that of the old man, as an earnest of fidelity, and remained standing by him.

After a little while Claudia lifted her head from the bosom of Lady Hurstmonceux, and said:

"Oh, papa, this is dreadful!"

"Dreadful, indeed, my dear."

"That any human being should be driven to such a fate!"

"To such a crime, Claudia," gravely amended the judge.

"Crime, then, if you will call it so. But I do not wonder at it. May God in his infinite mercy forgive him!" fervently prayed Claudia.

"Amen!" deeply responded the judge.

"Papa, they say that suicides are never forgiven—can never be forgiven—because their sin is the last act of their life, affording no time for repentance. Yet who knows that for certain? Who knows but in the short interval between the deed and the death, there may not be repentance and pardon?"

"Who knows, indeed! 'With God all things are possible.'"

"Oh, papa, I hope he repented and is pardoned!"

"I hope so too, Claudia."

She dropped her head once more upon the bosom of Lady Hurstmonceux, in pity and in awe; but not in sorrow, for his death was an infinite relief to her and to all connected with him. After a little while she raised her head again, and in a low, hushed voice, inquired:

"Papa, at what hour did he die?"

"Between four and five o'clock this morning, my dear."

"Between four and five o'clock this morning! Good Heavens!" exclaimed Claudia and Berenice simultaneously, starting and gazing into each other's faces.

"What is the matter?" gravely inquired the judge.

"That was the very hour in which Claudia was awakened by her strange dream!" replied Lady Hurstmonceux.

"Oh, papa! that was the very hour in which I saw Lord Vincent standing at the foot of my bed!" exclaimed Claudia, with a shudder.

"How passing strange!" mused the judge.

"Oh, papa! can such things really be? can a parting spirit appear to us the moment it leaves the body?" inquired Claudia, in an awe-struck manner.

"My dear if anyone had related to me such a strange circumstance as this, of which we are all partly cognizant, I should have discredited the whole affair. As it is, I know not what to make of it. It may have been a dream; nay, it must have been a dream; yet, even as a dream, occurring just at the hour it did, it was certainly an astonishing and a most marvelous coincidence."

Again Claudia dropped her head upon the supporting bosom of Lady Hurstmonceux, but this time it was in weariness and in thought that she reposed there.

A few minutes passed, and then, without lifting her head, she murmured:

"Tell me all about it, papa; I must learn some time; as well now as any other."

"Can you bear to hear the story now, Claudia?"

"Better now, I think, than at a future time; I am in a measure prepared for it now. How did it happen, papa?"

The judge drew closer to his daughter, took her hand in his, and said:

"I will tell you, as McRae told me, my dear. You must know that from the time Lord Vincent read the published confession of Frisbie, in the afternoon papers, he became so much changed in all respects as to excite the attention, then the suspicion, and finally the alarm of his keepers. At six o'clock after the turnkey, Donald, had paid his last visit to his prisoner, and locked up the cell for the night, he reported the condition of Lord Vincent to the governor of the jail. Mr. Gra'ame, on hearing the account given by Donald, determined to curtail many of the privileges his lordship had hitherto, as an untried prisoner, enjoyed. Among the rest he determined that nothing more should be carried to his lordship in his cell that he, the governor, had not first examined, as a precautionary measure against drugs or tools, with which the prisoner might do himself a mischief."

"I should think they ought to have taken that precaution from the first," said Claudia.

"It is not usual in the case of an untried prisoner; but, however, the governor of Banff jail seemed to think as you do, for he farther determined to make a special visit to the prisoner that night, to search his cell and remove from it everything with which he might possibly injure himself. And accordingly the governor, accompanied by the turnkey, went to the cell and made a thorough search. They found nothing suspicious, however. But in their late though excessive caution they carried away, not only the prisoner's razor, but his pen-knife and scissors. And then they left him."

"And after all, left him with the means of self-destruction," exclaimed Claudia.

"No, they did not. You shall hear. About eight o'clock that night, as the watchman of that ward was pacing his rounds, he heard deep groans issuing from Lord Vincent's cell. He went and gave the alarm. The warden, the physician, and the turnkey entered the cell together. They found the viscount in the agonies of death."

"Great Heavens! Alone and dying in his cell!"

"Yes; and suffering even more distress of mind than of body. When it was too late, he regretted his rash deed. For he freely confessed that being driven to despair and almost if not quite to madness, by the desperate state of his affairs, he had procured laudanum through the agency of his servant, having persuaded the old man that he merely wanted the medicine to allay pain."

"Poor, poor soul!"

"Cuthbert, simple and unsuspicious, and as easily deceived as a child, brought the laudanum to him and bid him adieu for the night. And it was in the interval between the last visit of the turnkey and the special visit of the governor that the prisoner drank the whole of the laudanum. And then to prevent suspicion he washed the label from the bottle and poured in a little ink from his inkstand. So that when the governor made his visit of inspection, although he actually handled that bottle, he took it for nothing else but a receptacle for ink."

"Oh, how dreadful! how dreadful, that anyone should exercise so much calculation, cunning, and foresight for the destruction of his own soul!" moaned Claudia.

"Yes; he himself thought so at last; for no sooner did the poison begin to do its work, no sooner did he feel death approaching, than he was seized with horror at the enormity of his own crime, and with remorse for the sins of his whole life. It would seem that in that hour his eyes were opened for the first time, and he saw himself as he really was, a rampant rebel against all the laws of God and on the brink of eternal perdition. It was the great agony of mind produced by this view of himself and his condition that forced from him those deep groans that were heard by the night-watch, who brought the relief to him."

"Then he must have repented. Oh! I hope that God forgave him!" prayed Claudia, with earnest tones and clasped hands.

"You may be sure that God did forgive him if he truly repented! Certainly it seemed that he repented; for he begged for antidotes, declaring that he wished to live to atone for the sins of his past. Antidotes were administered, but without the least good effect. And when he repeated his earnest wish to be permitted to live that he might 'atone by his future life for the sins of his past,' the physician, who is a good man, sent for the chaplain of the jail, a fervent Christian, who told the prisoner how impossible it was for him, should he have a new lease of life, to atone, by years of penance, for the smallest sin of his soul; but pointed him at the same time to the One Divine Atoner, who is able to save to the uttermost. The chaplain remained praying with the dying man until half-past four o'clock this morning, when he breathed his last. That is all, Claudia."

"Oh, papa, you see he did repent; and I will hope that God has pardoned him," said Claudia earnestly; but she was very pale and faint, and she leaned heavily upon the shoulder of Lady Hurstmonceux.

"My dearest Claudia, let me lead you to your room; you require repose after this excitement," said the countess, giving her arm to the new widow.

Claudia arose; but the judge gently arrested her progress.

"Stay, my dear! One word before you go. The business of McRae here was not only to announce the death of Lord Vincent, but also the approaching trial of Faustina Dugald. It comes on at ten o'clock to-morrow morning. You are summoned as a witness for the prosecution. Therefore, my dear, we must leave Edinboro' for Banff by the afternoon express train."

"Oh, papa! to appear in a public court at such a time!" exclaimed Claudia, with a shudder.

"I know it is hard, my dear. I know it must be dreadful; but I also know that the way of Justice is like the progress of the Car of Juggernaut. It stops for nothing; it rolls on in its irresistible course, crushing under its iron wheels all conventionalities, all proprieties, all sensibilities. And I know also, my daughter, that you are equal to the duties, the exertions, and the sacrifices that Justice requires of you. There, go now! take what repose you can for the next few hours, to be ready for the train at six o'clock," said the judge, stooping, and pressing a kiss upon his daughter's brow, before the countess led her away.

"Ishmael," said the judge, as soon as they were alone, "do you know what you and I have got to do now?"

"Yes, sir," said the young man solemnly, "I know."

"That poor, unhappy man in yonder prison has no friend or relative to claim his body, his father being absent; and if we do not claim it, it will be ignominiously buried by the prison authorities within the prison walls."

"I thought of that, but waited for your suggestion. If you please I will see the proper authorities to-morrow and make arrangements with them."

"Do, my dear young friend," said the judge, wringing his hand as he left him.

Amid the great crises of life its small proprieties must still be observed. This the Countess of Hurstmonceux knew. And, therefore, as soon as she had seen Claudia reposing on her comfortable sofa in her chamber, she ordered her carriage and drove to Edinboro', and to a celebrated mourning warehouse where they got up outfits on the shortest notice, and there she procured a widow's complete dress, including the gown, mantle, bonnet, veil, and gloves, and took them home to Claudia. For she knew that if Lady Vincent were compelled to appear in the public courtroom the next day, she must wear widow's weeds.

When she took these articles into Claudia's room and showed them to her, the latter said:

"My dear Berenice, I thank you very much for your thoughtful care. But do you know that it would seem like hypocrisy in me to wear this mourning?"

"My dearest Claudia, conventionalities must be observed though the heavens fall. You owe this to yourself, to society, and even to the dead—for in his death he has atoned for much to you."

"I will wear them then," said Claudia.

And there the matter ended.

Meanwhile, the news of Lord Vincent's death had got about among the servants. Katie and Sally also had heard of it.

So that when Lady Vincent rang for her women to come and pack up her traveling trunk to go to Banff, Katie entered full of the subject.

"So my lordship has gone to his account, and all from takin' of an overdose of laudamy drops. How careful people ought to be when they meddles long o' dat sort o' truck. Well, laws! long as he's dead and gone I forgibs him for heavin' of me down to lib long o' de rats, and den sellin' ob me to de barbariums in de Stingy Isles. 'Deed does I forgibs him good too. and likewise de shamwally while I'se got my hand in at forgibness," she said.

"That's right, Katie. Never let your hatred follow a man to the grave," said Claudia.

"I wouldn't forgib 'em if dey wasn't dead, dough. 'Deed wouldn't I. I tell you all good too. And if dey was to come back to life I would just take my forgibness back again. And it should all be just like it was before," said Katie, sharply defining her position.

Claudia sadly shook her head.

"That is a very questionable species of forgiveness, Katie," she said.

That afternoon the whole party, including the Countess of Hurstmonceux, who declared her intention of supporting Claudia through the approaching ordeal, left Cameron Court for Edinboro', where they took the six o'clock train for Banff, where they arrived at ten the same evening.

They went to the "Highlander," where they engaged comfortable apartments and settled themselves for a few days.

CHAPTER XLIX

THE FATE OF FAUSTINA.

Oh, what a fate is guilt! How wild, how wretched!

When apprehension can form naught but fears.

—Howard.

Early the next morning Ishmael went over to the prison to see the governor relative to the removal of the body of the unhappy Vincent. But he was told that the old Earl of Hurstmonceux had arrived at noon on the previous day and had claimed the body of his son and had it removed from the prison in a close hearse at the dead of night, to escape the observation of the mob, and conveyed to Castle Cragg, where, without any funeral pomp, it would be quietly deposited in the family vault.

With this intelligence Ishmael came back to Judge Merlin.

"That is well! That is a great relief to my mind, Ishmael," said the judge, and he went to convey the news to Lady Vincent and the countess.

At nine o'clock Katie, Sally, and Jim, who were all witnesses for the prosecution in the approaching trial of Faustina Dugald, were dispatched to the courthouse, under the escort of the professor.

At half-past nine Judge Merlin, Ishmael Worth, Lady Vincent, and the Countess of Hurstmonceux entered a close carriage and drove to the same place.

What a crowd!

It is not every day that a woman of high rank stands at the bar of a criminal court to answer to a charge of felony. And Faustina was a woman of high rank, at least by marriage. She was the Honorable Mrs. Dugald; and she was about to be arraigned upon several charges, the lightest one of which, if proved, would consign her to penal servitude for years.

The world had got wind of this trial, and hence the great crowd that blocked up every approach to the courthouse.

Two policemen had to clear a way for the carriage containing the witnesses for the prosecution to draw up. And when it stopped and its party alighted, the same two policemen had to walk before them to open a path for their entrance into the courthouse.

Here every lobby, staircase, passage, and anteroom was full of curious people, pressed against each other. These people could not get into the courtroom, which was already crowded as full as it could be packed; nor could they see or hear anything from where they stood; and yet they persisted in standing there, crowding each other nearly to death, and stretching their necks and straining their eyes and ears after sensational sights and sounds.

Through this consolidated mass of human beings the policemen found great difficulty in forcing a passage for the witnesses. But at length they succeeded, and ushered the party into the courtroom, and seated them upon the bench appointed to the use of the witnesses for the prosecution.

The courtroom was even more densely packed than the approaches to it had been. It was scarcely possible to breathe the air laden with the breath of so many human beings. But for the inconvenience of the great crowd and the fetid air, this was an interesting place to pass a few hours in.

The Lord Chief Baron, Sir Archibald Alexander, presided on the bench. He was supported on the right and left by Justices Knox and Blair. Some of the most distinguished advocates of the Scottish bar were present.

The prisoner had not yet been brought into court. A few minutes passed, however, and then, by the commotion near the door and by the turning simultaneously of hundreds of heads in one direction, it was discovered that she was approaching in custody of the proper officers. Room was readily made for her by the crowd dividing right and left and pressing back upon itself, like the waves of the Red Sea, when the Israelites passed over it dryshod. And she was led up between two bailiffs and placed in the dock. Then for the first time the crowd got a good view of her, for the dock was raised some three or four feet above the level of the floor.

She was well dressed for the occasion, for if there was one thing this woman understood better than another, it was the science of the toilet. She wore a dark-brown silk dress and a dark-brown velvet bonnet, and a Russian sable cloak, and cuffs, and muff, and her face was shaded by a delicate black lace veil.

Mrs. MacDonald, who had followed her into the court, was allowed to sit beside her; a privilege that the lady availed herself of, at some considerable damage to her own personal dignity; for at least one-half of the strangers in the room, judging from her position beside the criminal, mistook her for an accomplice in the crime.

After the usual preliminary forms had been observed, the prisoner was duly arraigned at the bar.

When asked by the clerk of arraignments whether she were guilty or not guilty, she answered vehemently:

"I am not guilty of anything at all; no, not I! I never did conspire against any lady! My Lord Viscount Vincent and his valet Frisbie did that! And I never did abduct and sell into slavery any negro persons! My Lord Vincent and his valet did that also! It was all the doings of my lord and his valet, as you may know, since the valet has been guillotined and my lord has suffocated himself with charcoal! And it is a great infamy to persecute a poor little woman for what gross big men did! And I tell you, messieurs—"

"That will do! This is no time for making your defense, but only for entering your plea," said the clerk, cutting short her oration.

She threw herself into a chair and burst into tears, and sobbed aloud while the Queen's Solicitor, Counselor Birnie, got up to open the indictment setting forth the charges upon which the prisoner at the bar had been arraigned.

At the end of the opening speech he proceeded to call the witnesses, and the first called to the stand was:

"Claudia Dugald, Viscountess Vincent."

Judge Merlin arose and led his daughter to the stand, and then retired.

Claudia threw aside her deep mourning veil, revealing her beautiful pale face, at the sight of which a murmur of admiration ran through the crowded courtroom.

The oath was duly administered, Claudia following the words of the formula, in a low, but clear and firm voice.

Oh! but her position was a painful one! Gladly would she have retired from it; but the exactions of justice are inexorable. It was distressing to her to stand there and give testimony against the prisoner, which should cast such shame upon the grave of the dumb, defenseless dead; yet it was inevitable that she must do it. She was under oath, and so she must testify to "the truth, the whole truth, and nothing but the truth!"

Then being questioned, she spoke of the sinful league between. Faustina Dugald, the prisoner at the bar, and the deceased Viscount Vincent; she then related the conversation she had overheard between these two accomplices on the very night of her first arrival home at Castle Cragg; that momentous conversation in which the first germ of the conspiracy against her honor was formed; being further questioned, she acknowledged the complete estrangement between herself and her husband, and the actual state of widowhood in which she had lived in his house, while his time and attention were all devoted to her rival, the prisoner at the bar.

Here Claudia begged leave to retire from the stand; but of course she was not permitted to do so; the Queen's Solicitor had not done with her yet. She was required to relate the incidents of that evening when the valet Frisbie was dragged from his hiding-place in her boudoir by the Viscount Vincent. And amid fiery blushes Claudia detailed all the circumstances of that scene. She was but slightly cross-questioned by the counsel for the prisoner, and without effect, and was finally permitted to retire. Her father came and led her back to her seat.

The housekeeper of Castle Cragg was the next witness called, and she testified with a marked reluctance, that only served to give additional weight to her statement, to the sinful intimacy between the deceased viscount and the prisoner at the bar.

Following her came old Cuthbert, who sadly corroborated her testimony in all respects.

Next came other servants of the castle, all with much dislike to do the duty, speaking to the one point of the fatal attachment that had existed between Lord Vincent and Mrs. Dugald.

And then at length came Katie. Now we all know the facts to which Katie would bear testimony, and the style in which she would do it; and so we need not repeat her statement here. It was sufficiently conclusive to insure the conviction of the prisoner, even if there had been nothing to support it.

But the most fatal evidence was yet to be produced: The Reverend Christian Godfree, chaplain of the jail, was called to the stand and duly sworn. And then a manuscript was placed in his hand, and he was asked if he could identify that as the veritable last confession made by the convict,

Alick Frisbie, in his cell, on the night previous to his execution. Mr. Godfree carefully examined it and promptly identified it.

But here the counsel for the prisoner interposed, and would have had the confession ruled out as evidence; and a controversy arose between the prosecution and the defense, which was at last decided by the bench, who ordered that the confession of Alick Frisbie should be received as evidence in the case of Faustina Dugald.

And then the Queen's Solicitor, taking the paper from the witness, proceeded to read the confession with all its deeply disgraceful revelations. From it, the complicity of Faustina Dugald in the conspiracy against Lady Vincent was clearly shown. Having read it through, the solicitor called several witnesses from among the servants of the castle, who swore to the signature at the bottom of the confession as the handwriting of Alick Frisbie. And then the solicitor passed the paper to the foreman of the jury, that he might circulate it among his colleagues for their examination and satisfaction. The solicitor then summed up the evidence for the prosecution and rested the case.

Mr. Brace, leading counsel for the prisoner, arose and made the best defense that the bad case admitted of. He tried to pull to pieces, destroy, and discredit the evidence that had been given in; but all to no purpose. He next tried to engage the sympathy of the judge and jury for the beauty and misfortunes of his client; but in vain. Finally, he called a number of paid witnesses, who testified chiefly to the excellent moral character of Mrs. Faustina Dugald, seeking to make it appear quite impossible that she should do any wrong whatever, much less commit the crimes for which she stood arraigned; and also to the malignant envy, hatred, and malice felt by every servant at Castle Cragg and every witness for the prosecution against the injured and unhappy prisoner at the bar, seeking to make it appear that all their testimony was nothing but malignant calumny leveled against injured innocence.

But, unfortunately for the defense, the only impression these witnesses made upon the judge and the jury was that they—the witnesses—were about the most shameless falsifiers of the truth that ever perjured themselves before a court of justice.

The counsel for the prisoner went over the evidence for the defense in an eloquent speech, which was worse than wasted in such evil service.

The Queen's Solicitor had, as usual, the last word.

The Lord Chief Baron then summed up the evidence on either side and charged the jury. And the charge amounted in effect to an instruction to them to bring in a verdict against the prisoner. And accordingly the jury retired and consulted about twenty minutes, and then returned with the verdict: "Guilty."

The Lord Chief Baron arose to pronounce the sentence of the law.

The clerk of the arraigns ordered the prisoner to stand up.

"What are they going to do now?" nervously inquired Faustina, who did not in the least understand what was going on.

"Nothing much, my dear; his lordship the judge is going to speak to you from the bench. That is all," said Mrs. MacDonald, as she helped the prisoner to her feet; for Mrs. MacDonald never hesitated to tell a falsehood for the sake of keeping the peace.

Faustina stood up, looking towards the bench with curiosity, distrust, and fear.

The Lord Chief Baron began the usual prosing preamble to the sentence, telling the prisoner of the enormity of the crime of which she had been accused; of the perfect impartiality of the trial to which she had been subjected; the complete conclusiveness of the evidence on which she had been convicted; and so forth. He gave her to understand that the court might easily sentence her to fifteen or twenty years' imprisonment; but that, in consideration of her early youth and of her utter failure to carry out her felonious purposes to their completion, he would assign her a milder penalty. And he proceeded to sentence her to penal servitude for the term of ten years. The Lord Chief Baron resumed his seat.

Faustina threw a wild, perplexed, appealing glance around the courtroom, and then, as the truth of her doom entered her soul, she uttered a piercing shriek and fell into violent hysterics. And in this condition she was removed from the court to the jail, there to remain until she should be transported to the scene of her punishment.

"We have nothing more to do here, Judge Merlin. Had you not better take Lady Vincent back to the hotel?" suggested Ishmael.

The judge, who had been sitting as if spellbound, started up, gave his arm to his daughter, and led her out of the court and to the fly that was in attendance to convey them back to the "Highlander." Ishmael followed, with the countess on his arm. And the professor, having the three negroes in charge, brought up the rear. Judge Merlin, Ishmael, Claudia and the countess entered the fly. The professor and his charges walked. And thus they reached the "Highlander," where the news of Faustina Dugald's conviction had preceded them.

The trial had occupied the whole day. It was now late in the evening; too late for our party to think of going on to Edinboro' that night. Besides, they all needed rest after the exciting scenes of the day; and so they determined to remain in Banff that night.

CHAPTER L

LADY HURSTMONCEUX'S REVELATION.

For life, I prize it,

As I weigh grief which I would spare; for honor,

'Tis a derivative from me to mine,

And only that I stand for.

—Shakspeare.

That same evening, while our party was assembled at tea in their private parlor, at the "Highlander," a letter was brought to Judge Merlin.

It was a formidable-looking letter, with a black border an inch wide running around the envelope, and sealed with a great round of black wax, impressed with an earl's coronet. The judge opened it and read it and passed it to Ishmael.

It proved to be a letter from the Earl of Hurstmonceux and addressed to Judge Merlin. I have not space to give the contents of this letter word for word.

It set forth, in effect, that under the recent distressing circumstances it would be too painful to the Earl of Hurstmonceux to meet Judge Merlin in a personal interview, but that the earl wished to make an act of restitution, and so, if Judge Merlin would dispatch his solicitor to London to the chambers of the Messrs. Hudson, in Burton Street, Piccadilly, those gentlemen, who were the solicitors of his lordship, would be prepared to restore to Lady Vincent the fortune she had brought in marriage to her husband, the late Lord Vincent.

"You will go to London and attend to this matter for me, Ishmael?" inquired the Judge, as he received the letter back, after the young man had read it.

"Why, certainly, Judge Merlin. Who should act for you but myself?" said Ishmael, with an affectionate smile.

"But it may be inconvenient for you to go just now?" suggested the judge.

"Oh, no, not at all! In fact, judge, I was intending to go up to London to join Mr. Brudenell there in a very few days. I was only waiting for this trial to be concluded before setting out," smiled Ishmael.

"Papa, what is it that you are talking about? What letter is that?" inquired Claudia, while Lady Hurstmonceux looked the question she forbore to ask.

For all answer the judge placed the letter in the hands of his daughter, and then, turning to the countess, said:

"It is a communication from Lord Hurstmonceux, referring us to his solicitors in London, whom he has instructed to make restitution of the whole of my daughter's fortune."

"The Earl of Hurstmonceux is an honorable man. But he has been singularly unfortunate in his family. His brother and his sons, who seem to have taken more after their uncle than their father, have all turned out badly and given him much trouble," said the countess.

"His brother? I know of course the career of his sons; but I did not know anything about his brother," said Judge Merlin.

"He was the Honorable Dromlie Dugald, Captain in the Tenth Highlanders, a man whose society was avoided by all good women. And yet I had cause to know him well," answered the countess, as a cloud passed over her beautiful face.

"You, Berenice!" said Claudia, looking up in surprise; for it was passing strange to hear that pure and noble woman acknowledge an acquaintance with a man of whom she had just said that every good woman avoided his society.

"I!" repeated the counters solemnly.

There was certainly fate in the next words she spoke:

"This Captain Dugald was a near relative and great favorite with my first husband, the old Earl of Hurstmonceux; chiefly, I think, for the exuberant gayety of temper and disposition of the young man, that always kept the old one amused. But after the earl married me he turned a cold shoulder to the captain, and complimented me by being jealous of him. This occasioned gossip, in which my good name suffered some injustice."

The countess paused, and turned her beautiful eyes appealingly to Ishmael, saying:

"When you shall become one of the lawgivers of your native country, young gentleman, I hope that the crime of slander will be made a felony, indictable before your criminal courts."

"If I had the remodeling of the laws," said Ishmael earnestly, "slander should be made felonious and punishable as theft is."

"But, dear Berenice, the gossip of which you speak could have done you no lasting injury," said Claudia.

"'No lasting injury.' Well, no eternal injury, I hope, if you mean that," sighed the countess.

"No, I mean to say that a woman like yourself lives down calumny."

"Ah! but in the living it down, how much of heartwasting."

The countess dropped her head upon her hand for a moment, while all her long black ringlets fell around and veiled her pale and thoughtful face. Then, looking up, she said:

"I think I will tell you all about it. Something, I know not what, impels me to speak tonight, in this little circle of select friends, on a theme on which I have been silent for years. Claudia, my dearest, if the jealousy of my old husband and the gossip of my envious rivals had been all, that would not have hurt me so much. But there was worse to come. The wretch, denied admittance to our house, pursued me with his attentions elsewhere; whenever and wherever I walked or rode out he would be sure to join me. I have said such was his evil reputation, that his society would have brought reproach to any woman, under any circumstances; judge you, then, what it must have brought upon me, the young wife of an old man!"

"Had you no male relative to chastise the villain and send him about his business?" inquired the judge.

Berenice smiled sadly and shook her head.

"My husband and my father were both very old men," she said; "I had but one resource—to confine myself to the house and deny myself to visitors. We were then living in our town house in Edinboro'. There my old husband died, and there I spent the year of my widowhood. There my father came to me, and also my kinsman Isaacs."

"Isaacs!" impulsively exclaimed Ishmael, as his thoughts flew back to his Hebrew fellow-passenger.

"Yes; did you know him?"

"I knew a Jew of that name; most probably the same; but I beg your pardon, dear lady; pray proceed with your narrative."

"I mentioned my kinsman Isaacs, because I always suspected him to be a party to a stratagem formed by Captain Dugald at that time to get me into his power. Captain Dugald scarcely let the first six months of my widowhood pass by before he began to lay siege to my house; not to me personally; for I always denied myself to him. But he came on visits to my kinsman Isaacs, with whom he had struck up a great intimacy. He had much at stake, you see, for in the first place he did me the honor to approve of me personally, and in the second place he highly approved of my large fortune. So he persevered with all the zeal of a lover and all the tact of a fortune-hunter. Several times, through the connivance of my kinsman, he contrived to surprise me into an interview, and upon each occasion he urged his suit; but of course, in vain. Captain Dugald was what is called a 'dare-devil,' and I think he rather gloried in that name. He acted upon the maxim that 'all stratagems are fair in love as in war.' And he resorted to a stratagem to get me into his power, and reduce me to the alternative of marrying him or losing my good name forever."

"Good Heaven! he did not attempt to carry you off by violence," exclaimed Claudia.

The countess laughed.

"Oh, no, my dear! Such things are never attempted in this age of the world. Captain Dugald was far too astute to break the laws. I will tell you just how it was, as it came to my knowledge. My town house fronted immediately on Prince's Street. You know what a thoroughfare that is? My bedroom and dressing room were on the second floor—the bedroom being at the back, and the dressing room in front, with three large windows overlooking the street. Large double doors connected the bedroom with the dressing room. I am thus particular in describing the locality that you may better understand the villainy of the stratagem," said the countess, looking around upon her friends.

They nodded assent, and she resumed:

"From some peculiar sensitiveness of temperament, I can never sleep unless every ray of light is shut out from my chamber. Thus, at bedtime I have all my windows closed, their shutters fastened and their curtains drawn, lest the first dawn of morning should awaken me prematurely. Another constitutional idiosyncrasy of mine is the necessity of a great deal of air. Therefore I always had the doors between my bedroom and my dressing room left open."

"After all, that is like my own need; I require a great deal of air also," said Claudia.

"Well, now to my story. On a certain spring morning, in the beginning of the second year of my widowhood, I was awakened very early by a glare of light in my bedroom. On looking up, I saw through the open doors connecting my bedroom with my dressing room that the three front windows of the dressing room, overlooking the street, were open, and all the morning sunlight was pouring in. My first emotion was anger with my maid for opening them so soon to wake me up. I got out of bed, slipped on a dressing-gown and went into the front room. Now judge what my feelings must have been to see there Captain Dugald in his shirt-sleeves, standing before one of the front windows deliberately brushing his hair, in the full view of all the passengers of the street below."

"Great Heaven!" exclaimed Claudia.

"I could not speak," continued the countess. "I could only stand and gaze at the man in speechless amazement. But he was not dismayed. He burst into a loud laugh, and laughed himself out of breath—for he was a great laugher. When he found his tongue, he said to me:

"'You had as well give in now, my lady. The fortress is sapped, the mine is exploded. The city is taken. Hundreds of people, passing up and down the street before this house, have looked up at these windows and seen me standing here half-dressed. And they have formed their opinions, and made their comments, and circulated their news accordingly; and so, if our marriage be not published this morning, you may judge what the consequences will be—to yourself.'"

"What a villain!" said Judge Merlin.

"Astonishment had struck me dumb in the first instance; and anger kept me silent," continued the countess. "I know what I ought to have done. I know that I ought to have summoned the police and given the man in charge on the spot, as a common burglar and housebreaker: only you see I did not think of it at the time. I only rang the bell, and then, without waiting the arrival of my servant, I opened the door and pointed silently to it. He made no motion to go; on the contrary, he began to defend his act, to plead his cause, and to urge his suit. He said 'that all stratagems were fair in love and war'; that it was now absolutely necessary for my fair name that we should be immediately married; that the bride he had won by fraud should be worn with faithfulness. But, with an unmoved countenance, I only pointed to the door, until my servant came in answer to the bell. Then I told that servant to show Captain Dugald out, and if he refused to go to summon assistance and eject him. Seeing that I was determined to be rid of him, he put on his coat, and, laughing at my discomfiture, took his departure. Then I instituted inquiries; but failed to gain any information respecting his means of entrance and concealment in my apartments. I strongly suspected my kinsman Isaacs of being the accomplice of Captain Dugald; but I had no means of ascertaining the fact by questioning him, as he went away that same morning and never returned. The adventure, of course, did me some harm at the time; but the unprincipled hero of it reaped no advantage. He doubtless thought me another Lucretia, who would sacrifice the reality to preserve the semblance of honor. He hoped to find in me one who, in the base fear of being falsely condemned, would marry a man I despised, and thus really deserve condemnation. He was disappointed! From that hour I forbade him the house, and I have never seen him since. A year later I married another," added the countess, in a voice so subdued that, at the close of the sentence, it gradually sank into silence.

Ishmael's beautiful eyes had been bent upon her all the time; now his whole face lighted up with a smile as of a newly inspired, benevolent hope.

"You were right-entirely right, Lady Hurstmonceux, in thus vindicating the dignity of womanhood. And I do not believe that any lasting blame, growing out of a misunderstanding of the circumstances, could have attached to you," said Ishmael earnestly.

"No, indeed, there was not. And soon after that event I left Edinboro' for the south coast of England, and at Brighton"—here the voice of the countess sank almost to an inaudible whisper—"at Brighton I met and married another. And now let us talk of something else, Ishmael," she concluded, turning an affectionate glance upon the sympathetic face of the young man. For there was a wonderful depth of sympathy between this queenly woman of forty-five and this princely young man of twenty-two. On her side there was the royal, benignant, tender friendship with which such sovereign ladies regard such young men; while, on his side, there was the loyal devotion with which such young men worship such divinities. Such a friendship is a blessing when it is understood; a curse when it is misapprehended.

Ishmael turned the conversation to the subject of the act of restitution proposed by the Earl of Hurstmonceux.

Ishmael now possessed the only clear, cool, and undisturbed intelligence of the whole party, who were all more or less shaken by the terrible events of the last few days. He had to think for them all. He announced his intention of departing for London on the ensuing Friday morning, and warned the judge that he should require his final instructions for acting in concert with the solicitors of the Earl of Hurstmonceux.

The judge promised that these should be ready, in writing, to place in his hands at the moment of his departure.

"And while I am in London, had I not better see the agents of the ocean steamers, and ascertain how soon we can obtain a passage home for our whole party? The termination of these trials, and the restitution of Lady Vincent's estate, really leave us nothing to do here; and we know that Lady Vincent is pining for the repose of her native home," said Ishmael.

"Certainly, certainly, Ishmael! The execution of Frisbie, the death of the viscount, the conviction of Mrs. Dugald, and the act of the Earl of Hurstmonceux, really, as you say, leave us free to go home. I myself, as well as Claudia, pine for my home. And you, Ishmael, though you have not said so, have sacrificed already too much of your professional interests to our necessities. You should be at your office. What on earth is becoming of your clients all this time?"

"I dare say they are taken good care of, sir. Do not think of me. Believe me, I have no interests dearer to my heart than the welfare and happiness of my friends. Then I shall engage a passage for us all, in the first available steamer?"

"I—I think so, Ishmael. There is nothing to keep us here longer that I know of; we have nothing to do," said the judge hesitatingly.

"I have something yet to do, before I return home," smiled Ishmael, with a quick and quickly withdrawn glance in the direction of the countess; "but I shall do it before we go, or if not I can remain behind for another steamer."

"No, no, Ishmael! You have stayed long with us; we will wait for you. What do you say, Claudia?"

Claudia said nothing.

Ishmael replied:

"I shall endeavor to accomplish all that I propose in time to accompany you, Judge Merlin. But if I should not be able to do so, still I think that you had better all go by the first steamer in which you can get a passage. You should, if possible, cross the ocean before March sets in, if you would have anything like a comfortable voyage."

"Heavens, yes! you are right, Ishmael. Our late voyage should teach me a lesson. I must not expose Claudia to the chances of such shipwreck as we suffered," said the judge gravely.

Ishmael turned and looked at Claudia. She had not once spoken since her name had been introduced into the conversation. She had sat there with her elbow on the table and her head bowed upon her hand, in mournful silence. She was looking perfectly beautiful in her widow's dress and cap—perfectly beautiful with that last divine, perfecting touch that sorrow gives to beauty. Surely Ishmael thought so as he looked at her. She lifted her drooping lids. Their eyes met; hers were suffused with tears; his were full of earnest sympathy.

"You shall not be exposed to shipwreck, Lady Vincent," he said, in a voice rich with tenderness.

Slowly and mournfully she shook her head.

"There are other wrecks," she said:

The last words were breathed in a scarcely audible voice, and her head sank low upon her hand.

With a profound sigh, that seemed to come from the very depths of his soul, Ishmael turned away. Passing near the Countess of Hurstmonceux, he bent his head and murmured:

"Lady Vincent seems very weary."

The countess took the hint and rang for the bedroom candles, and when they were brought, the party bade each other goodnight, separated, and retired.

Early the next morning they set out for Edinboro', where they arrived about midday.

The Countess of Hurstmonceux's servants, who had received telegraphic orders from her ladyship, were waiting at the station with carriages. The whole party entered these and drove to Cameron Court, where they arrived in time for an early dinner.

After this, Ishmael and Judge Merlin were closeted in the library, and engaged upon the preliminary measures for a final arrangement with the Earl of Hurstmonceux's solicitors.

The judge, in his good opinion of the earl, would have trusted to a simple, informal rendition of his daughter's fortune; but Ishmael, the ever-watchful guardian of her interests, warned her father that every legal form must be scrupulously observed in the restoration of the property, lest in the event of the death of the Earl of Hurstmonceux his brother and successor, the disreputable Captain Dugald, should attempt to disturb her in its possession.

The judge acquiesced, and this business occupied the friends the whole of that afternoon. In the evening they joined the ladies at their tea-table, in the little drawing room. After tea, when the service was removed, they gathered around the table in social converse.

A servant brought in a small parcel that looked like a case of jewelry done up in paper, and laid it before the countess.

She smiled, with a deprecating look, as she took it up and opened it and passed it around to her friends for inspection. It was a miniature of the countess herself, painted on ivory. It was a faithful likeness, apparently very recently taken; for, on looking at it, you seemed to see the beautiful countess herself on a diminished scale, or through an inverted telescope.

"It has been making a visit," smiled the countess. "A poor young artist in Edinboro' is getting up a 'Book of Beauty' on his own account. He came here in person to beg the loan of one of my portraits to engrave from. I gave him this, because it was the last I had taken. I gave it to him because a refusal from me would have wounded his feelings and discouraged his enterprise. Otherwise, I assure you, I should not have let him have it for any such purpose as he designed. For the idea of putting my portrait in a 'Book of Beauty' is a rich absurdity."

"Pardon me; I do not see the absurdity at all," said Ishmael earnestly, as in his turn he received the miniature and gazed with admiration on its beautiful features.

"Young gentleman, I am forty-five," said the countess.

Ishmael gave a genuine start of surprise. He knew of course that she must have been of that age, but he had forgotten the flight of time, and the announcement startled him. He soon recovered himself, however, and answered with his honest smile:

"Well, my lady, if you are still beautiful at forty-five, you cannot help it, and you cannot prevent artistic eyes from seeing it. I, as one of your friends, am glad and grateful for it. And I hope you will remain as beautiful in form as in spirit even to the age of seventy-five, or as long after that as you may live in this world."

"Thank you, Mr. Worth. I really do value praise from you, because I know that it is sincere on your part, if not merited on mine," said Lady Hurstmonceux.

Ishmael bowed low and in silence. Then he resumed his contemplation of the picture. And presently he looked up and said:

"Lady Hurstmonceux, I am going to ask you a favor. Will you lend me this picture for a week?"

The countess was a little surprised at the request. She looked up at Ishmael before answering it.

Their eyes met. Some mutual intelligence passed in those meeting glances. And she then answered:

"Yes, Mr. Worth. I will intrust it to you as long as you would like to keep it; without reserve, and without even asking you what you wish to do with it."

Again Ishmael bowed, and then he closed the case of the miniature and deposited it in his breast-pocket.

"I hope that youth is not falling in love with his grandmother. I have heard of such things in my life," thought the judge crossly within himself, for the judge was growing jealous for Claudia. He had apparently forgotten the existence of Bee.

As Ishmael was to leave Cameron Court at a very early hour of the morning, before any of the family would be likely to be up to see him off, he took leave of his friends upon this evening, and retired early to his room to complete his preparations for the journey.

CHAPTER L

ISHMAEL'S ERRAND.

I tell thee, friend, I have not seen

So likely an ambassador of love;

A day in April never came so sweet,

To show that costly summer was at hand.

—Shakespeare.

Ishmael left Edinboro' by the earliest express train for London, where he arrived at nightfall.

He took a cab and drove immediately to Morley's Hotel in the Strand, where Herman Brudenell was stopping.

Carpet-bag in hand, Ishmael was shown into that gentleman's sitting room.

Mr. Brudenell sat writing at a table, but on hearing Mr. Worth announced and seeing him enter, he started up, threw down his pen, and rushed to welcome the traveler.

"My dear, dear boy, a thousand welcomes!" he exclaimed, heartily shaking Ishmael's hands.

"I am very glad to come and see you again, sir. I hope that you are quite well?" said Ishmael, cordially responding to this warm welcome.

"As well as a solitary man can be, my dear boy. How did you leave our friends? In good health, I trust,"

"Yes; in tolerably good health, considering the circumstances. They are of course somewhat shaken by the terrible events of the last few days."

"I should think so. Heaven! what an ordeal to have passed through. Poor Claudia. How has she borne it all?"

"With the most admirable firmness. Claudia-Lady Vincent, I should say—has come out of her fiery trial like refined gold," said Ishmael warmly.

"A fiery trial, indeed. Ishmael, I have read the full account of the Banff tragedy, as they call it, in all the morning papers; no two of them agreeing in all particulars. The account in the 'Times' I hold to be the most reliable; it is at least the fullest—it occupies nearly two pages of that great paper."

"You are right; the account in the 'Times' is the true one."

"But, bless my life, I am keeping you standing here, carpet-bag in hand, all this time! Have you engaged your room?"

"No; they say the house is full."

"Not quite! Mine is a double-bedded chamber. You shall share it with me, if you like. What do you say?"

"Thank you, I should like it very much."

"Come in, then, and have a wash and a change of clothes; after which we will have supper. What would you like?"

"Anything at all. I know they cannot send up a bad one here."

Mr. Brudenell touched the bell. The waiter speedily answered it.

"Supper directly, James. Four dozen oysters; a roast fowl; baked potatoes; muffins; a bottle of sherry; and, and, black tea!—that is your milksop beverage, I believe, Ishmael," added Mr. Brudenell, in a low voice, turning to his guest.

"That is my milksop beverage," replied Ishmael good-humoredly.

The waiter went away on his errand. And Mr. Brudenell conducted Ishmael into the adjoining chamber, where the young man found an opportunity of renovating his toilet. When they returned to the sitting room they found the supper served and the waiter in attendance, but it was not until the traveler had done full justice to this meal, and the service was removed, and the waiter was gone, and the father and son were alone together, that they entered upon the confidential topics.

Mr. Brudenell questioned Ishmael minutely upon all the details of the Banff tragedy. And Ishmael satisfied him in every particular. One circumstance in these communications was noticeable—Mr. Brudenell, in all his questionings, never once mentioned the name of the Countess of Hurstmonceux. And even Ishmael avoided bringing it into his answers.

When Mr. Brudenell had learned all that he wanted to know, Ishmael in his turn said:

"I hope, sir, that the business which brought you to England has been satisfactorily settled?"

Mr. Brudenell sighed heavily.

"It has been settled, not very satisfactorily, but after a fashion, Ishmael. I never told you exactly what that business was. I intended to do so; and I will do it now."

Mr. Brudenell paused as if he were embarrassed, and doubtful in what terms to tell so unpleasant a story. Ishmael settled himself to attend.

"It was connected with my mother and sisters, Ishmael. They have been living abroad here for many years, as you have perhaps heard."

"Yes."

"And they have been living far above their means and far above mine. And consequently debts and difficulties and embarrassments have come. Again and again I have made large sacrifices and settled all claims against them. I am sorry to say it of my mother and sisters, Ishmael; but if the truth must be told, their pride and extravagance have ruined them and me, so far as financial ruin goes. If that had been all, it might have been borne. But there was worse to come. About a year ago my sister Eleanor—who had reached an age when single women begin to despair of marriage—formed the acquaintance of a disreputable scoundrel, one Captain Dugald, a younger brother, I hear, of the present Earl of Hurstmonceux—"

"Captain Dugald! I have heard of him!" exclaimed Ishmael.

"No doubt, most people have. He is rather a notorious character. Well, my infatuated sister took a fancy to the fellow; misled him into the belief that she was the mistress of a large fortune; and played her cards so skillfully that—well, in a word, the handsome scamp ran off with her, or rather she ran off with him; for she seems all through to have taken the initiative in her own ruin."

"But I do not understand why she should have run off? She was of ripe age and her own mistress. Who was there to run from?"

"Her mother, her mother; who could not endure the sight of Captain Dugald, and who had forbidden him her house."

"Ah!"

"Well, they were married at Liverpool. He took her to the United States. At my mother's request I followed them there to reclaim my sister, for report said that the captain had already another wife when he married Eleanor. This report, however, I have ascertained to be without foundation. I could not find them in the United States, and soon gave up the search. Captain Dugald had no love for my sister. He appears to have treated her brutally from the first hour that he got her into his power. And when he learned that she had deceived him,—deceived him in every way, in regard to her fortune, in regard to her age, in regard to her very beauty, which was but the effect of skillful dress,—he conceived a disgust for her, abused her shamefully, and finally abandoned her in poverty, in sickness, and in debt."

"Poor, unhappy lady; what else could she have expected? She must have been mad," said Ishmael.

"Mad—madness don't begin to explain it. She must have been possessed of a devil. When thus left, she sold a few miserable trinkets of jewelry his cupidity had spared her, and took a steerage passage in one of our steamers and followed him back to England; but here lost sight of him, for it seems that he is somewhere on the Continent. She came to my mother's house in London in the condition of a beggar, knowing that she was a pauper, and fearing that she was not a wife. In this state of affairs my mother wrote, summoning me to her assistance. I came over as you know. I have ascertained that my sister's marriage is a perfectly legal one; but I have not succeeded in finding her scoundrel of a husband and bringing him to book. He is still on the Continent somewhere; hiding from his creditors, it is said."

"And his unhappy wife?"

"Is on her voyage to America. I have sent them all home, Ishmael. They must live quietly at Brudenell Hall."

"But now that the Viscount Vincent is dead, and Captain Dugald becomes the heir presumptive to the earldom of Hurstmonceux, his prospects are so much improved that I should think he would return to England without fear of annoyance from his creditors; such gentry being usually very complaisant to the heirs of rich earldoms."

"I doubt if he will live to inherit the title and estate, Ishmael. He is nearly eaten up by alcohol. Eleanor, I know, will not live long. She is in the last stage of consumption. Her repose at Brudenell Hall may alleviate her sufferings, but cannot save her life," said Mr. Brudenell sadly. "I have only waited until your business here should be concluded, Ishmael, in order to return thither myself. You have nothing more to do. however, but to act for Judge Merlin in this matter of restitution, and then you will be ready to go, I presume."

"Yes; I have something else to do, sir. I have to expose a villain, to vindicate a lady, and to reconcile a long-estranged pair," replied Ishmael, in a nervous tone, yet with smiling eyes.

"Why, what have you been doing but just those things? What was Lord Vincent? What was Claudia? What was your part in that affair? Never, since the renowned Knight of Mancha, the great Don Quixote, lived and died, has there been so devoted a squire of dames, so brave a champion of the wronged, as yourself, Ishmael," said Mr. Brudenell.

"You may laugh, but you shall not laugh me out of my next enterprise, or 'adventure,' as the illustrious personage you have quoted would call it. And, by the way, do you know anything of a fellow-passenger of ours in the late voyage, the German Jew, Ezra Isaacs?"

"No; why?"

"I need him in the prosecution of this adventure."

"I have not seen him since we parted at Liverpool. I know nothing whatever about him."

"Well, then, after I have been at the chambers of Messrs. Hudson, I must go to Scotland Yard, and put the affair in the hands of the detectives, for have Isaacs hunted up I must."

"Is he the villain you are about to expose?"

"No; but he has been the tool of that villain, and I want him for a sort of state's evidence against his principal."

"Ah! I wish you joy of your adventure, Ishmael. It reminds one forcibly of the windmills," said Mr. Brudenell.

Ishmael laughed good-humoredly.

"I think it will do so, sir, when you find that the objects that you have been mistaking for giants are only windmills after all," he said.

"I do not understand you, my dear fellow."

Ishmael took from his breast-pocket the miniature of the Countess of Hurstmonceux, and opening it and gazing upon it, he said:

"This is the likeness of the injured lady whose honor I have sworn to vindicate."

"Is it Claudia's?" inquired Mr. Brudenell, stretching his hand for it.

"No. it is not Lady Vincent's. Pardon me, upon second thoughts, sir. I wish to tell you this lady's story before I show you her portrait," answered Ishmael, shutting the case and returning it to his pocket.

Mr. Brudenell sat back, looking puzzled and attentive.

"This lady was the young and beautiful widow of an aged peer. She was as pure and noble as she was fair and lovely. She was sought in marriage by many attractive suitors; but in vain, for she would not bestow her hand where she could not bestow her heart. Among the most persevering of these suitors was a profligate fortune-hunter, who, as the near relative of her late husband, had the entre into her house—"

"Ah! I think I have heard this story before," said Mr. Brudenell, with the slightest possible sneer on his handsome lip.

"One side of it, sir, the false side. Hear the other, and the true one. The beautiful widow repulsed this suitor in disgust, and peremptorily forbade him the house. Determined not to be baffled, he resorted to a stratagem that should have sent him to the hulks—that did, in fact, banish him from all decent society. Are you listening, sir?"

"With all my soul," said Mr. Brudenell, whose mocking sneer had disappeared before an earnest interest.

"By tempting the cupidity of a poor kinsman, who was a member of the young widow's family, he managed to get himself secretly admitted to her house and concealed in her dressing room, whose front windows overlooked the street. In the morning this man opened one of these windows, and stood before it half-dressed, in full view of the street, brushing his hair for the entertainment of the passers-by. The glare of light from the open window, shining through the open door into the adjoining bedchamber of the sleeping beauty, awakened her. At sight of the sacrilegious intruder, she was so struck with consternation that she could not speak. He took advantage of his position and her panic, to press his repugnant suit. He plead that his ardent passion and her icy coldness had driven him to desperation and to extremity. He argued that all stratagems were fair in love. He begged her to forgive him and to marry him, and warned her that her reputation was irretrievably compromised if she did not do so."

Ishmael paused, and looked to see what effect this story was having upon Mr. Brudenell. Herman Brudenell was listening with breathless interest.

Ishmael continued, speaking earnestly, for his heart was in his theme:

"But the beautiful and spirited young widow was not one to be terrified into a measure that her soul abhorred. Her first act, on recovering the possession of her senses, was to ring the bell and order the ejectment of the intruder; and despite his attempts at explanation and remonstrance, this order was promptly obeyed, and the lady never saw him afterward. Soon after this she left Edinboro' for the south of England. At Brighton she met with a gentleman who afterward became her husband. But ah! this gentleman, some time subsequent to their marriage, received a one-sided account of that affair in Edinboro'. He was then young, sensitive, and jealous. He believed all that was told him; he asked no explanation of his young wife; he silently abandoned her. And she—faithful to the one love of her life—has lived through all her budding youth and blooming womanhood in loneliness and seclusion, passing her days in acts of charity and devotion. Circumstances have lately placed in my power the means of vindicating this lady's honor, even to the satisfaction of her unbelieving husband."

Ishmael paused, and looked earnestly into the troubled face of Herman Brudenell.

"Ishmael," he exclaimed, "of course I have known all along that you have been speaking of my wife, Lady Hurstmonceux. If you have not been deceived; if the truth is just what it has been represented to you to be; if she was indeed innocent of all complicity in that nocturnal visit; then, Ishmael, I have done her a great, an unpardonable, an irreparable wrong."

"You have done that lovely lady great wrong indeed, sir; but not an unpardonable, not an irreparable one. She will be as ready to pardon as you to offer reparation. And in her lovely humility she will never know that there has been anything to pardon. Angels are not implacable, sir. If you doubt my judgment in this matter, look on her portrait now," said Ishmael, taking her miniature once more from his coat-pocket, opening it, and laying it before Herman Brudenell.

Mr. Brudenell slowly raised it, and wistfully gazed upon it.

"Is it a faithful portrait, Ishmael?" he asked.

"So faithful that it is like herself seen through a diminishing glass."

"She is very, very beautiful—more beautiful even than she was in her early youth," said Mr. Brudenell, thoughtfully gazing upon the miniature.

"Yes, I can imagine that she is more beautiful now than she was in her early youth; more beautiful with the heavenly beauty of the spirit added to the earthly beauty of the flesh. Look at that picture, dear sir; fancy those charming features, living, smiling, speaking, and you will be better able to judge how beautiful is your wife. Oh, sir! I think that in the times past you never loved that sweet lady as she deserved to be loved; but if you were to meet her now, you would love her as you never loved her before."

"If I were to meet her? Why, supposing that I have wronged her as much as you say, how could I ever venture to present myself before her?"

"How could you ever venture? Oh, sir! because she loves you. There are women, sir, who love but once in all their lives, and then love forever. The Countess of Hurstmonceux is one of these. Sir, since I have lived in daily companionship with her, I have been led to study her with affectionate interest. I have read her life as a wondrous poem. Her soul has been filled with one love. Her heart is the shrine of one idol. And oh, sir! believe me the future holds no hope of happiness so sweet to that lovely lady as a reunion with the husband of her youth."

"Ah, Ishmael! if I could believe this, my own youth would be restored; I should have a motive to live. You said, just now, that in the old sad times I had not loved this lady as she deserved to be loved. No—I married her hastily, impulsively—flattered by her evident preference for me; and just as I was beginning to know all her worth and beauty, lo! this fact of the nocturnal sojourn of the profligate Captain Dugald came to my knowledge—came to my knowledge with a convincing power, beyond all possibility of questioning. Oh, you see, I discovered the bare fact, without the explanation of it! I believed myself the dupe of a clever adventuress, and my love was nipped in the bud. If I could believe otherwise now,—if I could believe that she was innocent in that affair, and that she has loved me all these years, and been true to that love, and is ready and willing to forgive and forget the long, sorrowful past,—Ishmael, instead of being the most desolate, I should be the most contented man alive. I should feel like a shipwrecked sailor, long tossed about on the stormy sea, arriving safe at home at last!" said Mr. Brudenell, gazing most longingly upon the picture he held in his hand.

Ishmael was too wise to interrupt that contemplation by a single word at this moment.

"The thought that such a woman as this, Ishmael,—so richly endowed in beauty of form and mind and heart,—should be my loving companion for life, seems to me too great a hope for mortal man to indulge."

Ishmael did not speak.

"But here is the dilemma, my dear boy! either she did deceive me, or she did not. If she did deceive me, lovely as she is, I wish never to see her again. If she did not deceive me, then I have wronged her so long and so bitterly that she must wish never to see me again!" sighed Mr. Brudenell, as he mournfully closed the case of the miniature.

Then Ishmael spoke:

"Oh, sir! I have resolved to vindicate the honor of this lady, and I will do it. Soon I will have the German Jew, Ezra Isaacs, looked up; for he it was who, tempted by the false representations of Captain Dugald, secretly admitted him to her house and concealed him in her dressing room. And he shall be brought to confess it. Then you will see, sir, the perfect innocence of the countess. And for the rest, if you wish to prove her undiminished love; her perfect willingness to forget the past; her eagerness for a reconciliation—go to her, prove it all; and, oh, sir, be happier in your sober, middle age than ever you hoped to be, even in your sanguine youth."

The young man spoke so fervently, so strongly, so earnestly that Mr. Brudenell seized his hand, and gazing affectionately in his eloquent face, said:

"What a woman's advocate you are, Ishmael!" "It is because a woman's spirit has hovered over me, from the beginning of my life, I think."

"Your angel mother's spirit, Ishmael. Ah, brighter, and sweeter and dearer than all things in my life, is the memory of that pastoral poem of my boyish love. It is the one oasis in the desert of my life."

"Forget it, dear sir; forget it all. Think of your boyhood love as an angel in heaven, and love her only so. Do this for the sake of that sweet lady who has a right to your exclusive earthly devotion."

"Oh strange, and passing strange, that Nora's son should advocate the cause of Nora's rival!" said Herman Brudenell wonderingly.

"Not Nora's rival, sir. An angel in heaven, beaming in the light of God's smile, can never have a rival—least of all, a rival in a pilgrim of this earth. For the rest, if Nora's son speaks, it is because Nora's spirit inspires him," said Ishmael solemnly.

"Your life, indeed, seems to have been angel-guided, and your counsels angel-inspired, Ishmael; and they shall guide me. Yes, Nora's son; in this crisis of my fate your hand shall lead me. And I know that it will lead me into a haven of rest."

Soon after this the father and son retired for the night.

Ishmael, secure in his own happy love and easy in his blameless conscience, soon fell asleep.

Herman Brudenell lay awake, thinking over all that he had heard; blaming himself for his share of the sorrowful past, and seeing always the figure of the beautiful countess in her years of lonely widowhood. It is something for a solitary and homeless man, like Herman Brudenell, to discover suddenly that he has for years been the sole object of a good and beautiful woman's love, and to know that a home as happy and a wife as lovely as his youthful imagination ever pictured were now waiting to receive him, if he would come and take possession.

Early the next morning Ishmael arose, refreshed, from a good night's rest; but Mr. Brudenell got up, weary, from a sleepless pillow.

It was to be a busy day with Ishmael, so, after a hasty breakfast, he took a temporary leave of Mr. Brudenell and set out. His first visit was to the chambers of the Messrs. Hudson, solicitors, Burton Street, Piccadilly. Where all parties are agreed business must be promptly dispatched, despite of even the law's proverbial delays. The Earl of Hurstmonceux and Judge Merlin were quite agreed in this affair of restitution, and therefore their attorneys could have little trouble.

As the reader knows, upon the marriage of the Viscount Vincent and Claudia Merlin, there had been no settlements; therefore the whole of the bride's fortune became the absolute property of the bridegroom. Subsequently, Lord Vincent had died intestate; therefore Claudia as his widow would have been legally entitled to but a portion of that very fortune she herself had brought to him in marriage; all the rest falling to the viscount's family, or rather to its representative, the Earl of Hurstmonceux. It was this legal injustice that the earl wished to rectify, by making over to Lady Vincent all his right, title, and interest in the estate left by the deceased Lord Vincent. This business he had intrusted to his solicitors, giving them full power to act in his name, and Ishmael, with the concurrence of Judge Merlin, made it his business to see that every binding, legal form was observed in the transfer, so that Lady Vincent should rest undisturbed in her possessions by any grasping heir that might succeed the Earl of Hurstmonceux.

When this arrangement with the Messrs. Hudson was satisfactorily completed, Ishmael entered a cab and drove to Scotland Yard. He succeeded in obtaining an immediate interview with Inspector Meadows, to whose hands he committed the task of looking up the German Jew, Ezra Isaacs. Next he drove to Broad Street, to the agency of a celebrated line of ocean steamers. After looking over their programme of steamers advertised to sail, and reading the list of passengers booked for each, he found that he could engage berths for his whole party in a fine steamer to sail that day fortnight, from Liverpool for New York. He secured the berths by paying the passage money down and taking tickets at once. Finally, he re- entered the cab and drove back to his hotel. He found that Mr. Brudenell had walked out. That did not surprise Ishmael. Mr. Brudenell generally did walk out. Like all homeless, solitary, and unoccupied men, Mr. Brudenell had formed rambling habits; and had he been a degree or so lower in the social scale, he must have been classed among the vagrants.

Ishmael sat down in the unoccupied parlor to write to Judge Merlin. He told the judge of the satisfactory completion of his business with the solicitors of the Earl of Hurstmonceux; and that he had the documents effecting the restitution of Lady Vincent's property in his own safe-keeping; that he did not like to trust them to the mail, but would bring them in person when. he should return to Edinboro', which would be as soon as a little affair that he had in hand could be arranged; and he hinted that Mr. Brudenell would probably accompany him to Scotland. Finally, he informed the judge that he had engaged passages for their party in the ocean mail steamer "Columbus," to sail on Saturday, the 15th, from Liverpool for New York. He ended with sending affectionate respects to Lady Vincent and the Countess of Hurstmonceux. Being anxious to catch the afternoon mail at the last moment, Ishmael did not intrust the delivery of this letter to the waiters of the hotel, but took his hat and hurried out to post it himself. By paying the extra penny exacted for late letters he got it into the mail and then walked back to the hotel.

Mr. Brudenell had returned, and at the moment of Ishmael's entrance he was in solemn consultation with the waiter about the dinner. After dinner that day Ishmael went out to visit the tower of London, to him the most interesting of all the ancient buildings in that ancient city. At night he went with Mr. Brudenell to the old classic Drury Lane Theater to see Kean in "Richard III." After that intellectual festival they returned to Morley's to supper and to bed. On Sunday morning they attended divine service at St. Paul's. The next morning, Ishmael, with Mr. Brudenell, paid a visit to Westminster Abbey, where the tombs of the ancient kings and warriors engaged their attention nearly the whole day. It was late in the afternoon when they returned to Morley's, where the first thing Ishmael heard was that a person was waiting for him in the parlor.

Mr. Brudenell went directly to his chamber to change his dress, but Ishmael repaired to the parlor, where he expected to see someone from Scotland Yard.

He found the German Jew sitting there.

"Why, Isaacs? Is this you, already? I am very glad to see you! Mr. Meadows sent you, I suppose?" said Ishmael, advancing and shaking hands with his visitor.

"Mishter Meators? Who is he? No, Mishter Meators tit not zend me here; no one tit; I gome myzelf. I saw your name in te list of arrivals at dish house, bublished in tish morningsh babers. Ant I zaid—dish is te name of von drue shentlemans; ant I'll gall to see him; and here I am," replied the Jew, cordially returning Ishmael's shake of the hand.

"Thank you, Isaacs, for your good opinion of me. Sit down. I have been very anxious to see you, to speak to you on a subject that I must broach at once, lest we should be interrupted before we have discussed it," said Ishmael, who was desirous of bringing Isaacs to confession before the entrance of Mr. Brudenell.

"Sbeak ten!" said the Jew, settling himself in the big armchair.

"Isaacs, you had a beautiful kinswoman of whom you used to speak to me on our voyage; but you never told me her name," said Ishmael gravely, seating himself near the Jew.

"Titn't I, verily? Vell, her name vas Berenice, daughter of Zillah; Zillah vas mine moder's shister, and vas very fair to look upon. She marriet mit a rish Lonton Shew, and tiet leafing von fair daughter Berenice, mine kinsvoman, who marriet mit an English lort; very olt, very boor, put very mush in love mit my kinsvoman. He marriet her pecause zhe vas fair to look upon and very rish; her fader made her marry him pecause he vas a lort; he zoon tied and left her a witow, ant zhe never marriet again; zhe left te country and vas away many years ant I have nod zeen her zince. My fair kinswoman! Zhe hat a great wrong done her!" said the Jew, dropping his chin upon his chest and falling into sad and penitential reverie.

"Yes, Isaacs," said Ishmael, rising and laying his hand solemnly on the breast of the Jew. "Yes, Isaacs, she had a great wrong done her, a greater wrong than even you can imagine; a wrong so great in its devastating effects upon her life that you cannot even estimate its enormity! But, Isaacs, you can do something to right this wrong!"

"I! Fader Abraham, what can I?" exclaimed the Jew, impressed and frightened by the earnestness of Ishmael's words.

"You can make a full disclosure of the circumstances under which the miscreant Dromlie Dugald obtained access to Lady Hurstmonceux's private apartments."

The Jew gazed up in the young man's face, as though he was unable to withdraw his eyes; he seemed to be held spellbound by the powerful magnetism of Ishmael's spirit.

"Isaacs," continued the young man, "whatever may be the nature of these disclosures, I promise you that you shall be held free of consequences-I promise you; and you know the value of my promise."

The Jew did not answer and did not remove his eyes from the earnest, eloquent face of Ishmael.

"So you see, Isaacs, that your disclosures, while they will deliver the countess from the suspicions under which her happiness has drooped for so many years, can do you no injury And now, Isaacs, I ask you, as man speaking to man, a question that I adjure you to answer, as you shall answer at that great day of account, when quick and dead shall stand before the bar of God, and the secret of all hearts shall be revealed—did you admit Dromlie Dugald to the private apartments of the Countess of Hurstmonceux, without the knowledge or the consent of her ladyship?"

"Cot forgive me, I tit!" exclaimed the Jew, in a low terrified voice.

"That will do, Isaacs," said Ishmael, ringing the bell.

A waiter came.

"Is there an unoccupied sitting room that I can have the use of for a short time?" inquired Ishmael.

"Yes, sir."

"Show me to it immediately, then."

The waiter led the way, and Ishmael, beckoning the Israelite to accompany him, followed to a comfortable little parlor, warmed by a bright little fire, such as they kept always ready for chance guests.

"Writing materials, James," said Ishmael.

The man went for them; and while he was gone, Ishmael said:

"We might have been interrupted in the other room, Isaacs; that is the reason why I have brought you here."

When the waiter had returned with the writing materials, and arranged them on the table, and again had withdrawn from the room, Ishmael drew a chair to the table, seated himself, took a pen, and said:

"Now Isaacs, sit down near me, and relate, as faithfully as you can, all the circumstances attending the concealment of Dromlie Dugald in Lady Hurstmonceux's apartments."

The Jew, as if acting under the spell of a powerful spirit, did as he was ordered. He drew a chair to the table, seated himself opposite Ishmael, and—to use a common phrase—"made a clean breast of it."

I will not attempt to give his confession in detail. I will only give the epitome of it. He acknowledged that he had been bribed by Captain Dugald to favor his (the captain's) addresses to the beautiful young widow. But he solemnly declared that he had supposed himself to be acting as much for the lady's good as for his own interest, when he took the captain's money and admitted him freely to the house of his kinswoman, where he himself was staying, a temporary guest, and where he received her suitor as his visitor.

Farther, he more solemnly declared that on that fatal evening when he secretly admitted the captain to the house, and guided him to the boudoir of the countess, he had not the remotest suspicion of the nefarious purpose of the suitor. He thought Dugald merely wished for an opportunity for pressing his suit. He had no idea that the unscrupulous villain designed to conceal himself in the closet of the dressing room, and so pass the night in Lady Hurstmonceux's apartments, and show himself in the morning in dishabille at her open window, for the benefit of all the passengers through the street.

He affirmed that when in the morning he heard of this infamous abuse of confidence on the part of his patron, he had not had courage to meet his kinswoman at breakfast, but had decamped from the house in great haste, and had never seen the countess since that eventful day.

He said that he had heard how much she had suffered from the affair, at least for a short time; and that afterwards he had heard she had left the country; that he had since supposed the whole circumstance had been forgotten, and he did not even now understand how his disclosures should serve her, since no one now remembered the escapade of Captain Dugald.

As Isaacs spoke, Ishmael took down the statement in writing. When it was finished he turned to the Jew and said:

"You are mistaken in one thing—nay, indeed, in two things, Isaacs! The first is, in the supposition that your disclosures cannot now serve the countess, since the world has long ago done her full justice. It is true that the world has done her full justice, for there is no lady living more highly esteemed than is the Countess of Hurstmonceux. So if the world were only in question, Isaacs, I need never have troubled you to speak. But there is an individual in question; and this brings me to your second mistake in the matter; namely, in the supposition that the countess never married again. She did marry again; hut, a few months subsequent to her marriage, her husband heard the story of Captain Dugald's adventure, as it was then circulated and believed; and he thought himself the dupe of a cunning adventuress, and estranged himself from his wife from that day until this."

"Fader Abraham!" exclaimed the Jew, raising both his hands in consternation.

"Providence has lately put me in possession of all the facts in this case, and has enabled me to pave the way for a reconciliation between the long-severed pair—supposing that you will have the moral courage to do your kinswoman justice."

"Fader Abraham, I vill do her shustice! I vill do her more as shustice. I vill tell te whole truth. I vill tell more as te whole truth, and shwear to it. I vill do anyding. I vould do anyding alt te time, if I had known it," said the Jew earnestly.

"Thank you, Isaacs, I only want the simple truth; more than that would do us harm instead of good. This is the simple truth, I hope, that I have taken down from your lips?"

"Yesh, tat ish te zimple truth!"

"I will read the whole statement to you, Isaacs, and then you will be able to see whether I have taken down your words correctly," said Ishmael. And he took up the manuscript and read it carefully through, pausing frequently to give the Jew an opportunity of correcting him, if necessary.

"Dat ish all right," said Isaacs, when the reading was finished.

"Now sign it, Isaacs."

The Jew affixed his signature.

"Now, Isaacs that is all I want of you for the present; but should you be required to make oath to the truth of this, I suppose that you will be found ready to do so."

"Fader Abraham! yes, I vill do anyding at all, or anyding else, to serve mine kinswoman," said the Jew, rising.

"Thank you, Isaacs. Now tell me where I shall find you, in case you shall be wanted?"

"I am lotging mit mine frient, Samuel Phineas, Butter Lane, Burrough."

"I will remember. Thank you, Isaacs. You have done your kinswoman and her friends good service. She will be grateful to you. I have no doubt she will send for you. Would you like to come to her?"

"Mit all my feet. Vere ish she?"

"At her country-seat, Cameron Court, near Edinboro'."

"I ton't know id."

"No, you don't know it. It is a comparatively recent purchase of her ladyship, I believe," said Ishmael, rising to accompany the Jew from the room.

As they went out they rang the bell, to warn the waiter that they had evacuated the apartment. In the hall Isaacs bade him good-afternoon, and Ishmael turned into the sitting room occupied in common by himself and Mr. Brudenell. He found the table laid for dinner and Mr. Brudenell walking impatiently up and down the floor.

"Ah, you are there! I was afraid you would be late, and the fish and the soup would be spoiled, but here you are in the very nick of time," he said, as he touched the bell. "Dinner immediately," he continued, addressing himself to the waiter, who answered his summons. But it was not until after dinner was over, and the cloth removed, and Mr. Brudenell had finished his bottle of claret and smoked out his principe, that Ishmael told him of his interview with Isaacs, and laid the written statement of the Jew before him. Mr. Brudenell read it carefully through, with the deepest interest. When he had finished it, he slowly folded it up and placed it in his breast pocket, dropped his head upon his chest, and remained in deep thought and perfect silence.

After the lapse of a few moments Ishmael spoke:

"If you think it needful, sir, Isaacs is ready to go before a magistrate and make oath to the truth of that statement."

"It is not needful, Ishmael; I have not the least doubt of its perfect truth. It is not of that I am thinking; but—of my wife. How will she receive me? One thing is certain, that having deeply injured her, I must go to her and acknowledge the wrong and ask her forgiveness. But, oh, Ishmael, what atonement will that be for years of cruel injustice and abandonment? None, none! No, I feel that I can make her no atonement," said Mr. Brudenell bitterly.

"No, sir; you can make her no atonement, but—you can make her happy. And that is all she will need," said Ishmael gravely and sweetly.

"If I thought I could, Ishmael, I would hasten to her at once. In any case, however, I must go to her, acknowledge the wrong I have done her and ask for pardon. But, ah! how will she receive me?"

"Only go and see for yourself, sir, I implore you," said Ishmael earnestly.

"When do you return to Scotland, Ishmael?"

"When you are ready to accompany me, sir; I am waiting only for you," answered Ishmael, smiling.

"Then we will go by the early express train to-morrow morning," said Mr. Brudenell.

"Very well, sir; I shall be ready," smiled Ishmael.

Mr. Brudenell rang for tea. And when it was set on the table he ordered the waiter to call him at five o'clock the next morning, to have his bill ready, and get a fly to the door to take them to the Great Northern Railroad Station in time to meet the six o'clock express train for Edinboro'.

After tea the two gentlemen remained conversing some little time longer, and then retired to their bed-chamber, where, being without the help and hindrance of a valet, they packed their own portmanteaus. And then they went to bed early in order to secure a long and good night's rest, preparatory to their proposed journey of the next morning.

CHAPTER LII

THE MEETING OF THE SEVERED PAIR.

For she is wise, if I can judge of her;

And fair she is, if that mine eyes be true;

And true she is as she hath proved herself;

And therefore like herself, wise, fair, and true

She shall be placed within my constant soul.

—Shakspeare

Ishmael and Mr. Brudenell arose before the waiter called them. They dressed quickly, rang, and ordered breakfast, and had time to eat it leisurely before the hour at which the cab was ordered to take them to the railway station. They caught the six o'clock express on the point of starting, and had just settled themselves comfortably in a first-class carriage when the train moved.

There is a difference in the time kept even by express trains. This one seemed to be the fastest among the fast, since it steamed out of the London station at six in the morning and steamed into the Edinboro' station at four in the afternoon.

Ishmael called a cab for himself and fellow-traveler. And when they had taken their seats in it, he gave the order, "To Magruder's Hotel." And the cab started.

"I think, sir," said the young man to the elder, "as we are in such good time, we had better go to my rooms at Magruder's and renovate our toilets before driving out to Cameron Court and presenting ourselves to Lady Hurstmonceux."

"Yes, yes, certainly, Ishmael; for really I think after that dusty, smoky, cindery day's journey we should be all the better for soap and water and clean clothes. I don't know how I look, my dear fellow, but, not to flatter you, you present the appearance of a very interesting master chimney-sweep!" replied Mr. Brudenell.

Ishmael laughed.

Ah, yes; Herman Brudenell jested on the same principle that people are said to jest on their way to execution. Now, when he was so near Cameron Court and the Countess of Hurstmonceux, how ill at ease he had become; how he dreaded, yet desired, the interview that was to decide his fate.

The distance between the railway station and Magruder's Hotel was so short that it was passed over in a few minutes. Ishmael paid and dismissed the cab, and the two gentlemen went in. Ishmael's rooms in that house had never been given up; they had been kept for the use of his party, on their journeyings through the city. He conducted Mr. Brudenell to these rooms, and then ordered luncheon as soon as it could be served, and a fly in half an hour. Twenty minutes they gave to that "renovation" of the toilet advised by Ishmael, ten minutes to a simple luncheon of cold meat and bread, and then they entered the fly.

Ishmael gave the order, "To Cameron Court."

As they moved on Mr. Brudenell said:

"There are several points upon which I would like to consult you, before presenting myself to the countess.'

"Yes, sir," said Ishmael, looking up with a smile full of earnest encouragement.

"But, like all procrastinating natures, I have deferred the task until the last moment."

"There has been no better opportunity than the present, sir."

"That is true. Well, Ishmael, the first doubt that troubles me is this: That I should not, perhaps, intrude upon the countess, without first writing and apprising her of my intended visit. My appearance will be unexpected, startling, even embarrassing to her."

"No, sir, no; trust me it will not. If I have read that gentle lady's heart aright, she has been always hoping to see you; and, with the expectation that is born of hope, she has been always looking for you. No strange, unnatural appearance will you seem to Lady Hurstmonceux, believe me, sir. And, moreover, she has reason to expect you now. Listen, sir. It was on the day after I heard her story of Captain Dugald's midnight visit and the evil it brought her, I begged from her the loan of that miniature which I showed you. And I do think she half suspected the use that I was about to put it to. She loaned it to me freely, without question and without reserve, and she knew at the time that I was going directly to your presence; and finally, on the day before yesterday, when writing to Judge Merlin, I mentioned my hope that you would accompany me to Edinboro'. So you see, sir, Lady Hurstmonceux is not entirely unprepared to receive you."

"Ah, but how will she receive me, Ishmael? And how, indeed, shall I present myself to her?"

"She will welcome you with joy, sir; believe it. But you need not take her by surprise, sir, even supposing that she does not expect you. Indeed, in no event would it be well that you should risk doing so. When we reach Cameron Court you can remain in the fly, while I go in, and to her ladyship alone announce your arrival."

"Thank you, Ishmael. Your plan is a good one and I will adopt it. And now another thing, my dear boy. Ishmael, you have always refused to be publicly acknowledged as my son—"

"You know why, sir; I will not have unmerited reproach thrown upon my sainted mother's memory. She was a martyr to your mistake; it must never be supposed that she was a victim to her own weakness."

"Enough, Ishmael, enough! I will not urge the point, although Heaven only knows how great is the sacrifice I make in resigning the hope that you would take my name and inherit what is left of the family estates. But, there, Ishmael, I will say no more upon that point. You will continue to bear your mother's name—the name that you have already made famous, and that, I feel sure, you will make illustrious. So no more of that. But what I wished particularly to consult you about is the propriety of confiding to the countess the secret of our relationship. Ishmael, it shall be just as you please."

"Then, sir, tell her all. Have no secrets from the countess, she merits all your confidence; but tell her the circumstances under which you married my dear mother, that Nora Worth may be held blameless by her forever," said Ishmael solemnly.

It was strange to hear this middle-aged gentleman seeking counsel from this young man; but so it was that all who were brought within the circle of Ishmael's influence consulted him as an early Christian might have consulted a young St. John. Ishmael had not the experience that only age can bring; but he had that clear, strong, moral and intellectual insight which only purity of heart and life can give, and hence his counsels were always wise and good.

It was six o'clock when the carriage reached Cameron Court. When the carriage drew up before the principal entrance Ishmael observed that Mr. Brudenell had become very much agitated.

"Compose yourself, dear sir; compose yourself with the reflection that it is only a loving woman you are about to meet; a woman who loves you constantly and will welcome you with delight.

Remain here until I go in and announce your visit; then I will return for you," he said, pressing Mr. Brudenell's hand as he left the carriage.

The professor opened the door for Mr. Worth. There was no regular porter at Cameron Court, but Dr. James Morris was acting in that capacity.

"All well, professor?"

"All well, sir. The judge and Lady Vincent have gone out for an airing in the close carriage. We expect them, back to dinner, which will be served presently. You are just in time, sir."

Ishmael was for once glad to hear that the judge and his daughter were absent and that the countess was alone. But then, suddenly he reflected that this latter supposition was not so certain, and he anxiously inquired:

"Is the countess at home, professor?"

"Yes, sir; her ladyship is in the library, reading."

"Alone?"

"Quite alone, sir."

"That will do; I can find her," said Ishmael, ascending the stairs and turning in the direction of the library, which was situated on the first floor.

Berenice, dressed in a rich, but simply made, black velvet robe, with delicate white lace under-sleeves and collar, sat near the centre table before the fire, reading. Her head was bent over her book, and her rich black ringlets fell forward, half shading her beautiful dark face. She raised her eyes when Ishmael entered, and seeing who it was, she threw aside her book and started up to meet him.

"Welcome, Mr. Worth; welcome back again," she said, offering her hand.

Ishmael took that beautiful little brown hand and held it within his own as he said:

"Thank you, Lady Hurstmonceux. I am really very glad to get back. But—"

"What, Mr. Worth?"

"I do not come alone, Lady Hurstmonceux!"

Her countenance suddenly changed. Her voice sank to at whisper as she inquired:

"Who is with you?"

Dropping his voice to the low tone of hers, Ishmael answered:

"Mr. Brudenell."

The countess snatched her hand from his grasp, threw herself into the nearest chair, covered her face with her hands, and so remained for several minutes. At last Ishmael approached and leaned over her, and, speaking in a subdued and gentle voice, said:

"This visit is not wholly unexpected, Lady Hurstmonceux?"

"No, no, Mr. Worth," she murmured, without removing the shield of her hands.

"Nor unwelcome, I hope?"

"No, oh, no!" she said, dropping her hands now and looking up, pale, and faintly smiling.

"You will see him then?" said Ishmael, speaking, as he had spoken throughout the interview, in a low, gentle tone.

"Presently. Give me a little time. Oh, I have waited for him so long, Ishmael," she said, with an involuntary burst of confidence. But then everyone, even the most reserved, confided in Ishmael Worth.

"I have waited for him so long, so long!" she repeated.

"He has come at last, dearest lady; come to devote his life to you, if you will accept the offering," Ishmael murmured, bending over her.

"Oh, Mr. Worth, I am sure that I owe this happiness to you," the countess exclaimed fervently, clasping his hand and holding it while she repeated, "' Blessed are the peacemakers, for they shall be called the children of God.'"

Lowly and reverently Ishmael bowed his head at the hearing of these words.

"Where is he, Mr. Worth?" at length breathed Berenice.

"In the carriage outside, awaiting your pleasure."

"Bring him to me, then," she said, pressing his hand warmly before she relinquished it.

Ishmael returned that pressure, and then went out to speak to Mr. Brudenell.

"Come in, sir. She invites you," he said.

Herman Brudenell stepped out of the carriage and entered with Ishmael. He threw his eyes around upon the magnificence that surrounded him. Was all this really to be his own? the gift of that sweet lady's slighted love? He could scarcely believe it.

Ishmael led him through the halls and upstairs to the library.

"She is in there alone," he whispered.

"Go in with me, Ishmael," whispered the other. But Ishmael shook his head, smiled, opened the door, announced, "Mr. Brudenell, Lady Hurstmonceux," shut it and retired.

Herman Brudenell found himself alone in the library with his long-neglected wife. She was sitting in the armchair, where Ishmael had left her. She arose to meet her visitor; then suddenly turned deadly pale and sunk back in her chair, overcome by her emotions, but even in so sinking she stretched her hands out to him in welcome, in invitation, in entreaty.

Slowly and deferentially he approached this woman, so holy in her immortal love. And dropping on one knee, beside her chair, he bent his head and murmured in a broken voice:

"Berenice, Berenice—can you forgive all these long, long years of cruel injustice?"

"Oh, bless you; bless you, Herman, for coming at last. I am so glad to see you!" she said, drawing his bowed head to her bosom, dropping her face caressingly upon it and bursting into tears. A few minutes passed and he was sitting by her side, with her hand clasped in his, telling her the story of the sinful and sorrowful past, and imploring her forgiveness.

Would she forgive him?

Reader, Berenice was one of those women whom the wisdom of this world can never understand; one of those women who love purely and passionately; who love but once and love forever. She loved Herman Brudenell; and in saying this I answer all questions. She would not acknowledge that she had anything to forgive; she was glad to give him herself and all that she possessed; she was glad to make him the absolute master of her person and her fortune. And in giving all she received all, for as she loved she was happy. After some little time had elapsed, and they had both recovered from the agitation of the meeting, the countess looked up at him and inquired:

"Who is Ishmael Worth? Who is this young man, so stately, yet so gracious? so commanding, yet so meek? who walks among other men as a young king should, but as a young king never does. Who is he?"

"He is my son," said Herman Brudenell, proudly but shyly; "my son, the child of that unfortunate marriage contracted when I supposed that you were lost to me; lost to me in every way, my Berenice. That marriage of which I have already told you. Do you forgive me, for him also, Berenice?"

"I congratulate you on him, for he is a son to be very proud of. I glory in him, for he is now my son also," said this generous woman fervently.

Herman Brudenell raised her hand and pressed it to his lips.

"Oh, Herman, I knew it! I knew it twenty years ago, when I went to the Hill Hut and begged the babe to bring up as my own," she said.

"You did, Berenice? How divinely good you are."

"Good! Why, I only sought my own comfort in the babe. You were lost to me for the time, and your child was the best consolation I could have found. However, his stern kinswoman would not let me have him; would not even let me help him; denied that he was yours, and almost turned me out of doors."

"That was so like Hannah."

"But now at last he is mine; my gifted son. How I shall rejoice in him."

"He is yours, Berenice, as far as the most profound esteem and love can make him yours. But Ishmael will never consent to be publicly acknowledged by me," said Herman Brudenell sorrowfully.

"But why?" inquired the countess, in astonishment.

"For his mother's sake. Ishmael cherishes the most chivalric devotion for his angel mother, and I think also for all mortal women, for her sake. He bears her name, and is fond of it and will ever bear it, that whatever fame he may win in this world may be identified with it. He has vowed, with the blessing of Heaven, to make the name of Worth illustrious, and he will do so."

"A chivalric devotion, truly; and how beautiful it is. He is already, though so young, a distinguished member of the Washington bar, I hear. How did he get his education and his profession—that poor boy, whom I remember in his childhood as tramping the country with the old odd-job man—that very 'professor' who attends him as his servant now? You found him and educated him at last, I suppose, Herman?"

A fiery flush arose to Mr. Brudenell's brow, displacing its habitual paleness.

"No, Berenice, no! Not to me, not to any human being does Ishmael owe education or profession; but to God and to himself alone. Never was a boy born in this world under more adverse circumstances. His birth, in its utter destitution, reminds me (I speak it with the deepest reverence) of that other birth in the manger of Bethlehem. His infancy was a struggle for the very breath of life; his childhood for bread; his youth for education; and nobly, nobly has he sustained this struggle and gloriously has he succeeded. We are yet in our prime, my dear Berenice, and I feel sure that, if we live out the three-score years and ten allotted as the term of human life, we shall see Ishmael at the zenith of human greatness."

So carried away had Mr. Brudenell been in making this tribute to Ishmael that he had forgotten to explain the circumstances that would have exonerated him from the suspicion of having culpably neglected his child. Berenice brought him back to his recollection by saying:

"But I am sure you must have made some provision for this boy; how was it then that he never derived any benefit from it? How was it that he was left from the hour of his birth to suffer the cruelest privations, until the age of seven years, when he began to support himself, and to help support his aunt!"

"You are right, Berenice; I made a provision for him; but I left the country, and he never had the good of it. I will explain how that was by and by; but I believe the loss of it was providential. I believe it was intended from the first that Ishmael should 'owe no man anything,' for life, or bread, or education, or profession; but all to God and God's blessing on his own efforts. He is self-made. I know no other man in history to whom the term can be so perfectly well applied."

"Will you tell me all you know of his early struggles? I am so interested in this stately son of yours," said Berenice, who, while admiring Ishmael herself, saw also that he was the theme above all others that Mr. Brudenell loved to dwell upon.

Herman Brudenell told the story of Ishmael's heroic young life, as he had gathered it from many sources. And Berenice listened in admiration, in wonder, and sometimes in tears. And yet it was only the plain story of a poor boy who struggled up out of the depths of poverty, shame, and ignorance, to competence, honor, and distinction; a story that may be repeated again in the person of the obscurest boy that reads these lines.

After a little while, given to meditation on what she had heard, Berenice, with her hand still clasped in that of Herman Brudenell, looked up at him and said:

"Your mother and sisters?"

Slowly and sadly Mr. Brudenell shook his head:

"Ah, Berenice! I shall have to tell you now of a family self marred, as a set-off to the boy self-made."

And then he told the grievous story of the decadence of the Brudenell ladies, not, of course, forgetting the mad marriage of Eleanor Brudenell with the profligate Captain Dugald.

While Bernice was still wondering over these family mistakes and misfortunes, a footman opened the door and said:

"My lady, dinner is served."

"Have Judge Merlin and Lady Vincent returned from their drive?" inquired the countess.

"Yes, my lady; the judge and her ladyship are in the drawing room with Mr. Worth."

"Mr. Brudenell, will you give me your arm?" said the countess, rising, with a smile.

Herman Brudenell bowed and complied. And they left the library and passed on to the little drawing room. As they entered they saw Judge Merlin, Ishmael, and Claudia standing, grouped in conversation, near the fire.

The situation of this long-severed and suddenly reunited pair was certainly rather embarassing, especially to the lady; and to almost any other one it would have been overwhelming. But Berenice was a refined, cultivated, and dignified woman of society; such a woman never loses her self-possession; she is always mistress of the situation. Berenice was so now. But for the bright light in her usually pensive dark eyes, and the rosy flush on her habitually pale cheeks, there was no difference in her aspect, as, with her hand lightly resting on Mr. Brudenell's arm, she advanced towards the group.

Claudia turned around, not altogether in surprise, for Ishmael had thoughtfully prepared them all for this new addition to the family circle.

"Lady Vincent, I believe you have already met my husband, Mr. Brudenell," said the countess, gravely presenting him to her guest. And the form of her words purposely revealed the reconciliation that had just been sealed.

"Oh, yes, I know Mr. Brudenell well, and I am very glad to see him again," said Claudia, offering her hand.

"I had the honor of passing some weeks in Lady Vincent's company at her father's house in Washington," said Mr. Brudenell, gravely bowing. He next turned and shook hands with Judge Merlin. But the old man retained his hand, and took also that of the countess, and as the tears sprang to his aged eyes, he said:

"Dear Brudenell, and dearest lady, I sympathize with you in this reunion with all my heart. May you be very happy; God bless you!" and pressing both their hands, he relinquished them.

Mr. Brudenell and the countess simultaneously bowed in silent acknowledgment of this benediction.

Claudia involuntarily looked up to Ishmael's face; their eyes met—hers betraying the yearning anguish of a famishing heart, and his the most earnest sympathy, the most reverential compassion. Why did Claudia look at him so? Ah! because she could not help it. What was she dreaming of? Perhaps of another possible reunion, that should compensate her for all the woeful past, and bless her in all the happy future.

A moment more, and the folding doors connecting The drawing room with the dining room were thrown open.

"Mr. Brudenell, will you take Lady Vincent in to dinner?" said the countess, with a smile, as she herself gave her hand to Ishmael.

And thus they passed into the dining room.

But for the sadness of one mourning spirit present, the dinner was a pleasant one. And the reunion in the drawing room that evening was calmly happy.

CHAPTER LII

HOME AGAIN.

Home again! home again!

From a foreign shore!

And oh, it fills my heart with joy

To greet my friends once more.

Music sweet! music soft!

Lingers round the place;

And oh, I feel the childhood's charm,

That time cannot efface!

It had been decided in consultation between Judge Merlin and Ishmael that, under existing circumstances, it would be proper for their party to shorten their visit to Cameron Court, and leave the recently reconciled pair to the enjoyment of their own exclusive company.

And accordingly, while they were all seated at luncheon the next day, Wednesday, Judge Merlin announced their departure for Thursday morning.

This announcement was met by a storm of hospitable expostulation. Both the countess and Mr. Brudenell strongly objected to the early departure of their visitors, and urged their prolonged stay.

But, to all this friendly solicitation, the judge replied:

"My dear countess, painful as it will be for us all to leave Cameron Court, there are imperative reasons for our doing so. It is not only that we have engaged our passages on the steamer that sails on the 15th of this month of February, but that unless we really do sail on that day, we shall not have sufficient time to cross the ocean and get into port before the stormy month of March sets in."

"But this is only Wednesday. The 'Columbus' does not sail until Saturday after next. You might stay with us a week longer, and then have abundant time to run down to Liverpool and get comfortably embarked," said the countess.

"Thank you, dear lady; but the truth is, I wish to show my daughter London before we sail," replied the judge.

"The truth is," said the countess, smiling, "that you are all weary of Cameron Court. Well, so I will no longer oppose your departure. Very early in life I learned the twofold duty of hospitality: 'to greet the coming, speed the parting guest.'"

"Lady Hurstmonceux, we are not weary of Cameron Court. On the contrary we are attached to it, warmly attached to it; we have been happier here than we could have been anywhere else, while under our adverse circumstances. And we shall take leave of you, madam, with the deepest regret—regret only to be softened by the hope of seeing you some time in America," said the judge gravely.

The countess bowed and smiled, but did not in any other manner reply.

"Oh, Berenice; dear Berenice! You will come out to see us, some time, will you not?" urged Claudia.

The countess looked toward her husband with that proud, fond deference which loving wives glory in bestowing, and she said:

"When Mr. Brudenell visits his mother and sisters I shall of course accompany him, and we shall spend a portion of our time at Tanglewood, if you will permit us."

"Berenice, Berenice; what words you use! We know how happy we should be to see you," said Claudia.

"And how honored," said the judge.

Lady Hurstmonceux smiled on Claudia and bowed to the judge. And then the circle arose from the luncheon table and dispersed.

That day Ishmael wrote to Bee, announcing the speedy return of himself and his party, and Judge Merlin wrote to his manager, Reuben Gray, to have the house at Tanglewood prepared for the reception of himself and daughter on or before the 1st of March.

Early on Thursday morning our party took a most affectionate leave of their friends at Cameron Court, and set out in one of the countess' carriages for the railway station at Edinboro', which they reached in time to catch the ten o'clock express for London.

A twelve hours' flight southward brought them into that city. It was ten o'clock, therefore, when they ran into the King's Cross Station. There they took a fly to Morley's Hotel, in the Strand, where they arrived about eleven o'clock. They engaged a suite of apartments, and settled themselves there for a week. A very brief epitome must describe their life in London during that short period.

It was Thursday night when they arrived.

On Friday morning they visited the Tower, taking the whole day for the study of that ancient fortress and its awful traditions; and in the evening they went to Drury Lane, to see Kean in "Macbeth."

On Saturday morning they went to Westminster Abbey, and in the evening to Covent Garden.

On Sunday they attended divine service at St. Paul's, morning and afternoon, and they spent the evening at home.

On Monday they visited the two Houses of Parliament, and in the evening they wed to the Polytechnic.

On Tuesday they went over the old prison of Newgate, and in the evening they heard a celebrated philanthropist lecture at Exeter Hall.

On Wednesday they went down to Windsor and went over Windsor Castle, park, and forest, and they spent the evening looking over the illustrated guidebooks that described these places.

On Thursday morning they returned to London, and employed the day in shopping and other preparations for their homeward voyage; and Ishmael, among his more important purchases, did not forget the dolls for little Molly, nor the box of miniature carpenter's tools for Johnny. They passed this last evening of their stay quietly at home.

On Friday morning they left London for Liverpool, where they arrived at nightfall. They put up at the "Adelphi," the hotel favored by all American travelers, and where they found all their national tastes gratified.

Early on Saturday morning they embarked on their homeward-bound steamer and sailed from England. They were blessed with one of the most favorable voyages on record; the wind was fair, the sky was blue, and the sea smooth from the beginning to the end of their voyage, and on the evening of the tenth day out they ran safely into the harbor of New York. This was Thursday, the 25th of February.

The evening mail for the South had not yet gone; and, while waiting in the office of the Custom House, Ishmael wrote to Bee, announcing the safe arrival of his party; and the judge dashed off a few lines to Reuben Gray, warning him to have all things ready to receive the returning voyagers.

Only one night they rested in the city, and then on Friday morning they left New York, taking the shortest route to Tanglewood—namely, by railroad as far as Baltimore, and then by steamboat to Shelton, on the Potomac.

Our whole party landed at Shelton on Saturday evening. The judge dispatched a messenger on horseback from the little hotel to Tanglewood, to order Reuben Gray to have the fires kindled and supper ready against their arrival, and then, after some little search,—for the hamlet boasted few hackney coaches,—they found a carriage for the judge and his companions and a wagon for the servants and the luggage. It was nine o'clock when they reached Tanglewood.

Hannah and Reuben were standing out under the starlight, listening for the sound of wheels, and they ran forward to greet them as they alighted from the carriage.

"Oh, welcome; welcome home, sir! Thank God, I receive you safe again!" exclaimed Reuben Gray, as he grasped the judge's extended hand and wept for joy.

"Thank you, thank you, Gray. I'm happy to be home once more."

"Oh, my boy; my boy! Do I see you again? Do I really see you again? Thank Heaven; oh, thank Heaven!" cried Hannah, bursting into a passion of tears, as she threw her arms around Ishmael's neck and was pressed to his affectionate heart.

"God bless you, dear Aunt Hannah! I am very glad to come to you again? How are the little ones?"

"Oh, as well as possible, dear."

"Speak to Lady Vincent," whispered Ishmael.

"Madam, I am very glad to see you home once more, but sorry to see you in such deep mourning," said Hannah respectfully.

Judge Merlin then hurried the whole party out of the biting winter air into the house. Here they found all ready for them; the fires kindled, the rooms warmed, the tables set in the comfortable parlor, and the supper ready to be dished. They took time only to make a very slight toilet in their well-warmed chambers, and then they went down to supper. The judge insisted that Hannah and Reuben should join them on this occasion and remain their guests for the evening. And what a happy evening it was. After all their weary wanderings, perils and sorrows in foreign lands, how delightful to be at home once more in their dear native country, gathered together under one beloved roof, and lovingly served by their own affectionate domestics. Ah! one must lose all these blessings for a while, in order to truly to enjoy them.

How earnest was the thanksgiving in the grace uttered by the judge as they all gathered around the supper table! How earnest was the amen silently responded by each heart!

After supper they all went into the well warmed and lighted crimson drawing room. And Claudia sat down before her grand piano, and tried its keys. From long disuse it was somewhat out of tune, certainly; but her fingers evoked from those keys a beautiful prelude, and her voice rose in that simple, but soul-stirring little ballad, "Home Again."

As she sang Ishmael came up behind her, turned the leaves of her music book, and accompanied her in his rich bass voice. At the end of that one song she arose and closed her piano.

"Thank you, my dear," said the judge, drawing his daughter to him and kissing her cheek. "Your song was very appropriate; there is not one here who could not enter into its sentiment with all his heart."

Slowly and sadly Claudia bowed her head; and then she passed on to one of the side tables, took up a lighted bedroom candle, bade them all good-night and retired.

Reuben and Hannah, who on this occasion, at Judge Merlin's request, had remained in the drawing room, now arose and took a respectful leave. And soon after this, Ishmael and the judge separated and retired to their respective chambers.

Ishmael was shown into that one which he had occupied during that eventful first sojourn at Tanglewood. How full of the most interesting associations, the most tender memories, that chamber was. There was the bed upon which he had lain for weeks, a mangled sufferer for Claudia's sake. There was the very same armchair she had sat in hour after hour by his side, beguiling the tedious days of convalescence by talking with him, reading to him, or singing and playing to him on her guitar. Sigh after sigh burst from Ishmael's bosom as he remembered these times. He went to bed, but could not sleep; he lay awake, meditating and praying.

While Ishmael in his lonely chamber prayed, another scene was going on in another part of the house.

Old Katie was holding a reception in the kitchen. All the house servants, all the field laborers, and all the neighboring negroes—bond and free, male and female—were assembled at Tanglewood that night to welcome Katie and her companions home and hear their wondrous adventures in foreign lands.

Katie, in the most gorgeous dress of Scotch plaid, that displayed the most brilliant tints of scarlet, blue and yellow, purple, orange, and green, with a snow-white turban on her head and a snow-white kerchief around her neck, with broad gold ear-rings in her ears and thick gold finger-rings on her fingers—sat in the seat of honor, the chip-bottom armchair, and, for the benefit of the natives, delivered a lecture on the manners and customs of foreign nations, illustrated by her own experiences among them.

Now, if Katie had only related the plain facts of her life in Scotland and in the West India Islands, they had been sufficiently interesting to her simple hearers, but Katie exaggerated her adventures, wrongs, and sufferings beyond all hope of pardon.

"I seen the Queen," she said. "She rode about in a silver coach drawed by a hundred milk-white hosses, wid a golden, crown on her head a yard and a half high, and more niggers to wait on her, chillun, dan you could shake sticks at."

The least of her fictions was this:

"Chillun, I was fust kilt dead, den buried alibe, and kept so till wanted; den fotch to life ag'in, and sold to pirates, and took off to de Stingy Isles, and sold ag'in into slabery; arter which Marster Ishmael Worf drapped right down out'n de clear sky inter de middle ob de street, and if you don't beliebe it jes go ax Marse Ishmael hisse'f, as nebber told a falsehood in his life."

"And so he brought you away, Katie?" inquired Reuben's Sam, who was, of course, present.

"Well, I jes reckon he did some! He made dem Stingy Island barbariums stan' roun' now, I tell you, chillun."

Katie went on with her lecture. Her version of the fate of Lord Vincent, Mrs. Dugald, and Frisbie was rather a free one.

"I walked myse'f right 'traight up to de Queen soon as ebber I totched English ground, and told her all about dem gran' willians, and de Queen ordered de execution ob de whole lot. Which dey was all hung up by de neck till dey was dead de berry next mornin'," she said.

"What, all hung so quick, Katie!" exclaimed Sam, in astonishment.

"All hung; ebery single one ob dem. My lordship and de ehamwally and de whited saltpeter. All hung up by de neck till dey was dead, in de middle ob de street, right in de sight ob ebberybody going along, and serbe 'em right and hopes it did 'em good," said Katie emphatically.

"That was quick work, though," said Sam dubiously.

"Quick work? Dey deserbed it quick, and quicker dan dat. Hi, boy, what you talkin' 'bout? Didn't dey kill me dead, and bury me alibe, amd sell me inter slabery? You'spect how de Queen gwine let sich going on go on while she's de mis'tess ob England? No,'deed; not arter she see all dey made me suffer," exploded Katie.

"'Deed, Aunt Katie, you did see heep o' trouble, didn't you?" said one of her amazed hearers.

"Yes; but, you see, Aunt Katie wanted to see de worl'! "'Member how she used to tell us how she wasn't a tree as couldn't be transplanted, and how she was a libin' soul, and a p'og'essive sperrit, and how she wanted to see somefin' ob dis worl' she libbed in afore she parted hence and beed no more," said another.

"Well, I reckon you has seed 'nough ob de worl' now. Hasn't you, Aunt Katie?" inquired a third.

"Well, I jes reckon I has, chillun. I nebber wants to see no more ob dis worl' long as ebber I libs on dis yeth, dere. I be satisfied to settle down here at Tanglewood for de 'mainder ob my mortal days, and thank my 'Vine Marster down on my knees as I has got here safe," said Katie.

"If I was you, Aunt Katie, I'd publish my travels," said Sam.

"I gwine to, honey, 'deed is I. I gwine to publish um good, too. I gwine to get my extinguish friend, de professor dere, to write um all down fur me; and I gwine to publish um good. And now, Sam, chile, as de kettle is b'iling, I wish you jes' make de hot punch, 'cause I'se dead tired, and arter I drinks it I wants to go to bed."

And when the punch was made and served around, this circle also separated for the night.

The next morning, before breakfast, Ishmael walked through the forest to Woodside to see the little children of whom he was so fond. They were already up and waiting for him at the gate. On seeing him they rushed out to meet him with acclamations of joy, and laid hold of his overcoat and began to pull him towards the house.

Ishmael smiled on them, and talked to them, and would have taken them up in his arms, but that his arms were already full, for under one was Molly's family of dolls and under the other Johnny's box of tools. Smilingly he suffered them to pull him into the house, and push him into the arm-chair, and climb up on his knees and seize and search his parcels.

Molly knew her parcel by the feet of the dolls protruding through the end of the paper, and she quickly laid hands on it, sat down flat on the floor and tore it to pieces, revealing to her delighted eyes:

"Dolls, and more dolls, and so many dolls!" as she ecstatically expressed it. Then in the midst of her bliss, she suddenly remembered her benefactor, dropped all her treasures, jumped into his lap, threw her arms around his neck, and said:

"Oh, Cousin Ishmael, what pretty dolls! I will pray to the Lord to give you a great many things for giving me theses."

Ishmael kissed her very gravely and said:

"Pray to the lord to give me wisdom, Molly, for that is the best of all gifts, and I would rather a child should ask it for me than a bishop should."

And he sat Molly down again to enjoy her treasures.

Meanwhile Johnny had torn open his box of miniature carpenter's tools and run out to try their edges on the fences and out-houses; and all without one word of thanks to the donor. Boys, you know, are about as grateful as pigs, who devour the acorns without ever once looking up to see whence they come.

At the moment that Ishmael sat Molly down upon the floor, Hannah came in from a back room, where she had been at work.

On seeing the dolls she lifted both her hands and cried out:

"Oh, Ishmael, Ishmael, what extravagance!"

"Not at all, aunt. Look at little Molly! See how much happiness has been purchased at a trifling outlay, and talk no more of extravagance," said Ishmael, rising and taking his hat.

"Where are you going now? You have not been here a minute," said Hannah.

"Pardon me, I have been here half an hour, and now I must go back to Tanglewood, because they will wait breakfast for me there."

"Well, I declare!" wrathfully began Hannah, but Ishmael gently interrupted her:

"I have bought a fine Scotch tartan shawl for you, Aunt Hannah, and a heavy shepherd's maud for Uncle Reuben. They are such articles as you cannot purchase in this country. I will send them to you by one of the servants. I would have brought them myself, only you see my arms were full."

"Well, I should think so. Thank you, Ishmael! Thank you very much indeed. But when are you coming here to stop a bit?"

"Just as soon as I can, Aunt Hannah. This morning I must go to The Beacon. You may well suppose how anxious I am to be there."

"Humph! I thought now Mrs. Lord Vincent was a widder, all that was over."

"Aunt Hannah, what do you take me for?" exclaimed the young man, in sorrowful astonishment.

"Well, Ishmael, I didn't mean to insult you, so you needn't bite my head off," snapped Mrs. Gray.

"Good-by, Aunt Hannah," said Ishmael, stooping and kissing her cheek.

He hurried away and walked briskly through the woods and reached the house in good time for breakfast; and a happy breakfast it was, but for one sad face there. The old man was so delighted to be home again, under his own forest-shaded roof, seated at his own table, attended by his own affectionate servants, that it seemed as though the years had rolled back in their course and restored to him all the freshness of his youth.

After breakfast Ishmael arose and announced his departure for The Beacon, and requested of the judge the loan of two saddle horses.

"Ishmael, you have refused all compensation beyond your traveling expenses for your services; and I know, indeed, they were of a nature that money could not repay. Yet I do wish to make you some more substantial acknowledgment than empty words of my indebtedness to you. Now there is my Arabian courser, Mahomet. He is a gift worthy of even your acceptance, Ishmael. He has not his equal in America. I refused three thousand dollars for him before I went to Europe. I will not lend him to you, Ishmael! I will beg your acceptance of him—there, now don't refuse! I shall never use him again, and Claudia cannot, for he is not a lady's horse, you know."

"I shall never ride again," here put in Claudia, in a sorrowful voice.

Ishmael started and turned towards her; but she had arisen from the table and withdrawn to the window-seat.

Judge Merlin continued to press his gift upon the young man. But though Ishmael had almost a passion for fine horses, he hesitated to accept this munificent present until he saw that his refusal would give the judge great pain. Then, with sincere expressions of gratitude, he frankly accepted it.

The judge rang a bell and ordered Mahomet saddled and brought around for Mr. Worth, and a groom's horse for his servant.

Ishmael put on his riding-coat and took his hat and gloves. When the horses were announced, Ishmael went and shook hands with his host.

"God bless you, Ishmael; God bless you, my dear boy, for all that you have done for me and for mine! Yea, God bless you, and speed the time when you shall be nearer to me than at present," said the judge, pressing both Ishmael's hands before be dropped them.

Ishmael then crossed the room to take leave of Claudia. She was sitting in the armchair, within the recess of the bay window; her elbow rested on a little stand at her side, and her head was bowed upon her hand; this was her usual attitude now.

"Farewell, Lady Vincent," said Ishmael, in a grave, sweet voice, as he stood before her. She raised her head and looked at him. Oh, what a world of grief, despair, and passionate remorse was expressed in those large, dark, tearless eyes!

"Farewell, Lady Vincent," said Ishmael, deferentially taking her hand.

Her fingers closed spasmodically upon his, as though she would have held him to her side forever.

"Oh, must it be indeed farewell, Ishmael?" she breathed in a voice expiring with anguish.

"Farewell," he repeated gravely, kindly, reverentially; bowing low over the throbbing hand he held; and then he turned and softly left the room.

"It is his sense of honor. Oh, it is his chivalric, nay, his fanatical sense of honor that is ruining us! Unless Bee has the good taste and modesty to release him voluntarily, he will sacrifice me, himself, and her, to the Moloch, Honor," wailed Claudia, as she dropped her head upon her hands in a grief too deep for tears.

Was she right?

CHAPTER LIV

WHICH IS THE BRIDE?

His horse went on, hoof after hoof,

Went on and never stopped,

Till down behind the Mansion roof,

At once, the red sun dropped.

What fond and wayward thoughts will slide

Into a lover's head!—

"Oh, Heaven!" to himself he cried,

"If—if she should be dead!"

—Wordsworth.

Ishmael galloped along the road leading to The Beacon, followed at a short distance by the professor, who found some difficulty in keeping up with his master.

Ishmael's aspect was not altogether that of a happy lover going to see his beloved; for his countenance was thoughtful, grave, and sad. How could it be otherwise with him, after the scene he had left? His thoughts, his sympathies, his regrets were with Claudia, the earliest friend of his friendless childhood; with Claudia, grand, noble, and beautiful, even in the wreck of her happiness; with Claudia, loving now as she had never loved before. Yes, his thoughts, his regrets, his sympathies were with her, but where were his love, his esteem, and his admiration?

As he rode on the figure of Claudia, in her woe, became lost in a shadow that was gradually stealing over his soul-one of those mysterious shadows that approaching misfortunes are said to cast before them. In vain he tried by reason to dispel this gloom. The nearer he approached The Beacon, the deeper it settled upon his spirit!

What could it mean? Was all well at The Beacon? Was all well with Bee?

Reuben Gray, when questioned, had said that he had not heard from them in a week. And what might not have happened in a week? At that thought a pang like death shot through his heart, and he put spurs to his horse and urged him forward at his best speed, but with all his haste, the short February day was drawing to its close, and the descending sun was sinking behind the mansion-house and its group of out-buildings when Ishmael rode into the front yard, followed closely by his servant. It was but the work of a moment to spring from his horse, throw the reins to the professor, bound Tip the steps to the front door and ring the bell. The door was opened by Mr. Middleton in person. This was an unprecedented, and ominous circumstance.

Bee's father looked very grave as he held out his hand, saying:

"How do you do, Ishmael? I am glad that you have all returned safely."

"How do you do, Mr. Middleton? I hope—I hope that I find you all well?" said Ishmael, striving to speak composedly.

"Y-yes. Come into the library, my young friend; I wish to speak with you alone before you see any other member of the family," said Mr. Middleton.

Nearly overwhelmed with his emotions, dreading, he knew not what, Ishmael followed Mr. Middleton into the library and dropped into the chair that gentleman pushed towards him.

"Bee-Bee! For Heaven's sake tell me? Is she well?" he asked.

"Y-yes," answered Mr. Middleton hesitatingly, gravely. "Bee is well."

"Good Heaven, sir, can you not speak plainly? We say of the sainted dead that they are well; that it is well with them. Oh, tell me, tell me, is Bee alive and well?" exclaimed the young man, as drops of sweat, forced forth by his great agony of suspense, started from his brow.

"Yes, yes! Bee is alive and well."

Ishmael dropped his head upon his hands and breathed a fervent:

"Thanks be to God!"

"I have given you unintentional alarm, Ishmael."

"Oh, sir, alarm does not begin to express what I have suffered. You have wrung my heart. But let that pass, sir. What is it that you wished to say to me?" said Ishmael, raising his head.

"Take a glass of wine first," said Mr. Middleton, bringing a decanter and glasses from a side-table.

"Thank you, sir, I never touch it. Pray do not regard me; but go on with what you were about to say."

"I will then, Ishmael. And I hope you will forgive me if I speak very plainly."

"Speak then, sir; Bee's father has a holy right to speak plainly to Bee's betrothed," replied Ishmael, wondering what portentous communication these words prefaced.

"It is as Bee's father, and no less as your friend, Ishmael, that I do speak. Ishmael," continued Mr. Middleton solemnly, "we all knew your strong, your very strong attachment to Claudia Merlin before she became Lady Vincent—'

"Well, sir?" said the young man gravely.

"We all knew how nearly heart-broken you were for a considerable time after her marriage, and indeed until you found consolation and healing in the sympathy and affection of my daughter Beatrice."

"Yes, sir," said Ishmael, speaking low and bending his head.

"You possibly mistook this sisterly love of the companion of your childhood for that deeper love that should bind husband and wife together for time and for eternity. And you asked me to give you Bee, and I, rashly perhaps, consented—for who could foresee the end?"

Ishmael grew very pale, but compressed his lips, and governed his strong emotions.

Mr. Middleton continued:

"Lady Vincent fell into trouble. She needed the help of a man with a strong arm, wise head, and pure heart. You were that man, Ishmael. At her first cry for help wafted across the Atlantic, you threw up all your professional prospects, left your office and your clients to take care of themselves, and flew to her relief. It was to your wonderful intelligence, inspired, no doubt, by your pure love, that she owed her deliverance from all the snares laid for her destruction. You have rescued her and brought her safely home. Are you listening, Ishmael?"

"I am listening, sir," answered the young man very gravely. By this time he had begun to understand the drift of Mr. Middleton's discourse, and had recovered his composure, and his look was somewhat stern.

"Well, then, in a word—Lord Vincent is dead, Claudia is free, you have been her constant companion since her widowhood. Now, then, Ishmael, if in these days of close companionship with Lady Vincent your love for Claudia Merlin has revived—"

"Mr. Middleton, how can you speak to me thus?" interrupted Ishmael, in a stern voice, and with flashing eyes, and in very righteous indignation. The next instant, however, he recovered himself. "I beg your pardon, sir," he said sorrowfully. "I should not have spoken so to the father of my betrothed—to my own father, I might almost say. I beg your pardon sincerely."

"Compose yourself, Ishmael, and listen to me. I speak the words of truth and soberness, and you must hear them. I say if in these days of intimate association with Lady Vincent your love for Claudia Merlin has revived, you must break with Bee."

"Mr. Middleton!"

"Gently, Ishmael! If this is so, it cannot be helped, and none of us blame you. The human heart should be free. Nay, it will be free. So—"

"But, Mr. Middleton—"

"Gently, gently, Ishmael, I beg; hear me out. I know what you were about to say. You were about to talk of your plighted word, of fidelity, and of honor. But I think, Ishmael, that, if it is as I suppose, there would be more honor in frankly stating the case to Bee, and asking for the release that she would surely give you than there would be in marrying her while you love another. You should not offer her a divided love. Bee is worthy of a whole heart."

"Do I not know it?" broke forth Ishmael, in strong emotion. "Oh, do I not know it? And do I not give her my whole, unwavering, undivided heart? Mr. Middleton, look at me," said the young man, fixing his truthful, earnest, eloquent eyes upon that gentleman's face. "Look at me! It is true that I once cherished a boyish passion for Lady Vincent—unreasoning, ardent, vehement as such boyish passions are apt to be. But, sir, her marriage with Lord Vincent killed that passion quite. It was dead and buried, without the possibility of resurrection. It was impossible for me to love another man's wife. Every honorable principle, every delicate instinct of my nature forbade it. On her marriage day my boyish flame burned to ashes; and, sir, such ashes as are never rekindled again. Never, under any circumstances. It is true that I have felt the deepest sympathy for Lady Vincent in her sorrows; but not more, sir, than it is my nature to feel for any suffering woman; not more, sir, I assure you, than I felt for that poor, little middle-aged widow who was my first client; not more, scarcely so much, as I felt for Lady Hurstmonceux in her desertion. Oh, sir, the love that I gave to Bee is not the transient passion of a boy, it is the steadfast affection of a man. And since the blessed day of our betrothal my heart has known no shadow of turning from its fidelity to her. Sir, do you believe me?"

"I do, I do, Ishmael, and I beg you to forgive me for my doubts of you."

"For myself, I have nothing to forgive. But, sir, I hope, I trust, that you have not disturbed Bee with these doubts."

"Well, Ishmael, you know, I felt it my duty gradually to prepare her mind for the shock that she might have received had those old coals of yours been rekindled."

"Then Heaven forgive you, Mr. Middleton! Where is she? Can I see her now?"

"Of course you can, Ishmael. In any case, you should have seen her once more. If you had been going to break with her, you would have had to see her to ask from her own lips your release."

"Where is she—where?"

"In the drawing room—waiting, like the good girl that she is, to give you your freedom, should you desire it of her."

"I say—God forgive you, Mr. Middleton!" said Ishmael, starting off.

Suddenly he stopped; he was very much agitated, and he did not wish to break in on Bee in that disturbed state. He poured out a large glass of water and drank it off; stood still a minute to recover his composure, and then went quietly to the drawing room. Very softly he opened the door.

There she was. Ah, it seemed ages since he had seen her last. And now he stood for a moment looking at her, before he advanced into the room.

She was standing at the west window, apparently looking out at the wintry, red sunset. Although it was afternoon, she still wore a long, flowing, white merino morning dress, and her bright golden brown hair was unwound, hanging loose upon her shoulders. The beams of the setting sun, streaming in full upon her, illumined the outlines of her beautiful head and graceful form. A lovely picture she made as she stood there like some fair spirit.

Ishmael advanced softly towards her, stood behind her.

"Bee; dear, dear Bee!" he said, putting his arms around her.

She turned in a moment, exclaiming:

"Dear Ishmael; dearest brother!" and was caught to his bosom. She dropped her head upon his shoulder, and burst into a flood of tears. She wept long and convulsively, and he held her closely to his heart, and soothed her with loving words. It seemed she did not take in the full purport of those words, for presently she ceased weeping, gently disengaged herself from his embrace, and sat down upon the corner of the sofa, with her elbow resting on his arm, and her head leaning upon her hand. And then, as he looked at her, Ishmael saw for the first time how changed, how sadly changed she was.

Bee's face had always been fair, clear, and delicate, but now it was so white, wan, and shadowy that her sweet blue eyes seemed preternaturally large, bright, and hollow. She began to speak, but with an effort that was very perceptible:

"Dear Ishmael, dearest and ever dearest brother, I did not mean to weep so; it was very foolish; but then you know we girls weep for almost anything, or nothing; so you—"

Her voice sank into silence.

"My darling, why should you weep at all? and why do you call me brother?" whispered Ishmael, sitting down beside her, and drawing her towards him.

But again she gently withdrew herself from him, and looking into his face with her clear eyes and sweet smile, she said:

"Why? Because, dear Ishmael, though we shall never meet again after to-day—though it would not be right that we should—yet I shall always hold you as the dearest among my brothers. Oh, did you think; did you think it could be otherwise? Did you think this dispensation could turn me against you? Oh, no, no, no, Ishmael; it could not. Nothing that you could do could turn me against you, because you would do no wrong. You have not done wrong now, dear; do not imagine that any of us think so. We do not presume to blame you—none of us; not my father, not my mother—least of all myself. It was—-"

Again her sinking voice dropped into silence. "Bee; darling, darling Bee, you do not know what you are talking about. I love you, Bee; I love you," said Ishmael earnestly, again trying to draw her to his heart; but again she gently prevented him, as with a wan smile, and in a low voice, she answered:

"I know you do, dear; I never doubted that you did. You always loved me as if I were your own little sister. But not as you loved her, Ishmael."

"Bee—-"

"Hush, dear, let me speak while I have strength to do so. She was your first love, Ishmael; your first friend, you remember. With all her faults—and they are but as the spots upon the sun—she is a glorious creature, and worthy of you. I always knew that I was not to be compared to her."

"No, Heaven knows that you were not," breathed Ishmael inaudibly, as he watched Bee.

"All your friends, Ishmael—all who love you and who are interested in your welfare—if they could influence your choice, would direct it to her, rather than to me. You are making your name illustrious; you will some time attain a high station in society. And who is there so worthy to bear your name and share your station as that queenly woman?"

"Bee, Bee, you almost break my heart. I tell you I love you, Bee. I love you!"

"I know you do, dear; I have said that you do; and you are distressed about me; but do not be so, dear. Indeed I shall be very well; I shall have work to occupy me and duties to interest me; indeed I shall be happy, Ishmael; indeed I shall; and I shall always love you, as a little sister loves her dearest brother; so take your trothplight back again, dear, and with it take my prayers for your happiness," said Bee, beginning to draw the engagement ring from her finger.

"Bee, Bee, what are you doing? You will not listen to me. I love you, Bee! I love you. Hear me! There is no woman in the world that can rival you for an instant in my heart; no, not one; and there has never been one. That boyish passion I once cherished for another, and that haunts your imagination so fatally, was but a blaze of straw that quickly burned out. It was a fever common to boyhood. Few men, arrived at years of discretion, Bee, would like to marry their first follies—for it is a misnomer to call them first loves. Yes, very few men would like to do so, Bee, least of all would I. What I give you, Bee, is a constant, steadfast love, a love for time and for eternity. Oh, my dearest, hear me, and believe me," he said, speaking fervently, earnestly, forcibly.

She had started and caught her breath; and now she was looking and listening, as though she doubted the evidence of her own eyes and ears.

He had taken her hand and was resetting the ring more firmly on the finger, from which, indeed, she had not quite withdrawn it.

"Do you believe me now, dear Bee?" he softly inquired.

"Believe you? Why, Ishmael, I never doubted your word in all my life. But—but I cannot realize it. I cannot bring it home to my heart yet. How is it possible it should be true? How is it possible you should choose me, when you might marry her?" said Bee, with large, wondering eyes.

"How is it possible, my darling one, that you should not know how much more lovely you are than any other girl, or woman, I have ever seen—except one."

"Except one, Ishmael?" she inquired, with a faint smile.

"Except the Countess of Hurstmonceux, who is almost as good and as beautiful as you. Bee, my darling, are you satisfied now?"

"Oh, Ishmael, I cannot realize it. I have been schooling my heart so long, so long, to resign you."

"So long? How long, my dearest?"

"Oh, ever since we heard that she was free. And that has been—let me see—why, indeed, it has been but a week. But oh, Ishmael, it seems to me that years and years have passed since my father told me to prepare for a disappointment."

"Heaven pardon him; I scarcely can," said Ishmael to himself.

"But is it indeed true? Do you really love me best of all? And can you be satisfied with me, with me?"

"'Satisfied' with you, dearest? Well, I suppose that is the best word after all. Yes, dearest; yes, perfectly, eternally satisfied with you, Bee," he said, drawing her to his heart. And this time she did not withdraw herself from his embrace; but, with a soft sob of joy, she dropped her head upon his bosom.

"You believe my love now, Bee?" he stooped and whispered.

"Oh, yes, yes, yes, Ishmael; and I am so happy," she murmured.

"Now then listen to me, dearest, for I have something to say to you. Do you remember, love, that day you came to me in the arbor? I was sleeping the heavy sleep of inebriation; and you wept over me and veiled my humbled head with your own dear handkerchief, and glided away as softly as you came. Do you remember, dear, that night you sat up at your window, watching and waiting to let me in with your own dear hand, that none should witness my humiliation? Bee, apparently that was a compassionate sister, trying to save from obloquy an earing brother. But really, Bee, as the truth stands in the spiritual world, it is this: A sinner was sleeping upon one of the foulest gulfs in the depths of perdition. A single turn in his sleep and he would have been eternally lost; but an angel came from Heaven, and with her gentle hand softly aroused him and drew him out of danger. Bee, I was that sinner on the brink of eternal woe, and you that angel from Heaven who saved him. Bee, from that day I knew that God had sent you to be my guardian spirit through this world. And when I forget that day, Bee, may the Lord forget me. And when I cease to adore you for it, Bee, may the Lord cease to love me. But as love of Heaven is sure, Bee, so is my love for you. And both are eternal. Oh, love, bride, wife; hear me; believe me; love me!"

"Oh, I do, I do, Ishmael, and I am so happy. And the very spring of my happiness in the thought that I content you."

"With an infinite content, Bee."

"And now let us go to my dear mother; she will be so glad; she loves you so much, you know, Ishmael," said Bee, gently releasing herself—and looking up, her fair face now rosy with delicate bloom and the tones of her voice thrilling with subdued joy.

Ishmael arose and gave her his arm, and they passed out of the drawing room and entered the morning room, where Mrs. Middleton sat among her younger children.

"Mamma," said Bee, "we were none of us right; here is Ishmael to speak for himself."

"I know it, dear; your papa has just been in here, and told me all about it. How do you do, Ishmael? Welcome home, my son," said Mrs. Middleton, rising and holding out her arms.

Ishmael warmly embraced Bee's mother.

But by this time the children had gathered around him, clamorous for recognition. All children were very fond of Ishmael.

While he was shaking hands with the boys, kissing the little girls, and lifting the youngest up in his arms, Mr. Middleton came in, and the evening passed happily.

Ishmael remained one happy week with Bee, and then leaving her, recovered, blooming, and happy, he returned to Washington, where he was affectionately welcomed by the two fair and gentle old ladies, who had put his rooms in holiday order to receive him. He returned in good time for the opening of the spring term of the circuit court, and soon found himself surrounded with clients, and the business of his office prospered greatly.

CHAPTER LV

CONCLUSION.

How saidst thou!-Labor:-why his work is pleasure;

His days are pleasantness, his nights are peace;

He drinks of joys that neither cloy, nor cease,

A well that gushes blessings without measure;

Yea, and to crown the cup of peace with praise,

Both God and man approve his works and ways.

—Martin F. Tupper.

Early in the spring of the following year a great distinction awaited Ishmael Worth. Young as he then was, he had won the admiration and confidence of the greatest statesmen and politicians of the day. And there were statesmen as well as politicians then. "There were giants in those days." And from among all the profound lawyers and learned judges of the country, young Ishmael Worth was selected by our government as their especial ambassador to the Court of France, to settle with the French ministry some knotty point of international law about which the two countries were in danger of going to war.

Ishmael was to sail in May. His marriage with Bee had been deferred upon different pretexts by her family; for not very willingly do parents part with such a daughter as Bee, even to a husband so well beloved and highly esteemed as Ishmael; and Ishmael and Bee had reluctantly, but dutifully, submitted to their wishes, but not again would Ishmael cross the Atlantic without Bee. So, on the 1st of May they were very quietly married in the parish church that the family attended. Judge Merlin and his daughter were, of course, invited to be present at the ceremony; but both sent excuses, with best wishes for the happiness of the young pair. Not yet could Claudia look calmly on the marriage of Ishmael and Bee.

On the 7th of May Ishmael and his bride sailed from New York to Havre, for Paris. There he satisfactorily concluded the important business upon which he had been sent, and it is supposed to have been owing to his wise diplomacy alone, under Divine Providence, that a war was averted, and the disputed question settled upon an amicable and permanent basis. Having thus performed his mission, he devoted himself exclusively to his bride. She was presented at the French court, where her beauty, resplendent now with perfect love and joy, made a great sensation, even in that court of beauties. She went to some of the most select and exclusive of the ambassadors' balls, and everywhere, without seeking or desiring such distinction, she became the cynosure of all eyes. When the season was over in Paris they made the tour of Europe, seeing the best that was to be seen, stopping at all the principal capitals, and, through our ministers, entering into all the court circles; and everywhere the handsome person, courtly address, and brilliant intellect of Ishmael, and the beauty, grace, and amiability of Bee, inspired admiration and respect. They came last to England. In London they were the guests of our minister. Here also Bee was presented at court, where, as elsewhere, her rare loveliness was the theme of every tongue.

Meanwhile, Claudia, living in widowhood and seclusion, learned all of Bee's transatlantic triumphs through the "court circulars" and "fashionable intelligence" of the English papers; and through the gossiping foreign letter writers of the New York journals; all of which in a morbid curiosity she took, and in a self-tormenting spirit studied. In what bitterness of soul she read of all these triumphs! This was exactly what she had marked out for herself, when she sold her soul to the fiend, in becoming the wife of Lord Vincent! And how the fiend had cheated her! Here she was at an obscure country house, wearing out the days of her youth in hopeless widowhood and loneliness. This splendid career of Bee was the very thing to attain which she had sacrificed the struggling young lawyer, and taken the noble viscount. And now it was that very young lawyer who introduced his bride to all these triumphs; while that very viscount had left her to a widowhood of obscurity and reproach! In eagerly, recklessly, sinfully snatching at these social honors she had lost them all, while Bee, without seeking or desiring them, by simply walking forward in her path of love and duty, had found them in her way. But for her own wicked pride and mental short- sightedness, she might be occupying that very station now so gracefully adorned by Bee.

What a lesson it was! Claudia bowed her haughty head and took it well to heart. "It is bitter, it is bitter; but it is just, and I accept it. I will learn of it. I cannot be happy; but I can be dutiful. I have but my father left in this world. I will devote myself to him and to God," she said, and she kept her word.

There is one incident in the travels of Ishmael and Bee that should be recorded here, since it concerns a lady(?) that figured rather conspicuously in this history. The young pair were at Cameron Court, on a visit to the Countess of Hurstmonceux and Mr. Brudenell, whom they found enjoying much calm domestic happiness. Making Cameron Court their headquarters, Ishmael and Bee went on many excursions through the country and visited many interesting places. Among the rest, they inspected the model Reformatory Female Prison at Ballmornock. While they were going through one of the workrooms, Bee suddenly pressed her husband's arm and whispered:

"Ishmael, dear, observe that poor young woman sitting there binding shoes. How pretty and lady-like she seems, to be in such a place as this, poor thing!"

Ishmael looked as desired; and at the same moment the female prisoner raised her head; and their eyes met.

"Come away, Bee, my darling," said Ishmael, suddenly turn his wife around and leading her from the room.

"She really seemed to know you, Ishmael," said Bee, as they left the prison.

"She did, love; it was Mrs. Dugald."

Bee's blue eyes opened wide, in wonder and sorrow, and she walked on in silence and in thought.

Yes, the female prisoner, in the coarse gray woolen gown and close white linen cap, who sat on the wooden bench binding shoes, was Katie's "whited sepulcher." She had been sent first to the Bridewell, where for a few days she had been very violent and ungovernable, but she soon learned that her best interests lay in submission; and for months afterwards she behaved so well that at length she was sent to the milder Reformatory, to work out her ten years of penal servitude. Here she was supplied with food, clothing, and shelter—all of a good, coarse, substantial sort. But she was compelled to work very steadily all the week, and to hear two good sermons on Sunday, and as she had never in her life before enjoyed such excellent moral training as this, let us hope that the Reformatory really reformed her.

Ishmael and Bee returned home in the early autumn. Almost immediately upon his arrival in Washington, Ishmael was made district attorney. The emoluments of this office, added to the income from his private practice, brought him in a revenue that justified him in taking an elegant little suburban villa, situated within its own beautiful grounds and within an easy distance from his office. Here he lived with Bee, as happy, and making her as happy, as they both deserved to be.

It was in the third winter of Claudia's widowhood that the health of her father began to fail. A warmer climate was recommended to him as the only condition of his prolonged life. He went to

Cuba, attended by Claudia, now his devoted nurse. In that more genial atmosphere his health improved so much that he entered moderately into the society of the capital, and renewed some of his old acquaintance. He found that Philip Tourneysee had succeeded at last in winning the heart of the pretty Creole widow, Senora Donna Eleanora Pacheco, to whom he had been married a year. He met again that magnificent old grandee of Castile, Senor Don Filipo Martinez, Marquis de la Santo Espirito, who at first sight became an ardent admirer of Claudia, and the more the Castilian nobleman of this pale pensive beauty, the more he admired her; and the more he observed her devotion to her father, the more he esteemed her. At length he formally proposed to her and was accepted. And at about the same time the marquis received the high official appointment he had been so long expecting. Claudia, in marrying him, became the wife of the Captain General of Cuba, and the first lady on the island. But, mark you! she had not sought nor expected this distinction. She simply found it in the performance of her duties; and if she did not love her stately husband with the ardor of her youth, she admired and revered him. In his private life she made him a good wife; in his public career an intelligent counselor; in everything a faithful companion. Judge Merlin spent all his winters with them in Havana; and all his summers at Tanglewood, taken care of by Katie.

A few words about the other characters of our story.

Old Mrs. Brudenell and her daughters vegetated on at Brudenell Hall, in a monotony that was broken by only three incidents in as many years. The first was the death of poor Eleanor, whose worthless husband had died of excess some months before; the second incident was the marriage of Elizabeth Brudenell to the old pastor of her parish, who repented of his celibacy because he had become infirm, and took a wife because he required a nurse; and the third was the visit of the Countess of Hurstmonceux and Mr. Brudenell, who came and spent a few months among their friends in America, and then returned to their delightful home in Scotland.

The Middletons continued to live at The Beacon, but every winter they spent a month at The Bee-Hive, which was the name of the Worths' villa; and every summer Ishmael, Bee, and their lovely little daughter, Nora, passed a few weeks amid the invigorating sea-breezes at The Beacon.

The professor lived with Ishmael, in the enjoyment of a vigorous and happy old age.

Reuben and Hannah Gray continued to reside at Woodside, cultivating the Tanglewood estate and bringing up their two children.

Alfred Burghe was cashiered for "conduct unworthy of an officer and a gentleman," as the charge against him on his trial set forth; and he and his brother have passed into forgetfulness.

Sally and Jim were united, of course, and lived as servants at Tanglewood, where old Katie, as housekeeper, reigned supreme.

What else?

Ishmael loved, prayed, and worked—worked more than ever, for he knew that though it was hard to win, it was harder to secure fame. He went on from success to success. He became illustrious.

THE END

Made in the USA
Columbia, SC
10 December 2024

48928404R00267